Obses.

Susan Lewis is the bestselling author of twenty-two novels. She is also the author of *Just One More Day*, a moving memoir of her childhood in Bristol. She lives in France. Her website address is www.susanlewis.com

Acclaim for Susan Lewis

'One of the best around' *Independent on Sunday*

'Spellbinding! . . . you just keep turning the pages, with the atmosphere growing more and more intense as the story leads to its dramatic climax' *Daily Mail*

'Mystery and romance *par excellence*' *Sun*

'Deliciously dramatic and positively oozing with tension, this is another wonderfully absorbing novel from the *Sunday Times* bestseller Susan Lewis . . . Expertly written to brew an atmosphere of foreboding, this story is an irresistible blend of intrigue and passion, and the consequences of secrets and betrayal' *Woman*

'A multi-faceted tear jerker' *heat*

Susan LEWIS

Obsession

arrow books

Published by Arrow Books 2009

6 8 10 9 7

First published in Great Britain in 1993 by
William Heinemann
Random House, 20 Vauxhall Bridge Road,
London SW1V 2SA

www.randomhouse.co.uk

Addresses for companies within The Random House Group Limited can be
found at: www.randomhouse.co.uk/offices.htm

The Random House Group Limited Reg. No. 954009

A CIP catalogue record for this book
is available from the British Library

ISBN 9780099534297

The Random House Group Limited supports The Forest Stewardship
Council (FSC®), the leading international forest certification organisation.
Our books carrying the FSC label are printed on FSC® certified paper.
FSC is the only forest certification scheme endorsed by the leading
environmental organisations, including Greenpeace. Our
paper procurement policy can be found at
www.randomhouse.co.uk/environment

MIX
Paper from
responsible sources
FSC® C016897

Printed and bound in Great Britain by Clays Ltd, St Ives PLC

For Gary, Jill and Grace Elizabeth Lewis
and
for Denise Hastie

– Acknowledgements –

To begin with I should like to thank Dr Martin Atkinson-Barr, his wife, Sue, and Kevin and Jo Connor for their hospitality during my stay in Los Angeles. Also I should like to express my gratitude to Matthew Snyder of CAA for the invaluable contacts he gave me. A very special thank you to director, Jonathan Kaplan and producer, Chuck Gordon, who allowed me to spend so much time on their set and patiently answered an endless string of questions. To Di McClure for taking me to that delightful monstrosity of a Beverly Hills house and to David Rousell of Universal for giving me the benefit of so much knowledge.

My thanks also to the staff of the Castle Combe Manor House Hotel in Castle Combe and to Bridget Anderson for helping me with so much in the South of France.

And lastly, a very special thank you to my friends Lesley Morgan and Elaine Matthews for the contacts they gave me.

An entire world of sin lived in her eyes, a whole universe of pleasure in her body. Her pale lips spoke silently and unmovingly of excesses unknown, her skin glistened with a vibrancy that set his very soul on fire.

As he watched her, watching him, through a forest of glittering, baubled humanity he could feel her sensuality as though it were lazily curling itself around the heated core of his lust. It was as though he was being sucked in by her wild immorality, consumed by a stormy sea of intemperance. Her limpid eyes swam with the promise of unimaginable carnality, her exquisite mouth curved with a smile of untold depravity and wantonness.

Suddenly he was afraid. Memories started to dig into the chaos of his mind. Images of the past ballooned grotesquely before his eyes; the terror, the screams, the pain, the nightmare of endless violence ripped through him.

'Darling, are you feeling all right?'

He turned, as though in a trance, to see the aging and concerned face of the woman who adored him. Thirty years his senior, she could so easily have been his mother. He wished she were his mother, that she would rescue him from the fear that now blighted him. Dear God, if only she would rescue him, for his real mother never had.

'You're awfully pale, darling. Is something the matter?'

He loved her voice. He loved her kindness and selflessness. He cherished her.

'Everyone's talking about you,' she giggled.

He hated her. She didn't understand, would never understand. All she saw was an eighteen-year-old boy, a plaything, a stud, an ornament for her fleshy arm. He needed to be loved, not worshipped for his beauty, nor adored for the prowess of his young body. He needed her kindness to extend a hand of compassion; instead it bought him with riches beyond his comprehension. She had housed him, fed him, groomed him and educated him. She had shown him a world he might never have known, a world that glittered, a world so far from the pain. For that he would always be grateful.

Together they moved through the party. He smiled at her girlishness though inside he was repulsed. He laughed at her coquettishness while his heart contracted with pity. He was here to impress her friends, to instill in them a jealousy that would reassert her status in their society. Her self-doubt, her fear of growing old and her pathetic loss of worth, touched him. All she had now was a tremulous hand on a dead husband's past glories – and him. She could no longer stand alone in this cocoon of sybaritic strangers, not even her wealth could save her. He was her only hope, without him she would fall; she would descend into the abyss of ignominy and nonentity she so dreaded.

He felt the clutch of her need as though her hands were encasing his heart. He knew the stifling desperation of her fear as though she breathed with his lungs. Yet he felt a tenderness for her that surpassed all else.

Her bejewelled fingers slipped from his as someone led her away. He was alone, and the eyes of the she-devil still watched him. An arcane shiver of memory juddered through him once again, but the pull of her gaze was too strong and he found himself turning. Then, as his eyes came to rest on her, it was as though every fibre of his being was melting in shock. Her glorious white gold hair glistened and sparkled like the blurred light of a halo. It was as though she were looking right through him, into the very depths of his heart. He felt the touch of her empathy as though it were healing fingers reaching out for his pain.

She knew, she understood, and her earlier look had been meant to show him. He felt himself start to sway at the staggering realization of what was happening. She had come in the guise of a demon, letting him see in her eyes, her lips, her skin the reflection of his torment, and now, as though she were an angel from God, she was showing him his salvation.

He waited as she moved towards him, every part of his body responding to the divine illusion of her sensuousness. Her perfume reached him, an ephemeral fragrance, that made him lightheaded, almost drunk, and her hand slipped between their bodies, lovingly stroking his genitals.

She took his hand, leading him beneath the chandeliers to the wide, sweeping staircase. At the top she turned and, like a celestial being, surveyed the sinful world of plenty below. He watched her, unexpurgated love pounding through every pulse. His desire was excruciating, his fear sublime.

The bathroom was made for a Roman goddess. Marble and gold and onyx. As she turned from the door the light fell upon her; she was an ethereal vision of Elysian radiance. He wanted to fall to his knees in reverence, but it was she who dropped to her knees, then to her back until she was lying before him.

'I am yours,' she whispered. 'Do as you will.'

He took her, and the extremity of pleasure transcended everything. He had prayed that one day God would send someone to save him, and now He had.

Three weeks passed by. Each day saw the coming together of their bodies and the enmeshing of their minds. He knew nothing about her beyond the majesty of her beauty and the sublime sorcery of her body. She controlled him, consumed him, fornicated with him and revered him, until at last he knew he could do it. At last he could confess the atrocities, and she, as God's own messenger, would absolve him.

She listened, her youthful head bent in concentration as he spoke. It was a long story, as painful in the hearing as it was in the telling. Not until he had finished, had expunged his soul of every torment and abomination of his short life, did she look up. And it was in that instant, as her eyes moved to his, that he discovered she was not his salvation at all; she was his damnation.

'What! You've got to be joking!' Corrie cried, swinging round from the fire and brandishing the toasting fork with its smouldering slice of toast.

'I don't see why. In fact I think it's a bloody good idea, don't you Edwina?' Paula said, turning to Corrie's mother for support.

Edwina's pale brown eyes were swimming in mirth, her cheeks rosy red from the fire.

'If you agree with her . . .' Corrie warned.

'Why don't you just give it a shot?' Paula said, wincing as she tried to make herself more comfortable. 'I mean, what have you got to lose? Not your virginity, that's for sure.'

Corrie eyed her dangerously and Edwina laughed out loud. All three of them were very well aware that Corrie had lost her virginity to Paula's husband, Dave. Of course Paula and Dave hadn't been married then, but they had been seeing each other. And in a way it was Paula's fault, for if she hadn't started giving Dave the run around then he and Corrie might never have got it together. As it was, in an attempt to make Paula jealous Dave had switched his interest to Corrie. Paula had insisted that she couldn't care less, so Corrie, who was twenty-one at the time, and simply dying to be rid of the virginity that was threatening to become a permanent fixture, had set about seducing their old school-friend, who was by now the local car mechanic. It hadn't been a particularly memorable occasion, both of them had been too drunk to remember much about it, but Corrie did recall not feeling too good about herself after, particularly when Dave took it upon himself to tell Paula what had happened. Wasn't it just like a man to go and confess? If he'd kept it to himself Paula might never have known, but he didn't, and Corrie and Paula, who had been as close as, if not closer than sisters all their lives, hadn't spoken for three months. Now, five years later, they all, including Edwina, laughed about it.

'All you have to do,' Paula said, settling her plate on the mound of her heavily pregnant belly and sinking her teeth into a succulent slice of toast, 'is answer an ad. No one's asking you to put one in yourself. Well, you couldn't really could you? I mean, if they were to ring here Edwina might get arrested for pimping.'

From where she was sitting on the floor Corrie looked up at her mother, who, still laughing, was easing herself out of the chair to empty more coal onto the fire. While her back was turned Corrie and Paula exchanged glances. Paula winked and Corrie smiled.

'Mind you,' Paula said, yawning as the warmth of the small sitting room enveloped her, 'perhaps your own ad is a better idea. That way you can specify your requirements. To begin with, a nice big willie . . .' she broke off as Corrie threw a cushion at her. 'What's the matter with that?' she said, her pretty blue eyes rounded with seriousness. 'I can assure you it's an essential . . .'

'You're an outrage,' Corrie laughed. 'And big willie, small willie or no willie at all, I don't want a man.'

'Huh!' Paula snorted.

'Then tell us what you do want, sweetheart,' Edwina said. She was still standing in front of the fire, her back turned to the room, but Corrie could see her flushed, though tired face reflected in the mirror in front of her.

'Nothing,' she answered, perhaps a touch too brightly. 'I don't want anything. I'm quite happy here in Amberside with you and . . .'

'Pppht!' Paula interjected. 'Pull the other one. We all

know how you can't wait to get away from this . . .' she stopped suddenly as Corrie shot her a warning look, and her face instantly burned with misery.

Smiling, Edwina turned round and surveilled the two of them. So different in appearance, so different in ambition, yet so alike in character. They were devoted to each other. Devoted too, to her.

Her eyes rested on Paula. Everything about Paula, with the exception of her pregnant belly, was small. Her elfin face with those lovely mischievous blue eyes rarely failed to make Edwina smile. And the fluffy white blonde curls that bobbed around her face were almost the same now as they had been when she was a child. Though her beauty now, as a young woman, owed as much to her internal contentment as it did to her angelic features. It was a contentment, Edwina knew, Corrie was far from feeling.

'The world is out there waiting for Corrie,' Edwina said, 'if only she would go to meet it.'

'The world, at least for me,' Corrie answered, 'is right here in Amberside.'

Edwina cocked a disbelieving eyebrow. 'Living in a little cottage, in a little village, running a little dress shop? Some might be satisfied with that, but it's not enough for you.'

'Says who? And if this is your way of trying to get me to advertise for a man to change my life, then forget it. I don't want to meet a man that way. In fact I don't know that I want to meet a man at all.' Her head turned sharply at a loud clattering sound outside. 'What on earth was that?'

'If you think it's Mr Right coming down the square on his white charger on this cold winter night, you might be in for a disappointment,' Paula said, as Corrie walked to the window.

'It's next-door's bin, blown over in the wind,' Corrie said, letting the curtain drop back into place. 'Now enough about finding me a man. Tell us about the baby.'

'What, how I'm going to squeeze that great big head out of my tiny little bits? It's giving me nightmares. Let's change the subject. Are you going to join the aerobics class they're starting up down at the village hall on Tuesdays? Should be good for a laugh if nothing else, Di Robinson's running it and you know what she's like once she gets into a leotard. It's only two pounds to get in. Say you will, Corrie 'cos I couldn't bear to go alone with all those geriatric women, but I'll need to do something when the baby comes to get back in shape.'

'Oh, God,' Corrie groaned, 'do I have to? The very idea of bouncing around that draughty old hall with the likes of Mrs Willis while that backstabbing old cow Linda Morris inspects the current size of my thighs . . .'

Edwina and Paula exchanged looks.

'All right, I know what you're thinking,' Corrie said. 'And yes, I could do with losing some weight.'

'Oh, here we go again,' Paula sighed. 'Just which bit of your anatomy are you running a hate campaign for now?'

'How about all of it?'

'There's not an ounce of spare flesh on you.'

'What! Look at me! I mean you could hardly call me svelte, could you?'

'Not a word that comes instantly to mind, no,' Paula agreed. 'You're more . . .'

'If you say voluptuous I'll see to it that that baby starts squeezing through the small bits right now.'

Paula looked to Edwina for help. 'What do you say to the girl?'

'I've tried,' Edwina said. 'Corrie, sweetheart, you're just a big build. But you're tall enough to carry it off. If you were any slimmer you'd be skinny, lanky. You wouldn't look nearly so good as you do.'

'I don't suppose, as my mother, you might be just a touch biased?' Corrie replied. 'I'm fat.'

'Full-figured,' Paula corrected. 'And you should let

Harriet do your hair more often. She made a really good job of it for Kathy and Steve's wedding and don't deny it.'

'Aunt Harriet is a miracle worker with everyone's hair,' Corrie retorted, 'but I have to admit it did look good.'

She looked at her mother, from whom she had inherited her gleaming chestnut brown hair, and felt a sudden jolt of such painful anguish that her next words caught in her throat.

'So, aerobics it is,' Paula said, reading the situation perfectly. 'We'll go down to the hall and enroll as soon as I'm out of the hospital – which surely can't be more than two weeks now.'

Laughing, Edwina said: 'I don't think you'll be ready for aerobics quite that soon, Paula.'

'No,' Paula sighed, suddenly glum. 'I suppose you're right. No sex either. I'm mad for it, but Dave won't. He says he's afraid he'll poke the baby's eye out. And speaking of Dave, I guess his darts match'll be over by now, so I'd better be getting home, you know how he can't stand to be left with my mum and dad on his own. But he'll have to manage when I'm in hospital. Thanks,' she said, as Corrie took her hands and heaved her out of the squashy sofa. 'Now, remember, I'm doing the veg for lunch tomorrow. I'll clean it at home and bring it over here. All right? What time?'

'I'll put the chicken in about twelve,' Corrie answered, 'so come then. Then we can all go off down the pub for a drink.'

'Right you are.' Paula turned to Edwina. 'Sleep well,' she said, kissing her cheek, 'see you in the morning.'

As Corrie walked Paula out to the hall she closed the sitting-room door behind her.

'Sorry,' Paula said, before Corrie could speak. 'I just didn't think.'

'It doesn't matter,' Corrie assured her. 'She knows only

too well how badly I want to get out and do something with my life. I just wish I bloody well didn't.'

'Well you do, and trying to deny it is only making it worse. But I didn't mean to bring it up in front of Edwina.'

'It would make life so much easier if I could only meet someone and be happy the way you are.'

Paula shook her head. 'It wouldn't work. It's not enough for you here, and you know it. It never will be.'

'It'll have to be,' Corrie said, then smiled at the concern in Paula's eyes. It was a smile that all but transformed her otherwise homely face; a face that wasn't beautiful, but could be made so much more striking if Corrie only made the effort.

'What, darts on a Saturday night, roast chicken on Sundays and aerobics on Tuesdays?' Paula said. 'I don't think you're up to all that excitement, Corrie.' Her expression became serious. 'You will meet someone, though, I know you will. And he'll be really special, you see if I'm not right. And you'll have the career too. It'll all work out for you in the end.'

Shaking her head, Corrie said, 'if I could do a deal with God I'd live the rest of my life with my frustrations, if only He'd . . .'

Paula took Corrie's hand and squeezed it. 'I know,' she whispered, looking up into Corrie's face.

Corrie remained at the door, watching Paula battle her way through the wet and windy night until she reached the end of the street and turned into her parents' garden gate, the last house before the village square.

When Corrie returned to the sitting room Edwina was sitting on the sofa. The soft light shining through the fringes of the lamp, which stood behind the comfy fireside chair, cast an amber circle across the worn patterned carpet at her feet and over the cluttered bookshelves behind her. There was an odd flicker of a shadow as the wind howled outside and blew a draft around the curtains, and as it whistled down the chimney the fire, in its small cast-iron hearth, shifted and resettled.

'Come and sit here,' Edwina said, patting the cushion beside her.

Corrie looked up in surprise, then seeing the expression on her mother's face she gave a short smile.

'I know what's on your mind, sweetheart,' Edwina said. 'So come along, let's talk.'

Corrie shook her head. She had never hidden anything from Edwina, there had never been any reason to since theirs was a very special relationship, making them as much friends as they were mother and daughter, but Corrie didn't want to have this conversation. They'd had it many times before and it served no purpose. No matter how frustrated, confused and, yes, different to those she had grown up with, Corrie felt inside, nothing in the world would persuade her to leave her mother; to go away from the little Suffolk village of Amberside to find the life she almost constantly dreamed of. And that, she knew, was what her mother was about to do. And she in turn would fob Edwina off with her usual excuse that if she were to take herself and her ambitions out into the world she would be sure to end up making a fool of herself, trying to be something she wasn't.

Tonight she didn't feel like going through the charade, and neither, she guessed, did Edwina. But Edwina's concern tore at her heart, for in truth they both knew that the way Corrie felt about herself really had nothing at all to do with the reason she wouldn't leave this grey little village with its infernally dull routine and colourless people.

Taking the hand her mother held out Corrie stooped to kiss the once beautiful face, now bloated and pale. The eyes, a young woman's eyes, might have lost their sparkle now, but not the tenderness Corrie had known all her twenty-six years.

'You look tired,' she said.

Edwina squeezed Corrie's hand. In her heart she longed to tell her daughter to go, to stop wasting her young years on a dying mother, who might yet live to see fifty. By then Corrie would be past thirty. But she knew that nothing she said or did would persuade Corrie to leave her. They were devoted to each other, and how Edwina despised the illness that was ruining both their lives.

For a while they talked about Paula, missing her sparkle now she'd gone. Then, sensing that her mother was once again going to try broaching the subject of her illness, of how Corrie mustn't take it upon herself and get on with her own life, Corrie went to the cramped kitchen at the back of the cottage to make a hot drink before bed.

She filled a saucepan with milk, wiped down the draining board, then set out their two mugs. Too soon there would be only one mug to lay out, and she didn't know if she could bear it. It was five years now since Edwina had first discovered she had cancer. Five terrible years during which the tumour had been removed from her breast and they had thought she was cured. That had given them a two year reprieve. Two years during which Edwina had seemed younger and more vivacious than ever. They had made so many plans. But now there was a secondary cancer. The one that in five days, five months, maybe five years from now, would finally claim her.

As she moved about the kitchen Corrie found herself reflecting, as she had so often in these past few years, on how much easier life would be, not only on her, but on Edwina too, were she only able to settle down to wanting the same things as Paula. A husband, a baby, a part-time job in the local Spar and a life as safe and secure as it was predictable. She knew how happy it would make Edwina to see her married, to know that when she died Corrie wouldn't be all alone. But life was never that straightforward and though Corrie had a very real fondness for some of the boys, now men, she had been to school with, she couldn't begin to imagine being married to any one of them. Not even Bob, the only real boyfriend she'd had, who was now married to Maureen Dennis, and with whom she had thought herself in love before he'd two-timed her with Maureen, had even come close to quenching this damnable, burning desire for a life that she hardly dared to imagine. For a while though she had thought Bob her saviour, that at last she had met someone who could stifle her restlessness. And she would have married him, had he asked her, had he not met Maureen and got her pregnant.

There were no regrets now though, for she knew, had things been different with Edwina, that she would consider Maureen Dennis to have done her a favour. A man who had grown up in Amberside, whose idea of fun was darts on a Saturday night and an occasional visit to Ipswich when they were playing at home, just wasn't for her. No more than a life spent running her mother's dress shop in the village square, and the odd knees up at the bingo hall was the life for her. She had taken now to living her life in her dreams, letting them run away with her until she found herself living the fast, glamorous and demanding life of a career woman, like those she read about in magazines. Almost any career would do, but to be able to work in television, to rush about the country – the world – filming dramas or documentaries or even news, well that would be the ultimate. Occasionally she would envisage her leisure hours too, what few she would have given the demands of her career, spent like the sons and daughters of the families who lived in the grand houses in the nearby countryside, who came on summer weekends to throw parties while their parents were away on holiday. All last summer she had watched them from the window of the dress shop, pressing buttons into the wrong button holes as she dressed a mannequin, and more often than not she had found herself smiling through tears of frustration at the fun they all seemed to be having as they sped through the village in their open-topped cars, music blaring and hair flying in the wind. She had no idea what any of their names were, the people in the big houses had very little to do with the village, except an occasional visit to the pub or a rushed trip to the grocer's. None of them ever came into the dress shop. They'd probably never even noticed it the displays were so dull and styles so sober compared to the glittering designer creations they wore. She imagined them returning to London on Sunday evenings to resume their jet-set existence by night, and pursue their high-powered, demanding jobs by day; how she longed to go with them, to be one of them.

'By the way,' Edwina said, as she took the cup of hot chocolate Corrie was handing her. 'I know you and Paula like to tease me, but you wouldn't really consider advertising for a man, would you?'

Corrie who was stoking the fire, turned slowly to show her mother a look of mock surprise and confusion. 'Well I was thinking of putting a note in Norman the newsagent's window offering French lessons. Why, don't you think I should?'

'Not really, sweetheart, apart from anything else you can't speak French.'

'I don't think one has actually to *speak* it,' Corrie said, with more feigned innocence.

'In Amberside that's just what they would expect,' Edwina laughed. 'Now, turn on the TV, let's spoil ourselves and snuggle up on the couch in front of the late night movie.'

'Ooooh,' Corrie thrilled, 'just let me get my slippers on first.'

— 2 —

When Paula's baby girl was born two weeks later Corrie and her mother took the bus into Ipswich. A few minutes after they arrived at the hospital with their gifts of flowers, champagne and baby paraphernalia Dave came bustling down the ward, having just returned from taking his parents home. Corrie and Edwina stood to one side and watched as he lifted the baby into his arms, gazing down at her with such awe and devotion that both women were very nearly moved to tears – until Corrie saw the expression on Paula's face and they both burst out laughing.

Dave took their teasing in good spirit, but still, even when she started to whimper, wouldn't be parted from his daughter.

'She's hungry, you idiot,' Paula said.

Dave looked up at Corrie and Edwina with a grin so wide it looked painful. 'Amazing isn't it? She knows when she's hungry.'

Paula's face was a picture as reluctantly he handed the baby over. Then he proceeded to watch, mesmerized, as little Beth started to suckle.

'She's brilliant, isn't she?' Dave cried in triumph. 'Look she can even . . .'

'Dave! Shut up!' Paula said. Then turning to Edwina and Corrie. 'You should have seen him when I was giving birth. If it hadn't been for the fact a head was on its way down, he'd have had his head up there. Got in everyone's way, including his own. Then when it started getting really bad, what does he do? He starts cracking jokes! Tell them what you said to the midwife. Go on.'

Dave's face was all innocence.

'Well there's me,' Paula said, 'holding onto his hand for grim death, screaming my head off, and feeling like I'm giving birth to a table, and he *he* can't stand the pain. "God, you've got one hell of a squeeze," he says to me. Then he turns to the midwife and says, "Do you think I'll ever play the piano again?","Oh, I'm sure you will," she tells him. "Funny," he says, "I couldn't before." '

Dave looked so stupidly pleased with himself, that despite the laughter Corrie was hard put not to show how moved she was at how deeply Paula and Dave loved each other. Her own mother and father had been that much in love and she wondered if Edwina was thinking of that now and remembering the times when they had looked down at their new-born baby the way Dave and Paula were looking at theirs.

The introspection was fleeting and with Paula teasing Dave so relentlessly while he sat there beaming with pride, Corrie couldn't resist a few jibes of her own. She and Dave were always scoring points off each other, and today, with the heady combination of champagne and euphoria, they surpassed themselves. In the end they caused so much hilarity on the ward that they managed to attract quite a crowd around the bed.

Finally Edwina and Corrie made their farewells. When they got out onto the street Corrie was still animated, so much so that as they walked towards the bus stop and she chattered on to Edwina about the baby she ended up walking, smack! bang! into a lamp-post. She saw stars.

Edwina caught hold of her arm, but as dazed as Corrie was she could see her mother was trying very hard not to laugh.

'Oh, my God! Was anyone looking?' Corrie gasped. 'Please, tell me no one saw.'

'No one saw,' Edwina assured her, laughing as a grinning news vendor quickly averted his eyes.

'I shouldn't be allowed out,' Corrie wailed. 'Something like this always happens to me. And ow, it bloody well hurts.'

'Come on, I'll treat you to a cup of tea somewhere,' Edwina chuckled.

With no reason to rush home since Auntie Harriet was minding the shop, Corrie was about to agree, when she got a clear look at Edwina's face – just these couple of hours away from the house had taken their toll. But Edwina wouldn't hear of going home straight away.

'It makes a nice change to be in the cut and thrust of a town,' she said cheerfully, looking around her. 'It's been so long since I saw traffic and high buildings, and so many people.' Suddenly she shrieked and her hands flew to her head as a gust of wind nearly took her from her feet. 'My wig!' she cried. 'I nearly lost my wig!'

Laughing, Corrie straightened it, then lifted the scarf from Edwina's neck to tie it around her head. Edwina often made sport of her wig, but other than the doctors Corrie was the only person alive to have seen Edwina without it.

'What a pair we are,' Corrie laughed as she tied the scarf under Edwina's chin. 'Oh God, I don't believe it!' she cried, as a bus swerved dangerously close to them and splashed a puddle right up to their knees. 'Well, that's settled it anyway, straight home now. We can't have you hanging about with wet feet, you'll catch your death of cold.'

All the way home on the bus Corrie made Edwina laugh by bemoaning the fate that seemed intent on fashioning a life of pratfalls and *faux pas* for her, when she was doing her best to be so adult and sophisticated. 'If ever I write my autobiography,' she said, as they alighted from the bus in the village square, 'I shall be compelled to call it "The Confessions of an Eternally Embarrassed Woman." ' And with that they both exploded into laughter as Corrie hit the button of her umbrella and it flew off the end of the stick.

Five minutes later they were in the dimly lit hallway of their cottage, taking off their coats.

'Tell you what,' Corrie said, shrugging her coat back on, 'why don't I pop back up to the square and get us a couple . . .' Her words suddenly dried as she turned to look at her mother. 'Mum!' she cried. 'Mum! What's happening? Mum, are you all right?'

'Yes,' Edwina said faintly, hanging onto the stair rail. 'Yes, just a bit dizzy, that's all.'

Corrie looked at her watch. 'Oh Mum! You should have taken your medication half an hour ago. Come on now, come and sit down, I'll get it for you.'

She led Edwina into the sitting room, then raced upstairs to the bathroom. Her heart was pounding, her mind a vortex of terror. She stood over the wash basin, gripping the edge. She took several deep breaths, let them out slowly and waited. But when the fear finally left her, she was submerged in anger. A deep, violent rage that made her shake all over. That hideous disease! It was always there, waiting to spoil what little fun they had. Like a monstrous child it would never allow itself to be starved of attention. She looked down at the pills in her hands and had to fight the urge to scream. She wanted to hurl them at the window, smash the glass, destroy the bottles. Lash out and hurt . . . Hurt what? There was nothing she could hurt. Nothing she could do. For no reason a sudden image of Dave, holding little Beth in his arms, flashed through her mind, and she squeezed her eyes tightly, not wanting to face again the emotions it stirred in her. But she couldn't deny it. She wanted her father now. She wanted him for herself because she felt so alone and helpless. She wanted him for Edwina because he was the only man Edwina had ever loved . . . They needed him now . . .

Stop it! she told herself vehemently. Just stop! And tearing herself from the encroaching arms of self-pity she ran back down the stairs with her mother's pills.

It was later that evening, after Edwina had taken a nap, and Corrie had been to check on Auntie Hattie at the shop, that Edwina walked into the kitchen and found Corrie in the darkness staring out at the rain.

'Sweetheart?' she said softly.

Corrie turned around. For a while they simply looked at each other and Corrie's heart twisted inside her. Her mother was so soft, so gentle, so ethereal. Then Edwina lifted her arms and Corrie went to her, laying her head on her shoulder.

'There, there,' Edwina soothed as Corrie's tears flowed down her cheeks. 'That's it, let it all out now.'

'Oh, Mum, it's just so awful,' Corrie choked. 'It's so unfair. You're so young, and I love you so much.'

'And I love you too.'

They held one another tightly for a long time, until Corrie said, 'I can't help it, Mum, but I keep thinking of Dave, you know, when he held the baby. I keep thinking of what it was like for you then – I mean, when I was born.'

'Ah, yes,' Edwina sighed, smiling as she stroked Corrie's hair, 'I thought you were thinking about your father at the time.'

'Will you tell me about him?' Corrie sniffed. 'I mean, I know I've heard it before, but . . .'

'Of course, sweetheart. Now come on, it's chilly out here, let's go and sit by the fire.'

Corrie nodded, and forcing a smile as she ripped a piece of kitchen towel from the roll, she said, 'I'm behaving like a great big baby, aren't I? Sorry.'

'You'll always be my baby,' Edwina said, touching her cheek.

'Oh, yuk!' Corrie said, but laughing she pulled her mother back into her arms.

'So,' Edwina said, a few minutes later. 'Would you like me to start with how we met?'

Corrie nodded.

'That far back, mm? OK. Well, I was nineteen and working in one of the *better* dress shops in Brighton. I had a little bedsitter above it that the proprietress rented to me and a bicycle I rode around the town on my days off. I was always hoping, of course, that I would meet someone, make some friends, but I was too shy to go into the coffee bars alone. Then, would you know it, the shop door opened one day and Phillip walked into my life.'

'You've missed out the bit about Great-Granny,' Corrie protested.

'So I have. Well, she had been into the shop the week before to buy a new frock, which had needed altering. Dreadful woman she was, frightened me half to death. Mrs Browne,' Edwina said, affecting a deep resonant tone. 'Mrs Cornelia Browne. Gosh, she was awful, over-bearing, sharp-tongued and turned out to have the kindest heart imaginable. Anyway, she had to return for her dress, and when she did, her grandson came with her.' Edwina was watching Corrie's face closely. Then smiling and knowing that this next was one of the bits Corrie had always loved to hear as a teenager, she said, 'The bell over the door rang, I looked up and there he was. It was love at first sight.'

Grimacing, Corrie imitated the playing of a violin.

'Of course neither of us admitted to it straight away,' Edwina chuckled, 'it took about a week for Phillip to pluck up the courage to tell me, and then of course I told him I felt the same way. After that we spent all our free time together, mostly in my bedsit, talking and listening to music. One of our favourite songs, as I recall, was "Dedicated to the One I love", by the Mamas and Papas. It was the first record I ever bought. We used to sing it at the tops of our voices.' She paused for a moment, smiling, then went on. 'We had a lot of fun then, in those first few weeks, but, well, it was a difficult time too. You see he very much wanted to make love to me, and I wanted him to, but because I was still a virgin he wouldn't.'

Corrie looked up. 'You never told me that before.'

'You weren't twenty-six before.'

'So did you? In the end?'

Edwina shook her head. 'No. Not until we were married. But as you know, we married within three months of meeting each other. We went to see Cornelia first. Since I didn't have a family and Phillip only had his grandmother . . . Well, he was very fond of the old lady and wanted her blessing. She was horrified. Left us in no doubt as to her opinion on the matter. A shop assistant as a wife for her precious university educated grandson! Unthinkable! But as soon as she'd had her say, a teasing light leapt to her eyes, and we married the following week.

'We went to Spain for our honeymoon. I'd never been on a plane before, it was so exciting. We stayed in an awful hotel, building works going on all around us, but we didn't really notice. Your father, Phillip, he was so gentle, he treated me . . .' she laughed, 'it was as though he thought I would break. He had quite a shock I can tell you when I, a virgin, started to get adventurous. I made him do things I don't think he'd ever done before. But it was such fun finding out together. And once he realized he wasn't in any danger of hurting me . . . Well, I'll spare you the details – suffice it to say we were never long out of the bedroom.

'Anyway, just a week after we came back from our honeymoon Cornelia died. It was a shock for us both, Phillip most of all, naturally. And an even bigger shock was the amount of money she had left to Phillip. With it we bought a tiny flat just off the King's Road in London. It was the place to be then, in the late sixties, probably still is. Then, two months after we moved in I discovered I was pregnant.

I was horrified. Phillip was delighted. By then he had a job in a City bank and was earning quite good money, so we could afford a family, he insisted. And once I realized how happy he was I was happy too. And eight months later the proudest moment of his life occurred when the midwife handed him his baby daughter.'

Corrie pulled a face.

'Ten days later Phillip collected us, you and me, from the hospital, and to my amazement, when we got back to the flat there was a For Sale notice outside. "Yes," Phillip said, "we're moving. We're going to buy a palace for our princess!" '

Corrie moved forward and took her mother's hands as swallowing hard Edwina looked down at the handkerchief she was wringing in her lap.

'It's all right, you don't have to go on,' Corrie said gently.

Edwina shook her head. 'As you know,' she continued, 'we never did get the "palace". One evening, while returning home from work, Phillip stepped out in front of a car and was killed instantly. You were three months old.'

Corrie looked at her mother, desperately regretting having forced her back into the past. Over twenty-four years Edwina's pain and loss were still very much with her.

'Phillip's lawyer took over from there,' Edwina said, huskily. 'He sold the flat – I couldn't live there without him, the memories, you know . . .'

Yes, Corrie knew. The only memory her mother had now was one photograph of the wedding, a photograph which sat beside Edwina's bed, and from which Corrie knew she resembled her father much more than she did her mother.

'So we, you and I, came here to Amberside,' Edwina said, 'and though I have been happy here, I often wonder whether, for your sake, it might not have been better had we stayed in London.'

'I've been happy here too,' Corrie assured her.

'But you're not now, sweetheart. And I want to see you happy, as happy and as in love as your father and I were.'

Later that night, after Edwina had gone to bed, Corrie called up Kevin Foreman, the local butcher's son. Kevin had been keen on her since they were in school, and though he didn't exactly make her heart pound with desire she had always quite liked him. She had been out on dates with him before, he really could be quite good company sometimes, and now, perhaps, if she worked on it, she could more than like him.

'Got anything special you want to do?' he asked, when she told him why she was calling.

Corrie thought for a moment, trying not to be irritated that she always had to make the decisions. Oh, to be swept off into the night; to be wined and dined, danced and adored, seduced into the arms of untold passions and pleasures. 'How about the cinema?' she suggested, remembering the South Bank show she'd seen the week before on the Hollywood film director, Cristos Bennati. She and Paula were avid followers of showbiz gossip and Corrie wouldn't mind having a closer look at the woman Bennati was supposed to be having an affair with. 'We can go to see that new film with Angelique Warne in,' she said.

'Just so as long as it's not slushy.'

'It's a Bennati film,' Corrie said tightly.

'Oh, what the guy who made *Stranger*? That was a good movie. Yeah, let's go see his new one then. I'll pick you up around six thirty tomorrow night.'

Corrie was momentarily impressed that Kevin had heard of Bennati, but then felt she was doing him a disservice since Bennati's name and reputation were as well known as Scorcese's or Coppola's.

The following evening, as Kevin drove them into town in his father's Volvo, Corrie kept stealing quick glances at him from the corner of her eye. She was both surprised, and impressed, that he appeared to have made a special effort to look good for her. She hadn't seen that leather jacket before, it padded out his meagre shoulders rather cleverly, she thought. And those baggy trousers disguised his skinny legs well. At six foot three he towered over Corrie, which was one of the things she liked best about him, since at five foot nine she was taller than most of the boys she had been to school with. Shame Kevin wasn't better looking, though tonight his thin, normally pallid face, seemed to have a little more colour than usual and he'd obviously splashed his dimpled chin liberally with Eau Savage before leaving home. Smiling to herself Corrie wondered how long he had stood in front of the mirror combing the immaculate tawny hair he was so proud of, before pronouncing himself 'ready for the kill.'

For her part Corrie had made a bit of an effort too, having coiled her abundant hair, which she normally wore loose, into a French plait, and circled her eyes with a khol pencil. A few dabs of powder were concealing the freckles on her nose, but the lipstick she'd wiped off before leaving, she'd never been too fond of the stuff, perhaps she just didn't buy the right colours. Her navy, knee-length shorts and thick tights were sensible, but quite trendy too, she thought, though she already regretted not wearing a sweater over her burgundy and navy striped shirt since it was 'bloody freezing,' as she remarked to Kevin when they were getting out of the car.

'Yeah, real brass monkey weather,' he said, pocketing the car keys and walking round the car to join her. She looked up at him, waited a moment or two for something a little more erudite, perhaps even a compliment, but as neither was forthcoming, she flashed him a quick smile, pulled her scarf up around her ears, and they walked off towards the cinema. Kevin was chuntering on about some hilarious occurrence down at the abattoir earlier in the week, to which Corrie faked rapt attention while allowing her mind to wander. The mislaying of a pig's intestines didn't do much for her sense of romance, and though she hadn't decided exactly what was going to happen between her and Kevin once the film was over she didn't want her hopes of something amorous being destroyed by his butcher talk. A self-generated tingle of anticipation suddenly warmed her, and she gave his arm a squeeze.

'Popcorn?' he said, after he'd paid for the tickets and hesitated over taking Corrie's money.

Corrie shrugged. 'Why not?'

He bought her a giant-sized carton, himself a choc-ice, then they settled down to watch the film.

Almost from the start Corrie's concentration was poor. She'd seen Angelique Warne in a couple of films before this one, and had always thought that everyone made too much of her. But seeing her tonight, up there on the screen in glorious Technicolor, all Corrie could think of was how wonderful it must be to look like her, to have a lover like Cristos Bennati, and live in a Bel Air mansion – which was where she presumed Angelique Warne lived. What it must be like to be so successful, so adored by the public and have a man like Cristos Bennati too, Corrie was thinking to herself, when Kevin slipped an arm around her, and began nuzzling her ear. She put her head back, closed her eyes and pretended that it was Bennati, or de Niro, or Redford, sitting beside her. After a while she became so lost in her fantasy that she gave a severe start when Kevin suddenly took out his handkerchief and trumpeted into it.

Corrie turned away, rolling her eyes, but grinning all the same at the crude return to reality. Then, stuffing his handkerchief back in his pocket Kevin put his arm around her again and made to take up where he'd left off. Corrie sat straighter in her seat and whispered for him to watch the film.

On the way home, having overcome his fit of pique at being rebuffed, Kevin became surprisingly articulate with a sudden rush of compliments. Didn't she know that she, Corrie, was sexier even than Angelique Warne? 'Her tits are so small it'd be like feeling up yourself,' he said. 'Your figure could knock spots off hers, do you know that?'

'Yes, but it's such a bore having to fight off so many men all the time,' Corrie complained, running a finger over her eyebrows and pouting her lips. Inside she was laughing. She knew only too well what Kevin was leading up to – and this was his way of putting her in the mood.

After a while he fell silent and when Corrie glanced at him and saw his glum face she felt instantly contrite. He'd guessed she wasn't taken in by his compliments and was now hurt and embarrassed that she was teasing him. She was sorry and wanted in some way to make amends. What she'd like even more was to fall for him, to discover that he was all she wanted in a man – in life.

A few minutes later he stopped the Volvo in the same secluded spot they always stopped at after their visits to the cinema, and then began their ritual necking and fumbling.

Despite the cold it was a clear night, and catching a glimpse of Kevin's face Corrie found herself hoping that the moonlight wasn't as cruel on her as it was on poor Kevin's ghostly pallor. But his next comment, as predictable as all the others so far, told her it wasn't her face he was looking at.

'You got the most fantastic tits, Corrie, do you know that?' he said, wrestling the D cup of her reinforced cross-your-heart up over her left breast. Not for her a lacy scrap of nothing, she was far too well endowed for such fripperies.

Corrie let him fondle her a while, idly wondering whether she should replace some of the spring stock in the shop with more winter stuff since it had turned so cold again, when she surprised herself by giving a moan of genuine pleasure as Kevin lowered his mouth to her nipple. Try to concentrate, she chided herself. It wasn't difficult, not now, since the sensations Kevin was evoking were so pleasurable that she found herself freeing her other breast herself. And, as Kevin's hand closed over it, she felt the unmistakable warmth of lust starting to surge through her.

'Oh, Corrie,' he groaned savagely, his voice muffled somewhere in her cleavage. 'Corrie, they're so fantastic. They're so big and soft, and . . . Shit! Just looking at them I could come. Let me take my cock out,' he said, pressing her hand to his groin. 'Just for a few minutes.'

Corrie could feel his erection straining beneath his trousers and pushed her hand hard against it.

Kevin choked. 'Fuck me!' he cried. 'Let me take it out, Corrie. Please!' He was already fumbling with his zip. 'Oh Corrie, your tits, your great big tits. A man could . . . Ooooh!' he groaned, as he pulled his penis free. Quickly he caught Corrie's hand, and as she wrapped her fingers around it he seemed to go wild. 'Oh yes,' he groaned, moving his hand back and forth over hers. 'Yes, yes, yes. Squeeze it, Corrie, go on, squeeze it hard. Wank me. Oh yes.' He let her hand go, scooped up her breasts and pushed his tongue deep into her mouth. 'Let me put it in you,' he begged. 'Just a little way. Just for a minute.'

He asked every time if he could put it in her, and every time Corrie said no. But now, not giving herself any time to think, she said, 'Have you got any condoms?'

Kevin pulled away from her and stared at her in disbelief. 'Do you mean . . . ?' he gasped. 'Are you saying . . . ?' And then he started to tremble. 'Oh, shit, Corrie, I don't believe it. Yes, I got plenty of johnnies. They're here.' He lifted his hips to delve into his back pocket then swore violently as he squashed his penis against the steering wheel.

Corrie sucked in her cheeks so he wouldn't see her laughing. She still wasn't too sure she really wanted to do this, but . . . what the hell? It had been so long since she'd had sex and maybe this would form a bond between her and Kevin. After all, that was the whole point of tonight, wasn't it?

'Shall we get in the back?' he said, struggling with the wrapping on his condoms.

'I think we'd better.'

They both stepped out into the biting night air. A low mist drifted across the countryside and the wind whined gently through the nearby wood.

'God, it's fucking freezing out here,' Kevin shivered, pushing his trousers down to his knees. He pulled open the back door, plonked his bare bottom on the seat then proceeded to roll on his condom, his teeth chattering.

Grimacing, Corrie slid into the back seat, and watched as Kevin swung his legs into the car and slammed the door. 'Take your knickers off then,' he said.

For a moment or two Corrie simply stared at him, then shrugging she started to unfasten her shorts.

'No! No!'

'What's the matter?' Corrie looked at him, bewildered.

'I want to pull your knickers down myself,' he said, hardly able to speak his breath was so laboured. 'Let me pull them down.'

Corrie parted her hands, as if to say, be my guest, then she raised her hips as he started to tug.

It was a farce. His thumb got twisted up in the elastic of her knickers, he slipped off the seat and cracked his knee on the floor, then he couldn't get up because his trousers were restricting his movements. Corrie's arm was jammed painfully against the door, and she really didn't know whether she wanted to laugh or cry.

Eventually he managed to get himself back on the seat, and to her surprise she saw that his erection had lost none of its ardour. By now she was wearing only her raincoat and blouse, which were both open, and her bra which was clamped tightly over the top of her breasts.

'Lie down,' he said, raising himself up to make room for her.

Corrie wriggled beneath him, holding her raincoat together as she spread her legs either side of him.

'That's it,' he said, somehow twisting himself onto his knees between her legs. 'Are you ready?'

'Well, I guess so,' Corrie mumbled.

He leaned forward, resting his hands either side of her head. Then he lowered his hips and started to stab about.

'That's my navel,' Corrie told him.

'I know it's your bloody navel,' he said tightly, 'you'll have to move up a bit.'

'I can't. There's no room.'

'Oh God! Well, I'll just have to open the door.'

'Are you mad? It's freezing out there.'

'Well I can't get it in like this, can I?' he barked, and reaching behind him he threw open the door.

Surely this was happening to someone else, it couldn't be her lying here on the back seat of a Volvo, gales of icy air blowing around her most intimate places, with a man whose trousers were at half mast and whose technique regarding foreplay . . .

'Ooooh!' she grunted, as Kevin collapsed onto her.

'Sorry,' he mumbled.

Suddenly Corrie could feel herself brinking on hysteria. This was just too absurd to be true. But even more absurd were Kevin's legs, now jutting out of the door, his trousers dangling about his ankles. Come to that her own didn't look too dignified, one hooked up over the front seat, the other jammed up against the back. Then suddenly everything went black as Kevin moved himself forward. His chest was covering her face and as he shoved his hand between their bodies she tried to gulp for air.

'You'll have to put it in for me,' he muttered.

'I can't breathe,' Corrie cried.

'What? Oh, sorry,' he said, lifting himself up on his arms.

With more fumbling, twisting of hips and plenty of swearing, Corrie eventually managed to guide him into her.

'Phaaaw! In he goes,' he virtually sang, as he reached full penetration. Then he started lunging in and out of her. 'Oh this is good! This is gooood!'

Corrie looked up at him, then turned away quickly as he gave a particularly vigorous thrust and bashed his head against the window. But, after a while, they managed to get a rhythm going, and with Kevin huffing and puffing away on top of her, despite the fact that she was freezing, Corrie started to throw herself into it, making all the noises she had heard Angelique Warne make in the film.

'Baby, you're something else,' Kevin cried, holding himself up on one hand while with the other he lifted up his shirt and jumper. 'I gotta feel your tits up against me,' he said, lowering himself onto her. Then, 'Oh, yeah, yeah, yeah!' And he started to pump away again, grunting and groaning and rubbing his chest over hers. Then to Corrie's alarm he started to squeal and writhe so madly that she thought some animal had come out of the night and was attacking his bum.

'I'm gonna come! I'm gonna come!' he wheezed, then swearing viciously through his teeth, he gave a series of rapid jerks and fell panting on top of her.

It was a good five minutes before he managed to regain his breath, during which Corrie all but suffocated. At last he rolled off her and sat awkwardly across her legs. Then followed the nasty business of disposing of the condom, which, pinned to the seat as she was, Corrie was compelled to watch.

They drove home in virtual silence. Corrie wasn't at all sure how she felt. Stunned, that was for sure, and probably appalled. However, she could hardly wait to tell Paula. Paula would just roar with laughter, which Corrie felt apt to do herself right now. But in truth, for a while there, when the rhythm was good, it hadn't been so bad. And in a bed it would surely be better. Perhaps they should give it a go.

When they arrived back at the village Kevin pulled up outside the cottage, but didn't, Corrie noticed immediately, turn off the engine. 'It was a great night,' he said, turning to look at her. 'We'll have to do it again some time.'

'Would you like to come in for a coffee?' Corrie offered.

'No. Better not. Not with your mum being ill, like.'

'It's not catching.'

He made a noise that sounded vaguely like a laugh. 'Well, give us a ring if you fancy a repeat performance,' he said. 'Next time I'll bring the van. A joke,' he added when he saw Corrie's face.

For some reason his tongue felt revoltingly dry when he put it in her mouth this time, and Corrie pulled away.

'I don't suppose you'd let us have another feel of those tits before you go in, would you?' he said, making a grab for them.

'I don't think so,' Corrie said, pulling her coat together and opening the door.

'Suit yourself,' he shrugged as she got out. Then he called after her. 'Don't forget, just give me a ring if you fancy doing it again. Any time.'

The door slammed on his last word, and before Corrie even reached the gate he was reversing back up to the square.

Heaving a deep sigh she took out her key and inserted it in the lock. But instead of turning it, she let her head fall forward against the door. 'What a fool,' she murmured to herself. 'What a bloody fool I am.'

'Yes, I think I would agree with that,' her mother said, some ten minutes later when Corrie told her what had happened. Edwina had already retired for the night, and Corrie was sitting on the bed, hugging her knees to her chest. 'What in heaven's name got into you?' Edwina went on. 'It'll be all over the village by tomorrow night. I didn't bring you up to behave like that, my girl, and . . . No, you come back here, I haven't finished with you yet. Corrie! Come back here now!'

Corrie turned around and looked at her mother.

'I hope you took precautions,' Edwina snapped.

Corrie winced at the image of Kevin grinning as he draped his used condom over a bush. 'Yes, we took precautions,' she sighed. Then, 'Oh Mum, I only told you because I thought it would make you laugh. Now you're having a go at me. But you won't make me feel any worse than I already do I can promise you that.' She shuddered. 'God, he's so gross. "In he goes," ' she mimicked.

A light flickered deep in Edwina's eyes, and Corrie started to grin.

'I'm not laughing,' Edwina said, the bubble in her voice belying her words.

'Yes you are.'

Edwina was biting her lips. 'I'm really very angry with you, young lady.'

'Love you, Mum.'

'Don't try getting around me that way.' She slapped her hand against the bed. 'Kevin Foreman! Of all the uncouth . . . He's not the boy for you, and you know it. So what on earth were you trying to prove?'

Corrie simply looked at her.

'Yes, well I guess I know the answer to that,' Edwina sighed. 'Oh Corrie! What about your self-respect? How could you have demeaned yourself like that?'

'You already said, you know the answer to that,' Corrie said tightly.

'Don't take that attitude with me,' Edwina said. 'You behaved like a common little slut . . .'

'All right, I did. But what am I supposed to do, stay here in this Godforsaken place all on my own, never having anyone to love or to love me . . .'

'Doing what you did is no answer,' Edwina interrupted. 'And self-pity I won't tolerate. I've told you a hundred times to get out there and find a life of your own. Do what you want to do . . .'

'And leave you here to die on your own. How can I do that? And don't you dare to call me a slut again, because it's your fault. It's all your fault. I'd have a life of my own if it weren't for you. But I'm trapped. I'm stuck here with the likes of Kevin Foreman, and I was trying to make something of it. Trying to make a go of what little I do have. I wanted you to see me happy and settled. I thought it would make you happy. And now you've got the bloody nerve to call me a slut. Well perhaps I am, but it's you who's made me one. How do you think I felt, sacrificing myself to a pig like that?'

Edwina was out of bed, reaching for her daughter.

'No! Don't touch me!' Corrie cried. 'I don't want you near me. I just want you to die. I want you to get this over with because I can't stand any more.'

She ran sobbing from the room and Edwina, her face ashen-white and her whole body trembling, stood in the middle of her room trying to decide what she should do. In the end, though she ached to go to Corrie, to hold her and try to soothe her pain, she decided to leave her. Smothering her now was not the answer.

Late the following morning Ted Braithwaite, the solicitor who lived in one of the larger houses in the village, strode quickly through the rain, past Edwina's dress shop, around the war memorial at the centre of the square and down the little side street to Edwina's cottage. Edwina was waiting at the door, her face showing all the anguish he had heard on the phone, but when she saw him relief softened her expression, and as she smiled, for a fleeting moment, he was reminded of the young girl she had once been.

'OK, Eddie,' he said, using his own special name for her, 'what's all this about?'

'Come inside,' she said, taking his coat and giving him

a big hug. 'The kettle's just boiled and I've got some of your favourite almond cake. Corrie's at the shop so we won't be disturbed.'

In fact Corrie had gone off early that morning, before Edwina was up. Edwina knew that she'd be feeling terrible about all she'd said the night before, that it was only pride, and the fear she would break down again that was making her avoid her mother now, but Edwina would go over to the shop later to deal with that. First she needed to speak to Ted.

Ted was nearing seventy. He was a portly man with sparse grey hair and the kindest blue eyes Edwina had ever seen. It was his eyes that had first drawn her to him, all those years ago, when she'd first come to Amberside; that had given her the courage to take him into her confidence – though of course he'd known most of it already.

He still had his practice in Ipswich, though he rarely went in more than three times a week now, leaving the bulk of his work to his younger partners. 'Time to take life easy,' he would often be heard to say as he pottered about his garden, or, as often as he could, fussed over Edwina and Corrie. He and his wife Hattie looked upon Edwina as the daughter they had never had, and knowing that she was going to die so young was almost as hard on them as it was on Corrie. However, Ted rarely showed his emotions where Edwina's illness was concerned, at least not to Edwina, she had enough to cope with trying to ease the burden for herself and Corrie.

Now, as he sat back in the comfy chair and sipped his tea, he listened in silence to what Edwina had to say. Outside the rain grew harder and thunder rumbled through the heavens. The room was dark, and the fire crackled lazily in the hearth. Once in a while, as Edwina paused, he became aware of the grandfather clock, ticking loudly in the corner. The cake Edwina had placed in front of him went untouched, a constricting knot of grief was tightening his throat.

It was past midday by the time Edwina had finished, and as she looked up she seemed surprised at the tears in Ted's eyes. She smiled.

'Well,' he said, clearing his throat as he leaned forward to replace his cup on the coffee table, 'I can't say I'm surprised. Hattie and I have always thought you might ask me to do this one day. But I have to tell you Eddie, that I had hoped that . . .'

'I know,' Edwina interrupted. 'I know what you're going to say, but I can't do it, Ted. I can't tell her. Which is why I'm asking you. But only after, you understand that, don't you?'

'I don't know that I do,' he said, removing his wire spectacles and rubbing his eyes. 'I'm not saying I won't do it, but I do think you should tell her yourself.'

'No!' Edwina snapped.

It had been some time since Ted had seen her spirit, that same spirit that lived so recklessly in Corrie, but there it was now, and despite what she was asking him to do, it cheered him to see it.

'I know it's selfish of me,' she went on, 'but there it is. Corrie will understand.'

'I'm not so sure,' Ted said, picking up the fire guard and rattling more coal onto the fire. 'You've never had any secrets from one another, apart from this, I mean. You should tell her yourself. You should have told her a long time ago.'

'Perhaps you're right,' Edwina said. The defiance was still there in her eyes as she stood up. 'But what if I had? Tell me that! What if I'd told her the truth when she was a child, what then? I'll tell you what. I would have lost her. She's all I have Ted. She's all I have, and that's why she will understand.'

Ted looked across the room to the sideboard where there

were any number of pictures of Corrie in silver frames.
There were some of Edwina too, and of Paula. There was
even one there of him and Hattie. Her only wedding photograph, he knew, was upstairs beside the bed.

'I know you think I've ruined her life,' Edwina said
savagely. 'I know what . . .'

'I don't think anything of the sort,' Ted barked. 'You've
been . . .'

'I've been selfish. I came here to Amberside when I
should have stayed in London. She'd have had a life in
London. That's what she's always wanted, what she still
wants. I should have stayed there. After Phillip . . . I should
have stayed. But I didn't, and you know why I didn't. You
can sit in judgement on me all you like, Ted, but for God's
sake promise me you'll help her. When I'm gone. Be there
for her.'

'Edwina,' he said deliberately. 'You don't have to ask
that, we'll always be there for her. I'd give my life for that
girl, and you know it. I'd give my life for you. God, that I
could give my life for you.'

Edwina lowered her head at the note of defeat in his
voice. 'I'm sorry,' she whispered. 'I never wanted to take
advantage of the way you and Hattie feel about Corrie and
me, and if you feel you can't do it, that you don't want to
tell her . . . Well, I've written her a letter. It's all there . . .
It's just that, coming from you, with you there to . . .'

'Come here,' Ted said, holding out his hand. Edwina
went to him and taking her hand he held it between his
own. 'I'll do as you ask,' he said softly. 'But just tell me
why I can't tell her before you die.'

'Because I'm a coward. And . . .' She looked sadly into
his face, 'because I have my dreams too. Just like Corrie.
I want to keep them, Ted. Corrie will understand that.'

'I daresay she will,' he sighed. 'But you're not making
this easy on her.'

Suddenly Edwina was angry again, but with herself, Ted

knew that. 'None of this is easy for any of us,' she cried. 'I've devoted my life to her, Ted. What more could I have done?'

'No more.'

For a moment or two she looked into his eyes, her own glittering a challenge, waiting for his accusations. He merely looked back, his gentle blue eyes crinkled at the corners in a fatherly smile. Finally, laughing at herself, Edwina lifted his hand to her face and kissed it. 'Would you like some more tea?' she said.

'Yes, why not?'

She picked up the tray and carried it into the kitchen.

'I'd like to discuss this with Hattie,' he said, following her out.

Edwina nodded. 'Of course.'

'When would you like me to tell Corrie? I mean, how soon after?'

Edwina turned on the tap and waited for the pilot light to ignite the boiler so she could rinse out the tea cups. 'When you tell her about the money,' she said. 'You'll have to tell her then.'

Ted walked over to the back door and leaned against it so he could see Edwina's face. 'Is there something you're not telling me?' he asked carefully.

She looked at him in surprise.

'Has the doctor told you? Has he said when?'

Edwina shook her head.

Ted sighed. 'I thought maybe that was why you had called me over now.'

'Oh, I see,' Edwina said with a dry laugh. 'No. It's not that. Though God knows I wish it were. It would be so much easier if I could die now. It would set Corrie free. At last she . . .'

'No! Don't ever say that! Never! Do you hear me?'

Both Edwina and Ted spun round to find Corrie standing at the door.

— 37 —

'Corrie!' Edwina gasped.

'Don't ever let me hear you talk like that again,' Corrie raged. 'I didn't mean what I said last night, you know I didn't. I love you more than anyone else in the world. And you're not going to die. You're not! I'm not going to let you.'

She hugged her mother fiercely and Ted looked on. Then a cold feeling rose from the pit of his stomach as he caught Edwina's eye. It was too late. Edwina would die soon, it was there in her eyes.

'No, she won't kill herself,' he said later to Hattie. 'At least not in the way you're thinking. But she's willing herself to die, my love, and it won't be long now. It won't be long at all.'

– 3 –

Within a month the weather had changed completely. It was still early March, yet the sun was strong enough to make it feel like early summer. When Corrie had crossed the square that morning she had listened to the birds singing, and had felt, as she always did at the outset of spring, a combined sadness and happiness at the passing of time. The church bells had been ringing then, though no one, when she asked, knew why, since there was no wedding that day. She'd noticed that only the old ladies were wearing their coats, and Paul Smith, the local builder's son, had the roof down on his second-hand Golf. Now, much later in the morning, the Salvation Army band was playing beside the war memorial, and Fred Pinker had put two tables and chairs outside his café-cum-grocery. Paula was in the shop with Corrie. They were sipping the coffee Paula had brought over from Fred's and reading the newspaper lying on the counter between them. At that moment they were engrossed in the story of the prostitute murders taking place in London. The killer had now claimed his fourth victim, and though there were no actual details of what he did to them their imaginations had no trouble filling in the gaps.

'And you want to live in London?' Paula shivered.

'That's not all that happens in London,' Corrie retorted. 'And desperate as I am to become a high-flying career woman, being a prostitute wasn't quite what I had in mind.'

'The trouble is you don't know what you do have in mind,' Paula told her.

'I know,' Corrie said, and turned over the page to carry on reading as Paula picked up the baby and put her to the breast.

'I wouldn't mind working in films,' Corrie said after a while.

Paula was amazed. 'You mean as an actress?'

'What, and end up like her?' Corrie shuddered. 'No thanks.'

'Like who?'

'Angelique Warne.'

'Is there more about her then?' Paula asked, leaning towards the paper. The story of Angelique Warne's suicide was now a couple of weeks old, but was still gripping the public, both sides of the Atlantic since it was almost as rife with rumour and speculation as the death of Monroe. There were pictures of the senators she had 'known' in that morning's paper, and above the picture of Cristos Bennati was the headline, 'Did she jump, or was she pushed?'

'I'd freeze my bum off in the back seat of a car for him any day,' Corrie sighed, wistfully.

'Just so long as he doesn't push you out of the window after,' Paula remarked.

'You don't really think he pushed her, do you?'

Paula shrugged, 'Who knows?' She winced as Beth bit

hard on her nipple. 'So you reckon you'd like to work in films do you?'

'Why not?'

'What, over there in America?'

Corrie thought about that for a minute, then turned up her nose. 'Not in America, no. The place is full of nutters and psychos.'

'What about London?' Paula interrupted, laughing. 'You've just been reading about what's going on there.'

'True. But they've got all those dreadful women in America too. You know, with their Hollywood legs and silicone boobs, I could never compete. Besides, from all you read about them they're about as skilled at being real people as Kevin Foreman is at foreplay. So, no, I've no desire to go to America. London would do me just fine, thank you.'

She turned back to the story on Angelique Warne.

'Speaking of Kevin,' Paula said, trying to arrange Beth a little more comfortably, 'I saw Linda Farrow in Safeway's earlier. Did you know she was going out with Kevin?'

Corrie shook her head. She was looking at the picture of Bennati again. 'Good luck to her, is all I can say,' she mumbled.

'She told me they're getting engaged next month.' Paula waited for a reaction from Corrie.

'Bit quick, isn't it?' Corrie remarked, still not paying much attention.

'Well apparently she's been going out with him for ages, they just haven't told anyone until now. She didn't want Jerry to find out, you know what he's like. He beat Kevin up before, remember, when we were at the disco in the village hall? That was just for looking at Linda. Anyway, it seems like Jerry's got himself someone else now, someone he met in Benidorm last summer.'

'Just a minute,' Corrie said, looking up at last. 'Are you

telling me that Kevin Foreman was going out with Linda Farrow when he and I . . . ?'

Paula nodded.

'The bastard! The filthy, lying cheat . . . To think that that revolting goose-pimpled little wart had the gall to tell me to give him a call if I ever fancied doing it again. Anyone would think he was the superstud of the century. Ugh! He makes me want to vomit. Those spindly legs and concave chest. And all the time he's been sticking it up Linda Farrow. Look after the shop for me will you, I'm going over there to put his willie through the mincer.'

Laughing, Paula handed her the baby and tucked herself back into her bra. 'Sorry, I've got to go,' she said. 'It's Saturday and Ipswich are playing at home.'

Corrie grinned, knowing all too well the relevance of Saturday afternoons and Ipswich's home games to Paula. While her Dad was at the match and her mother was out shopping, Paula and Dave would have the house to themselves.

When Paula left Corrie retrieved the three outsize dresses Mrs Cunliffe had left in the changing room earlier and put them back on the rack. Then, glancing at the photograph of Cristos Bennati again, she muttered to herself, 'I'll bet he did push her. He's a man. All men are bastards.' Closing the paper and tossing it in the bin she went into the office at the back of the shop to wrestle with the new computer she'd bought a few days before to do the paperwork on. The damned thing was driving her insane, but what a sense of triumph when she got it to do something she wanted it to. 'Oh, the little highs of life,' she said chirpily, making herself laugh.

After a while the bell rang and she went back into the shop to find a woman who, given her appearance, and the chauffeur outside, could only be from one of the big houses nearby. Corrie hid her surprise well, but immediately felt shabby and parochial beside this elegant woman even though she must have been twice Corrie's age. To her unutterable disgust Corrie heard herself putting on a voice that made her sound like a prize idiot, and unable to stop herself she began treating the woman as though she were some kind of royalty.

The woman was there because a zip on a dress she'd bought in London, which she wanted to wear that night to the Denbys' ball had broken. Could Corrie fix it?

'Of course,' Corrie answered, after she'd given a sublime rendition of orphan Annie in admiring the dress. 'Well, actually my mother can. If I did it I'd be sure to leave a pin in somewhere, and the last thing we want is you getting a prick in the bum.' She looked at the woman aghast, unable to believe what she'd just said. '*Pin* in your bum,' she said quickly.

The woman laughed uncomfortably, and said she'd send the Denbys' chauffeur back to the shop around six that evening. Corrie walked her to the door, held it open for her, refrained from bowing, then watched through the window as the chauffeur helped the woman into the limousine. As they drove away Corrie, despite wanting to groan with undying embarrassment, was trying very hard not to laugh.

Half an hour later Auntie Hattie came in to mind the shop while Corrie went home for her lunch, taking the dress with her. When she arrived back at the cottage it was to find Doctor Sands just leaving.

'How is she?' Corrie asked.

The doctor smiled and patted her hand. 'A little better today, I think.'

Corrie knew he was being kind, but after stopping off in the kitchen and checking on the delicious aroma coming from the stove, she went outside to find her mother in the garden tidying up her rose bushes. She saw straight away that Edwina had a good deal more colour than usual in her cheeks and since Edwina hadn't heard her come in, she watched her curiously for a moment. Yes, there was no doubt about it, she did look better, and there was a smile on Edwina's face that Corrie felt reflecting on her own.

'You look wonderful,' Corrie told her.

Edwina looked up in surprise. 'Thank you,' she said.

'So, what's happened?'

'Happened? Nothing's happened. Except the sun is shining and I love my daughter more than anyone else in the world.'

Corrie pulled a face. 'God, you're slushy sometimes. Still I have to tell you it's a relief to know that's all it is. For one minute there I thought you'd been bouncing about the bedroom with Doctor Sands.'

Edwina laughed. She really did seem happy today.

Corrie handed her the bag with the dress in then went to put the kettle on. When she came out again Edwina's gardening gloves were lying on the table and she was holding up the dress admiringly.

'This isn't one of ours,' she said.

Corrie explained whose it was, then as she went back inside to make the tea she added. 'She wants it for a ball tonight at the Denbys'. The chauffeur's coming back for it, if you please.' Since her mother was standing quite near the door she kept up her chatter as she made the tea. 'You should have heard me in the shop with this woman,' she said. 'God, it was disgusting. There I was fawning around her like Uriah Heep, then you'll never guess what I said . . .' She was laughing away as she told her mother about her *faux pas*, by which time the tea was made and she carried it out into the garden. One look at her mother's face and the laughter died on her lips.

Corrie rushed to her side and asked what was wrong. Edwina said it was nothing, but Corrie was insistent. 'You're so pale all of a sudden.'

Edwina looked into Corrie's eyes and for a moment

seemed about to tell her something, but then she shook her head and turned back to the dress.

'Are you in pain, Mum?' Corrie asked.

'Not now, sweetheart. It's passed. Now go on telling me about the lady in the shop . . .'

At six o'clock the chauffeur returned for the dress, and Corrie, who was waiting impatiently by the door, handed it over and immediately locked up the shop. She all but ran back across the square, trying all the time to suppress the horrible foreboding that was threatening to explode into panic. She didn't want to admit it, even to herself, but she'd heard how sometimes people with cancer seemed better in the days before they died.

A week later Edwina was in bed. Corrie and Paula had spent the evening in her room with her, but Edwina was tired so Paula had left early. Around ten Corrie went in to wish her mother good night.

Edwina held out her hand and Corrie took it.

'Would you like me to read to you for a while?' Corrie asked.

'Mm, yes. Why not?' Edwina said. 'But in case I fall asleep I'll say good night now, sweetheart. And God bless.'

Corrie started to read, but Edwina fell asleep very soon. It was in the early hours of the morning, with Corrie still sitting beside the bed, that Edwina died.

– 4 –

It was a week after Edwina's funeral that Ted Braithwaite asked Corrie to come and see him. She'd been expecting the call and was surprised Ted had waited this long. For her part she could have waited a lot longer.

Since Edwina's death she had been coping with each day as it came. She never allowed herself to think beyond what she was doing at any given moment; she wouldn't allow herself to cry for more than a few minutes at a time; neither would she permit herself to be drawn into the vacuum of overwhelming senselessness that constantly threatened to engulf her. She made tea for the seemingly never-ending stream of visitors, comforted Paula and Auntie Hattie, who were as distressed, she knew, by her remoteness as they were by Edwina's death, and listened patiently, silently, to Reverend Fox's words of comfort.

The truth was that Corrie, even though she had known for a long time that her mother was going to die, was, now that it had finally happened, so devastated, so paralysed by shock and torn apart with grief that she didn't dare even to attempt to fathom the depth of her loss for fear she would drown in it.

She never minded talking about Edwina though, but only did so with Paula or Auntie Hattie, sharing her memories with them and more often than not laughing at some little thing she remembered that had been so characteristic of her mother. She pored over old photographs, giving many of them away to those who had loved Edwina, but keeping the special ones for herself. At night she would lie alone in the house wondering if her mother was happy now. She wondered too if Edwina could see her, could hear her speaking to her. She liked to think she could.

Edwina's clothes were already packed, and would soon be taken to the charity shop; her medicine cabinet had been cleared and the detestable wigs and breast pads disposed of. So it wasn't as though Corrie was refusing to accept that Edwina had gone, it was simply that she was too calm, too self-possessed, and altogether too brave, for either Hattie or Paula to rest easy.

But now Corrie had to face perhaps the most difficult test of all. Uncle Ted, she knew, had asked her to come over to tell her the contents of her mother's will. To Corrie's mind this, not the funeral, would be the final contact with her mother. After today there would be nothing more, Edwina would be gone forever. And Corrie knew, because she had known her mother so well, that there would be a special message for her in the will, and she wasn't sure she could bear to hear it. Already, as she put on her coat to cross the square, she could feel tears of desolation and loneliness simmering dangerously close to the surface.

Uncle Ted was waiting for her at the door, ready to pull her in out of the rain and fold her into his warm embrace. Corrie rested in his arms for a moment, then kissed him on the cheek and handed her umbrella to Auntie Hattie, before following them into Uncle Ted's library. As she sat down on the upright chair in front of his desk Ted glanced at Harriet. Her mournful expression reflected Ted's own. She knew how difficult this meeting was going to be for her husband, yet how much worse it was going to be for Corrie. They neither of them, Ted nor Harriet, could even begin to guess how Corrie was going to take what Ted had to tell her, but both were more than a little afraid. And seeing the glassy look in Corrie's eyes, the innocence in her wind-reddened cheeks Harriet's heart swelled with such pity that she had to stop herself sweeping Corrie into her arms.

Corrie watched Uncle Ted as he took his pocket watch from his waistcoat, glanced at it nervously then settled into the vast leather chair behind his desk. She waited quietly for him to begin, her eyes never leaving his face, but by now a faint shadow of confusion was creasing her brow. It was unlike Uncle Ted to be at a loss for words, but he seemed so now. He smiled awkwardly, then his eyes strayed to the leaded windows, staring out at the rain spattered garden.

Leaning forward Corrie covered his hands with her own. 'We can always do this another time,' she smiled. 'I mean, I guess Mum has left everything to me, so there's no real need . . .'

Her voice hung in the warm air as Ted looked at her.

Corrie put her head quizzically to one side, then with a glint of uncertain humour in her hazel eyes said,

'I take it I'm not in debt?'

At last Ted laughed. 'No. No, my dear, you're certainly not in debt.'

'Now there's a relief.'

'But I think you should prepare yourself for a bit of a – surprise.'

Instantly the humour retreated. 'What kind of surprise?'

Ted opened a file on the desk in front of him and stared down at it.

'Uncle Ted?'

He looked up, smiled briefly, then bracing himself, he once again lowered his eyes as he said, 'Well, my dear, apart from the shop and the cottage, your mother has left you something in the region of a quarter of a million pounds.'

He looked up and found the very expression he had expected – stunned disbelief.

For a moment or two Corrie simply blinked. Then she laughed. 'But the dress shop could never have made that much money. It didn't. I know it didn't, I do the accounts myself.'

'You're right,' Ted told her. 'It didn't. The money, with the exception of twenty thousand pounds, has come from your father.'

'My father! You mean. . . . But Mum never said anything about this. Uncle Ted, are you sure you have it right? I mean if Dad had left all that money for Mum when he died she would have told me.'

Ted shook his head. 'No, she wouldn't have told you. She didn't tell you. I think she wanted to, many times, but . . . well . . . The truth is, Corrie, your father didn't leave the money when he died. You see, he isn't dead.'

Again Corrie stared at him, her cruelly bitten lips trembling with shock. Then to Ted's dismay she started to recoil, as though he was playing her a cruel and tasteless joke.

'As I said,' Ted began, 'I think your mother wanted very much to tell you the truth, but . . .'

'What are you talking about? The truth is that he died. He died when I . . .' she stopped as again Ted shook his head.

'Your father is very much alive, Corrie. You don't know how sorry I am that you have to find out like this . . .'

'No! Stop, stop!' Corrie cried. 'You've made a mistake. My mother would have told me if he was alive. I know she would. I mean why would she keep it from me?'

'She had her reasons, Corrie. I don't think she was proud of them, but it was a decision she took before you were born.'

'No, I don't believe it. She wouldn't have kept . . . We told each other everything.'

Ted merely looked at her, his round blue eyes imbued with sympathy. Corrie turned away, absently shaking her head. Then suddenly her head snapped up and the look of anger and betrayal in her eyes was unbearable. 'So she lied! All those stories she told me about him, none of them were true?'

Taking a deep breath Ted removed his spectacles and rubbed a hand over his jaw. He suddenly looked very old and very tired. 'They were true,' he said, 'at least partly, but . . .'

'Why would she tell you and not tell me?' Corrie cried. 'I just can't believe . . .'

'She didn't tell me, my dear. At least not at first. It was your father who told me what happened.'

'You mean you *know* him?'

'Yes. I was his solicitor – more accurately his father's solicitor. Only here, of course, in the country, they had someone else to take care of affairs in London, but the matter of Edwina came to me.'

'The matter of Edwina! Oh God, I can't believe this is happening? Are you trying to tell me he deserted her, that he paid her off? Are you saying she's loved him all these years when all the time . . .' Corrie couldn't go on. Her eyes darted about the room, as though searching the shadows for the sense of all this. She felt suddenly weightless with the shock, lightheaded. It was as though she were drifting through the tangled, menacing branches of a dream – a nightmare.

Ted waited for her to look at him again. She struggled to see him, to hear him, but her mother's face, her mother's words were besieging her. She stood up, circled the chair and went to press her head against the soothing coolness of the window. She looked out at the village she had known all her life but now looked so alien. 'What, what did you say?' she said, distantly aware that Ted was speaking.

'I said that I am willing to tell you what really happened. But maybe we should wait . . .'

Corrie shook her head. Her eyes were absorbed by the heavy grey clouds hanging oppressively over the village. 'No, I don't want to wait,' she said flatly. 'Tell me now.'

Ted heaved himself to his feet and walked to the door. 'Hattie!' he called, 'bring us some tea.'

When a few minutes later Hattie brought in the tray Corrie was sitting down again. She looked up at Auntie Hattie's anxious face. 'Did you know?' she said quietly.

Swallowing hard Hattie nodded, and once again Corrie was aware of that strange feeling of weightlessness.

'So,' she said, when Hattie closed the door behind her.

'So,' Ted repeated. He handed Corrie a cup of tea then sat down with his own. For a moment or two he studied Corrie's face, loving her and admiring the inner strength that shone so clearly now in her eyes. These past few years had not been easy for her, the past two weeks must have been hell. And now here he was, adding to her distress, and there she sat, perfectly under control again, chin raised, and the only sign of the strain she was under showing in the faint shadows beneath her eyes. He could wish that perhaps she weren't so brave, that she would let go of her emotions and allow herself the release she needed. But that would happen in time, he told himself, he just hoped it would be sooner rather than later.

He took a sip of his tea then set the cup back in the saucer. 'I'm aware of the story your mother told you,' he began on a long breath, 'and it is true that she was working in a Brighton dress shop when she met Phillip – your father. It's also true that they fell in love at first sight. In your father's own words, Edwina wasn't like all the other girls he'd met. She had no affectations, no guile, just innocence and, as you know, a great beauty. She trusted him and loved him, and in a fit of youthful romanticism Phillip decided that he should marry her before deflowering her. Which is what he did.

'They told no one until after the honeymoon was over. It was then that the trouble began. When he took her home.

'Phillip's mother and father were furious. Phillip was only just out of University and they had a great future planned for him, which included hopes of a brilliant marriage to Octavia Farrington, the daughter of a close friend of the family.

'Serena, Phillip's mother, was, I believe, right from the start, inordinately cruel to Edwina, and from what I remember of Serena, I have no problem in believing that. She treated your mother as though she were incapable of normal human sensitivities. She was also behind Harold, your grandfather's, threat to cut Phillip off if he didn't end the marriage immediately. The only person who showed Edwina any kindness at all was Cornelia, Phillip's grandmother. Your mother named you after Cornelia,' he smiled.

Corrie didn't say anything.

'In no time at all Serena set about convincing Phillip

that Edwina was doing nothing to advance him either socially, or professionally,' Ted continued, 'if anything she was holding him back. Phillip himself was confused, and, remember, very young. I think initially he stood up to her, but Serena was a formidable woman, and clever. It took only a matter of weeks for her to show Phillip just how inept his new wife was when it came to holding her own in their world. Of course Edwina could have managed, given the chance, but Serena saw to it that she was never given the chance. It would be better all round, Serena insisted, if Phillip were to leave Edwina at home rather than introduce her into their élite circle of friends. It was for Edwina's own good, since she was so painfully shy with those who were her superiors she would be sure to embarrass not only herself, but him too. To keep the peace with his mother Phillip started to do as she said. Whether Edwina fought back I don't know. All I do know is that in the end neither of them could stand up to Serena, so Edwina decided to leave. She still loved Phillip, despite his weakness, but she knew he wasn't happy. And of course neither was she. When Cornelia found out that Edwina was planning to go she offered to intervene, but Edwina wouldn't let her. She didn't want a family feud to start because of her. So it was Cornelia, not long before her death, who called me and asked me to deal with matters. Harold and Phillip came to see me and we arranged for a lump sum, which Edwina and I have invested over the years, to be paid to Edwina to get her started somewhere new. The divorce followed not long after.

'Edwina chose to live in Amberside because the Denbys – your father's family – have a country estate nearby.' He paused for a moment as a flicker of recognition dulled Corrie's eyes. He waited for her to speak, but she said nothing. 'Edwina believed,' he went on, 'that in Amberside she would always feel a closeness to Phillip, even though she knew she would probably never see him. And in all these years I don't think she ever did. Except once. A year after you were born. It was the day Phillip married Octavia Farrington. He married her here, at St. Mary's, and Edwina, like everyone else from the village, went to watch. She took you with her, in your pushchair, and stood on the edge of the crowd until the bride and groom came out of the church, then she left. She didn't want him to see her. I think most particularly of all she didn't want him to see you. Whether Philip knew that Edwina lived here in Amberside I can't say, but I doubt it. He never asked me what happened to her, she never asked me to tell him. All I do know, as you do yourself, is that your mother never really stopped loving him.' What he wanted to add was that it was a tragedy that Edwina had wasted her love on a man like Phillip Denby, who, to his mind, had never been worthy of Edwina. Instead, he merely took another deep breath, then letting it out slowly said, 'I'm sorry I've had to be the one to tell you, Corrie, but it was the way Edwina wanted it.'

A long silence followed his words. The strange weightlessness had left Corrie now, in its place she felt the heaviness of betrayal and pain; she felt anger that both her parents had been so weak, and she felt hatred too, for Serena, a grandmother she had never known.

Her voice was hoarse when finally she spoke. 'Does my father know . . . ? Does he know I exist?'

Ted shook his head.

'I see.' Corrie put a hand to her mouth and started to chew her nails, something she hadn't done since she was a child. Suddenly realizing what she was doing she snatched her hand away and looked at Ted again. 'Is there anything else I should know?'

'No, I think you have it all.'

Corrie nodded. 'My grandparents, are either of them still alive?'

'No.'

'Do you know where my father is now?'

'Yes.'

'Are you in touch with him?'

'Not often.'

Corrie's face was hard. 'I see. Well, it looks like I've got a lot of thinking to do, so I'll go home now if you don't mind.'

'Auntie Hattie and I were hoping you'd stay for dinner.'

'No. I'd rather be alone, if you don't mind.'

'Corrie,' Ted said softly, as he was helping her into her coat, 'I know you're angry, but please, don't be too hard on your mother. None of this has been easy for her.'

'No, I don't suppose it has,' Corrie answered stiffly. 'I'll call you tomorrow,' and she ran out into the fading afternoon.

'How could she have allowed me to believe he was so bloody wonderful when he treated her like that?' she raged to Paula later. 'How could he have been so weak, so spineless as to have let her go so easily? Uncle Ted said they were in love, at the beginning, so why didn't he stand by her? God I hate him! I hate him so much I'd like to kill him. And my own mother! How could she have wasted her life like that – on someone like that!'

'Oh come on now,' Paula said. 'You're making judgements on two people you don't even know.'

'She was my mother!'

'Yes. But she was also once a young girl. A young bride. You didn't know that person. You didn't know what it was like to be her. How much she had to suffer at the hands of his mother.'

'But why did she live this lie? Why didn't she ever tell me the truth?'

'Probably because she didn't want to hurt you.'

'But I had a right to know my father. He had a right to know me. She denied us that.'

'How do you know? Maybe she did tell him. Maybe

he didn't want to know.' Paula groaned inwardly at her insensitivity. 'She's not denying you now though is she? She wanted you to know about him, otherwise she'd never have asked Ted . . .'

'But what about all the years I was growing up? Even if he didn't want me, she still should have told me.'

'Corrie, what would you have done in her shoes? I mean what if she had told your father and he hadn't wanted to know? Knowing you you'd have wanted to meet him anyway, and I can't imagine for one minute that Edwina would have wanted you to face that rejection. Or worse. What if he had wanted you? She could never have stood up to a powerful family like that alone. She'd have lost you and you were all she had.'

'I'd never have left her!' Corrie cried, kicking the fire guard. 'She must have known that. Oh why isn't she here, damn it?'

Paula sat quietly for a minute or two feeling, because she loved her, some of the pain that showed in Corrie's stricken face. 'I know this might not be what you want to hear right now,' she said finally, 'but I don't think your father can be all bad. I mean, Edwina would never have loved him as deeply as she did, for as long as she did, if he were.'

'I want to hate him, thank you very much,' Corrie snapped. She looked at her watch. 'I expect Beth will be wanting her feed, won't she?'

With a sigh of resignation Paula stood up. 'Won't you come over and have some dinner with us?'

'No. No thank you,' Corrie said tersely.

'So you're going to sit here on your own and fester over all this?'

'Yes.'

Paula looked at her sadly, but knew there was no point in trying to coax her out of it. 'Well, you know where I am,' she said, as they walked out into the hall, 'you only have to pick up the phone. I'll always be there for you, you know that.'

'No, I don't know it. I don't know who I can trust anymore. I mean if my own mother can let me down like this . . .' Her voice broke, but catching herself in time, she pulled open the front door, 'Yes, I know you'll always be there for me. Thanks.'

Corrie stood at the door watching Paula walk away. She was numb, devoid of all feeling. But then, as those familiar, precious blonde curls started to bob about in the wind she suddenly wanted to call Paula back. She opened her mouth, but no sound came.

She closed the door and sank down onto the bottom stair burying her head in her hands. All around her the house was silent, so agonizingly still and silent. She sat there for a long time, holding herself tense, hardly daring to breathe, suffocating in the engulfing emptiness. Everything inside her was welling so wildly, so uncontrollably that she didn't dare to move. She must hold on, mustn't let go. To do that would be to admit, finally to surrender . . . But it was all right, everything was all right . . . She could bear this, her anger would hold her together. Slowly she lifted her head. A familiar colour seemed to twitch in the corner of her eye. She turned and saw the sleeve of her mother's coat, hanging beneath her own on the end of the bannister. Unthinkingly, she reached out to touch it, then edging closer she rested her face against it. She could smell her mother; it was as though Edwina were standing right there beside her.

Suddenly her heart heaved in her chest, pushing the pain into her throat. She cried out. Then the sobs started to tear through her body, and she clung to the sleeve as though it were Edwina's own hand. 'Oh Mum,' she choked, 'Mum, why didn't you tell me? You didn't need to protect me so much, you know? Oh Mum, Mum, what am I going to do without you? You're all alone now. I can't bear to think of you all alone in the darkness. Come back to me, please.'

A week later Corrie was once again in Uncle Ted's library. Her hair was scraped back in a pony tail, her face was still pale, and the smattering of freckles on her nose stood out vividly. She seemed calm, but no longer frighteningly so, and as Ted listened to the decisions she had reached he was again impressed by the inner strength that he knew she had not inherited from either of her parents. She was going to move to London, soon, she was telling him, just as she'd always wanted. Paula and Dave were going to rent the cottage, and would Auntie Hattie like to run the shop? They both smiled at that, since they knew that Hattie would jump at the chance.

For a moment or two Ted's mind wandered. He could suddenly see Corrie's new, though fragile, self-confidence at the mercy of London and it bothered him. So many young people still believed London to be the land of golden opportunity, but those days had long gone – if they had ever even existed. Now it was a rat-race the like of which terrified even him. It wasn't that he didn't believe Corrie could survive it, he was simply afraid of the cost. Unlike her, the men in the village, the women too, he imagined, were not ignorant of the way Corrie looked. She considered herself too tall, too large, and lamentably plain. True, she was no beauty, but her body was surely a gift from the gods. Round and firm and rippling sensuality in a way he had rarely seen in any other woman. What kind of trouble would that lead her into? There were so many who were just waiting to prey on the innocence of a young girl – and a girl such as Corrie would be manna from heaven. But she had money, he reassured himself, and she had him to help her get started.

She had a streak of her great-grandmother in her, he was thinking happily, when she suddenly said something that brought him up sharply. He'd been expecting it, of course, but not quite this soon.

'Are you sure?' he said. 'Have you thought it through?'

'I think so,' Corrie answered. 'Besides, what is there to think through? I have a father. I'd like to meet him. I take it he does live in London?'

Ted nodded. 'Yes. Yes he does.'

'Naturally I don't want to go to his home. That would cause all sorts of problems, I'm sure, since he's married again. I can't say that I have any feelings for him, not after the way he treated my mother, but I'm prepared to give him a chance. Let's just hope he's prepared to give me one.' When Ted made no comment she went on. 'Paula accused me of sitting in judgement on him, and my mother. She's right, I am. At least I was. Now all I want to do is meet Phillip Denby for myself. So, will you arrange it for me, Uncle Ted?'

Ted pursed his lips thoughtfully and rocked back and forth in his chair. 'Yes. I can arrange it,' he answered. 'If you're absolutely sure that's what you want.'

'I'm sure. I would prefer that he didn't know who I am, though. At least not at first. I guess that makes things more difficult for you?'

'A little. But not impossible. I'll give it some thought.'

'I already have,' Corrie said, sitting back in her chair and crossing her legs.

A twinkle shot to Ted's eyes. 'And what would you have me do?' he said.

Corrie's burst of assertiveness seemed to flounder for a moment, but taking heart from the affection in Ted's eyes she said, 'I will need a job when I get to London so perhaps you could ask my father to help. I'm not suggesting that he should give me a job, rather that he might be able to put me in touch with someone who can. I know I'm not qualified for much more than running a shop, but I'm willing to start at the bottom and work my way up.'

Ted grinned. 'Up to what? A take over?'

Corrie grinned too. 'Don't rule it out.'

'And in which particular field would you be interested?'

Corrie eyed him sheepishly as she pushed out her cheek with her tongue.

'The media,' he answered for her.

'All right, I know I'm asking for the moon, the stars, the whole galaxy, I guess . . .'

'You are. Particularly these days. So few jobs and so many contenders. Much more qualified than you. Nevertheless, I might be able to work something out for you. Better still, your father might. He's a banker, bankers know a lot of people. He might be a little more willing to help though if he knew you were his daughter.'

'I do intend to tell him, but I'd like to meet him first. See what kind of a man he is.'

'OK. Just let me know when you're ready to go. Have you thought about somewhere to live?'

'I'll rent somewhere for a while, until I find a place to buy. A quarter of a million pounds should get me something decent, even in London, shouldn't it?'

'Oh, it will. But what about sharing? It's a way of meeting people.'

'Paula suggested that too, but I'm not sure. I'll think about it.'

'Do that. It's a dangerous city, I won't be too happy thinking about you there alone. Auntie Hattie certainly won't.'

Corrie rolled her eyes. 'Now I don't want you two sitting here worrying about me. I'll call you regularly, let you know what's happening. And you can always come to visit, you know.'

'We did think you might consider taking a holiday,' Ted said. 'Recharge yourself before you set off to seek your fortune.'

'I already have one,' Corrie laughed. 'And besides, I just want to get on with things now.'

Corrie spent the next two weeks in torment. Now she had

made the decision to leave, Amberside had suddenly become so dear to her that she really didn't think she could tear herself away. She felt safe and secure there; she knew everyone and everyone knew her. Having ambitions to go out into the big wide world was one thing, she realized, but fulfilling them was quite another. And as the day of her departure grew closer she became so nervous at the prospect of what lay ahead that had it not been for the fact that she had promised Paula the cottage she might just have called the whole thing off. On the other hand she couldn't bear to think of staying.

Though she said nothing of her feelings to anyone Paula sensed them, which was why, at the last minute she decided to go to London with Corrie for a few days to lend moral support. She had to take the baby as well of course, but since Ted had arranged for Corrie to stay in his company's Regent's Park flat, Dave insisted he didn't mind, and even offered to drive them down himself.

The first few days in London were all rather bewildering. Dave stayed only for Saturday night, and not until he went to bed did he stop voicing his awe and appreciation of the luxury flat with its plush grey carpets, formal leather furniture and *two* bathrooms. Corrie and Paula were more impressed by the view over Regent's Park, and the dish-washer which neither of them could work.

Now Dave had gone, and left to their own devices, neither Corrie nor Paula knew quite what to do, or where to go.

They decided to set about exploring the Underground first. Though Corrie had visited London before, as a teen-ager, she soon realized that this was not the town that had lived all these years in her memory. What had happened, she wondered, to all the bright lights? Where was the vibrancy, the exhilaration that had seemed to charge every particle of air the last time she was here? And how on earth would she ever get to know anyone, when just about every face she saw was so blank, so unreceptive, and everyone was in such a hurry to get somewhere? The whoop and wail of police sirens, coupled with the hostile blasting of car horns seemed unsettlingly constant, and the overcrowded streets, clustered, dour-looking buildings and the unrelenting greyness were almost as menacing as the daily headlines of violent crime.

Trying not to be daunted Corrie was slightly cheered when they visited Covent Garden and roamed about the weird and wonderful stalls packed with hand-carved wooden toys, ornately embroidered cushions and exotic jewellery. They went to a concert at the Albert Hall, where they spent as much time laughing at the way the baby sat curiously wide-eyed in her sling while seeming to tap her foot to the rhythm, as they did listening to the music. They visited Hyde Park, Buckingham Palace and on Paula's last night they went to the cinema where Beth slept through Cristos Bennati's film starring Angelique Warne.

'It's funny how it all seemed somehow attainable when I was in Amberside, just dreaming about it,' Corrie said when they came out into Curzon Street. 'Now, even standing here, smack in the middle of it all, it feels like a zillion light years away. Am I doing the right thing? Or am I completely insane?'

'Both,' Paula laughed. 'But you have to give it a try. And once you find a job, well, you'll have more friends than you can handle, you see. And you can always come home at weekends, if you get lonely. It's not far on the train.'

'I don't suppose you and Dave would consider moving down as well, would you?' Corrie asked glumly.

'Strap-hanging on the tube's not for me,' Paula winced. 'In case you hadn't noticed I'm just the right height for my nose to fit comfortably into the nearest armpit. I'd end up suffocating in BO.'

Laughing, Corrie hugged her. 'Just be thankful you're

not a midget,' she said. 'Oh, I'm going to miss you.' She didn't add how terrified she was of Paula leaving tomorrow.

'I'm going to miss you too,' Paula said, swallowing the lump in her throat. She'd never said so to Corrie, but the very idea of life without her seemed intolerable. Dave knew that, which was why he had let her come to London, but how on earth was she going to say good-bye? Even worse, how could she let Corrie stay here alone in this dreadful place?

When Corrie got up the next morning Paula was on the telephone to Dave.

'I've just asked him if I can stay until the end of the week,' she said when she put the phone down. 'Until after you've met your father. He said it was OK, but I have to go back at the weekend.'

'Oh Paula,' Corrie gasped. 'That's terrific. I was really dreading you leaving.'

'I thought you might be,' Paula laughed, and taking the toast Corrie had buttered for her she sat down at the gleaming white formica-topped breakfast table. She watched Corrie as she made more tea. Behind her the windows were steamy and a drizzly rain trickled down the outside. Paula had thought it rained a lot in Amberside, it seemed never to stop in London.

'Corrie,' she said after a while, 'you don't *have* to stay here you know. I mean no one will think any the worse of you if you change your mind.'

Corrie turned round, pulling the belt of her dressing gown tighter then stuffing her hands in the pockets. 'It really is bloody awful, isn't it?' she said. 'It's so gloomy, so depressed.'

'It's the recession,' Paula said. 'Not a good time to be looking for a job either.'

'Just what I've been thinking. You know ninety per cent of me wants to go home with you – ninety-five per cent. But the rest of me would never forgive me if I didn't at least give it a try now I'm here. But I'm not up for flogging a dead horse. I'll give Uncle Ted a call, get him to set up a meeting with my father, then I'll take it from there.'

'Meaning if your father doesn't come up with a job for you you'll come home?'

'Probably.' Corrie laughed then at the look of relief on Paula's face. 'You're supposed to be supporting me in this adventure,' she said, 'not willing my father to come up with zilch.' She pulled a face. 'I wonder what he's going to be like?'

'Do you think you'll tell him who you are?'

'That very much depends on him. On what my instincts tell me at the time.' She pulled out a chair and sat down. 'I've been thinking about Mum a lot these past few days,' she said, resting her chin on her hands. 'Well, I don't suppose that comes as any surprise, but I've been thinking about her life – about all of our lives really. I mean we're all of us striving for the same thing really, aren't we? A happy ending. But is there such a thing? There wasn't for her, was there? I wonder if there is for anyone. I guess though that we have to keep believing in it or there would be no point in anything, would there?'

'This dismal town is beginning to rub off on you already,' Paula shivered.

'No, but think about it. Is there such a thing as a happy ending? I mean we all die in the end, don't we? Is that such a happy ending?'

'Oh, Corrie!'

Corrie laughed. 'Well who knows? Death might just be the ultimate experience. And if it is, what does it really matter what we do in life?'

'What are you getting at?'

'I'm trying to be philosophical about going to see my father – a man who's destroyed at least one happy ending in his life.'

'I'd say don't think too hard. Don't expect too much,

and just hope that he's not the lily-livered mother's boy he was when he knew Edwina.'

'God forbid,' Corrie shuddered. 'But we'll see.'

Three days later Corrie was in Threadneedle Street with only a thin, but steady stream of traffic and a giant bolt of nerves between her and the imposing Victorian façade of the merchant bank of which her father was now a director. Beneath her coat she was wearing a new bottle-green suit from Next, white shirt and black low-heeled shoes. Her hair was loose, and held back by a black velvet Alice band. She wore no make-up or jewellery.

For the first time since she'd arrived in London it wasn't raining, though the air was dank and the gutters still filled with murky puddles. She glanced at her watch. She was early, but decided that she must go in now before her nerve deserted her altogether.

She had started out optimistically, reminding herself that so far her move to London had in truth gone so smoothly – mainly thanks to Ted – that perhaps fate was telling her that this was right for her after all. 'I mean,' she had said to Paula that morning, 'who else gets a best friend come to help them settle, an uncle who arranges for them to stay in a luxurious flat, and a father who might fix them up with a job?' It was only the weather, she told herself now, that made things seem so bleak – and the fact that she missed her mother more as each day passed.

Uncle Ted had told her nothing of his telephone conversation with Phillip, so, as she was taken up to the fourth floor in a lift that one usually only saw in a 1940s film these days, Corrie had no idea that she was not only extremely lucky to be seeing her father at such short notice, but was extremely honoured to be seeing him at all. Ordinarily a man in Phillip's position would never even have entertained the idea of giving fifteen minutes of his precious time to a doe-eyed girl from the sticks, who, along with thousands of others, had decided to try her luck in London. Indeed, when Ted had called and put his request Phillip Denby had refused, saying he was far too busy. Ted had persisted, so Phillip had offered the services of one of the bank's personnel officers. Still Ted wouldn't be put off, saying that he and Hattie would deem it a great personal favour if Phillip were to see the girl himself. Even then Phillip hadn't been easy to talk round, which had momentarily surprised Ted, until he remembered the reputation Phillip had earned for himself over the years. But ruthless and highly respected as he was in business, Ted – or more accurately Hattie – had it on the best authority, that of Phillip's wife, that Phillip remained an emotionally weak man. Using that to his advantage Ted had finally got Phillip to agree.

The lift clanged to a halt, and the wiry young man who had ridden up with her led Corrie along the central aisle of a computer boffin's paradise, where a dozen or more people were going quietly about their business and didn't even look up as they passed. She was shown into an office at the end, where she found more computers – a whole bank of them across one wall and several more on trolleys. They seemed so at odds with the austere, Victorian decor, Corrie was thinking, when a woman, in a neat navy suit got up from behind an enormous oak desk, and with a smile that transformed her otherwise homely face, held out her hand and introduced herself as Pam, Mr Denby's personal secretary.

By now Corrie felt as though she was in a trance. It was the way she wanted to stay, since it was too late to turn back and the thought that her father, the man who had given her life, whose blood ran in her veins, was very likely sitting behind that ominous closed door to her right was too terrifying to contemplate.

'. . . just through here,' the woman was saying, and before Corrie could even think about fleeing to the safety of the street outside, she was being shown into her father's office and the woman had closed the door behind her.

The office, with its high ceiling, antique furniture and desk top lighting was even more imposing than she'd imagined. Every wall was a bookcase containing leather-bound volumes of . . . what? She had no idea. In truth she barely saw them, since her eyes were transfixed by the figure sitting behind the mahogany desk, head bowed as he wrote.

She stood there awkwardly, clutching her handbag to her chest and feeling lamentably dowdy in her brown tweed coat. His hair was thick and glossy, she noticed, and was the exact same colour as her own – brown. She'd expected him to be grey. His hands looked nice, artistic, she thought, watching them move across the page, and his face . . . Corrie's heart turned over. He had lifted his head and was now looking at her – with her own hazel eyes. He was smiling with her own lips, even his nose, his cheekbones and chin were hers. The resemblance was so striking that she felt sure he must see it too. She felt momentarily cheated, since the almost masculine features she had lived with all her life and considered so plain were unbelievably handsome on him.

'Corrie?' he said, getting to his feet and holding out his hand. 'Corrie Browne?'

'That's right,' she mumbled, moving to the desk and taking his hand. The limpness of his grasp made her feel faintly odd.

'Please, sit down,' he said, waving her into a chair.

'Thank you.'

'Ted tells me you're looking for a job,' he said, sitting down too and resting his forearms on the desk. 'I'm afraid I don't know if I can be of any help, but perhaps if you tell me what you're qualified to do I can make a few phone . . .'

'Do you know who I am?' Corrie said. She was so

shocked by the words that she very nearly looked behind her to see who had spoken them. But her eyes remained fixed on her father, as her heart burned painfully across her chest. He stared back, impassively, but for one moment, so fleeting she couldn't even be sure she'd seen it, a hunted look passed over his eyes.

And then it hit her. Of course he knew who she was, and now she was sitting here she couldn't imagine why it had never occurred to her before. Ted Braithwaite calling him up, asking him to see a young woman by the name of Corrie Browne. Whatever else Phillip Denby was, he wasn't stupid. He would have worked out who she was long before she arrived. But he was going to pretend he didn't know.

The seconds ticked by, and with each one Corrie felt a hostility fill the air.

'Should I?' he said at last, his generous lips now compressed in a thin line.

Had he shown any surprise at her question, had there been even a glimmer of emotion in his eyes, Corrie's response might have been different. As it was, feeling herself go hot and cold all over, she said, 'I think you should. In fact I think you do.'

His eyes bored into hers. Corrie felt herself weaken under their pressure, but nothing in the world was going to make her look away now.

Phillip had used this look so many times in business, almost always to great advantage, but faced with the fervent challenge in Corrie's eyes, the bitter accusation in the curl of her lips, he was the first to give up the battle. 'You're a friend of Ted and Hattie Braithwaite's,' he said, no longer looking at her.

Corrie knew she was breathing too fast. Her voice was being strangled in her throat, but she forced the words out. 'I'm more than that,' she said. 'I'm Edwina Browne's daughter. And you know it.'

There it was again, that look of persecution, and of . . .

was it? Yes it was – a look of repulsion. He was very nearly physically recoiling.

The longest and most excruciating silence Corrie had ever known, followed – another of Phillip's ploys. But Corrie held her own, determined that he should be the first to speak. When he did she immediately heard the higher pitch to his voice. 'Then why don't we come straight to the point?' he said. 'What exactly do you want from me?'

Corrie almost reeled with the brutality of his words. She didn't know what to say. The question was so unexpected she had no answer. 'I want an explanation,' she heard herself say. She was far from feeling the confidence her voice portrayed, but thanked God that he had no way of knowing that.

'For what?' he asked.

'What do you think?'

'You tell me.'

'*I* am your daughter, that makes *you* my father, just so that this is spelled out. Now, I rather think that means it's for *you* to tell *me*.'

With a gesture of impatience he sat back in his chair. 'What do you want?' he repeated. 'Or should I say, how much? As I recall your mother's price was a hundred thousand . . .'

'How dare you!' Corrie seethed. 'I didn't come here for money, I came here to give us a chance to know each other. Perhaps to catch up on all the years we missed. I now find myself thanking God that we did miss them. Just what kind of a father would . . .'

'Your mother ran out on me! She took my father's money and left. What kind of mother . . .'

'If I were you I'd be very careful what I said next,' Corrie warned. She drew breath to speak again, but amazement snatched her words as with no warning at all he suddenly seemed to slump before her very eyes.

'Blackmail,' he groaned. 'You've come here to blackmail

me. You want to destroy my life, to make me pay for what I did to your mother. Well you won't get away with it, do you hear me? I'll pay you once, but if you think . . .'

'I don't want your money,' Corrie shouted, but he wasn't listening.

'I always knew this would happen,' he was muttering. 'I knew you'd come one day. I thought you were a boy. I always believed Edwina had given me a boy. But you! You're not . . .'

'Just a minute!' Corrie interrupted. 'Are you telling me that you *knew* my mother was pregnant when she left? That you . . .'

'You don't even look like her,' he rambled. He rubbed his hands across his face. 'I thought she'd come back to me. That she'd bring me my son . . . But she hated me, she never forgave me, and now she's sent you to torment me . . . Doesn't she understand? Won't you tell her . . .'

'My mother is dead!' Corrie cried.

Phillip's face turned white. He stared at Corrie, but she knew he wasn't seeing her. 'Edwina,' he murmured. 'Edwina, dead?' His eyes focused on Corrie. 'Oh God, if only you knew how difficult this is for me.'

Corrie eyed him with disgust. Not a thought for her, his daughter, that she had lost her mother. Not a trace of compassion, only pity for himself. And suddenly she found herself wanting to hurt him as deeply as she could.

'How did she die?' he asked dully. 'When? Oh God, I can't believe it. Did she ask for me? Did she . . . ?'

'I don't think you have a right to any answers,' Corrie sneered. 'I've wasted my time coming here today, I won't bother you again.'

'No! No, wait,' he cried, as she started for the door.

Corrie spun round, a very real temper flashing in her eyes. 'There's nothing to wait for,' she seethed. 'You won't be hearing from me again. As far as I'm concerned you really are dead.'

Seconds after the door slammed behind Corrie Phillip heard Pam let herself quietly into his office. He was slumped against the desk, his head buried in his hands. For the moment he was too stunned by what had happened to look up. All he could think about was Edwina – and his guilt, which, over the years had grown to monstrous proportions. He had always hoped, prayed, that one day she would come back to him. That she would tell him she forgave him, and give him the courage to tell Octavia that he had never loved her, that he had only ever loved one woman in his life, a woman Octavia had never even heard of – Edwina Browne. It was what had kept him going throughout the misery of his marriage. But now Edwina was dead. He couldn't believe it. He didn't want to believe it. If he did, there would be nothing to hope for anymore. Nothing to dream of. He would be stuck forever with Octavia – Octavia who was so like his mother . . .

But Corrie had come, she had sat there across his desk and told him that Edwina was dead. And all he had seen then was the person responsible for killing his dreams. In those fleeting moments he had hated Corrie. Even now he didn't want to believe she was his daughter. Edwina had given him a son, he was sure of it. The son he had always wanted. But she hadn't. She had given him Corrie, and he had been unable to disguise his resentment not only that she hadn't been a boy, but that she hadn't even looked like her mother. Corrie had cheated him. Corrie had annihilated his dreams.

But then he had seen the pain in Corrie's eyes. Had suddenly felt an overriding compassion for what she must have suffered since her mother had died. His heart had gone out to her, but it was already too late. He had seen, had heard, the contempt as she'd told him she wouldn't bother him again. And she wouldn't, he knew that, and already it was breaking his heart.

'Oh Edwina,' he cried silently. 'Edwina, forgive me.'

He felt a hand on his shoulder and looked up into Pam's face. Pam, a woman who cared for him deeply, who never sat in judgement of him, who wanted only what made him happy.

A sudden blinding rage surged through his veins. He looked at Pam again.

'Lock the door!' he snarled.

Obediently Pam crossed the room and turned the key in the lock. By the time she turned round again Phillip was on his feet. Already his trousers were unbuttoned. Her smile was one of understanding and sadness as she lifted her skirt up over her hips, removed her panties and tights and walked towards him. His mouth crushed brutally down on hers, his hands dug painfully into her buttocks. He knew he shouldn't do this to Pam, but was unable to stop himself as pushing her back across the desk, he entered her.

He took her savagely, almost delirious with the excitement of being in control of a woman. Of having her do exactly as he wanted. He grunted and groaned his way to ejaculation, hatred for Octavia firing his every thrust. When he was with Pam he wasn't a failure. With her he could fuck his inadequacy out of his system. But the guilt – the guilt over what he had done to Edwina, and now to Corrie, could he ever be rid of that?

He withdrew abruptly, rearranged his clothes and turned to the window. He stared silently down at the street, until Pam came to stand beside him. He flinched as her hands touched his face, but he allowed her to turn him to her. For a long while they simply looked at each other, then gathering him into her arms she held him as he wept.

Paula was waiting when Corrie returned to the Regent's Park flat. One look at Corrie's face told her all she needed to know. 'I'll start packing,' she said.

'No!'

Paula turned back.

'He's the weak, spineless, lily-livered excuse of a man we were afraid of,' Corrie said. 'But I don't need him. I can do it alone. I'll get there, wherever there is. I'll get right to the top and I'll show him that I never did need him.'

Paula watched her, then feeling all the pain and devastation of the grief locked inside her friend, she held out her arms. And with a barely audible sob, Corrie walked into them.

'That was Corrie,' Ted said, replacing the receiver.

Hattie was standing behind him. 'I guessed,' she smiled.

He shrugged, then putting an arm round his wife he led her into the sitting room.

'I take it things didn't go too well with Phillip,' Hattie said, as they each moved to their own chairs.

'No. She told him who she was.'

'I see. Are you going to speak to him?'

'No. She doesn't want me to. She's staying in London though.'

Hattie looked surprised.

'She doesn't want any more help, she says.'

'Pfff!' Hattie exclaimed. 'You don't want to take any notice of that. Everyone needs help when they're getting started.'

'I don't know how she'd view the interference right now though,' Ted said uncertainly.

'Did you tell her about Annalise?'

'No. I didn't think now was the right time. Besides, I'd like to speak to Annalise first.'

'Well if you can set it up, then believe me, Ted Braithwaite, there'll be no one happier than Corrie. Television is one of the most difficult industries to get into these days – she won't succeed without your contacts. And you know in her heart that's what she wants. She tried with her father and failed. That's not your fault, neither is it hers, but she deserves a *real* break now, so give it to her.'

Ted still looked doubtful.

'Ted, you can hardly be accused of interfering for making one phone call. And after that it's up to Corrie.'

Ted's eyebrows arched.

Ignoring his irony, Hattie said, 'Go on out there now and call Annalise Kapsakis. Go along with you, because if you don't, I will.'

– 5 –

Annalise Kapsakis stalked through the crowded production office and flung herself down in her chair. The other producers and researchers were too busy to notice, but the secretaries, grouped around their word processors in a corner, exchanged knowing smiles. The beautiful, spoiled child had just had a programme idea rejected by Luke Fitzpatrick – the chief executive of TW Productions, and anchorman of the one programme TW made – *The World This Week*. It was a current affairs programme broadcast each Tuesday on the ITV Network.

Seeing the secretaries watching her, Annalise tossed her crinkly blonde hair haughtily over her shoulder, pouted her caramel lips and turned to look out of the window. A moment or two later she looked sheepishly back at them and broke into a grin. The secretaries laughed too. At twenty-four Annalise was by far the youngest of the producers at TW, and undeniably the most popular.

Annalise shrugged then yelled above the office din for her researcher, Pippa. She'd done her best to talk Luke round, but she'd failed. Now she and Pippa had to come up with another idea, or they might lose their slot for that month to another producer.

When Pippa didn't materialize Annalise yelled again while rummaging through the mountain of files on her desk. Gareth, another producer, put his hand over the mouthpiece of the phone, 'Pippa's in the edit suite,' he barked, 'now keep it down I can't hear a thing.'

Annalise poked her tongue out at him, then picked up the phone to call the edit suite.

'Line five for you, Annalise,' a researcher called across the office.

'Another call for you Annalise,' a secretary shouted. 'Line three.'

'One at a time,' Annalise cried. 'Tell three I'll call them back.' She pressed the keypad in front of her and picked up line five. 'Annalise Kapsakis.'

'Annalise. It's Ted Braithwaite.'

'Ted, you old rogue!' she squealed. 'How are you? How's Hattie?'

'We're fine, my dear. You?'

'Pissed off. But that's fairly normal around here. What can I do for you? Or is this just a social call?'

Knowing that Annalise was always busy Ted came straight to the point. Annalise, with a finger pressed over one ear to block out the noise of the faxes, PA machines, TV sets and other phone calls, listened to what he was saying with mounting amusement. She toyed with coming right out and asking if this Corrie Browne was one of Ted's byblows, but decided it might be a bit tactless.

'I know it's a long shot,' Ted finished, 'and I don't suppose you've got any vacancies anyway, but I'd be grateful if you'd meet her. She doesn't know anyone in London . . .'

'It's all right, Ted, I don't need the whole sob story. And since it's you asking I'll see her. Where's she living?'

'Regent's Park – at the moment.'

'Very swish.' She took out her diary. 'Now let me see. Yes, here we are. Tell her to meet me at the Dôme in King's Road on Thursday morning. There's no point her coming here, you can't hear yourself think. How old is she by the way?'

'Twenty-six.'

'Qualifications?'

'I'm not sure. She has some O levels, or whatever they're called these days. She's incredibly bright though. The kind of bright that doesn't need qualifications.'

Annalise grinned at the pride in Ted's voice. 'OK, big boy, I'll see what I can do. Must rush now, lots to do and all that. Give Hattie my love, tell her I'll be in touch soon,' and she rang off.

Luke Fitzpatrick stood at the door of his office, surveilling the chaos. His dark blond hair was dishevelled from the harassment of the morning, his tie was loose and the top button of his shirt undone. The bone structure of his face was immaculate, so that no matter what expression he held he could never be described as anything other than devastatingly handsome. His body, all five feet eleven of it, was in perfect shape, something he didn't have to work at, but did nevertheless. In the past two years, since TW had started, he had become one of the nation's heart-throbs. It was a status he enjoyed. He had been voted the thinking woman's crumpet twice, was continually listed as one of the most eligible bachelors about town, and received fanmail by the sackload every day.

The mayhem around him, he knew, would continue right up until that night's transmission since news was coming in by the minute of the terrifying events going on out there on the streets of South London. Gangs of youths had begun rioting the night before, setting shops, houses and cars alight. Several of them had guns, others carried weaponry far outclassing anything rioters had ever laid their hands on before and so far four policemen had been shot. One was known to be dead. Seven rioters were at the morgue, fifty-eight more were in custody. And still the battle raged.

TW had four camera crews down at the scene, three on the ground, the other in a helicopter. An hour ago one of the sound men had been injured and had had to be replaced.

Here, in the office, every available researcher was busy lining up potential interviewees for that night's hour long special. They'd been granted the further half hour first thing this morning, when the seriousness of what had happened overnight was finally acknowledged. Luke would chair the debate, which would be interjected with scenes from the riot.

For the moment there was nothing for him to do, except delegate. Scripts were offered for his approval, but events were changing by the minute and the reporters who weren't at the scene were frantically rewriting. Footage was arriving every half hour by courier, and editors were manically trying to make sense of what was coming in.

It would be a great show, Luke was thinking, and already he could feel the adrenalin mounting. *The World This Week* was fast becoming one of the most respected current affairs programmes on broadcast television. Even ITN had been refused more than a fifteen minute extension to their *News at Ten* that night, in favour of the TW special. And this was the company that he had built, almost single-handedly in less than two years.

Of course he couldn't have done it without Annalise – or more precisely her disgustingly rich family. Her father was Luke's partner, her cousin was the TV accountant. Even her mother was on the board of directors. But the day to day running of the company was under Luke's control. He'd known, right from the start that the reason Annalise had talked her father into raising the money for TW wasn't only because of her ambition to become a producer; it was because of the way she felt about him. As to his feelings for her . . . This was a subject he never dwelt on for long – he couldn't, wouldn't, for the guilt he felt at what he was doing disturbed him so profoundly it was in danger of affecting his mind. He should have given her up long before now since the consequences of them staying together wouldn't only be disastrous they'd be devastating. But he couldn't bring himself to let her go. She was so beautiful, so desirable, it almost hurt his eyes to look at her, but what it did to his heart, even his mind, was agonizing. Perhaps if she weren't so in love with him it would have been easier, but she was, and each time he tried to end it between them and she begged him not to, he just couldn't go through with it.

He caught her watching him now and held her eyes. She had been downstairs in the foyer when he'd arrived that morning and had taken the lift to the fourth floor with him. No sooner had the lift doors closed, than she had taken his hand and put it under her mini-skirt. All she'd been wearing underneath was suspenders holding up her black woollen stockings. Within seconds his erection was straining against his trousers. On reaching the fourth floor he had taken her straight to the nearby stationery cupboard, but once inside Annalise had resisted him, saying she was far too busy now, but would come to his office later when she would discuss a great programme idea with him. Luke's laughter had echoed around the shelves of headed notepaper. This was her way of trying to manipulate him, but it wouldn't work. And now she knew it wouldn't work. Had her idea been a good one, then naturally he would have accepted it, but yet another crack in the Government's economic policy on Europe was virtually guaranteed to send the nation rushing for the remote control.

He grinned as Annalise screwed up her nose, slammed her eyes shut and turned away. There were times, he thought, when she looked no more than fourteen years old. But it wasn't only there, in those Lolita eyes and pout, that the danger lay. If he could, he would fire her, just to get her out of his life. But he couldn't – apart from being the boss's daughter, she was a good producer. Not the best, by any means, but she was a hard worker and tenacious to the point of obsession when she got her teeth into a hot story. Perhaps even more important though, was that despite being the spoiled rich kid she was, everyone adored her. It made for a good working atmosphere – and when everyone was under the kind of pressure they were, things like that mattered.

'Luke!'

He turned to see his secretary getting up from her desk.

'Gordon wants you in the edit suite,' she said.

'Which one is he in?'

'Two.'

'Tell him I'm on my way.'

Rolling up his sleeves Luke crossed to Annalise's desk, put his hand over the receiver she was speaking into and told her he wanted to see her in an hour. He would take her back to the stationery cupboard and finish what she had started that morning.

Corrie arrived at the Dôme half an hour early. She could hardly keep the smile from her face she was so excited – and nervous. An interview with a TV producer! Of course there was no guarantee of a job, but Uncle Ted had said that Annalise Kapsakis was a very special person, that she was lots of fun, generous, kind-hearted, perhaps a little wild at times, but would be sure to give Corrie some contacts even if she couldn't offer her a job herself.

As Corrie waited she scolded herself ruthlessly, telling herself that there was nothing to be nervous about, that Annalise was a person, just like her, and . . . Well, if it didn't work out, then it didn't work out, she'd just have to try something else. The important thing, as Paula had told her on the phone that morning, was to be herself.

Dave had come to collect Paula at the weekend. The parting had not been easy for either of them, but not until

Paula had gone had Corrie allowed herself to cry. Why she was being so stubborn about going home she didn't know, since London held little appeal for her now, and all she'd done after Paula had gone was stay in the flat watching TV and feeling sorry for herself. She was on the point of admitting defeat and packing up her things to go back to Amberside when Uncle Ted had called to tell her he had arranged for her to meet a TV producer in two days' time.

And now here she was, in the new clothes she'd bought the day before in Oxford Street, waiting for Annalise Kapsakis to arrive.

When she came in Corrie knew instinctively that it was her. Though Uncle Ted hadn't made too much of how beautiful Annalise was, Corrie had guessed she would be, and with her mane of crinkly blonde hair, vast blue eyes and exquisite figure, Annalise was breathtaking. And so young, Corrie thought. She looks no more than twenty, but Ted had said she was twenty-four. She was wearing a black jacket with military style buttons, square shoulders and an excessive flare from the tapered waist. Beneath that was a tight black mini-skirt showing her endlessly long slender legs and outrageously sexy thigh length boots.

Corrie smiled as she approached, forcing herself not to think of how dowdy she must look in her plain navy V-neck sweater with white shirt, and navy skirt and Alice band.

'Hello,' Corrie said shyly as Annalise made to walk right past her. 'Are you Annalise?'

Annalise looked down. 'Corrie?'

Corrie nodded and Annalise's face seemed to light up, which momentarily threw Corrie.

'It's great to meet you,' Annalise said, holding out her hand. 'Sorry I didn't recognize you, but Ted didn't tell me too much about you. Still, we're here to put that to rights, aren't we? Hi, John, a cappuccino for me, thanks. Make it a strong one. Anything else for you, Corrie?'

Corrie turned to John. 'The same again, please,' she said, nonchalantly.

'What was that?' John asked.

Corrie looked at Annalise and pulled a face. 'And I was trying to be so cool,' she said and felt suddenly lightheaded at the way Annalise laughed. 'An espresso, please,' she reminded John.

Annalise pulled out a chair and sat down. 'So,' she said, searching Corrie's face with her luminous blue eyes, 'you want to work in telly.'

Corrie winced and nodded. 'Now tell me I'm dreaming of the impossible.'

'I won't lie to you, it's hellishly difficult to get in.'

'Do qualifications help?'

Annalise shrugged. 'Depends where you're applying, and what you're applying for, I guess. Any idea what you want to do in telly?'

'Not really. To be honest I don't have the first idea what happens. But I can learn.'

Annalise laughed. 'Sure, we all have to learn.' She wrinkled her nose, 'Especially me, according to Luke, our chief exec.'

'You mean Luke Fitzpatrick?'

'That's the man. Gorgeous, isn't he?'

Corrie looked startled, then grinned at Annalise's frankness.

'Go on, admit it,' Annalise prompted, 'you wouldn't kick him out of bed.'

Corrie started to laugh. 'Chance would be a fine thing.'

Annalise seemed impressed with this answer, not one she'd have expected from someone who looked like Corrie.

'So, how did you get into TV?' Corrie asked.

'Me? Oh that's easy. Daddy bought me a production company.'

Corrie's eyes rounded. 'He *bought* you a company?'

'Sure. TW. He and Luke own it. I work for them. Well

for Luke, really, Daddy just put up the money. Luke put some up too. But the whole thing was my idea. Trouble is neither Daddy nor Luke will let me have any say in the running of things. I'm too young, still got a lot to learn, they keep telling me. But I managed to wangle myself a producer's job. And I'm a bloody good one too, even if I do say so myself. Well, I suppose I do go off the rails every now and then, late nights and all that. But Luke's pretty tolerant and I work hard most of the time. I know what you're thinking now, what a spoiled brat she is.'

Corrie was still laughing. 'I was thinking how lucky you are. So how did it all start? I mean what made you decide on TV?'

'When the world was my oyster, you mean? The answer is Luke Fitzpatrick. I met him a couple of years ago at some night club or other, both of us were pissed out of our minds, not unusual for me, I'm afraid. Anyway, I knew who he was because I'd already seen him on telly. He's a *bona fide* journalist, in case you didn't know. Meaning that he is well qualified for this work, unlike me. He was in newspapers in Ireland first, that's where he's from, then on local telly as a reporter somewhere in the north of England, or maybe it was Scotland, who knows? Anyway, he came to London and got a job with Thames News, then Thames lost their franchise. So he was about to be out of work, and that's when we met. I'm telling you Corrie, you might think he's good looking on the screen, but if you saw him, shit! The man is drop dead gorgeous. Anyway, to cut a long story short I introduced him to Daddy, they hit it off, *et voilà!* TW productions was born. Our offices are just across Battersea Bridge, we research and edit the programmes there, and they're transmitted from Euston Centre.'

'Just like that?'

'Sure. Just like that.'

'And you and Luke?' Corrie blushed. 'Sorry, I'm being nosy.'

'We screw ourselves silly as often as possible.' For a brief moment a cloud passed over Annalise's eyes, from which Corrie correctly deduced that this might not be as often as Annalise would like. But then she was smiling again, as infectiously as ever, and Corrie thought she had never felt so comfortable with a stranger in her life.

'Now, about you,' Annalise said. 'Can you type?'

Corrie grimaced. 'Not brilliantly.'

'Doesn't matter. Can you use a word processor?'

'Almost.'

'Shorthand?'

'I write fast.'

Annalise looked thoughtful. 'It could be that you're over-qualified,' she said at last.

Again Corrie laughed. 'What qualifications do you have?'

'Oh, I scraped a couple of A levels out of St. Paul's.'

'You went to school in England?'

'Sure. Where else?'

'I just thought ... Well, with your name being Kapsakis ...'

'Oh that! Kapsakis is my married name.'

Corrie was stunned. 'You're married?'

'Sort of. We've been separated for about three years now. I dropped out of University when I was twenty, went off around the world, got as far as Rhodes, met Thomas – he taught me to sail, actually – and I married him. Seemed like a good idea at the time.' She laughed. 'It lasted six weeks. Yet another mess Daddy managed to get me out of.'

'And what about you and Luke? Do you think you two will ever get married?'

'Oh God I hope so. The man is just to die for, Corrie. Well you'll see for yourself. When can you start?'

'Start?' Corrie repeated.

'Sure. I'll speak to Luke, but there shouldn't be a problem. We're in need of a research assistant and I think you fit the bill.'

'A research assistant?' Corrie gasped, feeling a silly grin spread across her face.

'Don't get carried away. It's just a high-faluting title for a dogsbody.'

'Just as long as I'm not expected to bark and wag my tail,' Corrie quipped, 'and OK, I'll work on my jokes before Monday.'

'Then Monday it is. Welcome aboard, Corrie Browne, I think I'm going to like having you around.'

Corrie left the Dôme on such a high that it was all she could do to stop herself smiling at strangers in the street and gushing out her good fortune. Even better the sun had come out, the first time she'd seen it since she'd arrived in London.

Unable to wait she dived into the nearest phone box and called first Paula, then Uncle Ted. After, she shopped for more clothes until it was time for her appointment with an estate agent, who was going to show her a studio flat just off the King's Road. She knew now of course that her mother and father had never lived there, but nonetheless it made her feel closer to Edwina to think that she was fulfilling at least a part of Edwina's dream. That was if the studio worked out of course, she reminded herself. Already she and Paula had seen some pretty grotty places – and the fact that most of them cost close on two hundred thousand was horrifying. But she had a good feeling about this studio, and since, as Paula had put it, she seemed to be on a roll, she was sure it would be just what she was looking for.

It was.

From the minute she stepped in the door she knew that this was her home. The room itself was a good size, not too big, not too small. The walls could do with a lick of paint, the light fittings would have to change and the carpet was an offence to the eyes. But the tiny marble fireplace, cosy kitchenette in an alcove and lemon and green bathroom were altogether perfect. However, the *pièce de résistance* was without a doubt the gallery overhanging the room and its vast skylight – the only window, but it was enough to light up the entire place. A plain wooden staircase led up to the gallery, which, apart from the splashes of brightly coloured paint on the tiled floor, was bare. It would make the most wonderful bedroom. And all this, coupled with its proximity to Battersea Bridge, well, it was just too good to be true. She made an offer instantly, but knew that if came to it she would pay over the odds to make sure she got it. For a fleeting moment her heart softened towards Phillip Denby, for in truth, were it not for him, she wouldn't have been able to afford anywhere – not without selling the cottage and the shop, which was something she'd never even contemplate.

Monday morning she turned up at the TW offices at nine thirty sharp – the time Annalise had told her to. Unfortunately it was raining again, and still not too sure which bus to take Corrie had decided to walk from the stop in the King's Road. As a result she was not exactly looking her best. Still, with a pounding excitement she pushed through the revolving door into the stark reception of the new building, and gave her name to the security man. He sent her up to the fourth floor, where the TW offices were located and as the lift doors opened she found herself in reception.

The receptionist was on the telephone, and looked up as the lift doors opened. When she saw Corrie she went back to her call, and Corrie had to wait over five minutes, frequently stepping out of the way as people whizzed back and forth, before the receptionist rang off and reluctantly gave her attention.

'I'm Corrie Browne,' Corrie said. 'I'm starting work here today.'

'Yeah. Annalise told me to expect you. Go on in. It's through there.'

Surprised by the lack of formality – not to mention cordiality – Corrie pushed open the door the receptionist had indicated and found herself in the middle of what seemed utter bedlam. In no time at all she realized what all the fuss was about. She'd heard on the news that morning that the IRA had blown up an MP's car somewhere on the outskirts of London, and it would appear that the following night's programme was on terrorism. This latest monstrosity naturally had to be included.

Everyone was talking at once.

'Any news on Jacobs yet?'

'No.'

'Well is the bastard dead or alive?'

'I don't know,' a woman screamed back. 'They're not saying.'

'Then he must be alive.'

'Shit! *I don't know!*'

'Get onto Scotland Yard again! Have you found a crew?'

'They're already on the way.'

'Colin's on the phone,' someone else yelled, 'says they've just arrived in Iran.'

'Has anyone seen the carnet I left on this desk?'

'Which reporter is handling it?'

'Gavin.'

'Sharon, get onto the cuttings library and get all the info you can on Jacobs. Do it *now* before some other bastard gets there. Then send a bike over for it. Perkin stop scratching your ass and sit on it. You can start writing a script.'

'You're in the way there,' someone said, pushing Corrie to one side as she flew past.

'Bob! Luke's on line three for you!'

The man who'd been asking most of the questions and

dishing out all the instructions disappeared into another office, but the pandemonium continued, and Corrie looked round helplessly, wondering who she should introduce herself to. Then to her relief Annalise rushed in behind her.

'Oh Corrie!' she cried, as they collided. 'You're here. Great. Follow me.'

She took Corrie to an over-laden desk in the corner, yelled out, 'Everyone, this is Corrie Browne, the new research assistant,' then promptly disappeared.

'What did you say your name was?' a woman asked her.

'Corrie.'

'OK, Corrie, get me twenty copies of these run off will you?' the woman handed her a pile of notes then returned to her phone call.

Corrie hunted around for the photocopier.

'It's in reception,' the woman shouted.

Corrie waved her thanks and went through the door. The minute she began copying someone pushed her to one side telling her to make room for more urgent business. Corrie waited, then started again. Within minutes someone else was pushing her out of the way, so again she waited. At the next attempt she managed four copies before the machine jammed.

'Oh no!' she groaned.

'Not a problem, just something caught up,' a man behind her said. 'I'm Alan Fox, by the way, one of the reporters.'

'Yes, I recognize you,' Corrie smiled. 'I'm Corrie Browne,' and she stood aside for him to sort the copier.

As he was bending down his hand touched her leg. Corrie couldn't be sure, but she thought he had done it purposely.

Once the machine was clear Alan stayed to chat. Corrie wished he would go away since she was trying to recollate what she'd already copied. But he stayed, and she wasn't too sure she liked the way he was looking at her. She was in quite a mess by the time someone else came and made her give way again.

She stood back and Alan slipped an arm round her, telling her not to worry, she'd soon get the hang of it. Corrie edged away as his hand was under her arm unmistakably fumbling for her breast. Thankfully he went then, and Corrie decided to dump what she'd done so far and start again. At that point the woman who sent her to do the photocopying came out.

'Oh for God's sake!' she cried. 'Why don't you go and get everyone some coffee, I'll do this myself.'

Dismally Corrie went back into the office. Seeing the secretaries she went over to ask where the coffee was.

'In the machine,' one of them answered, not even looking up from what she was doing. But Corrie didn't miss the quick glance that passed between the four girls.

She took a deep breath. 'Where is the machine?'

One of them pointed her in the right direction, and she went back to the over-laden desk Annalise had assigned her, found a pen and paper and started taking orders.

The rest of the morning she spent filing newspapers, getting shouted at for removing those that were still in use, and dreading that she would be asked to operate the fax. Annalise came back for half an hour, and managed a minute to ask her how she was getting on.

Corrie assured her that everything was OK, asked if there was anything she could do for her and promptly found herself in an edit suite logging the time codes an editor called out to her.

It was in the middle of the afternoon, on her fourth trip to the coffee machine, that Alan Fox found her again. 'Thought I'd come and give you a hand,' he said.

'That's very kind of you,' Corrie smiled. 'But really, I can manage.' She stooped to take another cup from the machine and almost dropped it as Alan quite blatantly put his hand on her bottom.

Gritting her teeth, Corrie put the cup on the tray and pushed the buttons for the next one.

'So you're new to London,' Alan said. 'We'll have to see what we can do to initiate you, won't we?'

'That's very kind of you,' Corrie repeated, not knowing what else she could say. The next coffee was ready and again she stooped to take it. Again Alan's hand found her bottom.

I don't believe this, Corrie was thinking to herself, *I haven't been in the place five minutes and already I've found the office groper.*

She took a sideways step away from him, flashed him a quick smile and pressed more buttons. 'I saw your programme on the Animal Liberation Front the week before last,' she said. 'It was very good.'

'Did you think so?' he said, his narrow eyes, as grey as his hair, seeming to slide all over her body. 'Perhaps we could look at it together sometime, I'll show you how it was put together. You said yourself, you've got a lot to learn.' The *double entendre* gleamed in his eyes as they seemed to rake her face, so deeply that she felt sure the lines on his own were now etched indelibly on hers.

God, is he sleezy, Corrie was thinking, trying not to curl her lip as she removed her eyes from his moistened lips.

The next cup of coffee was ready. This time he didn't touch her with his hand, instead he stood behind her and rubbed himself against her.

Corrie straightened abruptly, almost knocking him off balance. 'Please, don't do that again,' she said tersely.

Alan's nostrils flared. 'Do what?'

'Rub yourself against me.'

The blood rushed to his face, turning it purple. 'You flatter yourself, darling,' he spat. 'And let me tell you this, looking like you do you should be grateful anyone would want to,' and before Corrie could as much as draw breath he stormed off.

For a minute Corrie wanted to cry. Why was everyone so hostile? she wondered. Then quickly pulling herself together she got on with dishing out the coffee.

She didn't see Annalise again that day and by six o'clock she was exhausted, dazed and in a way exhilarated. The fact that she had been treated like a leper all day she put down to how busy everyone was and started to pack up her bag.

'Where are you going?' someone said.

Corrie looked up to see Perkin glaring at her across the office.

'Well, I thought . . .' She glanced at the secretaries' empty desks. 'I was going home,' she said, 'but if you need me to stay . . .'

'I want this voice-over put on the WP,' Perkin told her, handing her reams of handwritten notes. 'Luke will need a copy in the studio first thing in the morning.'

'Of course,' Corrie said.

By nine o'clock she was the only one left in the debris-strewn office and was still only half way through deciphering Perkin's handwriting. She could hardly believe that a half hour commentary could take up so many pages. But at least she'd got the hang of the WP by now. She went out to the coffee machine, got herself a drink then came back to start again.

By one o'clock in the morning, feeling as though her eyes were hanging from her head, she had finished. She got up to put Perkin's notes back on his desk and at that moment the power failed. Within seconds it was back on, but those seconds were all it took. She had forgotten to press the save button – the whole voice over had been wiped.

She wanted to cry, scream, shout, throw the machine out of the window, nuke the electricity board. But taking a deep breath she sat back down again. She finally left the office just after four in the morning. Oswald, the nightshift security man downstairs, called a cab to take her home.

She was back in the office for nine thirty. Perkin was screaming because one of the secretaries couldn't find the voice-over on the computer. Corrie's insides went to jelly.

She rushed over to the secretary, and told her she had stored it under VO.

'What!' the secretary screeched. 'VO? Who told you to put it under VO?'

'Well, I thought, as it's a voice-over . . .' Corrie began.

'You've created a document called VO?'

Corrie nodded.

The secretary turned to Perkin. 'Well you've got your commentary, Perk, but she's only gone and wiped . . .'

Corrie never did find out what she'd wiped since Luke Fitzpatrick came in then and Perkin shouted at the secretary to get printing. The secretary gave Corrie a filthy look and Corrie went off to her desk.

Her second day turned out to be even worse than her first, mainly, she told herself, because she was so tired. But at the end of the day, when she watched everyone go off to the wine bar for a quick drink before transmission, and she wasn't invited, she had to admit that her difficulties were mounting. Nevertheless, she assured herself she didn't care that she wasn't invited, besides which, she couldn't have gone anyway since she had an appointment with the estate agent who was coming with her to the studio to measure up for a blind.

The front door to the studio was at the top of an iron staircase which ran up the side of the Victorian house where the studio was situated. When Corrie arrived Nicholas, the agent, was hauling a step-ladder up to the front door. Corrie was glad to see him for when she'd first met him he had been extremely friendly, and she was much in need of a friendly face right now. But Nicholas seemed impatient with how long she was taking with her tape measure, and when Corrie tried to make conversation he answered in monosyllables, clearly preoccupied with something else. When they were leaving Corrie invited him for a drink. He refused, saying he had to dash off somewhere, so she was left to wend her way back to Regent's Park, through a rush hour that seemed endless. She looked at the faces around her on the tube, wondering where they were going and who they were going home to. She imagined their cosy homes, the nights out they might be planning, and felt the loneliness seep into her heart.

When she got home she turned on the TV to watch the TW programme, then called Paula to tell her about her first couple of days, making it all sound a good deal more successful and exciting than it really was. She didn't want Paula to worry, and besides, her pride wouldn't allow her to admit that things were heading rapidly down the road to disaster.

Beth was crying in the background, so Paula was distracted enough not to pick up the despondent note in Corrie's voice. She did ask, however, if Corrie had spoken to Luke Fitzpatrick yet, but Corrie hadn't. She was able to confirm that Annalise was right, though. Luke Fitzpatrick was even more gorgeous in the flesh than he was on TV. This seemed to satisfy Paula, and since Beth's wails had grown even louder, she had to ring off.

The next morning there was a production meeting. Corrie sat on the edge listening intently to everything that was said and making notes. When it was over Bob, the exec. producer, called her into his office.

As Corrie got up from her chair she didn't see Alan Fox behind her until it was too late. She bumped into him, knocking the cup of scalding hot coffee he was carrying all over him.

'Cunt!' he seethed.

Corrie gasped.

The secretaries giggled.

Corrie turned away quickly, damned if she was going to apologize now, and went into Bob's office.

'It's customary, Corrie,' Bob began, 'for the research team to stay in the office to watch transmission. Your absence was noted last night.'

Corrie's cheeks blazed. 'I'm sorry,' she mumbled, 'I didn't realize. It won't happen again.'

'Good.'

'Is that all?' she said, when he didn't continue.

He sighed. 'No. I'm afraid it's not.'

Corrie's heart churned. Whatever else he had to say she knew she wasn't going to like it.

'I know you've only been here a couple of days,' he said, 'but several people have already remarked on your attitude. Personally speaking I think you're doing a grand job, it's not easy dealing with all those egos out there, but try to remember your position – and have a little more respect, eh?'

Boiling with indignation Corrie managed a brief, though polite, 'Of course,' and left the office.

– 6 –

Six weeks later things still hadn't improved. Annalise was the only one who spoke civilly to Corrie, but Annalise was rarely in the office. She was either out filming, closeted in the edit suite or at home recovering from a hangover.

By now Corrie had discovered the reason behind the secretaries' animosity. They believed that they should have been offered the job as research assistant and felt that Corrie had come in over their heads. There were times when Corrie was tempted to tell them to have the bloody job, but she managed to bite her tongue and got on with whatever task she had been asked to do. As for the others, Alan Fox, she now realized, was governing their hostility. He was much older than the other reporters, had been in the game a lot longer, fancied himself as a bit of a Romeo, and, due to the fact that he presented the programme when Luke wasn't around, was treated, and behaved, as though he were king pin. Whether it was because of his seniority and track record, or his caustic wit, Corrie wasn't sure, but it seemed that everyone, producers, researchers and reporters alike, were all apt, like puppets, to dance to any tune he called. And, at the end of the day when he invited people over to the wine bar for a drink, Corrie noticed that no one ever refused, just as she noticed that she was never included.

She lived for the days when he was out on a story, when at least she felt she could breathe. She had now become the butt of his jokes, which were all the more painful for being so subtly delivered that she didn't always understand them. At least when he wasn't there people left her alone.

Some of the worst times though were when the office was full, but quiet, and she had nothing to do. Unless Annalise was there she was never included in the conversation, so she had no choice but to sit in her isolated chair staring out of the window of the tower block, gazing down onto the rooftops below and the River Thames. Occasionally she would try to alleviate her acute self-consciousness by reading a newspaper, but it seemed that every paper she picked up was suddenly wanted by someone else. Corrie simply smiled and handed it over. Not for a minute did she give any indication of how much they were hurting her, nor of how sickened she was by the way none of them had the guts to go against Alan. She simply took it, was always polite, then returned each evening to the loneliness of the Regent's Park flat and cried herself to sleep.

When Annalise was there things in truth weren't so much better, but at least Annalise was the centre of attention then, instead of Alan Fox. Annalise was so bubbly and lively and outrageous everyone seemed to love her. And no one could blame them for that, since apart from her mischievous sense of humour, refreshing honesty and wit, she had a remarkable capacity for being teased, and an equally remarkable talent for making everyone feel quite special.

The strange thing was that she didn't seem to notice Corrie's misery at all. She simply behaved as though everything was wonderful, like Corrie was having a marvellous time working for TW and wasn't life just terrific? Everyone was aware of her relationship with Luke – Annalise did nothing to hide it – but what anyone thought about it Corrie had no idea, she was not privy to office gossip. For her part she did wonder from time to time about the dark circles which sometimes appeared under Annalise's eyes. Annalise unfailingly attributed them to a hangover, but Corrie wasn't always convinced, since there were days when Annalise's intrinsic jubilation of life didn't quite ring true. Corrie was certain this had something to do with Luke, and wondered what his relationship with Annalise really meant to him – she guessed not as much as it did to Annalise.

She'd never yet spoken to Luke Fitzpatrick, and doubted he even knew she was there. His office, like Bob's, was off the main production unit, but unlike Bob's it had no window onto the comings and goings of the team. He wasn't there every day either, but when he was she loved to watch the way he joked around with everyone, or reshaped their ideas to something that invariably worked better. She liked him, instinctively, mainly because of the way he sent himself up over his popularity with the viewing public. Corrie was astounded to discover that some adoring fans actually sent him nude photographs of themselves, along with shockingly explicit descriptions of what they would like to do to him. When these photographs circulated the office they never reached Corrie, but she knew from the comments and hilarity that not all the photographs were of women. Julia, Luke's secretary, had the thankless task of replying to his fan mail, popping a signed photograph of him into each envelope. Paula wanted one, but Corrie didn't have the nerve to ask.

For the most part she kept herself to herself and observed everything quietly from the wings. On the whole it was hell, but she had now reached the point where she would rather die than allow herself to give in. She was going to use this time to learn. She was already absorbing all the information that came her way and studying how the programmes were made, from research to transmission. She listened hard to all the production meetings that took place in the general office, and tried to figure out for herself why some things worked and others didn't. She had started buying her own newspapers to bone up on what was going on in the world, and when the time was right she was going to say to hell with TW and find herself a job in another production company. One where she would be given an opportunity to excel. Where she might even yet rise to the top. And where, please God, she might one day find herself in a position to employ – or not – Alan Fox and his sycophants. Then it would be her turn to watch them suffer. She could hardly wait for the day.

'Your heart isn't hard enough to carry a grudge like that,' Paula told her when Corrie finally came clean as to how things really were at TW.

'Don't bet on it,' Corrie snapped.

'I will. I know you, remember. You're not capable of hatred, or revenge, much as you might like to think you are.'

'I've changed.'

'Not that much. OK, this might be toughening you up a bit, and who knows, maybe you need it. But being tough doesn't have to mean being hardbitten and vicious. It means standing up for yourself and showing them that you're bigger, better than them. The last thing you want is to be like them, to stoop to their level.'

'But you don't know what it's like,' Corrie protested.

'I know I don't. But listen, Corrie, if I were you I'd find a way to disarm them. Do something to *make* them like you. After all you're not a horrible person, and in the end that'll be a much more satisfying, not to mention healthy, victory than festering away there on how you're going to chew them up and spit out their bones – and you can do it if you put your mind to it.'

'Since when did you get to be so wise?'

'Since I was old enough to understand the advice Edwina always gave us. You reap what you feel. And if you feel bitter and lonely, hard done by and sorry for yourself, then that's the way you'll end up, no matter how successful you become. Don't let them do that to you, Corrie, they're not worth it – and you're worth a great deal more.'

There was a long pause before Corrie grudgingly whispered, 'I suppose you're right,' and Paula instantly heard the tears in her voice. She knew it had been the mention of Edwina that had done it.

'We all love you, Corrie,' she said softly. 'We're rooting for you. You can do it, you can get there. But just bear this in mind. All you're thinking of at the moment is material success, of "getting there." But a fat lot of good that's going to do you without personal success. That is the kind of success it is impossible to be happy without. So don't be too proud to forgive, and think before you go blindly into some kind of revenge trip. Ask yourself, who are you going to end up hurting? You. That's who. So, for your own sake, don't do it.'

'I wish it were as easy as that,' Corrie sniffed.

'I know. But just promise me that you won't go getting yourself all screwed up over this, over them, and how you'd like to pay them back – at least not until you've tried another way.'

Paula waited, and finally Corrie's voice came across the line, 'OK, I'll give it a go,' she said. 'But if doesn't work then I'm telling you now, I'll . . .'

'Save the threats,' Paula interrupted. 'You don't know what might be around the corner. And let's face it, since things can't get much worse . . .'

'I know, they can only get better. You just better be right, that's all I can say, because this is going right against the grain with me, putting myself out on a limb to be nice to those fuckheads.'

'You can do it,' Paula laughed. 'You can do anything.'

'Says who?'

'Me. Who else?'

'My mother, who seems to be living on in you,' Corrie smiled. 'That's who else.'

Phillip Denby was watching his wife. From where he stood, in front of the mirror arranging his bow tie, he could see only her profile, until she tilted her face to the light. She moved her head from side to side before discarding yet another pair of priceless earrings replacing them with another. Again she raised her face to the light, and his eyes followed the curve of her long, slender neck to her delicately bronzed shoulders. Her complexion was as flawless as the diamonds clipped to her ears, her ice-blue eyes as hard and translucent.

She was sitting at her own mirror, in her dressing room. The door was open, Phillip had left it that way after being summoned inside a few minutes ago for his opinion on the dress she had chosen for their cocktail party. As usual her taste was impeccable. She was wearing an off-the-shoulder, knee length black velvet creation from an Italian designer, with matching long gloves and black suede stiletto heels with fake diamond clusters. Her silvery blonde hair had been dressed earlier in the day, semi-precious stones studding the black lace snood holding the chignon. At her throat was the peardrop diamond he had given her three weeks before on their wedding anniversary.

Catching him watching her Octavia stood up and turned

to face him. 'What do you think?' she said, smoothing her hands over her hips.

'Very nice,' Phillip answered, assuming, correctly, that she meant the earrings.

'Yes, aren't they?' she purred, turning back to the mirror and pouting her lips. His face was expressionless as he continued to watch her. She was probably as beautiful now – at forty-six – as she had been the day he married her. She should be, the surgery had cost him a fortune. Was there an area of her body that hadn't yet been subjected to the surgeon's knife, he wondered. Probably not. Everything that could be tucked had been. That could be lifted, replaced or rebuilt was, that needed to be removed had vanished. Her hair was highlighted regularly, she took a sunbed once a week, had her nails manicured twice a week and worked out every morning with her personal trainer in the gymnasium Phillip had had installed in the basement of their Chelsea home.

How many times during the evening ahead, he wondered idly, would he be told what a beautiful couple they made? Friends and strangers alike remarked on it, with tedious regularity. The perfect couple, was how they had been written up in *Harpers* a few months ago, and if one judged them by looks and material wealth alone, then he couldn't deny that they did appear to have everything. Even they never discussed what was missing from their lives – he guessed that as far as Octavia was concerned nothing was. She was incapable of love, he'd discovered that only weeks after they were married, just as she was incapable of understanding the bitterness he felt on the occasions she demanded he make love to her.

She had never had an orgasm, at least not with him, and Phillip had given up trying when she'd told him she really didn't want one – it was undignified, she'd said.

She was dabbing herself with expensive perfume as he walked into her dressing room. Standing behind her he put his hands on her hips and looked at their reflections in the mirror. 'Mmm, smells good,' he murmured.

'Phillip, please,' she said, wriggling away, 'you'll muss up my hair.'

'Sorry,' he mumbled, not quite sure why he had touched her anyway.

'Shouldn't you be going downstairs to check on things?' she said, replacing her perfume on the dressing table and picking up a lip brush.

Swallowing the urge to sweep his fist across the dressing table and smash every bottle on it, he nodded. 'Is there anything I can get you before I go?' he said. 'Anything I can do for you?'

'No. Nothing,' she answered, seeming hardly to have heard him.

Why, oh why, he asked himself savagely as he crossed the room, was he so servile with her? Why couldn't he find it in himself to stand up to her, to tell her what he really thought of her and get the hell out of this farce of a marriage?

As he reached the door his nerves started churning up his stomach. For the past two hours he had been trying to pluck up the courage to tell her he was going away the following week for a few days, but as yet he'd been unable to. He frequently travelled on business, and she never minded, the trouble was, the trip he had planned for next week wasn't business and he was very much afraid that she was going to say she wanted to come too.

He was almost out the door when suddenly the words tumbled from his mouth. 'Oh darling, I almost forgot to tell you. I'm going to Spain for a couple of days next week.'

'Really?' she said, retouching her lips. 'What's in Spain?'

'Golf.' He smiled nonchalantly, but his hand had tightened on the door handle.

Her lip brush stopped in mid-air, and she turned slowly to face him. 'Golf?' she repeated, almost allowing a frown to crease her perfect brow. 'You're going to Spain to play golf?'

Phillip laughed awkwardly. 'Well it's not unheard of,' he said. 'Plenty of others do it, all the time.'

'I'm sure they do,' she said, 'but you don't. At least you never have before. So why suddenly now?'

It was over. There would be no trip to Spain. She was suspicious, she would never allow him to go when she didn't believe his reason for going. He felt a quick stab of sadness – and resentment – that he would have to let Pam down, yet again. 'A few of the chaps from the bank are going,' he said dismally. 'They've invited me along – it seemed like a good idea.'

When he looked up to his amazement he saw that she was smiling, and his hopes suddenly soared.

'How nice that you have some leisure time available to you,' she drawled. 'I'm so pleased, Phillip.'

He could hardly believe his ears and for one fleeting moment was tempted to thank her, but her next words stopped him.

'The de Whitneys have invited us to their cabin in Gstaad next week for a spot of skiing,' she said. 'Of course, I told them it was out of the question, with you being so busy. But now . . . Well, I'll get right on the phone and tell them we'll be there next Tuesday. Oh, darling, how simply splendid. You didn't really want to play golf, did you? No, of course you didn't. Such a dull game. And aren't I clever, I've managed to rescue you from all those middle-class oafs who will insist . . .'

'Actually,' Phillip interrupted, 'I didn't need rescuing. I rather *wanted* to go.'

'Oh don't be silly, Phillip. You hate golf.'

'I enjoy golf, Octavia.'

'No, no, no. You detest it, and Gstaad will be such fun, even though skiing is a bit of a bore. But you know how hospitable the de Whitneys are. One can't fail to have a good time with dear Ramona as one's hostess. And you adore skiing, don't you darling? You're so adept at it.'

It was true, Phillip was a good skier, and of their countless number of friends he probably like Ramona and Ivan de Whitney the most. But right now he wanted to go to Spain.

'I've already booked the flights to Barcelona,' he protested weakly.

'Flights?' Octavia said, giving a little shake of her head indicating confusion.

Phillip coloured and was about to attempt an explanation when Octavia's face lit up.

'Oh, I see,' she cried. 'You were intending to take me with you? How sweet of you, darling. But really, I'm not cut out to be a golf widow, and I would so much prefer to go to Gstaad. You can always cancel the flights, can't you? Yes, of course you can. Get that stupendously efficient little secretary of yours to see to it. Pauline, or whatever her name is.'

'You know very well that her name is Pam,' Phillip retorted.

'So it is. Well get her to handle things. She can book us onto the flight to Switzerland at the same time. Oh, Phillip, you've quite made my day. I'll start shopping first thing in the morning.'

She watched him, and he knew she was waiting for him to object further, but there was no point. She'd already guessed he was planning to take Pam away, the suggestion that Pam could change the flights told him that. Whether the de Whitneys' invitation was genuine he had no idea, but it hardly mattered, they would be going to Gstaad now, come what may. He would arrange the flights himself however, asking Pam to do it would be vindictive and cruel, which was probably what Octavia had intended.

'I'll get onto it first thing in the morning,' he said, and turned to leave the room.

By nature he was not a violent man, but there were times

when the fantasy of feeling his hands tighten around that repellently exquisite neck was so vivid, so compelling it frightened him. It was only the thought of Pam that steadied him, as it did now. How often, since knowing her, had he thanked God for Pam? With her he felt like a man. Pam allowed him to love her, to cherish her, to lavish her with all the kindness he was afraid to show his wife, for Octavia regarded his tenderness and generosity as the most tiresome of all his weaknesses. What was more there were times when Pam actively encouraged him to dominate her, knowing that he needed to feel in control of a woman in order to reassert the manhood that Octavia's indifference had all but destroyed.

He didn't deserve such devotion, he knew it, but Pam insisted he did. She knew him in a way that Octavia never had, and never would. She knew how he longed to love someone, to feel that he could give his whole heart without fear of it being abused and ridiculed. Only with Pam had he ever really allowed himself to open up, to give of himself in a way that ordinarily would have shamed him.

He had been there for Pam when her husband died, had supported her through the worst months of her life, and most of all he had listened when she had needed to talk. She had seen, even then, during her darkest days of grief, what pleasure it had given him to be needed; to feel for once in his life that he had nothing to fear from a woman. Throughout that time she had come to understand him, to care for him, then eventually to love him – deeply and unconditionally. And now, following Corrie's visit to the office, she wanted to help him.

Phillip sighed. It wasn't going to be easy for him to come to terms with Edwina's death, not when he had been carrying such a burden of guilt for so long – a guilt he had always believed that one day he could assuage by somehow making it up to her. Until Pam the only woman he had ever loved was Edwina, and Pam had tried so many times to persuade him to find her. But he was so bitterly ashamed of the way he had deserted her, he had been afraid to face her. He knew he couldn't have stood it if she'd refused to forgive him, but worse was his terror that she would deny him access to their child. The child that had grown through the years in his dreams, the son – his and Edwina's son – who, unbeknownst to Octavia, stood to inherit everything Phillip owned when Phillip died.

But now everything had changed – the son wasn't a son at all. The shock and disappointment had been almost too much to bear. But before Corrie had come to his office, in the days following Ted Braithwaite's telephone call, Phillip had done all he could to suppress the resentment and fear he had felt that there was now another woman in his life. Another woman to turn on him and despise him. He hadn't succeeded: his guilt had overwhelmed him and he had used it as a weapon with which to hurt Edwina's – his own – daughter.

Since Corrie had slammed out of his office that day Phillip had known such despair that Pam had started to become concerned for his health – which was why they had planned to go to Spain. Phillip needed to talk, to sort out in his mind what he must do about Corrie – the daughter he now realized he desperately wanted to know. But how could he when his life was such a mess? He couldn't allow Corrie to become embroiled in the nightmare that dogged his every move, his every thought. As her father he had to protect her from that, just as, by not telling her, he was protecting Pam.

– 7 –

'Corrie Browne's giving a party!' Perkin cried, waving his invitation in the air.

'Oh my God!' one of the secretaries gasped, clutching her own invitation to her chest, 'a rave-up at Corrie Browne's!'

It was the production manager's turn next. 'Come to Corrie Browne, for the most exciting thrills in town!' Billy Jones barked through his cupped hands.

Corrie sat at her desk quietly watching them. Their sarcasm was cruel and unnecessary, but she refused to drop her smile.

'Capers and cavorts, cunnilingus and cookies, all at Corrie the Coward's!'

Everyone laughed uproariously, and Alan Fox took a bow.

At that Corrie turned away, tears of humiliation and fury stinging her eyes. She didn't dare to speak, if she did she knew she would break down, and she would almost rather die than let them see that they had got to her.

From behind her word processor Prue, one of the secretaries, watched Corrie – she was the only one not laughing.

The weekend before Paula and Dave had come up to London to help Corrie move into her new studio. It had been Corrie's idea – following Paula's advice that she should try to win her colleagues over – to throw a house-warming party. Paula had helped her word the invitations that were now sitting on everyone's desks, and Corrie fervently wished that Paula could have been there to see the response for herself – perhaps then Paula would understand how futile any effort was to befriend these people. Had she been anywhere else in the world then Paula's philosophy might have worked, but Corrie knew by now that people in London were different. She didn't know why, they just were – and she hated them, every last one of them. The question now was, did she want to become like them in order to survive, or should she just give up and go home to Amberside? Whatever, it didn't look like there was going to be a party. And as much as it hurt her, it baffled her that anyone could throw a person's kindness back in their face this way.

Picking up her scissors she started to cut a story from the newspaper on the current European summit. Her eyes were so full she could barely see the words. Annalise had asked her to collect together everything she could find on this summit for a programme she was hoping to persuade Luke to do later in the month. Right now Annalise was off the coast of Scotland filming an oil rig. What Corrie wouldn't have given to be with her – or better still that Annalise should be here in the office. The acid remarks, mockery and practical jokes were put on hold when Annalise was around.

An hour later, as she usually did mid-morning, Corrie put on her coat and went out to get sandwiches for those who wanted them. Almost four months had passed now since she'd moved to London and she was still no closer to finding a friend than she had been the day she arrived. The loneliness was by now so overwhelming that she really didn't think she could stand anymore. She missed her mother desperately, and for that reason was afraid to go back to Amberside. Her failure in London, coupled with all the memories of Edwina in Suffolk, could just about finish her altogether. Sometimes it felt as though she had no place to go in the world – she just didn't belong anywhere anymore.

But that wasn't true, she told herself as she handed over her order in the sandwich bar. She had her little studio in Chelsea. For a moment her heart lifted at the thought of its welcoming walls, its friendly air and the way her quirky furniture seemed so at home there. Never mind that everyone had smashed to pieces the pleasure she'd felt inside at the opportunity to show it off, it was still hers and she loved it.

When she returned to the office it was deserted – with

the exception of one of the secretaries. 'They're all in the studio,' Prue told her, 'looking at the new set.'

Corrie's eyes showed her surprise as she turned to look at Prue. Someone had actually spoken civilly to her.

Prue smiled. 'Take a look on your desk,' she said.

Corrie turned to her desk half afraid that there was another cruel trick coming up, but all she saw was a pile of handwritten notes. Dreading what might be written on them she put the sandwiches down and picked up the first page. She read it, blinked hard, then read it again. It was from Perkin, accepting her party invitation. She turned to the next one, aware that her heart was starting an unnatural rhythm. It was from Cindy Thompson, a producer, also accepting her invitation.

Corrie sat down. Her hands were shaking as she leafed through the rest of the notes. Every one of them was an acceptance. 'I should be delighted to come . . .' 'Really looking forward to Friday . . .' '. . . so kind of you to invite me . . .' '. . . do we bring a bottle?'

Corrie looked up, but Prue had gone. Then she heard voices and guessed everyone was on their way back from the studio. Quickly picking up her bag she ran out to the ladies. She didn't want to face them right now. Part of her was burning with resentment that they had been so scathing about her party an hour ago, but another part of her was starting to simmer with euphoria. It was going to work! The olive branch she'd held out had been taken. She could hardly wait to tell Paula.

She left early that Friday to get things ready. Since she'd received their acceptances no one had actually mentioned the party again, but although their aloofness was still apparent, the jibes and jokes at her expense had mercifully stopped. Before leaving that afternoon she made a shy announcement that no one needed to bring a bottle, she had plenty – and she was looking forward to seeing them all later.

Her first stop was at Marks and Spencer where she bought quiche and pâté, french bread and cheese, crisps and nuts, all kinds of dips and chopped vegetables, cocktail sausages, olives and a gâteau. The wine merchant on the King's Road helped her to the studio with the glasses, ice and drink she had ordered – and even offered to help her put up the balloons. As a gesture of thanks Corrie invited him to come along too, but he had other plans, he said. Maybe next time.

'Definitely next time,' Corrie smiled, only just resisting the urge to hug him as he left. Perhaps Londoners weren't so bad after all.

By seven o'clock the food was laid out on the antique pine dining table she'd got from a Sunday auction at Lots Road, and the drink and glasses were set up in the kitchen and on a dilapidated Welsh dresser she'd bought at the same auction. The furniture, a cosy cottage sofa, an old arm chair, a glass topped coffee table supported by two wooden elephants and her TV and video, was all pushed up against the walls with her potted plants and vases of ostentatious ferns and feathers. There was plenty of room for dancing, she'd taken the oriental rugs off the wooden floor to make it easier and she'd bought over a hundred pounds worth of CDs earlier in the week. Selecting one by T'Pau, she turned it up good and loud while she went off to take a shower.

An hour later she was wearing her new tight black dress with a scooped neck and a frill just above the knee, black high heels and tights, a pair of enormous jet earrings and her hair was coiled into a bun on the top of her head. She grinned as she looked at herself in the mirror, twisting and turning to get herself from all angles. She didn't look at all bad, she decided. Even the thick brown eye-liner she'd carefully circled her eyes with didn't look as tarty as she'd expected. And the freckles across her nose barely showed beneath the heavy Revlon foundation cream. She pouted her caramel lips – the same colour as Annalise wore – and giggled. She'd left a message on Annalise's answerphone telling her about the party, but she hadn't heard from her yet. Annalise wasn't due back from Scotland until eight o'clock though, so she probably wouldn't arrive until much later.

Draping her dressing gown over the end of the brass bed, she picked up her glass of wine and went to lean over the balcony to survey the room below. It looked perfect. Balloons bobbed from the stair rail, bowls of crisps and nuts were scattered about, and the two peculiarly shaped candle lamps either end of the mantlepiece cast a rosy, romantic glow over the room.

Michael Jackson was playing on the CD now and Corrie danced her way down the stairs, clicking her fingers and singing along at the top of her voice as she went to help herself to more wine. She'd almost forgotten what it was like to feel happy.

She glanced at her watch. Eight thirty she'd put on the invitations, ten minutes to go. She'd give Paula a quick call to fill in the time.

By nine thirty she was still sitting alone. She was feeling slightly sick, which she put down to the four glasses of wine she'd already drunk.

'No one ever turns up to a party on time,' Paula had tried to reassure her when she'd called her for the second time, just over half an hour ago.

Corrie wandered outside, stood at the top of the steps and looked up and down the street. There was no one in sight.

At ten o'clock she turned off the CD and went to sit on the bottom of the stairs. As she sat there, still hoping beyond hope for someone to arrive, she listened to the police sirens wailing in the distance and the sound of the occasional car as it seemed to slow outside her studio then drive on. At ten fifteen she looked at her watch again and as the last flicker of hope died despondency and defeat washed over her.

She should have known. She should have realized they would do something like this. But why? What did they get out of being so mindlessly cruel? Why did they need to do it? She knew the answer of course, they did it for sport. Because Alan Fox enjoyed victimizing someone. And she, the naive little girl from the country, was that someone. There couldn't be any other answer, since not one of them knew her well enough to have any other motive. So often over the past weeks she had wondered how they would all feel if they knew the pain she was trying to hide, the pain of losing her mother, of being rejected by her father and now the pain of the way they were treating her. But even if they did know, would they care? Of course they wouldn't, and why should they? She was nothing to them, and what was she looking for anyway, their pity to go along with her own self-pity?

Pulling herself to her feet she crossed the room and started to clear the table. All this food, wasted, she was thinking to herself as a single fat tear splashed onto the back of her hand.

'How can they be so mean?' she asked aloud, biting her lips to stop herself crying any more. She picked up the quiche and carried it to the refrigerator. When she went back into the room she started gathering up the bowls of nuts and crisps and then she saw the photograph of her mother, smiling up at her from the coffee table.

'No!' she sobbed, turning away quickly. 'No, no.'

Grief and loneliness swelled so heavily through her chest she could barely breathe. She was locked into a welter of such overwhelming unhappiness that the only movement she could make was to bring her hands to her face. She had tried, had tried so hard . . .

'Oh Corrie!' Annalise cried, when Corrie opened the

door. 'Corrie look at you,' and she wrapped her arms around her.

'They were going to come,' Annalise said, 'I promise you they were. And it was a wonderful idea of yours, it shows a generosity they just don't deserve.'

Corrie pulled away from her, rubbing her fingers under her eyes to wipe away the kohl-blackened tears. 'So why didn't they come?' she asked, still shaking from the way she had jumped when Annalise had knocked on the door.

'Because apparently, just after you left the office this afternoon, Luke called up and invited everyone to a party at the Royal Garden.'

'I see.' Corrie didn't bother to point out that someone could have called her to let her know – what did it matter now? And she could hardly blame Luke when he probably didn't even know about her party since she hadn't invited him. It had seemed a bit presumptuous inviting the boss, she'd thought, especially when she'd never actually spoken to him.

'So why are you here?' she asked Annalise.

'Because when I turned up at the other party half an hour ago, straight from the airport, and Prue told me about your party I guessed you'd be sitting here all alone.'

Corrie forced a smile. 'Thanks, it was nice of you to come. But you don't have to stay. I expect you want to be with Luke.'

'Sure I do. But why don't you come along too? This'll keep, well most of it will, and you can throw your party tomorrow. Come on, we'll hop in a cab.'

'To be honest I don't really feel in the party mood any more,' Corrie said.

Annalise looked around the room. 'Oh you've gone to so much trouble,' she sighed. 'And this is such a lovely place, Corrie. Oh please say you'll come to the other party, I can't bear to think of you sitting here all by yourself.'

'No, really, I'd rather not,' Corrie answered. She didn't

add that she'd taken all the humiliation she could handle for one night – maybe for one lifetime. And as she showed Annalise back to the door she was already composing her letter of resignation.

On Monday morning Corrie was at the office early. Alan Fox was already there, so too were Billy Jones, two of the secretaries and Perkin. They all looked up as Corrie walked in, but no one spoke.

Corrie's face was pale, her lips compressed in a thin tight line as she crossed the office, hung up her coat, then marched straight over to Alan Fox. He looked up in surprise, but before he could utter a word Corrie's fist smashed into his face.

'You are a fucking asshole!' she spat, and turning on her heel she marched back out of the office and into the ladies.

It took her several moments to get her breath back, but by the time she had splashed her face with cold water and dried it she was grinning. God, that had been worth it, just to see the look on his face. She'd never done anything like it before in her life, but she'd do it again just for the sheer satisfaction she was feeling now. She'd even made his nose bleed.

Of course she had to go back in there and face them all again, but what the hell, she was going to hand in her resignation today anyway.

By the time she returned to the office several others had arrived. Their whispering stopped as she walked in the door and they all turned to stare at her. Ignoring them Corrie walked over to her desk. The mail was piled high, and taking the letter opener out of her drawer she sat down to open it.

She hit the floor with a resounding thud! It was several seconds before she realized she had forgotten to pull up her chair.

There was a loud guffaw from the other side of the office,

and even her own lips started to twitch. Of all the moments to pratfall this had to be just about the worst!

'Corrie! Corrie! Is Corrie here?' It was Luke's secretary.

'Yes, I'm here,' Corrie answered, poking her head up over the desk.

Judy frowned, then shrugging she said, 'Luke would like to see you. Can you come in a moment please?'

'Of course,' Corrie mumbled, picking herself up from the floor.

She turned straight to her handbag, knowing that everyone was still watching her, and laughing. She was shaking now, with the shock of the fall, her own suppressed laughter, and nerves at being summoned by Luke Fitzpatrick. Obviously Alan Fox had already told him what she'd done. She just hoped she wasn't going to be up on an assault charge now.

She took her resignation from her bag and walked towards Luke's office. As she passed Perkin he cowered away from her,

'Don't hit me!' he pleaded. 'Please don't hit me!'

The others laughed, Corrie kept going.

Luke Fitzpatrick closed the door behind Corrie and waved her to a chair. 'I think I owe you an apology,' he said, walking around his desk.

Corrie looked at him in amazement, but as his eyes met hers she turned quickly away, colouring to the roots of her hair. He was smiling at her and her sudden rush of self-consciousness was only heightened by an acute awareness of how very handsome he was.

'I stole all your party guests, Annalise told me,' he went on. 'It was unintentional, I assure you. And,' he added with an unmistakable twinkle in his eye, 'I shall overlook the fact that you didn't see fit to invite me. Nevertheless, you really should have come on to the Royal Garden with Annalise, you'd have had a good time.'

Corrie had to pull herself together rapidly. In the excitement of the past few minutes she'd all but forgotten about Friday night. 'Uh, well, I wasn't exactly in the mood for a party by then,' she answered, feeling herself responding to his smile.

'No, I don't imagine you were,' he said. 'And unless I'm greatly mistaken you've probably spent the entire weekend alone in your apartment wondering how you can tell the whole lot of us to go to hell. Or worse?'

Corrie grinned. 'Worse,' she said, realizing that he didn't as yet know she had biffed Alan Fox.

Luke laughed, then folding his arms on the desk he looked at her quite seriously. 'From what I can gather,' he said, 'things haven't exactly been easy for you since you started at TW.' He held up his hand as Corrie made to interrupt. 'I don't know too much about what has been going on,' he continued, 'but I know enough. Now, I can't tell them out there how to behave every minute of the day, and my guess is you wouldn't take too kindly to me ordering them to be nice to you anyway. But I could have helped this situation a long time ago just by showing you a little congeniality myself. I didn't, and for that I'm sorry. We will put that to rights starting now. I had a chat with Bob over the weekend and he tells me your work is of a very high standard, so if that's a resignation you're clutching in your hand there, can I ask you to put it on hold for a few weeks?'

Corrie looked at him. Any answer she might have given was unable to get past the lump that had suddenly risen in her throat.

The corners of Luke's incredible blue eyes crinkled in a smile. 'I hope that lip tremble was a yes,' he said.

Corrie laughed and choked on a sob.

'And,' he continued, 'I should like to make amends for Friday by inviting you out to dinner one night this week. It's about time we got to know each other.'

Corrie was stunned. Why on earth would he want to get to know someone as lowly as her? *And* over dinner? She'd better tell him about Alan Fox now, before anyone else did. He might well change his mind once he knew.

'I just punched Alan Fox on the nose,' she said flatly.

Luke's eyes widened. Then, to her unutterable delight, he burst out laughing. 'I'm sure he more than deserved it,' he said.

'Yes, he did,' Corrie beamed, feeling slightly delirious. 'I just thought I should tell you, because it's probably a sackable offence.'

'In some circumstances,' Luke admitted. 'But I daresay not these. I've watched you these past weeks,' he went on, 'so has Bob. Bob much more closely, of course. He is of the opinion that you are nurturing an ambition to become a researcher – perhaps a reporter . . .'

'Producer, actually,' Corrie blurted out.

'Producer then,' Luke laughed. 'Well, I admire people with ambition, and I admire people with guts. You clearly have both. There aren't many who would have been able to keep their heads above water faced with what you've been faced with since you started here. Most would have gone scuttling back home to mother by now. Is that what you intend, by resigning?'

Corrie shook her head. 'No. I was going to look for another job.' She didn't tell him her mother was dead, had died only five months ago, she hadn't told anyone – not even Annalise.

Luke was clearly impressed by her answer. 'Still weren't going to give up, eh? Now there's tenacity. So, what do you say? Will you let me take you to dinner?'

'Yes. Yes, I'd like that very much,' Corrie answered, already feeling slightly dizzy at the prospect of being seen in public with Luke Fitzpatrick. Just wait till she told Paula! God, did she have a lot to tell Paula.

Luke's eyes were on hers, and she could feel herself

starting to blush again. His magnetism was so all-pervading it was almost tangible.

'I don't suppose you have your diary with you,' he said, opening his own. 'But let me see, tomorrow night's good for me. Let me know if it's OK with you.'

'Oh, that's fine with me.' The words practically gushed from her mouth. 'I'm free all the time.' Oh God! she groaned inwardly, what an idiot I must sound.

Laughing, Luke stood up and walked around his desk. 'Then I'll make a reservation at San Frediano's in Fulham Road for eight o'clock. Do you know it?'

Corrie shook her head.

'It's Italian,' he said, opening the door. He was on the point of saying something else when he saw Annalise coming towards him.

'I thought you were going back to Scotland this morning,' he said.

'I was.' She smiled at Corrie as she passed, and flicked out her mane of foaming blonde curls. 'Pippa called last night, they won't let us back on the rig again until tomorrow, so I'm flying up there tonight.'

Corrie looked at her curiously. There was something odd about her, she thought. Her confidence was too bright, too brittle, and her movements seemed awkward.

Luke stood to one side as Annalise sailed into his office and Corrie started back to her desk.

Before closing the door Luke glanced across at Corrie. She was on the point of answering the telephone when she looked up and caught him watching her. She smiled, and laughing at yet another flood of colour to her cheeks, Luke disappeared back into his office.

'So?' Annalise said, as he walked behind his desk.

'I've apologized to her.'

Annalise waved a hand impatiently. 'I'm not talking about Corrie, and you know it. I'm talking about Saturday night. Remember Saturday night?'

Sighing deeply Luke sank into his chair. He hadn't missed the red rings around her eyes. 'I seem to be doing a lot of apologizing this morning,' he grumbled.

'I waited in,' Annalise retorted. 'I waited all night.'

'I'm sorry.'

Annalise held his eyes, but when it became clear he wasn't going to give her an explanation she gritted her teeth and asked for one.

'I didn't call because I wasn't in London,' he said.

'Then where were you?'

Luke's eyes narrowed with annoyance. He glanced at his watch. 'Annalise, this is hardly the time or the place to be having this discussion. I've said I'm sorry, now if you don't mind, I've . . .'

'I *do* mind,' she said, petulantly.

'I've got an important telephone call to make,' he said deliberately.

'But you distinctly told me on Friday night, when I was in your bed,' she was biting out the words, but her voice was thick with tears, 'that we were going out on Saturday. You didn't even call to say you couldn't make it. You owe me an explanation for that, you bastard, and don't think I'm . . .'

'Annalise, please leave this office now, before we both say something we'll only regret later. Now!' he barked, as she made to protest again.

Annalise started at the harshness of his tone. 'Why do you keep treating me like this?' she cried. 'One minute you're telling me you can't get me out of your mind, the next you're trying to throw me out of your office. I just don't know where I stand with you, Luke. I feel like I'm going out of my mind.'

'We'll talk about this when you get back from Scotland,' he answered, standing up and heading towards the door.

'No! Wait!' she cried before he could open it.

He turned back, his face expressionless.

— 115 —

'Oh, God, I hate it when you look like that,' she said, covering her face with her hands. 'Luke, just tell me, please! Tell me what is going on with us.' When she looked up her eyes were steeped in desperation. 'You know how I feel about you,' she said. 'I don't make any secret of it. Perhaps I should. Should I? I don't know. I don't know anything any more. I tried to call you all day yesterday . . .'

As the tears started to run down her face Luke let go of the door and pulled her into his arms. 'Don't cry,' he said, resting her head on his shoulder. 'Please, don't cry.' Again he looked at his watch.

'Then tell me how you feel,' she sobbed.

'You know how I feel. I'm crazy about you, but I'm just not convinced it can work. I . . .'

'But why? Tell me why.' She was looking up into his face, her eyes pleading for the reassurance she craved.

'You know why. I'm almost twenty years older than you to begin with, and I'm your boss. *And* your father's my partner. It's all too . . . It makes me feel trapped.'

'But Daddy hardly ever comes here. He told you himself that he'd leave the running of the place to you. And he does. And as for being my boss, if it make a difference, if you really want me to, I'll leave. I'll find a job somewhere else. If it means . . .'

'Annalise,' he groaned.

'If it means you won't feel trapped any more. I'll do anything, Luke. Anything you want me to.'

'I know you will,' he sighed. 'That's half the problem.'

'What do you mean?'

He shook his head. 'Nothing. Forget it.'

For a long time she searched his eyes with her own, trying to find the answers he couldn't, or wouldn't give. In the end she said, 'Luke, there's no one else, is there? Tell me there's no one else.'

She sounded so pathetic that he couldn't help smiling.

'You always ask me that,' he said softly, 'and the answer is still the same. No, there's no one else. Just you.'

'Are you sure?'

'Quite sure.'

She attempted a smile. 'Can we talk, when I get back from Scotland?'

'If that's what you want.'

When she had gone Luke buzzed through to his secretary to tell her he didn't want any more interruptions, then he picked up the telephone and dialled a long distance number.

'It's Luke Fitzpatrick here,' he said, when a voice answered at the other end.

'Ah, yes. I'll put you straight through, Mr Fitzpatrick,' the voice said.

The conversation didn't last long, but by the time Luke replaced the receiver the furrow between his brows had visibly deepened.

He got up and walked across to the window. If only there was someone he could confide in, someone to help him support this insupportable burden. A quick smile crossed his lips as an image of Corrie sprang to his mind. It was something like uncorking a genie, he thought wryly. And yes, he probably could tell her. Not that he expected her to have the answers, but he knew instinctively that she would care, that she would try to understand and do everything she could to help. She was that sort of person. Yes, he probably could tell her, but of course he never would.

Corrie spent the next twenty-four hours in agony. She was nervous, excited, talked for hours on the phone to Paula, and panicked incessantly about what she was going to wear for her dinner with Luke. She was longing to thank Annalise, who she was sure had put Luke up to it, but Annalise had returned to Scotland.

The atmosphere in the office seemed, Corrie thought, slightly better than before, though still no one spoke to her unless they had to. Alan Fox had let up on the practical jokes and insults since his whack on the nose, now he was going about the place snarling and scowling at her like some Walt Disney villain. But what did any of that matter? With Luke Fitzpatrick and Bob Churchill behind her she couldn't fail.

Throughout the day leading up to their dinner Corrie went through all kinds of scenarios in her mind as to how she was going to handle herself that night. What kind of sparkling conversation could she make, what should she do or say to make a good impression, and, if she dared, what little anecdotes could she tell him that might make him laugh?

At lunchtime she tore off to the King's Road, bought herself an electric blue suit in Wallis, then in a rash moment dashed up to Peter Jones where she treated herself to a dark red Dior lipstick.

When she was finally ready that evening she wasn't too sure about the way she looked. It didn't look much like her gazing back from the mirror, perhaps her skin was too pale for such a bright lipstick, but the freckles didn't show too much and she managed to convince herself that she looked a little more sophisticated than usual, even though the suit was a bit tight.

Luke had sent a taxi to pick her up and was waiting when she arrived at the restaurant. He ordered them both an aperitif and they talked for a while about TW. Corrie was trying very hard to pay attention, but she couldn't help noticing the way everyone was looking at them. Two women even came up and asked for Luke's autograph, while Corrie sat by nearly bursting with pride. Then the menus arrived. Corrie decided to go for the spaghetti.

'Not one of my more brilliant ideas,' she laughed nervously as she wiped the front of her suit.

Laughing, Luke gave her some of his lamb to taste. In return Corrie wound some spaghetti round her fork and offered it to him. He seemed highly entertained by this, but leaned forward for her to feed him. Before it reached his mouth, the spaghetti slid off the fork onto the edge of his plate, then slithered into his lap.

'Well, I guess you probably want to go home now,' Corrie said. 'I know I do.'

Luke was laughing so hard that for a while he didn't answer. In the end he picked up his wine and saluted her. 'Come on, we've got a dessert to get through yet.'

'No. I have no intention of leaving this restaurant wearing a chocolate mousse as well as spaghetti,' Corrie declared. 'You have the dessert, I'll drink some more wine. And when I've finished here, I'll go home and drown my disgrace in all that I was left with last Friday – thanks to you stealing all my party guests.'

She couldn't believe how outspoken she was being, but seemed unable to stop. Of course she knew that at any minute she was likely to say something so hideously embarrassing she'd want to stick her head in the oven later, but that he was so clearly enjoying himself was more intoxicating than the wine itself and there was no controlling her exuberance. She even warned him that she was quite capable of coming out with some outrageous *faux pas*, and gave him the example of the woman who had come into her mother's dress shop in Amberside, who, she explained, was going to a ball at her father's house that night, but she hadn't known that he was her father then, and anyway it had no significance really to her story. 'But I heard myself telling this woman that she might end up with a prick in her bum. Her face was a picture. I, of course wanted to die on the spot.'

Again Luke was laughing, but it wasn't that particular confession that made her want to hop up and down with embarrassment the next morning, it was the next one.

'You know what, Luke?' she said, resting her wine glass on her chin, 'you are just to drop dead for.'

'I think you mean to die for,' he corrected her, 'and you've been talking to Annalise. Anyway, tell me some more about where you grew up. Amberside, did you say? Where is it?'

Her humiliation had not yet reached her, so she chattered on quite happily, not thinking for a moment that she might be boring him – that only occurred to her later. Much later.

'Anyway,' she finally finished, at last realizing that she'd been rattling on for hours, 'my mother died just over five months ago and it was soon after that that I came to London. How about you, where did you grow up?'

Luke looked around and only then did Corrie notice that the waiters were putting chairs on the tables. She turned back to Luke in dismay.

'Come on, I'll take you home,' he chuckled, 'and if you ask very nicely I might come in and help you out with some of that wine I so rudely left you with last week.'

But as they were driving towards the King's Road the car phone rang and Luke told her that he'd have to take a rain check.

Corrie swallowed her disappointment, and when he had driven away ran inside to ring Paula. It was only when she was half way through dialling that she remembered how late it was.

The next morning her hangover tormented her with memories of all she'd said and done the night before. 'I just want to die,' she told Paula. 'Oh God, when I think of all the things I said. I spent hours telling him all about Amberside and there's nothing to tell. I tried to be so cool when I told him he was to die for, or drop dead gorgeous, but I got the two confused and I think I told him to drop dead. Oh, Paula, how can I ever face him again?'

'Oh, I'm sure you'll find a way,' Paula laughed.

But it was Luke who found the way, as later, in the office, after asking Eileen, one of the secretaries to book him a car to take him to the airport in the morning, he turned to Corrie and asked if she was free again that night.

With an extremely red face Corrie told him she was. Her embarrassment wasn't only for the night before, but because she was acutely aware that everyone had heard. It was only when Luke glanced about the room, before disappearing back into his own office, that she realized he had intended them to.

He came to pick her up that night. Corrie was so thrilled with his appreciation of her studio that she suggested they might just stay there and have a drink.

'I've plenty of food too,' she said eagerly. 'Unless of course you want to go out.'

'Here sounds great to me,' he said, settling himself onto the sofa and stretching an arm along the back.

Corrie couldn't hide her delight. It was really quite unbelievable that Luke Fitzpatrick should be her first proper guest.

'Would you like to choose some music?' she offered, pointing him towards the CD player. 'I'll just go and rustle something up in the kitchen.'

'That your bedroom up there?' Luke asked, nodding towards the balcony.

Corrie nodded, then blushed at the comical way he raised his eyebrows.

Five minutes later she brought in a tray laden with nuts, olives, crisps, wine and two glasses. Luke was back on the sofa, Phil Collins was playing on the CD.

They finished the first bottle of wine and started on another. All the time Corrie was listening with mounting horror and sympathy to what he was telling her about his family and childhood. He had grown up on a small farm in Southern Ireland, the youngest of three sons. There was a gap of fifteen years between him and the middle brother, he had been a mistake, and though he was never in any doubt that his mother had loved him, he couldn't even begin to say the same for his father. The old man, since he was old enough to remember, had been consistently cruel to him. He didn't go into detail, but Corrie could imagine the terror of a little boy being bullied by the father he tried so hard to please.

'It wasn't only me,' he sighed, 'he led my mother a hell of a life too. I think it's that more than what he did to me that's had such an effect on me.' He held out his glass as Corrie offered him more wine. 'Some women really do need protecting from men, even the men they love. Maybe especially the men they love. That was the odd thing, you know, she loved my father. I never did understand that. Just like you can't understand why your mother loved your father for all those years. Strange isn't it? Perhaps it's protection from themselves, women need. Who knows?'

'Did you have many friends as a child?' Corrie asked.

'A few. One in particular, I suppose. He was a couple of years younger than me, but we've lost touch now.'

'And your mother and father and brothers, where are they now?'

'My mother's dead, my father and eldest brother still live in Ireland, and before you ask, no I don't visit them. My other brother is married and lives in Australia. I've visited him once or twice, but we're not what you might call close. It's a shame really, I'd like to belong to a close family.' He smiled. 'Looks like I'll have to create one of my own.'

'Have you ever been married?'

'No. I guess I've never met the right woman.'

It was on the tip of Corrie's tongue to ask about Annalise, but she managed to bite it back. It was none of her business.

He looked at his watch. 'Well, I guess I'd better be going. I've got an early start tomorrow.'

'Are you flying to Scotland to join Annalise?' Corrie asked.

'Good God no. I'm off to LA to spend some time with an old friend of mine. Cristos Bennati. I expect you've heard of him.'

'*Heard* of him!' Corrie gasped. 'Oh, I've heard of him all right. You do mean *the* Cristos Bennati, don't you? The film director?'

Luke laughed. 'I do.'

'But how do you know him?'

Luke frowned thoughtfully. 'Let me see,' he said, 'I've known him so long . . . Oh, I remember, it was at a party in the South of France. Neither of us were much more than about twenty at the time. I don't recall too much about that, probably had a lot to drink, but a couple of months later Cristos turned up here in London, at the National Film School, and he gave me a call. We've kept in touch, on and off, ever since. And if your eyes get any rounder I'll fall into them.'

'I'm stunned,' Corrie said.

'He's just a man,' Luke chuckled, 'like the rest of us.'

'I know, but . . . Cristos Bennati!'

'Time really is getting on,' Luke said, chucking her under the chin, 'thanks for a great evening.'

Corrie laughed. 'Thanks for coming round, I've really enjoyed it.'

'Me too. We must do it again when I get back.'

When Luke got out onto the street he pocketed the keys to his car and walked in the direction of the King's Road to flag down a taxi. He didn't want to risk losing his licence, he'd get someone from the office to pick up his car in the morning. That should set the tongues wagging, he laughed to himself, as he flagged down a cab.

What would set them wagging even more was if he were to dump Annalise for Corrie. Now what kind of hornet's nest would that stir up? He grinned. At this precise moment in time he was probably the only one who could come even close to guessing the answer to that. And it sure as hell could be an answer to a whole lot of problems for him.

It wasn't until the middle of the next day that Cindy Thompson finally came right out and confronted Corrie with what was on everyone's mind. Corrie had been aware of the gossip all morning, of course. Sam, the odd job man, had made no secret of the fact that he'd had to go over to her place to pick up Luke's car. Predictably everyone had jumped to the conclusion that she and Luke had spent the night together. Corrie was in no position to put them right, since no one had had the guts yet to accuse her. That was until Cindy sauntered over to pick up her coat at lunchtime.

'Corrie,' she said.

Corrie looked up from her desk.

'You might have forgotten that it was Annalise who got you your job here,' Cindy began, 'but I can assure you that none of us have. And if this is the way you repay her then all I can say is you're a crafty, conniving, two-faced little cow.'

For a second or two Corrie merely looked at her, but gone were the days of letting them get away with their vicious, small-minded victimization. She got slowly and deliberately to her feet, looked Cindy straight in the eye, and said, 'Not that it's any of your damned business, but just for the record Luke Fitzpatrick did not spend the night with me last night, he merely came round for a drink. It was a gesture of friendship on his part, which is a damned sight more than any of you sycophantic hypocrites have ever made.'

'Oh, so the cat really has got claws,' one of the researchers meeeowed.

'She'll need more than claws once Annalise finds out about this,' Alan Fox chipped in. 'I hope old Luke remembered to use a condom, there's no knowing what a chap might catch . . .'

'Stop right there!' Corrie hissed.

'Watch out Alan, I think she's going to wallop you again,' Perkin snickered.

'Oh drop dead the lot of you!' Corrie snapped, and stormed out of the office.

She returned after a lunch hour spent wandering Battersea Park to a note on her desk asking her to go to the edit suite to log some tapes for one of the editors. The office was buzzing with the latest news in from Eastern Europe, something that was going to affect that night's programme, so no one paid much attention to Corrie as she picked up her notepad and pen and left the office again.

As she was walking down the corridor she heard footsteps coming after her, then someone calling her name. She turned round.

'Corrie,' Prue said in a hushed voice, 'I just thought I ought to let you know that while you were out Annalise called.'

'Yes?' Corrie said.

'Well, Eileen told her that you'd spent the night with Luke.'

'What!' Corrie gasped. 'But I told them . . . Oh God! What did Annalise say?'

'I don't know. But we both know how she feels about Luke. Anyway, I just thought I ought to warn you. Don't tell the others I did, will you?'

Corrie shook her head. 'No. OK. And thanks, Prue.'

That Thursday evening Corrie was sitting at home watching the TV when there was a knock on the door. To her dismay it was Annalise, who, judging by the holdall at the top of the stairs, had come straight from the airport.

Leaving her bag where it was Annalise swept past Corrie into the studio without so much as a hello. 'I do hope I'm not interrupting anything,' she said, her voice dripping with sarcasm.

Corrie sighed. 'No, you're not interrupting anything,' she said, with exaggerated patience.

'No, of course not, he's in LA, isn't he? Didn't you ask to go with him?'

It was on the tip of Corrie's tongue to tell Annalise to grow up, but despite the fact that Annalise was younger than her, she was still a producer. Instead she said, 'Of course not. Why on earth would I?'

'Well you can't tell me you don't fancy him.'

'I'm not telling you anything. There's nothing to tell.'

'Are you quite sure about that?'

'Of course I am. For God's sake . . .'

'Did you sleep with him?'

'No!'

'Liar!'

'Annalise, I did *not* sleep with Luke. I didn't even kiss him. But if you choose not to believe me then remember, it'll only be yourself you're hurting – and for no reason.'

'But you wanted to sleep with him.'

'For God's sake! We had dinner together, we had a drink together, that's all.'

'Didn't he try to get you into bed?'

'No!'

'You're a lying little bitch. I know Luke Fitzpatrick. He can't resist an easy lay.'

'I resent that remark,' Corrie snapped.

'Resent it all you like. You're an ungrateful little whore. I gave you your job, Ted Braithwaite's bastard child that you are . . .'

'What!'

'. . . and the minute my back is turned you're opening your legs for my boyfriend.'

'Annalise, if you don't trust Luke then that's your problem. But don't come round here . . .'

'You make me sick, people like you,' Annalise spat. 'You're common! A working-class slut going around with a massive chip . . . I suppose you managed to find out that Luke is working class too. Nice and cosy that, eh? Let's all us plebs stick together, a nice exclusive little club to fuck the ruling classes . . .'

'I don't know which century you're living in, Annalise, but it's clearly not this one. But all right I am common, if that's what you want to call it. I am working class, but my behaviour, my manners, are so far and away superior to yours, to those fuckheads you call colleagues who wouldn't know a scrap of human decency if it jumped up and bit them . . .'

'They know loyalty,' Annalise yelled, 'which is more than I can say for you, you two-faced little bitch. Now you keep your hands off Luke Fitzpatrick, do you hear me. Because if you don't you're going to be extremely sorry you ever clapped eyes on him.' And with that she slammed out of the door.

– 8 –

Luke was sitting on the pool deck at Cristos Bennati's home in Beverly Hills sipping a martini. Actually it wasn't Beverly Hills, Luke reminded himself, it was the Holmby Hills, one of the most exclusive addresses in Los Angeles. However, Bennati's Italian style villa, set well back from the highway at the centre of its own three acres of palm trees, landscaped gardens, swimming pool and tennis courts, was modest by American standards. But Bennati never had gone in for ostentation. Simple and functional, was how Luke would describe the house, just like the annexe where Bennati had a suite of offices, two Steenbecks and a screening room. This was as well as the facilities reserved exclusively for him on the lot at Universal, but Bennati preferred to work at home whenever he could.

He had been closeted in the annexe with a bunch of screenwriters since he had arrived back from Pennsylvania two days ago, meaning that Luke had seen very little of him. This didn't surprise Luke, neither was he put out about it, he'd always known how seriously Bennati took his art.

He wandered over to the bar to help himself to another martini. As he passed he idly fondled the breast of a luscious young starlet who had been keeping him company this past week. She giggled, then purred as she ran her glossy nails along the inside of his thigh. Luke wondered if he could summon the energy for another session between the sheets. He decided he couldn't and moved on to the bar.

A few minutes later, back on his lounger in the shade of the pool deck, Luke looked up as he heard a car start, and guessed that the screenwriters must be leaving. Just after he heard Cristos's voice coming from inside the house, and grinned.

'Who the hell are you?' Cristos barked.

Obviously he had come across Luke's other bed partner in the sitting room.

'I'm with Luke,' the girl simpered. 'He said it'd . . .'

'Out!' Cristos said. 'Get your clothes and out.'

'Well there's no need to take that attitude.'

'You too,' Luke said to the starlet. 'Time to go. Call yourself a cab.'

She pouted sulkily, but when Cristos came out onto the deck she pulled back her shoulders and gave him a dazzling smile. Topless as she was Cristos didn't even seem to notice her as he went to pour himself a drink.

Not long after they heard the girls leaving and exchanged looks. 'Sorry,' Luke said. 'I meant to get rid of them before you finished. I didn't notice the time.'

Cristos simply looked at him then wandered across to the pool. Unlike Luke he was fully dressed, if you could call Levi jeans and a faded denim shirt fully dressed. His sleeves were rolled back, revealing the dark hair on his forearms and the silver and gold wrist band of his watch. With one hand he swept the unruly jet black curls away from his forehead and with the other he held his drink against his chest. He stared down at the water, his handsomely rugged features taut with concentration.

From where he was standing Luke could see the thick curl of his eyelashes and the dark shadow on his chin. On Luke's last visit, six months or so ago, the two of them had laughed long and hard at the fact that some idiot magazine had just voted Bennati the world's sexiest man. His physique alone could have won him the accolade, but they both knew that it was his reputation that had clinched it. Bennati himself never discussed the women he dated, the women themselves weren't quite so discreet. But it was quite something that they still raved about his prowess in the sack when he had dumped them, Luke thought admiringly.

He lifted his glass as Cristos turned to look at him.

'OK, let's have it,' Cristos said, 'what you doing here, Fitzpatrick?' He looked at his watch. 'You got thirty minutes before my next appointment.'

From the window of Cristos's office Jeannie Feldman, Cristos's personal assistant, was watching them with mounting curiosity. Her round, happy face was at that moment drawn in a frown, and a tuft of her short spiky hair was on end from where she had scratched her head. She was not at all sure she liked the look of what was going on out there, in fact, if pushed she'd have to admit that she had gotten the distinct impression these past couple of days that Cristos's liking for Luke Fitzpatrick was running out of fuel. But it wasn't Cristos's style to have someone around he didn't like. Still, the two of them went back a long way, and she knew Luke had put Cristos up plenty of times in London, maybe Cristos felt obligated. Still didn't sound like Cristos.

She watched as Luke started to laugh at something Cristos was saying. Cristos had his back to her so she couldn't see if he was laughing too, but somehow she didn't think he was. The phone rang then and she moved away from the window to answer it. When she returned both Cristos and Luke were still standing beside the pool, drinks in hand.

She'd be hard put, she mused to herself, to decide which of them was the more gorgeous, but guessed that in the end she'd have to say it was Luke. Not that she personally would go for him, since she was extremely happily married to Cristos's friend and director of photography, Richard Feldman. But, if she had to make a choice, it probably would be Luke. She liked Luke. She'd enjoyed having him around while Cristos was visiting his folks in Pennsylvania. He had a great sense of humour, knew how to have a good time unlike most Brits, and she didn't even mind the way he teased her about her occasional lisp. She experienced a sudden pang of disloyalty then as she looked at Cristos, and decided that OK, perhaps his features weren't quite so regular as Luke's, and perhaps his manner could be abrupt sometimes, but with his mixed Italian and French blood, his moody eyes and, when he decided to use it, that devastating smile, she could see what everyone made all the fuss about. And he was taller than Luke. She liked tall men.

She was so engrossed in her assessment of them that it came as a shock when Cristos suddenly flung his glass down on the terrace, smashing it to smithereens. She caught a glimpse of his face then, boy did he look mad. She couldn't see Luke's face now, but he was waving his arm in the air and . . . Thsshit! Jeannie muttered, as Cristos's fist connected with Luke's jaw and Luke went crashing into the pool.

'Now what do you suppose that's all about?'

Jeannie jumped and turned to find her husband, Richard, standing behind her.

'Search me,' she answered. 'But something's going on. Cristos was . . . Holy shit! Look! Do you think he's going to hit him again?'

'Nah,' Richard answered. 'They're laughing, look at them.'

Jeannie pulled a face. 'Luke is laughing . . .'

'Hi there, anyone at home?'

They both turned round to see Paige Spencer, an actress made famous by her role as Edith Pargiter on TV, standing at the door. She was Cristos's five o'clock appointment.

Jeannie blinked. 'How did you get in?'

'The casting guy let me in, honey,' Paige answered, sounding for all the world as though she'd already got the part. If she did manage to clinch it then she was going to be a very lucky girl, since it was the lead in Cristos's next movie she was up for. But this was only a preliminary meeting before he started screen-testing, so she wasn't a star yet, and Jeannie never had had much time for TV actors who thought too highly of themselves.

Paige sauntered over to the window and looked out to where Cristos and Luke were standing. 'Gee, who'd have thought they'd still be fighting over li'l ol' Angelique Warne after all this time?'

Jeannie glanced at Richard in amazement. Then turning back to – God, what was her name? – 'Were you eavesdropping out there?' she demanded, angrily.

'Aw no, honey. They was a-shout'n, and I was a-coming on in. Just heard Angelique's name mentioned, noth'n more.'

Suddenly Richard grabbed Jeannie's arm and pulled her away from the window. She looked back over her shoulder and saw Cristos coming across the garden towards them.

'Oh my, is he gorgeous?' the actress drooled.

'If I were you I wouldn't repeat that in his hearing,' Jeannie snapped.

'Richard!' Cristos cried as he walked into the office. 'I'm glad you're here, there's something in the latest rewrites I want you to take a look at. Get them for him, will you Jeannie?'

Miraculous, Jeannie thought. The scowl had completely vanished from his face and looking at him now, as he greeted Paige Spencer, no one would ever have known that he had just thumped someone into the swimming pool. Charm itself. But unlike Jeannie, Cristos had a high regard for actors, whatever their medium. Providing they had talent, naturally. And, Jeannie guessed, Paige did have talent.

She turfed out the rewrites for her husband, sat him down to read them then wandered across to the house to find Luke. He was in the kitchen holding an ice-pack to his face and reading the *New York Times*.

'You OK?' she asked.

Luke looked up. 'Oh sure,' he said. 'Just a misunderstanding.'

'About Angelique Warne?'

'You were listening?'

'Only caught her name. Cristos is very touchy on that thubject.'

'Tho I discovered. I won't mention it again.'

Jeannie smiled. 'You staying for dinner?'

'No, he's not.'

Jeannie spun round to find Cristos standing at the door.

'Get these copied for me, Jeannie,' he said, handing her a sheaf of typewritten pages, 'then get onto Bud Winters and tell him I'll be down at the lot tomorrow, around four. I want to take a look at David Easton's profile again, tell him. I'll have the casting directors with me, it'd be good if he was there too.' He turned to Luke. 'Isn't it time you were on your way, Fitzpatrick?'

'Cristos,' Luke protested, 'if I'd known you felt that way . . .'

'You mean if you'd known the Chief of Detectives was in that room with me,' Cristos interrupted.

'Who?' Jeannie said. 'What's going on here?'

'You don't wanna know, Jeannie, believe me,' Cristos answered, his livid black eyes still fixed unyieldingly on Luke.

'Now, come on Cristos,' Luke began, 'there's no need to take . . .'

'Just get the fuck out of here, Fitzpatrick,' Cristos barked, and walked out again.

Two weeks had passed since Corrie's showdown with Annalise. Neither of them had spoken, and neither it seemed was going to back down. Corrie had fully expected, when she'd turned up for work the next day, to find herself out of a job. In fact she'd been waiting this past fortnight for Bob to call her into his office and tell her *adieu*, but he hadn't. In fact he was the only one speaking to her, insofar as Bob spoke to anyone, more often than not he was shouting.

Though Corrie had done nothing to heal it, the rift between her and Annalise bothered her much more than she'd have expected. It wasn't only that she had lost the one friend she had at TW, it was that she sensed a vulnerability in Annalise that disturbed her. She'd seen it several times since she'd started at TW, but lately – and particularly the night she had stormed into Corrie's studio – she had seemed almost paranoid. There was little doubt that it was to do with Luke, and though Corrie had never experienced it herself she knew enough to know that unrequited love could unbalance the most stable of people. It was only a guess that Annalise's feelings were unrequited, but piecing together just the few things both Annalise and Luke had told her, she knew it was probably a pretty accurate one. Of course it was none of her business, and even if it were there was precious little she could do about it, but she cared enough for Annalise not to want to add to her distress. And therein lay the guilt, for she couldn't deny that she was strongly attracted to Luke herself. Not that she stood a chance with him, it just seemed so unforgivably disloyal after all Annalise had done for her. And there was no denying that Annalise was as upset by the quarrel as Corrie was. She did everything she could to hide it, but Corrie had caught the sadness in her eyes only that morning. She'd been on the point of saying something to her, but Annalise had simply walked away. She was also encouraging everyone else to be as cruel to Corrie as ever, even joining in herself now, but Corrie could see that it was hurting Annalise even more than it was hurting her. She was so like a child at times that it made Corrie want to reach out and take her in her arms. But what then? She couldn't make the pain and insecurity go away. Only Luke could do that.

It was Tuesday morning now, the day of transmission. And, as it so frequently did, new information was coming in which drastically affected that night's programme, which happened to be one of Annalise's.

Chaos ruled. New computer graphics had to be designed, scripts had to be rewritten, stringer footage had to be bought in, plus more library footage, and the video itself had to be recut. Not only that, both video editors were off with the flu and the assistant who had taken over didn't seem able to cope.

The day passed in a blur, and more than once Corrie reflected that if only everyone were to calm down a bit then they might actually get somewhere without putting themselves on the short list for a heart attack. Of course she kept her thoughts to herself, and dashed about the place with everyone else, trying to pull things together. Alan Fox was presenting the programme in Luke's absence, and it was just after everyone disappeared into the links studio to record the programme's opening and closing, that Corrie took the call from British Telecom. There was a major computer failure at the Telecom tower, meaning that they were not going to be able to send the programme down the line to the transmission centre that evening.

Corrie knew only too well how serious this was, but seeing no reason to panic anyone yet, she got straight on the phone to the Despatch Rider company to take the transmission tape to Euston. But their regular company didn't have any riders available.

'I'll ring round some of the stand-by companies,' Eileen shouted, having guessed what was happening. 'You go to the studio and tell Annalise the bad news.'

'What!' Annalise shrieked. 'You're kidding me! That means we'll have to finish by seven. We're losing forty-five minutes editing time here.'

'They said they'd get right back to us if the situation changes,' Corrie told her. 'Meanwhile, Eileen's trying some other DR companies.'

'Nothing doing,' Eileen said when Corrie went back into the office. 'But I'll keep trying. Perkin's been screaming for you, he wants the cuttings on that Manchester MP.'

'Any luck?' Annalise asked, coming into the office ten minutes later.

Corrie looked at Eileen.

'Nothing,' Eileen answered.

'OK, the studio's ready to roll,' Annalise said, 'you go outside Corrie and flag down a taxi.'

Half an hour later, with the links recorded and edited onto the programme, Corrie was packed off with the tape to the transmission centre. 'I don't care how you get it there, just get it there,' Annalise shouted after her. She saw Annalise glance at one of the researchers, and knew instantly that they didn't trust her.

But that was ridiculous, she told herself, as the cab

nudged its way into the logjam of traffic on Battersea Bridge, they'd never have given her the tape if that was the case. But of all the times to be trying to cross London . . . The traffic was so bad that at Sloane Square she abandoned the cab and went into the tube station. The minutes were ticking by, the station was crowded, and there was no sign of a train.

Eventually it came. Corrie fought her way viciously on board, hugging the tape to her. The programme was due for transmission at eight o'clock, it was now seven forty-three and she'd got four stations to go, with a change of line in the middle. She'd never make it!

At last she arrived at Warren Street, tore across the Euston road and with minutes to spare raced into the transmission centre. Someone was waiting for her in reception, snatched the tape from her and ran off down the corridor telling her to follow.

Still panting, she watched as he loaded the tape into the machine. The commercials were playing on the off-air monitor in front of them, and Corrie was nearly sick with relief when she saw the TW logo come up on the VTR monitor. The man flicked several switches, all the monitors around her went to black, then she heard the transmission controller telling the operator to roll. He did.

Corrie looked on in panic. Nothing was happening. Then, in one blinding flash, she remembered the horror story she'd once heard about a tape being wiped by the magnetic forces on the underground train.

Her face was completely white as she looked at the man in terror. He was frantically pushing buttons and yelling down the talk back that yes, he'd 'got the fucking tape, but nothing's happening.'

He turned to Corrie.

'I came by tube,' she said in a broken voice. And only then did the real horror of the situation grasp her. It was eight o'clock, no time to line up a fill-in programme, what the Independent Television network was faced with now was half an hour of blank screen. And it was her fault.

She looked at the man, then heard herself mumbling that she was sorry, that she realized it was too late now, that she wished there was something she could do, but there wasn't, and then she dashed out of the building.

Seeing a cab she hailed it and went back to her studio. Her humiliation and misery were complete. She couldn't even bring herself to ring Paula to tell her what had happened.

She made herself go in to work the following morning. It was her error and she must face it. Of course they would fire her, and now any chance she might have of finding a job elsewhere was destroyed.

When she arrived a deathly silence greeted her. Everyone was looking at her. Annalise got up from her desk and came to stand in front of her. Corrie willed herself to meet Annalise's eyes. But before either of them could speak, Corrie's misery was compounded by Luke walking out of his office. She hadn't even known he was back.

He looked at her. Corrie tried to speak, but found she couldn't. Then before she knew what was happening Annalise was flinging her arms round her, laughing, and saying she was sorry.

Somehow, through the confusion of the next few minutes, Corrie finally realized what was going on. She had been set up. The phone call from Telecom was a hoax, the tape Annalise had given her had been blank to start with, even the men in the transmission centre had been in on the joke. The real tape had been sent down the line minutes after Corrie had left the office.

For a while Corrie was too dazed to respond. All around her everyone was laughing, even Luke, and though she tried to see the funny side herself, she couldn't. She wanted to strangle Annalise for the hell she had put her through. In the end she turned and headed for the door.

'Hey! Come on!' Annalise called after her. 'Where's your sense of humour?'

Corrie spun round. 'I don't know, perhaps *it* got wiped on the tube, yesterday. But what I do know is that I've had enough. You've, all of you, laughed at me, ridiculed me, snubbed me, slandered me, you've even molested me,' she added glaring at Alan Fox, 'and I can't take any more. I've got feelings too, believe it or not, and quite frankly I wouldn't treat *anyone* the way you've treated me.' And with that she slammed out of the office.

Annalise caught up with her in the street outside. 'Corrie, please, wait,' she cried, taking Corrie's arm.

'Just forget it,' Corrie snapped, tugging her arm away.

'Corrie, don't be like this, please. I'm sorry. You're right, it was mean of me. I shouldn't have done it and I'm sorry. Truly I'm sorry.'

'It's too late,' Corrie said.

'No, it's not. Look, I've behaved badly – all right, atrociously,' she admitted when Corrie threw her a look, 'but I'll make it up to you. Somehow I'll make it up to you. Don't go. Please.' When Corrie didn't answer Annalise took her arm again and pulled her to a halt on Battersea Bridge.

Corrie heaved a deep sigh and gazed past Annalise towards the cluttered houses of Chelsea Embankment.

'I should congratulate you actually,' Annalise said. 'You passed your initiation test.'

'What's that supposed to mean?' Corrie enquired, still not looking at her.

'It means that when you thought there was a real emergency you acted coolly and responsibly by trying to fix things before throwing everyone else into a panic. Not many of us can keep our heads in a crisis. I expect you've noticed. You did brilliantly.'

'But there was no crisis.'

'I know, but that's not the point I'm trying to make. You're doing really well at TW you know.'

Corrie wondered if Annalise had any idea just how bad it really had been for her.

'And I owe you an apology too, for all the dreadful things I said, you know, the night I came round,' Annalise went on. 'I didn't mean any of them. I was half out of my mind with jealousy. The trouble is, where Luke is concerned, I can't help it. I know it's no excuse, but I am irrational about him I know I am. I've never been like it with any other man, but then I guess I've never had such trouble in hooking any other man.'

Corrie looked down at her and Annalise smiled.

'He's back from LA early because he missed me,' she said, 'or so he tells me. I don't really believe him, but it's nice hearing it. And last night he told me all about you, and what you talked about together, which, incidentally, is why I didn't call you last night to tell you that all that business with the tape was a joke. Luke rang me from the airport and everything else just went clean out of my mind.'

Corrie was still silent. Annalise looked into her eyes and Corrie could see the nervous strain in every contour of her lovely face.

'Corrie, I couldn't bear it if you went,' Annalise said quietly. 'Say you forgive me, please. I know I don't deserve it, but . . .'

'It's all right, I forgive you,' Corrie sighed. 'At least for the hoax. But you really are going to have to do something about the jealousy, Annalise.'

'I know.' Suddenly Annalise grinned. 'You sound so maternal when you say things like that.'

'Ugh!' Corrie said. 'That's the last thing I want to sound. I think I'll stick to common, thank you.'

'Oh please,' Annalise groaned, 'can't we forget everything I said, and start again?'

'Yes, I suppose so,' Corrie laughed.

Annalise smiled, then lowering her eyes she turned to lean against the bridge. Corrie watched her for a moment or two then went to join her. She couldn't see her face, her disorderly mass of white blonde hair was falling like a curtain between them. Eventually Corrie lifted her hand and pulled it back. She wasn't surprised when she saw the tears on Annalise's cheeks.

'Do you want to tell me about it?' Corrie asked gently.

Annalise shook her head. 'No. No, it'll be fine.' After a while she turned to look at Corrie. 'I'm glad you're here,' she whispered. 'I don't know why, I just am.'

Corrie smiled. 'I'm glad I am too.'

When they returned to the office everyone carried on as though that morning's outburst had never happened. But at six o'clock, when they were all packing up to go, Alan Fox called over to Corrie to ask if she would like to join them all for a drink at the wine bar.

– 9 –

Phillip Denby leaned forward in his seat and told the taxi driver to pull up outside the Dorchester. It was three thirty in the afternoon, his appointment was at four.

He was generally early for these meetings, and would often while away the time sipping coffee inside the Dorchester. It was half an hour he relished, sitting quietly by himself, watching the affluent world go by, while reflecting on the sordid purpose of his visit. Today was no exception. He ordered his coffee, took a newspaper from his briefcase and settled back to make a pretence of reading.

He only ever came when things had got particularly bad with Octavia, and last night they had. She had decided, as she did every now and again, that she wanted him to make love to her – if one could call the things Octavia wanted, making love. Her idea of foreplay was to get him to paint her toe and finger nails, an exercise she insisted got her in the mood, though he knew it was the act of belittling him that did it. Once the polish was on, he then had to blow it dry himself, and though with some women this might have been a nonsense they could laugh about together, he couldn't remember the last time he and Octavia had shared anything remotely approaching fun.

What invariably came after the routine with the nail polish repelled him to the point of utter disgust. But it wasn't only disgust at the fact that his wife so shamelessly indulged in sado-masochistic practices and gained such malicious pleasure in making him partake when she knew how he hated it, it was disgust at himself for the violence it generated in him that gave him an erection the like of which he never achieved otherwise.

More often than not he faked his orgasm, knowing that he had to get away from her as fast as he could. To stay would be dangerous, for it was all he could do to keep his hands from her throat, to stop himself squeezing the very life from that artificially exquisite body. Which was why the following day would find him sipping coffee at the Dorchester before paying a visit to a prostitute.

In his briefcase was a bottle of Octavia's perfume. There was a photograph of her too, one that he could look at while he thrust himself in and out of a nameless, faceless woman he could pretend was his wife. The rope he didn't need to carry with him, prostitutes always kept that sort of thing – just as they kept their silence while he tied them face down to the bed. Their bodies, of course, were never as good as Octavia's, but that hardly mattered. What he craved was to hear their screams as he beat them, screams he would never get from Octavia, her pleasure in mindless pain was too intense for her to disguise.

He guessed that if he asked Pam to do this for him she would. She would do anything for him. But what he had with Pam was pure. He didn't want to sully it with his hatred for Octavia, which was why he chose to exorcise his abhorrent feelings of violence on a whore.

Glancing at his watch he saw the time was approaching four o'clock. He summoned the waiter, paid his bill and got up to leave. As he walked out into the bright afternoon sunlight, heading towards the heart of London's red-light district, his erection was already beginning to grow. He kept his eyes fixed straight ahead, neither seeing nor acknowledging anyone else in the street. He felt good about what he was doing, for in a perverse way he saw it as protecting his wife. A man was expected to protect his wife, even though there were times when she might fill him with a rage so murderous that to control it was almost imposs-ible. This way no harm would come to anyone.

From the Village Café, where he was drinking coffee with Bob Churchill and two of the TW reporters, Luke Fitzpatrick was watching the banker, Phillip Denby, the man Corrie had told him was her father, as he rang a doorbell opposite.

With mild amusement Luke continued to look out of the window until Denby disappeared inside the house. A man in Denby's position should be more careful, Luke was thinking to himself. Being seen going into the home of a known hooker would do nothing at all to enhance his career, never mind his reputation. He didn't imagine Corrie would be too impressed either, were he to tell her. But from what she had told him Denby wouldn't be much concerned about that. Or would he?

Due to the live coverage of a European football match there was no transmission that week, so on Tuesday morning Bob took the opportunity to convene a special production meeting, which was held in the general office. The ratings for the programme were down and he, Bob, had received instructions from Luke that they were to put their heads together and come up with something to remedy the situation.

It was probably the first time the entire team had been together since Corrie had started, and having been fore-warned of the meeting the day before ideas were instantly thrown into the forum, discussed and discarded, or listed for action. It was a healthy debate with much humour and much furrowing of brows, and Corrie was more than a little pleased to discover that she was as up to date with what was going on in the world as any of them.

There was no mistaking the fact that she was, at last, being made to feel a part of the unit. A space had been made for her at the meeting, she was sitting between Cindy Thompson and Perkin, and though she didn't quite have the courage to speak up as yet, she was listening so intently to the ideas Richard Taylor – one of the reporters – had to offer, that it was only when a secretary called out that Lorna, the receptionist, needed a researcher down in the lobby, that Corrie even realized the telephone had rung. Apparently Lorna was downstairs with Bill, the security man, trying to help control a bunch of women who were insisting they see someone.

'She says they're getting violent,' Prue added.

Bob looked straight at Corrie. Corrie nodded, flicked over to a clean page in her notepad and left the meeting.

When she got downstairs she could hardly believe her eyes. She had never seen women like it in her life. Their hair was every colour of the rainbow, their make-up was as thick as grease paint and their skirts were so short she thought for a minute that some weren't even wearing one. But even worse was the noise they were making.

'Who are they?' she whispered to Lorna.

'Prostitutes. Can't you tell?'

Corrie looked at them round-eyed. 'What do they want?'

'They want locking up, that's what,' Bill said, going after one who was heading for the lift. 'Come on, out on the streets where you belong,' he growled, hauling her out by her hair.

The woman screeched, and started to attack him. She was cheered on by the others, who were yelling such lewd and obscene remarks about certain parts of his anatomy that Corrie had to turn away before Bill saw she was laughing.

'Grab his goolies!' one woman cried.

'What do you mean, he hasn't got any.'

'Look at that face, it looks like your pussy, Sherry.' This to a woman whose hair was as blazingly red as Bill's beard.

'We want to talk to someone, asshole,' an Amazonian purple-haired woman snarled. 'And we ain't leaving here till we do.'

'You're out now!' Bill shouted.

'Oi! Rancid dick! You get someone down here now or this radio goes so far up your ass you'll be farting the breakfast show for a month.'

Bill swung round to make a grab for his radio. A scrawny little harpy with green and yellow hair ducked under his arm and dashed for the lift. Bill was after her like a shot, picked her up and all but threw her back into the crowd.

Corrie watched the mêlée with horror and fascination. She knew she should do something, but wasn't quite sure what. It occurred to her to try to speak to one of them, but as she stepped forward Bill pushed her aside.

'It's all right, I know how to handle this lot,' he told her. 'They've been here before.' Corrie saw him going for the fire extinguisher, but the women hastily blocked his way.

The purple-haired woman caught Corrie's eye and winked, and Corrie was just on the point of going over to her when the revolving doors spun and in walked Felicity Burridge.

Felicity was well known to them all. Not only because she was an actress, but because of her recent divorce from a rock star who had been made to stand trial for raping her. Corrie hardly had time to wonder what she was doing there before Felicity took charge of the situation. She was, Corrie realized with amazement, a part of this prostitute lobby.

'Are you a researcher?' Felicity asked her, and before Corrie could answer Felicity took her by the arm and marched her over to the sofas. Once there she proceeded to tell Corrie why she, and the other women, were there. In light of the recent spate of grotesque and violent murders around the Shepherd Market area they were campaigning for prostitutes' rights. 'More particularly for brothels to be legalized,' she said. 'I, and many other women in the public eye, have decided to lend our support. You know they found another body just over an hour ago?'

'No,' Corrie answered. 'I didn't.'

'Well they have. Floating in the Thames, just like all the others. I won't tell you what she looked like, just suffice it to say there is a psychopathic maniac at large and these women are his target. He's got to be caught. There's got to be some pressure brought to bear on the police and society to recognize that these women, just like any others, need protecting. The psychos nearly always go after prostitutes, and most of us choose to ignore the fact that they feel terror, and pain just like the rest of us. Like it or not, they perform a vital role in society, and a part of that role is *not* to be ripped to pieces by a lunatic's knife. They've got to be made to feel safe. They need brothels. Legalized, clinicized, brothels.'

Her large, unpainted face was quivering with passion as she went on. Throughout her monologue the prostitutes themselves remained silent and though Corrie heard every word Felicity was saying, her eyes frequently roamed to the bizarre faces surrounding her. Like many other women before her she found herself totally overawed by her first encounter with a prostitute. The reality of their occupation kept racing through her mind's eye and she found herself revolted, fascinated, excited and horrified, but most of all, she realized, she was moved – deeply. For, abrasive and brash as they appeared, she could see the fear in their eyes. She could sense their vulnerability, their unquestioning trust in Felicity and their desperate need for help. Occasionally one of them met her eyes, and though some seemed almost childlike in their eagerness to win her over, most, she could tell, regarded her with cynicism. They didn't believe she would help, and why should they when no one else had?

When Felicity had finished Corrie took her number and told her she would contact her very soon. Quite what her next move should be, she wasn't too sure, but she knew she wasn't going to let them down.

She gave herself a day or two to think it through, made copious notes, spoke several times on the phone to Felicity and Carol, the woman with purple hair who was the prostitutes' spokeswoman, then went to see Luke.

'Until I met them I had no idea just how important their role was in society,' she told him. 'I, like everyone else, just took it for granted that they were there, never even bothered to consider them as human beings. As women, like myself.'

'Not quite like you, Corrie,' Luke smiled.

'Yes, like me. The only difference between us is our professions. But whereas both are valid, theirs is vital. Carol, their spokeswoman, told me only yesterday about one of her clients. About his fantasy. I can see you smiling, Luke, but no, I'm not going to tell you the old story of the cream cakes or hooplah with doughnuts, neither am I going to tell you about the man who likes to have cologne poured over fresh cuts in his penis. Those are sick, but they're harmless. What I'm going to tell you is something that chilled me right to the bone. The kind of story none of us wants to hear. This man, who visits her at least twice a week, does so because he can only reach his climax by fantasizing about strangling his children. He brings dolls with him, lifesize baby dolls, and the violence he inflicts on those dolls is so horrifying that Carol has already reported him to the authorities twice in an attempt to protect his children. Two kids she doesn't even know. The authorities won't listen, they have done nothing about it simply because of who, *what* Carol is.'

Luke's face had paled, and only then did Corrie recall the abuse he had known himself as a child.

'That's not the only story Carol told me,' she continued more gently now. 'There are others, equally as hideous, equally as frightening and some that could almost break your heart. Like the man who can't even masturbate because he has no arms. Where would he be without someone like Carol? But that's not the point really. The point is that some men will go to any lengths, and I mean any, in order to achieve orgasm. And if Carol and women like her weren't there, then God only knows who might be the victim of these appalling perversions. For God's sake, these women do every bit as much for society as any social worker, very often more. We need them, and because we need them we must protect them. We must do everything we can to ensure that they too are safe. Safe from the psychopathic maniacs who make them their targets. They must have legalized brothels – and established links with the authorities.'

'You feel very passionately about this, don't you?' Luke said.

'Yes, I do. And if you were to listen to them you would too.'

'I daresay if men spent a lot more time listening to women then this society we live in would take a turn for the better.'

Corrie smiled. 'I'm glad you feel that way,' she said, 'because it leads me quite neatly onto what I want to say next.'

Luke looked at his watch. 'Let's go and discuss it over a spot of lunch, eh?'

Corrie would have preferred to stay in the office, since she didn't want any more unfounded suspicions reaching Annalise, but this was important and she needed Luke on her side.

They went to a wine bar in the King's Road, and once Luke had ordered a steak sandwich and Corrie – on yet another soon to be discarded diet – a salad, Luke said, 'I have to tell you that in principle I'm for doing a programme to support these women. You're right, they do need help, and we're in a position to give it. However, you said there was more.'

'Not specifically to do with that programme,' Corrie answered, forking then discarding a limp lettuce leaf, 'it's more to do with women in general. And the ratings of the programme. I thought, well how would it be if we devoted one half hour in the month to women? No other hard hitting current affairs programme does it. I'm not talking about a Woman's Hour type thing. Well actually, that's pretty good, but it's on Radio 4, a lot of women don't get to hear it. And TV has so much more power. I'm talking about real issues. Real controversy. Things that affect the nation as a whole, and how women have created it, are subjected to it, are repressed by it, whatever, and how much better things might – or might not – be were there more women in Parliament. More women as captains of industry. Let's give women a voice, let them shout as loud as they like about the chauvinism they have to suffer – and let the men answer, of course. Anyway, the possibilities are endless . . . I've prepared some notes on it which I can let you have, but in principle what do you think? It could bring in a lot more women viewers, and all the surveys show that in the main it's they who control the on-off switch.'

Luke's eyes were brimming with laughter. 'My, you

really have been working hard, haven't you?' he said. 'Well, I shall be glad to read your notes. I'm not promising anything,' he added, when Corrie's face lit up, 'but if I think it's worth a shot I'll certainly talk it through with Bob and the producers. If they like it either Annalise or Cindy could take it on.' He paused, and gave Corrie a look from the corner of his eye. 'The question is, though, if it does look like a goer, who is going to research it? With Pippa leaving we'll only have three researchers on the team and they're all men.' He frowned. 'On the other hand it might be a good idea to give it to a man, to strike the balance.'

'Well actually,' Corrie said, her fingernails digging weals into her palms, 'I was hoping you might let me research it.'

Luke nodded thoughtfully. 'Mmm, it's possible,' he said. 'I'll give it some thought. Again I'll have to discuss it with the others.'

'I can do it,' Corrie said eagerly. 'I know I can. I mean, I know I haven't had any actual experience, but, well, we all have to start somewhere, and you could always give me a trial run. If I don't work out then you haven't really lost anything, have you?'

'I guess not,' Luke laughed. 'Leave it with me, I'll see what can be done. Now, that's enough shop, what's all this with the new look?'

Corrie grinned self-consciously and looked away so that he wouldn't see her blushing. No one else had remarked on her attempts to vamp up her appearance, so she had assumed no one had noticed. But Luke had, and she felt suddenly foolish.

'Don't tell me,' she said, 'I've got it all wrong. I didn't like my hair when they cut it, but at least they didn't take too much off. And these clothes look ridiculous, don't they? I was trying to look a bit more sophisticated. There was no point trying to look trendy, like Annalise, that just wouldn't suit me, but . . .'

Luke hooked his fingers under her chin and lifted her face to look at him. 'What you've achieved,' he said gently, 'is something between the two.'

'So what you're saying is, I look like a clown?'

'No,' he laughed, 'But if you'd let me help . . .'

'Oh no, no, I couldn't do that,' Corrie interrupted, thinking immediately of Annalise. 'Really, I couldn't take up your time.'

'It won't be my time,' he said, smiling right into her eyes, 'I was thinking of putting you in touch with a stylist I know.'

'Oh.' She didn't say anymore than that, since she was afraid of how her voice might sound once it had broken through the all too disturbing feelings his eyes were evoking in her.

Later that afternoon, as Corrie was finishing off yet another revealing telephone conversation with Carol, Luke called her into his office.

'Here you are,' he said, 'Georgina's telephone number. The stylist,' he explained, when Corrie looked at him blankly. 'She's expecting to hear from you in the next half an hour.'

'Half an hour!' Corrie gasped.

'Why not? You want a new image, so go get yourself one. Take a few days off then we'll see if we recognize you when you come back.'

Corrie took a breath to speak then stopped herself. It would seem churlish to object when he was being so kind, but the last thing she wanted right now was to take time off. What she wanted was to get to work.

However, between beauty salons, make-up counters, image consultants, colour co-ordinators and dress designers she was able to make even more notes, and took the opportunity to see a little more of Felicity whom she was coming to like, and respect, a great deal. She hardly had time to reflect on what exalted company she was now moving in, with friends like Felicity Burridge and Svengalis like Luke Fitzpatrick, though Paula was always there to remind her, and Corrie almost burst with pride at the way she seemed to be taking her new friendships in her stride.

'Well, I think you're done,' Georgina, the stylist said just four days after they first met. 'What do you think?'

They were in the hairdressers where Corrie had just had her shoulder length hair completely restyled, highlighted and permed. Now it was just beneath her chin and framed her face with such an abundant cascade of coppery curls that when Georgina spun her towards the mirror she actually gasped. Her hair had always been thick, but she had never imagined that it could look so wildly abandoned yet chic at the same time. And her face! Her features looked so much smaller than before, yet somehow more defined. There was just a whisper of brown eye-shadow on her lids, a double coat of mascara on her lashes, the merest hint of blusher lifting her cheekbones and a soft glossy amber lipstick coating her lips.

She broke into a smile, but still she couldn't speak as she stood up to take in her whole appearance. She was wearing a creamy cashmere dress which came to just above the knee, pale coloured tights and black pumps, all of which she'd bought under Georgina's guidance.

'I can hardly believe it,' she finally breathed, peering suspiciously at the mirror. 'I mean it's me, but . . . My God! It really is possible to make a silk purse out of a sow's ear.' Laughing, she turned to Georgina. 'Of course, I'll never be a raving beauty, but . . . What can I say, Georgie? You've performed a miracle. I even look quite slim.'

'You're not fat,' Georgie laughed. 'You're just big-boned.'

'Ugh! You make me sound like Rambo.'

'Then think of it this way. You've got good strong

features, great ankles, good legs all round actually, terrific tits, small waist – in fact, my dear, you're the regular hour glass. And believe it or not you'd photograph beautifully.'

'So I take it you've told them to hold the front cover of *Vogue?*'

'Not quite. But don't rule it out.'

'I know my limitations,' Corrie laughed. 'Now, how much do I owe you for all this.'

'Brace yourself.'

Corrie winced. 'It's the Saint Laurent suit isn't it?'

'And the Lagerfeld. And all the Nicole Farhi stuff. Not to mention all the accessories and the . . .'

'No, don't go on, I can't bear it. Just tell me, and be ready with the smelling salts.'

'OK. Stand by.'

Corrie closed her eyes.

'Five quid.'

'What!'

'Five quid. A tip for the hairdresser.'

'But . . .'

'Luke's footing the bill for the rest.'

Corrie stared at her open-mouthed. 'Oh no,' she said at last. 'No, I can't let him do that. I have some savings, Georgie, and I want to . . .'

'Too late, he's already paid. You want to argue, take it up with him. He's waiting for your call by the way. He says you can get him at the office.'

Corrie was already heading towards the phone. 'May I?' she said to the receptionist.

The receptionist waved her on and Corrie dialled the number, tapping her foot as she waited for someone to answer and stealing disbelieving glances at herself in the mirror.

'Am I speaking to Henry Higgins?' she said, when Luke came onto the line.

'Speaking,' he laughed.

'Well it's Eliza Doolittle here, and I really am grateful, please don't think I'm not, but I just can't . . .'

'Save it, Corrie. Just come and have dinner at my place tonight. Let me see the new you. And if you're worried about the money, think of it as a payment for coming up with a brilliant idea.'

'You mean you're going to take it,' she gasped. 'The women's thing?'

'I've discussed it with Bob and the producers, and we're all agreed. We'll start with the prostitutes. Now, I'll expect you around eight this evening.'

He'd rung off before Corrie could protest, but in truth she was relieved she didn't have to. She didn't want to upset Annalise again, but Luke had been so kind that it would seem downright ungrateful of her to turn him down.

By the time she arrived at his Knightsbridge apartment she was on such a high that she couldn't keep the smile from her face. She had changed from the cashmere dress into a simple black dress with a wide round neck, short sleeves and black and gold buttons which finished mid-thigh. She'd thought it a bit daring when she'd bought it, since it revealed so much of her legs, but Georgie had been so insistent that she had great legs and should show them off that she had given in. She was glad she had now, for one look in the mirror before she'd left had told her how good she looked in it – though if the truth were known she really had no idea just how good.

When Luke opened the door and saw her standing there, it was all he could do to keep his mouth from falling open.

Corrie grinned, 'Well I wasn't that bad before, was I?' she quipped.

'No,' he laughed, 'But I have to confess you . . .'

'No spare me, please. I'm no good at handling compliments.'

'Then you'd better get used to it. You look terrific.'

He watched her walk into the apartment, still slightly

taken aback by such a transformation. She might never, as Corrie herself had remarked, be a raving beauty, but she sure as hell had something. And unlike Corrie Luke was only too aware what that something was. He had rarely seen such potent sensuality, or such unadulterated eroticism in the curves of one body. Did she have any idea what it could do to a man just to watch her move? He'd noticed it before, of course, they all had, but now . . . Well, he could almost feel her writhing beneath him, panting for him to take her. And that hair! He could just see it, tumbling over the pillows, falling into her eyes, pasting itself to her lips. The odd thing was though, that she seemed totally unaware of the effect she created, and he wondered if it wasn't that that somehow made it all the more powerful.

He let her chatter on over the dinner he had cooked himself. She made him laugh a lot at the faces she pulled and expressions she used, and all the while he was reflecting on how all too easy it was to change someone on the outside, but thank God no one could tamper with the inside. She really was quite unique.

When they finished the meal they moved to the sofa. Corrie immediately noticed the file of newspaper cuttings on the coffee table about the murdered prostitutes and was delighted to think that he was involving himself personally in the first programme.

'But of course I am,' he laughed. 'I interest myself in every programme TW makes, though I have to admit this one is somewhat special. After all, I can't have my very own Eliza going off the rails before she even gets started, now can I?'

Flustered by the possessiveness of his remark Corrie felt her pulses start to race. He was smiling, and again his eyes were penetrating hers, the way they had in the wine bar. His body was turned towards her, with one arm resting along the back of the Chesterfield. There was a space between them, but if he were to move his hand it would be touching the back of her neck. Corrie was half-turned to him, the hem of her dress riding up her thighs and she was acutely aware of the disturbing sensations spreading heat through her body.

'Did you . . . ? Have you . . . ? Well, is there any chance I might be able to research it myself?' she finally blurted out.

'Yes,' he said, 'I think there could be every chance.'

'You mean . . . ? Have you discussed it with the others?' She sounded so breathless, and felt sure he must have noticed the way her chest was rising and falling beneath her dress.

'We talked about it, yes.'

'And?'

His eyebrows arched ironically. 'The casting vote lies with me.'

Corrie smiled and looked down at her hands. 'And have you come to a decision?' she asked, quietly.

'I have.'

She lifted her eyes back to his face. 'Please don't keep me in suspense,' she said. 'Am I going to be a researcher, or aren't I?'

'Is that what you want?' he asked, the unmistakable ring of laughter in his voice.

'Oh Luke, you know it is.'

Laughing, he pulled her into his arms and kissed her gently on the mouth. 'You're not being quite honest with me,' he told her. 'You want to produce the slot, is the real truth.'

Though her heart was pounding Corrie's eyes widened with disbelief. 'Do you mean . . . ? Are you saying . . . ?'

'What I'm saying,' he said, 'is that you want to produce the slot, which is not beyond the bounds of possibility. I've read your notes, we all have, and we're all in agreement that you've got quite a future ahead of you. You're an asset we don't want to lose.' All the time he was talking he was unfastening the buttons on her dress.

Corrie's head was spinning. This was all happening so fast that she could barely comprehend what he was saying or doing. She was looking into his eyes, and though a dim and distant voice was telling her she should make him stop, she said nothing. She felt vaguely as though she was hypnotized, and her eyes fluttered closed as he pushed her head gently into the crook of his arm and kissed her again.

His hand moved to her knee and started to slide slowly along her thigh. At the same time his tongue entered her mouth. This shouldn't be happening, she knew it shouldn't, she must make him stop, but dear God it felt so good.

He lifted his head and looked down into her face.

She smiled awkwardly and put her hand on his to stop it going any further.

'By the way,' she said, throatily, 'how was your trip to LA?'

'Great.'

'Did you see Cristos Bennati?'

'Mmm. I stayed with him.'

'Oh.' His hand was moving inside her dress, over her breast. 'How come you – you came back early?' she faltered.

'We fell out.'

'What about?' she mumbled, as he took the weight of her breast in his hand.

'I mistakenly opened an old wound of his. I tried to apologize, but he's pretty fiery is Cristos.'

'Oh, I see.' She sucked in her breath as he took her nipple between his fingers and looked down at what he was doing. He lifted her chin and kissed her again. 'You really want to be a producer, don't you?' he said.

'Yes,' she breathed. 'Yes I do.'

Taking her hands he pulled her to her feet. She looked at him tentatively, knowing what was going to happen and powerless to stop it. He slipped her dress over her shoulders and let if fall to the floor. She stood before him in her black teddy and black hold up stockings. She was rigid. She had never felt so vulnerable, so embarrassed nor so nervous in her life.

'Look at you,' he groaned, running his fingers lightly over her waist. The teddy was cut high on her hips so that his fingers soon found the ample flesh of her buttocks. He squeezed hard, lowering his mouth to her neck and kissing it. She had never known her body capable of such voracious desire, but she was afraid to move, terrified lest she should do something wrong.

Taking her hand he led her into the darkened bedroom. For a while they stood in the moonlight, simply kissing until Luke's fingers found the join in her legs and pressed hard against the flimsy fabric of her teddy. When he let her go he lifted his fingers to his mouth and licked them. Corrie watched him, feeling so unworldly, so out of her depth, that she wanted to run away. Yet at the same time she wanted nothing more than for this to continue. He pulled her hard against him. She could feel the strength of his erection, and was by now so weak with her own desire she could barely stand.

He pushed her back onto the bed, pulled the straps of her teddy down over shoulders, her hips, her legs until he was holding it in his hand.

Corrie looked up at him, wanting desperately to cover herself, but when she lifted her arms he took them and laid them back on the pillows.

'Ssh,' he said, 'just stay like that.'

She watched as he stripped away his own clothes. His skin glowed bluish-white in the moonlight, and she could see the powerful muscles of his legs, his arms, his shoulders, his . . .

He was holding himself, and watching his hand as it moved gently back and forth. 'Open your legs,' he whispered.

Obediently Corrie parted her legs, trying to ignore the wave of embarrassment that swept through her. She looked up at him, waiting for him to lie down with her, but he was still watching himself.

'What do you want now?' he asked softly.

'I want you,' she croaked.

She saw him smile. 'Which part of me?'

Not quite sure if she was doing what he expected of her she reached out and touched his penis. 'This part,' she answered shyly.

'Say it,' he said, watching her hand.

Say what? Oh God, she was going to make a fool of herself, she just knew it. 'I want this part of you,' she said.

'Tell me you want my cock.'

Corrie felt the heat rise in her cheeks, but mustering her courage she whispered, 'I want your cock.'

'Where do you want my cock?'

'Here,' she said, shyly touching herself.

He didn't look. 'In your cunt,' he whispered. 'Tell me you want my cock right up inside your cunt.'

Misery engulfed her as her tongue recoiled from the words, but, feeling utterly naive and inept, she forced herself to repeat them. He was still speaking, so softly she couldn't make out what he was saying. Then he lowered his head again and watched his fingers massaging his penis.

'Ask me to suck your tits,' he moaned.

Corrie did, trying desperately to remind herself that he was a man of the world. Of course things would be different with him, his tastes would be so much more sophisticated than those of the men she'd known before, but she didn't like this coarseness – she hated it. His eyes moved to hers and she felt herself tense even more. It was as though he was seeing someone else, or perhaps no one at all. His eyes were glazed, and his urgency seemed so contained, somehow so personal, as though this arcane foreplay was something he was doing for himself, and himself alone.

As he sat down on the bed a stream of unbelievable obscenities issued from his mouth. His hand was fumbling for her breasts, but he wasn't watching what he was doing, his eyes were focused on his hand. He was asking her again to repeat what he was saying, but the profanities were coming so thick and fast from his own lips he wasn't giving her the chance. 'Tell me, tell me, tell me,' he gasped. 'Fucking tell me.'

Corrie didn't know what to say, though for one horrifying moment she suddenly wanted to giggle. 'Luke,' she whispered tentatively, 'don't you think we should . . . Well, that we should use, you know, something?'

Both his hands stopped moving as he lifted his eyes to her face. She could see that he wasn't quite sure what she meant.

'A condom,' she said in a hushed voice. 'Do you have any?'

His lip curled with laughter. 'Sure, if you insist,' he said, and leaning forward he opened a drawer beside the bed.

'Now,' he said, as he rolled the diaphanous rubber lovingly over his penis, 'let me hear you tell me how much you want my cock. How you're going to take it in your mouth, up your cunt – up your ass.'

Corrie's eyes rounded with horror. She didn't want to be here anymore. She didn't want him to think her unworldly, or a prude, but all this talk was making her feel distinctly uncomfortable – even afraid. And as he went on to describe in graphic detail what he was going to do to her, she said,

'Luke. Luke I don't think . . . I mean, well I've never done anything like that before . . .'

'Easy, easy,' he soothed, lying down beside her. 'It'll be all right. Mmmm, you are sensational,' he murmured, running a hand over her belly. 'I want you now. I want you right up here.' His fingers were inside her, his lips touching hers. 'Don't be afraid,' he whispered, 'I won't do anything you don't want me to. I promise.'

He rolled onto her then and kissed her so tenderly that her fears started to ebb. She felt his hand move between them, felt the tip of his penis start to penetrate her.

'You're so soft,' he said, moving slowly in and out of her. 'So soft.'

He started to move faster, not hard, just faster. There was none of the violence in his movements that there had been in his words and Corrie felt herself start to relax. Then his breathing started to quicken, and with surprise Corrie realized he was nearing ejaculation.

'Tell me where my cock is,' he groaned in her ear. 'Tell me where it is.'

'Inside me,' she mumbled.

'In your cunt. Say it.'

Corrie said it.

'Again.'

She said it again, and again.

'Holy shit!' he choked, and ground his hips into hers as the semen flooded from his body.

'Carry on like that,' he said as he rolled off her, 'and I'll be making you more than a producer.'

'What?' Corrie said, not at all sure she liked the sound of that. 'What do you mean?'

He chuckled softly and took her face between his hands. 'Let's just wait and see, shall we?' he said.

Within minutes he was fast asleep. Corrie lay in the darkness for a long time, thinking back over the past half an hour. For a while she couldn't be rid of the feeling that he had used her body to exact the price of her producership, but no, that was nonsense, she'd have slept with him anyway and he knew it. She turned to look at him and seeing his exquisite face so gentle and so vulnerable in sleep she started to smile. What an idiot she was to have been so shocked by the way he had talked himself – had got her to talk him – to climax, for that was all it had been – talk. He hadn't hurt her, just as he'd promised, neither had he even attempted to make her do anything he'd suggested. It was merely the thought of it that had excited him. But then remembering what the prostitute Carol had told her about the sometimes uncontrollable power of fantasy she started to feel uncomfortable again.

But Carol hadn't omitted to explain the importance of the imagination during sex. Very often, she'd said, a shared fantasy was the most erotic thing in the world. She had given, as an example, the number of women who fantasized about being raped. With the right man there was no harm in it at all, with the wrong man, when fantasy became reality, well that was a different matter altogether. No woman in her right mind wanted the actuality of rape, any more, Corrie guessed, than Luke had wanted to do the things he had spoken of. And as Corrie contemplated it now, as she voiced in her mind all the things he had made her say, she found herself becoming aroused by it too. She still, she realized, had so much to learn about her own body, her own fantasies, and what it might take in order for her to reach a climax.

It was just after one in the morning when the telephone rang. The answerphone picked up the call, but not before the ringing had woken Luke. The two of them lay there listening through the open door to Annalise's slurred voice telling Luke that she knew he was there, that she had waited all night for him to call.

'If you don't ring me back in the next five minutes,' she ended, 'then I'm warning you I'll swallow every one of these pills . . . See how you can live with yourself then, you bastard.'

The line went dead and Corrie turned to Luke. 'Aren't you going to call her?' she asked when he didn't move.

'No.'

'But you heard what she said.'

'I did. And it's the third time she's threatened it this month.'

His voice sounded harsh, angry even, but Corrie could sense his anguish and didn't know which of them she felt the most sorry for. It must be terrible to be subjected to that kind of blackmail, but wasn't it even worse to be so desperately in love with someone that you could even consider killing yourself over it.

'What if she isn't crying wolf?' Corrie asked.

'She is, believe me. And I have no intention of letting her rule my life with her hysterical threats.'

'But Luke . . .'

'Sssh,' he said, putting his arms around her. 'She'll probably have passed out by now, and if it'll make you feel any better then I promise to go round and see her in the morning. Now go back to sleep,' and snuggling her deeper into his arms he wrapped his legs around her. 'Mmm, you feel so good,' he murmured squeezing her, and Corrie could hardly believe it when only minutes later he was snoring softly in her ear.

It wasn't until past three o'clock, when he had rolled away from her and Corrie was convinced he was fast asleep that she gingerly got up from the bed, picked up her teddy and crept into the sitting room.

Once she was dressed she scribbled a note, thanking him for a lovely evening, and saying she would see him on Monday. She didn't know whether she hoped he would call her over the weekend, because she didn't know how she felt. Except to say that the disloyalty she had shown Annalise was already weighing heavily on her conscience.

Whether or not he did call was in the end irrelevant, since, for the first time since she'd left, she summoned the courage to go home to Amberside. But before she set out on Saturday morning she called Annalise. The phone rang for a long time until finally a disgruntled voice came onto the line. It was clear that Annalise was struggling with a near comatose hangover, but Corrie didn't regret calling, she had needed to reassure herself that Annalise hadn't done anything stupid. She could go off to Amberside with an easy mind now, at least as far as her fears for Annalise went she could. As to her feelings for Luke . . . Not even now, in the cold light of day could she say what she truly felt, which was why she was on her way to see Paula.

'I'm speechless,' Paula cried, as she took in Corrie's new look. 'Absolutely speechless.'

'Oh good,' Corrie laughed, 'that's the kind of compliment I can handle.'

'Isn't she a picture?' Uncle Ted, who had picked her up from the station, was grinning with pride.

'You look bloody fantastic,' Dave declared, as he embraced Corrie. 'What's happened? You fallen in love, or something?'

'Or something,' Corrie answered with a mischievous twinkle.

'Dinner at our place tonight then,' Uncle Ted said, getting back into his car. 'Hattie's looking forward to seeing you. Incidentally, how's Annalise? You two hitting it off, are you?'

'Oh, uh, yes,' Corrie assured him, unable to meet his eyes. 'Yes. Just great.'

'Good. Now, we're expecting you around seven thirty. Don't for heaven's sake be late, Hattie's been preparing for this all day.'

'You mean she abandoned the shop?' Corrie gasped, with mock horror.

'I was in charge today,' Paula answered. She turned to Ted, 'so tell Hattie from me that it'd better be a banquet she's rustling up over there. I've been rushed off my feet.'

'No?' Corrie cried.

Laughing, Paula shook her head. 'Same steady old flow.

Now come on in, we've got your old room all ready for you.'

'But that's Beth's room now,' Corrie protested, trying to ignore the clenching of nerves in her stomach as she followed Paula into the cottage. It still smelt of Edwina and as Corrie looked around she felt a sudden rush of tears.

'I guessed it might take you a bit like this,' Paula said, hugging her. 'But it's all right to cry, you know. After all, she hasn't been dead that long.'

'In some ways it feels like a lifetime,' Corrie sniffed. 'So much seems to have happened in such a short time.' She suddenly grinned through her tears and Paula looked at her curiously. 'Boy have I got a lot to tell you,' Corrie said.

It wasn't until they had returned from Hattie and Ted's and Dave had decided to go off down the pub for a last beer, that she and Paula were finally alone together.

'Oh my God!' Paula cried, when Corrie made her confession. 'Tell me every detail. No, no. Wait! I think I'm going to faint. *Luke Fitzpatrick*! I can hardly believe it. What was it like?'

'Well, it was . . . OK.'

'OK? *OK*! You go to bed with a man as gorgeous as Luke Fitzpatrick . . . I was expecting fireworks at the very least.'

'To tell you the truth so was I. But . . . Well, let's just say it wasn't exactly what I . . .'

'No, don't let's just say anything. Let's have the whole story! From the beginning.'

Paula was listening with such rapt attention as Corrie told her about her night with Luke that it was all Corrie could do not to laugh. Clearly Paula was even more overwhelmed by it than she was. Though Paula did frown a little when Corrie told her about the telephone call from Annalise.

'He probably did the right thing,' Paula said. 'I mean, what else *could* he do? You were there, and it wouldn't have been very nice if he'd just got up and left you to go to see another woman, would it?'

'I wouldn't have minded.'

'Liar.'

'Seriously, I wouldn't have. Remember, I got up and left myself in the end. Anyway, what do you reckon to all that dirty talk?'

Paula's eyes rolled back in ecstacy. 'Sounds like heaven,' she drooled. 'Mind you, I have to admit I'd have been a bit shocked myself, what with it being the first time. I mean, usually that kind of thing only happens when you know someone quite well. Still, if you move in those circles I guess anything goes. It must have blown your mind.'

'Well, yes, I suppose it did in a way, but I still didn't . . . Paula, tell me honestly, you don't think there's something wrong with me, do you?'

'What on earth are you talking about?'

'Well, I mean, you read so much about sex and all that's supposed to happen, you know the earth moving and all that, and I end up going to bed with someone like him and . . . Well, as I said, it was OK, but . . . I think I must be doing something wrong.'

'Why?'

'Well I don't seem to be able to, you know.'

'Come?'

'Yeah. You don't think all these women who write about these mind-blowing orgasms are just making it up do you?'

Paula shook her head.

'I thought you might say that,' Corrie said dismally. 'So tell me where I'm going wrong.'

'You're not. It just takes time. It was ages before Dave could make me come, I had to show him how to do it.'

'What!' Corrie said aghast. 'Are you seriously suggesting I tell Luke Fitzpatrick how to make me come?'

'Why not?'

'Because I'd die of embarrassment, that's why not.'

'No you wouldn't. Once you get to know him better he'll probably guess that you're faking it anyway, then he'll ask what it is that turns you on. You did fake it, didn't you.'

'It was an Oscar winner,' Corrie lied, not wanting to admit that there hadn't appeared to be any need for it. 'Anyway, we might as well leave this conversation right here, because there won't be a next time.'

'You've got to be kidding! Why not?'

'Annalise.'

'Oh yes. Well, you know what they say about all's fair . . .'

'But I'm not going to war for it. So let's change the subject because I've got some even more amazing news.'

'More amazing than hitting the sack with Luke Fitzpatrick! I can't even begin to imagine.'

'Then hold on,' Corrie beamed, ''cos you really aren't going to believe this. I'm not even sure I do myself. But I am going to be a producer.'

'*What?*'

Corrie nodded. 'You know the woman's angle thing I was telling you about, well they've bought it. They're going to do it, and Luke more or less said that he is going to let me produce it.'

'You're right, I don't believe it!' Paula said incredulously. 'I thought you were angling to research it.'

'I was. But they've read my notes and well, they reckon I've got a great future ahead of me. They consider me an asset they can't afford to lose, and, might I add, who can blame them?'

Her exaggerated immodesty was making Paula laugh. 'So when do you start?'

'I'm not sure yet. I guess they'll let me know on Monday. But it's amazing isn't it, from dogsbody to producer in one clean jump.'

'You're dead right it's amazing. Those notes must have

been quite something to have earned you a promotion like that.'

Corrie's eyes narrowed as she looked sceptically at Paula. Was Paula thinking along the same lines as her, or was that just an innocent remark? Whichever, it was with her again, that unpalatable feeling of having prostituted herself.

'Well, if you have,' Paula said once Corrie had confided in her, 'it's too late now to do anything about it. You'll just have to hope he never tells anyone. Anyway, I'm sure you've got it wrong. Some men get off on treating women like whores, could be that he's one. But I wonder what he meant about making you more than a producer?'

'I don't know,' Corrie answered. 'And right now I'm not sure that I want to.'

The humid night air blew a gentle breeze in through the open window of Annalise's basement flat where Annalise was lying sleepily in Luke's arms. He was spreading her hair over her shoulders, stroking it, then lifting it to his mouth and kissing it, while whispering the words of his favourite poem. His voice was imbued with the soft Irish lilt he affected especially for her and as she listened she felt herself dreamily drifting into sleep.

They hadn't made love that night, and they wouldn't. Tonight he just wanted to hold her, to feel her close and to love her. Annalise cherished these moments more than any others she spent with him. Sometimes she thought she wouldn't mind if they never made love at all, for she never felt as close to him then as she did when they were like this. His gentleness gave her the feeling that she was the most precious thing in the world to him, just as he was to her. And when he was holding her so lovingly she forgot the times that he beat her, forgave him for the rage that frightened her, all that mattered was that he loved her.

He hugged her closer, then rolled onto her lifting himself on his elbows. It was a prelude to nothing more than a look. Annalise smiled up into his eyes, wanting him to read in her own how very deeply her love ran. He smiled too and kissed her gently on the lips.

'Why are you here?' he murmured. 'I don't understand. How can you still be here?'

She lifted her hands to his face and circled his mouth with her forefinger. 'I'm here because I love you,' she whispered.

His head came down, burying his face in her neck. 'I love you too. Oh God, I love you.'

She ran her fingers through his hair, her own eyes filling with tears as she felt his on her shoulder.

'Why are you doing this to me?' he said. 'Why don't you just leave me?'

'You know I'll never do that,' she answered, tightening her arms around him and feeling as though her heart might break. 'Please say you don't want me to.'

'I can't live without you,' he murmured. 'You know that.'

He drew himself up and looked at her again. When she saw the pain in his eyes she tried to pull him back, but he wouldn't let her. She knew he was looking at the cut on her lip and wished there was some way she could hide it.

'I'm sorry,' he whispered. 'I didn't mean . . .'

'Sssh, I know you didn't. It was an accident. Now let me hold you, let me make it go away.'

'I wish you could,' he said, lying over her again. 'Oh, Annalise, I wish you could.'

Annalise cradled him in her arms, soothing him, kissing him and caressing him. It was all she could do, for whatever it was he was holding deep inside she knew he was never going to tell her. She'd tried so many times in the past to draw it from him, but she'd learned now that she only hurt herself by pressing him. It hurt him too, for his anger at her prying rarely failed to manifest itself in violence. And whenever he hurt her, he seemed to hurt himself more. But whereas Annalise's injuries were physical, his scored across his mind in way that seemed somehow indelible. And the deeper his scars ran the worse it became.

It always happened after he had disappeared for a weekend. Where he went Annalise had no idea, though she could be in no doubt that it was to another woman, for on more than one occasion he had called her by the woman's name. To tell him he had done so provoked his anger to such a degree that he would lash out, as he had done earlier. Invariably Annalise backed down, assuring him she had made a mistake, but she knew she hadn't. His denials were so vehement that all she could do was keep the pain of her confusion hidden, for fear that he would strike her again.

He started to move from the bed and Annalise reached out a hand to stop him. Taking it, he lifted it to his mouth and kissed it.

'I'm not going anywhere,' he smiled down at her. 'I just need to sit alone for a while.'

Annalise let him go and lay staring out at the new moon through the trees. She longed to know what the hold was that this woman had over him, but since he insisted that she didn't exist there seemed no way of finding out. And in truth, it was screwing him up so badly that Annalise was half-afraid to know.

She tried to reassure herself with the comfort of knowing that every time he left the woman he came straight to her, but tonight, just like all the other times, Annalise had sensed that he didn't really want to be there. She wondered why he came when he felt that way, but whatever his reasons she would never tell him to go. She wanted him to know that she was there for him, that no matter what, she loved him more than anyone else ever would. She didn't care that her obsession with him, her terror of losing him, was already affecting her so badly that others were beginning to notice. She loved him and would never stop trying to get through to him. She truly believed she was strong enough to give him the support he needed, even though those who loved her, her family, her friends, not only seriously doubted it, but were already showing grave concern for what it was doing to her.

After a while she went to look for him and found him sitting in the darkened kitchen, resting his head on his arms. She watched him, feeling a knot of unbearable emotion tightening in her throat. She thought that he was probably crying and was afraid that if he caught her standing there the violence would erupt again. But as she started to turn away he said, 'No, don't go.'

He lifted his head to look at her and Annalise looked nervously down at her hands.

'Hold me,' he said softly.

Going to him Annalise sat on his lap and rested his head on her shoulder.

'Don't ever leave me,' he whispered.

'No,' she said. 'I'll never leave you.'

When Corrie went in to work on Monday morning it was to discover that Luke had given her idea to Annalise to produce. He informed her of this decision during a meeting at which Annalise was present.

Despite the cut on her lip, which Annalise had playfully told everyone Luke had given her, she looked radiant, almost too radiant, Corrie thought, and wasn't too sure whether it was jealousy she was feeling that it had probably been a weekend spent with Luke that had done it.

But whatever she was feeling, Corrie was dumbfounded by the way he was behaving; it was as though Friday night and his half-promises had never happened.

She waited until the meeting was over then steeled herself to speak to him. She knew she had no right to, that he would probably be furious that she, a mere dogsbody, was daring to criticize him, but she felt used and cheated and

was going to speak up for herself no matter what the consequences.

As it turned out Luke wasn't angry at all, if anything he
seemed surprised – and hurt.

'My God, I had no idea I'd made you feel like that,' he
said when she had finished. 'What can I say? I guess I just
came on too strong for a first date. I should have realized
that it would have been too heavy for you ... But that you
should have felt like that ... Shit, Corrie, I can't apologize
enough. And as for having misled you into thinking I would
make you a producer straight away ... Oh God, what a
mess I made of things. But thank God you felt able to tell
me. And what the hell have you been thinking of me all
weekend? No, perhaps you'd better not answer that, I'm
not sure I want to know. Would it help if I told you that
I have every intention of making you a producer – one of
these days?'

Corrie shrugged, already beginning to feel slightly ridiculous.

'But you must understand why it isn't possible right
now?' Luke went on. 'I'm afraid, just like the rest of us you
have to earn your stripes. And you don't earn them in my
bed.' He smiled. 'That's not how I run this operation. And
you, young lady, shouldn't have such a low sense of self-
esteem. You don't need to be sleeping with the boss to get
on. You can, and will, do it anyway, believe me.' He sighed
and shook his head. 'I was hoping you'd be pleased when
I told you that we're going to make you Annalise's
researcher, but in light of your astronomic hopes of clinch-
ing a producership I imagine it seems pretty second rate
now.'

Corrie was grinning sheepishly. 'Looks like I've made a
proper fool of myself, doesn't it?' she said.

Luke was laughing. 'A bit,' he said. 'But there's no
harm done. So, are you going to accept the position of
researcher?'

'Of course. And . . . I'm sorry . . .'

'Forget it.' He got up from his desk and started walking to the door with her. 'Before you go,' he said, 'you can do one thing for me. You can promise me that the next time we spend the night together you'll tell me if I'm making you feel that way.'

Corrie's cheeks flushed hot with confusion. How on earth could she promise him that now that she and Annalise were going to be working so closely together? But how could she deny him either, when right at that minute she wanted nothing more than for him to take her in his arms and kiss him?

Fortunately she was saved from answering by a loud knock on the door.

Luke pulled it open.

'Fucking hell!' Alan Fox exclaimed when he saw Corrie. 'Just look at you. You undergone some kind of metamorphosis at the weekend, or something? You look fantastic!'

'Control yourself, Fox,' Luke laughed, 'and keep your groping hands off her too. We don't want you up on a sexual harassment charge, though how you've got away with it this long beats me. Anyway, I've just given her the news that she's to be a researcher, so you can be the first to congratulate her.'

'And some,' Fox grinned. 'You deserve it babe, you've worked hard, put up with a lot of shit around here and survived.'

Corrie was smiling. Since the set up with the transmission tape it was as if nothing had gone before, and though she guessed she'd never really like Alan Fox too much, there seemed little point in bearing a grudge now. The main thing was that she was at last accepted. Her colleagues spoke to her, laughed and joked with her, and even invited her to the cinema or parties they were going to. Life really had changed so much for the better these past couple of weeks, that what was the point in dwelling

on the pyrrhic victory of revenge? What she needed now
was to concentrate her energies on the new hurdles already
confronting her – hurdles that were every bit as emotional
as they were professional.

– 10 –

Corrie and Annalise were shooting interviews all over the
country with prostitutes, MPs, policemen, health and social
workers and campaigners for women's rights. Carol had
given them plenty of names and already they had some
excellent footage in the can. They'd even been to Amster-
dam and Hamburg to take a look at the way the laws
governing prostitution and brothels worked there. Not that
they saw much of either city, they simply weren't there
long enough. And while they were there they spent their
time either in a brothel, or in law offices or a hotel room.
The only language Corrie learned – other than the colourful
jargon used by the prostitutes – was film language, and she
was quite proud of the way it was already beginning to slip
so easily off her tongue. Though she had little choice but
to learn fast, since Annalise was proving something of a
problem.

It had been Corrie's idea that Felicity Burridge should
conduct all the interviews, and it was one, everyone agreed,
that was working well. However, Annalise was jealous of
the friendship Corrie had struck up with Felicity, and the
fact that both Felicity and the crew were starting to look
to Corrie for instructions irritated Annalise even more.
Corrie was in no position to point out to Annalise that if
she would only exert a little authority of her own, shake
herself out of this stupor she seemed to have fallen into,
and concentrate a little harder on what she was supposed
to be doing, then there would be no reason for everyone to

turn to her. Annalise was the producer, but not only that she was so unpredictable in her moods lately, was all too often hungover and so clearly resented spending so much time away from London, that Corrie was afraid of an irreparable flare up if she so much as uttered one word of criticism. Instead she went out of her way to stress to Felicity that she must consult with Annalise, and if the cameraman conferred with her on anything she made sure to steer him in Annalise's direction too.

Understanding the problem, Felicity did all she could to make things easier on Corrie, but still there was no doubt whom both she and the camera crew respected. Corrie might have been flattered, and in a way she was, but the trouble was, as far as the technical aspect of making the programme was concerned, she was blatantly inexperienced. The content she could handle, without any problem, she knew the message she wanted to get across, but she needed Annalise to tell her how to shoot it.

They were now nine days into filming, and again, as the crew set up outside one of the more dilapidated buildings in a Birmingham street, Annalise was nowhere to be found. Corrie, tucked in behind her sunglasses and a woollen scarf, was looking at their notes as the camera crew, Felicity and two prostitutes waited.

'Well,' she said, looking up at last, 'I think perhaps we should see the girls walking down the street here first – they can start somewhere up there, by the pub, I'll time the shot to forty-five seconds and Felicity can fill it with voice over.' She glanced at Felicity who smiled her encouragement. 'Then perhaps we can go in for singles for the interview,' she added, looking at the cameraman hopefully. He nodded. 'Then come round here to do the reverses on Felicity?'

Darren, the cameraman, shook his head. 'You'll be crossing the line doing it that way. But if this is just your standard interview you can leave it to me.'

'Crossing the line?' Corrie mouthed to Felicity.

Felicity shrugged.

'Oh, just one other thing,' Corrie said, turning back to Darren who was readjusting his tripod. 'I think we'll want to intersperse the interview with shots of where the girls work.' She paused. 'Will that make a difference to the line?'

Darren laughed. 'It very nearly makes it redundant,' he told her. 'But not quite.'

'OK, Polly and Danielle, if you can take up your positions,' she said to the prostitutes, 'we'll get to it. I'll just run through your questions with you, Felicity, before we turn over.'

'You should be getting paid a producer's salary for this,' Felicity remarked, as Corrie took her to one side.

Corrie pulled a face and continued flicking through her notebook.

'Where is she?' Felicity asked.

Corrie was now stealing sidelong glances at the crowd starting to gather across the street. She hoped they wouldn't start bawling and shouting once the camera was rolling, like the people of Newcastle had. Or come beetling over to ask Felicity for her autograph half way through a take. 'I'm not sure,' she answered, distractedly. 'Anyway, let's go through this, and once it's done you can go back to the hotel. No reason for you to stay for the cutaways. I wonder if the line matters with them? I'll have to get Darren to explain to me what it is. Oh, by the way, the sound guy asked me earlier if we wanted to record your voice wild. What the hell does that mean?'

'I think it means do we want to do it here, on location, or do you want to dub it on in editing?'

'Editing sounds safer. But I'll have to come clean and tell him I don't know. He's a grumpy old sod, but hopefully he'll give me the benefit of his advice. Anyway, let's take a look at what we're doing here. The fact that two prostitutes sharing a house or a flat together constitutes a brothel in the eyes of the law we'll handle in the voice over, so don't worry too much about that now. This is the list of questions you should ask for the interview, get one of them, Polly I think, she seems the better speaker, to explain why she and Danielle break the law by sharing the house, you know, about it being safer and all that. Then ask Danielle to tell you about the time she was beaten up and ended up in hospital for three weeks, which was why she and Polly decided to live and work together . . . Well, you can read what I've written. Run through it a minute and see if there's anything you want to add.'

An hour later, with mercifully little disruption from the crowd, the crew were ready to move their equipment inside the house, and Felicity took the hire car she and Corrie were sharing back to the hotel. The unit finally wrapped at five thirty, and though Corrie was buzzing, she was exhausted too and badly in need of a drink.

'I've found her,' Felicity said, when Corrie turned up in the hotel bar with the crew.

'Where is she?' Corrie asked, flopping down in a chair and unzipping her Barbour.

'Upstairs in her room. She's been on the phone to Luke again. Surprise, surprise.'

Corrie rolled her eyes, but as she made to get up again Felicity caught her arm and pulled her back. 'You can't keep covering for her like this,' she said. 'She's a big girl now, she should be facing up to her responsibilities, like everyone else has to.'

'I know,' Corrie sighed. 'But you've seen the state she gets herself into.'

'Oh yes, I've seen it all right. So has everyone else. But she's not a child, Corrie. She shouldn't be allowed to get away with it. OK, I know it sounds hard, and ordinarily I'd be the last person in the world not to sympathize with what she's going through, but there are times when one has to be professional, no matter what it's costing you personally. I mean, how the hell did she get the job in the first place behaving like that?'

'Connections,' Corrie answered. 'And besides, it's only recently that she's been as bad as this.'

Felicity raised an eyebrow, as if waiting for Corrie to explain, and Corrie found herself suddenly unable to meet Felicity's gaze. Had Felicity guessed that Corrie felt partly responsible?

'She's besotted with him, Fliss,' Corrie said, uncomfortably, 'you know she is, and I can't help feeling sorry for her.'

Felicity sighed with exasperation. 'You're too soft hearted for your own good, Corrie,' she said. 'And you're not doing her any favours, molly-coddling her, mark my words. She'll never pull herself out of it unless you make her.'

'It's not up to me, Fliss. I can't tell her what to do.'

'Like hell you can't. That girl hangs around you like a shadow. She thinks everything you say is gospel, that is, when she's not bitching about the way you're trying to steal her job. Jesus Christ, she'd never survive without you . . .'

'Oh, she'd survive without me all right,' Corrie smiled. 'It's Luke she couldn't survive without.'

'Then she'll have to learn. I mean the guy doesn't want to know. He's made that more than plain.'

'Has he? I don't think so. To be honest I think he's just as confused about their relationship as she is.'

'I can't think why. I mean, he must know the way she feels about him . . .'

'Yes, he does. But there are difficulties. Her father is his partner . . .'

'I don't call that a difficulty.'

'You and I might not, but according to Annalise Luke does.' She sighed. 'I have to admit though, that I think there's a lot more to it than Annalise is letting on.'

Felicity eyed Corrie knowingly. 'How about admitting,' she said, 'that there's a lot more to it than you're letting on?'

'I don't know what you mean,' Corrie laughed awkwardly. 'Anyway, I'd better go up and see her. I'll meet you back here in about an hour.'

As Corrie rode up in the lift she was still smarting from the way Felicity had so easily detected her guilt. She'd never told Felicity about the night she'd spent with Luke, but Felicity knew that while they had been out on the road filming, while Annalise had been waiting in vain for his calls, Luke had on several occasions found the time to call Corrie. They never discussed anything other than how the programme was shaping up, but Corrie could sense from the tone of his voice, that the instant she returned to London he would be wanting to see her.

As soon as Annalise let Corrie into her room Corrie knew she'd been drinking. Fortunately not too much, by the look of her, but she must have been crying for some time for her eyes to be so red. Corrie had intended, as gently as she could, to remind Annalise that she had a duty not only to everyone else to see this film through, but to herself too. But her words would have been wasted, she knew that immediately, for Annalise's mind was clearly a long way from the shoot.

'He's with her, I know he is,' Annalise exclaimed before Corrie even had a chance to close the door.

'Who?' Corrie asked.

'Her! Whatever her name is. Look!' Annalise dug into her bag and pulled out a birthday card. 'I found this, last night on his desk . . .'

'On his desk!' Corrie interrupted. 'Are you telling me you were in London last night?'

'Yes. I took the train back. I had to find him, Corrie. I just had to. Please try to understand. I know I've landed you in it here, but I can't think about anything else.'

'It's all right,' Corrie sighed. 'Go on. Did you find him?'

'No. But I found this, on his desk for all the world to see. I took it so he couldn't sent it, but he'll have sent another.' She opened the card and started to read, 'To my darling . . .' Suddenly she flung the card down. 'I can't even pronounce the bloody name.'

Corrie took the card and read the name Siobhan. 'It's pronounced Shevawn,' she said. 'It's Irish.'

'Oh God, I can't stand it!' Annalise cried, covering her ears with her hands. 'He's called me Siobhan, that's the name he calls me. He's even said it when we're making love. Oh God, when he's with me he's thinking about her. What am I going to do, Corrie? Tell me, for God's sake, what am I going to do?'

'Do you know who she is?' Corrie asked lamely.

Annalise shook her head. 'No. But it's her he goes to see. When he disappears, it's her he's with. I know it.'

Corrie was at a loss, and seeing the tears brimming in Annalise's eyes she put her arms around her. 'Come on,' she said, 'you're only making this worse for yourself by dwelling on it. Why don't you get into the shower then come and join us downstairs?'

'I can't face anyone,' Annalise sobbed. 'I've disgraced myself in front of everyone, I know I have, they're all talking about me. They all hate me. I know you do, and I don't blame you.'

'That's utter nonsense,' Corrie told her firmly. 'No one hates you. Least of all me.'

'Oh Corrie!' Annalise cried, suddenly clinging to Corrie so tightly it hurt. 'What am I going to do? Please tell me. I can't go on like this. I've got to make him understand that I love him. That I'll do anything for him.'

'I think he already knows,' Corrie said as gently as she could.

'Then why won't he give her up? Why does he have to keep seeing her? And why does he always come to me straight after? He's so cruel to me then . . . Oh Corrie, it's so awful. You just don't know what it's like. He hits me. Sometimes he hits me so hard . . .' Her voice broke off as she started to sob.

Having seen the bruises on Annalise's face this came as no surprise to Corrie at all. However, it was the first time Annalise had admitted to it. 'Why does he hit you?' she asked.

'I don't know. He just says that I ask for it. But I don't. I don't want him to hurt me, I just want him to love me. He says he does, he even makes me promise never to leave him. And I won't. Oh God, who is she, Corrie? What is she doing to him?'

Again Corrie didn't have an answer. All she could do was hold Annalise as she wept into her shoulder, stroke her hair and whisper that it would be all right, that they would work something out in the end.

'Stay with me while I shower,' Annalise choked. 'I don't want to be on my own.'

'All right,' Corrie smiled, looking at her watch. She had a whole list of telephone calls to get through that night to check that everything was set up for the next day, but it seemed they would have to wait. 'I told Felicity we'd meet her at seven, so you've got half an hour.'

When Annalise had gone into the shower Corrie picked up the birthday card again and opened it. *To my darling Siobhan on your birthday, with all my love, Luke.* So there was another woman, and Corrie could only feel relieved that it wasn't her. During the past two weeks her feelings for Luke had become confused; she would, naturally, always be grateful for the promotion he had given her, however she had earned it – and she still wasn't sure – but she couldn't be anything other than disturbed by the way he was treating Annalise. A man striking a woman was anathema to Corrie, something which just couldn't be forgiven, especially when that women was as fragile as Annalise. He knew how much Annalise loved him, how easy it was for him to hurt her, either physically or mentally, so why did he do it? Corrie herself had sensed the undercurrent of violence in him before he had made love to her that night, but even so she had come away still strongly attracted to him. She really didn't think she was now though, not having seen how badly Annalise was suffering, but in truth she couldn't say for sure how she felt.

The following night, after a long, tiring and frequently hysterical day of shooting in a 'torture' chamber, Corrie was again sitting in Annalise's room, this time listening to Luke yelling down the phone at her to get off his back and get on with her job. Annalise was pleading with him to listen, but Corrie heard him tell her to act her fucking age, before hanging up.

'If he doesn't want her,' Corrie said to Paula on the phone later, 'then why the hell doesn't he just let her go? I can't understand it. And if you could see her, she's lost so much weight, she's drunk half the time – he's really screwing up her mind. She just can't handle this, and I don't know how to advise her.'

'I think all you can do is listen,' Paula said. 'And think yourself lucky you're finding out what he's like before you got involved yourself.'

'Yes, you're right,' Corrie said, uncertainly.

'You're not involved, are you?'

'No, of course I'm not.'

'Mmm,' Paula grunted. 'Have you got any idea who this Siobhan might be?'

'No,' Corrie answered. 'It could be just a fling, though I doubt it. Annalise certainly doesn't seem to think so. My guess is, if he's keeping her under wraps like this, she must be married.'

'Could be,' Paula said. 'Oh no!' she groaned, 'can you hear that?'

Corrie could. The baby was crying, so their conversation,

as it so often was these days, was brought to an abrupt end.

The following day the crew moved on to Coventry to shoot an interview with Jack Watkins, a Labour MP, who was violently opposed not only to the idea of brothels, but to prostitution altogether. As far as he was concerned prostitutes actively encouraged unstable men to indulge their fantasies, unhinging them further and making them a danger to society. They were nothing short of vermin and should be swept from the streets, horsewhipped, jailed or, as Felicity suggested through gritted teeth, burned at the stake. Corrie had known from her telephone conversations with him that he wasn't going to be an easy man to deal with, and was now having to exercise every ounce of her diplomatic skills to prevent him and Felicity from coming to blows. But when he started to give the camera crew directions as to when they should turn over and cut, and then to tell Corrie which bits of what he was saying he wanted edited out, Corrie informed him politely but firmly, that if there was anything he didn't want broadcast then he should not say it. As it was, TW held the rights to the interview, he had even signed a form agreeing that they did, and therefore they would transmit the way they saw fit.

'Then you leave me no alternative but to call this interview to an end,' Watkins declared, getting up from his desk.

'As you like,' Corrie answered calmly, knowing that they already had what they'd come for. Watkins knew it too, and his long, pasty face began to twitch with anger. Corrie busied herself with her notes before he could see her smile; he was absolutely correct in thinking that he had not done himself any favours.

As the crew started to pack up Corrie watched the MP lumber about the room deliberately getting in their way. He was the oddest shape for a man, she was thinking, with his narrow, slightly stooped shoulders and bulging hips. His trousers were shiny, his sandals scuffed at the toe, and his hands, she had noticed earlier, were repulsively feminine. Then, to her horror, she found herself fantasizing about him sexually. She turned away quickly. This whole thing really was beginning to get to her and she wondered if she was ever going to be able to look at a man again without imagining him molesting her.

As they travelled back to the Holiday Inn, Corrie was surprised by how quiet Felicity was. But half an hour after they'd arrived back at the hotel she came banging on Corrie's door.

'I've just spoken to Carol,' she declared, with a triumphant grin, 'and it's just as I suspected. That fucking hypocrite Watkins is not only a bigot, he is a regular client of none other than Carol herself.'

'No!' Corrie gasped. 'You're kidding me.'

'Speak to Carol yourself if you like,' Felicity answered, waving a hand towards the telephone. 'It was why Carol gave us his name,' she added, laughing. 'She knew he'd end up fucking himself. She told me to tell you that in his case she's prepared to make an exception and reveal on camera that he's a client. So, what do you reckon?'

'I reckon we've got quite a scoop, is what I reckon,' Corrie grinned. 'This'll do more for their cause than anything else we've done so far. God, I can't believe it. To think that he had the nerve to sit there beating his puritanical drum when all the time he's getting his rocks off with Carol. What a fraud, and him a member of our estimable parliament! I'll have to get some advice though. I mean, I really don't know how to handle anything like this, and I'll have to make sure there aren't any legal problems. It could be that we should invite him to answer Carol's accusation. Let's hope he declines, that'll sink him even further. Anyway, whatever, this is a decision for the producer.'

'You're going to ask Annalise?' Felicity said incredulously.

'I'll have to. She's the producer.'

'And what the fuck does she know? She wasn't even there this afternoon.'

'Nevertheless . . .'

'Nevertheless shit!' Felicity cried. 'Get on the phone to London. It's Bob Churchill or Luke Fitzpatrick you should be asking, not little dolly day-dream.'

'It's Annalise who should be doing the asking,' Corrie reminded her, firmly, 'and I'm not about to drop her in it. Just give me a while to think about it though, I'll have to work out how to put it to her so she doesn't feel we're attacking her for not being there.'

Felicity shook her head. 'She doesn't deserve you, Corrie.'

'I know. I'm such a saint!' Corrie grinned.

'Yes, well just you look out that no one tries to use that halo to hang you with,' Felicity remarked seriously.

An hour later, having showered and dressed for dinner, Corrie was on the point of going to find Annalise when Annalise came barging into her room.

'I don't believe you could do this to me,' Annalise declared, as Corrie closed the door behind her.

'Do what?' Corrie asked in amazement.

Annalise sat down on the bed, wringing her hands, then turned her immense blue eyes to Corrie. Corrie didn't remember ever seeing her look so young, or so bewildered. Her wild blonde curls were tumbling about her face, her make-up was smudged and her lips were bitten and trembling. Worse, was the haunted expression in her eyes that Corrie couldn't yet fathom.

'Luke told me,' Annalise said shakily. 'He told me himself that you slept with him.'

Corrie closed her eyes as her heart froze. 'Oh my God,' she breathed.

'How could you?' Annalise cried. 'How could you have done that to me?'

All Corrie could do was look at her. Then Annalise started to cry.

'So it's true, you did sleep with him. I thought he was lying . . . I trusted you, Corrie,' she sobbed. 'I really trusted you. You were the only one who seemed to care, when all the time . . . Oh, Corrie, why? Why did you do it?'

'I don't know,' Corrie answered, dashing a hand through her hair. 'It just happened. But it didn't mean anything. Annalise, please believe that, it . . .'

'No, it didn't mean anything to Luke either,' Annalise interrupted. 'He told me that, you know, that he spent the night with you, but it didn't mean anything. I was just afraid it had meant something to you.'

'Well it didn't,' Corrie assured her.

'Oh, I'm so glad. You see, basically, Luke is a really kind man. He took pity on you when everyone else was giving you such a hard time. He wanted to comfort you.' She said through her tears. 'Isn't he a chauvinist!'

Corrie had several far more choice names she would like to call him right now, but managed to refrain.

'He's coming here, tonight,' Annalise said. 'I've just spoken to him in the car, he's on his way.'

'What for?'

'He said he was missing me. But I had to be sure that it wasn't you he was coming to see.' She reached out her hand to Corrie and pulled Corrie down beside her. 'I don't want you to think I blame you for sleeping with him,' she said, searching Corrie's eyes with her own. 'I mean, I know only too well how irresistible he is when he turns on the charm. Even when he doesn't,' she added with a sad smile. 'But . . . I don't suppose I've got any right to ask this, but you won't do it again, will you?'

Corrie shook her head. 'No, I won't,' she assured her. She wished there was a way she could persuade Annalise to stop seeing him too, but she knew she would be wasting her time. What she couldn't work out though was why Annalise had forgiven her so easily, but Felicity supplied the answer to that when Corrie met her in the bar later and told her what had happened.

'She has to forgive you,' Felicity said, 'for the same reason she feels she has to forgive him. If she didn't she'd lose you. And I've told you before, she can't survive without you – OK, either of you.'

Corrie stared down into her gin and tonic. 'She must be so lonely, so frightened,' she said.

'Yeah, poor kid.'

Corrie looked up in surprise and Felicity smiled.

'I know you think I'm an ogre with no heart,' Felicity said, 'but I'm not. And that girl is suffering. I don't admire her lack of professionalism, it's true, but I feel as sorry for her as you do. The point is though, that she's leaning very heavily on you and you are taking on the responsibility. I like you, Corrie, a lot, and I don't want to see you getting in so deep that it's you who ends up drowning in their problems.'

Corrie knew that what Felicity was saying made sense, she could already feel herself becoming submerged in something she had hardly begun to understand, but the idea of cutting herself loose from Annalise when Annalise so badly needed a friend and a shoulder, felt so disloyal, so selfish even, that she knew she'd never do it.

'So,' Felicity said suddenly. Corrie looked up and found that Felicity was laughing. 'You did sleep with him then. I guessed as much.'

'I thought you had,' Corrie answered with a wry smile. 'But as I said, it only happened once.'

'And the bastard had to go and tell Annalise. Now why do you suppose he did that?'

Corrie shrugged. 'Your guess is as good as mine.'

'I have to confess I wouldn't mind a roll in the hay with him myself,' Felicity grinned. 'He's a damned attractive man. I wonder if Annalise would be so quick to forgive me?'

'I don't know about that,' Corrie answered, 'but she'd forgive Luke, that's for sure. Anyway, the important thing now is that he's on his way here, and I was thinking that perhaps it would be better if you asked him what we should do about Jack Watkins. That way it won't look as though I've gone behind Annalise's back.'

'So we'll make me the villain of the piece, is that it?'

'Yep.'

Laughing Felicity got up from the bar. 'All right, I'll talk to him. What are you doing now?'

'I'm off for a Chinese with the crew, so I'll call in on you when I get back, find out how you got on.'

Later in the evening, when Corrie returned from the restaurant, she made a stop at reception to see if Luke had checked in yet. He had. They gave her his room number, but she went to Felicity's room first. It was empty. So too was Annalise's. Getting back into the lift she rode up another floor to Luke's room. She found the door slightly ajar, and hearing muffled voices she blithely walked in.

What confronted her stopped her dead in her tracks. Luke, Felicity and Annalise were all writhing naked about the bed.

Shocked, Corrie beat a hasty retreat and went back to her room. She couldn't even begin to imagine how the unlikely threesome had come about, but somehow it had, and already it was giving her an uneasy feeling in the pit of her stomach.

She hadn't had time to take in much more than their nudity, so she wasn't sure if she was imagining the fact that one of them, Annalise she thought, had been tied to the bed. The idea that Annalise had been put into such a vulnerable position didn't sit too well with her either, some-how it smacked of exploitation, and Corrie was more than a little tempted to go back and insist she was released. But she couldn't be sure about what she had seen, and besides, if Annalise had been tied up she certainly hadn't been screaming for help. Corrie smiled then, as she imagined their reaction to her descending upon them like some avenging angel, but the smile quickly faded. It was starting to seem to her that the whole world was obsessed with sex. Sex, lust and perverted fantasy. She was beginning to hate what it did to people, the way it made them behave. She already knew more than she wanted to about what lengths some men would go to in order to achieve the ultimate orgasm, and the knowledge alone felt like a violation. Her sympathy with the prostitutes was not in any way dented, she knew that, but her attitude towards sex was causing her a great deal of concern. She could no longer equate it with an act of love, instead she was seeing it as an act of violence, debauchery and depravity.

'Well that's hardly surprising,' Paula told her, when Corrie called her in the middle of the night. 'It's a horrible world out there, and right now you're staring it straight in the face.'

'Yes, but what about Luke, Felicity and Annalise? I have to tell you Paula, it's left me with a really bad taste.'

'Probably because you feel so protective about Annalise. But she's a grown woman, Corrie. And you said yourself, she wasn't objecting.'

'She wouldn't object to anything Luke wanted her to do.'

'Maybe not, but it's her life. And your trouble is, you're an incurable romantic. Sex for sex's sake can be every bit as erotic as sex with love, you know? Dave and I are always pretending we don't know one another, or acting out little roles that turn us both on. We call it dirty sex, and we love it!'

Corrie laughed. 'What would I do without you, Paula

Jeffries? You make everything sound so uncomplicated, so normal.'

'Well you can't tell me that you haven't had little fantasies of your own,' Paula remarked.

'Sure I have,' Corrie confessed, 'but don't you dare ask me what they are, because I'm not telling you.'

'That's all right. Just be sure to tell the right man when he comes along. It'll blow his mind – and yours.'

'And try to be a little more tolerant of what others are doing?'

'Yeah, I guess so. And ask yourself if you weren't just the tiniest bit jealous that you weren't on that bed with them.'

'I wasn't,' Corrie assured her. 'The idea of another woman being in the room does nothing for me. Now, if it were two men and me . . .'

Paula laughed. 'You see, you're a raver at heart, and don't know it. Anyway, I must go, it's getting cold standing here in this hall. Call me again soon and let me know all developments. I live my life vicariously through you, you understand?'

The following morning Luke was the only one of the three to show for breakfast. With momentary surprise Corrie noticed everyone look up as he walked into the restaurant, then remembered that of course they all knew who he was. She watched him weave a path through the tables towards her, and her heart very nearly turned over as he started to smile. There was no denying how incredibly handsome he was, nor how pleased she felt that his smile was directed at her. Nevertheless she was disappointed in herself for responding the way she was.

He joined her at her table, where she sat alone, and after they had exchanged good mornings Corrie casually asked if Felicity had spoken to him the night before.

Immediately Luke grinned and after ordering himself some coffee from the hovering waiter, he turned and looked

Corrie straight in the eye. 'I saw you come into the room last night,' he said.

Corrie blushed, and started to apologize for barging in like that.

'Why worry?' he shrugged. 'Unless of course it upset you.'

'Why would it upset me?' Corrie said, a little too defensively.

He treated her to a long, appraising look, then said, 'It's Annalise, you know. She really gets a kick out of bondage *and* troilism. And Felicity, we discover, gets her kicks out of swinging both ways.'

'And you? No, don't tell me, you were nothing more than the helpless victim of a female web of lust?' Immediately the words were out Corrie regretted them; they held the unmistakable ring of jealousy.

Luke was laughing. 'You should have stayed,' he said, 'we could have made quite a night of it, and helped you shed some of those inhibitions into the bargain.'

Corrie passed no comment as she looked down at the mug of tea cupped between her hands. What she was thinking was that it was more likely him who got a kick out of bondage and troilism, since it simply didn't add up where Annalise was concerned. As for Felicity swinging both ways . . . Well, what Felicity did was her own business.

'Anyway, what you really want to know,' Luke said, 'is did Felicity tell me about Watkins? And the answer is yes, she did.'

Corrie looked up, then started as Luke suddenly burst out laughing.

'What's so funny?' she asked uncertainly.

'You.' He put a hand over hers and squeezed it. 'I'm sorry if last night shocked you,' he said gently. 'And I'm sorry if I've upset you by talking about it this morning.'

'You haven't upset me,' Corrie protested.

He shrugged. 'OK, have it your way. But if you had seen your look of relief just then when I changed the subject . . .'

Corrie lowered her eyes, but Luke put his fingers under her chin and brought her face back up to look at him. 'Last night meant nothing to me,' he said softly. 'I want you to know that.'

It was on the tip of Corrie's tongue to remind him that he had said exactly that when he'd told Annalise about the night he had spent with her, but she bit it back. It wasn't something she wanted to discuss.

'It's you, Corrie,' he said, slipping his hand into her hair, 'you know that don't you? You're the one I want. And if you're afraid I'll ever ask you to do that sort of thing . . .'

'Please, let's change the subject again,' Corrie interrupted, her eyes darting towards the door for any sign of Annalise.

'No. Let's not. It's important to me that you understand that I'll never make you do anything you don't want to do. That I'll do all I can to make you care for me the way I care for you. I'll even give up Annalise if that's what you want.'

'No, no. That's not what I want at all. Apart from anything else it would break her heart . . .'

'And what about my heart? Or doesn't that matter?'

Overcome with confusion Corrie tried to turn away from him, but he held her there. 'You don't know me,' she said feebly, 'you don't know anything about me.'

'I know that I want you more than I've ever wanted any other woman. I know that I need you too.'

'How can you say that when . . .'

'I can say it, Corrie, because it's true,' and to her amazement there was such sincerity in his eyes that she almost believed him.

'But Annalise . . . You tell her you love her, she believes you love her . . .'

He looked away for a moment, but not before Corrie had seen a raw pain pass across his face.

'Corrie,' he said, almost in a whisper, 'Annalise is like an addiction with me. I don't know if what I feel for her is love, all I know is that there are times when she means more to me than life itself, and other times when I feel so stifled by her that it's as though I'm losing my mind. Our relationship isn't healthy, and it frightens me . . . I need to get away from her, Corrie. That's why I'm so cruel to her. I try to drive her away, but it only seems to make her want me all the more. And God help me, I don't seem able to resist her. I need you to help me, Corrie.'

'But I can't do that, Luke. I'm just not . . .'

'But you can, Corrie, because what I feel for you makes me feel so good, so . . . I don't know, I can't explain it, other than to say that it just feels right. Wholesome, I suppose. Whereas, what I feel for Annalise . . . Well, I can't explain that either . . .' He smiled, sadly, and seemed to withdraw into himself. 'I'm sorry,' he said, 'I'm confusing you. I don't mean to. If you like we can forget everything I've said. There's no reason in the world why you should share my feelings, it was presumptuous of me to think that you might. So, shall we talk about Watkins?'

Corrie looked at him, aware of a rising compassion for him that was making her want to understand what was going on in his heart, what was making him seem almost as lost and lonely as Annalise. But she knew she was in danger of saying or doing something she might regret later, so she said, as gently as she could, 'I think we'd better.'

He nodded. 'OK. Well, I've decided that I don't want TW becoming embroiled in a law suit, which it almost inevitably would if we revealed Watkins' hypocrisy, so I'm going to pass the scoop on to someone in Fleet Street.'

Corrie was stunned. 'I don't believe it! You're seriously going to let this go?'

He smiled at her surprise. 'Not exactly. I'll be asking

the newspaper to run the story the morning after our transmission. They're sure to agree, since the story doesn't mean much without his denigration of brothels and prostitution.'

'Well if we're going to handle it that way, then surely it would be better to get the paper to run the story the morning *of* transmission. We can give them quotes from the programme, making sure that they credit us, naturally, and that way it should help pull in even more viewers.'

Luke was watching her, and shaking his head. 'You really are starting to become quite invaluable,' he smiled. 'And don't think I'm blind to the fact that you've been running this show. Annalise has been in no fit state, I'm more than aware of that, just as I'm all too aware that it's my fault. I only wish I could make it up to you, Corrie, and give you the recognition you deserve for all you've done. But politically I'm afraid it's just not possible at this time. All I can offer is dinner, tonight, when we get back to London.'

'Oh, no, you don't have to do that,' Corrie said. 'I mean, it's very kind of you, but . . .'

'I'd really appreciate it if you'd accept,' he interrupted.

'I'm afraid I can't,' she said. 'I've promised Annalise I won't see you again, and if she were to find out . . .'

'She won't find out. She's going to spend the weekend with her parents. But of course if it's me that you object to . . .'

'No, it's not that. Please don't think that,' Corrie said hastily.

'Well I'm glad to hear that,' he smiled, and he really did look so very relieved that Corrie found herself smiling too. 'So you will come?' he said, cupping her chin in his hand and drawing her towards him; and despite desperately wanting to distance herself from both him and Annalise, if only for a few hours, Corrie heard herself saying she'd love to have dinner with him.

The betrayal of her promise to Annalise played on

Corrie's conscience all day after that, and it was only exacerbated by the fact that Luke had insisted on cooking dinner himself, at his apartment. The intimacy of a cosy meal at home was inescapable, and she only hoped to God that Luke didn't take it upon himself to tell Annalise about it later.

When she finally arrived back at her studio, early that evening, after a couple of nightmarish hours filming on the M1 into London, all she wanted to do was curl up in the safety and comfort of her own home. Paula, who called almost as soon as Corrie walked through the door, told her quite vehemently that that was just what she should do.

'You don't owe him anything, Corrie,' she said. 'He's just playing on your sympathy, and if you ask me you've got far too much of that for your own good.'

'But I didn't ask you,' Corrie snapped back.

'He's manipulating you, every bit as much as he is Annalise,' Paula went on, obviously unperturbed. 'You're going to have to learn when to put your foot down, Corrie. Now if you don't want to go, just call him up and say so.'

'I can't! If you'd seen him, Paula . . . Oh God, I don't know, I can't explain it, but believe me, I have to go.'

'Then I think you should ask yourself why – and try being honest with your answer.'

'And what's that supposed to mean?'

'It means that I think you want something to come of this relationship you're not admitting to. You still fancy him, Corrie, and don't bother to deny it because this is me you're talking to. You've got some crazy idea that you're the one to change him, to sort out all his problems, and that's just what he wants you to think. He's using you, surely you can see that . . .'

'Paula . . .'

'No, I'm not listening. Not until I hear you admit to the truth. You want to sleep with him again, don't you? You want to hear him tell you again how special you are. Well, I can't blame you for that, we none of us tire of . . .'

'Paula!'

'Just admit it, Corrie! For God's sake if you can't be honest with yourself you're going to end up in an even bigger mess than you're already in.'

'All right! All right! Part of me does want to go to bed with him again. Satisfied? He's an attractive man, so why shouldn't I? But it's only physical. I'm not emotionally involved with him at all.'

'That's what you think,' Paula said.

'I'm going to ring off now,' Corrie retorted, 'before I get really mad at you, because quite frankly you're getting on my nerves assuming you know better than I do what's going on inside my head.'

At eight o'clock Corrie turned up at Luke's apartment with the truth of all Paula had said still ringing in her ears. She was furious with herself for not being able to understand why she was still attracted to Luke, when she hadn't even really enjoyed sleeping with him on the one occasion she had. And to make matters even more confusing she was more than a little disturbed by the things he had said about his relationship with Annalise over breakfast that morning. She just knew that she was getting herself into something that was way beyond her, but simply didn't know how to pull back.

She rang again on the doorbell, and waited for his voice to come over the entryphone. Baffled by the silence she turned towards the square to see if she could spot his car. It was nowhere in sight, but in Knightsbridge that wasn't unusual, it was rare that anyone could park outside their own homes. She rang the bell again, but still there was no reply and not sure whether she was relieved or offended that he had stood her up, she started back down the steps.

At that very instant he drove around the corner and pulled up on the yellow line right in front of her. Though he apologized profusely for not being there when she'd arrived Corrie could see that he was agitated, barely even knew what he was saying. When they got into his flat he went instantly to his answerphone to replay his messages, and to Corrie's amazement she heard Jack Watkins' voice saying that he would be glad to meet Luke the following day.

Corrie didn't ask what it was about, but her curiosity showed, and laughing, Luke said, 'I thought it only fair that the man should be tipped off that we know about him before we inform someone in Fleet Street.'

'But why?' Corrie protested.

Luke shrugged. 'I guess because it's a pretty rotten thing having your name splashed all over the newspapers like that.'

'Well it's not as if he doesn't deserve it,' Corrie pointed out, heatedly.

'Oh come on, give the guy a break. The damage is done now, so it makes no difference whether he finds out sooner or later. I just thought it would be fairer to give him time to prepare himself for the flak. It's quite usual, you know, to tip off the subject of an exposé. Anyway, let me get you a drink. Name your poison.' He crossed to the drinks cabinet, then turned to look at her. 'By the way, you look gorgeous tonight.'

'Thank you,' Corrie answered, avoiding his eyes.

'Hey,' he said, 'you're not still mad at me about last night, are you? I told you, it meant nothing.'

'Like I meant nothing the last time I was here?'

'What are you talking about?'

'That's what you told Annalise, wasn't it? That I had meant nothing. And while we're on the subject, why in God's name did you tell her anyway?'

He sighed, and taking her by the hand led her to the sofa and sat her down. 'I thought I'd explained that this morning,' he said. 'I need to get her off my back, to make her stop idolizing me the way she does . . .'

'But telling her about me! Didn't you even stop to consider what it might have done to our friendship?'

'Your friendship with Annalise means that much to you?'

'Yes, as a matter of fact it does.'

'More than me?'

'That's not what we're talking about.'

Luke smiled. 'I can't say I'm sorry that you care so much for her. As a matter of fact, I'm glad. She needs a friend, badly, and I can't see you letting her down.'

'Except for the fact that I'm here,' Corrie pointed out.

'She'll never know. At least not from me, she won't.'

He was still holding Corrie's hand, and as his thumb started to circle her palm Corrie could feel his magnetism starting to draw her in. She tried to look away, there was still so much more she wanted to say, to demand that he explain, but he pulled her back and covered her lips gently with his own.

'I'm sorry,' he whispered, 'but I just had to kiss you.'

Corrie was never too sure later quite how she ended up in bed with him, but she did. And something else she was never able to figure out was how he managed to persuade her to let him tie her to the bed.

She hated it. The way she was spread-eagled across the sheets wasn't only demeaning, the feeling of helplessness it gave her was frightening. But there was no mistaking the fact that it was driving Luke crazy.

She tried to hold on, telling herself that he would come soon and it would be over. But in the end she couldn't stand anymore. 'Luke,' she whispered, as he pounded away on top of her, 'Luke, please untie me now.'

'Just a couple more minutes,' he gasped, his eyes fixed to the bonds on her wrists, 'I'm nearly there.'

Corrie closed her eyes, trying to disassociate herself from her own body, then suddenly she became aware that he had stopped. She looked up at him, then smiled weakly as she saw the deep concern in his eyes.

'You really don't like it, do you?' he said.

She shook her head.

'Oh God, I'm sorry,' he groaned. 'You should have said sooner,' and within seconds he had freed her.

'I told you before,' he said, as he cradled her in his arms, 'I don't want you to do anything you're not comfortable with. Please, don't ever say yes to anything just to please me, because that's not the way I want it with us.'

Corrie buried her face in his neck. 'I'm sorry,' she mumbled, 'I didn't want to let you down. I wanted to prove that I was as adventurous, as open-minded as you are, but I guess I'm just not.'

'Oh Corrie,' he said, finding her mouth and kissing her tenderly, 'I want you just the way you are. Please believe that.'

They lay quietly together for some time, until Corrie lifted her head and looked at him.

He smiled. 'Are you all right?' he asked, pulling a strand of hair from her lips.

'You didn't come,' she whispered.

'No. But it doesn't matter.'

'It does to me,' she said. Then swallowing hard she asked him to make love to her, using the words she knew he wanted to hear.

His erection was instant. 'Oh, baby,' he groaned, as he rolled onto her. And as he pushed himself inside her, he said, 'You just don't know what you do to me, Corrie.'

– 11 –

It was early one morning the following week, before anyone else arrived at the office, that Corrie was making her way down the corridor to the edit suite in order to view some police library footage for the prostitution programme. She knew already that a great deal of it would be unusable, since it contained explicit pictures of what had happened to the prostitutes from Shepherd Market who had been murdered. In fact she was not at all looking forward to viewing it herself.

With her programme file under one arm, and carrying a cup of coffee and a half-eaten pastry, she backed into the darkened edit suite, turned round and was momentarily stunned to find herself confronted by a bank of monitors all displaying horrific pictures of the mutilations the prostitutes had suffered both before and after death.

'Oh God!' she muttered, then glancing at her pastry she threw it into the bin.

Luke was at the controls, running the pictures through, frame by frame. Corrie wasn't surprised to see him, since it had been at his personal request that the police had released the footage. He glanced up as she came towards him and she noticed straight away how deathly pale he was.

'Jesus God,' he murmured, 'it's enough to turn a man's stomach. There's not much here we can use though, I'm afraid.'

Corrie sat down next to him and watched as he continued to screen the pictures. After only a few minutes he stopped. 'Look at it if you want to,' he said, 'I can't. I'll be in my office.'

As he stood up Corrie noticed him wince and as he turned into the light she saw a dark swelling above his eye. 'What happened to you?' she asked.

He grimaced. 'If I told you it was a cupboard door would you believe me?'

Corrie shrugged.

'Well it was.' He laughed then. 'If I were a woman you'd think my husband had been beating me up, wouldn't you?'

'Probably,' Corrie smiled. 'But that cut looks pretty deep, maybe you need stitches.'

'It'll be all right,' he answered, and was on the point of leaving when he turned back. 'By the way, I've invited a few people round to the flat for cocktails tonight. Would you like to come?'

Corrie was hesitant. She hadn't seen him since the Friday before, when they'd spent the night together, and she was still no closer to resolving the turmoil of her feelings for him.

'Annalise will be there too,' he said, 'so you don't have to feel you're being disloyal.'

'Does she know you're inviting me?'

'Of course.'

'Then OK, I'd love to come. Incidently, do you know where she is? She was supposed to meet me here at seven to go through this material.'

'If the telephone call I received at four this morning is anything to go by, then I think you'll find her tucked up in bed with a hangover.'

Corrie sighed and turned back to the controls. Annalise had called her around midnight looking for Luke, so she had expected something like this.

The next hour, spent viewing the police footage, she knew would live in her mind, probably for the rest of her life. That one human being could do such terrible things to another defied belief – except she was sitting there looking right at it. Each gaping knife wound, caked in blood and slime from the river bank, stared down at her from the playback monitors like grisly smiles. On three of the bodies most of the cuts were bone deep, but the fourth was by far the worst. On this one several of the internal organs were visible. Corrie couldn't even begin to imagine the depths of terror or pain either of them must have suffered in the minutes before they died, but it was there, even in death, frozen in their bulging eyes.

Detective Inspector Radcliffe who was leading the murder hunt, had told Corrie the day before, after they'd interviewed him, that he was only too aware that the prostitutes didn't believe the police were doing all they could.

'But I can assure you we are,' he'd said. 'And somehow we're going to nail that bastard, because no one on God's earth deserves to die like that.'

'Do you have any leads at all?' she had asked. Felicity had asked the same question on camera, so Corrie more or less knew what his answer would be.

'Not enough,' he said. 'All these women seem to have in common, aside from their profession, is blonde hair. We don't even know yet where the murders were carried out. If we did . . . Well, let's hope your programme will persuade someone to come forward.'

What was distressing Corrie most of all now, as she forced herself to look at the passing images which, in any sane world, should only have come from a slaughterhouse, was the way in which she was identifying with the victims. She had known, albeit for a short time, what it was to be tied up, to feel so helpless and afraid. The difference was of course, that she had been with Luke, who had been so sensitive to her fear that he had released her immediately. That hadn't been the case for these women, and it made her want to weep for the unfairness of it, when all they had set out to do was help a man release his pent up sexual desires.

In the end she selected some shots of the type of knife that had probably been used, some coils of rope and one rear shot of a prostitute who was tied up into the foetal position. Unless she was instructed otherwise she didn't want to use any shots of their faces – the only part of their bodies that had not been slashed by the knife. With the terror printed indelibly in their eyes it seemed an unforgivable intrusion, and would, she was very much afraid, incite some latent psychopath to try his own hand at forcing such an expression.

She spent the rest of the day with the editor, piecing together the interviews they had shot over the past two weeks. At midday she called Annalise, but as the phone was ringing Annalise walked into the office. There was a heated argument going on at the time between Alan Fox and Cindy Thompson, who were working on a programme about the recent clash between church and government. Corrie was paying very little attention, but Annalise, looking infinitely better than Corrie had seen her for some time, entered into the affray the minute she walked in the door and very soon had everyone laughing.

'You're looking mightily pleased with yourself,' Corrie remarked when Annalise came to perch on the edge of her desk. Now that summer had arrived Annalise was wearing even shorter skirts than usual, without tights, and Corrie glanced a touch wistfully at her slender brown thighs.

'And why shouldn't I be?' Annalise asked. 'No don't answer that, because you're angry with me that I didn't turn up this morning. Well, I'm here now, at your disposal. What do you want me to do?'

'You could go and view the editing we did this morning,' Corrie answered, 'and the shots I've selected from the police stuff. Grant has them all lined up.' She laughed as Annalise threw her arms around her and planted a loud kiss on her cheek.

'Thank you,' she whispered in Corrie's ear.

'What for?' Corrie asked.

Annalise shrugged. 'For being you,' and she skipped off across the office towards the edit suite. As Corrie watched her go she was frowning. She hadn't missed the bitter smell of alcohol on Annalise's breath.

Corrie and Annalise had been at Luke's apartment since seven o'clock, the time he'd told them to arrive, but as yet, there was no sign of anyone else. It was now past eight o'clock and Corrie was starting to feel lightheaded after two martinis on an empty stomach.

The hour had, in fact, passed quite pleasantly, until some five minutes ago when Corrie had got up from the sofa to go and look at an oil painting Luke had bought a couple of days before. At the same time Annalise had gone to the bathroom. Almost before she knew what was happening Luke had taken Corrie in his arms and was kissing her. For a moment or two Corrie found herself kissing him back, but then, hearing the bathroom door unlock she all but leapt away from him. Whether Annalise had noticed the guilty flush on her cheeks, Corrie didn't know, though she doubted it – Annalise would have been sure to say something if she had.

Now Corrie was in the drawing room alone, but from where she was sitting she could see Annalise and Luke in the kitchen together. He was whispering something to her and Annalise kept giggling, which was making Corrie feel more than a little uncomfortable. After a while she looked at them again, but turned away quickly as Luke met her eyes while slipping a hand between Annalise's legs.

Corrie turned hot with embarrassment and anger. The invitation to a cocktail party, she realized, was a sham. He had used it as an excuse to get them both into his apartment, and once there, into his bed. Well he could think again if he thought she was going to take part in his perverted sex games because she was leaving right this minute. Which she would have, had there not been a ring on the door bell, announcing the arrival of more guests.

While Luke went to let them in Annalise remained in the kitchen, and seeing her bend over to retrieve her knickers from her ankles, Corrie discreetly closed the door. She was half smiling to herself now, mainly with relief that she had been wrong in her surmise of the situation. But her relief was shattered the instant the new arrivals walked into the room.

She recognized her father immediately, as, from the expression of horror on his face, he did her. Corrie spun towards Luke, but he was already embracing the woman who had come in with Phillip. On the brink of panic Corrie looked at her father again, but though his face had paled he seemed to have himself back in control again.

'Corrie,' Luke said, taking her by the arm, 'let me introduce you to Phillip and Octavia Denby. Phillip and Octavia, this is Corrie Browne, TW's brightest and best researcher.'

Corrie's mind was in chaos. Surely Luke must know that this was her father. That the stupendously beautiful woman with him was her stepmother. Or did he? He certainly gave no sign of knowing, and Corrie just couldn't remember if she'd ever told him her father's name. Luke was looking at her now as if baffled by her reluctance to shake hands, and there was a smile in his eyes, as though encouraging her not to be shy.

Somehow Corrie managed to shake her father's hand. Both of them narrowly avoided eye contact, and Corrie could sense from his voice that he was as nervous as she was. Then it was time to shake Octavia's hand, and as Corrie turned towards her her heart suddenly froze with the shock of seeing such naked hunger in Octavia's eyes as she looked at Luke. *My God!* Corrie thought, *surely he can't be screwing her too.* Unable to stop herself Corrie glanced at her father, wondering if he too had noticed the look, but Phillip was already turning to the cocktail cabinet.

'It's very nice to meet you, Corrie,' Octavia was saying, and as Corrie felt her hand encircled by the slim, delicate fingers, and looked into the coldest blue eyes she'd ever seen, she almost felt herself recoil. Never would she have believed that beauty could be such an offence to the eyes, but it was; for the flawless, alabaster face looking so absurdly large on the stick-like neck, was so devoid of animation or warmth it could only be described as grotesque. Then suddenly Octavia was smiling – a smile designed not to crease her skin – and it was a second or two before Corrie realized it wasn't at her. Corrie turned to look behind her and suddenly it was as though the whole world had gone mad.

'Mummy, Daddy,' Annalise cried, coming across the room to embrace them.

Corrie took a step back. She was reeling. She felt faint, needed to sit down, better still to run away, but she could barely move. She turned to Luke again. There was nothing in his manner to suggest that he knew what was going on, he wasn't even looking in her direction. If only she could remember whether she had told him Phillip's name. Surely she must have, somewhere along the line, but if she had then why had he never said that he knew Phillip?

No, it was nothing more than a coincidence, she told herself, a terrible coincidence . . . But dear God, if Phillip was Annalise's father, that could only mean that she, Corrie, was . . . No, she couldn't think about it now. It was too much to take in. Again she looked at her father, and only then did it occur to her, that on top of everything else he was also her employer. He was Luke's partner – the man whose name, she realized now, had never been mentioned in her hearing, and whose name she had stupidly never thought to ask.

As if in a daze Corrie watched as Phillip handed his wife a drink, then turned back for his own. Taking a sip he settled himself in a chair beside the stereo, and seemed to absorb himself in the music. Behind her Annalise, Octavia and Luke were standing in front of the oil painting discussing its merits, so not knowing what else to do Corrie sat down on the sofa.

Somehow she managed to get through the next half an hour, but it was one of the worst half hours she'd ever had to endure. Keeping a check on her emotions was proving almost impossible, for as she watched her father from the corner of her eye, she could see quite plainly, from his jerky movements and the sweat on his brow, that he was deeply upset by her presence. Instead of feeling angry or sickened by the way he was behaving, she felt saddened by it. Just that one brief introduction to Octavia was enough for Corrie to guess at how intolerable his life must be married to someone like her; since they'd arrived Octavia's only acknowledgement that he was in the room had been a sneery smile when Luke had asked him, 'how's tricks?'

Phillip's answer had sounded confident enough, as he told Luke about a meeting he'd had that day with his nephew, the TW accountant, but the moment Luke returned his attention to Octavia Phillip had seemed to withdraw back into himself. Did he know, Corrie wondered again, that Luke was sleeping with his wife? It seemed blatantly obvious to her, but right now Phillip seemed more intent on avoiding any kind of communication with her. She wished she could reassure him that she had no intention of telling anyone who she was, but of course it was unthinkable. If only he didn't look so alone though, so utterly confined in the loneliness of his weak man's world. But he had Annalise, Corrie reminded herself, and any fool could see how much he doted on her. Nevertheless, after their initial greeting Phillip had appeared awkward with Annalise too, as though he was afraid she was going to hurt him in some way, and despite the fact that he was a big man Corrie could only watch helplessly as he very nearly cowered into his chair like a whipped puppy. For a moment she was almost overcome by the urge to shake him, to tell him to act like a man, but at the same time she couldn't help wondering why he was so afraid.

She turned her attention to the others again, watching Octavia with mounting revulsion. She was pawing Luke's arm as she asked him and Annalise all about the prostitute programme, and from the way her eyes were glittering Corrie could tell that she was already more than a little aroused. Corrie was very tempted at that point to describe in graphic detail the shots she had viewed earlier that day, just to shut Octavia up, but judged it better to remain silent for now.

It was no wonder, Corrie was thinking to herself, that Annalise was so unstable in her emotions when she had parents like these. Octavia wasn't even subtle about the way she was trying to capture all Luke's attention, and as they smiled deeply into each other's eyes, deliberately shutting Annalise out, Annalise, clearly as hurt as she was bewildered, fought bravely to make him notice her again. But each time she succeeded Octavia was ready.

'Just imagine,' she drawled now, 'having someone pay you for the privilege of fucking you.'

Corrie barely had time to be amazed by such a profane word coming out of such a clinical mouth before Octavia said something that shocked her beyond words.

'I'd just love to be bending over with a stranger's cock right up my cunt, and all the time look at the money he's left on the table.'

Corrie's head spun towards Phillip. Slumped in his chair as he was, he seemed not to have heard, but Annalise had.

'Mummy!' she declared, her face on fire, 'that's disgusting. I've never heard you talk like that before.'

From the look passing between Octavia and Luke, it was quite evident that Luke had.

'I'm sorry, darling,' Octavia was saying, patting Annalise's cheek. 'But you have to remember, sweetheart, that mothers are human too. Still, it was quite unforgivable to say such a thing in front of you, and I apologize.'

'I think you should apologize to Daddy too,' Annalise retorted. 'And Corrie. You've really embarrassed her.'

Octavia turned to Corrie with a look of mild surprise.

'Oh, but I'm sure Corrie's heard it all before,' she remarked smoothly.

Corrie felt like she was in the middle of a nightmare, and wanted nothing more than to get out of there. Obviously Octavia was letting her know that she knew about her relationship with Luke, but why? She was a vindictive bitch, that was for sure, the way she was treating her own daughter more than proved that. But what about the way she was treating her husband, pathetic cuckold that he was, sitting there huddled into his chair? And if Octavia knew so much about Corrie's relationship with Luke, did she also know about her own relationship to Corrie? Somehow Corrie didn't think so. The person pulling all the strings here, she felt sure, was Luke. He was sleeping with them all – Octavia, Annalise and Corrie. But what was he trying to prove by bringing them all here together like this? Suddenly Corrie's eyes rounded, and she turned slowly towards her father as the realization of what was happening started to dawn on her. She had no idea why Luke should want to humiliate Phillip like this, but there was little doubt in her mind that that was exactly what was going on.

Phillip's eyes flickered towards her, but seeing her looking at him he turned quickly away. Octavia's falsetto laugh suddenly grated through Corrie's ears, and when Corrie turned back she felt a near overriding nausea rush to her throat. Octavia was pressed so closely to Luke's arm that Annalise couldn't see the tiny, bejewelled hand carressing his buttocks, but Corrie could. So too could Phillip, if he'd cared to look. This grotesque pantomime was insufferable, and all Corrie wanted was to get outside, away from the overpowering stench of Octavia's perfume and breathe some fresh air into her lungs.

She was already on her feet when the doorbell rang again. Immediately Corrie looked at Luke, hardly daring to imagine what more chicanery was to come. As he turned his back on Octavia and Annalise he rolled his eyes at

Corrie, then went to answer the door. A few minutes later several people, all as immaculately dressed as Phillip and Octavia, filed in, and at last Phillip got up from his chair. Corrie could hardly believe the transformation in him as he greeted the newcomers, and started to mingle with all the confidence one might expect of a successful business-man who knew his importance in the world.

However, he continued to avoid Corrie like the plague, which upset Corrie more than she wanted to admit, for she was becoming increasingly aware, through the thin crowd, that Luke and Octavia were whispering, looking in her direction, then laughing. She was horribly unnerved by it, and found herself wishing that she could turn to Phillip for reassurance, after all he was her father. But she knew that she stood even less chance of success there than Annalise was having in trying to detach her mother from Luke. Watching him now Corrie was even more bitterly disap-pointed in Phillip than she had been the first time she met him, and for some reason this made her want to cry. He was letting both her and Annalise down, seemed to care nothing for what either of them might be suffering, yet somehow Corrie knew, that as oblivious as he wanted to appear to it, he wasn't. It was distressing him too, but even so he was going to do nothing to comfort either of them. She started to notice then, the furtive glances he kept throw-ing in Luke's direction. This had the effect of convincing Corrie even more that there was something going on between them that went far deeper than a mere power struggle, which was what she had assumed it to be at first.

'Do you think my mother's having an affair with Luke?'

Corrie turned round to find Annalise looking up at her with stricken eyes. Instantly Corrie's heart turned over. *She's my sister*, Corrie was thinking, *my own flesh and blood. And she's such a child still.* But what the hell could she do to comfort her? How could she even begin to explain to Annal-ise what was going on when she didn't even know herself?

It was likely that Annalise sensed something too, something beyond her mother's outrageous behaviour, though Corrie doubted very much that Annalise would even want it put into words. All she wanted was to be reassured. It was all, in her fragile state of mind, she could handle. But the tragedy of it was that Corrie could sense only too well the desperate need inside her. Annalise wanted to be loved. To feel that she mattered to someone more than anyone else in the world, and God help her, she had chosen a man like Luke to do it.

For a moment Corrie was so close to tears that she couldn't answer, then seeing the panic her silence had evoked in Annalise she smiled, lifted a hand to Annalise's cheek and lied.

'No,' she said softly, 'I don't think so. But what I do think is that you are paranoid where Luke is concerned.'

It was what Annalise wanted to hear, just the look on her face told Corrie that, but what Corrie had to decide now was what she was going to do about getting him out of their lives. And, if she could, find out what was going on between him and her father. There might well be nothing she could do about that, but she wanted at least to try, for as improbable as it might seem now, she was already harbouring a hope that one day, if only in a small way, she, Phillip and Annalise could become a family.

The next morning Corrie rang the office to say she would be in late, then settling herself down for what she knew would be a lengthy conversation with Paula, she reached out for the phone. As she did it rang. To her amazement it was her father.

'I'd like you to meet me tomorrow night,' he said. 'I'll be at the Man in the Moon pub at World's End. If you can, be there at eight thirty, if not I'll wait,' and before Corrie could utter a word he rang off.

Still somewhat dazed by the abrupt call Corrie dialled

Paula's number. It took quite some time to tell her all that had happened the night before, but the fact that her father had just called Corrie decided to hold back for the time being.

'I don't believe it,' Paula said in a hushed voice when Corrie had finished. 'I just don't believe it. My God, it must have blown your mind.'

'It did,' Corrie answered, 'but the question is, what am I going to do about it?'

'I don't know. I mean, do you think Luke knows?'

'I can't be sure. To be honest, I had so much to drink that first evening we went out, I don't remember what I told him.'

'Then I think you should confront him, ask him.'

'That's what I thought at first. But if he doesn't know that Phillip's my father, then quite frankly, I don't want him to know.'

'But you think there's something going on between him and Phillip, you said? That would suggest that he *does* know about you. I mean the way he lined you all up in front of Phillip . . . God, it's sick!'

'Isn't it? But I've more or less decided that it must be him who tells me what he knows. I want to hear it from his own lips, that way I might stand a chance of getting to know what's behind it. If I tell him Phillip's my father, then for some reason I feel as though he'll have me at a disadvantage. And if he doesn't know, and finds out from me, I sure as hell don't want him to be the one to tell Annalise.'

Corrie could hear the smile in Paula's voice as she said, 'Do I take it from this that you're no longer lusting after him yourself?'

'Do me a favour!' Corrie cried. 'The man's obviously some kind of pervert.' She shuddered. 'If you'd seen him with Octavia last night. I have to tell you Paula, I've seen and heard some pretty sickening things these past two weeks, but she, more than anyone or anything else, has left the worst taste in my mouth. There's something about her that makes the most sordid whore you can imagine seem pure by comparison.'

To Corrie's surprise Paula was silent. 'What's the matter?' she asked. 'What are you thinking?'

'I'm thinking about Ted Braithwaite,' Paula answered steadily. 'Has it occurred to you that he must have known who Annalise was when he put you in touch with her?'

'Yes,' Corrie answered, 'I've thought about that. But I'm pretty sure his motives were genuine.'

'Are you going to talk to him about it?'

'I don't think so. Not yet, anyway.'

'And what about Annalise? Are you going to tell her who you are?'

'No. That's for Phillip to do. Which brings me on to the telephone call I received just before I rang you.'

'Holy shit! What *is* going on?' Paula cried, when Corrie told her. 'It all sounds like one hell of a mess, Corrie, and I have to tell you that it frightens me a bit. At least, Luke does. I'm convinced he knows.'

'You could be right. But as I said, I'm not going to be the one to confirm it.'

'Doesn't it make you want to get out of there?' Paula said hopefully.

'You're dead right it does,' Corrie answered. 'And I would, believe me, if it weren't for Annalise. I'm more afraid for her than I am for anyone else.' Again she shuddered. 'I just don't understand how her own mother could have behaved the way she did right in front of her. And Phillip's not going to do anything about it, that much is obvious. She doesn't have anyone else, except me, and if I walked out now I'd never stop worrying about her.'

'Well, I can understand that. But for my part, I'm worried about you. Why should Octavia have wanted you to know that she knew about you and Luke?'

'To be truthful I don't think it's any more than that she got a kick out of it. She wanted me to know that she has more power over him than either me or Annalise. Well, she's welcome to it, if that's the case. But I don't think she has. I think Luke is calling all the shots, and she's just so wrapped up in herself, and her nauseating fantasies, she can't even see what he is doing to her husband.'

'There goes that word again,' Paula said.

'What, fantasy?' Corrie sighed. 'It's one that's starting to make me feel sick just to hear it. What ever happened to good old romantic dreams? Of meeting Mr Right and going off into the sunset together? These days my definition of fantasy is something that depraves the mind, makes you behave . . . Well, like Octavia. Anyway, I don't think she's the problem, I think Luke is, and I'm fascinated to know what he's going to say about last night.'

But when Corrie finally arrived at the office Luke didn't even mention it. Corrie played along with his silence, keeping to her decision to say nothing until he did. But maybe her father would throw some light onto things when she saw him the following night. But any hope she had of that was dashed the next morning, when Phillip's secretary called to tell Corrie that he couldn't make it.

Cristos Bennati, his hands stuffed into the pockets of his jeans and his thin, pale cotton shirt billowing in the warm California breeze, was strolling around his pool terrace listening to the lead actors discussing their roles.

As he paced he said very little himself, wanting, for the moment, only to glean how they saw their parts in this arcane story of *Past Lives Present*. It was going to be one difficult movie to shoot, with so many changes of period, special effects and stunts, not to mention the size of the cast, but what concerned him most was that the lead artists should have a clear and human concept of each character they were to play. That wasn't going to be easy for Paige

Spencer, who had never taken on a part so complex, nor so demanding before, but Cristos was certain that with the right help she would deliver. David Easton, on the other hand, who was unquestionably where the money was, Cristos knew he could rely on totally. Easton had a whole string of successes behind him, was as versatile an actor as Cristos had ever come across, and was one of the hardest workers, too.

He was watching Easton now, using a hand to shield his eyes from the dazzling sun as Easton patiently went over what he saw as Paige's character in her eighteenth century incarnation. Paige and the others were listening as intently as Cristos to Easton's views, and though they were different from Cristos's own, Cristos was more than ready to accept that Easton might have come up with an angle he'd not seen himself.

A few minutes later Cristos was grinning. Sure enough, Easton had yet again pulled a rabbit from the hat. Easton was looking at him, grinning too and knowing that he had just impressed the hell out of his director.

'You look like you're gonna piss your pants with excitement, Bennati,' Easton remarked, leaning back on his lounger and picking up the mineral water beside him.

'If I didn't think you'd do something to upstage me, I would,' Cristos laughed. 'Where the hell d'you get that idea from?'

Easton shrugged, the shrug that had helped make him famous the world over. 'Just came to me in the night, you know how it is. So what do you say, Paige, honey? Wanna try it my way?'

Paige glanced at Cristos, who nodded his encouragement, then he crouched down on one of the steps to watch them run through the lines. There were other actors in the scene, and one by one Cristos nodded to them to come in too.

When it was over Cristos roared with laughter and

applauded. 'Paige,' he declared, 'you could out-English Queen Elizabeth herself. The accent is terrific, babe, just terrific.'

Paige was beaming. Cristos and Easton exchanged glances, and Easton gave an almost imperceptible nod of his head. At the outset Easton hadn't been exactly over-whelmed by Cristos's choice of leading lady, now, not for the first time, he was letting Cristos know that he had changed his mind.

Cristos was pleased with his choice too. He liked Paige. She was easy to get along with, gratifyingly intelligent for a woman who coyly professed not to be, and, every bit as important as far as Cristos was concerned, never made the slightest attempt to seduce him – though both Cristos and Easton knew she was dying to. She'd have been wasting her time with Easton, for he was so happily married it was disgusting, but Paige had already made it more than plain that she wasn't attracted to short men. Easton had yelled with laughter at that, a response that Cristos was more than a tad relieved at, since it wasn't the most diplomatic thing Paige had ever said, and the whole world knew how sensitive Easton was concerning his lack of height.

'OK,' Cristos said, rubbing his hands together, as they finished, 'I reckon we've about cracked it for today guys. David, Paige, d'you get the books on English social history Jeannie sent? Good, then let's meet again Friday and talk about it some.'

'I think make-up are dragging this l'il ol' girl off to the wig-makers,' Easton said, mimicking Paige's drawl and mincing a path towards Cristos. 'Kissy, kissy,' he said, pouting his lips at Cristos.

'Get out of here,' Cristos laughed.

He saw how nervous Paige's laugh was and sensing that she was afraid they were making fun of her, he winked.

'What about you, honey?' he asked. 'You free on Friday?'

She pulled a face. 'Sorry, costume fittings.'

'OK, that's it then. All of you be ready to roll a fortnight Monday, you'll have your schedules by then, but if you wanna discuss anything beforehand someone in the production office will know where to get hold of me.'

'Got any idea yet when the shooting'll start in Britain?' Easton asked. 'The lady wife wants to bring the kids along too.'

'Sure. We'll be there mid-November through December. Home for Christmas – if we keep to schedule. D'you find yourself a new assistant yet, or d'you want Jeannie to check out renting a house for you?'

'Got myself someone,' Easton answered. 'She's already on the pay roll.'

'Good. What about you, Paige? Your assistant working out?'

'Just fine,' she answered. 'But maybe we could have a talk about make-up.'

'Sure.'

Cristos walked with the others to their cars, accepted Easton's invitation to dinner at his place that night, then stood in front of the house waiting until they had driven down through the gardens and out the gates. Easton was on his Harley Davidson, and hearing him roar off down Sunset Cristos smiled to himself. Easton was like a big kid with that bike, though Cristos might wish, just as Jane, Easton's wife, did, that Easton didn't ride it quite so fast. And Cristos wasn't just thinking about the movie. He liked Easton and loved Easton's kids, so he sure as hell wouldn't want to see anything happen to the man.

Cristos was still thinking about Easton as he wandered back round to the pool. Easton hadn't been the most obvious choice for this movie, but Cristos trusted his talent like few others in this town. He was a volatile man, for sure, though Easton preferred to think of himself as a perfectionist. Cristos couldn't argue with that, but he didn't relish the thought of too many explosions on the set, when the need to keep to schedule was more pressing on this movie than on any other he'd made. He never failed to calm Easton down, and to be fair Easton wasn't an actor to throw a scene unless he felt justified. But boy, when he threw one, he sure as hell threw one, and anyone in a twenty yard radius better run for cover. Cristos grinned. How many times had he heard the same thing said of himself? Paige, he knew, was already quaking in her boots at the prospect of becoming a target, either of himself or of Easton, which was probably why she had created a scene with the make-up guy earlier in the week. Nothing more than nerves, and now Cristos was going to smooth her ruffled feathers, just as he had Aidan's when Aidan had reported the incident to him. Cristos felt it important he let Paige know that Aidan Starr was, in his opinion, the best prosthetics guy in Hollywood. Sure, she would have her own personal make-up artist, but Aidan was the guy whose job it was to rebuild her face, her hands, and even, for one scene, her breasts. That was what had caused the problem. It was Paige's only topless scene in the movie, and she didn't want the public thinking she had wizened breasts. Well, there was one easy way of getting over that, which was to make her topless in another scene, when she was playing a young woman. It wasn't vital to the story that she did that, but Cristos guessed it would make her happy.

It did, and it was all Cristos could do to stop himself laughing when she thanked him so gushingly. There would be more fireworks to come in the make-up department, he was sure of that, but they'd get through it. Paige was a pussycat at heart, she'd just felt it necessary to show a few claws to begin; she'd soon have them eating out of her hand. What Cristos had to be careful of though, was that he didn't succumb to Paige himself. He sure was tempted, he couldn't deny that, especially when she turned on that sultry look of hers and tousled that mane of red hair about her face. The first time she'd done it for the camera, during her test, he'd damned near found himself with an erection. Since then he'd kept himself in better check, but she was still getting to him. If he gave in he knew he'd never hear the end of it from Easton, which was as good a deterrent as any Cristos could think of.

When Paige had gone, Cristos wandered up over the terrace, through the wide white arches of the villa and into the kitchen, to find Jeannie.

'What's cooking?' he said, slapping her bottom as he passed.

'Paige Spencer, that's who's a-cooking,' Jeannie grinned. 'Boy, has that lady got the hots for you.'

'How about telling me something I don't already know?' Cristos said. 'Like, how the location boys are getting on over there in Britain.'

Chuckling quietly Jeannie picked up her notebook from beside the salad washer, saying, 'They reckon they'll be ready by the time you arrive, but they need to know if the script revisions are going to affect anything. I told them I didn't reckon so – it's all dialogue stuff, isn't it?'

Cristos nodded.

'OK, I'll get back to them.' She looked down at her pad and began ticking off her list of messages. 'Casting have got a whole lot of talent lined up for you over there too. Freda, the line producer, is booking the British crew now, but she needs a list of who you want to take out from the States.'

'We'll get to work on that tomorrow, down at the lot with Freddy Burnside,' Cristos answered. 'What else?'

'Uh-uh,' Jeannie said, shaking her head. 'Our darlin' unit manager has just been diagnosed HIV.'

'And that prevents him from working?'

''Fraid so. The insurance guys won't buy it. I got onto Stan Rowlinson this afternoon, he's taking over tomorrow.'

Seeing little point in expressing his personal feelings

about the insurance jerks, Cristos picked up an apple and biting into it, said, 'Go on.'

'Still with the insurance boys, they wanna discuss stunts – *again*! And Con Rosenburg wants a meet about the special effects for the dancing scenes. He's got some problem with it, he says, and needs Richard to be there too, to discuss lights. And the costume designer. I've arranged it for Friday morning, unless you tell me otherwise. Oh yeah, and don't forget you've got a meeting at the Black Tower tomorrow with god.'

Cristos laughed. This was Jeannie's way of referring to Bud Winters, the exec. producer, who, like all the other men of power at Universal, had their offices in the giant tower just off Lankershim Boulevard. 'OK, is that it?' he said, already heading out towards the annexe where the two screenwriters had been at work all day.

'Just about,' Jeannie answered. 'Except Luke Fitzpatrick called to say he'd heard you were flying in to London next week and did you want to get together?'

'Don't bother to call him back,' Cristos said, 'And if he calls again, tell him I died.'

He could feel Jeannie's frown as he swung himself over the wall into the garden, but didn't look back. If she knew what had been behind Fitzpatrick's last visit she'd soon quit hassling him over the way he had treated the bastard. Perhaps he should tell her, after all, he had very few secrets from Jeannie and her husband, Richard. And he had nothing to hide. It was just that he didn't much like discussing Angelique Warne. The whole thing was still, after all these months, too painful.

Cristos had loved Angelique more than any other woman he'd known. And she had loved him – or so he'd thought. He wasn't so sure now. But at the beginning it had been good . . . No, for the whole two years it had been good. It had only turned bad at the end, and then so quickly that

Cristos could scarcely understand, even now, what had happened.

He'd known Angelique took drugs, hell, they both did from time to time. Nothing heavy, just something to help relax them when they felt they needed it. As far as he knew she only ever took them when she was with him, but he'd learned, the night she died, that that wasn't the case. It was also the night he'd found out about the other man.

He could only thank God now, that Hank Robarts, the Los Angeles Police Department's Chief of Detectives, was with him when Angelique had called from a hotel in Beverly Hills. Hank had been at the villa, advising him on the correct procedure for certain scenes in the movie, and had offered to drive him to the hotel. Once there, Hank had sheepishly asked if he could have an introduction to Angelique, so Cristos had taken him up to the room.

What had happened then was still pretty much a blur in Cristos's mind, though he guessed he'd never forget the things she'd said in the minutes before she'd thrown herself to her death. It had all been because of an interview the *Los Angeles Times* had run that day, in which Cristos had confirmed that Angelique was not to star in his new movie, and that no, they did not have any plans to marry either. It was true, they hadn't, though Cristos had known for months that he was the only reluctant party. Had it been up to Angelique they'd have been married long before, but Cristos just didn't want to be married. He didn't want to be another statistic on the Hollywood divorce annals, and that was the only way marriages headed in this town. They were happy as they were, he'd repeatedly told her, and saw no reason to change things. He knew now that the drugs had been responsible for inciting her paranoia, but that she should have taken matters to such an extreme . . . That she could have planned to hurt him as much as she had . . .

She had started by accusing him of publicly humiliating her in using the *LA Times* to throw her over. Cristos, stunned by her misconstruction of what he'd said, had responded by losing his temper too. As they fought Cristos totally forgot about Hank Robarts, who, he later discovered, only stayed because unlike Cristos, he had noticed the drug induced glaze in Angelique's eyes the minute they'd walked in the door. Like any good cop, he could sense when things were going to turn real nasty. And they had, pretty quick.

It was only thanks to Hank that none of it had come out after. That the public would never know that Angelique Warne had been pregnant when she died. Cristos himself would never know now whose the baby was, since during their showdown she had told him about the senator. The man she had been sleeping with to make Cristos jealous. The pitiful part of it was that until that moment Cristos had never even suspected there was another man. But there was, the senator himself confirmed it later, in the privacy of Hank Robarts' office.

Angelique hadn't known who the father was either. She told Cristos that. 'It could be any one of you,' she'd spat, 'and what the hell do I care anyway. But the whole world is gonna think it's yours Cristos. Everyone's gonna know what you've done to me, you bastard.' Her move to the window had been so fast that neither Cristos nor Robarts had chance even to grab her clothing before she threw herself from the balcony into the gardens fourteen floors below.

It was Robarts who had found the suicide note beside the hotel bed. In it she had announced to the world that the baby was Cristos's. That he had refused to marry her, even though she was carrying his child, and because of it, she was going to kill herself.

The rumour and speculation that followed her death was intolerable. The press just wouldn't let up. A bellhop had confirmed seeing Cristos going into Angelique's room before she'd died, but the fact that Hank Robarts was there too was never divulged. It was all part of the convoluted cover-up to save the senator's good name. But the police had made it clear in a statement they issued to the press that as far as they were concerned Cristos Bennati had no charge to answer.

Maybe not, at least not so far as the suicide was concerned, but for Cristos the guilt and grief he felt inside was so torturous that at times it was as though it might strangle him. He missed her real bad, not only because he had loved her, but because he had got so used to sharing his life with her. But what hurt more than anything else was the way she had turned on him at the end. Why in God's name should she have done that?

He guessed he would never know the answer to that, any more than he would ever be able to find out just how Luke Fitzpatrick had managed to learn so much about the case. But Fitzpatrick hadn't known everything, he'd been missing one vital piece of information – that Hank Robarts had been in the hotel room that night too.

Just what Fitzpatrick had been planning to do with the information he'd gathered was a mystery Cristos had no interest in solving. He guessed it had something to do with blackmail, though if he really thought about it he had to admit that there was something about Fitzpatrick's last visit that had smacked of something more than that. He had started by letting Cristos know that he knew Cristos had been in the room with Angelique when she died. Well that was common knowledge, not that Cristos had even bothered to point that out. But then Fitzpatrick had gotten onto the subject of children, using sly remarks and innuendo, but all the same letting Cristos know that he had somehow found out about the baby. That was when Cristos had punched him so hard he'd gone into the pool. Cristos had waited then for the blackmail threat, but it hadn't come. If anything Fitzpatrick had appeared contrite, but Cristos wasn't fooled. It was as though Fitzpatrick was using his knowledge to show Cristos which of them held the power. But the power for what?

Cristos didn't even want to know. There had always been something unhealthy about Fitzpatrick, and theirs was an association Cristos had tried to break off many times over the years. Fitzpatrick had never let go, kept turning up like the proverbial bad penny. Well this was the last. Fitzpatrick could find some other poor bastard to manipulate, extort, destroy or whatever sick game he was about these days, because if he were ever to come in swinging distance of Cristos again, then after the stunt he'd tried to pull over Angelique, Cristos might just murder the sonofabitch.

– 12 –

Phillip Denby was in his office. Luke was facing him across the mahogany desk, sipping the coffee Pam had just brought in. The sudden intensity of late summer meant that both men were in shirt sleeves, though Phillip's were long, as befitted a man in his position. The sash window behind him had been raised, though no idle breeze found its way into the room, just the roar of City traffic four floors below.

Neither man had spoken yet, but already there was an unmistakable tension beginning to build. Luke seemed at ease with it. Phillip, however, despite his efforts to appear composed, was sweating profusely.

He waited until Luke had replaced his china cup in the saucer, then with his eyes still focused on the cup, said, 'I've had Jack Watkins, the Labour MP, in here.'

'Oh?' Luke said with mild surprise.

Phillip ran a finger around his collar. 'He says you're . . .

That you're . . . Well, he wants us to take the prostitute's allegations concerning him out of the programme.'

Luke nodded thoughtfully. 'I see. Well, you can put his mind at rest and tell him it's as good as done.'

Phillip's eyes shifted back to the coffee tray. He knew only too well why Watkins' request had been granted so readily – Luke had only the day before received twenty thousand pounds for his co-operation. Twenty thousand pounds that Phillip himself had been forced to give the MP. If he hadn't then, with nothing else to lose, Watkins had threatened to report the extortion to the police, and Phillip was in no position to let that happen. Naturally Luke had known that, just as he had known that in the end it would be Phillip who would pay the money. But that wasn't the real issue here, and both men knew it.

'Incidentally,' Luke said chattily, 'we're transmitting the programme tomorrow night.'

Phillip's face was suddenly so taut and pale that it seemed he might be suffocating.

Luke shrugged. 'Just thought you'd like to know,' he said. 'Annalise and Corrie have done a great job on it. Corrie in particular.'

Phillip waited for Luke to tell him that he knew who Corrie was, but Luke didn't. 'Of course,' he went on, 'the main emphasis of the programme is on whether or not brothels should be legalized, but there's a powerful piece on the whores who have been murdered. The police are hoping that someone will come forward after the programme. What do you say? Do you think anyone will?'

He showed no surprise at all when Phillip slumped forward onto his desk and started to sob. 'For Christ's sake, Luke,' he choked, 'I didn't do it. I swear to God, I had nothing to do with it. I told you, I visited them. I had sex with them, but I didn't kill them. As God is my witness, I didn't kill them.'

Luke shook his head, as though confused, then helped

himself to more coffee. 'I don't recall ever saying that you did, Phillip,' he said. 'Now, try to pull yourself together, there's a good chap. After all, I'm sure you don't want Pam to know about this, now do you?'

'There's nothing *to* know,' Phillip cried, beating his hands against the desk.

Luke sighed. 'I'd like to believe you, Phillip,' he responded sadly, 'really I would. And I'm trying. But how on earth do you explain the fact that you were the last trick every one of them had before they died?'

'I don't know. I just don't know,' Phillip spluttered. 'But I didn't kill them. You've got to believe me, Luke, I didn't kill them.'

'Then who did?'

'*I don't know*! I wasn't with them when they died. I was with them before, I admit that. I paid them, I . . . I tied them up even, but I didn't . . . Oh God!' He clutched his hands to his head and started to shake it. 'I didn't mean them any harm,' he cried. 'I only wanted . . . I wanted . . .'

'Yes? What did you want?' Luke prompted, calmly.

'For mercy's sake, leave me alone,' Phillip begged.

'What you wanted,' Luke continued, as though Phillip hadn't spoken, 'was to punish Octavia, wasn't it? You want to make her suffer for the way she's emasculated you, but you don't have the balls to do it.' He grinned at the neatness of that. 'So instead, you take yourself off to a whore,' he concluded.

'No! No!' Phillip sobbed. 'It wasn't like that.'

'Then what was it like?'

'Why are you doing this to me?' Phillip cried. 'I've told you a thousand times, they were alive when I left them.'

'Then why don't you go to the police and tell them that? They're men of the world. I'm sure they'll understand why you spray your wife's favourite perfume over a hooker before you tie her up and screw her.'

Phillip's breath froze in his lungs, and as he looked back at Luke a blinding terror started to seep into his eyes.

Luke merely smiled and shrugged. 'The investigating officer is a friend of mine,' he explained. 'He told me, just the other day, that the forensic experts have now identified the perfume on each of the bodies. They're withholding the information from the public of course, they have to do that to sort out the headcases who keep confessing. Anyway, it would appear that it's the same brand of perfume as Octavia favours. Now isn't that a coincidence?'

Phillip was trembling so hard he could barely speak. 'No, no,' he mumbled. 'You're lying. You're making it up . . .' His eyes were darting about the room, as if seeking some means of escape. Finally they settled again on Luke and he flinched, as though Luke had struck him. 'All right,' he whispered, 'I did spray them with perfume, but I didn't kill them.'

'OK, if you say you didn't, then you didn't. I'm prepared to believe you. But have you considered that you might be suffering from some kind of black-out while you're chopping them up. That could serve you quite considerably in your defence,' he suggested helpfully. Then he shrugged again. 'Or it could be that you know only too well what you're doing, but just don't want to admit it. I can understand that. I mean, I've seen what happened to them, and if I were you I wouldn't want anyone to know what an animal I was either.'

Phillip regarded him with heavy, fearful eyes. 'What are you going to do?' he whispered eventually.

'Do?' Luke repeated, seeming surprised by the question. He cocked his head to one side and thought for a moment or two, then said, as though musing aloud, 'Just imagine what a sensation it would cause if it came out that the daughters of the very man who was with the prostitutes during their last hours had researched and produced the programme designed to help catch him. In fact, one could almost say that they would be guilty of screwing their own father.' He laughed at that, apparently liking the pun, but Phillip could only stare at him in mindless terror.

'Luke,' he said at last. 'I'll do anything. Anything you want, but for God's sake don't tell Annalise or Corrie what you know.'

'Ah, so we're admitting that Corrie's our daughter now, are we? Good. By the way, she didn't deserve the way you treated her when she came to see you. She told me all about it, you know. Of course she didn't know then that I knew you.'

'Just leave them alone, Luke, I'm begging you to leave them alone. Take Octavia, if that's what you want, but please, for pity's sake don't do anything to harm my daughters.'

'It's my guess that the fathers of those hookers probably felt much the same way about their daughters. That is,' he added, 'if any of them ever had a father. Still, let's address this little matter of Octavia, shall we, because that's where all this stems from, isn't it? I mean the fact that she whores around with your colleagues, yet can hardly stand you to touch her. She even screws them in your bed, doesn't she? I've often wondered why she felt the need to do that, but we both know what a bitch she is – it probably gives her an extra kick. Anyway, the point is, divorce is out of the question, if you even attempt it she's going to inform all those poor unsuspecting wives of where their husbands spend their free afternoons. That wouldn't leave you in any too healthy a position, now would it? But all the same, you want to be rid of her, and believe you me, Phillip, I can understand that. The problem is, you just can't bring yourself to do what it would take to get her out of your life for good. After all, the finger of suspicion would point straight at you if anything were to happen to her, wouldn't it? With a whore, a professional whore that is, you thought you'd get away with it. So you vent your frustration, your hatred I should call it, on an innocent woman.'

Phillip was crying again. The tears of desperation streamed unchecked down his face, and he was sobbing so hard he could hardly catch his breath. 'Luke, please, what more do you want from me? Already you're sleeping with my wife and both of my daughters, just tell me what more it'll take. I told you, I'll do anything.'

Luke pondered this for a moment, then suddenly his face lit up, as though he had only now come up with his price. 'I'll tell you what,' he said, 'you can quit hiring thugs to beat me up. That's what you can do.'

Phillip stared at him helplessly. He knew already that this wasn't enough, that the price was going to be far, far higher than that. 'I'll do it,' he mumbled.

Luke stood up. 'Good. Now, all that I have to decide is whether or not to do my duty as a law abiding citizen and inform the police of what I know. I might, but there again I might not. As a matter of fact I'm in a position to do you a great favour, but I haven't decided yet whether or not I will.' He walked to the door, pulled it open so that Pam could hear every word he was saying, then turned back to Phillip. 'So long, old friend,' he smiled cheerily, 'and try not to slash up any more hookers, won't you?'

Corrie was about to explode with fury. '*What*?' she screamed at the editor. 'He told you to do what?'

Keith, the editor, didn't much like being shouted at like this, so it was in a disgruntled voice that he repeated what Luke had told him on the telephone the night before. 'I have to take out all references to the MP Watkins.'

'But why?'

'Don't ask me! I just do as I'm told.'

'Well I take it you did point out that it's the most powerful stuff we have.'

'It's not my job,' Keith retorted.

'And what about the interview?'

'That has to go too, he said.'

'I don't believe it!' Corrie seethed. 'I just don't fucking believe it. He's destroying the programme and we transmit tonight! What the hell are we going to put in its place? We haven't got anything else like it! Does Annalise know about this?'

Keith shrugged. 'She was in here earlier, I told her.'

'Well what did she say?'

'That I should go ahead and cut it out.'

'Then why didn't she tell me?'

'I don't know,' Keith answered through gritted teeth. 'Now if you don't mind, I'd like to get on with it.'

'Corrie!'

She spun round to find Alan Fox standing at the door.

'I think you'd better come out here,' Fox said, 'there's something going on you should know about.'

'Damn right, there is!' Corrie snapped. 'Have you heard what Luke's done to our programme?'

'Whatever he's done isn't going to make a lot of difference now,' Fox replied. 'Come and see.'

Still fuming, Corrie followed him back into the office and over to the PA machines. Everyone was grouped round, but made way for Corrie when they saw her coming.

'Oh my God!' she muttered, as she read what was coming over the wire. She leaned in closer. 'Oh my God!' she said again. 'This is incredible!' She waited for the message to finish then ripped it off the machine, her heart beating such a wild rhythm she was panting for breath. 'Where's Annalise?' she said, her eyes still glued to the page in disbelief.

'Here I am!' Annalise cried, sailing in through the door.

Corrie passed her the PA message. 'They've caught the murderer,' she said. 'They have him in custody!'

'What!' Annalise gasped, her eyes racing over the page. 'Bloody hell! When did this come in?'

'Just,' Corrie answered.

'Well it changes everything – and we transmit tonight.'

'Precisely. So we'd better get our skates on.'

Both of them immediately moved to the phones. 'Who are you calling?' Annalise asked.

'Chelsea Police Station, see if Radcliffe will give us an interview.'

'Great. I'll get onto Felicity, tell her we need her.'

'Anything I can do?' another researcher asked.

'Yeah,' Corrie answered. 'Get onto Scotland Yard press office, see what other information they're giving out. Try, if you can, to get the name and address of the man they've arrested.'

'You got it,' the researcher answered.

'Awaiting instructions,' Perkin called out.

'Stand by to rewrite the entire script,' Annalise yelled.

'What's going on?' Bob Churchill asked, walking into the office at that moment.

Quickly Alan Fox filled him in.

'All right, get to it,' Bob said to the production manager. 'Line them up a crew, a car, a telephone. Any luck with Chelsea Police yet, Corrie?' he added when she put the phone down.

'Yeah, eleven o'clock, Radcliffe will give us first crack. They're doing a press conference at midday though, so it'll still be on the news before we hit the air.'

'Doesn't matter. What do we know about this guy?'

'Nothing yet. We're working on it.' She turned to the other researcher.

'All lines are busy right now,' Jennifer told her. 'I'll keep trying.'

'How are you doing with Felicity?' she asked Annalise.

'She's not there, I left a message on her answerphone.'

'Shit!' Corrie said, slapping her forehead. 'She's got an audition today. We'll never get hold of her. Anyway, let's get onto Carol, we want the prostitutes' reaction to this. Shit! What are we going to do about Felicity?'

'Alan, you'll have to do the interview,' Bob said.

'Can't,' Alan answered. 'I'm already booked out today with another crew.'

'This is an emergency.'

'Hands off!' Cindy, Alan's producer, yelled. 'I've moved heaven and earth getting this interview lined up with the Archbishop of Canterbury. It's today or not at all.'

'All right,' Bob winced. 'Where are the other reporters?'

'All out,' the production manager answered.

Bob turned back to Corrie. 'Get to work on the questions,' he barked, as Corrie picked up an incoming call, 'bring them to me when they're ready.'

'Hello?' Corrie said into the receiver, then put her hand over it as Annalise said.

'You'll have to conduct the interview yourself, Corrie.'

'Don't be ridiculous! I've never been in front of a camera in my life.'

'There isn't anyone else. You'll have to.' Annalise grinned. 'Your chance for stardom.'

'I don't want stardom,' Corrie snapped, and took her hand away from the mouthpiece.

'Corrie? Corrie, it's Luke. I just heard the news. What have you got lined up?'

'Chelsea Police. We're working on the prostitutes, and trying to find out who the guy is. Scotland Yard . . .'

'I can tell you who he is,' Luke interrupted. 'His name's Bobby McIver. Have you got a pen, I'll give you his address.'

'Fire away,' Corrie said.

She jotted down the address, signalling at the same time for the production manager to come and read over her shoulder. 'Hang on a second, Luke,' she said. Then to the production manager 'Can we get a crew over there to do some exterior shots of where he lives?'

'Leave it with me.'

'Luke, are you there?'

'Yeah. I'm on my way in.'

Corrie looked at her watch, and not giving herself a second to think of the impropriety of ordering Luke about, she said, 'No, don't do that. Meet us at Chelsea Police Station. We need someone to do the interview. Felicity's not available.'

'You've got it,' Luke said, and rang off.

Luke was in his car, only a few minutes' ride from Chelsea Police Station. He was chuckling quietly to himself as he listened to LBC chuntering out the few details they had on the arrest. Picking up his car phone he dialled a number, and pulled over to the side of the road.

'Phillip?' he said, as Phillip's voice came over the line. 'Have you heard the news?'

'No,' Phillip answered shortly.

Luke laughed. 'Well you will, soon enough,' he said, and rang off.

When Corrie and Annalise arrived at Chelsea Police Station Corrie immediately started briefing Luke on the questions needing to be asked. Meanwhile, Annalise was organizing the crew as they set up their equipment in DI Radcliffe's office.

'So remember,' Corrie said to Luke when Radcliffe went off to comb his hair before appearing on camera, 'we don't need any preliminaries, you can just start right in on the questions. Now, there's something I want to ask you.'

'About Watkins?' Luke suggested.

'Yes. About Watkins. Why do we have to take out . . .'

'Later,' Luke said, holding up his hand. 'I'll explain everything later. Now, it looks to me that we're about ready to roll.'

They were, so Corrie stood to one side as Radcliffe reappeared from the men's room and he and Luke sat either side of Radcliffe's desk, while the cameraman adjusted the lights.

'OK, Steve?' Annalise said.

The cameraman nodded.

'Then turn over.'

'Speed,' the cameraman said a few seconds later.

Annalise nodded to Luke, and clearing his throat Luke turned to Radcliffe.

The interview lasted no more than ten minutes, during which Radcliffe confirmed that a man by the name of Bobby McIver had been arrested in the early hours of the morning. At this stage the police weren't prepared to divulge much about McIver's background – probably, Corrie thought, because they didn't know anything. However, Radcliffe and his team were in no doubt that they had the right man.

'He has made a full confession,' Radcliffe said, 'giving us certain details unknown to the public at this stage. What's more a team of detectives are even now at his home, where they have found considerable evidence to back up McIver's claims.'

'And what led you to suspect McIver in the first place?' Luke asked.

'A tip-off from a neighbour,' Radcliffe answered. 'We would like that neighbour to come forward again, if they would, in complete confidence, naturally.'

'And what are your feelings now, Inspector Radcliffe, concerning the legalization of brothels?'

'They remain unchanged,' Radcliffe told him. 'The fact that we have caught one maniac does not mean that there won't be others. I believe we should have legalized brothels in this country.'

When he continued to elucidate his opinions Annalise looked at Corrie. Corrie nodded, and waiting until Radcliffe came to a natural end, Annalise said, 'OK, cut.'

'Thank you very much, Inspector,' Corrie said, moving into the light and handing both him and Luke handkerchiefs to wipe the sweat from their faces.

'He hasn't told us much,' Annalise whispered, when Luke and Radcliffe wandered outside into the corridor to give the crew some room to pack up.

'I know, but I think it's all we're going to get,' Corrie whispered back. 'They've only had him in custody a few hours remember.'

'If you don't need me for anything else I'm going to head off to the office,' Luke said, coming up behind them and draping an arm over each of their shoulders.

Annalise looked to Corrie for confirmation. 'Sure, that's fine,' Corrie answered. 'We'll just do a vox pop with the prostitutes over at Shepherd Market. Thanks for helping out, Luke.'

'The pleasure was all mine,' he grinned.

Corrie found Radcliffe a few minutes later, once again coming out of the men's room. She smiled as he came towards her and held out her hand. 'I was wondering,' she said, 'how a policeman feels on a day like today?'

Radcliffe chuckled. 'Exhausted, is your answer,' he said. 'Elated too, I suppose. And relieved. And several other things I'd better not tell you about.'

Corrie looked at him curiously, even a touch flirtatiously, but she could see he wasn't going to be drawn. 'Where's McIver now?' she asked.

To her surprise Radcliffe looked at her long and hard before answering. 'Safe,' he said at last.

'Safe?' Corrie echoed, her surprise showing. 'Safe from whom?'

'The press, of course.'

They both smiled, then Corrie, more or less repeating the question Luke had asked during the interview, said, 'So you don't know anything about his background yet?

Whether or not he has a mother, a wife, or any family at all come to that?'

Radcliffe shook his head.

'I suppose it's crazy to ask at this stage if you know *why* he did it?' Corrie ventured.

Radcliffe grimaced. 'Finding a motive can be a very long process, and even then we don't always succeed. In McIver's case it's going to be even more difficult.'

'Why do you say that?'

Again Radcliffe looked at her as though assessing her. 'McIver has the mental age of a ten year old,' he said carefully. 'The strength of an ox, of course, but the mind of a child.'

'Why didn't you say any of that in the interview?'

'Because we don't want to unleash a storm of criticism on the mentally incapable roaming our streets. Most of them are harmless, but . . . Government cut-backs, Miss Browne, I'm sure you understand what I'm saying.'

'You mean you've had instructions from the top to keep this quiet?' Corrie said, understanding perfectly but wanting it spelt out.

He looked at her. 'I'd prefer that you kept this to yourself for the time being. It'll come out eventually, but for now . . .'

'OK. If that's what you want. But tell me, are you prepared to say now what the evidence was that you were holding back?'

Radcliffe shook his head. 'Still too early for that. But I will tell you this much. There are two extremely peculiar things about this case, that only the murderer – and ourselves, of course – could know about. The first concerns a certain fragrance, as I told Mr Fitzpatrick myself, a week or so ago. You can put that into your programme, you probably already have.'

Corrie nodded. 'We don't know the brand name though.'

'No,' Radcliffe confirmed. 'But McIver does. The second

thing he's been doing is something which still has us all totally baffled. McIver's confessed to it, but refuses to give a reason why.' He looked up then as someone called out his name, and turning briefly back to Corrie he said, 'I'll be in touch, Miss Browne.'

When they left the police station Annalise and Corrie took the crew on to Shepherd Market to interview the prostitutes, and from there went on to McIver's flat in Camberwell to join up with the other crew. They shot what they could of the exterior through the crush of other photographers and press, then headed back to the office to begin a rushed re-edit of the programme.

It was a great relief to Corrie that for once Annalise seemed to be on the ball, since Corrie couldn't get the conversation with Radcliffe out of her mind. Why, she kept asking herself, had he told her things he'd refused to say on camera? And why, at the end, had he told her he'd be in touch? He'd made it sound as though he wanted her to know something else, but what? And this cover up about McIver's mental age. OK, if Radcliffe was being leaned on to keep it quiet, she could understand that, but why tell her? And why even trust her? After all, wasn't she one of the press Radcliffe had said he wanted to keep McIver 'safe' from?

In the end she decided to go and talk it over with Luke. She didn't feel she was breaking Radcliffe's confidence, since Radcliffe himself had told Luke about the fragrance, he'd even told Luke the brand name, though Luke had refused to tell either her or Annalise. But as she got up from the edit suite, leaving Annalise to it, one of the secretaries called out that there was a telephone call for her.

To Corrie's astonishment it was her father, asking if they could meet that night. As she was explaining that she wouldn't be able to make it until nine o'clock at the earliest she saw Luke walk out of the office.

'It's all right, I'll wait,' Phillip said. 'The Man in the Moon? Like before?'

'OK,' Corrie answered, distractedly. 'I'll see you there.'

By the time she rang off Luke had already gone down in the lift. Well he was sure to be back later, she'd try to speak to him then, if not it would just have to wait until tomorrow. In the meantime she had her very first transmission to sort out, so making a concerted effort to put Radcliffe's bewildering comments, and her father's cryptic meetings, out of her mind, she returned to the edit suite.

It was a frenzied afternoon, with new graphics being drawn up every few minutes, fresh material being inserted into the main body of the programme and a miraculous re-jig of the main interviews to make them more pertinent. At four o'clock there was a deafening cheer when one of the secretaries managed to get hold of Felicity, who took a fast car from St John's Wood to come and record a new voice over. By six thirty the dubbing was finished and they were ready to go into the studio for Luke to top and tail the programme. It only remained now for it to be sent down the line to the transmission centre. At seven forty-three they received the all clear from Euston and just as Corrie and Annalise were heaving a great sigh of relief, Luke came into the studio to congratulate them.

'I watched it going through from my office,' he told them, 'you've done a great job. And someone somewhere is smiling on you, that we should be transmitting the very day the murderer was arrested. Quite a coup! How about some champagne in my office to celebrate?'

Annalise and Corrie, both pale and harassed, looked at each other, then broke into a grin. 'And why not?' Annalise said. 'We'll drink to Corrie, because the whole thing was her idea in the first place. And if I were a truly generous person I'd have given up my producer's credit for her. But I didn't. Not because I'm not a truly generous person, you understand, but because I only just thought of it.'

Laughing, Corrie hugged her. 'I couldn't have done it without you,' she said.

'Which is why,' Luke added, 'I am taking you both – and Felicity too – out to dinner the minute the programme ends.'

'Ah, now that could be difficult,' Corrie said. 'Felicity has already left, off on some hot date somewhere, and I have a date too, I'm afraid.'

'Cancel it!' Annalise cried.

'I can't.'

'Then bring him along,' Luke said.

'That wouldn't work either, I'm afraid. No, you two go along and drink a few glasses for me.'

'But you'll have some before you go?' Luke insisted. 'In fact, you can't go until the programme's been transmitted.'

'Just lead me to it,' Corrie said, holding out her arms to both of them, and suddenly realizing she was already slightly drunk on adrenalin.

'Are you sure you won't come for dinner with us?' Luke said, a few minutes later, as he poured champagne into Corrie's glass. Annalise had slipped out to the ladies, so Corrie and Luke, for the moment, were in the office alone.

'Quite sure, thank you,' she said, looking up at him and smiling.

He smiled too, but to her surprise she saw that he looked genuinely hurt. She lifted a hand, intending to take his, but then stopped herself. It was too intimate a gesture should Annalise come back, and besides, Corrie didn't want him to think that he still meant anything to her.

She'd done a lot of thinking since the night she'd met her father at Luke's, and had now attributed her reaction to shock. Nonetheless, she still didn't quite trust Luke. Though suspecting him of all that she had, and deciding to guard Annalise against him, now seemed to Corrie an extreme over-reaction on her part. Besides which, when a woman was as obsessed with a man as Annalise was with

Luke there was little anyone could do. And Corrie had finally come to the conclusion that Luke probably didn't know that Phillip was her father, since if he did, he would have been sure to have said something by now. Or at least to have given himself away somehow. But his only reference to that evening had been to tell Corrie how upset he had been that Annalise had got so drunk in front of her parents.

'She thinks her mother and I are having an affair,' he'd gone on to say, 'and I guess I can hardly blame her for that. Of course, you don't know Octavia, but she's like that with just about every man she meets. Especially any man who shows an interest in Annalise.'

There had been plenty Corrie had wanted to say to that, but since they were standing in the corridor at TW at the time, she'd judged it wiser to remain silent.

As for their own relationship, such that it was, Corrie could only hope that it was over. Luke had neither called her, nor invited her out since the night of the cocktail party, though Corrie had caught him watching her from time to time, with a strange expression in his eyes.

He was looking at her that way now, and again, like all the other times, Corrie felt that he was trying in some way to reach out to her. She wasn't proud of herself for turning away, she hated to do that to anyone, but it was her own sense of self-preservation that made her do it. She truly didn't want to get caught up in any part of his life.

'What is it about you that makes me feel I can trust you, Corrie?' Luke said quietly.

'Trust me with what?' she asked.

He shook his head. 'I don't know. It's just a feeling I get when I look at you. You don't trust me though, do you?'

'No,' she confessed. 'You've never really given me any reason to.'

'I gave you your promotion.'

'Yes.'

'But that's not what we're talking about, is it?'

'No. Or perhaps, yes. Sometimes, Luke, you give me the impression that you're playing games with us all. Will you explain now about Watkins?'

He smiled, then putting down his drink he walked around his desk and took a buff file from the drawer. 'It's quite simple really,' he said. 'I told Watkins that if he were prepared to pay me twenty thousand pounds then I would see to it that his name was removed from the programme. He paid.'

Corrie's eyes dilated. 'You mean . . . Are you saying that you blackmailed him?'

Luke nodded. 'Yes, I blackmailed him. But only after he had made me an offer himself.'

'But Luke, that's illegal.'

Luke laughed. 'My darling, innocent Corrie. Of course it's illegal. Now, aren't you going to ask me what I did with the money?'

Corrie watched him suspiciously as he started towards her. 'No,' she said, when he took two pieces of paper from the file and handed them to her. 'No, I don't think I want to know.'

'OK, then I'll read it to you myself.' He glanced up as Annalise walked in, and holding out a hand towards her he pulled her into the circle of his arm. 'I was just about to tell Corrie how we gave Carol a cheque for twenty thousand pounds to help with the prostitutes' cause,' he told her.

Annalise turned to Corrie, but Corrie was still looking at Luke, shaking her head in disbelief.

'This here,' Luke said, indicating the top page, 'is a letter to Watkins telling him precisely what I did with his money. And this one here, is a letter from Carol to the Editor of the *Sun* newspaper informing him of Watkins' most generous donation.'

Annalise laughed. 'Isn't he a genius, Corrie?' she said, gazing up at Luke.

Luke's eyes were still on Corrie.

'Yes,' Corrie mumbled, 'isn't he?' Then standing up she excused herself, saying she must powder her nose before the programme began.

It wasn't so much that she completely disagreed with the ethics behind what Luke had done, it was more that she couldn't bear the way he was looking at her, as though seeking her approval. She didn't want to feel responsible for his actions, and much less did she want to feel that he had tricked Watkins to please her. But that was the way he'd made her feel.

Making a supreme effort she tried to shrug it off, what Luke did was his business, she just wished he wouldn't make it hers by telling her about it. Maybe she'd discuss it with her father, after all he was the chairman of TW, and surely wouldn't approve of what Luke had done either. A quick fantasy flashed through her mind, of seeing Luke pushed out of TW and she and Annalise appointed joint-heads. What a miracle that would be, she and her half-sister heading up their own TV company under the guiding hand of their father. She almost laughed aloud then, as she thought about all those hours she'd spent in Amberside, dreaming of what her life could be like, but never had she imagined that she might one day succeed with a father and a sister. There was a long way to go though, before anything like that could happen, but tonight was going to be a first step in that direction. Blood ties, she now realized, really did mean something, for it didn't seem to matter about the way Phillip had treated her, she still wanted, more than anything else in the world, for him to accept her as his daughter – and Annalise's sister.

It was just after eight o'clock when Phillip Denby pushed his way from the bar of The Man in the Moon to a seat in the corner of the lounge. He set his glass of Guinness down on the round table, then took out a packet of cigarettes. It would be at least an hour before Corrie arrived, but he'd needed to get out of the house, not only because he couldn't bring himself to watch the programme, but to get away from Octavia. God, how he hated her. Every vein in her body ran with venom, and there were times when it seemed to seep through the very pores of her skin. She was so corrupt that he could feel soiled just to have her eyes look upon him. She had destroyed his life, totally, he couldn't even call himself a man anymore. Now, all he wanted was to lose himself, if only for a while, in the anonymity of a public house, where crowds of young people shouted and swilled their pints, flirted and popped their Ecstacy. He watched them spilling out onto the pavement of World's End, and felt an overwhelming sadness at how rotten the world had become. Children, getting drunk, taking drugs and living day after day with the ever-encroaching threat of AIDS.

He took a quick gulp of his Guinness then lit a cigarette. The panic was threatening to engulf him again, but he must force himself to stay calm. Corrie would be here soon, Corrie would make it all right. He wasn't quite sure when he had reached that conclusion, but it had happened some time over the past week, after he had seen her at Luke's. But even now he couldn't be sure if he was right, if he really had felt . . . Felt what? He didn't know. Was it sympathy he had sensed in her? Perhaps it was strength. Whatever it was, he knew, deep down in his heart, that she was the only one he could turn to. Not Pam, though God knew he'd wanted to, and he'd tried so many times, but in the end he just hadn't been able to bear the thought of her turning on him. Every woman he'd ever known had ended up despising him, and once she knew what he'd done Pam would prove no exception, no matter how much she claimed to love him. And who could blame her? But Corrie was different, she would help him, he was certain of it, she would help Annalise too. Corrie would find a way.

He drank some more Guinness then crushed out his half-smoked cigarette. His hands were shaking.

He pictured Corrie in his mind's eye and started to smile, then suddenly his face contorted with the agony he felt inside. Could he really do this to her? He was her father, he should be protecting her, not burdening her with the terrible tragedy of his life. And why should she want to help after the way he had treated her? He hadn't even had the guts to speak to her that night at Luke's. But if she knew the truth, if she knew what was really going on, surely she would understand.

Choking back a sob Phillip dug his fingers into the sockets of his eyes. For Christ's sake, he told himself bitterly, five prostitutes were dead and an innocent man had been arrested! How could she ever begin to understand that? How was he going to explain that he knew McIver was innocent without incriminating himself? Did he really want Corrie to know that he had been visiting whores, or what he had been doing to those whores? Did he want to see the suspicion, the accusation then, God forbid, the fear come into her eyes when he told her? And once he had told her, what then? The answer suddenly seemed so brutally clear that Phillip could hardly believe he was sitting there. But of course that was why he had let Corrie down before. He was afraid of what she would do once she knew. She would go to the police, she'd have to. It wouldn't matter that he was her father, she would do what was right. And then they would come for him.

It wasn't that he really minded for himself, he just wanted this torment to be over, it was the shame it would bring upon Annalise and Corrie that he couldn't accept. But maybe, just maybe, he could save Corrie. Yes, that's what he would do. He would save her from the shame. It was too late for Annalise, but not for Corrie. Tears welled in his eyes. It would probably be the only thing in his entire life he would ever do for Edwina's daughter, and it would be worse than tearing out his own heart, but he was going to do it. He had to, for Corrie's sake.

When at last Corrie arrived Phillip was still sitting in the same seat, with the same glass of Guinness in front of him. He saw several heads turn as she glanced about the bar, trying to find him, he even heard one man ask her if she'd like to join his party. He didn't hear Corrie's response, but whatever it was it made the man laugh. Phillip felt a quick swell of pride, but when Corrie spotted him, he looked away. He didn't want to watch her walk towards him, he didn't want to acknowledge how astonishingly lovely she had become during these few short months in London, and neither did he want to read whatever expression there was in her eyes.

'Hello,' Corrie said.

Phillip nodded, but did not look up.

'Can I get you a drink?' Corrie offered.

'No. I won't be staying, thank you,' Phillip said curtly.

He felt Corrie bristle. 'Then what can I do for you?' she said, sitting down.

With his eyes still averted Phillip consciously tightened his jaw, and said, 'You can swear to me that you'll never tell Annalise who you are. I don't want her to know about you, I don't want anyone to know about you, do you understand? And no matter what you do, or whatever you might claim in the future, I want you to know that I will always deny that you're my daughter. Have you got that straight? You are no relation to me, you never have been, nor ever will be. And keep away from Luke Fitzpatrick. He's got Annalise, he doesn't need you too, so keep away from him.'

Still he didn't look at her as he jerked himself to his feet. He could feel her pain, but forced himself to move away. His legs were shaking so badly it was all he could do to get himself out of the pub and into his car. He knew he had just cut off any hope he'd ever had of being able to confide in anyone, but it was for the best. This way she would never have to suffer the humiliation of pointing fingers as she walked down the street, 'there goes the daughter of that psycho. You know, the one who chopped up the whores.' But, dear God, Annalise would, and he could only pray that Corrie would be there for her. He should have seen to that, *dammit* he should have seen to it! Instead he had made a mess of it, just like he did everything else in his life. But it was too late now. He couldn't go back. His only comfort was how mindful Corrie had seemed of Annalise that night at Luke's. Corrie knew Annalise was her sister, Corrie wouldn't let her down, she just wouldn't.

Now all he had to do was force himself to drive to the police station and give himself up.

— 13 —

'Sitting here all alone?'

Corrie looked up from her desk and smiled as she saw Luke coming in through the office door. 'All alone,' she confirmed.

'Where is everyone?'

'Lunch or filming.'

He nodded and Corrie watched him as he walked across the office and wondered how he managed to look so cool when it was so unbearably hot outside. His blond hair had been bleached almost white by the sun, and he was wearing a pair of faded denims with the sleeves of his red and white striped shirt rolled back to reveal his tanned forearms and the gold Rolex he always wore. He looked so at ease with himself, and Corrie could only wish that she could be so comfortable with herself. But summer was not a season she enjoyed – at least not so far as clothes were concerned. She didn't like to reveal too much of her pale skin, but it was unavoidable when the temperature was soaring so high. Nevertheless, T-shirts were out of the question, her breasts were too large and she was horribly self-conscious about the way her nipples always showed through. Georgie had helped out again though, choosing soft flowing cottons and muslins with silk camisoles to go underneath, tailored short-sleeved dresses and vivid flowery shirts to wear with her jeans. Right now Corrie's newly trimmed hair, which seemed to her thicker and heavier than ever, was curling happily about her neck and shoulders, though it felt like it was clinging to her skull.

Luke came to perch on the edge of her desk, and Corrie instantly tried to hide the newspaper she'd been reading, but she wasn't quick enough.

'So Bennati's in town, is he?' Luke grinned, spinning the newspaper round to get a better look at the picture of Cristos arriving at Heathrow airport. 'I heard he was coming.' He took a few moments to read the caption beside the photograph, then dismissing it turned back to Corrie. His smile faded rapidly as he saw her red-rimmed eyes, but as she made to look away he caught her chin to turn her back. 'Are you all right?' he asked.

'Of course,' she answered. 'Just a bit of a cold.' He was the last person she was about to tell that she had been awake half the night crying because of her father.

'So how did your date go last night?' Luke ventured.

'Oh, OK, thanks. And you and Annalise? Where did you go in the end?'

'We joined up with some friends at the Chelsea Arts Club. You should have come, we had a great time.'

Corrie smiled, but said nothing.

'So,' he said, 'have you two decided on your next project yet?'

'Transsexuals,' Corrie answered. 'Annalise is at lunch

with three of them now.' Corrie hadn't gone because she just didn't feel up to it after her disturbed night.

Luke looked doubtful. 'I'm sure you have your reasons,' he said. 'Did you bring them up at the meeting this morning?'

'Yes. There's a report due out in the next ten days or so to show that the number of operations, world-wide, has increased in the last year by seven per cent.'

'And Bob bought the idea?'

'Yep.'

'Then fair enough. By the way, did you see the write-up in the *Guardian* this morning, for last night's programme?'

Corrie nodded. 'Great, wasn't it?'

'It sure was. Can't wait to see the ratings.' He paused, watching Corrie as she looked everywhere but at him. 'Hey, come on,' he said, in the end, 'something's upsetting you. Why not tell me about it?'

'No, really. I'm fine.' She looked up and smiled.

'That's better,' he said, smoothing his fingers over her cheek.

She felt so vulnerable in that moment that she very nearly started to cry again. Instead, she swallowed hard and said, 'Luke, I'd like to talk to you about Bobby McIver.'

'Bobby?' he said curiously. 'What about him?'

'Well it was something DI Radcliffe told me yesterday. He said that Bobby McIver had the mental age of ten. Did he tell you that too?'

Luke shook his head. 'No. But I didn't get much chance to speak to him off camera.'

'Don't you think it's odd?' Corrie remarked. 'I mean that a man with a child's mind should visit a prostitute?'

Luke shrugged. 'I don't know. I guess he has a man's body, therefore a man's sexual appetite?'

'Maybe, but that's not the only thing is it? For instance, how on earth did he get them all the way from Shepherd

Market to Camberwell? And then their bodies from Camberwell to Chelsea Embankment?'

Luke pursed his lips thoughtfully. 'Beats me,' he said. 'But no doubt Radcliffe and his team will come up with the answers eventually – if they haven't already.'

'But I can't help wondering why Radcliffe told *me* about McIver's mental state. I've looked in all the papers this morning and there's no mention of it in any of them.' She paused, then said. 'Luke, you may think this sounds crazy, but I got the feeling Radcliffe was trying to tell me something – I mean something else.'

'Like what?'

'That's just it, I don't know. But before I left he told me he'd be in touch. Now why should he have said that?'

Luke shook his head, bewildered. 'Where are they holding Bobby, do you know?'

'No. All Radcliffe said was that he was safe.'

'Safe?'

'That's what I thought. He said from the press.'

'But anyone in custody is safe from the press.'

'I know. Do you think I should get in touch with Radcliffe again?'

Luke took some time to think that over. 'Give it a few days,' he said eventually. 'See if Radcliffe does contact you. If not, we'll talk again.'

'OK.'

Luke smiled affectionately, then standing up he took Corrie's hand and pulled her to her feet too. For some time he simply looked at her, searching her face with his eyes, apparently amused by the way she appeared so self-conscious. Then very softly he said, 'I'd like to kiss you, if I may?'

'Oh no, no, not here,' Corrie said, with a rush of alarm.

He was still gazing at her, waiting for her to meet his eyes, and when finally she did Corrie was surprised to see the depth of feeling in them. 'OK,' he said. 'But can I just hold you for a moment?'

Not knowing how she could object Corrie allowed him to pull her into his arms, all the time praying that no one would walk through the door. He held her for a long time, pressing the full length of his body against her, but to Corrie's relief there appeared to be nothing sexual in what he was doing. If anything, she was beginning to sense that terrible sadness in him again. She held him close and, as the seconds ticked by, started to feel her own tension ebb from her body; it felt so good to be held this way. He had such strong arms, and despite all her misgivings about him, in those few moments all she wanted was that he should just go on holding her.

'Sometimes,' Luke whispered, 'I think that you're the only good thing that's ever happened to me.'

Corrie remained silent, but found herself returning the pressure when he squeezed her even tighter.

'Oh God,' he sighed, when finally he let her go, 'I think I'm beginning to understand what it feels like to be Annalise.'

Corrie frowned, which made him smile.

'I mean to feel a certain way about a person and them not to feel the same way about you,' he explained.

Corrie lowered her eyes and started to turn back to her desk.

'It's OK,' Luke said, running his fingers through her hair, 'I'm not going to make you talk about it if you don't want to.'

'It's not that I don't want to talk about it,' Corrie said, 'it's just that I don't think you mean what you say.'

'I know you don't. But I do. Believe me, I do. But I'm not going to force you, Corrie.' He laughed quietly. 'I couldn't, even if I wanted to. Your feelings are your own, it's up to me to win them – if I can. Though I guess I haven't made too good a job of it so far, have I?'

'Let's discuss this another time, shall we?' Corrie said. 'Anyone could walk in, and I don't think either of us want . . .' She trailed off, not knowing quite how to finish the sentence.

'When can I see you?' he said.

'I don't know. I'm pretty booked up for the rest of this week.'

'And I'm away at the weekend.'

Unable to stop herself Corrie turned back to look at him. It was on the tip of her tongue to ask about Siobhan, something she'd been longing to do ever since Annalise had discovered her existence. But Corrie never had asked, nor would she now, for if she even so much as mentioned the name it would mean betraying Annalise. 'Where are you going?' she asked instead.

'To stay with a friend.'

'Oh.'

'It's no one you need worry yourself about,' he laughed. 'You've got enough on your plate fretting over Bobby McIver.'

He went off to his office then, and Corrie, puzzled by his last remark sat down in her chair, absently fanning herself with a newspaper.

She couldn't explain it, but all of a sudden she was thinking that Luke knew more about Bobby McIver than he was letting on. Perhaps it was the way he had referred to him twice as Bobby. Or was it something about the way he had brought him so abruptly back into the conversation? But no, it was more than that, it was something else he had said, something maybe not today, maybe yesterday, but what was it? She just couldn't think, then realizing that she was once again guilty of mistrusting him when he had just shown her nothing more than some badly needed affection, she turned back to her perusal of the papers.

Nevertheless, she couldn't get her suspicions out of her mind. She toyed with the idea of talking to Felicity about it when the two of them met up the following night to celebrate Felicity's success – she would soon be off to Hollywood to take the lead in a major film – but then Corrie remembered that it would entail breaking Radcliffe's confidence about McIver's mental age: and since that concerned the murdered prostitutes Felicity would be unlikely to keep it to herself. She did tell Felicity about the way Luke had held her in the office, however, and how disturbed she had been by her own reaction.

'I just don't understand myself sometimes,' she said, as they handed their menus back to the waiter. 'I mean, I don't trust him, how can I when he behaves the way he does? But, well this is going to sound really conceited I know, but sometimes I get the impression that he really does care for me. And I can't even say that I don't care for him, because, despite everything, he can still stir . . . well, you know, certain feelings in me.'

Felicity shrugged. 'He's an attractive man. Add to that a bit of mystery, a touch of unpredictability and you come up with a devastating combination. And let's not forget, he is single, so what greater challenge than to be the woman who finally hooks Luke Fitzpatrick?'

'But I don't see him as a challenge, not in the sense you mean it, anyway. To tell you the truth, and you're not to laugh at this, Felicity, but there have been times when I've actually felt afraid of him. I know it sounds a bit dramatic, but it's true. The feeling goes, pretty quickly, I have to say that, and I feel pretty stupid for it after, but nevertheless there's something about him that on the odd occasion very definitely unsettles me. I just wish I could put my finger on what it was.'

'Does it matter, if you don't want to get into a relationship with him?' Felicity said, tasting the wine then nodding for the waiter to carry on.

'No, I suppose not. Mind you, I'm finding that pretty difficult to fend off. But it does matter about Annalise. You remember I told you about Siobhan? Thank you,' she added to the waiter.

Felicity nodded, 'The woman he was sending the birthday card to?'

'That's her. Though more importantly it's the name Annalise claims he sometimes calls her by. Well, he's going away this weekend, and I reckon it's to see her.'

'So?'

'So, Annalise says that it's always after he's seen this Siobhan that he beats her up.'

'And you have some grand plan to stop this happening?'

'No, not really. You know what Annalise is like, she won't hear a bad thing said about him – unless she's saying it herself. I just think . . .'

'I just think we should change the subject,' Felicity interrupted. 'You're like a mother hen where that girl's concerned. Let her look after herself, and you, madam, start thinking about *your*self for a change. Like what Luke Fitzpatrick can do for you.'

'And what can he do for me?' Corrie grinned.

'Cristos Bennati.'

Immediately Corrie's heart turned over. 'What about Cristos Bennati?' she said.

'Oh come off it, he's in town and you know it.'

'So?'

'So, Luke knows him, doesn't he? And he's your everlasting heart-throb, or so you once confessed to me. So, get Luke to introduce you.'

'I can't do that,' Corrie said, not wanting to admit that this had crossed her mind more than once in the past twenty-four hours.

'Why ever not? Jesus Christ, there aren't many people who find themselves in a position to be introduced to Cristos Bennati. So go for it. What have you got to lose? And if you do, just remember, he's a mere man. He's made of flesh and blood like the rest of them, probably a bastard like the rest of them too. But you'd like to be able to say you've met him, wouldn't you?'

Corrie laughed. 'I'd die for it,' she admitted. 'But I think he and Luke have fallen out about something. Don't ask me what, but I recall Luke mentioning it.'

'So what? Ask anyway. You never know, this could be the start of something big.'

'Well now you've just gone and put the kiss of death on it,' Corrie complained. 'There you are ten years older than me and still you don't know that you should never voice your hopes. If you do, you might just as well kiss them good-bye.'

'You didn't voice them, I did. But if you *are* hoping for anything as far as Bennati's concerned, anything meaningful that is, then if I were you I'd kill it stone dead right now.'

'I know, he'd never look at anyone like me twice, and I'm fantasizing myself into a fairy tale.'

'I don't know about that, but what I do know is that he's Hollywood. Which means that he just wouldn't be good enough for you. You need a real man, Corrie, not a fake one, and that's all Hollywood produces – fake people. They're so up themselves it just isn't true. Get Luke to introduce you to Bennati, then you'll see what I mean. It'll be great for the first half an hour, you can look at him and lust after him all you like, then listen to what he's saying. Well, you'll have to because he won't stop talking – about himself. I say this because Hollywood people are all the same – me, me, me. It's all so phoney and *soooo* boring, you'll be crawling up the walls inside five minutes.'

Corrie was laughing. 'But what if I'm not?' she teased. 'What if I fall in love?'

'Then that'll make two of you in love with him, won't it?'

'What?'

'You and Bennati,' Felicity laughed. 'Come to think of

it, it'll probably make six million of you in love with him. Now come on, eat up, I'm starving.'

Luke was standing very still gazing out through the huge picture window overlooking the sea. The sun was dazzling, fusing the sea and sky into one. His hand was resting on the back of a chair and he could feel the warmth of her skin through the thin blouse she was wearing. There was the hint of a smile on his lips, but the sadness in his eyes was as unfathomable as the anguish in his heart. Even so, his voice was steady as he asked if she had received the flowers he'd sent.

After a while he turned, and looking down at her he lifted her hair in his hands. 'You look lovely today,' he said, and stooped to kiss the top of her head.

He pulled up a chair then and taking her hands said, 'I'm glad you liked the flowers. I'll send some more next week if you like.'

Siobhan stared unblinkingly out through the window, her gaze drowning somewhere in the vast expanse of brilliant white light. Her hands hung limply in Luke's.

'No walk today, I'm afraid,' he chuckled. 'But perhaps we could go for a drive. I've taken the roof off the car. No? OK, I guess it is a little too hot out.' He paused and put his head to one side. 'How are things at TW, did you ask? Oh, they're just great. The ratings are up again. The new researcher's working out just fine. I told you about her, didn't I? Her name's Corrie. Yes, of course I did.' He laughed. 'I'm getting pretty keen on her, you know. She's kind of special.' Again he paused as though listening. 'What about Annalise? Well, to be sure, I'm keen on her too.' He sighed. 'I wish you could see her, Siobhan, it would be such a surprise for you. Just like it was for me when I first saw her. Sorry, what was that you said? Oh, yes, she's very beautiful. And Corrie? Well, Corrie's different. She's more . . . Let me see, how would you describe Corrie?

She's striking. Yes, striking. And she's, well, untainted by life. I feel so good when I'm with her.' Again he chuckled. 'It's easy to forget how innocent she is when she looks the way she does . . . She has an amazing body. It seems to ooze sophistication, but at heart she's almost like a . . . yes, like a child.' He frowned then, and it was several minutes before he spoke again. 'Yes, you're right, my darling, she could be good for me. But, you know, she concerns me. Why? Oh, lots of reasons. For one thing she's never taken in by flattery, like most women, and you should see her when she's at work. She's been with us such a short time, but to listen to her you'd think she'd been there forever. I have a suspicion that she's nurturing an ambition to take over TW one of these days. Perhaps she could, given time, were it not for the fact that, as professional and single-minded as she can be, I think, no I believe, that beneath that bravado of hers, and that all too convincing act of self-confidence, she is fundamentally stupid. In what way?' He shrugged. 'Well, she's a romantic,' he answered, as though that explained everything. 'Her heart will always get the better of her in any situation, I'm certain of it. In fact I'm counting on it.

'But then of course there's Annalise. Corrie knows now that Annalise is her sister, and that sentimental heart of Corrie's means that she'll do anything she can to stop Annalise from being hurt. That's what Corrie's like. She's a decent human being. Which is basically what makes her stupid. She becomes confused when she's confronted by the seamier side of life. Though I have to give her credit for the way she tries to deal with it, she never runs away, but she hates it all the same. I admire her courage.' He paused, then his face hardened. 'I wish I could say the same for her father,' he growled. 'I thought he'd have given himself up by now, but he hasn't. He hasn't got the guts. I don't want to be the one to turn him in though, because then I won't be able to get to him. This way, while he's here, on the outside, I can make him suffer for all he's done . . . To you, Annalise . . .' He sighed heavily and let his eyes drift for a while. 'I don't want to hurt Annalise, you know that Siobhan, don't you? I love her. But Corrie is the woman I need. She could change everything for me . . . Yes, you're right, it is a dilemma, but I can see that you don't really want to hear about all this. Why don't you tell me what you've been doing since I was last here?'

A gentle breeze lifted Siobhan's hair and blew it across her mouth. Leaning forward Luke brushed it back into place. His face was very close to hers now, and he stayed like that, watching her, waiting patiently for her to speak.

Half an hour later he stood up, kissed her tenderly on the cheek, and left.

'Corrie! Corrie! It's me! Let me in. Please, let me in.'

Annalise was banging frantically on the door of Corrie's studio, and as Corrie pulled it open Annalise virtually fell into her arms.

'My God, what's happened?' Corrie cried when she saw Annalise's face. 'You look like you've seen a ghost.'

'I have. At least, he's like a ghost. Oh, Corrie, you've got to come. Please! You've got to come.'

'Come where?' Corrie asked, closing the door and stealing a quick look at the clock on the wall. It was one thirty in the morning.

'To Luke's. Oh Corrie, you should see him. It's terrible. I don't know what to do. I tried to talk to him, to make him tell me what was wrong, but he won't speak. He's just sitting there, like a zombie. It's horrible – it's as though . . . as though, he were dead. But he's breathing, his eyes are open, but he just won't speak. Oh Corrie, say you'll come. Please! I didn't know who else to turn to.'

'You'd better wait while I get dressed,' Corrie said. 'Have you got your car?'

'Yes, it's outside. I tried to ring you,' Annalise called up the stairs after Corrie, 'but your phone was engaged for so long.'

'Yes, I took it off the hook earlier,' Corrie shouted over the balcony, not adding that it was so she could get some uninterrupted sleep.

Twenty minutes later Annalise was letting them into Luke's apartment. Annalise seemed confused to find it in total darkness, and as they crept in through the door Corrie felt a sudden chill of unease.

'You don't think he's gone out again, do you?' she whispered to Annalise.

'I don't know. I shouldn't think so. His car was downstairs. Shall I turn on the light?'

'Yes, yes of course,' Corrie said, sounding a lot more courageous than she felt. She started as the hall flooded with light, and looking at Annalise she could see that Annalise was every bit as nervous as she was. 'Where was he when you left?' Corrie asked.

'In the sitting room.'

Corrie peeked round the door. 'Well he isn't there now,' she said, surveilling the empty, moonlit shadows.

'Perhaps he's gone to bed?' Annalise suggested.

'Then we ought to go.'

'But hadn't we better check first? I mean, make sure he's all right.'

Corrie looked hard at Annalise as she thought what to do. Then suddenly they leapt into each other's arms as the bedroom door creaked open.

'Oh my God!' Corrie breathed, as an ominous shadow stole across the sitting-room floor. She looked up to see Luke's silhouette framed in the bedroom door, and didn't know whether it was her own or Annalise's heart that started to thunder through her ears.

'Luke?' Annalise said tentatively. 'Luke, it's us. Are you . . .'

She stopped as Luke flicked on the light, and Corrie's heart seemed to plunge to her knees.

'What the hell are you playing at?' Luke said, half shouting. 'I thought you were burglars creeping about the place like that.'

'But Luke, are you all right?' Annalise cried, running to him.

Tightening the tie of his bathrobe he put an arm around her. 'Of course I'm all right,' he said. 'Why shouldn't I be?'

Annalise turned helplessly to Corrie, clearly hoping she would explain.

Corrie glared at her, then looking back to Luke she shrugged awkwardly. 'Well, I guess I'd better be getting home,' she said, feeling extremely embarrassed.

'Oh no you don't,' Luke said. 'I want an explanation from you two. Annalise, go and put the kettle on. Better still, get out the brandy. Not for you though, you're to have tea.'

'But Luke . . .'

'Tea! Or orange juice. No more alcohol tonight.'

Meekly Annalise lowered her eyes and went off to the kitchen. Luke walked to the cocktail cabinet and took down a bottle of brandy. He grimaced when he saw it was empty, and put it back on the shelf.

'That bottle was full when I left here on Friday,' he said to Corrie, who was still standing in the hall. 'When I got back tonight Annalise was here, waiting for me – well, there's no need for me to explain what a state she was in, the empty bottle says it all. Did she drive over to your place?'

Corrie nodded.

'Jesus, she's going to kill herself one of these days.' He smiled then. 'You can come in, you know, I won't bite.'

'Did she really drink all that brandy?' Corrie said, going

to sit on a hard-backed chair between the two sash windows.

Luke shrugged. 'She must have done. No one else has been here. So what did she tell you that brought you rushing over here in the middle of the night?'

'Well, not much really,' Corrie confessed. 'I mean she was a bit hysterical, I didn't stop to think that she might have been drinking. She said that you wouldn't speak to her. That you were just sitting there, saying nothing.'

Luke laughed. 'She's right, I was. And she knows why, but I don't suppose she told you that.'

Corrie shook her head.

'I wouldn't speak to her because she has some fixation that I have another woman. That when I go away for the weekend I go to be with this woman. She drives me so mad with her paranoia sometimes that it's all I can do to stop myself hitting her. Well, actually, I have hit her before now. It's the only way I can bring her hysteria under control.'

'Luke?'

Both Corrie and Luke turned to see Annalise standing at the door. Sighing Luke held out his arms. 'Come here,' he said.

Annalise all but ran to him, and as he held her Corrie was struck by how tiny she looked in his arms. And his tenderness was so enveloping that it was almost like watching a father with his child.

'I should be angry with you,' he said, gently stroking her hair. 'I've told you a hundred times not to drive that car when you've been drinking. Still, you're safe now, so I guess that's all that matters.'

'I've made some tea,' she said, gazing up at him with tears in her eyes.

'Then you take yours to bed. I'll be in shortly.'

Again Annalise went off to do as she was told and Luke turned back to Corrie. 'Would you like some tea?'

Corrie shook her head. 'No, I'd better be getting back.'

'You've welcome to stay here. You can share the bed with Annalise. I'll sleep on the sofa.'

'No, it's all right. Besides, I think she'd prefer that you slept with her tonight.'

'How will you get home?' he asked, as he walked her to the front door.

'I'll get a cab.'

'At this time of night?' He reached down for the handbag Annalise had left on the floor. 'Here,' he said, handing Corrie a set of keys, 'take Annalise's car. I'll drive her to the office in the morning.'

As Corrie took the keys she looked into Luke's face, but he bowed his head, as though not wanting to meet her eyes. Instinctively Corrie put a hand on his arm, but Luke merely reached out to open the door.

'Thanks for bringing her back,' he said.

As Corrie gingerly drove the Mercedes sports car through the deserted streets of Knightsbridge she suddenly found that she was fighting the urge to cry. This was a stupid reaction, she kept telling herself, but she just couldn't help it. It was upsetting her that Annalise hadn't denied she'd been drinking, when Corrie was convinced she hadn't been. At least not an entire bottle of brandy. Corrie just couldn't understand why she hadn't defended herself, and neither could she understand that dreadful sadness she had once again sensed in Luke. What was going on between them, she wondered. What really had happened to make Annalise come running to her like that? And why, for those few moments after she and Annalise had entered his flat, had she, Corrie, felt such an overpowering sense of fear?

Three days later, during a break in filming, Corrie and Annalise were strolling through Richmond Park. Annalise was giggling and kept digging Corrie in the ribs, trying to tickle her.

'Will you behave?' Corrie laughed, pulling Annalise's arms behind her and pushing her away.

'I can't! I can't! I can't!' Annalise cried, waving her arms in the air.

'People are staring at you,' Corrie told her.

'Oh good! I want them to, and maybe one of these days, when Luke and I go public, they'll remember seeing me in Richmond Park, screaming my head off with joy.'

'Now don't get carried away,' Corrie said, not much liking being the voice of caution. 'He's only said he's thinking about asking you to marry him.'

'Oh, don't be such a killjoy! If he's thinking about it, that means he's going to do it.'

Corrie was shaking her head in exasperation, but smiling nevertheless. The fact that Sunday night had not even been mentioned since didn't even strike her as odd, she was getting used to these convenient silences by now. And now surely wasn't the time to point out to Annalise that she really did have a whole heap of problems to sort out with Luke before she should even consider marrying him. Siobhan for one, whoever Siobhan was. Whether or not Luke had spent the weekend with her Corrie had no idea, but she rather suspected he had. Still, at least he hadn't hit Annalise this time. And why not let Annalise be happy while she could, God knew she'd known enough misery at Luke's hands. Corrie could wish though that she was able to shake off this dogged sense of foreboding – she hated being pessimistic, but try as she would she just couldn't bring herself to trust Luke.

Those niggling doubts she'd had concerning Bobby McIver were once again bothering her. For the past three mornings, before leaving the office to join up with the crew, Corrie had noticed Prue, who'd been made the new research assistant, cutting out all the news stories regarding McIver. There was nothing unusual in that, files were kept on everything, but what was unusual was the sixth sense that had made Corrie check if they were being booked out to anyone. They were. Luke had a standing requisition that everything concerning the murdered prostitutes was to be left on his desk each morning. And to make matters worse Corrie had at last remembered what it was that had first made her suspect that Luke knew more about McIver than he was saying. It was the fact that Luke had given her McIver's name and address over his car phone only minutes after the story had broken. Sure, he had contacts in the police force, which could easily have explained his prior knowledge, but Corrie might have felt a little more satisfied with that explanation had Luke not then started referring to McIver as Bobby.

'You're not listening to me!' Annalise declared.

'Because you're not making any sense, that's why,' Corrie answered, watching several deer scuttle off into the trees.

'You don't even know what I said!'

'Then what did you say?'

'I said that Felicity Burridge called me last night.'

'Oh?' Corrie said, surprised.

'And I told her I'd do it.'

'Do what?'

'See, I told you you weren't listening. I said I'd get Luke to introduce you to Cristos Bennati!'

'Oh, no, Annalise! Don't do that, I should die of embarrassment.'

'Too late, I'm afraid. I've already asked him and he said he'd see what he could do.'

'Oh God!' Corrie groaned. 'You didn't tell Luke it was for me did you?'

'No. I said we both wanted to meet him. But I'm afraid Luke did guess it was for you.'

'Yes, well he would, wouldn't he? It seems the whole world knows I've got a crush on Cristos Bennati, and now he's going to know too. Oh, yuk, I don't think I can bear it. Let's just hope Luke can't pull it off, 'cos if he does I'm just bound to make a complete prat of myself.' And with that her foot twisted into a dip in the ground and she took a long, stooping run towards a park bench. When she turned back it was to find Annalise convulse with laughter. Corrie was laughing too, but then, as she looked around to see who else had seen, the smile froze on her lips.

– 14 –

'It was the third time this week,' Corrie said, taking the glass of wine Paula was handing her and curling her feet under her on the sofa. 'He just keeps turning up. I thought at first that it was to see Annalise, but I'm not so sure now.'

'Why?'

'Well he spends most of his time talking to me, treating me as though I were the producer, and Annalise just goes along with it. It's as if she's absolved herself of all responsibilities now, but she's only copy-catting Luke. Anything he says goes. I'm convinced that if he told her he wanted her to give up work altogether and stay at home to look after him, she'd do it. To be frank she might just as well for all the commitment she has to the programme these days. She's like a love-struck teenager! Well, she always has been I suppose, but there are so many stars in her eyes now he's considering asking her to marry him, that they're blinding her. To such an extent that she doesn't even seem to notice that when she's making up to him around the set he's almost always watching me. It makes me feel really spooked.'

'Does he ever say anything to you?'

'No, at least not on the set. But I have to tell you what happened last night. I was on my way out to meet a couple of the secretaries to go to the cinema, when I opened my front door and he was standing there. I can tell you, he gave me the fright of my life. He hadn't rung the bell or anything, well he might just have arrived, but I got the feeling he'd been standing there, just waiting for me to come out.' She gave an involuntary shudder. 'It was horrible.'

'Well, what did he say?'

'That he was looking for Annalise. But Annalise was at home, I knew that because I'd just spoken to her on the phone. Then he asked me if the police had been in touch with me about Bobby McIver – the man who was arrested. I said no, then he offered me a lift to the cinema. I didn't accept because it's only at the end of the road, so he walked along with me. He kept asking me then how I felt about him marrying Annalise, whether or not I minded, or if I thought he was doing the right thing. I told him I didn't think it was any of my business, and he seemed to find that quite funny. It was such a strange reaction, and if you could have seen his face when he laughed . . .' Again she shivered. 'He's really giving me the creeps these days, Paula. I just wish Annalise weren't so obsessed with him, perhaps then I could get us both out of there. But she is, so what can I do?'

Paula shook her head, as defeated by the question as Corrie was herself. 'I guess Felicity's right,' she sighed in the end, 'Annalise is old enough to look after herself.'

'In years maybe, but certainly not in her mind. And what about this Siobhan? From what I can tell Luke goes to see her most weekends – and Annalise knows it. She gets herself into a hell of a state about it, and, well, it's true, I've never actually seen the way Luke behaves when he gets back, but I know one thing for sure, it's not normal.'

'If Annalise is to be believed.'

'I've seen the bruises myself. OK, perhaps he is trying to control her hysteria, but what's he doing that gets her into that state in the first place? Yes, I know, he calls her by this woman's name. But why? It's as though he's deliberately tormenting her. OK, I know, you're going to remind me that Annalise is a woman obsessed, possessed, more like, that she could be imagining things, but remember I've seen that birthday card too.' Corrie sighed and shook her head. 'Their relationship just isn't healthy, Paula, and the way Annalise is heading she's going to end up in the funny farm. And what really bothers me, is that Luke knows that.'

'He does?'

'He's not stupid, Paula, if I can see it then he sure as hell can.'

'And what about her – your, father? Surely he can see it too. I mean if it's that obvious. Why doesn't he do something about it?'

'He couldn't piss his pants if he was on fire,' Corrie snorted. 'But I'm beginning to wonder if my initial instincts weren't right, you know. There could be something going on between him and Luke. Luke's never mentioned that night again since, you know when we were all at his flat, but what if he *was* parading us all under Phillip's nose, like I thought?'

'I don't know why you ever stopped thinking it,' Paula said, 'because speaking personally, I'm convinced of it. Not that I can offer you any theories as to why, but I reckon that was what he was doing, letting Phillip know that he was screwing all three of you. Which of course means that he knows Phillip is your father. And I don't care what you say, I'm convinced of that too.'

'So why hasn't he said anything?'

'Search me, but from the things you've told me about him I wouldn't trust the man an inch. I mean, look at all that business in the office, wanting to hold you, then telling you that you're the only good thing ever to happen to him. Now what was all that about, when he's supposed to be in love with Annalise?'

'Oh God, it's all such a mess,' Corrie groaned.

'You're dead right it is, and you're getting in deeper and deeper by the minute. Which, if you ask me, is exactly what Luke Fitzpatrick wants, because, remember, you too are Phillip Denby's daughter. As far as I'm concerned that's just too much of a coincidence. OK, Luke hasn't got you eating out of his hand the way he has Annalise, but boy he's sure working on it.' She paused, watching Corrie's anxious face looking about the room. 'I think it's about time you started asking yourself some pretty serious questions, Corrie,' she said in a quiet voice. 'Like where is all this going to end? I know you won't leave TW because of Annalise, but, well, I don't want to sound too dramatic about this, but I think that man's dangerous. Very dangerous in fact. You said yourself Annalise is heading for the loony bin . . . You want to try and stop that happening, and I understand that, but for God's sake be careful yourself. I mean, like you say, it's bloody weird the way he's been hanging around these past few days.'

It was a long time before Corrie spoke again. There were so many thoughts going round in her head and she just didn't know if she wanted to burden Paula with anything else. But she had to. She couldn't keep it to herself any longer. 'I think,' she began hesitantly, 'that Luke knows something about those murdered prostitutes.'

Paula's eyes dilated. 'What do you mean?' she whispered.

Corrie shook her head. 'I'm not sure. Please keep this to yourself, Paula, but Detective Inspector Radcliffe told me that Bobby McIver has the mental age of a ten year old. To me, that just doesn't add up to what happened to those women.'

'But McIver confessed, didn't he? Anyway, what's that got to do with Luke?'

Corrie looked into Paula's bewildered and already fearful eyes, and dug her nails into her palms. 'Brace yourself,' she said. 'I think Luke knows Bobby McIver.'

'Oh my God! Paula cried. 'Corrie, you've got to get out of there. I mean, if he knows that man, if he's in some way involved . . . Jesus Christ, this is worse than I thought. I mean, what if this is all tied in somehow with what's happening between him and your father? Corrie!' she gasped, as Corrie suddenly turned away. 'Corrie, that's what you think, isn't it? That somehow your father's mixed up in this?'

Corrie looked down at her hands. 'I don't know what to think,' she said. 'All I know is that Phillip's a very frightened man. He said to me, that night I saw him, he told me to keep away from Luke. He said, "he's got Annalise, he doesn't need you too, so keep away from him." At the time I thought he was telling me . . . Well, you know what I thought, but now . . .'

'Corrie, are you telling me that you think Luke Fitzpatrick might have murdered those women?'

'No, of course I'm not. I'm just saying . . . I'm saying that I think he knows more than he's letting on.'

'Have you told anyone else about this?'

Corrie shook her head.

'Then you must! You've got to tell the police.'

'Radcliffe is a friend of Luke's.'

'Not that good a friend, I'll bet. I heard what Radcliffe said on your programme, and he meant it. You have to go and see him, Corrie. Promise me, promise me now, that you'll go as soon as you get back to London.'

For the past few minutes Detective Inspector Radcliffe had been sitting quietly behind his desk, listening intently to what Corrie was telling him. She'd said only that she thought Luke Fitzpatrick knew Bobby McIver, but wasn't making much sense in backing up her claims. But there was something else troubling her, Radcliffe was pretty sure of that, and he could hazard a fairly accurate guess what it was. If he was right then he knew already it would annoy him. Too many people came in here wasting his time trying to frame someone in order to avenge their personal grievances.

Sensing that Corrie was on the point of repeating herself again, Radcliffe leaned forward in his chair and held up his hand. 'What's your relationship with Mr Fitzpatrick, Miss Browne?' he asked, bluntly.

'He's my boss,' Corrie answered, feeling herself start to blush. Radcliffe was quite aware of that, but they both knew that that wasn't the question he'd asked. The colour in Corrie's cheeks deepened even further then as she saw Radcliffe's eyes wander momentarily to the female DC sitting beside her. Corrie didn't see the brief smile DC Archer gave in response.

'Can I tell you something, Miss Browne?' Radcliffe said, standing up and leaning against the wall behind him.

Corrie was wide-eyed as she nodded.

'I'm going to tell you that you're absolutely right in thinking that there was someone else behind these murders, since of course, a man like Bobby McIver could never have managed it alone – if indeed he could manage it at all. We now, as I told you before, have McIver in a secure place where he's being well taken care of. Naturally, it's our hope that at some point he will tell us the name of the man we're really looking for. Now, are you trying to tell me that you know who that man is?'

'No! No,' Corrie answered hastily. 'I'm just saying that I think Luke Fitzpatrick might know Bobby McIver.' The way she was saying it didn't even sound convincing to her own ears, so was it any wonder that Radcliffe was looking at her so sceptically?

'Because he referred to him twice as Bobby, and gave you his name and address?'

'Yes.'

Radcliffe shook his head, but as he made to speak again Corrie interrupted him.

'Why aren't you making this public?' she asked. 'I mean about the other man?'

'We have our reasons.'

'So why are you telling me?'

Radcliffe was looking at DC Archer as he answered. 'Again, we have our reasons,' he said. 'But now, I'd like to thank you for coming here today and if we need to speak to you again, I imagine we can contact you at TW?'

'Yes, yes, of course,' Corrie said, picking up her bag. 'Um, if you do speak to Luke Fitzpatrick,' she added, as she and DC Archer reached the door, 'then I'd be grateful if you didn't mention anything about me.'

'Of course,' Radcliffe assured her, and yet again, he and Archer exchanged glances.

'Are you thinking what I'm thinking?' Radcliffe asked, when Archer had dispensed Corrie into the care of a PC.

'That hell hath no fury?' Archer smiled.

Radcliffe nodded. 'Funny she didn't strike me as that type when I first met her. Still, I think she's to be trusted with the information I've given her. She's naive enough to keep it to herself for now, and professional enough to do the right thing with it when the time comes.'

'What about Fitzpatrick?'

Radcliffe shrugged. 'We might as well get him in, find out what's behind it all. But do it tomorrow, I've just about had it with this place for one day.'

Having worked off his fury in the hotel gym, Cristos Bennati was now upstairs in his room taking a shower. The cool water was helping calm him even further, but that asshole location manager just better not show his face again today.

Cristos had been in London for four days now, and each one had gotten progressively worse. To begin with it was hotter than hell, and matters hadn't been helped any by the fact that Richard, his DP, had gone down with flu, meaning that Jeannie's loyalties were split. Well that he could handle, it was the dragging round useless locations, like a general at the head of a bewildered army, that was eating him. The designer was working his butt off with what they'd been shown so far, but even his awesome talent couldn't make anything of it. Not one single fucking thing was going to work, thanks to Joe, the assistant director, and Peter the jerk of a location manager. Cristos was so mad at them that an hour ago he'd had to leave them on the side of the street before he turned violent. To think he'd spent the past two years of his life working with the screenwriters to get the script in shape and those schmucks hadn't even read it! At least if what they'd found so far was anything to go by, they hadn't.

But Cristos was as mad at himself as he was at them. He should have stuck to his guns when he'd told Bud Winters he didn't want Dreamboat Joe as his first assistant. And he would have if his regular AD had been available, but he wasn't, so Bud Winters had seized the opportunity to ease in his fuckhead of a nephew. And somehow the nephew had managed to work in his boyfriend as location manager.

Cristos was well used to having family and faggots foisted on him, not that he had any objections to either so long as they were good at their jobs, but on his last couple of movies he'd had all parasites removed. He'd do it again, he suddenly decided, and he'd start now, by putting in a call to LA and demanding that the location manager be replaced inside twenty-four hours or he, Cristos, was on the next plane out of here. The jerk was costing money and there was nothing like hitting an exec. where it hurt most, he grinned savagely.

Still dripping from the shower he padded into the bed-room and picked up his watch. Winters would still be in bed. Well he could just get the hell out of bed.

'Boy, you sure got a hair up your ass,' Winters remarked,

when Cristos had finished yelling down the phone at him. 'Try to be tolerant, my friend . . .'

'I'm not known for it,' Cristos reminded him. 'I told you before those fuckwits flew out here that we needed a Brit to find these locations. Someone familiar with the terrain. Sure, they did OK in LA, but over here they've well and truly screwed up. They don't know what they're doing, and they're wasting my fucking time. Now I want them off this movie and someone who knows what they're doing on.'

'But what can I do, Cristos? You're out there now . . .'

'You tell Dreamboat Joe that the party's over, that's what you do,' Cristos interrupted. 'And I'll find myself a location manager here in London.'

'But if the location manager's the problem, I don't see why Joe has to go,' Winters protested.

'They're running as a team, they both go. No, you listen to me,' he barked, when Winters made to interrupt. 'I don't want anyone hanging around my set sulking because their fancy boy's been fired. He's off, Bud. I gave him a chance and he's fucked up. Jeannie'll be speaking to Rowlinson later to line up a new AD. I'll handle the other.'

'OK, OK, have it your way,' Winters sighed. 'But I don't know what I'm gonna tell my sister.'

'Yeah, well maybe you'd better work out what you're gonna tell your nephew first . . .'

'But . . .'

'You hired him, you fire him.'

Cristos felt a whole lot better by the time he put the phone down. You turned in as many million dollars as he did then it was easy to get those power junkies hopping about their Black Tower. But this just better not cost him any time, 'cos time was the one commodity he could not afford. This movie had to be ready for the Cannes festival, or Bud Winters was going to have a whole lot more than a hair up his ass.

He picked up the phone again and dialled Jeannie's

room. 'Get yourself up here, babe,' he said, 'we got a lot to do tonight.'

He was about to go find himself a towel when the phone rang. He sure as hell hoped it wasn't either of the Goddammed faggots, he'd had about all he could take of them for one day.

'Bennati,' he barked into the receiver, then stiffened as he heard the voice at the other end. 'Fitzpatrick! I thought I made myself clear last time . . .'

'Cristos, just hear me out, will you?'

'You got nothing to say that . . .'

'Cristos, it was all a misunderstanding. You just got the wrong end of the stick. Now why don't you stop by my place for a couple of drinks and we'll talk.'

'You heard what I said, Fitzpatrick. Now just get the hell . . .'

'Cristos, I'm not asking for myself, I'm asking for someone who works at my office. She's dying to meet you, and once you see her . . .'

Cristos had already taken a breath to tell Luke to go fuck himself, when suddenly he remembered that right now he was in sore need of a location manager. If Fitzpatrick was good for nothing else he was good for a few contacts. 'I can spare an hour tomorrow between seven and eight,' he snapped, and rang off.

The minute he put the phone down he winced. Cocktails, a doe-eyed dimbo, or bimbo, or whatever they called them these days, and Luke Fitzpatrick! Wasn't he just having one hell of a time in good old London town!

There was a knock on the door and he yelled for whoever it was to get lost. The door opened and when Cristos turned to see Jeannie's raised eyebrows his thunderous face immediately broke into a grin.

'You could at least have the decency to turn your back,' Jeannie grumbled.

'It's nothing you didn't see before, so quit playing coy,'

Cristos told her, grabbing a towel. 'Well, come in, get it all out and let's get on with it,' he added, when she continued to hover at the door.

Jeannie walked timidly across the room, opened the lid of her portable computer then looked at him demurely. 'Is thith how you want me, thir?' she said.

At last Cristos laughed. Thank God for Jeannie, she could always make him laugh. And were it not for Richard, her husband, he might just have the hots for Jeannie – if for no other reason than sometimes she seemed the only woman alive who didn't have the hots for him.

'Ah, Corrie, there you are,' Luke said, seeing that she had at last returned to her desk. 'Where have you been all afternoon?'

'Talking to the mother of a transsexual,' Corrie lied, avoiding his eyes by picking up the messages piled on her desk.

'Right. Well, you'll be pleased to know that I've just spoken to Bennati and he's coming to my place tomorrow night at seven. I take it you're free?'

'Yes, I'm free,' Corrie answered, wishing she had the courage to say she wasn't. But bad as she felt about going to see Radcliffe, she just couldn't pass up the opportunity of meeting Cristos Bennati. Already her stomach was churning at the very thought of it, she just wished, for all sorts of reasons, that it wasn't Luke who was doing her such an enormous favour.

The following morning DC Archer managed to get hold of Luke at home and asked him to come in to the station. Luke's immediate thought was that Denby had given himself up. If he had . . . But no, the police wouldn't be asking him to come in if they'd interviewed Denby, they'd be banging on his door and dragging him in. Besides, Denby didn't have the guts to give himself up, Luke would stake his life on that.

When he arrived at the station, instead of taking him to the CID office, a WPC led him straight to an interview room. This too unnerved Luke, not that he let it show.

'Luke, good to see you,' Radcliffe said, standing up as Luke walked into the room. 'How's tricks?'

'As ever,' Luke answered, shaking Radcliffe's hand and nodding at Archer.

They all sat down, and when a few more pleasantries were out of the way, Radcliffe came to the point. 'I believe,' he began, 'that you are aware of Bobby McIver's mental state.'

Luke raised his eyebrows, letting his surprise show. 'Yes, I am,' he answered.

'Can I ask how you came by that knowledge?'

'Oh, come on, Paul. How do you think I know? You told one of my researchers.'

Radcliffe's face was inscrutable. 'In your opinion, Luke, do you think a man such as McIver could have carried out the murders?'

Luke was visibly unsettled by the question. 'Why are you asking me?' he said. 'I don't know enough about mental illness, or to what extent McIver is retarded. Anyway, he confessed, didn't he?'

'Yes, he confessed all right. The trouble is, we don't believe him.'

'But I thought he gave you all the details . . . Those you'd been holding back.'

'He did. But I think someone else told him what we wanted to know. Someone who has got to him. I don't suppose you have any idea who that someone might be?'

At first Luke's eyes widened with shock, then slowly they started to narrow as he glanced several times between Radcliffe and Archer. 'That's a mighty peculiar question,

Inspector,' he remarked. 'How would I know who's been getting to McIver?'

'Do you?'

'No.'

'Are you sure about that?'

'Look, is this some kind of joke, or . . .' Luke stopped and frowned heavily as suddenly the pieces started to fall into place. 'Oh, I get it,' he said, suddenly starting to grin.

Radcliffe's silence was a clear sign that he was waiting for Luke to elaborate.

Luke's grin was very wide indeed by now, since he understood only too well what was going on. For some reason, Corrie, and it could only have been Corrie, had come here to tell Radcliffe that her boss knew Bobby McIver. Exactly what he had done to betray himself, Luke wasn't sure, but he had obviously under-estimated her somewhere along the line, for she clearly wasn't as stupid as he'd thought. Well, the situation wasn't irretrievable by any means – at least not so far as he was concerned. As far as Corrie was concerned, well that was a different matter altogether. 'Have you ever spurned a woman?' he asked Radcliffe.

'Not for many years.' Radcliffe's eyes flicked towards Archer. Their suspicions, it seemed, were about to be confirmed.

Luke couldn't have been more delighted by that exchange of glances. 'Well unfortunately, in my position,' he said, 'I frequently find myself having to turn women down. Chiefly because I have a girlfriend who means a great deal to me. She works at TW, in fact you've met her, Annalise Kapsakis. But between ourselves, Inspector, I have made the mistake of sleeping with other women, one in particular, and perhaps I didn't handle it quite as tactfully as I might.' He waited, but when it was evident that Radcliffe wasn't going to say anything, he added. 'I think we both know who I'm talking about.'

Radcliffe cleared his throat, and getting to his feet said,

'Thank you for coming in, Luke. Miss Archer here will see you out,' and after shaking Luke by the hand he left the room.

On the pavement outside Chelsea Police Station Luke waved a cheery goodbye to DC Archer, and trotted off towards his car. Only now that his back was turned could he allow his face to contort with all the rage he'd managed to keep bottled inside. With every step he took his body jarred. He slowed down, but it was no good, the stiffness in his legs had spread to his lungs. He could barely move. The rage was now so intense it was clawing at every bone in his body.

He all but fell into his car, coughing and spluttering, gasping urgently for air. His fury was squeezing him, gripping his throat with choking, slithering tentacles. But it would be all right. He would control it, he would make himself. He'd go see a whore, that's what he'd do. He'd screw this frenzied rage into the ass of a woman – and all the time he'd remember. He'd let the memories haunt him, crowd in on him, torture him and all the time he'd remember. And after, when he had pumped the vile poison from his veins, he would decide what must be done about Corrie.

The office was almost empty now, but earlier everyone had been there for the regular post-mortem of the previous night's programme. Bob had taken the meeting, as he usually did in Luke's absence, but when Luke still hadn't shown by midday, Corrie was starting to feel extremely nervous.

She'd come away from Radcliffe's office the previous afternoon with the distinct impression that she hadn't been taken seriously. It was that thought which had enabled her to sleep the night before, since by now she was feeling so guilty, not to mention ridiculous, about what she had done, that she just wanted to forget all about it. But as the morning wore on and there was still no sign of Luke, Corrie was fast approaching the point of panic. In the end, unable to stand the suspense, she asked Julia, Luke's secretary, if she knew where Luke was.

'He's gone to see DI Radcliffe,' Julia answered.

Corrie's heart dropped like a stone. It was the reply she had dreaded.

'I thought he'd have been here by now,' Julia said, eyeing Corrie curiously. 'Anything I can help with?'

'No. No, it can wait,' Corrie mumbled, and returned to her desk. He probably knew by now that she had been there herself the day before. But Radcliffe had promised not to mention her name. What difference did that make though, Luke would know that it was she who had told Radcliffe about McIver, after all who else could it be? She tried to imagine how he would react once he found out, and nothing she came up with made her feel any better. If anything her nerves were becoming edged with fear.

By the middle of the afternoon Corrie was almost beside herself. She and Annalise were sorting through some surgeon's stills, laid out on Annalise's desk, most of which, if screened, were guaranteed to get legs crossing in a national wince, but some, picked out by Annalise, were usable. However, Corrie simply couldn't concentrate. She kept reminding herself that Luke's absence was nothing unusual, he kept his own hours, and sometimes they didn't see him for days at a time. Which meant that this mounting unease was merely paranoia, or guilty conscience more like, but every time she envisaged Luke with Radcliffe she felt almost sick with apprehension.

'Look, if you're that nervous about meeting Cristos Bennati tonight,' Annalise laughed, when for the fifth time Corrie returned a question with a blank stare, 'why don't you just go home, make yourself glamorous and I'll finish up here.'

'No, no, it's all right, I'll stay,' Corrie answered, spinning towards the door as it opened. It was the production manager, spouting off his grievances to a cameraman about a facility house.

Luke had left Chelsea Police Station hours ago, Corrie knew that because she had called Radcliffe herself to find out what had happened. She had spoken to DC Archer, who had assured Corrie that they were quite satisfied with what Luke had told them, and that no, her name had never been mentioned.

So why, Corrie kept asking herself, was she feeling like this? For sure, she was nervous about meeting Bennati that night, but that had nothing to do with the way her heart kept leaping to her throat every time there was a phone call for her.

It wasn't until she and Annalise were leaving the office around five, that Corrie finally admitted to herself that she was afraid. Truly afraid. She was experiencing the kind of fear that on the face of it was irrational, for the fact that Luke hadn't turned up at the office in itself said nothing, but to Corrie it was saying everything. He was absolutely bloody furious with her for going to the police the way she had, and this was his way of letting her know. For now he was merely letting her sweat it out, but he was going to have something to say about it, Corrie was convinced of that. Just as convinced as she was that he was going to do it that night – right in front of Cristos Bennati.

By now Annalise had dropped Corrie at her studio and Corrie was on the point of getting into the shower. However, this sudden added fear stopped her in her tracks. She could suffer just about anything for what she had done, but to be humiliated in front of Cristos Bennati was unthinkable. She couldn't, wouldn't let Luke do it. He could shout her off all he liked in front of anyone else, but dear God, not in front of Bennati.

Immediately she turned to the phone and dialled Luke's number. She didn't know yet what excuse she was going to give, but whatever it turned out to be she wasn't going to his place that night. She tapped her foot impatiently as the phone rang at the other end. It rang and rang, but no one picked it up – not even the answerphone.

'Damn it!' Corrie cried, slamming the receiver back in the cradle. All right then, she'd go, but she'd get there early so that they could get it over with before Bennati arrived.

She wandered back to the shower then, feeling thoroughly miserable that this was spoiling what should have been one of the most exciting nights of her life.

By the time Corrie arrived at Luke's she had rehearsed so many apologies, accusations and defences that she couldn't hold a single coherent thought in her head. On top of that she was racking her brains trying to come up with some sparkling wit or intellectual profundity with which she might entertain or enthral Cristos Bennati. But first things first, she reminded herself. Luke would want a damned good reason as to why she had gone to the police before speaking to him, so she'd just better come up with something fast or they'd still be at it when Cristos arrived.

She was so engrossed in her panicked thoughts that she didn't even realize that Luke had now pressed the buzzer three times to let her in through the downstairs door.

'Corrie!' he cried, when she was only half way up the stairs. 'Thank God you've come early. I've only just realized what the time is. The place is a mess, come and give me a hand to clear up will you?'

Corrie was caught completely off guard, and before she knew what she was doing was racing up the stairs to help. It wasn't until she arrived at the door that she suddenly remembered that she had dressed herself in a very expensive suit – after discarding all her sexier dresses for fear of making a fool of herself – and was not in the least impressed by having to throw herself into housework.

Luke looked comically hurt when she told him this. 'Can't you take pity on a poor single man just this once,' he pleaded.

Corrie eyed him for a moment, then tossing her head she marched past him into the flat.

'You look lovely,' he said, closing the door behind her.

'It's all right, I'll help,' she said, still not quite daring to believe that the showdown wasn't going to happen. 'What have you been doing all day, anyway? I thought you were coming into the office.'

'Can I take it from that that you missed me?' Luke grinned.

Corrie pursed her lips and turned away. She couldn't believe this! She was going to get away with it, he wasn't going to say a word. Or, God bless Radcliffe, he really hadn't given her away after all. 'You've been smoking,' she said, turning her nose up at the full ashtray on the coffee table.

'I do sometimes,' he confessed, 'when I've got a lot on my mind.'

Here it comes. He's going to bring it up right now. But when she turned round he was stuffing a pile of newspapers into the bottom of the bookcase, so she simply picked up the ashtray and carried it into the kitchen.

His laundry was scattered all over the floor, and kicking it to one side, Corrie started to make her way towards the bin. Then she stopped, so abruptly that the ashtray jolted in her hand spilling its contents onto the shirt she was staring at. Her heart was slowly pounding into an unnatural rhythm, and her head began to swim.

She took a step back, her eyes darting about the kitchen as though expecting to see more. But there was nothing, it was only the shirt . . . She shook her head, trying to clear it. She was over-reacting, it was nothing to be afraid of . . . It was just blood . . . OK, a lot of blood, but . . . She nearly leapt from her skin as she heard the door close behind her.

She spun round to find Luke standing very close, so close she could feel the heat of his body. She looked into his face and for one blinding second knew abject terror.

'What is it?' Luke gasped, taking her by the arms. 'Corrie, what's the matter?'

'Nothing. No, nothing,' Corrie mumbled. 'It was – you just startled me, coming in like that.'

He pulled her against him, hugging her tight.

The fear was rapidly beginning to subside now, but she was badly confused and could feel the sweat on her body turning cold with the breeze coming in through the open window. Then something strange started to happen, and it was a while before she realized that the odd vibrations against her body were coming from Luke.

Corrie moved away, and watched, as still laughing, Luke stooped to pick up the shirt. 'It was this, wasn't it?' he said. 'You thought it was blood.'

Corrie raised her eyes slowly to his, trying very hard to keep her head.

Luke threw the shirt back to the floor. 'You think I did it, don't you?' he smirked. 'You think I killed them.'

Corrie's heart was hammering so strenuously she couldn't even breathe. It was as though her skin was tightening across her face, so hard that she couldn't move her lips. She hadn't said anything about suspecting him of murder, not to him, not to Radcliffe, not even to Paula. She'd never even said it to herself . . .

'Oh, I know all about your little visit to the police,' Luke said, taking her ice-cold hands in his. 'And you think I'm angry with you, don't you? Well you're wrong. I was at first, I have to admit, but then I got to thinking, and reminded myself that most people over-react to things when they are close to murders – especially the first time they come into contact with one.' He put his head to one side and looked searchingly into her eyes. 'That there, on my shirt, Corrie, is paint.'

'Paint?' she echoed, unable to take her eyes from his.

'Yes, paint. Oil paint. Have I never told you about my little hobby?'

She shook her head.

'Come with me,' he smiled.

A few minutes later they were standing inside a small studio at the rear of the flat that Corrie hadn't even known existed until now. She didn't want to be there, she wanted only to get away from him, but her eyes moved slowly over the artist's paraphernalia scattered about the room, until they finally came to rest on a chair in front of an empty easel. On it was a palette daubed with red paint.

She knew Luke was watching her, waiting for her to speak, but she just didn't know what to say. Inside her head there was only an amorphous jumble of thoughts which just refused to take shape.

To her unutterable relief the doorbell rang then and he left her alone to go and answer it.

A few seconds later, after quietly closing the studio door behind her, Corrie stood in the narrow stone corridor leading back into the flat. She was making an effort to pull herself together. Annalise had obviously arrived, and she should go to say hello, but she couldn't, not yet anyway. She had to think. She had to ask herself why on earth she had responded the way she had to the paint-encrusted shirt, and, more importantly, why Luke thought she suspected him of murder? She didn't, at least she hadn't – until now. But she still didn't, did she? No, of course not, though if she really thought about it, she was now, tonight, convinced that he knew who *had* done it. She squeezed her eyes tightly. There was a thought, somewhere at the back of her mind, pushing wildly against all the others trying to get to the front. But every time it so much as probed her consciousness every other thought in her head seemed to knit into such a solid mass that there was no way it could get through.

Hearing voices she lifted her head, then her heart somersaulted so violently that she actually felt the blood drain from her face, and at the same time her mind emptied of everything but the fact that it wasn't Annalise who had arrived at all, for that voice she could hear, the one with the American accent, could only be Cristos Bennati's. Any minute now she was going to meet the man who lit up just about every fantasy she'd ever had. For one panic-stricken moment she wanted to run. There seemed to be so much happening at once that she just couldn't handle it.

She took a deep breath, tried to make herself move and found that she couldn't. 'For God's sake, grow up!' she muttered angrily to herself. Her fists were clenching and unclenching and she was breathing very heavily now. Then all of a sudden the absurdity of her behaviour struck her and she started to grin. Were either Paula or Felicity able to see her now, trapped here in a stone hallway trying to pluck up the courage to meet Bennati, they would just die laughing. But Corrie couldn't laugh herself, she was too sick with nerves.

Placing her fingers against her temples she willed herself to keep the past few minutes out of her mind, to concentrate now on what she felt to be the most important event of her life.

Finally she was ready to push the door open. She did, and walked into the sitting room. Cristos and Luke were standing close together over Luke's desk, and Cristos was writing something down on a pad he was holding. They both turned as Corrie came in, and Corrie, who had a happy smile planted on her face, felt the corners start to droop as her entire body threatened to go limp.

He was so much darker than she'd expected – and taller, taller even than Luke. His long, jet black hair was an unruly mess, his jeans were worn and torn, and his pale blue cotton shirt had seen better days too. That he had neither showered nor changed before coming here was obvious, not only from his clothes, but from the dark shadow on his chin. But what Corrie couldn't believe, what was holding her rooted to the spot, were his incredible eyes. They looked . . . well, they were so absorbing she felt as though she was sinking right into them. She tried to pull herself together, but all she could do was gape in blind adoration as she asked herself how on earth it was possible for one man to be so sensationally attractive.

'Corrie! Come and meet Cristos Bennati,' Luke said.

In a state of sublime unreality Corrie crossed the room. She knew Cristos was still watching her, but now she was unable to meet his eyes.

'Cristos, this is Corrie Browne, the one I was telling you about,' Luke chuckled. 'She's been dying to meet you so be nice to her, won't you?'

This was just what Corrie needed to bring her crashing back to earth. 'Luke is very good at embarrassing people,' she said, sending him a daggered look. 'It's very nice to meet you, Mr Bennati.'

'Cristos. It's good to meet you too, Corrie.'

He shook her hand and she tried not to be overwhelmed by the fact that he was actually touching her.

'I've seen all your films,' she said, trying to sound breezy but only succeeding in sounding trite. 'I particularly liked the one with David Easton in . . . Well, you've done a couple of films with him, haven't you? It was the one . . . I know, it was called *Never Too Far*. You remember the one, it was where he operated . . . What am I talking about, you know your own films.' Why was God doing this to her? Why was He denying her control of her own tongue? 'I saw your latest film twice,' she went on. 'It was amazing. It must be so wonderful to have a talent like yours.' Oh yuk! Did she really say that? But it didn't seem she was finished yet. 'You're absolutely my favourite director. Well, of course, I'm not the only one to think that. You've got such an enormous following. I imagine that's because you're so dedicated to what you do. I know you are, because it's probably the most consistent thing I've read about you. Anyway, it shows in your films . . .'

As she rambled on and on Cristos was smiling politely, but it was obvious, even to Corrie, that he was no longer listening, and eventually she managed to rein in her tongue. Almost immediately Cristos turned his attention back to Luke.

Corrie sat down, so hot with embarrassment it seemed to be oozing from her pores. It was some while before she could bring herself to look at him again, though she was registering vaguely what he was telling Luke about some jerk of a location manager. When eventually her embarrassment started to abate, she began to feel annoyed, as though it was Cristos's fault that she had made a fool of herself. But the evening wasn't over yet, she could, and would, try again as soon as she got the chance. For the moment, both he and Luke seemed to have forgotten she was in the room.

She lifted her head to look at him again, but didn't get very far before she found her eyes glued to the bulge at the front of his jeans. She couldn't believe it. She'd never looked at a man that way before. But his physique was so compelling she just couldn't tear her eyes away. She forced herself to, and standing up wandered shakily across to the drinks cabinet.

'Can I get either of you a drink?' she shouted.

They both turned to her in amazement, and she felt herself turn almost purple with embarrassment. She couldn't even seem to control the level of her voice.

She had her back to them now, but caught the amusement in Luke's voice as he told her what he wanted.

'And I'll have a scotch,' Cristos added.

As she poured the drinks she was giving herself the stiffest talking to, but a few minutes later, after she had given them their drinks and was once again back on the sofa, she found herself studying his shoulders, his hands, his legs until she suddenly realized that she was in the middle of the most astonishingly erotic fantasy she'd ever had. She was so shocked that she actually burst out laughing. Both Luke and Cristos, who were now sitting down too, looked at her. Cristos seemed irritated, as though he had been forced to remember the presence of a giggly schoolgirl and Corrie's laughter died instantly. How dare he look at her like that! Just who the hell did he think he was anyway? Her head spun towards Luke then, as he actually laughed out loud at the outrage gleaming in Corrie's eyes.

'So what do you do?' Cristos asked, as Luke got up to answer the door.

Corrie eyed him with marked hostility. 'You mean when I'm not having sexual fantasies about you?' she responded haughtily. 'That was what made me laugh, you know.'

The corner of Cristos's mouth lifted, along with one eyebrow. Then he swept an unhurried look the entire length of her body. 'Was I good?' he asked.

Oh my God, what was she going to say to that? 'As you heard,' she replied smoothly, 'it made me laugh.'

'Is that all?'

'Actually, it robbed me of the urge to tear off all my clothes and beg you to make love to me on the instant.'

He grinned and Corrie, who simply couldn't believe what was coming out of her mouth, melted.

'To answer your question,' she said, much gratified by the fact that she hadn't yet – at least during this conversation – blushed, 'I'm a programme researcher. In other words I find and develop the ideas . . .'

'I know what a researcher does,' he interrupted. Then he smiled again and this time, to her dismay, Corrie felt her colour rising.

'Have you found *any* locations yet?' she asked, crossing her legs and bouncing her hair with her fingers.

'Not one.'

'What is the film about?'

He was about to answer when Annalise and Luke came into the room.

'So sorry I'm late,' Annalise gushed, crossing the room to embrace Corrie. 'Daddy called in and I just couldn't get away.'

She turned to Cristos, and as Luke introduced her Corrie noticed immediately the spark of appreciation in his eyes as he shook Annalise's hand. Oh well, Corrie told herself, swallowing hard on her jealousy, she was insane to have thought she could impress a man like Bennati in the first place.

Miserably she watched him as he sat back down again, then to her surprise, as her eyes reached his, she found that he was watching her. But there was such a knowing smile on his lips, as though he could read her thoughts, that before Corrie could stop herself she had slammed her eyes closed and looked away.

'You were asking what the film was about,' he reminded her.

Corrie felt sick. 'Mmm,' she grunted, tossing her head. 'So I was.' If he preferred Annalise to her then that was up to him, but she was going to wipe that smug smile off his face as far as she was concerned. He might like to think that every woman in the world fancied the pants off him, well now he was going to find one who didn't!

'Did you still want to know, or did you go off the idea?' he asked.

'Oh no, no,' she said, wishing that Annalise and Luke weren't watching her with such evident delight. 'I'd like to hear.'

'Well it's kind of a difficult story to explain, but it's based on the book *Past Lives Present*,' he said. 'I guess you won't have read it, since it's not published here in Britain yet. If you're interested, though, I'll have my assistant mail you a copy.'

'That's very kind of you,' Corrie said, appalling herself by how off-hand she sounded. Then to compound matters even further she added, 'I'll try to get round to reading it sometime, but I'm so busy these days I don't get a lot of time for reading.'

Annalise was gawping at her in amazement, and Corrie's expression was much the same as she looked back. She just couldn't believe this was happening. She'd never been so rude to anyone in her life, but words were just spurting out of her mouth like anarchic missiles.

She turned back to Cristos. 'Of course,' she said, with her eyebrows arched so high they were half way to her hairline, 'I'll make a special effort for this book – now that I've met you!'

She sounded so unbelievably patronizing that she longed to smack herself across the face. A bubble of laughter escaped her at that, as she imagined how they might all react if she actually did. But, deciding that the only thing she could do now was keep her lips firmly clamped together, she stared down at her drink feeling more wretched and more angry with each passing minute. She had so desperately wanted to make an impression on him, but she could see now that he was so well used to dealing with star-struck females like her that even her rudeness was commonplace, and it was unlikely he'd get even as far as the front door before forgetting her very existence.

It was ten minutes or more before Corrie spoke again. 'Is it a problem for you?' she suddenly blurted out. 'I mean being so good-looking.'

When Cristos turned to look at her she saw straight away that he was trying very hard not to laugh. Luke was less successful, for Corrie heard him snigger before he covered his mouth with his hand. Corrie was on fire.

'How do you mean, a problem?' Cristos asked.

Corrie shrugged. 'Well, I was just thinking that women

who are very good-looking find it hard to get themselves taken seriously. I wondered if it was the same for a man.'

'Not so's I've noticed,' Cristos answered.

'Well, I guess you wouldn't in your position,' Corrie said.

Not long after that Cristos announced he was leaving. Corrie immediately looked at her watch and claimed that she too must be getting along. Cristos glanced at her with mild surprise, and she wanted to die. Obviously he thought she was engineering their joint departure, and already in his mind he was probably working out a way to be rid of her. Well, it was too late now, she'd only end up in an even bigger mess if she tried to backtrack.

As they walked down the stairs together Cristos was ahead of her, and Corrie prayed that he hadn't heard the yell of laughter coming from Luke's flat as Luke closed the door. But he was sure to have, and Corrie felt so totally foolish that for a moment she wanted to cry. But, as they rounded a corner of the stairs, and she watched him adoringly from behind, her spirits underwent a sudden lift. Perhaps they would get a few minutes together walking along the street. If nothing else it might give her a chance to redeem herself.

'Uh, um, Cristos?' she said, as he walked out through the front door.

'What's that?' he asked, not even looking back.

'Well, I'm sorry if I sounded ... Back there, in Luke's ...'

'Forget it,' he told her.

'Well, you see, I'm not normally ...'

'Taxi!' he shouted, and to Corrie's unutterable frustration a cab pulled right alongside them.

'It's all right,' she told him loftily, as he started to get in, 'I'll take the next one.'

'I'm sorry,' he said, 'can I give you a ride somewhere?'

'No. It's quite all right. I don't mind waiting.'

He shrugged. 'Suit yourself,' and with that he slammed the door and the taxi drove away.

Twenty minutes later Corrie was back at her studio and on the phone to Paula.

'It was a disaster,' she cried, gulping at a glass of wine. 'An unmitigated disaster.'

'So what happened?' Paula demanded. 'What did you do?'

By the time Corrie had finished relating the brief hour she'd spent in Cristos Bennati's company Paula was beside herself laughing. 'And you reckon you didn't make an impression?' she gasped. 'Oh, what I wouldn't give to have been there.'

'Well apart from my mortification you didn't miss much,' Corrie told her. 'I mean he's not what I expected at all. Oh, he's good-looking all right, too damned good-looking if you ask me, and God, does he know it! He didn't really impress me though, I mean not as much as I thought he would . . .'

'Corrie, this is me you're talking to.'

'I know who I'm talking to,' Corrie retorted. 'And I'm telling you that I didn't fancy him after all . . .'

'Corrie!'

'I didn't. Well, OK, I did, but he made me feel such a prat . . . All right, it was me who did that . . . But it was his fault. He made me say things I didn't mean . . .'

'Well how did he do that?'

'He just looked at me, that's how he did it.'

There was a silence at the end of the line, and Corrie took a deep breath which she eventually let go on a long sigh of resignation. 'Paula,' she said mournfully, 'I think I've fallen in love. I hate him, I detest him, I never want to see him again in my life . . . But he's the sexiest man alive, and I wanted to tear his clothes off right there and then and beg him to take me. The trouble was he fancied Annalise, well at least he looked at her like he did – he just looked at me as though he wished I would go away. I'm in agony, Paula. He's the only man I've ever met who's had anything like that effect on me.'

'Well at least you've met him,' Paula reminded her.

'Yes, at least I've met him.'

'Oh come on, don't sound so dejected. I mean what else were you expecting? That he'd fall at your feet and declare undying love?'

'It would have done for starters.'

'You shouldn't aim so high,' Paula laughed. 'He's a major film director, Corrie, he's probably got women chasing him all over the world.'

'I know, and I'm nothing special. But he's ruined me now for any other man. Do you think I should write to him and apologize for the way I behaved?'

'No I don't.'

'No, I suppose you're right. He probably wouldn't read it anyway. Oh, Paula, why has God blessed me with a taste in men beyond my capacity to pull? You can make that my epitaph when I die, if you like. Here lies Corrie Browne, spinster of this parish, God blessed her with a taste in men beyond her capacity to pull.'

'Oh shut up, Corrie. He's probably a bastard anyway. Now, tell me about Luke. Did you find out what happened when he went to see Radcliffe?'

'Yes. He doesn't know Bobby McIver, it was all a figment of my imagination.'

'You don't believe that, surely?'

'Yes, I do. All right, no I don't. But I can't think about anything other than Cristos Bennati right now.'

'Stop being such a wimp! Does Luke know that it was you who went to see Radcliffe?'

'Yes. And we talked about it, before Cristos arrived. He was furious at first, he said, but then he explained why . . . Oh, Paula, don't bug me about this now. My nerves have been in such a state all day, what with one thing and another, and as a result I've over-reacted about everything. I just want to forget about Luke Fitzpatrick now.'

And with her humiliating experience with Cristos Bennati to occupy her thoughts, that was precisely what Corrie did. For, she told herself, if Inspector Radcliffe was satisfied with what Luke had told him, then who was she to doubt it? OK, Luke's behaviour was odd sometimes, but her imagination was even odder. She read things into situations that just weren't there, like mistaking paint for blood, and frightened herself half to death doing it. What Luke had said about her first encounter with murder made sense; it had clearly spooked her to such a degree that she was starting to become obsessed by it. So it was time now, she decided, that they all, she in particular, put it behind them and stopped trying to play amateur detectives.

– 15 –

Phillip Denby was standing in the porch outside a small terraced house in Twickenham. He had rung the bell twice now, but there was still no answer. She was in there though, he was certain of it, she simply didn't want to let him in.

His handsome face was pinched and white as he turned to look up and down the suburban, tree-lined street. It was early in the evening and several people were about, mowing their lawns or washing their cars. A group of boys was playing in the garden three doors away, kicking a ball around and swearing like Irish navvies. Phillip winced to hear it.

He turned back to the front door. He should leave now, he told himself, he should just go away and leave her alone. It was what she wanted, and the thought almost broke his heart.

He walked the few paces down the garden path, pulled

open the gate and dug into his pocket for his car keys. He was on the point of getting into his car when he took one last look at the house and his heart contracted as he saw her standing at the door.

For a long time they simply looked at each other, until finally Pam stood back and held the door wide. Phillip's relief was so great that he started to shake. She was going to let him in, she was waiting there for him . . . He mustn't jump to any conclusions, he didn't know yet what she was thinking, or how she was feeling.

As he walked back up the garden path he was looking straight into her eyes. He thought she had aged in the past three days, but as he reached her she smiled, weakly, and he realized the tiredness in her eyes wasn't tiredness at all – it was anguish.

'I wondered if you would come,' she said.

'I had to. I had to know . . .' He looked away. 'If you'd prefer that I went . . .'

'No. I wanted you to come. You've just come sooner than I expected. I needed some time to think, you understand that, don't you?'

'Of course.'

'It's why I haven't been at the office,' she added. 'But I'm glad you've come now.' She closed the door behind him, then walked through to her sitting room. Phillip followed, all the time thinking of how much he had always loved this cluttered little house and the woman who lived in it. They had shared such wonderful times here, but now he felt awkward, as though he no longer belonged. His tension, his fear, was so great that it was difficult for him to move – he simply stood at the centre of the room and waited as Pam poured him a drink.

When she handed it to him Phillip gazed down into her deep, hazel eyes, wanting her to know how much he loved her, but that he would understand if things could never be the same between them now.

'It's all right,' she said softly. 'I know you didn't do it.'

For a brief moment Phillip's face froze, then suddenly his chest started to heave. He could barely catch his breath, the relief was so intense. 'Oh God,' he murmured, 'if you only knew how it felt to hear you say that.'

'Come here,' she whispered, and holding out her arms she drew him to her.

It was a long time before they broke their embrace, and both had tears on their cheeks when they did. Phillip looked again into her eyes and he knew that his love for this tiny woman, with her pretty face and enormous heart was now more precious to him than ever.

'I was so afraid,' he said. 'I still am, but knowing that you believe me . . . Oh Pam, how can I ever begin to tell you what that means to me?'

She smiled and taking him by the hand led him to the sofa beneath an open window. 'Have you decided what you're going to do?' she asked him.

He shook his head. 'I know I should go to the police, tell them everything . . . I intended to, but . . . It's Annalise and Corrie. It's the shame, I can't–let them suffer, Pam, please try to understand that.'

'But you didn't do it, Phillip.'

He let his head fall back. 'Oh, keep saying that, just keep saying it. If only you knew what it's been like, how at times I've even wondered myself if I did it. But I didn't, I couldn't . . .'

'I know you couldn't. That's why I believe you. You know that you didn't need to go to a prostitute for what you wanted, don't you? You could have come to me.'

Looking at her he cupped her cheek gently in his hand. 'And defile you with what I feel for Octavia? I could never have done that, Pam. I never will.'

She smiled and kissed his palm. 'Just in case you were wondering,' she said, 'I still love you. This hasn't changed anything – except perhaps that I love you more for trusting me.'

'I don't deserve you,' he whispered.

She laughed quietly and kissed him gently on the mouth. 'I still think you should go to the police,' she told him. 'In fact, you must.'

Phillip shook his head. 'We have to remember, Pam, that all the evidence points to me. That I could be convicted for this, even though I didn't do it. These things happen . . . The trouble is, they're holding an innocent man.'

'How do you know he's innocent?'

'Because Fitzpatrick is behind this. I don't know how he managed it, for all I know McIver could be some other poor bastard that Luke has got to, the same way he's got to me.'

'Phillip,' Pam said, after a pause, 'have you ever asked yourself how Luke knows so much about these murders?'

'The police tell him. The inspector in charge of the case is a friend of his.'

'Yes, but how does Luke know that you were the last person to see those girls alive?'

'If they smelt of Octavia's perfume, then I probably was.'

Pam shook her head. 'You couldn't have been. The murderer was the last person to see them alive. Now either he went to see them immediately after you, which in itself is a coincidence that stretches belief . . . OK, if there had only been one of them, but five! It's just not credible. Or the murderer is using this perfume too. Which is another coincidence I find very hard to swallow. Does Luke Fitzpatrick know when you go to see these women?'

'Not as far as I know.'

'But he might.'

They sat in thoughtful silence for some time, sipping their drinks and holding each other's hands. In the end, Pam said, 'I think Luke killed those women, Phillip.'

Phillip immediately got to his feet and went to stand in

front of the empty hearth. His back was turned so that Pam couldn't see his face, but she didn't have to to know what had made him stand up like that.

'You think so too, don't you?' she said.

'I can't prove it.'

'You don't have to. That's for the police to do. That's why you have to go and see them. Unless they know about the way Luke is blackmailing you, manipulating you or whatever other vile little game he's playing, then . . .'

'I can't do it, Pam! If I do then God only knows what he'll do to Annalise and Corrie.'

'But they're in far more danger from him if you don't. Oh, Phillip, I'm not trying to frighten you, but if Luke Fitzpatrick is killing those women, then you have to get him locked up as quickly as you can – before he does it again.'

'He won't, unless he can frame me. And if I don't go to see any more prostitutes . . .'

'It might not be as simple as that. Besides, five women are dead already, we can't forget that.'

Phillip was pressing his hands to his head. 'I don't know what to do, Pam. I just can't think straight anymore. He has my daughters, he has my wife . . . Jesus Christ, why is he doing this to me? What have I done to make him hate me like this?'

There was no answer Pam could give, so going to him she started to rub his shoulders, trying to ease his tension. 'Has he been to see you at all recently?' she asked.

'No. But he's spending more and more time with Annalise. Every time I call in to see her lately she's either with him or on her way to him.'

'And Corrie?'

Beneath her soothing fingers Pam had started to feel Phillip relax, but at the mention of Corrie's name his muscles tightened again. 'I don't know,' he answered. 'She works with him, of course, but anything more than that . . .

God, I'd like to kill that man for what he's doing to us. He's made me alienate my own daughter, Edwina's daughter. I owe Edwina so much . . . If only I could get him out of their lives.' He slammed a fist hard against the wall. 'Dear God, what does he want from me?'

'Not that you go to prison,' Pam answered. 'If he did, he'd have told the police what he knows himself by now.'

'So what *does* he want? He's got me, as they say, by the balls and I can't move. If it ever comes out that I might, just might, have been involved in what happened to those prostitutes then I'm finished.' He sighed. 'I wouldn't care, except for what it could do to Annalise and Corrie. I just can't drag them down with me.'

'Phillip, for heaven's sake, he's got you into such a state you're starting to talk as though you're guilty. OK, you visited the prostitutes, but there's no crime in that. Nothing is going to happen to you, or to Corrie and Annalise, if you confess . . .'

'Luke has other holds on me,' Phillip interrupted. 'You know that.'

'Octavia?'

Phillip nodded. 'Do you think I want Annalise to know what her mother's really like? If I go to the police it'll all come out, these things always do. And Fitzpatrick will see that they do. There's nothing I can do about that.'

'But if he did kill those women, Phillip, then something has to be done about that.'

The smirk on Luke's face was making Phillip feel sick. He'd only been here, in this coffee bar, a few minutes, and already he knew it was a mistake to have come. Confronting Luke Fitzpatrick was not the answer, especially when he didn't have one shred of evidence to back up what he knew deep down in his gut to be true. He waited with mounting impatience as Luke signed autographs for three middle-aged women, knowing full well that he was deliberately taking his time.

'I'm just asking you where all this is going to end?' Phillip repeated, when the women had at last returned to their own table. 'Can't you answer the question?'

'Where all what is going to end?' Luke said.

'You know what I'm talking about, man!' Phillip snapped.

Luke shrugged. 'It'll end, Phillip, when you give yourself up to the police.'

'For something I didn't do?'

'Didn't you?'

'You know damned well I didn't.'

'I'm afraid I don't know anything of the sort.'

'Then why aren't you telling the police yourself what you know?'

'I have my reasons.'

Phillip glared at him, knowing such hatred that his entire body ached with it. 'You do realize, don't you, that if I talk to the police then you will immediately be implicated yourself?' he said.

'How so?'

'Well, I should have to tell them about the way you've been harassing me, that it's because of that that I've decided to see them.'

'If you were to tell the police that,' Luke said, 'then I should have to make it public that I have been pimping for your wife. Oh, didn't you know that? Well, I have. It's stopped now, but for a while there she took a fancy to become a whore. I have the photographs, Octavia and I look at them together from time to time – they blow her mind. I could lend them to you if you like, perhaps you might get a little more success with her in the sack if you shared her fantasies.'

'You disgust me!' Phillip snarled. 'Almost as much as

she does. But I'm not here to talk about Octavia, I'm here to talk about those girls – and who killed them.'

'As far as I know, you did,' Luke grinned.

'Then who the hell is Bobby McIver?'

'A friend. One you should be extremely grateful to, since it looks like he's going to take the rap for you. Now, I have to be running along, I've got a date with one of your daughters.' He threw a handful of coins onto the table and stood up. 'Oh, and Phillip,' he said, as he picked up his jacket, 'I just thought you might like to know, that straight after the next time I screw Corrie, I'm going to ask Annalise to marry me.'

'Keep away from them!' Phillip cried. 'Just keep your filthy hands off my daughters!'

'But I'm only doing to them what you want to do yourself,' Luke said pleasantly.

Phillip gaped at him in horror. 'You're sick!' he gasped finally. 'You're insane.'

'But I'm not a murderer,' Luke grinned, and walked jauntily out of the coffee bar.

More than three weeks had gone by since Corrie had met Cristos Bennati, and still she couldn't get him out of her mind. It was making her so miserable and irritable that she was turning down all invitations to drinks, the cinema, private views or whatever else was on the agenda, for fear of boring everyone to tears. She was furious with herself for behaving like a spoiled brat who was sulking because it couldn't have what it wanted, but she just couldn't help feeling cheated.

'It wouldn't be so bad,' she told Paula on numerous occasions, 'if I didn't feel that someone up there was laughing at me. It's like God, or fate or whatever, has deliberately dangled him in front of my nose just to show me what I really want, then they've snatched him away. Ha! Ha! You can't have him!'

'Well if you didn't set your sights quite so high,' Paula told her.

'That's not my fault is it!' Corrie snapped back. 'I can't help the way I feel.'

She could hear the grin in Paula's voice as she answered. 'Were it anyone else, Corrie, I'd find it easier to sympathize with you, but you're living in the clouds. Cristos Bennati's an international movie director, one of the best in the world.'

'I know that!'

'OK, if you feel that strongly about him then get out there and do something about it.'

'Like what?'

'Don't ask me, you're the one with all the imagination.'

'All right then, I will,' Corrie retorted. The question was what?

The programme about transsexuals had now been transmitted, and Corrie and Annalise were currently investigating the increasing number of homosexual men, and the corresponding increase in the number of single women. This subject was depressing Corrie no end, since she was haunted night and day by the fact that she couldn't have Cristos, and if these horrendous statistics were anything to go by, there wasn't much hope of meeting anyone else.

'I'll be glad when we get this programme out of the way,' she grumbled to Annalise one Saturday afternoon when they were on their way back from a series of interviews in the north. 'Meeting all these single women is beginning to get on my nerves.'

'Well, if I have my way you'll be sharing a car with a married woman before much longer,' Annalise said chirpily. 'Anyway, we've only got the editing to do now, so you'd better start racking your brains as to what we do next.'

'Don't think I'm not trying,' Corrie sighed. Which she was, though that in itself was annoying her intensely, since she was trying – and failing – to conjure up a story that would take them to Los Angeles. Exactly what she thought she was going to achieve there as far as Cristos was concerned was a question she didn't care to answer, she simply scanned the newspapers every day in the hope that something in the vicinity of Hollywood would leap out at her begging to be made into a programme.

Annalise knew precisely what was going on in Corrie's mind, and the following morning when she called in to see Corrie at her studio, and found her submerged in the Sunday papers, Annalise burst out laughing.

'I can't believe I'm doing it,' Corrie wailed. 'I'm going off my head. I must be to think that I could stand a chance with a man like that, especially after what happened. What the hell would he ever see in me anyway, even if I hadn't behaved like a blithering idiot?'

'Corrie!' Annalise cried. 'I think it's about time you woke up to just how lovely you really are. Now stop putting yourself down and go and get me a cup of coffee.'

'Get it yourself,' Corrie said. 'You know where it is.'

'Oh, great hostess you are.'

'I'm depressed. You should be sympathetic.'

'Depressed because you can't have your wicked way with Cristos Bennati!'

'No, because no one else wants me either.'

'Corrie!' Annalise virtually screamed this time. 'Are you blind, or what? Just about every man on that crew up in Leeds had his tongue hanging out for you. You've only got to walk down the street to get heads turning . . .'

'If you think that then you've taken leave of your senses,' Corrie informed her. 'Besides which, we're not talking about your average man in the street, are we? We're talking about Cristos Bennati. A man who wouldn't even lift his eyelids never mind turn his head to look at me. Which he proved . . .'

'If you really believe that,' Annalise interrupted, 'then

why are you bothering to look for a story that will take you right to his doorstep?'

'Because I've taken leave of my senses too. Oh God, I need help. I mean just who do I think I am that I could actually . . . Everything's gone to my head. I'm working in telly, I've got a flat in London, I dress like a career woman, I look like a different person and now I'm a basket case. Well, as of this minute, I'm giving up my search for an LA hook on a story.'

'Good,' Annalise grinned.

'I mean it.'

'I don't disbelieve you. Now, can I get you a coffee?'

'Yes. By the way, why are you here? I thought you were spending the day with Luke.'

'I am. But I thought I'd call in and see you first. That's all right, isn't it?'

'It would be if I hadn't seen you yesterday. I'm getting bored with you.'

Hurling a cushion at her Annalise went off to the kitchen. 'Not half so bored as I am with Cristos Bennati,' she threw back over her shoulder.

'I don't want to hear his name mentioned again,' Corrie said loftily. 'Every time it is I promptly go and make a fool of myself. So that's it! Over!'

Ten days later Annalise threw an envelope onto Corrie's desk. 'OK, hot shot kid,' she said, 'you want to contrive a trip to Hollywood, then there's your material.'

Corrie would have liked nothing better than to have been able to throw the envelope back, but already tiny fireworks of excitement were exploding into life. Pulling a wry face at Annalise she emptied the envelope onto her desk and picked up the documents that spilled out. Since they contained so much legal jargon it took her some time to read them, but when she'd finished she was still none the wiser. She looked across at Annalise, who was now sitting at her own desk facing Corrie's.

'Let's do a programme about rape,' Annalise said.

'Yes, why not,' Corrie answered. 'But what has that got to do with Hollywood?'

'Don't you know a rather famous person in Hollywood who was raped by her husband?' Annalise replied.

Corrie's eyes widened.

'Precisely. Felicity! She'll be sure to give us an interview, and no doubt a few colourful opinions on the fact that there are now moves afoot to protect the man's identity as well as the woman's when it comes to trial.'

Corrie was looking thoughtful. 'And while we're in the States,' she added, 'we can try to get an interview with William Kennedy Smith. You remember, the guy who was cleared of raping that girl at the Kennedy mansion in Palm Springs. Yes, he's just the guy we want. He might have been cleared, but mud sticks, we could find out what he has to say about it. Annalise, you're a genius. Do you think we'll get it past Luke?'

'We can but try,' Annalise answered. 'He's in his office now, why don't we go and ask.'

Corrie shook her head. 'Put it forward as your idea, otherwise he'll think it's just a ruse for me to get to Hollywood.'

'Well that's what it is, isn't it?'

Corrie pursed her lips. 'Sometimes, Annalise Kapsakis . . .'

By the time Annalise had finished Luke was already laughing. 'If you think I can't see through that,' he said, 'then you must . . . Corrie!' he shouted, seeing her walk past his door. 'Corrie, come in here a moment, will you?'

Looking distinctly uncomfortable Corrie walked into his office.

'I'd like to talk to Corrie alone for a moment, if you don't mind, Annalise,' Luke said.

Annalise shrugged, then winking at Corrie she went back to her desk.

'So,' Luke said, getting up and walking round Corrie to close the door, 'you want to do a story on rape and you want to do it in Hollywood. This wouldn't, by any chance, have anything to do with one Cristos Bennati, would it?'

'No, of course not,' Corrie denied hotly. 'Annalise and I just thought that this proposed Amendment would make a good programme. And that Felicity would make a good interviewee.'

Luke was nodding. 'So would Kennedy Smith,' he said. 'Did you think about him?'

'Yes.'

'Have you managed to contact him?'

'Annalise only told me about it ten minutes ago.'

'Right. Well, it's a good idea, it'll make a good programme, with or without Felicity Burridge. So, if you want her included in the hope of getting to see Bennati again, I'll sanction it – on one condition.'

Corrie waited.

'That you sleep with me tonight.'

Outwardly Corrie barely even flinched, but as she stared back at him, for the moment bereft of speech, a swell of unmitigated fury rushed through her. Since the night she had met Cristos Luke had seemed so close to Annalise that Corrie had truly believed that his infatuation, or whatever it was, with her was at an end. The profound relief Corrie had felt at that was immeasurable, since it had not only enabled her to sleep a lot easier at night, but it had had a dramatic effect on Annalise too. But now here he was asking her, no blackmailing her, into going to bed with him.

She knew her disgust showed, but she didn't care. 'Felicity will make a good interviewee,' she spat, slapping his hand away as he tried to touch her, 'but you're right, we can do it without her.'

'But you wouldn't get to see Bennati then,' Luke reminded her.

Corrie's eyes blazed furiously into his.

'Oh?' Luke commented with surprise. 'I thought you might have had something to say about that.'

Still Corrie refused to speak. In truth she didn't dare go any further. He was her boss, after all, no matter that he was behaving like a prize bastard.

'Well,' he sighed, going to sit back in his chair, 'I think the programme would benefit from Felicity's input, as it happens. And I also think that you should see Bennati again, since you obviously need convincing that he's just not interested in you. So I'll sanction the programme anyway.'

'Don't do me any favours,' Corrie muttered under her breath.

'You can hire a crew locally,' he went on, 'I'll give you some contacts before you go and you can take Peter Fredericks as your reporter/interviewer.'

'Why him?'

'Why not him?'

Corrie shrugged. 'OK, Peter Fredericks.'

'Unless Felicity can put you up,' he continued, 'you should stay at the Four Seasons on South Doheny. Hire yourself a car at the airport, you'll need it. Justify your stay in Los Angeles by finding other interviewees besides Felicity, then, if you do manage to get Kennedy Smith you can fly down to Florida – or wherever he's to be found these days. Make sure to draw yourself a decent float, you'll have to tip all the way out there, particularly if you're staying in a hotel. Now go and speak to Billy and have him book your flights.'

'I need more time,' Corrie pointed out. 'I haven't made one phone call yet.'

'Do it when you get there, the time difference will only hamper you here. I'll give you some contacts for people who might be able to help.'

'Thank you,' she said flatly. 'Is that all?'

He nodded.

'Oh Corrie,' he said, as she was opening the door. She turned back. 'With regard to the other matter.' From his expression there was no doubt in her mind as to what he was referring to. 'You'll come to me in the end, you know.'

'Don't hold your breath,' she hissed.

Luke grinned. 'Oh, you will,' he said. 'And shall I tell you why?'

Corrie simply glared at him.

'Ask Annalise to come in again, will you?'

After Corrie had given Annalise the message she took herself off to the ladies to be alone. She was badly shaken by those few minutes with Luke – it was the first time he'd actually shown her the side to him that she'd always believed existed, and she was still reeling from the way he had done it so openly. And that underlying threat in his words, if she was reading him correctly, was not a threat directed only at her, it was directed at Annalise too.

Luke and Siobhan were walking along the beach. Siobhan's hair was covered by a scarf, and despite the sunshine she was huddled into her coat. Luke was holding her hand, swinging it gently as they walked and talked.

'So Annalise and Corrie are to be off to LÁ on Monday,' he was saying, and frowned at the way his voice was being submerged in an Irish brogue. 'Corrie's wanting to see Cristos Bennati again. She'll end up making a fool of herself, to be sure, like she did the last time, but why should I worry? Whatever else she does, she'll be making a good programme.'

He lifted Siobhan's hand to his mouth and kissed it tenderly, all the while gazing out to sea. 'No, I haven't forgiven her yet for what she did,' he said, 'it made me very angry, as you know. Her father came to see me, you know. He thinks I killed the whores. Oh, he didn't say so in so many words, but that's what he thinks.' Luke started to laugh then, but there was no one to see the way his lips curled back over his gums baring his teeth like a snarling dog. The air around him was thick and clammy and clung to his face in tiny globules of sweat. 'We know who killed them, don't we, Siobhan?' he sniggered. 'Oh, to be sure, we know who killed them. He killed the whores! Phillip Denby, Phillip Fitzpatrick Denby killed the whores!'

'Actually,' he continued, as though the brief and sudden outburst had never occurred – yet still his voice was shifting between an English and an Irish accent, 'I'm considering making Corrie a producer before very much longer . . . Yes, you're right, we'll be having all the producers we need, but I'll be sorting something out.' He gave a sad smile and pulled Siobhan to a halt. 'It'll mean hurting Annalise again,' he told her, 'you don't like it when I do that, do you? Oh, Annalise will forgive me in the end, she always does. Am I worried about Corrie's crush on Bennati, did you say?' He shrugged. 'To be sure I am.' He laughed again, a deep resonant sound vibrating balefully through his jowls. 'Yes, you're right, that is why I'll be making her a producer, to see if I can be winning her over. I'm not thinking she can be bought so easily though, but I have a plan. I'll be flying out to LA in the middle of the week to join them.' He lifted Siobhan's face in his hands and looked searchingly into her empty blue eyes. The pain in his own was as infinite and as deep as the murky grey sea pushing waves onto the shore. 'It means I won't see you for a couple of weeks, my darling,' he murmured. 'Do you mind? To be sure, I'll be thinking about you all the time. I love you, Siobhan,' he whispered. 'You believe that don't you? Yes, to be sure you do.'

They walked on in silence, their feet sinking into the sand as they went. Apart from a man and his dog, way in the distance, the beach was deserted. Every now and again Luke used his fingers to comb the thick, blond hair away from his face; he didn't appear to notice the way the surf was lapping over Siobhan's sandals, saturating her ankle socks with salt water and curling seaweed about her ankles. His face was turned into the breeze, his mind was bent on the nightmarish past.

Finally he stopped again and took Siobhan in his arms. 'They none of them mean anything compared to you, Siobhan,' he told her gently, 'but I have to do this, you understand that don't you? I have to find love elsewhere. And yes, in the end it will be Corrie. She can help me, Siobhan, it was you who made me see that. But you and Annalise will always be the ones I love. You, Siobhan, most of all.'

– 16 –

Wearing her cut-off jeans, a bikini top and a muslin scarf around her hair Felicity was waiting to greet Corrie and Annalise when they finally drew up in their hire car outside the colonial style mansion on Alpine Drive. Felicity was sitting the six million dollar house for a friend and was just dying to show it off to someone, especially someone English.

'Welcome to the Sunshine State,' she cried, as Corrie leapt from the car and hugged her with, Felicity remarked wryly, a disgusting amount of energy for someone who'd just undergone an eleven hour flight.

'I thought we'd never get here,' Annalise grumbled as she climbed out of the car to embrace Felicity herself. 'It's like a jungle out there.'

'Oh, stop moaning,' Corrie laughed, sweeping her awe-struck eyes across the imposing red-brick façade of the house. 'She's been like that ever since we got off the plane.'

'Well, you didn't have to do the driving, did you?' Annalise pointed out. 'She's so excited,' she added in a whisper to Felicity, 'she's like a dog with two tails.'

'I heard that,' Corrie called out. She was standing at the foot of the front steps now, using a hand to shield her eyes as she looked up and down the Ionic columns flanking a porch the height of the house. 'If I stay here long enough,' she said, 'I'll start thinking I'm Scarlett O'Hara. It's amazing!' Then spotting the security camera to one side of the front door she peered up at it and pulled a face.

'Don't do that, you'll frighten the maid,' Felicity told her, as she helped Annalise drag the luggage from the boot.

'Maid!' Corrie squealed. 'You've got a maid?'

'Everyone has, darling,' Felicity drawled. 'By the way, where's this reporter chappie you mentioned on the phone?'

'Gone to stay with a boyfriend in Sherman Oaks,' Annalise answered with raised eyebrows. 'Shit, this is heavy. What have you got in here, Corrie? Corrie! Come and help with the luggage, will you?'

But Corrie was already inside the house. 'I don't believe it,' she murmured, as Felicity and Annalise came in behind her. 'It's . . . Well, it's . . .' She looked at Annalise, waiting for her to supply the words, but after Annalise had taken a good look round the vast entrance hall, with its flowered velvet and silk wallpaper, rococo framed paintings, oak floor with marble inlay, and black lacquered staircase sporting a zebra stripe carpet, she turned back to Corrie at a loss.

'Fucking awful?' Felicity suggested.

Corrie looked warily at Felicity, but when she saw the laughter in Felicity's eyes she allowed herself a grin. But the hall was nothing compared with what was to come.

After zig-zagging them back and forth across the hall to visit a study the size of a boardroom which was crammed full of mind-boggling technology, the family room with its immense white leather sofas, ankle-deep carpet and carved ivory and brass fireplace, the television room with four VCRs, a TV set that could easily double as a small movie screen and a whole library of video tapes, Felicity led them into the dining room. Actually it was more like a banqueting hall and had the most perplexing mix of modern and antique furnishings. Then came the den, followed by the breakfast room and from there into the biggest kitchen Corrie had ever seen. In it were things she'd never seen before, like double sub-zero refrigerators and a butler's pantry.

'It's kosher compatible too,' Felicity boasted, not without irony, and pulled open two doors to reveal two dish-washers, then waved an arm towards the double salad-washer in the central unit.

'Come and see this,' Annalise called out, and following the direction of her voice Corrie walked out through a set of French windows into a conservatory which ran the whole width of the house. In it she counted no less than eight wicker sofas and five marble coffee tables, all of which were surrounded by a forest of potted plants and a bar as big as a single-decker bus.

'It's called a solarium here, not a conservatory,' Felicity told them, kicking one of the deep pile white rugs back into place.

'Oh!' Corrie exclaimed, and started backing away from an assortment of stuffed animal heads peering down at her from the wall.

Next came the kidney-shaped swimming pool, complete with Jacuzzi, which was squashed onto the first terrace of the garden with just a small paved area for a twelve-seater table and twelve padded arm-chairs. There were changing rooms and a sauna to one side, and a life-size replica of the Trevi fountain the other. A small army of gnomes were fishing in the fountain! The entire garden, with its occasional perfect flower bed and towering palm trees was a blaze of vivid colours which seemed to be melting at the edges into the shimmering heat. 'Can you smell the pollution?' Annalise asked Corrie, turning up her nose. 'Ugh! You can taste it even.'

Down on the next terrace was the tennis court. Both

Corrie and Annalise gaped with frank incredulity when they walked onto it, since an audience had been created on all four sides by a life-size mural.

'This place is a joke, isn't it?' Corrie whispered to Felicity. 'It has to be. I mean, no one in their right mind . . .'

'You wait till you see upstairs,' Felicity laughed. 'It gets worse.'

And she wasn't kidding. But the opulence, the sheer luxury of it all was awesome. After wading through yet more carpets to the games room with its one-armed bandits, snooker table, antique juke-box, card tables and Leroy Newman sketches of the stars, came the bedrooms. The one Felicity had assigned Corrie would have swallowed Corrie's entire studio, and Corrie, who was beginning to recover from her initial shock and starting to enjoy herself, knew that she was just going to love sleeping in that king-size bed and pressing all the buttons around it to find out what they did. There were walk-in, *walk-in!*, wardrobes which could have housed more clothes than she'd probably ever own in her life, and a separate room for shoes! But it was the bathroom that finally did for Corrie. She simply couldn't believe what her own eyes were seeing. Everything in it, right down to the loo roll holder, was of red-veined marble, or brass, or both. There were mirrors everywhere, and Corrie wasn't at all sure she was going to enjoy looking at herself from so many angles. The bath was made for four people, Felicity told her, but the shower only for one. There was even a telephone on the wall next to the bath, and a portable TV with remote control.

'This is nothing,' Felicity said, as Corrie looked like she didn't know whether to laugh or throw up. 'There are two bathrooms off my room, they call them his and hers bathrooms. Both of them are as big as this one, but I have to say, slightly more subtle in decor.'

'Is this an orgasm giver?' Annalise said, bending over to turn on the bidet. A fountain of water shot out, and squealing with delight, Annalise cried, 'Oh it is! Corrie, you're not going to know yourself.'

'You can borrow it if you like,' Corrie said, generously.

'She's got one of her own,' Felicity said, and took them off to see Annalise's room.

'It's hideous,' Annalise gasped, flinging herself onto the bed, 'and I'm going to love it. By the way, who owns this place, Felicity?'

'A friend,' Felicity answered. 'He's a TV producer.'

'With a wild sense of humour?' Corrie added.

'No. All this is absolutely for real. It might not appeal to your taste, but you have to understand that out here it's a must to display your wealth in every way possible. They wear it too. And drive it. And talk about it all the time. To us poor, uptight Brits this way of life might be seriously grotesque, but you have to admit it's bloody fascinating. Thank God not all of America is like it though, but Los Angeles isn't like the rest of America. You'll either love it here, or hate it. Personally I love it – for a visit. No way could I live here all the time. Anyway, I'll leave you two to clean up and meet you downstairs when you're ready. It's too hot to have a drink outside so we'll have it in the solarium.'

Ten minutes later, since she didn't have three more people to help fill up her bath, Corrie was standing in the shower tentatively turning the knobs in the hope of finding some water. Nothing was happening, so she pushed the button above them, and to her amazement no less than five shower heads suddenly sprang into life, pounding her blissfully from all directions.

I could get used to this, she grinned to herself as she started to twirl, and letting the water cascade luxuriously over her she started fantasizing herself towards the dizzy heights of movie stardom. She didn't get too far though before she found herself wondering if Cristos's house was anything like this one. The very idea that it might be took the smile from her face – the thought of him having so much money, together with his talent and his fame, was just too daunting to contemplate. But he had to be worth millions, and this, to Corrie's surprise, was the first time that had actually occurred to her. It was a distressingly uncomfortable realization, for that, probably more than anything else, was at last bringing home to her the utter hopelessness of her situation. But it wasn't only the money, it was the fact that he lived here, in this dreadful town, that he was a part of this society! Never before had it occurred to Corrie just how far apart their two worlds might be, but it was coming home to her now, and to her dismay she realized that after just these few short hours in Los Angeles she was already starting to feel like she was on another planet rather than in another country.

Fearing that she was becoming prejudiced before even giving herself a chance to get to know the place, Corrie made a supreme effort to banish Cristos from her mind and entered into the spirit of things by trying out the bidet.

Yes, she decided a little while later, she should very definitely think about getting one installed. But those few moments of pleasure were quickly displaced by the dismal reality that never in her life had she reached an orgasm with a man. Inevitably Cristos returned to her mind then, making her feel gloomier still.

A little later she found Felicity in the solarium, going over the scenes she was shooting the following afternoon, and Annalise joined them almost immediately.

'Right,' Annalise said, rubbing her hands together. 'Let's get down to what this is all about, shall we? Have you found out yet, Felicity, where Cristos is filming?'

Corrie's head snapped up. 'Have you been talking behind my back?' she demanded hotly.

'We most certainly have,' Felicity grinned. 'And to answer your question, Annalise, he's just this week moved from the lot to the Mayan Theatre downtown.'

'Good for him,' Corrie retorted. 'I hope he and his movie will be very happy together. Now, I'm going to sit out by the pool and read through the notes I've made for the programme *we have come here to make*. If you'll excuse me, ladies.'

'She's just embarrassed,' Annalise whispered to Felicity.

'Can't say I'm surprised,' Felicity remarked. 'This is a mighty big fish she's trying to land.' And shaking her head almost in wonder, she added, 'I only suggested she met him, you know, just to say she had, I never dreamt she'd take it this seriously.'

'Well, I'm afraid she has. I guess she's going to end up disappointed, well she must know that, but . . .'

'Maybe not that disappointed,' Felicity interrupted with a smile. 'A mate of mine is the unit publicist on *Past Lives Present*. I've already sounded him out about going along to take a look one day, he said he'll get back to me.'

'Well done you,' Annalise remarked. 'Do you think he'll swing it?'

Felicity shrugged. 'It should be easier now they're off the lot, but all major movies are closed sets no matter where they're shooting. Better not let Corrie know this, but the final decision as to whether we can visit will be down to Cristos himself. Ah,' she said as the doorbell sounded, 'that'll be Rita. She's an old friend of mine from way back. She writes one of the major American soaps, but I can't for the life of me remember what it's called. Anyway, I've invited her round for the evening, I hope you don't mind.'

As it turned out neither Corrie nor Annalise minded in the slightest, since Rita seemed to have missed her vocation as a writer – she should have been a comedienne. Nevertheless, as funny as her stories were about writing for television, both Corrie and Annalise were profoundly relieved that working in documentary television was nothing like the nightmare it sounded working in drama television. All that interference and committee decision-making – and sponsorship! It was a wonder anything ever got made at all.

Over the next few days Corrie and Annalise set about ringing round Luke's contacts and lining up a crew, while Felicity was gone most of the time, shooting her own movie on the lot at Universal. Corrie and Annalise managed to squeeze in a few touristy things too, like having their photographs taken with the Hollywood sign in the background, doing the Universal Studios' tour and a shopping trip on Rodeo Drive. It was there, browsing round the designer shops, that Corrie got some idea of what Felicity meant about people wearing their wealth. There was nothing simple to be found anywhere, everything just dripped sequins and glitter. But the night they went to the Four Seasons Hotel to meet up with some more friends of Felicity's Corrie really had her eyes opened.

There was no getting away from it, she realized despondently as she watched a sea of bejewelled and bewigged humanity ebb and flow before her, this really was a town of supreme superficiality. She was truly sorry she felt that way, since she wanted to like the place, more than anything else she wanted to love it, but it just wasn't happening. It was like looking into a swimming pool, she thought; it all looked so wonderful, as though there was nothing else in the world that could be more inviting than that pool, but every time you tried to immerse yourself in the water you found that it wasn't water at all, but glass. There was no way in because there was no depth, no reality, only illusion. She found it both touching and tragic to watch the grotesque grasping at a lost youth; women who simply made themselves ridiculous by wearing mini-skirts and high heels at the age of sixty or more; and sun dried old men who decorated their entourage with the youngest, blondest and leggiest females in town. But as depressing as Corrie found it all, Annalise, who had been there before, was frequently able to make her laugh about the sheer awfulness of it. And

Annalise making her laugh was something in itself that delighted Corrie, since she had been worried that Annalise might have started to become difficult, being so far from Luke. But if anything she and Annalise were developing a closeness that pleased Corrie no end, and at the same time Annalise seemed happier than Corrie had ever known her.

But Corrie soon discovered why Annalise was so happy when they returned late one afternoon from their first filmed interview down at Santa Monica to find Luke looking very much at home in the solarium.

'Just thought I'd pop out and see how you're getting along,' he laughed, as Annalise threw her arms around him. Corrie simply stood there, holding his eyes and allowing her anger to show. She realized of course, that Annalise had known he was coming, and she was intensely annoyed at Annalise for not telling her. She became even more irritated as the evening wore on and she was forced to watch them nuzzling and whispering and giggling like silly lovebirds.

'Jealous,' Felicity told her, 'not irritated, jealous. They're in love and so are you. But theirs is working out and yours isn't.'

'It's not as simple as that,' Corrie retorted. 'There are things I just don't want to go into that make his presence here . . . Well, unacceptable.'

'She's happy, I thought that was what you wanted.'

'Of course I do. But . . .'

'Then it's time now for your happiness, don't you think? You've got a free day the day after tomorrow haven't you? Good. So have I. So what about going to the set of *Past Lives Present?*'

Corrie instantly came over so hot and cold it was like she was having some kind of attack. 'No! No,' she said quickly. 'I can't do it. It's too humiliating, and I won't.'

'Oh yes you will. I've gone to a lot of trouble to get us onto that set, at least my friend Carl has, so you're going whether you like it or not.'

'Going where?' Luke enquired, strolling into the kitchen at that moment.

'Nowhere,' Corrie answered hastily. 'Actually, I'm glad you're here, Luke, because I wanted to talk to you about the Kennedy Smith interview. He doesn't want to do it.'

'Who did you speak to?' Luke asked.

'I'll leave you to it,' Felicity said. 'Dinner's in an hour, I'm having it sent in.'

She wandered outside to find Annalise swimming in the pool and sitting down on the edge with her drink, she allowed her legs to dangle in the water. 'I've set it up,' she told Annalise, as Annalise swam over to her.

'When for?'

'The day after tomorrow. The trouble is, Corrie says she won't go.'

'Oh, she will,' Annalise said, dismissively. 'She's just playing hard to get.'

'Yeah, well, all the same I think I'm going to need your help persuading her.'

'You got it,' Annalise grinned.

But when it came to it Annalise was no longer there to lend her help.

If there was one thing Corrie loved about Los Angeles it was the service. Nothing she'd ever encountered before came even close to it, and sending someone else to park the car seemed, to her, a luxury in the extreme. But even that was starting to wear a little thin now, as she and Annalise climbed out of their car at the Beverly Hills Hotel and handed their keys to a jockey.

'If one more person tells me to have a nice day I'm going to tell them to fuck off,' she declared.

'Oh, come on, don't be in a bad mood,' Annalise laughed, taking Corrie's arm as they strolled along the red carpet towards the hotel's front entrance. 'It's not your fault today's a foul up. You didn't have much time to set it up, did you?'

'That's not the point,' Corrie snapped. 'The crew and Peter Fredericks are half way to Pasadena and we're here!'

'Yes, but they're on their way back, aren't they?' Annalise reminded her. 'And look at it this way, it'll give you more time to prime the interviewee.'

'Stop being so reasonable!' Corrie stormed. 'As if there's not enough pleasantness going about this town, and now you're at it too. It's getting on my nerves.'

Annalise turned away before Corrie could see she was laughing. She knew only too well what was eating Corrie, but knew better than to bring up the subject of Cristos at that moment. Besides, now that they had some time to spare . . . 'I think,' she said, glancing at Corrie from the corner of her eye, 'that I might just pop back to the house for a while, see what Luke's doing with himself.'

'Yes, why don't you do that?' Corrie said. 'And leave me here to cope with everything.'

'You'll do it admirably,' Annalise replied, giving Corrie a resounding kiss on the cheek. 'Do you mind if I take the car?'

'No, you might as well. After all, I'm not going anywhere am I?'

Corrie's face was as sour as it could be as she turned to watch Annalise skip back down the canopied walkway. She knew that even if she hadn't messed up the addresses for today that Annalise would have cried off at some point, since she'd heard Luke tell her to as they were leaving that morning. And no doubt, the minute Annalise got into the car, she'd pick up the phone and call Luke to tell him she'd managed to pull it off.

Which was precisely what Annalise did, and only ten minutes after that she was parking the car in the mansion's crescent drive and taking out her set of house keys. As far as she could remember Felicity was filming today, so she and Luke were in for a long, luxurious and uninterrupted session of whatever Luke wanted to do. Already Annalise could feel herself starting to tingle.

As she was letting herself in through the front door though she started to frown. She really wished that Corrie liked Luke a bit more, not that Corrie had ever said that she didn't, but Annalise could tell. For a long time, knowing that Corrie had been to bed with Luke herself, Annalise had thought that Corrie was jealous, but she didn't think so any more. No, Corrie very definitely didn't like Luke, and that really bothered Annalise. For some reason what Corrie thought mattered. In fact, it mattered a lot. Annalise experienced a pang of guilt then, that she had left Corrie alone at the Beverly Hills, feeling, Annalise guessed, utterly wretched about Cristos. It just didn't seem fair, somehow, that she, Annalise, had everything she wanted, when Corrie was so alone. Corrie didn't even have a mother and father, but, Annalise reminded herself, she had plenty of friends who really cared about her. She wished that Corrie could get over this crush on Cristos though, it was really getting her down, and Annalise hated to see Corrie unhappy. But who could say, Corrie might pull it off in the end. OK, with Cristos being who he was the odds were stacked heavily against it, but stranger things . . . In fact, if she thought about it, if she really stretched her imagination, Annalise could actually see them together. Corrie's aversion to Los Angeles might prove a problem though, but Annalise guessed that Corrie had only taken a dislike to it in order to protect herself. If things were to work out with Cristos Corrie would no doubt fall instantly in love with the place.

By now Annalise had searched the entire downstairs and the garden, but there was no sign of Luke. Guessing that he was probably upstairs sleeping she decided to go and climb into bed beside him, snuggle up and wait for him to realize she was there.

Yes, she thought, trying not to wince at the zebra carpet

as she climbed the stairs, if miracles were to be believed in then Corrie really might find what she wanted with Cristos, and then she'd know what it was like to be in love. She'd understand how wonderful it felt to know that someone had flown half way round the world to be with her, the way Luke had, to see her. She was outside her bedroom now, and it suddenly occurred to her that if Luke was awake it would be a wonderful surprise for him if she were to walk into the room stark naked. So, with not much to take off, Annalise slipped quickly out of her clothes and dropped them in a pile at her feet.

Placing a hand on each of the handles she gingerly pushed the double doors open. She was being deliberately quiet in case Luke was asleep. Yes, he probably was, she decided, since the curtains were drawn and the room was in semi-darkness. Then she looked at the bed and what she saw there caused the blood to drain from her face.

'What the fuck!' Luke cried, looking back over his shoulder.

'Oh my God!' Felicity cried. She was on all fours and buried her head in her arms.

'Get out of here!' Luke yelled. 'Get the fuck out!'

But Annalise couldn't move. Her eyes were riveted to where Luke's body was joined with Felicity's. Briefly, the image of the three of them in bed together, all that time ago, passed through her mind. She hadn't wanted that, but Luke had insisted, and if Luke wanted it, as long as she was a part of it . . . But now was different. Now, he was shutting her out. He was telling her to go – she wasn't a part of this.

'What the fuck are you just standing there for?' Luke seethed. 'Didn't you hear me? Get out!'

'Luke!' Felicity cried. 'Luke, for God's sake!'

'You knew I was coming,' Annalise whispered, barely hearing her own voice over the thudding in her ears. 'Luke, I called you, I told you I was coming.'

But Luke wasn't listening.

'Luke!' Annalise murmured.

'*Get the fuck out of here!*' he yelled, still jerking himself in and out of Felicity.

Dully Annalise turned to pick up her clothes. In a daze she stumbled down over the stairs, pulling on her shorts and her T-shirt. When she got outside the car was still there, where she'd left it, for some reason that surprised her.

She got in, started it up, and drove slowly out into the street. It was all right, there was no need to panic, she told herself. She'd be with Corrie soon, Corrie would make it all right.

'Hi,' Corrie said, dropping her clipboard, stopwatch and heavy bag onto a chair in the hall. 'Where is everyone?'

'Luke's gone out,' Felicity answered.

'And Annalise?' Corrie grimaced as she inspected her sun-burned face in the mirror.

'I think I'd better get you a drink,' Felicity answered.

'God, I don't look that bad, do I?' Corrie asked, seriously.

Felicity didn't answer, she simply turned and walked through to the kitchen.

Corrie followed her, and picking up an apple from the fruit bowl she perched on the edge of a high stool. 'Annalise go out with Luke, did she?' she asked, biting into the apple.

'No. No, she didn't go out with Luke.'

There was something in Felicity's manner that made Corrie stop chewing and look at her. 'Then where is she?' Corrie asked.

'I was hoping you might be able to answer that question,' Felicity said.

Corrie's eyes were suddenly very narrow. 'What's happened?' she said. 'She was coming here. When I last saw her . . .'

'She came,' Felicity interrupted. 'She was here about two hours ago . . . I thought she might have come back to you.'

By now Corrie was trying very hard not to panic. 'Why? Why should she have come back to me?'

Felicity only looked at her.

'For God's sake, Fliss, *what happened*?'

Corrie listened then, in appalled silence, to what had taken place when Annalise had returned to the house.

'I'm sorry,' Felicity cried. 'I didn't know she was coming. I didn't . . . Oh shit! There's no excuse, I shouldn't have been in bed with him in the first place. But I thought . . .'

'It doesn't matter,' Corrie interrupted. 'All that matters is where she is now.'

Felicity shrugged. 'Like I said, I thought she'd come to you.'

'She might have,' Corrie answered, 'but I wasn't there. We switched locations at the last minute. Oh God, where can she have gone? Where's Luke?'

'I don't know. He just said he was going out. He left about half an hour ago.'

'I should have known something like this would happen,' Corrie cried, starting towards the phone.

'Look, Corrie, I know this is my fault, that . . .'

'No, don't blame yourself, Felicity. It's not your fault. Believe me, it's not. Did she take the car?'

Felicity nodded.

Corrie was dialling the number of the Beverly Hills Hotel. 'She might still be there,' she said, as she waited for someone to answer.

An hour later between them Corrie and Felicity had rung round just about every hotel in Beverly Hills, and every hospital too. No one had heard of Annalise Kapsakis. They tried all the airlines then to see if she'd flown back to London, but it didn't appear that she had.

'I don't know what else we can do,' Corrie cried frantically. 'She could be anywhere.'

'Like in a bar getting drunk,' Felicity suggested.

Corrie nodded. 'I'm afraid you're probably right. Come on, we'll have to go and look for her.'

It was approaching midnight by the time they gave up the search and returned home. They'd combed just about every bar on Sunset Strip and dozens of others too, but Los Angeles was such a big place they could go on for ever and still not find her. As Felicity closed the front door behind them Corrie heard a noise coming from the television room and running across the hall she burst in through the door to find Luke idly flicking through the channels.

'Where's Annalise?' Corrie demanded. 'Where is she?'

Luke shrugged. 'I presumed she was with you.'

'Have you heard from her?' Felicity asked. 'Has she called at all?'

'No,' he answered.

'Well don't you care where she might be?' Corrie stormed.

'She'll be out somewhere getting drunk, I expect,' Luke answered casually.

For a moment Corrie was speechless. She looked at Felicity, but as she turned back to Luke, obviously about to explode with rage, Felicity took her arm and drew her out into the hall. 'There's no point losing your rag with him,' she said. 'It's not going to get us anywhere. If I were you I'd go on to bed. You look all in. Annalise'll probably turn up sometime in the early hours.'

But when there was still no news of Annalise by the morning Corrie was almost out of her mind with worry.

'It's your fault, you bastard!' she screamed at Luke when he came down for breakfast. 'Why did you do it? You knew she was coming!'

'Don't be ridiculous,' Luke snapped. 'Do you think I'd have let her find me like that if I'd known?'

'Yes! Yes, I do! I heard you ask her to come back here

yesterday. You knew she was coming! What are you trying to do to her?' She was on her feet now, advancing towards him. 'Just what the fuck are you playing at? Why did you do it? What are you getting out of this? Tell me, you bastard! Tell me!' As she started to punch him Felicity caught her hands and pulled her away.

'Corrie, ssh,' she soothed. 'It's not going to do any good getting yourself in such a state.'

'But you don't understand!' Corrie sobbed. 'You don't know what he's like, Felicity. There's something going on with him – '

'Corrie, calm down,' Felicity said. 'You're . . .'

'He knows where she is!' Corrie screamed. 'I'm telling you he knows!'

Felicity looked at Luke, but Luke simply shook his head.

'If anything's happened to her!' Corrie yelled at him. 'I'm warning you, if . . .'

'Corrie, just stop it! Stop!' Felicity barked. 'She'll be all right. We'll find her, I promise . . .'

The telephone rang then, and before Felicity could stop her Corrie had dashed across the kitchen and snatched it up.

'Corrie? Is that you?'

'Annalise!' Corrie gasped. 'Oh, thank God! It's her,' she said to Felicity. 'Annalise! Are you all right? Where are you?'

'San Francisco.'

'*Where*? What are you doing there?'

'I'm with an old school friend. She lives here.'

'But why didn't you wait for me?'

'I couldn't. I came to find you, but you weren't there. Oh, Corrie, it was so awful . . .'

'I know. Annalise . . .'

'Is Luke there?'

'Yes,' Corrie answered, throwing him a filthy look.

'Has he said anything?'

'No.'

'Can you do this programme alone, Corrie? I can't come back, I just can't. Not with her there!'

'But you have to come back,' Corrie cried. 'We'll go and stay at a hotel if you prefer, but you have to come . . .'

'No. I can't come back, Corrie, not after the things he said to me. Please, try to understand . . .'

'All right,' Corrie said. 'OK. You just stay there . . .'

'Tell her if she walks out on this programme she's fired,' Luke shouted.

'Was that him?' Annalise said. 'What did he say?'

'It doesn't matter. You just stay where you are. Now give me the number.'

The second she put the phone down Corrie rounded on Luke, 'I hope you're pleased with yourself, you bastard! She . . .'

'It's you who should be pleased with yourself,' he interrupted. 'You're the producer now. It's what you wanted, isn't it? So why don't you stop yelling at me and just get on with it.'

He was almost at the door by the time Corrie spoke. 'You know where you can stick your job!' she hissed. 'If she's fired, then I'm resigning. As of now.'

'She's not fired.'

'But you said . . .'

'I know what I said, and I'm telling you she's not fired. How can she be when her father's who he is?' He looked straight into Corrie's eyes and grinned. 'You're the producer. Now, I'm going to the gym. I'll be back around lunchtime.'

Corrie turned to Felicity and Felicity gave a brief shake of her head, as if to say, let it go now, but as soon as Luke walked out the door Corrie started racking her brains to try and remember if she'd said where Annalise was. She hadn't, Felicity told her, and Annalise's telephone number was still in Corrie's hand. So whether he was lying or not about going to the gym, he couldn't be going after Annalise, which was all that mattered for now.

Since neither of them were filming that day Corrie and Felicity spent the morning in the pool, the Jacuzzi and the sauna. But it wasn't until they were chopping up a salad for lunch that Corrie had calmed down sufficiently for Felicity to dare to broach the subject of visiting Cristos's set.

'Oh no, Fliss,' Corrie said, trying to ignore the sudden dance her heart was performing. 'I'm just not in the mood now. Not after what's happened.'

'Then we'll just have to get you in the mood, won't we?' Felicity said, sneaking up behind her and poking her in the ribs.

Corrie squealed and managed to wriggle out of the way before Felicity could get her again. 'Felicity, no,' she laughed. 'I'm not going, so let's drop the subject.'

'So you're prepared to let this golden opportunity pass you by, are you?' Felicity demanded. 'Probably the only chance you'll ever get in your life to see him again?'

'You don't have to put it like that.'

'Well that's how it is,' Felicity shrugged. She turned back to her pile of chopped carrot, watching Corrie from the corner of her eye. A moment or two later she said, 'Would it help if I told you he knew you were coming? That he himself gave permission for us to visit the set? You don't want to let him down now, surely?' Whether or not Carl had actually mentioned Corrie's name Felicity had no idea, though she strongly doubted it. Probably all Cristos knew was that a couple of visitors from London were going to appear at some point in the day, but what harm would it do to bend the truth a little if it ended up getting Corrie what she wanted? And it sure seemed to have done the trick, because when Felicity looked up again Corrie was beaming all over her crimson face.

'OK, we're here,' Felicity declared, steering the car from Olympic Boulevard onto Hill Street. 'And somewhere around here . . . Yes, there it is, the Mayan Theatre. And, lo and behold, prop trucks, lighting trucks, generators and the whole caboodle.'

'I feel sick,' Corrie muttered. 'Let's turn back now, before anyone sees us.'

'Not on your life,' Felicity grinned. 'Luke, stick your head out and ask that cop where we should park.'

'Do you think he's a real one, or an actor?' Luke asked, winding down the window.

'He's real. All sets are guarded by the police out here.'

Corrie sat stiffly in her seat, thankful that no one could detect the almighty chaos going on in her chest, her stomach and her bowels. She was too nervous and embarrassed even to mind about Luke coming with them, though she had resolutely refused to speak to him.

A few minutes later their car was parked and they were walking back along the street towards the theatre. A few people, all it seemed in shorts, T-shirts and peaked caps, were milling about outside, and to Corrie's astonishment Felicity crept up behind one man and accosted him by the seat of his pants.

'Leonard Bloom!' she cried. 'How you doing you old rogue?'

The man spun round and the instant he saw Felicity his sun-weathered old face lit up. 'What you doing here, kid?' he laughed, throwing his arms round her in an enormous bear hug, 'Gee, this sure is one surprise. It's good to see you, babe.'

'I'm doing a movie out here, aren't I?' Felicity chuckled. 'Not this one. This one we're just visiting.' She turned to Corrie and Luke. 'This old reprobate here,' she told them, 'was a sparks on the last movie I did in Hollywood. He's a great guy, and . . .' she added turning back to Len, 'he's going to go inside and find Carl for us.'

'Sure,' he said. 'Just tell me who the guy is, I'll go get him.'

'He's the unit publicist,' Felicity laughed. 'Short fellow with a ginger moustache.'

'There's over two hundred people inside that theatre,' Len said, scratching his head. 'You'd better come along inside with me and point him out – if you can find him.'

As they walked from the blistering heat into the foyer of the decaying theatre Corrie was dimly aware that her hands and feet had turned to four blocks of ice, but despite how petrified she felt inside she knew, that had Felicity said they could turn back now she wouldn't have. Already she was starting to feel the excitement of drawing close to a major movie set, and as Felicity had pointed out herself, this was probably the only chance she was ever going to get to see Cristos again.

They came to a stop at the back of what had once been the auditorium. Now there was only a stage to say it had been a theatre in another life. An army of technicians were at work on it, rigging lights, a camera, microphones and all sorts of things Corrie didn't recognize. Everyone else was wandering about the space where there had once been audience seating, stepping over the tracks that were being laid, or huddled in groups having hair and make-up retouched. The actors were easy to spot, since they were wearing a spectacular variety of outlandish costumes; there were so many that Corrie guessed most must be walk-ons. The noise level was high as the crew rushed about shouting to make themselves heard above the hammering, sawing and drilling on the stage, then a voice yelled above the din to keep it down.

Corrie's eyes moved steadily through the crowd, and she very nearly jumped when she recognized David Easton, pacing up and down one wall of the theatre, seemingly muttering to himself.

She nudged Felicity who was still scanning the room for Carl, and nodded towards Easton.

'Bit short for us,' Felicity whispered, 'but he's kinda cute, don't you think?'

'He's talking to himself.'

'Rehearsing,' Felicity corrected. 'The guy with him is probably his dialogue coach.' She stood aside for two props men to pass with a towering alabaster statue. 'There's obviously a major re-set going on,' she added, 'but the fact that all the actors are inside must mean they can't be far off a take.'

Corrie nodded, and started once again to search the semi-darkness. It was some minutes later, when a tightly knit group over on the left seemed to dissolve, that her heart turned over so violently she thought it might have torn itself from the roots.

He had his back turned, but she'd have known it was him without having to see his name written on the back of the chair. It was a tall canvas chair, and he was balanced precariously against it, his legs, crossed at the ankles, stretched out in front of him, and his arms folded. For a moment Corrie felt so lightheaded it was as though she was dreaming. The strangeness of the lights, the heavily-painted faces and surging mass of people seemed like surreal, intangible obstacles put there to prevent her from reaching him. She could almost feel herself pushing through them, searching the glittering bodies, shrinking from the dazzling lamps, drowning in the noise. She was starting to smile to herself, imagining him coming to find her, when suddenly a walkie-talkie crackled on the hip of someone passing her and a voice yelled over it,

'Cut the crap, Brown! I'm coming up there to see for myself.'

In any other situation the coincidence might have struck

Corrie as funny, hilarious even, but in this instance the shock of hearing her own name like that brought her thundering back to reality.

'OK, let's go,' she hissed to Felicity. 'I've seen him, so let's go now.'

Felicity only laughed, and it didn't take long for Corrie to realize how absurd she was being, and finding herself laughing too she turned back to look at him again. He appeared to be wearing the same tatty jeans he'd worn in London, and a white T-shirt with *Past Lives Present* emblazoned across the back. His hair was just as untidy as it was before, though it seemed longer and blacker against the white of his T-shirt. She could see the powerful muscles in his arms as he rested his hands on his hips, then he turned his head to one side giving her a profile of his darkly rugged features.

'It's so humbling, isn't it?' she whispered to Felicity. 'I mean, to think that he's in charge of all this, that it's because of him . . .'

'Corrie,' Felicity warned. 'He's a director, not a god, remember?'

But to Corrie, he felt like a god. He was standing now, and she watched, mesmerized, as with his head tilted to one side, he listened intently to one of the actors standing in front of him. After a while he started to speak himself, then reaching out for an actress he took her into his arms, still speaking over his shoulder to the actor. Then he proceeded to demonstrate to the actor precisely what he wanted. A hot jealousy flared through Corrie as he lifted the actress right up into his arms, pressing his mouth to hers, and slowly rotating. Every now and again he stopped to give notes to the actress – everyone was hanging on his every word and there was a tension about the group that seemed to begin and end with him. She had never seen a director of his stature at work before, and now, witnessing the spell he seemed to weave over everyone around him, she felt gauche and parochial. He belonged to another world and that she, Corrie Browne from Amberside, should have the audacity to fantasize about him, to have actually come here today hoping to . . . No, she couldn't bear to think about it.

At last he put the actress down and Corrie noticed immediately how flushed she was. Cristos's attention however was back with the actor who was now preparing to emulate Cristos's performance. After a short discussion Cristos backed away and the actor moved in. Cristos's concentration was total as he watched them, and so too was Corrie's as she watched him. Finally, the actors broke apart and Cristos was laughing and applauding. It was only then that Corrie realized how aroused she had become.

'Look at you!' Felicity laughed. 'You look like you're about to wet your knickers.'

'I think I already have,' Corrie confessed with a grin. 'Felicity, I honestly didn't know anyone could feel this way just looking at a man. He did it to me before you know, in London, and he's bloody well doing it again . . . And with all these people around! I really think I ought to go before I do something rash.'

But even if she'd meant it, which she didn't, it was already too late, for, recognizing Luke, Jeannie, Cristos's assistant, was on her way over to say hello, at the very point that Carl materialized and swept Felicity into the crowd.

Corrie stood alone, not sure what to do. She wondered if Luke might introduce her to the woman he was talking to, and decided that she would break her silence with him if he did, because she was feeling exceedingly awkward just standing here like this. She stole another glance at Cristos, and to her profound alarm, found he was looking in her direction. He looked away, apparently not recognizing her and Corrie was able to breathe again.

'Hi.'

She looked up to see the woman who'd been speaking to Luke was holding out her hand.

'I'm Jeannie, Cristos's PA,' she smiled, as Corrie took the hand. 'You're over from London, I hear?'

'Yes, that's right,' Corrie answered, wondering just how personal an assistant this Jeannie was. 'I'm Corrie, by the way. A researcher with Luke's company.'

'Producer,' Luke corrected her. 'She was just promoted,' he explained to Jeannie.

'Well, congratulations,' Jeannie said. 'So, what do you think of LA, Corrie?'

'Um, uh, well, shall we just say it's not what I expected,' Corrie answered.

'Don't worry, I hate it myself,' Jeannie laughed. 'You off somewhere, Luke?'

'The little boys' room,' he grinned.

Jeannie turned back to Corrie and Corrie smiled. 'If you hate it here, then why do you live here?' she asked.

Jeannie shrugged. 'I guess I'm married to it. That's my husband up there on the stage giving the effects boys a hard time. He's the DP.'

'DP?'

'Director of Photography,' Jeannie explained. 'He always works with Cristos, that was how I came to get my job.'

'I see.' Corrie was much happier now she'd got that straight. 'What are the effects for?' she asked.

'A love scene, would you credit? One of Cristos's crazy arty shots that always work – almost always, anyhow.'

'What's the film actually about?' Corrie asked.

'Oh shit!' Jeannie laughed. 'That's one hell of a question. In a nutshell, it's this woman who lived all these lives before. It's a true story, she wrote a book about it. Anyway, her past lives keep cropping up in her present life, there you have the title. I met her, Muriel Bond, the author, oh, ages ago now, she blew my mind. She knows things like you just wouldn't credit. She's been checked out by the historians over there at Oxford, all over the world in fact, and she's ended up explaining things to them they didn't even know. It's kinda like she can see someone here, today, but she knows who they were before. Only if she knew them before though. And it's like all the things that didn't get resolved in one life, start getting resolved in the next one, and the next and so on ... For instance, she was some English Countess in one life, back in the seventeenth century, fell in love with this cute Italian soldier, but she was already married. She knew everyone who was anyone in Britain at that time, you just gotta read what she writes about it! Anyway, in the next life her and her soldier, and other people they knew too, were all Italian, but still those two couldn't be together. The second unit's going over to Italy to shoot that stuff in a couple of weeks. Anyhow, after that life they turn up on the Jarrow march, you know, back in the thirties over there in l'il ol' England, and they get married and go live in the west of the country where they meet all these people they knew before and all these incredible things start happening. The main unit's going to England for that. Anyway, he's dead now, the soldier, her husband, and Muriel Bond lives in New Hampshire ...' Jeannie shrugged, 'It doesn't sound too convincing the way I tell it, but boy, if you met her ...'

'And what's this scene all about, that you're setting up for now?'

'It's supposed to be in an opera house, back in the seventeenth century. You see David Easton over there, he's the soldier, I guess that's kind of obvious from his costume. Anyway, Paige Spencer is playing the part of Muriel Bond, Paige is over there somewhere ... Looks like she's disappeared ... Anyway, the man Paige, Muriel, was married to in the seventeenth century, the count, loved the opera. In this scene, he's in one of the boxes with his wife watching John Blow's *Venus and Adonis* – we shot that this morning so the box has been struck now – when he gets kind of passionate and starts kissing her. And as she's kissing him she starts thinking about her lover, and all the people on the stage are watching her, and then she finds herself in the middle of the stage with her husband and then with her lover, and everyone's dancing around them. Then she's like flying and all the walls cave in – it's kind of difficult to explain, Cristos does it better in the script. Take a look if you like.'

Corrie leaned forward to look at the paragraphs of stage direction Jeannie was showing her, so engrossed by the story now that she was on the point of asking if she might have a copy of the screenplay to read when a voice behind her said,

'Had any good sexual fantasies lately?'

Corrie spun round and found herself face to face with Cristos. In a split-second she knew so many emotions that she felt herself start to sway. She pulled herself together so quickly that no one could have noticed, but then felt so ridiculously elated that he actually remembered who she was that she only barely resisted the urge to hug him.

'About you in particular?' she heard herself counter.

'Why not?' he shrugged.

'As a matter of fact I have,' she told him.

'Am I still making you laugh?'

'Amongst other things.'

He raised his eyebrows humorously and, to Corrie's mind, very definitely flirtatiously.

'In fact, I almost came once,' she added.

It was only when Cristos's eyes rounded with astonishment that Corrie actually realized what she'd said.

'I'm sorry,' she gasped immediately. 'That wasn't what I meant to say . . . What I meant to say was . . .'

But Cristos wasn't listening. Jeannie's husband was talking to him now, wanting to go over something again and Richard had all of Cristos's attention. Watching them walk away Corrie knew only the utter misery of wanting the floor to open up and swallow her.

She turned to Jeannie, wretchedness written all over her face.

Jeannie was still laughing.

'I just don't know what came over me,' Corrie said. 'I never say things like that normally.'

'I wouldn't feel too bad,' Jeannie said, putting a comforting hand on Corrie's arm. 'He's heard a lot worse.'

She started then as Cristos yelled out her name, and excusing herself ran off across the theatre.

Corrie could concentrate on nothing now, even though some very peculiar things were starting to happen on the set. All she could see were Cristos's eyes when she'd said those hideously outrageous words.

It took what felt like ten years to find Felicity, but she did eventually, outside with the coffee.

'We have to go,' Corrie told her. 'I've disgraced myself and I just want to leave. Let Luke find his own way back.'

Felicity couldn't help laughing at such a doleful expression, but realizing that this time Corrie really meant it, she made her goodbyes and took Corrie off to the car. She screamed with laughter when Corrie told her what had happened. In fact she was still laughing when they pulled up outside the mansion, by which time even Corrie was starting to see the funny side.

'Well, at least I won't ever have to see him again,' she said, as they walked in through the front door. 'Now, just lead me to the bar, because I need one stiff drink.'

But she did see him again. That very night in fact, at Spagos. Luke was taking them out for a late dinner, and though Corrie really didn't want to go, she didn't much relish the idea of being left on her own.

She spotted Cristos the instant she walked into the restaurant. He was sitting alone at a table, not far from the door. Immediately Corrie made to head back outside, but when Felicity thwarted that, she tried to slink past him before he had chance to see her. However, to her intense annoyance, Luke not only stopped to speak to him, he actually sat down. And next thing he was waving her and Felicity back.

'I'll kill him!' Corrie hissed to Felicity. 'I'll fucking kill him!' Only once they were seated, did Luke inform them that he had invited Cristos to join them and Cristos had accepted.

'Because,' Cristos said quietly to Corrie, 'I like to consider myself too much a gentleman to leave a woman on the doorstep of an orgasm.'

'I would prefer it,' Corrie replied, 'if you didn't remind me of the embarrassing things I keep saying to you. You probably won't believe this, but I'm never like it with anyone else, and I've suffered a great deal since I first met you . . .' He was smiling right into her eyes, listening to everything she was saying, and suddenly her mouth fell open as what he had said actually began to sink in. Too much a gentleman to leave a woman on the doorstep of an orgasm . . . Did that mean . . . ? She turned away quickly, never more grateful for seeing a waiter in her life.

When they'd ordered Cristos turned his attention to Felicity and Luke. Corrie didn't mind in the slightest, in fact she was relieved. Provided she didn't have to talk to him there was little danger of her making a fool of herself.

It wasn't until their food arrived that Corrie realized the conversation around the table had somehow turned to her. Felicity was singing her praises for stepping into the breech, and Luke was adding to it by saying that he knew she was going to make a terrific producer. What made matters worse was that Cristos seemed bored. And Corrie was only slightly cheered when she realized that he didn't seem any more interested in the numerous women – half-clad airheads! – who were coming up to their table to speak to him. It was only when the second course arrived, and the conversation had thankfully run on to other topics, that Corrie realized Cristos wasn't bored at all, he was merely preoccupied. Of course he would be thinking about his film! She wished she could find something intelligent to ask him about it, but wasn't too sure whether she should risk it. Nevertheless, she began turning it over in her mind, and was drawing breath to ask how today's special effects shot had gone, when she suddenly realized he was watching her. The blood immediately rushed to her cheeks, and she was already half-turned to Felicity before she realized that she was being rude again. With a wry smile she turned back.

'You're pretty quiet,' he said.

'I think it's safer that way,' she answered.

It was a reply that succeeded in widening his smile, but before he could say anything Corrie tossed her hair back over her shoulder and changed the subject. 'Do you come here often?' she said.

Immediately the cliché was out she started to cringe, but when her eyes met his, they both started to laugh.

'What is it with you?' she said, shaking her head. 'You seem to turn my tongue into a little boat which sails the most banal or most outrageous things right out of my mouth before I can stop them.'

Again he laughed and picking up his fork took a mouthful of food.

'I'm afraid,' Corrie said, a few minutes later, 'that I didn't get to see the shot you were setting up today. Did it work?'

'Sure it worked,' he answered, putting his fork down again and picking up his wine. 'How come you didn't stay?'

'No, I'm not being drawn on that one,' Corrie told him. 'You know why I didn't stay.'

'I do?'

'Yes, you do. But now's my chance to apologize again. I really am sorry for what I said.'

'What did you say?' Luke asked.

Corrie looked across the table at him, unaware until then that he'd been listening. Without answering she turned back to Cristos. His eyes were dancing as he watched her discomfort, and knowing he was teasing her Corrie started to smile.

Someone else Cristos knew stopped at the table then, and when they'd gone Luke claimed Cristos's attention by asking about the location manager he'd recommended. Corrie listened as Cristos talked, and eventually, as the subject changed again she found herself speaking. She was talking about the rape programme they were making, and the interviews they'd done so far. Cristos appeared to be listening quite intently, apparently interested in the fact that she didn't blame Kennedy Smith for turning down an interview which would only put him back in the public eye for something he didn't do. She felt quite passionately about the rights of men in this situation, she told them, and was glad to be making a programme designed to help the Amendment through. She was really warming to her subject when Luke suddenly interrupted her.

'I wouldn't be taken in by all this fervour if I were you, Cristos,' he laughed. 'We're here in LA for one reason and one reason only. So that she could see you again, old chap.'

Corrie simply stared at him, knowing already that to say anything in her defence, right here in front of Cristos, would probably only make matters worse. So, with no more to say and no appetite either, she merely lowered her eyes to her plate, mumbling a thank you as Cristos poured her more wine and wishing that someone else would speak to break this unbearable silence. At last Felicity came to the rescue.

'Come on, let's get out of here,' Cristos whispered a few minutes later.

Corrie's fork clanged against her plate as she turned to him in amazement, but he was already standing up.

'Corrie and I are leaving,' he announced to the others.

Corrie threw a look at Felicity, whose eyes were out on stalks, and picking up her jacket and bag she followed Cristos out of the restaurant.

Neither of them spoke as they waited for his car to be brought round, and Corrie was so tense that she barely even registered surprise when she saw that it wasn't a Mercedes, or a Porsche, or any other kind of vehicle intended to depict his wealth. It was an enormous black and silver Toyota Jeep. He handed her into it, then walked round to the driver's side.

As they pulled out onto the busy highway Cristos was broodingly silent, and Corrie, who kept stealing glances at his hands on the wheel, was trying hard to keep her nerves under control.

'Where are we going?' she asked some time later as he turned the car off Sunset Boulevard towards the Holmby Hills – though Corrie had no idea where they were.

When he still hadn't answered a few minutes later Corrie presumed he hadn't heard, and was about to repeat the question when he slowed up in front of a set of huge wrought iron gates – which, she noticed with a sickening thud to her heart, were beginning to slide open.

The drive up to the house was a relatively short one and in the beam of headlights Corrie, who was in no doubt where she was now, could see a long, low, white building with shuttered windows, lots of arches and a red tiled roof. It was surrounded by palm trees, and the garden, from what she could see of it, sloped in semi-circular tiers down towards the boundary walls. This was obviously his home, and Corrie was stunned by the fact that he had brought her here.

As he drew the car to a halt outside the front door, the courtyard was flooded with light. Still he was silent as he got out, closed the door and came round to help her down. As she put her hand into his she could feel the strength in his fingers, and knew that she was shaking, that he could probably feel it, but there was nothing she could do to control it. As she stepped down in front of him she deliberately avoided his eyes, and still he didn't speak as he started to lead her towards the front door.

It wasn't until he let go of her hand to take out his keys that the sheer magnitude of what was about to happen hit her and for one insane moment she wanted to run away.

'Cristos,' she whispered.

He turned to look at her.

'I don't want you to think,' she began hesitantly, staring down at her hands, 'that I do this sort of thing with just anyone.'

Hooking his fingers under her chin he brought her face up to look at him. She could see the laughter in his eyes and her head started to swim.

'You don't?' he teased gently.

Her breath caught on a sob as what felt like a tidal wave of nerves crashed through her chest. He'd be so used to experienced women and she'd rather die than be found lacking . . .

He was still looking at her, and seeing how badly she was shaking he ran the backs of his fingers over her cheek. She gazed back at him, tears of utter hopelessness shining in her eyes.

'It'll be all right,' he whispered, and pulling her to him he kissed her, gently sucking her lips with his own, until he felt her start to relax. And as her arms went round him and he felt her heart hammering into his chest, he pushed his tongue deep into her mouth.

Still kissing her he managed to unlock the door but as he pulled her inside, he lifted his head to look at her. 'Well, there's one threshold you've already crossed tonight,' he smiled, his lips still very close to hers.

Oh please don't let me panic! Please, please! Corrie was crying inside. She could feel his arms around her, she could feel the hardness of his body and she knew she wanted him in a way she had never wanted anyone before. But she just didn't know what to do.

He was kissing her again and unbuttoning the front of her dress. She could feel her nipples throbbing with the need to be touched and as he slid the shoulder straps down over her arms and unhooked her bra he stood back to look at her. Corrie watched his face, panic rising in her again. He doesn't like big breasts! He's used to skinny women!

He lowered his head to take a nipple in his mouth. With his fingers he was massaging the other. Corrie was leaning back against the table behind her, desperately trying to reassure herself that there was nothing wrong with her body. She looked down at him, at his mop of jet black hair and his dark hand over her pale skin, and there was only one thought in her mind. This is Cristos Bennati. *The* Cristos Bennati!

She let her head fall back and started to moan loudly, the way she'd seen in films. She twisted her fingers through his hair, tugging at it and shaking her head back and forth. Then she started to oooh and aaah as though her life depended on it. 'Take me now!' she gasped, suddenly. 'Please, take me now.'

Listening to her Cristos could hardly stop himself laughing. He'd known other women whose nerves had made them turn on a performance like this, it was one of the hazards of being who he was. Normally it irritated him, but for some reason, with her, it didn't. Probably, he smiled to himself, because she was such a lousy actress. Well, he decided, he'd just have to give her something to oooh and aaah about.

Swallowing his laughter he stood up and pressed his mouth to hers. She helped him unbutton the rest of her dress, still groaning for all she was worth. Then, as the dress fell to the floor and he pushed his hand inside her knickers Corrie fell instantly silent. All she knew now was the movement of his fingers and the incredible sensations it was sending through her body. She held her breath, hardly daring to believe this could last, then opening her eyes she found him watching her.

He smiled. 'Feel good?'

She nodded, then her eyes closed as he leaned forward to kiss her. As he did he increased the pressure of his fingers and Corrie almost collapsed.

'Come on,' he said, gruffly, 'let's go upstairs.'

'No!' Corrie gasped as he started to remove his hand. His eyes shot to her face and what he saw there brought his mouth crushing down on hers.

He took her right there, against the table, his jeans around his knees and her legs around his waist. Corrie clung to him, hardly able to breathe. The way he was pushing into her was more erotic than anything she'd ever known. It was as though he knew every secret part of her, how to touch it, to stroke it then set it ablaze with unparalleled ecstasy.

He pushed her back, lifting her breasts in his hands. The power of his erection was incredible, he'd never dreamt she'd feel this good. He moved faster, and harder, feeling her abandon herself to him. She was driving him wild, but he made himself hold on.

'Jesus Christ!' he seethed, as the first grasp of her muscles tightened around him.

'Cristos,' she moaned, 'Oh, Cristos.' Tears were streaming down her face as she buried it in his shoulder. 'I can't,' she sobbed, 'Cristos, I can't.'

'It's all right,' he whispered. 'I'm right with you. Oh, babe!' he cried as his own orgasm threatened to explode.

He was holding her so close now that he could feel her rubbing against him. He ground himself savagely against her, burying himself so deep inside her until at last, as she cried out, he knew he had her.

'Let it go,' he whispered. 'Just let it go. That's it . . . Oh, yes . . .'

And as her climax erupted around him, pulling him into her, gripping him, kneading him and holding him, he felt the semen start to rush from his body. She cried out his name, and he pumped harder, prolonging the exquisite pain until eventually she turned limp in his arms and there was no strength left in his body.

It was a long time before he lifted his head to look at her, and seeing that she was still dazed he kissed her softly on the mouth, smoothing the hair from her face. Her lips parted in a whimper as he eased himself away, then she smiled shyly up into his eyes.

'You OK?' he whispered.

She nodded. But when her feet touched the floor she was still too weak to stand. He held her, kissing her and chuckling quietly while she waited for her strength to return.

'Coffee?' he said.

'Mm.'

He helped her dress, then taking her by the hand led her into the kitchen and sat her on a stool. She watched him moving about as he made the coffee, then blushed and looked away as he turned round. Folding his arms, and leaning back against the counter behind him, he looked at her with that all absorbing attention she'd seen him give the actors that day.

'Your face is like an open book,' he told her.

'Sorry.'

'What for?' he laughed. 'Because for the first time in your life a man has made you come?'

Corrie felt the blush sink right to the roots of her hair. 'How do you know that?' she whispered.

'I told you, it's in your eyes.' He turned away to pour the coffee, and knew she was still watching him with that same expression of awe. He threw her a look over his shoulder, and this time Corrie grinned, wryly.

'Was I . . . I mean, was it good for you too?' she asked quietly.

'Sure,' he said.

Corrie's face fell. She didn't really know what she'd been expecting him to say, but she'd hoped for more than that.

Bringing the coffee across to where she was, he perched on the stool next to her and lifted her face. 'It was better than good,' he said, 'now drink your coffee.'

'You're patronizing me,' she told him.

He grinned, then she laughed too as a sudden rush of happiness erupted inside her.

She sipped her coffee as he turned to play back the messages on the answerphone beside him, and feeling as though she was eavesdropping she started to concentrate on her surroundings. His kitchen, for all its stark whiteness, was every bit as well equipped as the one at the mansion, though nowhere near the size – and it wasn't kosher compatible either, she smiled to herself. The bar at which they were sitting opened out onto a sitting room, and though the only light came from the kitchen she could see the low, cushioned sofas haphazardly arranged around a neat grey marble fireplace, and the threadbare Oriental rugs scattered across the wooden floor. The whole of one wall was made up of French windows which led out onto a terrace, where a single coach lamp illuminated the Italian villa style arches. She imagined there was probably a swimming pool somewhere out there too, maybe even tennis courts, and she guessed that they would be as tastefully unadorned as everything else.

Eventually she looked back at him, and as she watched his hand move across the page, jotting down the names of his callers, Corrie could feel the dread mounting in her. Please God, don't let there be a woman's voice, she prayed silently. Please, don't let anything happen to spoil tonight.

But there was a woman's voice, the very last one on the tape, and Cristos turned to look at Corrie, grinning as the beautifully-accented voice told him that his mother was just calling to find out how the movie was coming along.

'She thinks of it as her movie,' he told Corrie, as he turned off the machine. 'She found the book, handed it to me and told me to go get her the Palme d'Or.'

'And are you going to?'

'I'm sure as hell gonna try,' he laughed.

Corrie felt herself smiling too. 'I take it you get along well with your mother,' she said.

'Sure I do. My father too. You're looking surprised.'

Corrie thought about that for a moment. 'Yes,' she said, 'I am. In England we only ever seem to hear about broken families in the States. Where do your parents live?'

'Philadelphia.'

'But they're not American?'

'Uh-uh. My mother's French, my father's Italian.'

As he got up to refill their cups, he began telling Corrie of how his parents had met, at the outbreak of World War II when the Italians had invaded the South of France. He made her laugh about his mother's horror at falling in love with the enemy, but it was a touching story too and Corrie listened raptly as he told it. Then she found herself telling him things about her own childhood, making him laugh with the way she described the people from Amberside and their little idiosyncrasies. Somehow then they got onto the subject of Los Angeles and it was evident that he found her views on it highly amusing. It was only when he got up to refill their cups for the third time that it occurred to Corrie he was probably only being polite, and was actually waiting for her to go. Immediately she started to look around for a telephone, trying hard to swallow the crushing disappointment she felt at having to leave. Surely there must be a phone next to the answering machine, but there didn't seem to be.

'You're not listening to me,' he said, coming to sit back down.

'I am,' she declared. 'You were telling me that you didn't know yet whether or not *Past Lives Present* was going to be selected for Cannes, and that someone from the Festival will be coming over here soon to take a look at the script and your dailies.'

He nodded, and Corrie saw that he was laughing at her.

She looked around again. 'Can I call a cab from here?' she asked.

'Why? You going some place?'

'Well, I thought that now we've ... I thought ...'

He leaned towards her and putting a finger under her chin lifted her face to look at him. 'Sleep with me tonight, Corrie Browne?' he said.

Corrie very nearly melted at the sonorous intimacy in his voice, and in truth Cristos himself was surprised by how badly he wanted her to stay. In fact right at that moment he just as badly wanted to hold her.

'What do you say?' he asked.

'Yes,' she whispered.

He smiled, and taking the cup from her hand he put it on the counter. Corrie was gazing deep into his eyes as he pulled her to her feet, then, at last finding the courage that had eluded her all night, she put a hand either side of his shadowed face and pulled his mouth down to hers.

'You know what you're doing to me?' he murmured, when she let him go.

Smiling, Corrie said, 'I think I'm getting an idea.'

'Are you gonna let me take you upstairs this time?'

She nodded.

When they walked into his bedroom and stood in the shadows of the moonlight coming through the unshuttered windows Corrie was looking down at the low, tapestry covered king-sized bed. There was such a sadness in her that it was as though she might drown in it. But, she told herself, she wasn't going to allow herself to think about the other women who had been there before, women far more beautiful and worldly than she would ever be. Women who had mattered to him, maybe still did. No, she wasn't going to let anything spoil tonight, because it was a night she wanted to remember for the rest of her life.

Cristos was standing behind her, and turning her into his arms he looked deeply into her eyes. He wasn't too sure what was happening here, but he did know that it was a whole lot more than he'd expected. He knew too that she was thinking of herself as a one night stand. He didn't want her to feel that way, but damn it, there was nothing he could say to reassure her, because she was right, that was all she was going to be.

'Is something the matter?' she asked, and when he saw the fear steal into her eyes he suddenly pulled her to him and held her very tight.

'This isn't only for tonight, you know that don't you?' he heard himself murmur, and then he was searching for her lips, wanting to kiss her so bad his whole body ached for it.

'I'd like you to make love to me now,' Corrie said shakily, when he let her go.

'You would?' he smiled, caressing her cheek with his fingers in a way she was already coming to love. 'Then how about we get into bed?'

As they undressed there was a choking knot of emotion tightening in Corrie's throat. She could hardly believe what he had said, or how deep her feelings were running because of it. Such joy and tenderness flowed through her veins that it seemed to melt the very core of her heart. She loved him, she knew that, she could feel it so strongly that there was nothing else in her.

Then he turned towards her and her lips parted as she saw the sheer beauty of his naked body. He wanted her – he wanted her every bit as much as she wanted him. She was still in her underwear and with movements that seemed almost fluid he turned her round and unfastened her bra. Letting it fall to the floor he took her breasts in his hands, then lifted the hair from her neck to kiss it.

Resting her head back on his shoulder, Corrie could feel his hardness pressing against her. His hands were so gentle, his breath so warm on her skin. Then he was turning her in his arms, and when he kissed her his mouth was so tender she though she might cry.

Taking her hand he led her to the bed and laid her down. The flicker of a smile seemed to pass through his eyes as he looked at her, and she lifted her hips for him to take down her knickers.

'You feel good here,' he said, touching a finger to the moist flesh between her legs.

Corrie murmured, and as he started to stroke her, her eyes closed and her knees drifted apart. He was still stroking her as he took each of her distended nipples in his mouth and sucked gently. Then his fingers took her nipples and his tongue was where his fingers had been.

A long time later he lifted his head and saw that her orgasm had exhausted her. But as he made to take her in his arms she pushed him away, and started to slide down the bed.

A groan escaped him as her mouth closed over him and as she started to suck his hands fell to his sides and his head was turning from side to side.

He didn't want to come in her mouth, but she made him. She stayed with him until every last drop had left him. Only then did she let him go, and sitting back on her knees in the strange silvery light she looked at him.

'Come here,' he said.

She lay down beside him, resting her head on his shoulder and listened to the beat of his heart. He wanted to say something to her, but he just didn't know what. So he held her, and stroked her, and kissed her.

When Corrie woke the next morning it was to find the bed empty beside her. There was a note though, telling her where to find everything, but saying nothing more than that. She tried not to mind, to reassure herself with the things he had said and done the night before, but she couldn't help feeling disappointed that he wasn't there, or that he hadn't put something a little more intimate in his note.

Then suddenly she noticed the time and shot out of bed. They were shooting at nine and already it was past eight o'clock. It wasn't until she stepped out of the shower though, and wrapped herself in his robe, that she started to wonder how the hell she was going to get back to Felicity's when she didn't even know where she was. She laughed at her mawkish romanticism then, as she reflected on how wonderful it would be to remain stranded here for ever. To spend her days pampering herself in that enormous caramel bath, or soaping his magnificent body beneath all those shower jets when he returned after a hard day.

She was touched to find that he had hung her dress in his closet, but slipped into it quickly, now really pressed for time.

She was running down the stairs, raking her fingers through her hair and reluctantly coming to the conclusion that only Luke could help her out, since he was the only one who knew where Cristos lived, when she thought she heard voices coming from the kitchen. She stopped. Yes, she definitely could, but neither of them were Cristos's.

'Hi there,' Jeannie said as Corrie walked into the kitchen, clearly not in the least surprised to see her there. 'Like some coffee?'

'Um, uh, yes, thank you,' Corrie answered, quickly realizing that the Mexican looking woman must be the maid.

'Cristos had me come back for you,' Jeannie explained, as she poured the coffee. 'He guessed you probably didn't know where you were, so I'm here to drive you wherever you gotta go.'

'Oh,' Corrie said, feeling so absurdly pleased that she

wanted to hug Jeannie for telling her. She managed not to however, and a few minutes later they were walking out of the door to Jeannie's car.

Corrie went through the morning as though in a trance. She had no idea, until the cameraman complained she was more dazzling than the sun, that she was grinning like the Cheshire Cat, but when she tried to stop she couldn't. Little snatches of all the things he had said or done the night before kept coming back to her, and though they were creating havoc with her insides, it was the most wonderful feeling in the world. She quickly realized though, how irreverent it must seem to look so happy when they were dealing with a subject that had caused such tragedy in people's lives, so she endeavoured to keep her thoughts from expressing themselves on her face by frowning. Unfortunately the frown didn't last long because she remembered those few minutes in the night when she had sleepily opened her eyes to find him watching her. He had kissed her then, so tenderly and so lovingly, that she had felt her whole heart might overflow with love.

Early in the afternoon Luke joined the unit down at the Los Angeles Police Department Headquarters to find out how Corrie's first day as a fully fledged producer was going. He was clearly amused by the undisguisable euphoria burning so brightly in Corrie's eyes, and as soon as he had a chance went over to speak to her.

'Do I take it you had a good time last night?' he laughed.

'Yes I did, thank you,' Corrie answered, finding it impossible to be angry even with him today.

'I'm glad,' he said. 'You deserve it.'

Corrie found that a rather curious remark coming from him, but said nothing as Peter Fredericks, the reporter, called out for her then, to ask her to go over again just what she wanted him to ask the policeman who was sitting with him.

Half an hour later the interview was done, and as they

waited for the camera to turn round for the reverses Corrie saw Luke beckoning her over.

He gave her a few suggestions as to how she might improve what had turned out to be a rather dull monologue from the policeman, then said, 'You're doing really well, you know?'

'Thank you,' Corrie answered.

They stood watching the crew for a while, then Luke said, 'Annalise called this morning.'

Corrie's eyes closed. She had been so wrapped up in herself these past twenty-four hours she'd almost forgotten about Annalise. Turning to Luke, she eyed him warily. 'What did she say?' she asked.

'She wanted to speak to you, but when I told her where you were and offered her Bennati's number she said she didn't want to disturb you.'

'I see. Did she say anything else? Is she coming back?'

He shook his head. 'No, at least she didn't say she was.'

'Luke,' Corrie said carefully, 'you didn't say anything to upset her again, did you?'

'No. In fact I tried to apologize, but she wouldn't listen. She hung up on me.'

Trying – and failing – not to show how pleased she was to hear that, Corrie said, 'So she didn't tell you where she was?'

He shook his head.

'Why did you do it, Luke?' Corrie asked after a pause. 'There must have been a reason, because you did know she was coming.'

'I did it to get her out of the way so I could make you the producer,' he answered simply.

'You can't possibly think I'd want the job based on that!' Corrie whispered angrily, hoping no one could hear.

'I'm afraid I did, but obviously I made a mistake. A very big mistake.'

'Yes, you did,' Corrie told him. 'I don't understand you, Luke. I thought you loved her.'

'I do,' he said in a broken voice. He turned away, but not before Corrie had seen the sadness that had suddenly filled his eyes. She noticed then how stooped his shoulders seemed, as though he could no longer support the unsupportable burden of misery and Corrie found her heart touched with compassion.

'Luke, what is it?' she said, putting a hand on his arm.

Briefly he shook his head. 'Nothing,' he answered. 'Nothing except that I might have lost her. I deserve to lose her, I know that, but . . .'

Corrie stepped round in front of him, and saw the tears shining in his eyes. 'Luke!' she gasped. She look quickly back over her shoulder to see how the crew were doing, then taking his arm, she said, 'Let me take you outside. The air's not too fresh,' she added in a lame joke, 'but . . . Come on, let's get out of here.'

'No, it's OK,' he said. 'I'll be all right. It just got to me for a minute, that's all.' He lifted his eyes then and looked so pleadingly into her face that Corrie tightened the hold on his arm. 'I know I've fucked everything, Corrie,' he said, 'and I know that you hate me for it . . . But will you . . . Oh God, I've no right to ask this, I know, but will you talk to her for me?'

For a long time Corrie simply looked at him, then very slowly she started to shake her head. 'I'm sorry, Luke,' she said, 'I can't do that. Even if I wanted to, I couldn't. You see, I don't trust you not to do it again.'

'But I won't,' he said, with such sincerity that had it been anyone else Corrie would have believed it.

'No, Luke,' she said. 'No. Because there's more to this than what happened with Felicity. A lot more. I don't know what, I'm not sure I even want to know, but . . .'

'You're talking about me making you a producer, aren't you?' he interrupted.

'Well, yes. That's part of it. I mean, why was it so important to you to do that?'

'I wanted to give you something you wanted,' he answered. 'OK, we've already agreed I went about it in the wrong way . . .'

'Corrie! Ready to rock-n-roll,' the cameraman called out.

'We'll continue this conversation later,' Corrie told Luke. 'Are you all right for now?'

He nodded. 'Yes. Thanks.'

Twenty minutes later they were done with the reverses and on their way to Mulholland up in the Hollywood Hills. Luke went with them, and seemed, to Corrie's profound relief as she watched him sparring with the sound man in the front of the car, to have pulled himself together. But when they reached Mulholland where she had intended they take some high wide panning shots of the city, the yellow green smog was so thick and so low that almost nothing was visible.

'We'll have to re-schedule,' Corrie told the crew, 'so we'll call it a day today. We'll pick up the other shots on Friday. I'll knock out a list for you, they're mainly to cover voice-overs.'

'I wanted to talk to you about the voice-overs,' Luke said as they rode back into Beverly Hills. 'Have you written them yet?'

'I've made some notes,' Corrie answered, 'I was going to let Perkin perfect them when we get back.'

'Good. But we might as well get something valuable going while we're here. You haven't written anything yourself yet, have you? I mean, not a complete script?'

'No.'

'Then we'll take a look at it when we get back,' he smiled. 'You never know, you might have a God-given talent for it.'

Half an hour later they were sitting next to the pool back at the mansion, involved in a healthy, witty and, Corrie realized, genuinely helpful debate on what the voice-overs should say. Felicity was in the solarium, reading through the scenes she was shooting that night, and kept yelling to them to keep the noise down.

'It's her big scene with the murderer tonight,' Corrie whispered to Luke.

Luke's lips curled in a smile, which, had Corrie seen it, would have sent a shiver down her spine. 'Then we ought to leave her to it,' he said, getting up. 'I'm off to take a shower. Maybe you'd like to call Annalise. No, not to speak up on my behalf, but because she wants you to.'

Corrie nodded. 'OK, I'll call her now,' she said.

But when she got through to Annalise's schoolfriend it was to discover that Annalise had taken herself off shopping. Corrie left a message to say she'd called, then went to ask Felicity if she could help by reading in for her. She'd never done it before, and really didn't know if she'd be any good, but she had to do something to stop herself fretting about whether or not Cristos would call.

By six o'clock she was so edgy that Felicity thanked her for her help, took the script back from her and told her to go pour herself a stiff drink. Corrie did, but it didn't seem to help, if anything it made the churning in her stomach worse. As she started to pace Felicity dropped her script in exasperation.

'What time's he due to wrap?' she said.

'I don't know,' Corrie answered.

'Then what the hell are you getting yourself into such a state about? He'll have dailies after he's wrapped as well, so if he is going to ring at all it won't be until nine thirty at the very . . .' She broke off as Corrie made a dash for the telephone.

'Hello?' Corrie gasped.

It was the third assistant on Felicity's film, telling Felicity that her call time had been put back by an hour.

'This is awful,' Corrie wailed an hour later, now pacing

around the pool. 'He said that it wasn't just for the night, but . . .'

'Hey, come on,' Felicity chuckled, 'you're a big girl now, you know better than to believe what a man tells you when you're in the sack with him.'

Corrie's face turned ashen white as she looked back at Felicity. 'You mean you think he was lying?' she said.

'Not lying, exactly,' Felicity answered uncomfortably. She hadn't expected Corrie to look quite that distraught. 'In fact he probably meant it when he said it.'

'But he doesn't now?'

Felicity sighed heavily. 'Corrie, you've got to face it honey, he's a big-time director. He'll have been in that same situation he was in with you last night a hundred times before. These things trip off the tongue real easy with men like him. They know all the lines. Jeez, they should, they wrote most of them,' and getting up from her chair she went to answer the phone which had started to ring again.

With a horrible paralysis in her heart, Corrie listened as Felicity repeated the number.

'Oh hi,' Felicity said. 'How are you? Yeah, yeah, I'm fine, just getting ready for my big scene tonight.'

Feeling the disappointment draw at every bone in her body Corrie started to walk away. But at that moment Felicity turned to look at her. 'It's him,' she mouthed.

Corrie's entire body turned so weak she couldn't move.

'Yeah, it's tonight,' Felicity was saying. 'Oh thanks, thanks very much. Yeah, she's right here, I'll put you on.'

As she handed the receiver to Corrie she put her hand over the mouthpiece, saying, 'OK, I made a mistake and I'm sorry.'

Kissing her on the cheek Corrie took the receiver and put it to her ear. 'Hello?' she said.

'Hi. How you doing?'

'Oh, I'm fine,' she said, feeling herself respond to the

dark intimacy in his voice. 'How are you? How was your day?'

'Pretty good. We wrapped early, I've just watched yesterday's dailies.'

'And?'

'They work.'

'Of course,' she laughed.

There was a pause, then he said, 'I'd kinda like to see you.'

'I'd like that too,' she whispered.

'Then how about I stop by?'

After she'd given him the address Corrie rushed straight out to the pool where Felicity had taken her script in search of what was proving unattainable peace.

'What time's he getting here?' she said when she saw Corrie's face.

'I don't know. I think he's coming straight away. But he didn't say where he was. Oh Fliss! Fliss! I just can't believe this is happening.'

Laughing, Felicity once again put down her script, then taking Corrie in her arms she danced her around the pool. 'Now,' she said, breathlessly when they'd finished, 'what do you say that we two take a swim to try and calm you down before he gets here?'

'You're on,' Corrie laughed.

Five minutes later she was running back down the stairs in her swimsuit and robe when the doorbell rang. 'I'll get it,' she called out to whoever was listening.

When she opened the door Cristos was leaning against the side of the porch, and when she saw the look that came into his eyes the smile froze on her lips.

'Hello,' she murmured as he took her in his arms.

'Hello yourself,' he said, and lowering his mouth to hers he started to suck gently on her lips. Then he was kissing her, pushing his tongue against hers and holding her so hard against him she knew that the desire she had seen in his eyes was very real. He stopped for a moment and looked down at her, then he was kissing her again.

'I've thought about you all day,' she laughed, between kisses. 'Have you thought about me?'

'From time to time,' he answered, running his hands over her bottom. He wasn't about to tell her the problems she'd given him, or that he wasn't even too sure he was happy about being here now, so he said, 'What are you wearing under this thing?'

'My swimsuit. Felicity and I were about to take a swim. Can you stay tonight?'

'Hey, you two,' Luke called out, 'are you going to stand out there all night, or are you going to come and join the party?'

'Go take that swim,' Cristos said. 'I'll watch.'

Corrie wasn't too sure she felt happy about that. The idea of Cristos seeing her in a swimsuit next to Felicity, who was so tall and slender and so . . . well, Hollywood, was disheartening to say the least . . . But then she reminded herself that he had already seen her in the nude, so it was a bit late to be thinking of modesty now. So, as they walked out to the pool she dropped her wrap on a chair, and with her shoulders held well back she marched over to the swimming pool – and belly flopped in.

When she resurfaced she could hear Cristos still laughing, but deciding to ignore it she swam on down the pool.

'She is one crazy lady,' Cristos murmured to himself as he watched her. He was startled when Luke agreed, since he hadn't known Luke was so close.

'So you had a good time with her last night then?' Luke said.

Immediately Cristos's jaw tightened.

Pretending not to notice Luke said, 'She's got one helluva body, don't you think? Yeah, she's got it all there, all right. Some might say too much of it, but not me. Can't get enough of her myself. Those tits of hers just drive me wild.'

By now Cristos's face had turned very dark, but feigning surprise Luke pressed on, 'Hey, she hasn't got to you, has she? Shit, I didn't think you'd fall for that, mate. I mean, didn't she tell you? Didn't she say one word about me? Well, I don't suppose she goes round advertising the fact that I've been screwing her ever since she joined TW, she wouldn't want everyone to know that's how she got her job. Mind you, I'd have screwed her anyway with a body like that. You know, come to think of it she wasn't too backward in telling us about you today. She rates you pretty high, you know? I've been wondering what she was thinking she might get out of you.' He shrugged. 'Who can say? Generally she's known as my property, but feel free to enjoy it. She's a star-fucker, and a bloody good one at that. You'll be quite a feather in her cap.'

Cristos was on his feet, a murderous rage blazing in his eyes, 'One of these days, Fitzpatrick,' he hissed, snatching up his keys.

But Luke kept going. And he kept on going until he heard the front door slam behind Cristos.

Corrie was out of the pool by now and had gone into the changing room to pick up a towel. When she came out she presumed that Cristos had gone inside for something and went to the bar to freshen her drink. When he still didn't materialize after five minutes she looked across at Luke and said, 'Where's Cristos?'

'He left.'

Corrie frowned. 'What do you mean, left?'

'He's gone. Said he had another appointment and went.'

Corrie's face was so strained she could barely move her lips. 'Without saying goodbye,' she whispered.

Luke shrugged, then seeing the way Corrie's eyes began to narrow he held up his hands, 'Now hang on a minute . . .'

'What did you say to him!' she yelled. 'What did you say, you bastard!'

'I didn't say anything. You were there, in the pool, you'd have known if I was talking to him.' But she hadn't been looking, and Luke knew that. 'He just sat here, watching you swim,' he went on, 'then when you got out he said something about having made a mistake and that he was leaving. And he left.'

'What do you mean, a mistake?'

'How do I know? That's all he said, that he'd made a mistake.'

'What's going on?' Felicity said, coming into the solarium in the briefest of swimsuits. 'Where's Cristos?'

'Gone,' Corrie stated.

'What? Gone where?'

'I don't know,' Corrie answered, verging on tears, and picking up her wrap she ran up to her room.

Felicity found her half an hour later, sitting on the edge of her bed, staring sightlessly out of the window. Apart from the red rings round her eyes, her whole face was drained of colour. Hearing the door open she looked round and seeing it was Felicity turned back to the window.

'How are you feeling now?' Felicity asked, going to sit beside her.

Lowering her eyes to her hands Corrie simply shook her head.

'Have you tried to call him?'

Corrie nodded. 'The answerphone's on.' She turned to look at Felicity then and Felicity felt her own heart turn over at the very real pain in her eyes. 'I don't understand, Fliss,' she whispered. 'I just don't understand. If he didn't want to see me, then why did he come? And what did he mean about making a mistake?'

Sighing heavily Felicity took her in her arms. 'I didn't want to tell you this, Corrie,' she said, 'but I think I'll have to. I mean, I don't know if it's got anything to do with the way he just left like that, or with what he said, but . . . Well, before you got here, to LA, there were rumours going around about him and Paige Spencer – the lead actress in his movie. I don't know if they're true, but there are those who think that it's pretty serious between him and Paige. I'm only telling you this so that you'll understand just what you're up against here.'

Corrie's heart was a red hot furnace of pain, and every word Felicity was saying was a torch making it burn all the hotter. Just the thought of him with another woman was so pure in its torment that Corrie didn't think she could stand it. It hurt too much even to cry.

'I have to go now,' Felicity said, a few minutes later. 'I just popped in to say goodbye. There are some sleeping pills next to my bed if you want them. Don't take any more than one though, will you? He's not worth it, babe, honestly. None of them are.'

When Felicity returned from her night shoot the following morning Corrie was already up and had breakfast waiting for her. Felicity was so tired she wanted nothing more than to collapse into bed, but not wanting to seem ungrateful she slumped into the chair Corrie pulled out, and dropped her bag on the floor.

'How are you feeling this morning?' she asked, stifling a yawn.

'Oh, I'm fine, thank you,' Corrie answered, brightly. 'How did last night go?'

Felicity sighed, 'Well, we got there in the end. I'm just about all in though. I'll eat this then get off to bed.'

Corrie went off to the kitchen to fetch the coffee, but from the breakfast room where she was sitting, Felicity saw how badly she tensed up when the telephone rang. She made no move to answer it though, so Felicity picked it up herself. It was her director, ringing to ask if she'd like to go see dailies that evening.

'Thanks,' she said to Corrie as she sat down again and

picked up the coffee Corrie had just poured. 'Aren't you having anything yourself?'

'No, I don't feel very hungry,' Corrie said.

'No man is worth starving yourself for,' Felicity remarked.

'I'm not starving myself, I'm just not hungry,' Corrie answered tersely.

Felicity watched her as she sat down with her own coffee and started to flick through the pages on her clipboard. Corrie's suffering was so near the surface it was plain for anyone to see, and Felicity knew precisely what was happening inside her. Last night the pain, today the anger, tomorrow the hurt, confusion and disillusion. It was the way it always went in situations like this. But during the endless hours of waiting for the moon to appear last night, Felicity had thought a lot about Corrie and Cristos and though it went right against the grain with her to give a man a second chance, since to her mind not one of the bastards was worth it, she was of the opinion that in this instance Corrie should. She couldn't say exactly why she felt that way, except that she just couldn't get it out of her head that in some way Luke Fitzpatrick was behind Cristos going off like that. Exactly what Fitzpatrick stood to gain from breaking them up, Felicity didn't know, but what she did know was that she'd rather rot in hell than sit back and watch some man screwing up the life of a friend of hers.

Putting her knife down and picking up her coffee, she looked across the table at Corrie. This wasn't going to be easy, she could sense that already, but to hell with it, she was going to give it a go anyway. 'Corrie,' she said, 'I think you should try calling him again.'

Not even the anger could disguise the hurt in Corrie's eyes as she looked up. 'Felicity, he walked out of here without even saying goodbye. Don't you think that means he should be the one to call me?'

'Yes, I do. But if he's worth it, Corrie, and I think as far as you're concerned he is, then you'll swallow that pride and ask him why the hell he did.'

'He made a mistake,' Corrie reminded her. 'He said that, he said he'd got it all wrong. So I don't need to ask, do I?'

'You're going to take Luke's word for that?'

'I don't have much choice, since he chose to say nothing to me. And even if Luke is lying, there's always Paige Spencer, isn't there? You told me about her yourself. I take it *you* weren't lying.'

Felicity sighed. 'No, I wasn't lying, but it's only gossip, Corrie. There might be nothing to it. Look, you're going home in a few days, why not give it one last shot before you leave?'

'Frankly, I don't see the point. Now can we change the subject, please?'

'No!' Realizing that her tiredness was in danger of making her sound fiercer than she intended, Felicity made an effort to soften her voice. 'Look,' she said, 'I can't explain this, and God knows, cynic that I am, I'm the last person on earth to romanticize a situation, but I saw the way he was watching you the other night at dinner, and we both know that he was only there because of you. Not only that, I saw the way you looked yesterday when he called. This is special between you two – at least I reckon it could be . . . Oh, I don't know what I'm trying to say really, except that I think he cares for you more than . . .'

'No!' Corrie shouted, leaping to her feet. 'I don't want to hear it, Felicity. I was taken in by it once, and it won't happen again. If he cared he'd have called me by now, but he hasn't, has he? Now, if you'll excuse me I have to get ready to meet the crew.'

Felicity watched her walk out, deciding not to go after her, as probably the last thing Corrie could handle right now was pity. She'd been there so many times herself in the past, so she knew that Corrie's hurt was still too raw to be comforted. Maybe, once the anger had gone, she could try again. Or was it really worth it, Felicity asked herself, stifling another yawn. If the rumours about Paige Spencer were true, then it probably wasn't.

For the next forty-eight hours Corrie threw herself single-mindedly into her work. At least it got her through the day, but the nights were a different matter altogether. Sleep continually eluded her, and as she lay there tossing and turning in the darkness, all she knew was the confusion and utter hopelessness she felt inside. She had believed, truly believed that she had meant something to him, and even now, after what had happened, a part of her was still refusing to accept that she hadn't. She couldn't forget his eyes when he'd looked at her, nor his tenderness when he touched her, but as Felicity had pointed out, he was a man well practised in the art of seducing women and how naive she was to have fallen for it so completely.

She spoke to no one about it, she didn't want to talk about him at all. She just wanted to try and forget, to get on with her life and put this stultifying pain and disappointment behind her.

But two nights before she was due to fly back to England she found herself picking up the phone and dialling his number. She hadn't really thought about what she was going to say, all she knew was that Felicity was right. If he was worth it then she would swallow her pride and give him another chance. And he was worth it, even though he had walked out on her and not even bothered to call to explain.

As the phone started to ring at the other end her nerves clawed at her stomach so cruelly she started to feel sick. If the answerphone picked up the call she knew she wouldn't leave a message, but the answerphone didn't. At first Corrie didn't know who it was, since all she could hear was music, then she heard a woman laugh and Cristos saying 'give me that phone!' Then the woman's voice said, 'Hi there, Cristos Bennati's residence.'

Corrie replaced the receiver, knowing that she would never feel so bad in her life as she did at that moment. But there was still worse to come, for the following morning when she opened the newspaper there, staring back at her, was a picture of Cristos with Paige Spencer. They were leaving Spagos together, Paige was gazing up into his face and Cristos looking straight into the lens, was laughing.

Luke was sitting at the mirror in his bathroom, staring at himself. His face was ravaged, but he didn't recognize the pain and sadness in his eyes, he saw only the diminishing light of rage that moments ago had reared up at him, mocking him, perverting him, sucking him into the hell he could never escape . . .

Thank God no one had seen him, were anyone ever to witness the rabid demon tormenting his soul it would be the end. Even now he could feel the great monster fidgeting within him. It was a like a separate being, a life force obliterating his own with an unslakeable thirst for vengeance. It governed him, mind, body and soul until he no longer knew who he was.

Then this morning he'd asked her to marry him. He'd got down on his knees and asked her to become his wife. She'd laughed. She hadn't said anything, not a single word had passed her lips, she had simply laughed. He knew of course that shock had provoked the response, so he had waited for her laughter to subside and asked again.

Of course he wasn't surprised when she turned him down, after all she still carried a torch for Bennati. Neither was he surprised that she had done it so spitefully. She'd guessed that he was behind Bennati walking out on her, but he, Luke, had wanted her to understand that he needed her far more than Bennati ever would. He couldn't do that while Bennati was around, and what a fool he had been ever to let her come here. He'd only done it so that she would see for herself that a man like Bennati would never be interested in someone like her. He'd wanted to be there to pick up the pieces, to take her battered ego and soothe it so that she would come to recognize his tenderness, but it hadn't worked out that way. At least not at first, but he had seen to matters, and now, with Bennati no longer an obstacle, he must make her understand that to marry him was the only thing she could do – for all their sakes.

He pressed his fingers to his eyes as though to push back the tears that had started. She was on her way to Annalise now, he knew that even though she hadn't admitted it. Annalise had called him herself, just after Corrie had left. Annalise, his darling, precious, Annalise. How he'd wanted to go to her, to hold her as she told him she forgave him. But he had stopped himself, and that was why the rage had come. It had nothing to do with Corrie, he felt only a desperation for Corrie that she should try to understand. But how could she when he couldn't find it in himself to tell her what he had done, or why it was that he did it?

He knew that she would try to talk Annalise out of ever seeing him again, and please God she would succeed. He had to let Annalise go; he had to end everything between them before he started doing to her what the bastard had done to Siobhan. But it was going to kill him to lose her, it would sap the very life from him to be without her now. He slumped forward, his body convulsing with sobs. But Corrie wouldn't succeed, would she? The sly, vindictive beast inside him had seen to that. It had spoken to Annalise and now Corrie wouldn't stand a chance.

'Corrie,' he gasped. 'Oh my God, Corrie! You've got to help me. Please, make it stop . . .'

'Luke! Are you all right?'

He spun round to find Felicity standing at the door.

'I thought I heard you in here,' she said, uncertainly.

'Annalise is still on the line, she'd like to speak to you again.'

Luke's eyes had narrowed. He could see her lips moving but barely heard what she was saying. The terror was suddenly with him again, yet he knew with a few last moments of clarity that the rage was closing in. There was nothing he could do to stop it, already it was blinding him to all else beyond Felicity the slag, who'd made him hurt Annalise. Felicity the slag, who had enticed Corrie here to Bennati. Felicity the slag, who must pay for what she'd done.

'Are you all right?' she said again, when he continued to stare at her.

He picked up a towel. 'I'm fine,' he said, wiping it over his tear-stained face. 'Just fine. Tell me, Felicity, would you be liking rabbits?'

– 18 –

'Corrie! Corrie!'

Corrie smiled as she saw Annalise leaping up and down to attract her attention through the crowd, and lifting an arm Corrie waved back. There could be no mistaking Annalise's joy to see her and suddenly feeling the need to hug Annalise she started to run.

'Oh, Corrie,' Annalise cried, as Corrie let go of her baggage trolley and swung her into her arms. 'Corrie, are you all right?'

'Of course I am,' Corrie laughed. 'Are you?'

'Yes. No. Yes, as long as you are. Felicity called me, she told me what happened – Oh, Corrie, what can I say to make you feel better?'

'You don't have to say anything,' Corrie told her, pulling

her trolley out of the path of other passengers. 'I'm fine, honestly. It happened, now it's over.'

'But Felicity said you were broken-hearted,' Annalise protested.

'Don't be silly, of course I'm not. How can I be? We only spent one night together. No, no, no,' she said, as Annalise started to protest again. 'Not another word on the subject. Felicity's just exaggerated everything out of all proportion and . . .'

'But you've lost weight, Corrie. I can tell.'

'And not a moment too soon,' Corrie grimaced, wishing more than anything else in the world that she felt even remotely as light-hearted as she sounded. 'Now come on, let's get out of here. I take it you've still got the hire car.'

As they drove along the 101 freeway into San Francisco Corrie was aware that Annalise, who kept looking at her and smiling brightly, was trying to work up the courage to tell her something. But, when she casually enquired if Annalise had any news Annalise immediately said,

'No, nothing's happened. I've just been sitting up here thinking, nothing else . . .'

'Thinking about what?' As if Corrie needed to ask.

'Things. By the way, I've booked us into the St. Francis overlooking Union Square. Diane's place is too small for us both to camp out in, and I wanted to be with you.'

Corrie smiled. 'That's good,' she said, 'because I wanted to be with you too.'

They talked for a while then about the programme and how the filming had gone, until Corrie suddenly gasped.

'My God, just look at it!' she cried, as they brinked a hill and the staggering panorama of San Francisco unexpectedly revealed itself before them. They were at the top of Pacific Heights where the roller coaster of a road they were on swept dramatically down towards the heart of the city. 'It's stupendous,' Corrie murmured, gazing at the maze of majestic towers rising through the rippling heat.

'You should see it by night,' Annalise told her, 'it takes your breath away.'

Corrie's eyes were circles of wonder as she watched the city unfold. Soon, too soon, they were entering the heart of it, but still she was transfixed. She was experiencing an almost overwhelming sense of relief and familiarity. Relief to discover that not everywhere in the United States was like Los Angeles: and familiarity because nestling in amongst the gleaming, spectacular sky-scrapers, was the unmistakable, though neglected, grandeur of bygone days. This town had a heart, more than that it had a soul. And, she realized with a jolt of pleasure, it had a past. She smiled to herself then, unaware until that moment just how much she had missed England these past two weeks. Its history was something she'd always taken for granted, barely even noticed was there it was so familiar. But in Los Angeles, she realized now, she had been uncomfortable without it.

'I thought,' Annalise said, as they approached Union Square, 'that since you're only staying two days we'd dump your bags at the hotel then take you off to see something of the city right away. How does that sound?'

'Perfect,' Corrie answered, and an hour later, after abandoning the car at the hotel, they were alighting from a taxi down at Fisherman's Wharf.

It was teaming with tourists and Corrie balked at the idea of having to spend even a few minutes in such heat with so many people. But, as they strolled from Ghirardelli Square, past the endless queues who were being entertained by buskers as they waited for cable cars, and approached the bay, she stopped being bothered by the masses. This was a wonderful place, so alive and thrumming with excitement, and so entrenched in reality that she was just happy to be there. And how lucky she was, Annalise told her, not to have arrived on a day when the infamous fog was masking it all.

On reaching Hyde Street Pier they rested their arms on

the wall and stared out across the water to the Golden Gate Bridge – and to Alcatraz.

'We can take a trip out there if you like,' Annalise said.

Corrie shook her head. She didn't want to visit a prison, not when just looking at it, even from this distance, was reminding her of what a prison her own body had become. All her feelings were locked deep inside her now, she would never be able to share them with him, never be able to let them go.

Hooking her arm through Annalise's they started along the Embarcadero, past the National Floating Park, through a battery of music and streetside dancing, heading towards the site where there had once been a double decker bridge, before it had been destroyed by the earthquake in which so many had perished.

So many gloomy thoughts, Corrie chided herself, and forcing a smile to her lips dragged Annalise over to look at the countless multi-coloured stalls which lined the street with handcrafted jewellery, caricature portraits, hats, T-shirts, sourdough bread and living sea-food. They bought tiny wooden cable cars which when wound up played *I left my Heart in San Francisco*, watched and laughed along with the one man juke-box who, in his Punch and Judy box, was playing a lively tune on his trumpet, and devoured ice-creams the size of a candy floss.

Eventually they reached the world famous Pier 39, and as they strolled arm in arm to where the seals were basking in the afternoon sun, and Corrie inhaled deeply of the tangy salt air, Annalise trespassed into her thoughts with the words, 'I've spoken to Luke, Corrie.'

Having already guessed this, Corrie was only surprised by how long it had taken Annalise to tell her. 'When?' was all she said.

'This morning, just after I talked to Felicity, while you were on your way here.'

'And?'

Annalise walked on ahead, pushing through the crowd to find them a spot where they could watch the seals. 'Corrie, please don't be angry,' she said, as Corrie joined her, 'but I've decided to go back to him. He wants me to, and it's what I want too.'

'Even after what he did, after the way he spoke to you?'

'Yes. Oh, Corrie, please try to understand. I love him, and part of loving someone is forgiving them, isn't it?'

Corrie watched as a huge grey seal rolled over and flopped into the water. Would she forgive Cristos if he ever did that to her, she was asking herself. She didn't think so, but she couldn't imagine him ever doing it. She squeezed her eyes tightly closed. What was she talking about? He had allowed his picture to be printed in the newspapers with Paige Spencer, knowing she would be sure to see it. She doubted though that it had even entered his head that it would hurt her so badly, if he had thought of her at all, which he most likely hadn't. And besides, she and Cristos didn't even have a relationship, they never had, unless one night constituted a relationship, which it didn't, so how could she compare her feelings with Annalise's?

'Did he explain why he did it?' Corrie asked, knowing already that whatever he had told Annalise wouldn't have been the truth. But she was wrong, and she could hardly believe her ears when Annalise said,

'He told me he wanted to make you the producer for this programme. That he thought it was the only way he could do it, and now he's begging me to forgive him.'

'Did he say why he wanted to make me the producer?'

'He thought that was what you wanted.'

'Not that way.'

'I know. He understands that now. He told me to tell you that once this programme has been transmitted you'll revert to being my researcher again.'

Corrie gave a dry laugh and stared sadly out at the chopping waves. 'So we all go back to where we were before

Los Angeles and pretend nothing ever happened? I only wish it were that easy.'

'Do you mean . . . ? Are you saying that you don't want to work with me again?'

'No,' Corrie said, shaking her head. 'I was thinking of something else.' She turned to look at Annalise, sweeping her face with her eyes, taking in every line, every pore, every tremor. It was such a pretty face, so young, so trusting and eager. But for how much longer? Already the depth of suffering she had known was beginning to take its toll. 'I wish you'd give him up, Annalise,' she said.

Annalise shook her head. 'I know you do, but I can't,' she whispered.

'But if you could only see what he's doing to you. You look awful, Annalise. No, ravaged is the word, and it's him who's doing it.'

'I know. But it's because I haven't been with him. I've missed him so badly while I've been here. But I made myself stay. I knew I had to think, to decide what to do for the best . . . Corrie, I can't live without him. I don't want to live without him. OK, I know he has his faults, but there are other things about him . . .'

'What things?'

Annalise shrugged. 'I don't know. I can't put it into words, but he means more to me than anyone else in the world.'

Corrie heaved a deep sigh and turned back to the seals. Should she tell Annalise what Luke had said to her before she'd left? How he'd asked her to marry him, that he needed her? She really didn't think it would do any good, that Annalise, in her desperation, would very likely find it in her heart to forgive even that, and Annalise's next words confirmed it.

'I told you,' she was saying, 'I've done a lot of thinking, and I realize now that Luke is never going to be faithful.

It's just something in him I'm going to have to condition myself to live with.'

'Oh Annalise,' Corrie groaned. 'Why should you do that when there are so many men out there who would be faithful? Who would love you every bit as much as you deserve to be loved, and who would treat you the way you should be treated.'

'But they're not Luke, are they?'

Corrie turned to face her, and lifting a hand to stroke her hair, said, 'Annalise, I know this is going to hurt you, that it'll hurt a great deal, but I have to tell you so that perhaps you'll start to understand what he's really like. Before I left Los Angeles this morning, Luke asked me to marry him.'

To her amazement Annalise simply nodded. 'I know,' she said. 'He told me. He asked you to try to make me jealous. He thought it would bring me back to him.'

Corrie turned away quickly before Annalise saw the fury in her eyes. The bastard! she was thinking to herself. He tells her everything, he never lies and because of it Corrie could see that she was never going to get through to Annalise. Well damn it, she wasn't going to give up yet.

'I think there's something wrong with Luke,' she said bluntly. 'I mean seriously wrong. I think his mind is disturbed.'

'Isn't everyone's, one way or another?'

'Annalise!' Corrie cried, barely able to resist the urge to shake her. 'Ask yourself, just ask yourself rationally, who in their right mind would do the things he does?'

'I don't see that he does anything so out of the ordinary,' Annalise answered. 'All right, sometimes he might, and I know he gets some very odd moods every now and again, but don't we all?'

Corrie turned away in exasperation.

'Come on,' Annalise said, taking her by the arm, 'you're getting angry now, and I don't want anything to spoil these two days, so let's walk on around the pier and talk about something else, shall we?'

Realizing that for now she was beaten Corrie allowed herself to be dragged away for more shopping and sight-seeing. It wasn't until much later in the evening, when they were sitting in McCormick & Kuleto's sipping white wine and tucking into the most succulent mussels, that Corrie broached the subject again.

'What do your parents think of your relationship with Luke?' she asked, as Annalise dipped her fingers in the lemon water.

There was just the briefest of hesitations before Annalise answered, but it was long enough for Corrie to know that she was going to lie. 'They never really say too much,' she shrugged. 'At least Mummy doesn't. Daddy thinks that I'm too young for him, but then Daddy would.'

'Meaning?'

'Daddy wouldn't approve of anyone, no matter who they were. He's always been over-protective of me, but he's beginning to understand now that I have to make my own decisions in life.'

'So your father doesn't really approve of Luke, is what you're saying?'

'Corrie, if you're thinking of ganging up with him against me then please don't. The last thing in the world I want is for us to fall out, but we will if you do anything to interfere in my relationship with Luke.'

'All right,' Corrie said crossly, 'then I'm going to tell you quite frankly that Luke Fitzpatrick frightens me. That I really think he's up to something that involves both you *and* your father. No, don't ask me to explain, because I can't. But it's a feeling I have, and I know I'm right. So, I want your solemn promise, Annalise, that if he ever does anything, anything at all, either to harm you or frighten you or anything that is in any way out of the ordinary, you will come straight to me.'

Annalise laughed uneasily. 'All right,' she said, 'if it makes you feel any better, then you have my solemn promise that I will come to you. Actually,' she added after a pause, and her voice was barely audible as she continued, 'there isn't anyone else I'd go to anyway.'

There was a lump in Corrie's throat as she reached out to squeeze Annalise's hand. 'I'm glad to hear it,' she said, but what she was even more glad to hear was that tiny whisper of acknowledgement that there might one day be cause to turn to someone. It was, she knew, the best she could do for now.

– 19 –

Phillip Denby was in his office staring down into the busy street. He'd been standing at the window for some time, quietly mulling over in his mind the many times he had come so close to ending it all by jumping into the constant flow of traffic below. It seemed crazy now, but then he had been crazy at the time. Not anymore though, thank God not anymore. Now he felt so free; so free that if he did jump he would probably fly.

Hearing a gentle tap on the door he turned to see Pam put her head round. Smiling he beckoned her in, and slipping an arm about her waist as she rested her head on his shoulder he said,

'I can't believe it, you know. I still just can't believe it.'

'Am I allowed to say I told you so?' Pam chuckled. She lifted her head then and looked into his face. He looked so handsome today, so carefree and ... yes, happy. It had been a long time since she'd seen him happy. But she still didn't yet know all the details of his visit to the police, and knowing him as she did she was concerned that he might not, even now, have told them everything. 'So,' she said, 'are you going to tell me what happened?'

'You can see for yourself,' he laughed, 'they let me go.'

'Of course. You didn't do it, remember?'

'But they believed me, Pam! They actually believed me.' Letting her go he walked back to his chair and collapsed into it. Pam followed, perching on the edge of the desk in front of him. 'I told them,' he said, looking up at her, 'about how I was the last person to visit the prostitutes, and about how I had tied them up. I even told them how worked up and angry I get about Octavia, which was why I dabbed her perfume over them. And then I told them . . . I said, "I didn't kill them," and they believed me.'

'As easily as that?' Pam said doubtfully.

'Well no. They asked me a lot of questions, naturally, like what made me think I was the last person to see them alive . . .'

'And what did you say?' Pam interrupted.

'I gave them the times I was there.'

Already Pam could feel her heart starting to sink. 'Go on,' she said.

'They asked me all sorts of things about sexual positions and the like. It was pretty embarrassing really, especially when they got me to tie knots in rope . . . They did ask me one strange thing though. They wanted to know if I could tell them the contents of the dead prostitutes' stomachs.'

'What did you say?' Pam asked, turning up her nose.

'I said I couldn't, of course. I mean, how could I? The last thing on my mind when I went to see them was food, which is what I told the police.'

Pam pondered on that for a moment, then said, 'Now don't take this the wrong way, Phillip, but for all they know you could have just been withholding information. So what made them believe you so readily?'

Phillip shook his head, 'I don't know. They just seemed to take my word for it.'

'It was probably the incredulous look on that wonderfully innocent face of yours that convinced them,' she teased, mussing up his hair. 'But you were gone a long time, so what else did they say?'

'Not much really. These things just take a long time. You know, going over and over every movement of the day, every word that was spoken – right down to the money that changed hands. Did I pay in cash, and if I did, did I use twenties or tens, or what did I use?'

'Didn't they want to know what had made you come forward now?'

It was the question Phillip had been dreading, from Pam, not from the police, and unable to meet her eyes he stood up again and walked over to the bookshelves. 'I told them that I had heard about the perfume, that I'd only just heard about it, and since I knew that the times of my visits coincided with the deaths too, that I should go and speak to them in order, as they put it, to eliminate myself from enquiries.'

'Didn't they want to know how you knew about the perfume?'

He still had his back to her, but now, knowing that he had to, he turned to face her. 'I explained about my contact with TW,' he answered lamely.

'Oh Phillip,' Pam groaned. 'In other words, you didn't tell them anything about Fitzpatrick. Is that what you're telling me?'

He nodded.

'Not even that it was him who told you about the perfume?'

Phillip shook his head. 'No. I said it was Annalise who told me. They were surprised that she knew the brand, but then assumed that probably most people at TW knew that by now, since they'd told Fitzpatrick themselves.'

'Phillip, *why* didn't you tell them about Luke?'

'You know why, Pam. It's Octavia. Clearing myself with the police doesn't change what he knows about her.'

'And it doesn't change what we know about him, either.'

'But what do we know? Nothing. Nothing that can be substantiated, anyway. It's all surmise on our part, Pam, and what if we're wrong? What if he didn't do it? If I told the police I thought he did, and I was wrong, then you know full well what he'd do. He'd make everything public about Octavia, and though I might not care about her, or even what it would probably do to me, I do care about what it would do to Annalise.'

'And what if he did do it, Phillip? Have you thought about that? It won't be scandal and heartbreak you'll have to worry about then, will it? And it won't just be Annalise either. It'll be Corrie too. Because if that man is a killer, Phillip, then you surely don't need me to remind you that he's very, very, dangerously close to both those girls. Think on that, Phillip. Think on it, then for God's sake go back to the police.'

When Corrie and Annalise arrived at Heathrow Airport Luke was in the arrivals lounge waiting for them. He greeted Annalise with such convincing contrition and devotion that it made Corrie feel ill. She noticed too all the people who passed by, staring at him, recognizing him and nudging each other with delight at having got an 'in the flesh' look at him. If only they knew what he was really like, she was thinking to herself. Would they be quite so impressed if they had any idea what was going on behind the public façade of that oh so handsome face?

When he finally let Annalise go it was as much as Corrie could do to say hello to him herself, but she tried, and she did accept his lift into London, where he dropped her at her studio before taking Annalise to his own flat, where they would no doubt spend what was left of the weekend making up.

As she closed her front door behind them Corrie turned to look around her studio. She'd always loved this little place, it was her sanctuary, her own personal haven where she could hide from the rest of the world when life was getting her down. One of the secretaries had been in to water the plants while she was away, and had even left a small bunch of freesias to welcome her home. And Corrie would have been glad to be home, were it not for the fact that she felt she had left an integral part of herself on the other side of the world. And as she moved across the room, registering the fact that nothing had changed, that everything was just as she had left it, she began to feel even more depressed. It was as though the past three weeks had never happened, and now she wished to God that they hadn't.

Even before she rewound the tape on her answerphone she could feel the blind hope building in her that he might have called. He could have got her number from Felicity . . . But of course, there was no message, and even though she hadn't really believed there would be, the disappointment wrenched cruelly at her heart.

There was, however, a message from Felicity. 'Call me the minute you get back to London,' she said urgently. 'I couldn't get hold of you in San Francisco, you didn't leave the number. But I need to speak to you, PDQ.'

Once again hope flared in Corrie's chest. Felicity had sounded so excited that it must be something to do with Cristos. But the very last message on the tape was again from Felicity.'

'Hi. Thought I'd better call back just to let you know that what I have to tell you is nothing to do with Cristos. Didn't want you getting your hopes up. But ring me, Corrie. Seriously! Get in touch as soon as you can.'

Corrie looked at her watch. It would be five o'clock in the morning in Los Angeles now. Well, Felicity had made it sound pretty pressing so she probably wouldn't mind being woken up. But when Corrie got through the answer-phone picked up her call, so she left a message saying she was back in London now, then made herself a cup of tea before calling Paula. God, how she'd missed speaking to Paula while she was away.

Ten minutes later she was curled up on the sofa with the telephone telling Paula that yes, she thought the pro-gramme was going to work, and that no, she hadn't liked Los Angeles very much, but San Francisco was wonderful.

Paula waited for more, but when it didn't come she said, 'You sound really down in the dumps, Corrie. Did something happen out there to upset you, or something? Or is it just jet lag?'

Corrie sighed. 'A bit of both I expect,' she answered. 'Oh God, Paula, so much happened out there I don't even know where to begin.'

'Well how about starting with the important bits? Like did you get to see Cristos Bennati again?'

'Yes, I got to see him. But listen, I'm coming down to see you next weekend, I'll tell you all about it then, OK?'

'That's cruel!' Paula cried. 'I shall die of curiosity between now and then.' But sensing that Corrie really was unhappy, she added, 'I missed you.'

'I missed you too,' Corrie said, her eyes filling up with tears. 'Oh God, I missed you. Anyway, I'm going to get some sleep now, I'll call you midweek, OK?'

Hating herself for doing it Corrie put down the phone, went upstairs to lie on her bed and cried herself to sleep.

To her relief though, she felt better in the morning, and since the date the Amendment was being debated in the House had, she discovered when she arrived at the office, been brought forward, Luke took the decision to postpone that week's programme in favour of the rape programme. This meant that Corrie had more than enough to occupy her mind over the next thirty-six hours. Every available minute there was she spent in the edit suite, and actually ended up working through the night piecing together all they'd shot in LA.

On Tuesday night the programme was transmitted, and everyone insisted that they must take Corrie out to celebrate her first credit as a producer. She went, carried along now by sheer adrenalin, and not a little euphoria that the programme, against all the odds, had come out so well. They took her to the Chelsea Arts Club where Annalise bought the first bottle of champagne, Luke the second, Alan Fox the third and she didn't have any idea who bought the fourth, fifth and sixth, all she knew was that she was drinking it like there was no tomorrow. She even had a good time, at least she thought she did, but she couldn't remember too much about it the next morning. But what was pretty certain was that she had once again cried herself to sleep – one look at her swollen eyes told her that.

Annalise arrived at nine o'clock to take her to the office, looking, Corrie told her, disgustingly healthy for someone who'd been out on the town half the night.

'That's because, unlike some, I didn't drink,' Annalise laughed.

'You didn't?'

'Nope. I don't need to when things are going well with Luke. And they are going well, Corrie. I mean really well.'

'I'm pleased for you,' Corrie lied.

'No you're not. But feeling the way you are about Cristos doesn't mean . . .'

'Who said anything about Cristos?'

'You did. Last night. No, it's all right, you didn't say it in front of anyone else. You just kept telling me that you understood why you couldn't reason with me, when you couldn't even reason with yourself.'

'I said that? What the hell was I talking about?'

'You were trying to make yourself believe that you were no more than a one night stand.'

'God! Remind me never to get drunk again.'

'Corrie,' Annalise said, as Corrie went to turn on the answerphone, 'if you are hurting, I mean, if you want to talk, then I'd be happy to listen, you know.'

'I'm not hurting,' Corrie snapped. 'I don't want to talk, and I wish bloody Felicity would stop leaving cryptic messages on my answerphone and not being there when I call back. Now come on, or we'll be late for the post-mortem.'

Corrie spent most of Saturday looking after Beth while Paula worked in the shop. Corrie had offered, and wanting more than anything that her best friend should establish a relationship with her daughter, Paula had agreed. But now Paula was at home, and though it saddened her to do it, since she knew that Dave had been longing to hear about America, she bundled him off down to the pub, settled the baby, then returned to the sitting room where Corrie was pouring them both some wine.

'OK, let's have it,' she said, closing the door behind her.

Corrie was standing in the middle of the room, and as her head dropped Paula realized straight away that she was crying. And not only was she crying, she was sobbing as though her heart would break.

'Oh, Corrie,' she cried, tears starting in her own eyes as she ran to take Corrie in her arms. 'Corrie, what is it? What happened?'

'Oh Paula, it hurts so much,' Corrie spluttered. 'It hurts and I just can't stop it. I thought by now that I'd be over it, but it just seems to get worse.'

'What does?' Paula said gently.

A bubble of laughter erupted through Corrie's tears then. 'It's going to blow your mind, Paula. You'd better sit down, because if you don't you'll probably fall down.'

It had never even occurred to Corrie how wonderful it might be to relive what she had known with Cristos in mere words, but it was. It was as though she was somehow transported back to the night and could see him, smell him, feel him – and most of all hear him and all the things he'd said, all over again. Throughout most of it Paula was open-mouthed, though she did not laugh when Corrie told her some of the things she'd said, like that day on the set when she'd told him how she almost came, and especially when she'd tried to act out a love scene with him. She whooped with joy to learn that Corrie had actually managed the elusive orgasm, but by the time Corrie finished there was a frown on Paula's face, and Corrie herself was angry.

'I was such a bloody fool to fall for it all,' she seethed. 'And to think that I'm sitting here actually hoping that he'll get in touch again! I can't believe I'm doing it! And even if he did, which obviously he won't, I'd tell him where to go.'

'Why? If you ask me it sounds like he was pretty keen.'

'Don't say things like that Paula, it only encourages me, and I can't get him out of my mind as it is. But he won't get in touch, because no matter what he said I was only for one night and I just have to learn to live with that. And if he does call me, then I'll bloody well let him know that it makes no difference to me who he is, I'm just not being messed around like that.'

'Are you *sure* Luke Fitzpatrick wasn't behind it all?' Paula asked.

'You're forgetting, I saw the pictures of Cristos and Paige Spencer together myself. Luke couldn't have arranged that. But yeah, I reckon he might have said something to Cristos that night, it would be just like him to. Felicity thinks he did too. She's been trying to reach me for days, but we just keep missing each other. I told her to call me at the office, but she said that she definitely didn't want to speak to me there. Anyway, it's not about Cristos, that much she has told me.'

'Which means, if she won't speak to you at the office, that it could be about Luke?'

'Or Annalise. Most likely Luke though. He was still with her when I left for San Francisco, so maybe something happened. Anyway, Luke Fitzpatrick in Los Angeles is another story in itself.'

'That man should have been strangled at birth,' Paula stated furiously when Corrie had finished telling her all that he'd done. 'And Annalise needs a damned good kick up the jacksie. I'm sorry, I know she's your sister . . .'

'Half-sister.'

'OK, half-sister – which is another thing, Corrie Browne, have you told her that yet?'

'No.'

'Then I think you should. If she knew that you were related she might be more inclined to listen to what you're telling her about Luke.'

'Believe me, Paula, knowing we're related isn't going to make any difference to Annalise. She's totally obsessed with the man. And remember what my father said, he'll deny all knowledge of me if I so much as mention it to anyone. Oh shit! I'm going to cry again. I never seem to stop bloody crying these days.' She took out her handkerchief and blew her nose, but the tears just wouldn't stop coming. 'Oh, Paula,' she sighed, 'I know it's pathetic but I wish Mum were here. I really miss her still.'

'I know you do.'

Corrie sniffed and tried again to stem the tears. 'Can you imagine what she'd say if I told her about Cristos?' she smiled. 'She'd just die. Oh God, what an expression to choose! She hasn't even been dead seven months and already I'm hob-nobbing around the world with any number of celebrities. It makes me feel so ashamed some-times, it's as though I couldn't wait for her to die.'

'Oh, Corrie, don't be so hard on yourself,' Paula said

sternly. 'It's what she wanted, that you should find a life for yourself.'

'I know. And look what a mess I'm making of it. Besides, there are times when none of it seems to matter without her here to share it.'

'It's understandable that you should feel that way right now,' Paula soothed. 'But I'm sure she knows what's going on, that she's up there somewhere, watching over you.'

'Do you think so?'

'I'm sure of it.'

'Oh, I wish I could speak to her. That I could hear her say something to me. Death is so final, isn't it?'

'Do you mean that?' Paula said. 'That you'd like to hear her speak to you?'

'Oh God, don't tell me you're thinking of sending me to a clairvoyant,' Corrie cried.

'No, it's not that,' Paula answered softly. 'It's . . . Look, I don't know if now is the right time to tell you this, it's probably not in fact, but . . . well I'm going to anyway. I found a letter, some time ago now, when I was turning the mattress. It's addressed to you, and it's from Edwina. I haven't read it, so I don't know what it says, but . . . Well, it's up to you . . .'

Corrie buried her face in her hands. 'I don't know. I'm not sure that I could handle it right now.'

'How about if I give it to you, then you can read it when you feel up to it?'

Corrie's distress was evident the moment she saw her mother's handwriting. 'It's no good,' she said, 'I'll have to read it now, do you mind?'

'Of course not.' Paula poured her some more wine then went to check on the baby so that Corrie could read the letter privately.

It was a very long letter, most of it telling Corrie the truth about her father, and begging forgiveness for not being honest when she was alive. She realized she should never have made the story up in the first place, but when Corrie was still a child and wanted so desperately to know about her father, had so badly wanted to be loved by her father she, Edwina, couldn't bring herself to disillusion her.

'Then, as the years went by,' she wrote, 'I too almost came to believe that Phillip was dead. It was better that way, because I was always afraid knowing about you would make no difference to him, that Phillip wouldn't want you, and I couldn't bear to think of you being so hurt. But there have been so many times when I have come so close to telling you, times when I knew you should leave me, that your own life was being ruined by mine. So often I have dreamed of the two of you being together, of you finding happiness with him, and having someone there to love and care for you when I died. May God forgive me that I never found the courage, Corrie, but please try to understand it was only because I love you so very, very much. If you do go to find him, sweetheart, then please try to be patient with him and don't judge him too harshly. He's a weak man, but he's a man of deep kindness and sensitivity too. He was the only man I ever loved, and as his daughter – our daughter – you have given me all the joy a woman could ever need in her life.

'This letter will be doubly hard for you to read because by the time you receive it I won't be with you anymore. But please know, my darling, that though you can't see me I am watching over you all the time, and that I love you very, very much.'

When Paula came back into the room and saw the tears running down Corrie's face, she simply took the letter, put an arm around Corrie and read it herself. By the time she had finished she too was crying.

They held one another for a long time, until Corrie said,

'I'm going to try again with Phillip, Paula. I know I could be wasting my time, but . . . Maybe I can reach him, if only for Annalise's sake.'

'Yes, I think you should,' Paula said, 'for both your sakes. But don't rush things. You're still pretty vulnerable right now and the last thing I want to see is you hurt again.'

'OK!' Jeannie cried, clapping her hands for quiet as she walked headlong into the pandemonium, 'let's have some quiet around here.'

Cristos came into the production office behind her and several of the production team watched him as he walked over to the schedule cards pinned over one wall of the office. They were in the process of planning the trip to England now, since the New Hampshire filming was through and the second unit had the cast out in Italy.

Jeannie waited until phone calls were finished and all mobile as well as land lines were turned off, then said, 'Just in case any of you didn't already know, the guy who's been watching dailies and rough cuts with Cristos this past week is Pierre Montbastion. He's the guy who's selecting the movies for the next festival in Cannes. And . . .' She paused, looking into each of their faces as they waited to hear the results, '*Past Lives Present* was just accepted for entry!' she announced triumphantly.

A cheer went up, and as everyone else applauded the two line-producers went over to shake Cristos by the hand. He accepted their congratulations cordially enough, but reminded them, as he continued to run his eyes over the editing schedule he was holding, that they weren't there yet.

'We still gotta lot to get through,' he added, looking round the office, 'and we don't have a lot of time. Getting finished is as much in your hands as mine, and I'm telling you now, I catch any one of you guys not pulling his – or her – weight around here then you're not gonna hit the floor with your hat. Have you got me?' As everyone nodded and murmured his eyes came to rest on Jeannie. 'A word.'

Almost instantly the noise erupted again as production managers, unit managers, line-producers, production co-ordinators, assistants and accountants got back on the phones, and Jeannie walked through the maze of desks to where Cristos was standing. One look at his face was enough for her to see that he was still as mad as hell.

'Don't you liaise with these boys out here?' he snapped. 'You got me editing when we're in England. How the fuck can I be in two places at once?'

'Lance is coming out to England,' Jeannie reminded him gently. 'You requested it yourself, so you could get ahead.'

Cristos glared at her, then turning back to the schedule board, said tightly, 'There's nothing here about Wiltshire.'

'Detailth going up this afternoon,' Jeannie said, pointing to a card at the bottom of the board, and if she didn't feel so sorry for him she might have laughed at the look on his face at being thwarted again.

'Do you have any preference which hotel you stay at in London, Cristos?' one of the production managers suddenly yelled out.

'No,' Cristos answered. He turned back to Jeannie. 'Get onto Fitzpatrick, find out if he knows of a house to rent for David Easton and his family. I'll be with Lance if anyone's looking for me,' and before Jeannie could make any comment he walked out of the room.

'For a guy who's got a lot to feel happy about he sure is sore about something,' one of the production managers remarked, when he was certain Cristos was no longer in earshot.

'Mmm, or someone,' Jeannie answered, still looking at the door.

'Oh?' Everyone was immediately interested, and laughing Jeannie followed Cristos out of the office leaving them, she knew, to speculate over his affair with Paige Spencer.

When she returned to her own office, adjoining Cristos's, Jeannie found her husband sitting at her desk using the phone. Hearing the voice at the other end, barking into the receiver, and seeing how twitchy it was making Richard she started to grin. Eventually Richard put the phone down, and taking him by the hand to pull him out of her chair, Jeannie said, 'Just get your head bitten off, did you?'

'Damned right I did,' Richard answered, glaring down at the telephone. 'What the hell's eating him anyway? He's been like this for days.'

'Who.' Jeannie corrected him. 'You mean *who* the hell's eating him? The answer is a woman.'

Richard waved a hand dismissively. 'Women never get to Cristos,' he snorted.

'Well this one has.'

Richard's eyes widened, then he started to shake his head. 'Nah, you got it wrong, Jeannie. This isn't about Paige Spencer, she just doesn't mean that much to him.'

'Did I say it was Paige Spencer?'

Richard eyed her suspiciously. 'Then who?' he said.

'Come on, guess. You said yourself he's been ticked this past week. And you got to have noticed, the closer we get to going to England the worse he's getting.'

'You're kidding? You're not telling me he's got himself hooked up on that English broad who was here with Fitzpatrick's outfit?'

'That's what I'm telling you. Her name's Corrie Browne by the way.'

Richard grinned. 'Well, I'll be darned. How do you know?'

'Let's just say I know Cristos.'

'What's he say about her?'

'He doesn't, that's not his style. But I'm telling you this is to do with her all right. I tried to talk to him about it the other day . . .'

'You did!' Richard interrupted in amazement. 'I didn't know you were so brave. What'd he say?'

'Just that it wasn't something he wanted to discuss. I

guess it was the way he said it that told me how bad it really was. It's driving him crazy . . .'

Richard was looking doubtful again. 'You sure you got this right, Jeannie? I mean, she's hardly his type, is she?'

'Meaning she doesn't have yards of blonde hair, a gap in her legs right up to her fanny and pouty little lips? Cristos has had his fill of women like that, Richard, honey. He crooks that little old finger of his and they just come a-running.'

'All right, then why doesn't he do something about this Corrie Browne instead of going about the place getting pissed at everyone?'

Jeannie shrugged. 'So he says, she's a star-fucker.'

At that Richard just roared with laughter. 'Cristos Bennati gets hooked on a star-fucker! I've heard it all now. Does she know?'

'What do you think?' Jeannie answered, kissing him on the nose. 'Besides she's no star-fucker. OK, I know what you're gonna say, and sure she leapt right into bed with him, but I've met her, and I'm telling you she's no star-fucker. And, despite what he says, Cristos knows it too. He's still raw over that business with Angelique,' she went on solemnly. 'And who can blame him? It'll be pretty damned difficult for him to trust a woman again after that. He doesn't want to get involved and he's mad as hell at himself 'cos he knows it's happening whether he likes it or not.'

'Shit! Your powers of deduction just leave me standing,' Richard groaned.

'I know, honey,' Jeannie grinned picking up the phone to answer it. Immediately she drew her head back as Bud Winters' voice bellowed down the line, 'Where the fuck's Bennati? I just heard the news. Tell him to get himself over here, we got champagne waiting for him.'

'I'll tell him,' Jeannie laughed, and hung up. 'I'll bet

Cristos is just in the mood to drink champagne with Bud Winters,' she remarked to Richard.

Richard was looking thoughtful. 'You know, if you're right about this, Jeannie, then it looks like we could be in for one bumpy ride over there in England.'

Jeannie shook her head. 'Not if I got anything do with it we won't.'

'Jeannie!' Richard warned.

'Yes?' she said, all innocence.

'You know what I'm talking about,' he told her. 'And who's to say you haven't got it wrong over this Corrie woman. I mean I don't care what you say, it sounds pretty unlikely to me. The man only spent one night with her.'

'Sometimes one night's all it takes,' Jeannie grinned. And winking at him, added, 'Remember?'

Richard laughed. 'All right, you got me convinced. But don't go getting involved there, Jeannie. You know what he's like about his private life. Besides, if I know Cristos, he'll get this sorted out before he lets it get in the way of the movie.'

'So? You were the one who was worried,' Jeannie reminded him. 'Anyway, he's waiting for you so you'd better run along.'

When Richard had gone Jeannie sat down at her desk intending to set about tidying the mess, but half an hour later she was still resting her chin in her hands, thinking about Cristos. She wasn't too worried about how he'd be when they got to England, Paige would be back by then, and though it was no romance made in heaven, Jeannie knew Cristos liked having Paige around. Ordinarily that sort of thing would make Jeannie mad, she hated the way men used women when something was eating them, but in this instance Paige was using Cristos too. It got her name in the papers and gave her a credibility she wouldn't find with many other men. And Cristos was no one's fool. He knew what Paige was about, just like he knew that one of these days he was going to call Corrie Browne – he just needed some time to come round to the idea. The question was, how did Corrie Browne feel about him now he'd walked out on her? Jeannie didn't know Corrie too well, but in her position Jeannie knew exactly what she'd do. She'd tell him to go straight to hell, that's what she'd do. And, she thought wryly to herself, she'd end up living to regret it. So, Jeannie decided, she just better make sure that didn't happen or they'd all be waiting for the next life to come round to get this resolved.

– 20 –

Phillip Denby was in a regular monthly board meeting when Pam let herself quietly into the mahogany panelled room, skirted round behind the other six directors of the bank and passed him a note. His face paled slightly as he read it, then nodding to Pam he tucked the note into a corner of his blotter and turned back to the meeting. It wasn't until early afternoon that he eventually returned to his office, where he buzzed immediately through for Pam.

'Did she say what she wanted?' he asked, as soon as Pam had closed the door.

Pam shook her head. 'Just that she wanted you to call her.'

Phillip looked distractedly about the office, trying to decide what he should do. It was probably because it was such an alien feeling to him that it was some time before he realized that the emotion unfurling itself inside him was only just short of pure joy, and as he turned to Pam he found that she too was smiling.

'Shall I get her on the line?' Pam asked.

'Yes, do that. Do it right now.'

A few minutes later Pam put the call through and Phillip

felt a sharp pang in his chest as he heard Corrie's voice, saying,

'Mr Denby?'

'Yes,' he said. 'What can I do for you, Corrie?' He hoped he sounded at the very least approachable, and wished he could tell her that she didn't have to call him that.

'I was hoping we could meet,' Corrie said. 'I have something important I'd like to discuss with you.'

'Are you free this evening?' Did she have any idea, he wondered, how very like her mother she sounded?

'Yes, as a matter of fact, I am,' Corrie said.

Smiling at the surprise in her voice, Phillip said, 'Then why don't we meet at the Ritz. In the cocktail bar at six thirty?' Was that the kind of treat she might enjoy?

'That should be fine,' Corrie said, and rang off.

Phillip wandered out to Pam. 'She says she's got something important to discuss with me,' he told her. Then, almost because it was second nature for him to respond that way, he was suddenly stricken with panic. 'Do you think she's planning to tell Annalise who she is?'

'Does it matter?' Pam asked.

'Yes. Yes it does.'

'Why?'

'Because then Octavia will find out . . .'

'I don't see that that matters either.'

'It does! Octavia has no idea that I was married before, she doesn't even know that Edwina existed . . . But she'll have to know, sooner or later, won't she?' he added, and he seemed quite pleased by the notion. 'But not right now,' he said. 'I have to think it through first. In fact, if I feel it's right to do so, I'll talk it over with Corrie.'

'That sounds like a good idea,' Pam chuckled. 'And while you're at it, why don't you tell her how worried you are about Annalise?'

'Oh, hang on,' Phillip said, holding up his hands. 'I want

to give her the chance to get used to being my daughter before I start loading her half-sister's problems onto her.'

'It wouldn't surprise me if she's already carrying them,' Pam remarked. 'Didn't you say they work as a team?'

'Mmm,' Phillip nodded thoughtfully. 'You know, I hope I'm right about this, that she is going to give me another chance. It's more than I deserve after the way I've treated her, I know, but now all that business with Luke is over there's nothing else in the world I want more than to get to know her.'

But it's not over is it! Pam wanted to scream, for love him as she did, the way he blinkered himself to situations made her want to strangle him at times. But she said nothing, since this was a subject they'd argued about too many times already. She could only hope now that Corrie would say something tonight that might persuade him to see sense. Because, if Pam's instincts were serving her aright, then Corrie wanted to talk to her father about Annalise, for what could be more important to Phillip than Annalise? And Corrie would know more than anyone else exactly what was going on between Annalise and Luke.

'I think,' Phillip said, 'that I might start by telling her how much I loved her mother. What do you think?'

Pam looked at him in despair. Sometimes, she thought, shaking her head in fond exasperation, the man was beyond all hope.

Corrie arrived at the Ritz early, hoping to calm her nerves with a drink before her father arrived. It had taken her a few weeks to pluck up the courage to make the call, feeling as vulnerable as she did lately she didn't think she could handle another rejection so close on Cristos. That pain still hadn't gone away, but she was coping with it better now, at least on the surface she was. What she felt inside she only ever discussed with Paula, like the way she still lay awake at nights, her whole body yearning for him to touch her and look at her again with that heartrending tenderness in his eyes. She knew that she was probably driving Paula as crazy as she was driving herself with her sudden swings in moods and incessant repeating of 'Why did it ever have to happen?' and she was going to make herself stop. Just as she was going to put an end to this nonsense of scanning the newspapers to find out if he was filming in England yet. He was, she'd read it only that day, but what difference did it make? She certainly wasn't going to ring him! And if he rang her . . . ? Well, he wouldn't so there was no point in thinking about that. But if he did . . . She'd tell him to go straight to hell, that's what she'd do. There were more important things in life than Cristos Bennati, like the frustration she'd started to feel lately about the programmes TW were making.

They were all right in their own way, but there was nothing innovative about them – they were just the same as all the other current affairs programmes going out on all the other channels. They were dry, sometimes pompous and very often boring. There was nothing in them to make people really sit up and listen, to motivate them into doing anything about changing a situation. And what did they themselves as programme makers do to improve the plight of those they made programmes about? Nothing. They just shot it, transmitted it, then forgot it. It wasn't good enough, Corrie felt, there had to be a way of really getting to the people, of doing something effective, worthwhile and vital.

She'd talked this over with Bob, who, to her surprise, agreed with her, but when he'd taken her suggestions to Luke, Luke had sneeringly reminded her that she wasn't running the company yet! It was that yet! that had made Corrie back off, remembering the way she'd got her promotion to producer. She didn't want anything like that happening again. But she wasn't going to give up that easily, in fact she was going to fight this and win! And what was more, she was going to get everyone else at TW on her side. It seemed that most were already, since other producers had started asking her to work with them, and her fellow researchers were lately spending quite a lot of time at her studio sounding her out on their own ideas.

So there *were* things in life more important than Cristos Bennati, and the very idea of spending her days pampering herself in his bathroom while waiting for him to come home was so ludicrous, so laughable as to make her no better than those Hollywood airheads even for thinking it. Not that she'd ever seriously thought that was the way their relationship would be . . . Were she and Cristos ever to be seriously involved . . .

Stop it! she told herself vehemently. Just stop! She knew what was happening, and it was making her angrier even than her unrelenting preoccupation with Cristos. For she was purposefully evading even thinking about the repellent, horrifying, even chilling problem she'd come here to discuss with her father. But she must! She had to go through it in her mind coherently and logically, make certain she overdramatized nothing, but still got across the seriousness of the situation, for, to Corrie's mind it most certainly had become serious now.

Since they'd returned from the States everything had been so 'blissfully wonderful,' to use Annalise's expression, between her and Luke, that Corrie had only just stopped short of yelling at her for being so stupid and so blind. Annalise had actually walked into Luke's office only two days before to find Luke trying to kiss her, Corrie. Of course Luke had twisted it round, saying that it was she who was trying to kiss him, and Annalise had actually said that she didn't blame Corrie; that she understood if Corrie still fancied Luke, and wasn't Corrie impressed by the way she was coming to terms with his lack of fidelity? It was enough to send Corrie screaming mad with frustration. But that was only the tip of the iceberg.

Annalise would never admit it, of course, but she was

violently jealous of any attention Luke paid to Corrie, and Corrie knew it. What was more, if Annalise even as much as mentioned the way she felt to Luke, he beat her. Corrie had seen Annalise's bruises for herself, and to her mind they were much worse than before. And now Luke was blaming her, Corrie, for what he was doing. He'd actually told her that it was because she was refusing to marry him that he beat Annalise, and until she agreed to be his wife he'd just keep right on doing it. For over two weeks he'd been bombarding Corrie with telephone calls and letters pleading with her to say yes, then just last night he'd come round to her studio.

It was approaching midnight when he'd arrived and Corrie had kept the chain on the door, refusing to let him in. He had simply stood outside, at the top of the steps, and spoken to her from there.

Corrie had listened, at first in disgust, then in mounting fear. He sounded so rational, so sane, yet what he was saying was crazy.

'But why me?' she'd cried when he'd finished explaining once again that she was the only one who could save Annalise from further pain.

'Because I love you,' he pleaded, pushing his fingers through the crack in the door. 'Don't you understand that? I love you, Corrie.'

'You don't!' she cried. 'And I don't love you. I don't want to marry you, Luke. Can't you understand that?'

'But you have to, Corrie,' he said. 'Now you be letting me in, like a good girl.'

It was that sudden and sinister introduction of the Irish brogue that had made Corrie think of what Felicity had told her when the two of them had finally caught up with each other.

'He's sick,' Felicity had proclaimed, 'I mean seriously sick. He thinks he's someone else, or he's pretending to, I don't know which, but he needs help, Corrie. You're right to try and keep him away from Annalise, but you can't do it alone.'

She'd gone on to tell Corrie then how Luke had asked her, Felicity, to tell him where he might find rabbits. He wanted her to eat them! And all the time he was asking he was speaking in an Irish accent. It had frightened Felicity half to death, so she'd just leapt in her car and driven to some friends where she'd stayed until she knew he was on the plane back to England.

But there was no such easy escape for Corrie, she was trapped inside her studio, and he was right there, outside, begging her to let him in.

'Corrie, Corrie, Corrie,' he sang. 'Corrie, be letting me in now. I won't be going away till you do.'

'Luke,' she cried, 'I'll call the police. I swear it, I'll call them if you don't go right now.'

'I don't want to be hurting you now, Corrie, I just want to be talking to you. Now please let me in, there's a good girl. If you don't I'll just be waiting here till you do.'

'Luke, didn't you hear me? I'm going to call the police. Now go. Please, just go!'

'And just what would you be telling the police?' he laughed softly. 'Now you don't want Annalise to be hurt anymore, do you? So you just be letting me in there.'

'Why are you doing this, Luke?' she cried. 'What's the matter with you? Why are you using that horrible voice?'

She hadn't been able to see him, he was standing in the shadows, but even though there was no answer she'd known he was still there. She listened, waited, her heart pounding thunderously through her ears. And then she heard him again. He wasn't speaking, neither was he laughing, but there was a sound coming from him that in her terror she just couldn't recognize.

Minutes later, in a voice totally his own, he said, 'You have to understand, Corrie. I want it to be you, because you're the only one it can be,' then she heard his footsteps running down the steps to the street.

And now here she was at the Ritz, not knowing how she was even going to begin to explain this to her father, but believing that he was the only person she could turn to now. Please God, he wouldn't let her down.

By the time Phillip arrived Corrie was already on her second Bellini. She saw him before he saw her, and thought straight away how different he looked to the last time they'd met. He seemed to be standing straighter, walking tall and there was an expression of something like eagerness in his eyes. Then, to her amazement, when he spotted her his whole face lit up.

Corrie was instantly annoyed. Though he had sounded friendly enough on the phone earlier, she certainly hadn't expected anything like this. But if something had happened to soften him then he could at least, she thought, show some remorse for the way he'd treated her before. She quickly pushed that to one side though, it hardly mattered now in light of what she had to tell him. If anything, she realized with inordinate relief, it was going to make it easier.

'Hello,' he said, sitting down on the small couch beside her. 'Am I late?'

'No,' Corrie told him. 'I was early. I needed to fortify myself before you got here in case you turned on me again.'

'I'm not going to do that,' Phillip assured her, with an immediate and very genuine sorrow in his eyes. 'I'm never going to do that again, Corrie. In fact, I was hoping, I mean, if you're agreeable, that we might turn back the clock and pretend that this is the first time we've ever met.'

Corrie was more than a little thrown by this, and found herself looking helplessly about the plush, dusky-pink room as though in its ornateness she might discover what she should say. She didn't want to sound churlish by telling him it was too late for that, yet on the other hand it just wasn't that easy to forget all that had gone before. Why, she wondered angrily, did she feel that if Cristos were here he could give her the answer? She was perfectly capable of finding it for herself! Except she couldn't. So she simply turned back to her father and forced herself to smile.

He smiled too, and then she saw the uncertainty in his eyes. He was afraid she would reject him, was even expecting her to, and because of it Corrie felt her heart starting to thaw.

'I'm a weak man,' he said frankly, 'I know that. And I have many other faults besides. But I am capable of love, and I want you to know, Corrie, that I loved your mother more than I've ever loved any woman.'

Then why did you abandon her the way you did? Corrie wanted to shout. Though deep in her inner-self she was asking herself if she should tell him that Edwina had loved him too — until the day she died. But fearing that would upset him, Corrie decided not to. And it was that decision which started her realizing that coming to him was going to be of no help at all. If anything, it was he who needed her help. He wanted her to ease him over his guilt, not only by forgiving him for what he'd done to her mother, but by telling him that she understood. Corrie could see it all written there in his earnestly imploring eyes. But she didn't understand! She could never understand a man who had allowed his child to grow up pretending he didn't even know she existed. And to think of all the pain he had caused her mother . . .

But then she remembered Luke, recalled vividly the night she had seen Phillip at Luke's apartment, and how certain she had been that Luke was somehow, for some reason, tormenting her father. Just like he was tormenting Annalise. And that, after all, was why she was here — to talk about Annalise, or, she realized now, more specifically about Luke. But, dear God, how to begin?

She did, somehow, but with more false starts than she'd

care to remember, until eventually she realized that she had her father's undivided attention. In fact, he was listening so intently to everything she was telling him, that Corrie could feel herself in danger of losing her concentration. She was suddenly reassessing him, thinking that perhaps he wasn't so spineless after all, because the look on his face was of such deep anger and concern that she just couldn't believe that he was incapable of acting now.

When Corrie had finished, sparing him nothing, right down to the way Luke had threatened the night before that he would hurt Annalise again if Corrie didn't agree to marry him, Phillip's face was so rigid that she really didn't know what he was thinking. But she found out soon enough, and if his response hadn't been so tragic it would have been laughable.

'Just tell me what you want me to do, Corrie,' he said, gravely. 'Just tell me and I'll do it.'

Unable to stop herself Corrie closed her eyes in exasperation. So the decisions were going to be hers. How tired she suddenly felt, and how responsible too. He was like a child, and just as though he were a child, she had no doubt that he meant every word he'd said. He would do anything she asked of him, it was just that he wouldn't, probably couldn't, take the responsibility himself.

'You could begin,' she said, wearily, 'by telling me what it is that Luke Fitzpatrick is holding over you.'

If she'd expected any reluctance, hesitation even, she'd have been wrong, because there was none. 'Oh, that's to do with my wife,' he said, and his eagerness in honesty was so touching that Corrie actually found herself moved by it. She listened, with no surprise, to what he then told her about Octavia. It was so frank, so utterly repulsive and revealing of himself, that it had to be true. No man would make up a story like that about his wife, most of all not about himself, and after all Corrie had met Octavia herself. The profligacy wasn't difficult to believe.

'But there's more, isn't there,' she said, when he'd finished. 'There has to be, or why else is Luke behaving the way he is with Annalise and me?'

'I really don't know the answer to that,' Phillip said helplessly. 'God knows, I wish I did.'

Corrie looked at him, then steeling herself to be brutal she began by saying, 'Luke must hate you to an almost unimaginable degree to be doing this to you, after all we are your daughters. So please, tell me, what have you done to him? Because you must have done something for . . .'

'I've done nothing, Corrie. I swear to you, nothing. I don't know why he's doing it, I don't even know what he's trying to achieve. All I know is that he's been terrorizing my family one way or another ever since I went into partnership with him. That was why I didn't want to get involved with you. I was afraid that if he knew who you were he'd start hurting you too.'

'But you're here now,' Corrie said. 'So what's happened to change that?'

Phillip bowed his head and Corrie could already sense there was another heart-wrenching confession to come. It saddened her to think that it had to be like this, but how else could she help him – any of them – unless he told her the entire truth?

It was some time before he spoke, but when he did it was only to ask if he could hold her hands. Had he not asked then things might have turned out very differently, but he did, and Corrie gave him her hands. And that was how, before Phillip could tell her anything about the prostitutes, Octavia discovered them.

The scene that followed was so staggering in its suddenness that Corrie simply sat rooted in horrified fascination. The true ugliness of Octavia's face was seeping through its mask of surgery. Corrie had never heard such invective, nor such venom in her life. It wasn't until Octavia suddenly started to strike Phillip that she finally came to her senses and jumped to her feet to defend him.

'Get your hands off me, you slut!' Octavia snarled, as Corrie started to drag her away. 'Get your filthy hands off of me. This is a whore!' she cried to an approaching waiter. 'A whore in the Ritz! What are you doing letting scum like her in the door? Get her out of here! Get the bitch . . .'

'Shut up!' Corrie hissed. 'Just shut up before I slap your face!'

'She's threatening me!' Octavia screamed to anyone who was listening, and everyone was. 'She's threatening me with violence, and that's my husband sitting there! She's got the audacity to threaten me while she's trying to procure money from my husband . . .'

Phillip was on his feet. 'Octavia!' he barked. 'Pull yourself together, now!' And to Corrie's amazement, he wrenched Octavia from her and started to march her out of the hotel.

Totally dumbfounded Corrie stood and watched them go, as stunned now by the sudden assertiveness in Phillip as she was by Octavia's outburst. It was only when the waiter touched her lightly on the arm to enquire if he could get her anything else that Corrie remembered where she was. She looked around to see that all eyes were still on her, and recalling all too vividly what Octavia had called her she hastily settled the bill and left.

But the degradation of Octavia's words that seemed to crawl out into the street after her was sufferable, if only for the fact that she had managed to get through to Phillip. To what degree she wasn't yet sure, but right at that moment she felt a strong desire to congratulate him for the way he had taken Octavia in hand. Corrie would lay odds that he had never done it before, she only hoped he had it in him to carry on doing it. Or better still, to leave Octavia altogether. But more pressing than that was what he was going to do about Annalise. Corrie already knew she'd have to decide that for him, but whatever she concluded he'd do it, of that she was certain. The question was, what *could* he do when neither of them had any idea what they were up against?

Phillip himself however, believed he had the answer, for early the next morning, unbeknownst to Corrie, he went to the police and told them everything he'd been holding back from them about Luke.

He was extremely pleased with himself when he left the station, but had he only known it, he'd made such a mess of what he'd told them, that after he'd left DI Radcliffe and DC Archer were of the opinion that somehow the father had now become embroiled in the love problems concerning his two daughters and Luke Fitzpatrick. However, with a certain weariness they did call Fitzpatrick back to the station.

'I don't believe this!' Luke stormed, when they repeated what Phillip Denby had disclosed to them. 'I told you before, I don't know anything about Bobby McIver or about those murdered women except what you've told me yourselves! And the reason I didn't come to you before about Denby was precisely because he is the father of the woman I'm in love with . . .'

'Who is?' Radcliffe enquired.

'Annalise Kapsakis.'

'But if you had suspicions, Luke,' Radcliffe pointed out, 'then you shouldn't have kept them to yourself. That's an offence, you know, withholding information.'

'But I tried everything I could to make the man come forward himself. And he did, didn't he? Surely you can give me credit for that.'

Radclife waited.

'Look,' Luke said, dashing a hand through his hair. 'I didn't want to tell you this, but it looks like I'll have to. That family is really screwed up. I mean seriously screwed up. If it weren't for Annalise I'd pull out right now. Shit, they're nearly taking me round the bend with them. If you only knew the half of it . . .'

'We've got time,' Radcliffe said.

'OK. Then here it is.' And Luke then told the police not only what Octavia was like, but that Phillip was trying to hide the fact that he had another daughter whom neither his wife nor Annalise knew about. 'On top of which,' he added, 'the bastard beats Annalise half out of her senses, has done all her life, which is why she spends as much time as she can with me. I'm the only one she has to protect her, and I'm trying to keep Corrie away from him now before he starts on her. So if you want to question anyone around here, I suggest you start over again with him.'

'But we only have your word for this, Luke,' Radcliffe reminded him.

'Then it's up to you whose word you take,' Luke said, 'because quite frankly I've had it up to here. And until somebody does something about that bastard then I'm quite prepared to accept that I'm on my own.'

'You're asking us to help?' Archer asked.

'Help, intervene, whatever you want to call it.' He laughed suddenly and bitterly. 'Oh, I know what you call it, you call it a domestic. You don't want to get involved, do you?'

'Don't we?' Radcliffe said. 'If he's beating up on either one of those girls then we want to know about that.'

'Well I've told you, so it's up to you now to do the rest,' Luke stated, only just able to disguise his triumph. They'd never find any evidence against Denby, and Denby could point the finger all he liked at him, he'd never get anywhere without Annalise to back him up. Which was something Annalise would never do, just so long as Luke asked her to marry him. He wouldn't marry her of course, he couldn't, he was going to marry Corrie – but it was vital that for now he kept Annalise on his side.

That wasn't going to be easy though, he was thinking to

himself as he walked back down the street. Corrie was proving almost impossible to control, but damn it, he'd work it out. Didn't he work everything out in the end. In fact, now he came to think of it, he knew precisely how he was going to handle Corrie, but he'd have to be exceptionally careful how he went about it, for Corrie was nobody's fool. In fact, on second thoughts, he wasn't too sure he should risk it. No, keeping Corrie occupied with Bennati wasn't such a good idea, since the last thing he wanted was for Bennati to whisk her out from under his nose. He wanted Corrie himself, he needed her, and the more he thought about it, the more convinced he became that, despite everything, he must do all he could to keep her and Bennati apart. Which might not be a problem at all were Bennati not right here in England, and just to think of that caused the demon of rage to heave to his throat. He was only sorry that he couldn't be taking Corrie, right now, but with the police breathing down his neck the way they were that just wasn't possible. But he'd be having her in the end, to be sure he would. But first there was Annalise to be dealing with ... Annalise, his darling Annalise, who was so like Siobhan it tore his heart apart just to look at her. And all the bastard had done to Siobhan he, Luke Fitzpatrick, was going to inflict on Annalise ... It was the only way, he knew that now – he only wondered why he'd never seen it before. All this time he'd been fighting to stop himself, but he knew he no longer could, or should. Because only then, once this devil inside him was exorcised, could he turn to Corrie. Corrie, his everlasting salvation, the perfect mother for his children, the only one of them he would never hurt ... Unless Bennati got in his way.

For now though, he must wait until this untimely business with the police cooled down. But all the time he would be watching Corrie, his Corrie, because she would be his in the end, of that he was in no doubt at all.

It was while Luke was on his way back from the police station that the telephone call Corrie had been dreading came through to the edit suite where she was viewing rushes with Annalise.

'Mummy! Mummy!' Annalise cried after only a few moments. 'You're not making any sense. No, no, listen! I'll go to a private office and call you back. Just hang on there.' She put the phone down and turned immediately to Corrie. 'Mummy sounds terribly upset about something,' she said. 'Do you mind carrying on without me for a while?'

Not knowing what else she could say, Corrie simply shook her head and turned back to the monitors. It was pointless even to pray that Octavia wouldn't tell Annalise anything about what had happened at the Ritz, it was quite obviously why she had called. And exactly what Octavia was going to tell Annalise was anyone's guess, though all that concerned Corrie right now was what excuse she was going to give for being there with Phillip in the first place.

It was some time before Annalise returned to the edit suite, and the minute the door opened Corrie started to brace herself. She turned round, and seeing Annalise's face her insides seemed to collapse. It was more than obvious that Octavia had done her very worst. Not that Corrie had thought for one minute that she wouldn't, nor that this was going to be easy, but without her father's permission to tell Annalise who she really was, she knew now that this was going to be impossible.

'Annalise,' she started, but Annalise immediately interrupted.

'Colin,' she said to the editor, 'would you mind leaving us alone for a while?'

Colin shrugged, hit a couple of buttons then got up to leave the room. Already the atmosphere was so tense he had no desire to stay.

Annalise waited only until the door had closed behind

him before rounding on Corrie. 'You two-faced, conniving, little bitch!' she spat. 'I know . . .'

'Annalise, please, just listen . . .'

'I don't want to hear anything you've got to say. Not one fucking word! I got you this job, Corrie Browne. without me you'd still be out there in the gutter grubbing around like the little scrubber you are! And how do you repay me? What do . . .'

'For God's sake, Annalise . . .'

'Shut up! Just shut the fuck up! I can't believe how stupid I've been all this time. I thought you were my friend, I trusted you, you bitch, and all the time you've been scheming behind my back. Not only have you tried to steal my job, you've tried everything you could to come between me and Luke, and now you're using my father to help you! What won't you stop at? Just what lengths . . .'

'Annalise, you've got it all wrong . . .'

'I don't know how you've got the fucking audacity to come in here and face me every morning when you're not only sleeping with my boyfriend, you're sleeping with my father too. Is there nothing you'll stop at to get what you want?'

'I'm not sleeping with your father, don't be so damned ridiculous. And neither am I sleeping with Luke!'

'You surely don't expect me to believe that,' Annalise yelled, 'when my own mother saw you parading yourself about the Ritz like the little . . .'

'It wasn't like that! I was there because . . .'

'I know why you were there, you whore! Holding his hands, canoodling with him . . .'

'For Christ's sake!' Corrie screamed. 'Is there no getting through to you? I was not canoodling with him, I was merely talking to . . .'

'About me! About how you want this company! Oh, I know all about your ideas to dramatize our documentaries, how you're trying to win everyone over to your side so that you can get rid of me and take over. Well it won't work, do you hear me? It just won't work!' And before Corrie could utter another word she turned and slammed out of the room.

As she stormed back up the corridor Luke was coming in through the door. Without saying a word Annalise walked straight into his office, waited for him to follow, then slammed the door.

'If you're in cahoots with Corrie Browne to get rid of me,' she hissed, 'then I want to know now.'

'What? What the hell are you talking about?' Luke laughed in amazement.

'I'm talking about her affair with you, *and* with my father. I'm talking about the way she's always . . .'

'Hang on! Hang on!' Luke said holding up a hand to stop her. 'Did you say her affair with your father?'

'Yes, with my father! And I notice you don't deny she's having one with you! So just what the hell is going on, Luke?'

'She's not having an affair with me,' Luke said. 'Hand on my heart, she's not. But your father . . .'

'Mummy caught them last night at the Ritz.'

'What *in flagrante delicto*! I don't believe it!'

'Then ask Mummy! She'll tell you. That bitch is trying to get my father to give her this company. She's using him to get to the top and get me out. We've got to stop her, Luke!'

Luke was still dazed. He was trying to think! To sort out what all this could mean. 'Yes,' he murmured, absently, 'yes, we've got to stop her. Shit! She's sleeping with your father?'

'I told you!' Annalise yelled. 'Mummy caught them!'

Luke shook his head in amazement. So the bastard was doing it again! But Corrie, he'd never have dreamt it of Corrie.

'I want you to fire her!' Annalise demanded.

Luke simply looked at her.

'I said, fire her!' Annalise screamed.

Luke shrugged. 'All right, Annalise,' he said, 'if that's what you want, then leave it with me.'

'All right, Jeannie, you guessed it,' Cristos said, throwing down his pencil and getting up from the drawing board where he'd been studying the designer's plans of Hyde Park.

Jeannie was barely able to disguise her grin. She'd been badgering him for ten minutes now and still he hadn't got mad. This was a good sign.

'Yeah, you're right, she got to me,' Cristos almost shouted when he saw the way Jeannie was looking at him, 'and, yeah, you're right again, I don't like it. But I'm not calling her . . . No! Save it, Jeannie I'm not doing it! I got a movie to shoot here, I got a star breathing down my neck, and we both know I don't mean Easton. The last thing I want right now is to upset Paige Spencer.'

'But it's OK to upset yourself?'

'That doesn't even come into it. All right, I know I've been kind of ticked lately, but . . .'

'Kind of!' Jeannie cried. 'You've been a regular pain in the butt, is what you've been. But we're here in England now, so why not just give her a call. She'll probably tell you where to get off anyway, but if she matters that much, and I reckon she does, you'll handle it.'

'And how is Paige gonna handle that? Jesus Christ, Jeannie, you know what she's like, she's more insecure than a man hanging from a cliff with one finger. She needs everything I can give her right now, and she's gonna get it.'

'You take those actors too damned serious,' Jeannie told him frankly. 'They're adults, not kids, let them take some responsibility for themselves.'

'The responsibility is mine!' Cristos snapped.

'Not twenty-four hours a day!'

'Yes, twenty-four hours a day.'

'Why, you gonna marry her or something?'

'I'm not gonna marry anyone, and you know it. After that business with Angelique . . . Jesus Christ, I don't believe we're having this conversation! I knew the girl for one night . . .'

'But she got to you?'

'Yeah, I said, she got to me. But there are other things more important right now.'

'But she got to you?'

'Will you just let up on that, Jeannie! I told you what you wanted to hear, now let's forget it! I'm seeing Paige in half an hour and I just don't need this.'

'OK,' Jeannie said. 'You go right ahead and screw up your life for the sake of your art. I won't stop you.'

Cristos eyed her threateningly and suddenly Jeannie fell backwards clutching her hands to her heart.

'Don't do that,' she gasped, 'I'm a married woman.'

Despite himself Cristos laughed, but as he left the room he said, 'Would it help if I promised to lay off the guys?'

'Sure, it would help them,' Jeannie told him. 'But will it help you?'

Her answer was the door closing behind him.

She waited a few minutes, wanting to make certain he'd gone, then digging into her pocket for her mobile phone and the scrap of paper with TW's number on it, she started to dial. She was half through when the door suddenly opened.

'Oh, it's you,' she said as Richard walked in, and pulling the phone out from behind her back she dialled again.

'These the plans of the park?' Richard asked, leaning over the drawing board.

'Mmm, yeah,' Jeannie answered. 'Oh, hi there, can I speak to Corrie Browne please?'

As Richard spun round Jeannie glared back at him, but as he made to wrest the phone from her she pushed him out of the way saying, 'Sorry. Could you repeat that please?' As she listened to the voice at the other end Richard watched her eyes grow wider by the second. 'Oh, she has,' Jeannie said in the end. 'When did this happen?' She nodded. 'Sure, I got you. OK, thanks for your help,' and she rang off.

'Jeannie, will you give the guy a break,' Richard barked. 'He's got enough on his mind right now without you stirring up his private life.'

'Mmm, yeah,' Jeannie said engrossed in thought.

Richard looked at her, then rolling his eyes, he said, 'OK, what you planning now?'

'Nothing,' Jeannie said. 'Nothing at all. You know, I could swear that was Luke Fitzpatrick I just spoke to, but he didn't say it was him. Now why do you reckon that was?'

'Don't ask me. But just leave it now, Jeannie. If Cristos wants to get in touch with her he'll do it himself.'

Jeannie shook her head. 'He can't. Or not so's I can see, unless he knows where she lives.'

'What are you talking about?'

'She's not working there any more. She's been fired.'

As Luke replaced the phone after speaking to Jeannie he picked up a London directory and started to search for a number. Not finding it, he checked his watch, then after slotting several programme files into his briefcase, walked out into the main office. It was past seven o'clock and only three people were left working: Perkin, Cindy Thompson – and Corrie. He watched her for a minute or two, a smile hovering around his lips, then saying a general good-night he left the office.

Lucky, he was thinking as he rode down in the lift, that he'd taken that call from Jeannie himself. She wouldn't ring back now, not after what he'd told her, and he knew for a fact that Corrie's number was unlisted – he'd just checked for himself.

Annalise was still after him to fire her, but the hell he would. He wanted Corrie Browne right where he could see her, at all times, and Annalise was just going to have to suffer it. But it had come in useful as an excuse to get rid of Jeannie – or more precisely, Bennati – and he felt strangely indebted to Annalise for planting the idea.

But Annalise would have to wait, he had more pressing matters to attend to right now, like the bastard screwing his own daughter! Old habits die hard he thought, bitterly savouring the cliché, and leaping into his Porsche he roared off across Battersea Bridge.

– 21 –

'Get out of here, man,' Cristos laughed, pushing David Easton away. 'Go rehearse it on someone else.'

Easton's face fell in mock devastation, and all those standing around the coffee urns set up in Hyde Park started to laugh. 'But I gotta know my gyrating hips are having the desired effect,' Easton complained, fluffing out the frilly cuffs of his Georgian costume. He knew without lifting his eyes that they were all waiting to see what he'd do next, and so's not to disappoint his audience he looked at Cristos through narrowed eyes, then pouting his lips sultrily as he let his hands go limp at the wrists, he squeaked, 'And I just fancy the pants off you, Cristos Bennati.'

'Get this jerk out of here,' Cristos told Easton's dresser. 'He's driving me crazy.'

As Cristos made to walk off through the snow, which had been brought in that morning, Easton minced along behind him, making a grab for Cristos's rear end. 'And you're just driving me crazy, honey love,' he trilled ecstatically, and to everyone's evident delight he started to chase Cristos through the trees.

'All right! That's enough!' Cristos said, eventually allowing Easton to catch him up. 'They gotta be about ready now, so back to work.'

Laughing, and panting for breath Easton threw an arm round Cristos's shoulders – which wasn't too comfortable given the discrepancy in height – and walked back towards the set with him.

'You joining us for dinner, tonight?' he asked. 'We're eating in. The kids'd love to see you.'

'Can I take a rain check?' Cristos said.

'Got another date with Paige? Bring her along too.'

Cristos shook his head. 'Can't. She wants to talk about her big scene on Friday.'

'That woman always wants to talk about something,' Easton grumbled. 'Can't she let you go, even for five minutes?'

'Come on,' Cristos chided, 'give her a break. You were there once yourself.'

Easton was thoughtful for a while, then said. 'You getting serious about her, man?'

Cristos threw up his hands. 'Shit! There sure is a lot of interest in my personal life going on round this place.'

'Cristos! Ready to roll!' the first assistant yelled, from the centre of the set.

'We OK with the snow?' Cristos called back, quickening his pace now as he weaved through the lamps the electricians were checking.

'We're set!' the man on the snow machine answered.

'OK, then let's see if we can get this baby in the can,' Cristos said, rubbing his hands together as he sat down on his chair. He looked at the small black and white monitor in front of him, waiting for the camera operator to line up for the first frame. When he was there Cristos raised a walkie-talkie and spoke into it, 'Don't forget, Kevin, we want to see the grass without snow over there and those buildings out on Park Lane before you come right off the Serpentine.'

'Got it!' Kevin responded from the crane.

'Actors in position?' Cristos asked the first.

'Right there,' the first responded.

Cristos nodded and the first bellowed into a megaphone, 'OK, Action snow!' Then, when the snow was falling to Cristos's satisfaction, 'Turn over!'

'Camera's rolling,' the follow focus announced over the radio.

'Mark it!'

'End board,' the clapper-loader called back.

Again Cristos nodded to the first.

'OK! And, *action everyone!*' the first roared, and a few seconds later the crane started to track the camera very slowly from the Serpentine, to swing over the trees and onto the set where the actors were waiting. Cristos's arm was in the air, ready to swing it down for their cue.

Knowing that this shot was never going to be done in one take, which meant they wouldn't be needing Paige Spencer for some time yet, Jeannie crept silently away heading for Paige's trailer.

Paige was inside, picking at the meagre salad one of the runners had delivered for her lunch and idly flicking through a magazine. 'Oh hi, honey,' she said, when Jeannie knocked and put her head round the door, 'come on in.'

'Can we talk?' Jeannie said, sitting down on the sofa opposite Paige. 'Privately,' she added, throwing a look at Paige's dresser.

'Sure,' Paige answered, and nodded a dismissal to the dresser. 'So what's on your mind, honey?' she said, when they were alone.

Ten minutes later Jeannie left Paige's trailer, walked back to the set and gave Cristos a beaming smile. If he ever got to find out about this he wouldn't just fire her, he'd kill her, she was thinking to herself, but it had to be done and done it sure as hell was.

The next three days proved trying on the entire unit – Cristos most of all. Watching him now Jeannie could see that his good humour was a thing of the distant past, and in a way she couldn't help feeling as responsible for that as the snow machine which had started to fire snow balls instead of flakes, the Simon tower which hadn't turned up and David Easton going down with a raging temperature. She couldn't say for certain of course, 'cos with so much else going on it was understandable he was in a bad mood, but earlier that morning, having waited for what she'd hoped was the right moment, she'd told him that Corrie had been fired from her job and that her telephone number wasn't listed in the directory.

'So I don't know how you're gonna find her,' she'd finished lamely seeing the look on his face.

'Jeannie, you're in danger of abusing our friendship here,' he'd told her. 'Now you just quit hassling me about Corrie Browne or . . .'

'Cristos, just listen . . .'

'No! You listen to me, 'cos we better get one thing straight here, Jeannie. If I wanted to find her I'd do it myself, without any help from you. So quit interfering in things that don't concern you! And if you bring this up again when I'm about to start shooting I really will fire you.'

As he stormed off towards the make-up trailers Richard had strolled up. 'Looks like you succeeded in putting him in a good mood,' he'd remarked jovially.

'Don't get smart. But you know, it kinda reminds me when you first fell in love with me. You didn't much want to be in love either, did you?'

'I still don't, but you don't give a man any say in the

matter,' and laughing he'd kissed her full on the mouth before going off to sort his lights.

That had been some hours ago, and Richard wasn't smiling anymore. None of them were, though Richard was closest to losing his cool, fighting like he was with those British electricians. Paige was a hot contender for second to blow, Jeannie noticed, turning round as Paige came bristling out of her trailer, telling the hairdresser she didn't care how long it had taken to make the fucking wig she wasn't wearing it!

Jeannie watched, as leaving Richard to sort his own problems Cristos went over to handle Paige. To Cristos's astonishment Paige seemed suddenly not to want to discuss it anymore – at least not with him – and flounced off to the make-up trailer, no doubt to wreak more havoc there.

Turning back Cristos was on the point of calling Jeannie over when Colin Walker, a British actor whose shooting days had been pulled forward to cover Easton, padded up to him.

Inwardly Cristos groaned. The guy had just joined them that morning and already he was proving one of the biggest jerks Cristos had ever worked with. He had three scenes in the entire movie, and this was now the fifth time he'd asked Cristos where he was supposed to be coming from. Cristos was sorely tempted to tell him to read the damned script instead of just picking out his own scenes, but since it wasn't his way to let off at the actors, he rounded up every shred of his fast disappearing patience and went over Walker's scenes with him one more time.

'If I were Cristos I'd tell the asshole to go screw himself,' the script girl remarked quietly to Jeannie.

'Me too,' Jeannie said. 'He's so anal!'

'Linda! Get over here and go through Colin's moves with him,' Cristos called out to the script girl. 'He wants to know which hand his handkerchief was in when he turned out of the last shot.'

'It was in his fucking pocket where we've never seen it,' Linda muttered, then smiling sweetly trotted off to do her duty.

After what seemed like an eternity the snow machine was functioning with flakes, the electricians had been sorted and Paige was wearing her wig. They were ready to roll.

'Five up!' the script girl called to the clapper-loader – and the first, waiting for his cue from Cristos stood poised with his megaphone. Cristos nodded, the camera started to roll and the first had just drawn breath to shout action when . . .

'Wait! Wait! Wait!' Colin Walker cried.

Gritting his teeth Cristos looked up from his monitor. 'What is it?' he said.

'I was just thinking, perhaps I should hit my hands to my head before hitting them to my heart. What do you think?'

'Cut the camera!' Cristos shouted.

'I'm sorry,' Colin giggled as Cristos walked over to him, 'I don't want to be a nuisance, but we do want to get it right, don't we?'

A few minutes later the camera was rolling again. Everyone was standing by, even Colin Walker, and this time Cristos was standing at the edge of the set to watch the action.

Jeannie's fingers crossed in her pockets. There was an explosion in the offing, she just knew it, but meanwhile the snow was falling, the wind was whipping it about, and the dry ice machines were breathing mist into the mayhem. The whole unit was holding its breath, and as the camera tracked forward through the snow and the electricians changed the lights from green to yellow to blue Walker, in his tattered Georgian costume, turned into shot, his eyes filled with tears, his false moustache and beard speckled with frost. Cristos brought his arm down and the background action began. Walker looked around – as directed.

He was lost, he was in the wrong place, the wrong time. Women and children in modern day summer costumes merged into the shot. Walker blinked. He was confused and frightened. A child ran past him, looked at him curiously – as directed. Then Walker clutched his hands to his chest, groaned in agony and fell sobbing to his knees.

'Cut!' Cristos roared.

Jeannie hid her face and Walker almost cowered behind a snowman as Cristos stormed towards him.

'What the fuck did you do that for?' Cristos yelled glaring down at him.

'I thought . . . It felt right . . . It . . .'

'We went over this five minutes ago! No hands! No knees! No sobs! This is a fucking movie. You're not playing to the back of the stalls, you're playing here!' He put his hand over the actor's face. He continued to glare at him, more angry with himself now for having lost it on the set. 'Reset!' he shouted. Then in a dangerously low voice, 'Do it the way we said. Just do it for me, all right?' He reached out a hand and pulled Walker to his feet. 'You're doing fine, you're great, just bring it down, OK? And don't be an asshole all your fucking life.'

Twenty minutes later, after five takes, the shot was in the can and the first assistant called a much needed break. Cristos went straight to his trailer, threw everyone out and slammed the door.

His anger was such that he couldn't sit down. He would never have tolerated that sort of outburst in anyone else and damned well wasn't going to tolerate it in himself. He paced the trailer, dashing a hand through his hair and slamming his fist against the wall. Never in his life had he spoken to an actor that way, and though Walker, with his wingeing pigheadedness and absurd theatrics probably deserved it, that was not the point. The point was that he, Cristos, was not in control of himself.

He looked out of the window and saw Jeannie hovering

not far away. He wrenched open the door to tell her to get the fuck away from him, but when she looked up and he saw the genuine anxiety in her face he slammed the door without saying a word.

He slumped down into a chair and put his head in his hands. There was no getting away from it, the more he tried not to think about her the more he thought about her. Corrie. Corrie Browne. He couldn't get her out of his mind. Three fucking times, he raged to himself, slamming his fist on the table. Three times I've seen her and she's turning my whole fucking life inside out. So far the days hadn't been so bad, but at night . . . at night she just tormented him. He couldn't sleep and now his tiredness and frustration was spilling into the day. He could hardly believe it was happening to him. He was a reasonable man, a man who dealt with life and got on with it. He knew all there was to know about love, he should, he'd shot it from every conceivable fucking angle, so what was this all about? He'd asked himself over and over what was so special about her? Why was it that she could do this to him when no other woman ever had? The crazy thing was that he could hardly picture her face now. But it wasn't her face, was it, it wasn't her body either, though God knows the need to touch her was driving him half out of his mind. It was her! It was that quirky naivety, those absurd remarks she came out with that she thought so smart, and the way things went wrong when she tried to be cool. He almost smiled then as he recalled the first time he'd made love to her and the way she'd made him laugh by trying so hard. Godammit, he didn't know how she'd done it, but she'd got to him right where it hurt. And now, knowing that Fitzpatrick had fired her from a job she cared passionately about, to think of her out there somewhere alone, Cristos was about ready to break.

It took some time for him to cool down, but even before

he did he knew what he was going to do. He just couldn't do it when he was this angry.

Everyone was well advanced into setting for the next shot by the time he got to his feet, and pulling open the trailer door again, he called out, 'Jeannie! I know you're hiding there somewhere, so get yourself in here.'

Immediately Jeannie put down her coffee and ran around to the front of the trailer.

'Let's have the TW number,' he said, as soon as she'd closed the door behind her.

'You gonna call her?' Jeannie beamed.

'No. I'm gonna call Fitzpatrick and find out where she is.'

'Oh gee, Cristos, am I sure glad to . . .' she broke off as the trailer door opened.

'Jeannie, honey, I saw you come in here . . .' Paige was saying.

'Ah, Paige,' Cristos said, throwing a look at Jeannie as he swung his legs up onto the table in front of him. Paige was a problem he'd have to sort before he saw Corrie. 'I wanna have a talk with you some time . . . Like tonight. Are you planning on . . .'

He stopped as, to his amazement, Paige started to back out the door. 'When this is through,' she hissed, 'I'm gonna have a lotta things to say to you, Bennati. Until then I'll do my job, but I don't want you to touch me, and I don't wanna be in the same room as you unless someone else is there. Have we got that straight?' Without waiting for a reply she slammed out the door.

Cristos turned to Jeannie, dumbfounded. 'What the hell was all that about?' he said.

'Search me,' Jeannie shrugged, hoping she wasn't over-doing the innocence. 'But looks like she's out of your hair, doesn't it? Now, about Corrie Browne.'

'Just give me the number Jeannie, then be on your way. OK?'

Corrie was on the point of going out filming. She really wasn't looking forward to it, not only because they'd be out there in a battered wives refuge until well past midnight, but because life had become so intolerable working with Annalise. Everything Corrie suggested was rejected, or even ridiculed, and were it not for the fact that she could see how badly Annalise was hurting inside, she'd have brought things to a head again.

She hadn't spoken to her father since the night at the Ritz either, except for one phone call when he'd rung to say that he thought they ought to let things calm down for a while. That hadn't surprised Corrie, though it infuriated her to think that once again he was backing away from a situation. She'd have to speak to him soon though, because if Annalise's attitude since having her engagement to Luke announced in yesterday's *Times* continued, then as far as Corrie could see she was heading for some kind of breakdown. Annalise's jubilation was so forcefully pronounced that Corrie knew she wasn't the only one who could see through it. Her eyes were too bright, her laughter too brittle, and the way she kept looking at Corrie was as though she had gone ahead with the engagement just to score some kind of victory over Corrie. And that in itself was leading Corrie to wonder if perhaps Annalise's feelings for Luke were at last starting to fragment. The problem was, with things as they stood right now, Annalise's pride would never allow her to admit that; certainly not to Corrie, but maybe she would to her father. Perhaps he could coax her out of this sham of an engagement. It wasn't very likely, Corrie knew that, but someone had to get through to Annalise, and though she had promised herself she would try again at the weekend when they were editing together, she felt quite strongly that Phillip should try too.

Right now the office was in chaos; a story had broken in the Middle East which meant getting a crew out there fast, and everyone was shouting, phones were ringing, the fax, photocopiers, PA machines and computer printers were all in full volume too, and as Corrie picked up her bag, unable to wait to get out of the noise, she found herself automatically picking up the phone.

'Hi, there,' said the voice at the other end. 'Is Luke Fitzpatrick around?'

Corrie's heart turned over, then seemed to stop beating altogether as she fell back into her chair.

'Hello?' the voice said again. 'I was wanting to speak to Luke Fitzpatrick. Is he there?'

'Cristos,' Corrie whispered tentatively, 'it's Corrie Browne here. I don't know if you remember me . . .'

'Corrie!'

'Yes.' Her heart suddenly flooded with joy. 'Oh, you do remember.'

'What the fuck are you talking about? Of course I remember. What are you doing there?'

'I work here,' she laughed, trying to remember what it was she'd promised herself she'd say if ever he did call. But he wasn't calling her, was he? He was calling Luke, and her heart immediately sank.

He was saying something, though Corrie couldn't hear what since someone was shouting in her ear.

'How are you?' she asked him, putting a hand over Perkin's mouth.

'Just fine,' he said and as his voice deepened into that sonorous intimacy she remembered only too well, her whole body seemed to turn liquid. 'How are you?' he asked.

'Oh, just fine. How's the film – movie, coming along?'

'Yeah, great. We got accepted for Cannes.'

'That's good news,' Corrie said, knowing it was inadequate but unable to think of anything else. 'Where are you? You sound very close.'

'In London.'

Even though she already knew that her heart still somersaulted to hear him confirm it. 'Oh, that's nice,' she said.

Annalise yelled for her.

'You got to go?' he said.

'I'm afraid so. Shall I put you onto Luke?'

'No.'

There was a pause as neither of them knew quite what to say. Cristos was the one to break it. 'Look, the reason I was calling Luke,' he told her, 'was to find your phone number. It was you I wanted to talk to.'

Corrie closed her eyes, not knowing if she could contain her joy it was so overwhelming. 'But you know I work here,' she laughed shakily.

'I thought you weren't there any more. Crossed wires. Anyway, I was trying to reach you 'cos I was thinking you might like to come over to Wiltshire at the weekend?'

'With you?' Corrie breathed, certain she was going to wake up any minute and find that this was all just a dream.

He laughed. 'And two hundred or so others.'

Corrie laughed too. 'Sounds irresistible. I take it you're filming there?'

'You got it. We leave tomorrow. So, you gonna come at the weekend?'

'Yeah. OK.' So much for telling him to go to hell.

'Right. I'll see you Friday night at the Castle Combe Manor House Hotel. That's where we're staying.'

'Oh hang on,' Corrie cried, suddenly remembering that she and Annalise were editing that weekend, 'I don't think I'm free. Oh damn it! Look, I'll try . . .'

'It's OK. You're not free, you're not free.'

'Cristos! I didn't say that. What I'm saying is that if I can get there I will, but . . .'

'It's OK, I understand,' he said. 'You got other commitments.'

'I'm editing, for Christ's sake,' she shouted, but the line had already gone dead.

Though she'd read in the papers which hotel he was staying

at Corrie didn't get a chance to call Cristos again until the following night. She had to explain why she might not make the weekend, she just couldn't let him think it was because she didn't want to see him. But when she did get through to the hotel he wasn't in his room.

'Would you like to leave a message?' the operator asked her.

'No, thanks,' Corrie said. Then suddenly remembering Jeannie she asked if she was in the hotel.

'Could you give a message to Cristos for me, please,' Corrie said, when Jeannie's voice came over the line. 'It's Corrie Browne here.'

'Sure, Corrie,' Jeannie grinned. 'What do you want me to tell him?'

'Just that I'm editing this weekend, which is why I can't make it to Wiltshire. But if I can get out of it, I'll be there – if he still wants me to come.'

'Oh, sure, he still wants you to come,' Jeannie laughed. 'And that's one message I'll be more than happy to pass on. As a matter of fact I was gonna call you myself, see if you could change your mind.'

'Were you?' Corrie said, surprised.

'Yeah. See, I thought you'd told him to go to hell, which is what I'd have done in your shoes. But seems if you did, you changed your mind.'

Corrie was laughing. 'I was going to,' she confessed, 'but somehow it just didn't come out.'

'I'm glad. Look, let me give you the number of my mobile, call me if you can make it 'cos Cristos is kind of hard to get hold of.'

Quickly Corrie jotted down the number, and was on the point of saying goodbye when Jeannie said,

'Before you go there's something I think you should know, Corrie . . . Cristos is a great guy and I love him to death, but he isn't too keen on being in love, get's kind of

antsy about it, you know? Well, you'll get used to that . . .
I just wanted to warn you not to take it too serious.'

Hardly able to speak through the shock, Corrie once
again assured Jeannie she would try to be there at the
weekend and rang off.

She was dreaming, she had to be, because Jeannie had
actually said that Cristos was in love. With her! Corrie
Browne! Did that mean that he'd been thinking about her
all this time too? Oh, God, if only she'd known . . . And
almost bursting with excitement she picked up the phone
to ring Paula.

'Oh Corrie,' Paula wailed, 'I'm sorry, can I call you
back? The baby's screaming blue murder here.'

'I can hear,' Corrie said, swallowing hard on her disappointment. 'What's the matter with her?'

'I don't know. But everything's all right with you, is it?'

'Yes, I just wanted to tell you . . .' she stopped unable
to hear herself as the baby's screaming got louder.

'What did you say?' Paula shouted.

'Nothing. Call me back when you can.'

Corrie hung up, and settling herself down with a glass
of wine set about trying to work out just how she was going
to avoid editing that weekend.

Over the next few days she tried everything short of
black magic to rearrange the editing, but the schedule was
such that if they didn't do it then the programme wouldn't
be ready on time. Finally, in desperation, she confided in
Annalise, and asked if she would mind doing the editing
alone.

'Sure, if you want to walk out on a programme half way
through,' Annalise replied frostily.

'I'm not saying that,' Corrie answered. 'What I'm saying
is . . .'

'That you are unprofessional,' Annalise interrupted.

It was on the tip of Corrie's tongue to remind Annalise
of the way she had behaved in the past, but knowing how

miserable Annalise was she bit it back – to fight with her now would get neither of them anywhere.

'You sure it's Cristos Bennati you want to see, not my father?' Annalise snapped nastily.

'Oh Annalise,' Corrie groaned, 'if only you knew what you were saying.' She was tempted to tell Annalise precisely who she was, but Annalise was in no mood to hear it. Besides, Corrie felt that Phillip should be the one to tell her.

'I don't think I'm interested. We start editing at nine on Saturday.'

It was later in the day that Corrie discovered the real truth behind Annalise's inflexibility – Luke wasn't going to be in London that weekend and Annalise didn't want to be alone.

Siobhan was in her chair by the window, her eyes fixed on the early morning horizon. Fingers of brilliant winter sunshine streamed through the blinds striping the Spartan furniture with bands of white light and grey shadow, and Siobhan's tender skin was blotched red across one cheek from where she'd sat so long in the sun. There was no sound in the room, there was only the monotonous and distant sough of the waves. She didn't move as the door opened, not even to blink.

Luke walked quietly across the room, watching her, silently begging her to register just this once that he was there, but of course she didn't.

'Here you are, see what I've brought you, Siobhan,' he said, holding up a large, square basket as he reached her. 'Would you like to know what's inside? Yes, to be sure you would,' and putting the basket on the window ledge in front of her he raised the lid and reached inside. 'See here,' he said, lifting the two baby rabbits onto his shoulder, 'aren't they lovely? You did want grey ones, didn't you?'

he asked. 'Like you had before? Good, I'm glad I got it right. Would you like to hold them?'

He placed the rabbits in Siobhan's lap. Siobhan blinked, once, twice, but her eyes didn't move from the murky horizon. Lifting her hand, Luke put it on one of the rabbits, showing her how to smooth it. Then he stood for a long time watching her, waiting for the explosion, but Siobhan merely sat gazing into space, mechanically running a hand over the rabbit's fur. It was more than evident from the vacant look on her face that she had no idea what they were.

Luke closed his eyes as blinding anger and frustration seared through his head. He turned away, trying to control himself, but this time he knew he couldn't. Memories were dancing before his eyes, the hideous nightmare images of the bastard, of all that had happened . . . The pain, the degradation; the terror, the screams . . . He pressed his hands to his ears, as though to keep in the terrible rage, but it was bursting from every orifice of his body. The sound of his own voice crashed over him like roaring waves in a storm, sending him into the nightmare of his past.

The door behind him opened, but pushing his way through he ran from the room, fled from the incubus closing its monstrous jaws around him . . . He ran and ran until there was no breath in his body, until his legs buckled with the pain, until he could see nothing more than the star-spangled sparks of exhaustion. Then, and only then, did he let Corrie into his mind, moaning helplessly as he felt the thought of her start to soothe him. But as he fell to the floor clasping his chest, blazing like a fire, the bastard was waiting for him. The bastard wrenched her from him, turned her away and then the bastard pressed his grinning face right into his mind. Recoiling savagely Luke tore at his head as though to pluck out the vile image. But the bastard's face stayed, distorting with laughter, twisting with glee, and then the bastard's eyes began to gleam with lust.

'No! No!' Luke roared, covering his head with his arms . . . But there was no escape. The bastard was still there, triumphantly tearing the rabbits limb from limb, letting the blood wash over his hands . . . And then, with deranged laughter bubbling from his throat, he took her . . . The bastard took his Siobhan, right there inside his head . . .

— 22 —

It was now approaching four on Saturday afternoon and Corrie and Annalise had, as yet, only managed to get seven and a half minutes of programme time edited. At this rate, Corrie knew, they didn't stand a hope in hell of getting away until ten at the very earliest and even then, catching the last train to the West Country was out of the question – women just couldn't travel alone late at night anymore.

The reason they were so behind with their schedule was because Annalise was being deliberately difficult to ensure that Corrie's weekend was spoiled. And Annalise's guilt at what she was doing wasn't helping too much either, since she continually snapped at Corrie, as though it were Corrie's fault she was behaving like this. All day long Corrie had bitten hard on her tongue, but an hour or so ago she had found herself starting to snap back, since it was then that she had finally admitted defeat and called Jeannie to say she wouldn't be able to make it down to Wiltshire. And, because she was so furious with Annalise for being so childish and selfish, Corrie had told Jeannie exactly why she couldn't make it.

'But there's nothing I can do,' she'd added, 'she's the producer. But you will explain to Cristos won't you, and make sure he knows that it isn't because I don't want to come?'

Jeannie had assured Corrie she'd do just that, and when Corrie had left the deserted production office to return to the semi-darkness of the edit suite she had found Annalise and the editor sitting there chatting with a bank of frozen images on the monitors in front of them.

'Oh,' Annalise said sarcastically, as Corrie walked in through the door, 'nice of you to join us, and we're so sorry if this is getting in the way of your love life, but we need the tape with the Bradshaw interview on it.'

Corrie had given the tape to Annalise first thing that morning, and Annalise knew it. Now, obviously, Annalise had hidden it in order to hold up proceedings further. Corrie found the tape eventually in the bottom of her own bag, and handing it to Annalise said,

'I'd appreciate it if you didn't go into my bag again without my permission.'

'Oh, so clever!' Annalise sneered. 'Blame me for everything, why don't you?'

'Yes, I will,' Corrie said, 'and I hope you're getting some pleasure out of this because if you're not your entire effort is being wasted,' and sitting down she turned to Colin and asked if he was ready to start again. Annalise was eyeing Corrie nastily, not quite sure whether or not she'd understood that remark, but as Colin was spooling through the Bradshaw tape she turned back to the monitors.

At five thirty Annalise suddenly announced that they *might* break for an hour at seven. Corrie glared at her furiously, knowing only too well that the reason even for taking a break at all, never mind such a long one, was so that Annalise could drive over to Luke's – if he was back. This, Corrie decided, was just going too far, and she was on the point of really laying into Annalise when the telephone rang. Fixing Annalise with a viciously daggered look Corrie snatched up the receiver.

'Hello!' she barked.

'Oh my, someone sure sounds ticked,' Cristos laughed.

On hearing that wonderful velvety voice Corrie immediately felt her tension start to ebb, and turning away from Annalise and Colin, said softly, 'Hi, how are you?'

'Just fine. How you doing with your difficult producer?'

'Not too well right at the moment,' Corrie smiled. 'I take it Jeannie explained?'

'Jeannie explained. And I guess I owe you an apology for ringing off like that the other day.'

'Apology accepted.'

'So, you can't get away, huh?'

'It doesn't look like it. I've tried everything I could think of, but she just won't wear it.'

'I see. Then it looks like I'm just gonna have to come to you, doesn't it?'

Corrie's eyes closed as her heart seemed to expand right across her chest. 'But . . . Are you sure?' she whispered. 'I mean, I really won't get off until late.'

'Then I'll just have to wait, won't I?'

'But what about your film? I mean, won't they say something if you just up and come to London?'

Cristos laughed, and then Corrie realized what a silly question that was.

'I'll come pick you up at TW,' he said. 'Just over the Battersea Bridge?'

'That's right,' Corrie answered, feeling as though she might just melt with sheer relief and joy.

'Corrie!' Annalise barked. 'Can we have your attention here, please?'

'I'd better go,' Corrie said quietly to Cristos.

'OK. See you in a coupla hours.'

The break at seven turned out to be for ten minutes only, when Colin ate the sandwiches his wife had packed for him that morning and Annalise and Corrie studiously ignored each other behind Saturday review magazines. Obviously

Luke hadn't returned from wherever he was, which was why Annalise was still there, but despite the fact that Cristos was on his way, Corrie was finding it very difficult to soften towards Annalise. She'd done all she could to ruin this weekend for Corrie, and spoiled brat that she was she was going to find no sympathy from Corrie tonight. Corrie didn't even tell her Cristos was on his way, she'd find out for herself soon enough.

Just before eight o'clock there was a tap on the door and Bill, the security man, came in, beaming all over his face. 'Corrie, you've got a visitor,' he announced, and standing back he held the door wide for Cristos to walk through, waving an arm and all but bowing, as though Cristos were some kind of royalty.

Corrie stood up, and the instant she saw the wry humour on Cristos's face her heart became so full that all she could do was smile at him. Whatever she'd thought she felt for him during these long months since Los Angeles was nothing to what she did now, she realized. And what was more it felt right for him to be there, just as it felt right for her to walk up to him and kiss him gently on the mouth.

'Hi,' he chuckled, looking so deeply into her eyes there might have been no one else in the room.

'Hi,' she said, a droll smile dancing around her lips. She couldn't be sure, but she thought she saw him wink, then following his eyes she turned to Annalise who was staring at him as though he were some kind of apparition. He walked over to her, holding out his hand, saying, 'How you doing there, Annalise? It's good to see you again.'

'Um, I'm fine,' Annalise mumbled, shaking his hand. 'Nice to see you, too.'

He turned to Colin then, who was looking at him curiously, obviously trying to remember where he'd seen him before. And when, shaking Colin's hand, Cristos introduced himself Corrie had to smother her laughter at the way Colin's eyes rounded with near divine reverence.

'Please, don't let me interrupt,' Cristos said, backing towards an empty chair to one side of Corrie. 'Do you mind if I sit down?' he said to Annalise.

Still slightly off balance Annalise shook her head.

'Thanks,' he said. 'I'll just wait until you're through here. You know, I've never seen TV editing done before, so I'm kinda interested to see what happens.'

In order to try and keep herself from laughing Corrie stuck her tongue into her cheek, and turning back to her notes suggested that they now take a look at the piece to camera outside the refuge. As she gave Colin the relevant time codes Cristos folded his arms and stretched out his legs to make himself more comfortable as he watched.

After fifteen minutes Corrie was in such pain trying not to laugh that she had to walk out into the corridor to catch her breath. She knew precisely what Cristos was up to, and what's more she was fairly certain he'd succeed, since Annalise was already showing signs of how intimidated she felt by his presence. He was being so outrageous in his absorption that Corrie could almost feel sorry for Annalise, after all, who the hell wanted a director of his stature looking over their shoulder when they were trying to make difficult decisions? Not that Cristos had said a word, he was just sitting there looking so rapt that even Corrie might have been convinced had he not just winked at her.

When she went back into the edit suite Cristos was sitting with his elbows on his knees frowning with concentration as Colin explained how he was storing up edit codes on the machine's computer system ready for the dub. Annalise, with a pencil behind her ear and another between her teeth, was searching through her notes, which was presumably what had brought proceedings to a halt once again. Seeing that Cristos was genuinely interested in what Colin was saying Corrie eased herself in front of him and sat down quietly. He could still see, but pulling himself forward he leaned an elbow on the back of Corrie's chair to watch from behind her. Corrie opened the transcript in front of her and started to ask Annalise what she was looking for, but the words dried on her lips as she felt Cristos's fingers brush lightly over her waist. Her response was so instant and so powerful she almost gasped. She knew he was still watching the monitors, and shooting a quick look at Annalise and Colin she saw that they were too. So, folding a hand beneath the desk she reached out for his. He took it, linking his fingers through hers and giving them a gentle squeeze.

It wasn't long after that, while Corrie's hand was still in Cristos's, that Annalise said, in a voice several notes higher than normal in its effort to sound casual, 'You can go now, Corrie, if you like. I can manage here alone with this next interview.'

'Are you sure?' Corrie said, having expected this but perhaps not quite so soon.

Annalise shrugged. 'I expect Cristos is hungry after filming all day. Why don't you take him somewhere for dinner now he's come all this way?'

'Oh, I'm doing just fine right here,' Cristos assured her, letting go of Corrie's hand and leaning back in his chair with his hands behind his head.

Corrie glared at him, but before she could speak he said, 'It's kinda fascinating watching all this technology at work, I could sit here all night.'

Catching the laughter in his eyes Corrie's own narrowed as she muttered through her teeth, 'Don't push it!'

His face broke into a grin, and rolling her eyes, Corrie started to pack up her things. 'I'll see you at nine in the morning, then,' she said to Annalise as she was leaving.

'On the dot,' Annalise answered, without turning round.

Corrie stood at the door, tapping her foot as she waited for Cristos, who was now standing with his hands in his pockets behind Colin having something else explained.

'You're incorrigible,' she told him when they eventually walked along the corridor to the darkened office.

'Me?' he said, all innocence.

'Yes you! You knew full well that you being here would browbeat Annalise into letting me go.'

'But I didn't say a word,' he protested.

'You didn't have to. And all that business about pretending not to know about TV editing . . .'

'But I don't,' he interrupted, taking her coat from her and holding it out for her to put it on, 'and it *was* kinda fascinating.'

She slid her arms into the sleeves, and as he hooked it up over her shoulders she was about to say something else when he bunched her collar in his hands and turned her to face him. 'It's great to see you,' he murmured, and using her collar to pull her closer he brought her mouth to his.

'It's great to see you too,' she whispered when he let her go, 'but if you do that again I don't know if I'm going to be able to walk out of here.'

He grinned. 'It was that good, huh?'

Laughing and shaking her head she heaved her bag up over her shoulder and pulled him out of the office.

'Hungry?' he asked, as they rode down in the lift.

'I'm not sure,' she answered, pursing her lips in a smile.

His eyes were dancing as he bent his head to kiss her again. 'What do you say we pick up a Chinese and take it back to your place?'

'Sounds good to me,' she said, wondering how much more of this euphoria she could take.

His hire car was right outside on double yellow lines, where, Corrie discovered, Bill had been guarding it with his life. Cristos thanked him, wanting to tip him, but Bill wouldn't hear of it.

'You've made his day, you know that, don't you?' Corrie remarked as they edged out into the traffic.

'I got a habit of doing that to people,' he grinned.

Corrie's mouth fell open. 'Oh! You conceited . . .'

'Conceited what?' he asked when she stopped.

'I don't know, but I'll think of something,' she laughed.

'You wanna tell me where we're heading?' he said, when they reached the lights at the Embankment.

'Straight ahead to the next lights,' she answered. 'Cristos . . .'

'Did I tell you yet how great you're looking?' he interrupted.

A mischievous light shot to Corrie's eyes. 'No, but you don't have to, I already know.'

With a shout of laughter Cristos put the car back into gear and drove on.

'Cristos,' she began again. 'I don't know if now is the time to bring this up, but I'm going to. I mean, this is all pretty difficult to take in when the last time I saw you you walked out without saying so much as a word. You never even called me after . . . Yet now here you are and . . .' She shook her head, 'I just don't understand. What happened?'

Though he was smiling as he glanced over at her as soon as he spoke Corrie heard the serious note in his voice. 'I don't know if now is the time to bring this up, but I'm going to,' he said, repeating her words with a touch of irony. 'What happened was, I couldn't get you out of my mind. When I told you that we weren't just for one night, I guess I meant it. There's something special happening here and we both know it. But the night I came round, when you were swimming in the pool, Fitzpatrick said something that kind of got to me. I didn't believe him, even when he said it, but back then I was looking for a way out so I used it. You got to understand, I didn't want to get involved, but you were getting to me and I could feel myself going along with it. Then when Fitzpatrick started in about how you were his property, that he was sleeping with you . . .'

'So that's what he told you!' Corrie interrupted. 'I always knew he'd said something.'

'We gotta make a decision here, Corrie.'

Bemused Corrie turned to look at him.

'Left or right?' he grinned.

'Right,' she chuckled. 'So,' she said, as they headed along the King's Road, 'you walked out because of what he told you? Meaning you believed it.'

'I walked out 'cos I could see things were going to start getting complicated,' he corrected.

Corrie was silent for a while, torn between her fury with Luke and the wonderful feelings Cristos's admissions were evoking in her.

'So,' he said, 'did you ever sleep with the guy?'

Corrie hesitated. 'Twice,' she confessed. 'I slept with him twice and ever since I've wished it never happened. Pull in over there.'

Following her directions Cristos stopped the car and turned off the engine.

'Do you mind?' Corrie said when he still made no response to her confession.

He sighed heavily. 'Hell, I knew you were no virgin when you came to me,' he said, 'but yeah, I mind it was Fitzpatrick. Was he the first?'

'No. I slept with two other men before him. 'And,' she continued, 'you're the only man I've ever slept with without using a condom, if that means anything.'

'Does it bother you?'

'I don't know. Should it?'

'No. I had to get tested for the movie. But I guess we were pretty irresponsible.' He turned to look at her. 'But if I'm clear and you're clear, what do you say we go on being irresponsible?'

'That calls for fidelity,' Corrie answered without even thinking about it.

He nodded. 'I'm up for that. How about you?'

Corrie simply looked at him, so full of stunned emotion the words would barely come. 'Yes,' she whispered, 'I'm up for that.'

Sliding his fingers under her hair Cristos began stroking her jaw with his thumb. 'What are you doing to me, Corrie Browne?' he whispered.

Corrie's answer was to turn her face and kiss the palm of his hand, all the time keeping her eyes on his.

'Let's go get this food and get back to your place,' he murmured.

Twenty minutes later Corrie was letting them into her studio and turning on the lights. 'If you just put the food on the table I'll get some plates,' she said, dropping her bag on the floor and starting to unbutton her coat.

Cristos walked over to the dining table, put down the cartons of Chinese then taking her hand as she made to pass him he pulled her into his arms.

'So this is home?' he said softly, looking around the place.

She smiled shakily. 'It's no villa in the Holmby Hills I know, but . . .'

He interrupted her with a kiss so gentle his lips barely touched hers. He pulled back to look into her eyes then brushed his mouth against hers again. Corrie gazed up at him and seeing the way his eyes were clouded with such feeling her own fluttered closed as her lips parted. Then he was kissing her again, moulding his lips slowly and tenderly to hers, bringing her whole body against his and supporting her as she clung to him in sheer need.

'Corrie, I want you so bad,' he whispered, his lips still touching hers. 'I want you now, here . . . Oh, Christ,' he moaned as she pressed herself even harder to him and this time when he kissed her he pushed his tongue deep into her mouth.

Somehow they managed to climb the stairs, and as they went, kissing all the time, his hands were under her dress and Corrie's fingers were seeking the hardness of him.

Cristos reached the top first and turned to stand over her, one hand on the wall the other on the banister, as she unzipped his jeans. He watched her as she lifted his erection free, then gave a long groan as, stooping to take him in her mouth, she pushed his jeans to the floor.

'Come here,' he murmured, pulling her up into his arms.

She was still one step lower than him as he bent to kiss her, and lifting her pale cashmere dress to her shoulders, he pulled back, tugged it over her head, then was kissing her again. And all the time Corrie was unbuttoning his shirt and spreading her hands over his chest, his abdomen, then gently caressing his testicles with her fingers.

The bed was so close that Cristos just let himself sink back onto it, pulling her on top of him and, still kissing her, kicked off his shoes, then his jeans. Corrie rolled onto her back, taking him with her, raking her fingers down over his buttocks.

'Sit up,' he whispered, moving off her, 'let me watch you undress.'

Corrie pulled herself up and as she reached behind herself to unhook her bra he gently eased her tights and knickers down over her thighs. In the lustrous moonlit glow coming from the skylight above them Corrie could see that his eyes were on hers, but as she peeled away the lace cups of her bra, revealing the heavy plumpness of her milky white breasts and succulent rosy nipples his eyes dropped from her face.

'Oh, Jesus Christ, just look at you,' he groaned, and letting her knickers and tights fall to the floor he rolled onto his back and all but lifted her onto him. She was up on her knees and his hands were around her waist as he rose to meet the nipple she lowered to his mouth. And as he sucked and kissed each one of them in turn his hands moved down over her buttocks and thighs teasing her to such a state of arousal that she was begging him to take her.

Looking up at her and smiling he shook his head, and breathless as she was Corrie smiled too. But as she sat back on his legs and lowered her head to take him in her mouth he stopped her and pulled her back up to her knees.

'OK, you win,' he murmured, 'I want to be inside you. Real deep inside you.'

His words sent a bolt of such exquisite eroticism through her that Corrie pushed her tongue into his mouth and moaned frantically as he continued to knead her breasts and evaded her searching lips. In the end, moving a hand between their bodies he guided his penis to her and pulled her very gently, very slowly, so that they could savour every moment of penetration, onto him.

'Sit back,' he whispered, drawing his knees up. 'Sit back and let me watch you,' and as Corrie rested against his legs he cupped his hand over her pubic mound and began to caress her with his thumb. At first she could only look at him, hardly able to breathe it felt so good, then as he started to rock his hips slowly back and forth her head fell back as she felt herself starting to lose control.

'Oh no,' she cried, 'Cristos I can't bear it.' And then he was sitting up too, taking her nipples in his mouth and biting hard as she ground herself onto him. He knew she was very close now, but suddenly he pulled himself out of her and covering her protests with his mouth, he pushed her onto her back. Lying over her he lifted himself up on his arms and entered her again. Corrie's legs circled his waist and she gazed up at him as he began moving in and out of her with long, tender strokes, letting her feel every inch of him.

'Yes, oh, yes,' she murmured, her head turning from side to side. Then she gasped and her eyes flew open as suddenly he jerked hard into her. He did it again and again, then he was rotating his hips gently and rubbing himself against the delicate bud at the join of her thighs.

Time after time he took her to the brink, watching her

face, feeling her body start to convulse until he knew she couldn't take anymore, and lifting her knees with his hands he forced her legs wider, then pushed every ounce of his strength into taking them both there.

'Oh, Cristos, Cristos,' she sobbed as a surge of such excruciating, debilitating sensation drove through her that her arms fell from his shoulders and she could only gasp and moan as her climax broke around him and he continued to thrust himself into the heart of it.

He was holding her very close, and began kissing her brutally as he felt the force of her uncontrolled muscles clench him and push him and draw him to her until the seed exploded from his body and she clung to him, whimpering and whispering, 'I can feel you. Oh God, Cristos, I can feel you there so deep inside me!'

When it was over she lay quietly beside him, her hand in his, staring up at the skylight, and as she allowed herself to relive every moment they had spent together, every word he had spoken since he had arrived at TW that night she felt her heart tightening with such immeasurable emotion that she knew it just wasn't possible to feel happier or more fulfilled than she did right at that moment.

She could hear him breathing, steadily now, but knew he wasn't sleeping even though his eyes were closed. She turned to him and looked down the full length of his perfect body lying there in the moonlight – it looked so dark and so masculine beside her own creamy fullness.

'What are you thinking?' she asked when her eyes returned to his face and she found him watching her.

Smiling, he closed his eyes again and bringing her hand to his lips, said, 'Jeannie figures I'm in love with you.'

Corrie's heart seemed to stop as, hardly daring to breathe she waited, until at last his eyes opened again and the smile faded from his lips. 'I figure she could be right,' he said huskily and drawing her to him he kissed her full on the mouth.

When he let her go and Corrie simply continued to look at him a teasing light sprang into his eyes. 'Don't you have anything to say?' he smiled.

Corrie lowered her eyes and resting her forehead on his shoulder, she murmured, 'I don't know what to say. I mean, it's all, well it all seems so unreal. You and me, and . . .'

He chuckled. 'For a minute there I thought you were going to say that it was all so sudden . . .'

'It is . . .'

'But how do you feel?' he asked kissing the top of her head.

'Confused suddenly.' And it was true, she did. Not that she wasn't sure about the way she felt, it was just that she didn't know how easily those words might come to him – or if they really meant as much to him as they did to her. She'd never realized this in herself before, but now she was confronted with it she knew that to tell him she loved him would mean everything. That to say those words would be for her the ultimate commitment. It was a commitment she could make, but if it didn't mean the same to him . . .

He hugged her. 'Hey, it's all right, sweetheart, I'm not going to rush you.'

Immediately Corrie's eyes filled with tears and laughing she said, 'Oh Cristos, that's what my mother used to call me.'

'It was?' he smiled, lifting her face back up to look at him. 'Then I guess that's why you're crying. You still miss her?'

Corrie nodded. 'All the time.'

'Why don't you tell me about her?'

'I can't, because right now I'm so full up with emotion I might never stop crying. And I look terrible when I cry.'

'Thanks for the warning,' he laughed. 'So, how about we have that food? I'm starving.'

'Do you want to eat it here?' she said, lifting herself up on one elbow. 'In bed.'

He nodded, but when Corrie got up and began to put on her robe, he caught it and pulled it away. 'Uh, uh,' he said, shaking his head. 'No clothes. You've got one sensational body, I want to look at it.'

Rolling her eyes and surprising herself by how unselfconscious she felt, Corrie padded off down the stairs to reheat the Chinese in the microwave. A few minutes later she looked up and saw that he was leaning his arms on the balcony watching her.

'I'm beginning to think you're kinky, Bennati,' she told him.

He laughed. 'Just get your ass back up here woman and quit messing about down there.'

'Messing about!' she declared.

'Don't think I don't know what you're about, keep bending over the refrigerator that way. You haven't taken a single thing out yet.'

Laughing Corrie raised a chopstick at him and turned away to load the cartons onto a tray.

When she carried them upstairs she found he had stacked the pillows against the brass head rail and opening his legs he pulled her between them so that she sat with her back resting against his chest as they tonged their food with chopsticks, fed each other, laughed, kissed, fought over the tastiest bits and kissed again. Then Cristos dipped a finger in sweet and sour sauce and after circling it around her nipple, pushed her back in his arms to lick it off.

As he did the same with her other nipple Corrie could feel his erection pressing against her, and lifting the tray onto the bedside table, she turned around, pushed him back against the pillows and sat astride him. Then, deliberately teasing him with her movements to reach for food, she began feeding him, sometimes putting the chopsticks straight to his mouth and sometimes smearing the sauce over her breasts and leaning over for him to take it from there. In the end he stopped her, and taking the chopsticks from her hand he said,

'I want you now, just you.'

This time, as they made love, he told her he loved her, he said the words right out, 'I love you,' but still Corrie couldn't bring herself to say them back. He didn't even comment on her silence, which only made Corrie feel that she was right to hold back. Now was simply too soon, and as certain as she felt about him right at that moment, there was no knowing what tomorrow would bring.

Later, they dozed in each other's arms and when Corrie woke and saw he was still sleeping she got up and went downstairs to make herself a coffee. It was ludicrous even to think she could sleep the night through – feeling as she did, it just wasn't possible.

'Smells good,' she heard him say a few minutes later. 'What time is it?'

She looked up to where he was leaning over the balcony. 'Just after midnight,' she answered, wondering if her heart would always contract this way when she looked at him.

Wrapping a towel round his waist he came down the stairs to join her on the sofa.

'I don't know how the hell I'm going to get through tomorrow,' he said, sipping his coffee.

'What time do you have to be up?'

'Around five.'

She nodded. Then sitting on one leg she turned to face him. 'Will I see you again after tonight?' she asked.

'Shit, Corrie!' he exclaimed, almost spilling his coffee. 'You have to ask?'

She grinned. 'No. I just wanted to hear you say so.'

'You wanna hear me tell you I love you again?'

Quickly she shook her head. 'No. I don't want you to wear the words out.'

'Well you sure as hell aren't,' he remarked.

She looked down at her coffee and he let the silence tick by until she said, 'I can't say it, Cristos, it's not because I don't feel it, it's just that . . . Oh, I don't know . . . It's just . . . Well, it's different for you. You've probably told a hundred women you love them, and more than a hundred have said it back. But I've never said it to anyone . . .'

'I've told one woman I love her before you,' he corrected. 'I'm only telling you that so's you know, not to try and force you in to telling me something you don't want to say.'

'Do you mind?' she asked.

'No.' He grinned. 'Because I know you do.'

'You're so Goddammed sure of yourself,' she laughed, punching him gently on the arm.

'Steady! You sounded almost American there.'

'Do you wish I were?'

'No. But I guess it would be easier if you were.' He reached out for the photograph on the table beside them. 'Is this your mother?' he asked.

'Yes.'

'She's beautiful.' After a while he put the photograph down and turned back to look at her.

'Will I see you next weekend?' she asked.

'If that's what you want,' he shrugged.

Corrie felt a sudden breath of cold air blow around her heart. 'Isn't it what you want?'

'Sure it is. But you'll have to come to Wiltshire.'

'I'll come,' she said, leaning forward to put her arms around his neck. He made no move to kiss her and Corrie felt a swift and irrational panic. What had suddenly happened to make him back off like this? 'Will Paige Spencer mind me being there?' she heard herself ask.

'That's over.'

'Are you sure? I mean, I don't want to cause any difficulties. After all she is your star.'

'I told you, it's history.'

'But there was something between you?'

'Yes.'

A sixth sense was already telling her that she should stop there, but she seemed unable to. 'Who was the other woman you told you loved her?' she asked.

'It doesn't matter.'

She could see how his face had darkened, but still she didn't stop. 'Was she another leading lady?' She laughed uneasily. 'Maybe you make love to all your leading ladies?'

'No.'

'But most.'

'No.'

'Then how many? Or have you lost count?'

'Look, Corrie,' he said, 'we both know I've been around the block a few times – Christ, I'm forty years old, but you've got your own history and I'm not questioning you about that . . .'

'I know. But tell me, have they all been as beautiful as Paige?'

'Let's go get some sleep.'

'Just tell me.'

'Corrie, leave it.'

'Are you hiding something from me?' she said, her heart twisting with sudden and irrepressible jealousy. 'Perhaps you're still in love with one of them.'

'Corrie, I said leave it. Now let's go to bed,' and putting his cup down he got to his feet and started up over the stairs.

Furious with herself, Corrie carried the cups to the kitchenette. She had no idea where that sudden rush of insecurity had come from, but it had been upon her and basking itself in the heat of her jealousy before she had known it.

'I'm sorry,' she said, as she sat down on the bed and picked up the alarm to set it.

'Forget it.'

Corrie turned out the light and pulling the duvet over herself she lay beside him in the darkness. After a few minuted he turned over and took her in his arms. 'How about we make a pact?' he said. 'You don't ask about my past, I don't ask about yours.'

'OK,' she said, hoping her misery didn't sound in her voice. But what chance did they stand together, she was asking herself, if they were already hiding things from each other?

It was only in the early hours of the morning when he was fast asleep and she was still lying awake in his arms that Corrie suddenly remembered his affair with Angelique Warne. Restlessly she turned away from him. So that was his raw nerve! It had to be, and she wanted to tear out her tongue for what she had said about leading ladies. Angelique Warne, she was convinced, had been the other woman he'd told he loved and now Angelique was dead. Corrie couldn't even begin to imagine how Cristos must feel about that, since she had no idea about the truth of their relationship. All she knew was that he must still feel something to be shying away from it the way he was, and she, in her ignorance and despicable jealousy, had managed to reopen the wound. But she hadn't intended to, it had been a genuine mistake on her part and because of it he had withdrawn from her. So much for loving her, she thought, angrily digging her fingers into her eyes to stop the tears. If he'd truly meant it he'd be honest with her and tell her what had really happened between him and Angelique. He was still in love with her, Corrie was certain of it, and realizing that she was right not to have told him the way she felt about him didn't make her feel any better, if anything it made her feel a whole lot worse.

She had no idea what time she finally fell asleep, but when she woke in the morning it was to find that Cristos had already left. She looked at the clock and saw that it was still a quarter to five. She felt wretched, and rolling over to the spot where he had lain buried her face in the pillow. Everything had been going so well before she'd started to antagonize him, and now he'd gone without even leaving a note. She tried to reassure herself by remembering all the things he'd said and done – if his feelings were that strong, surely she couldn't have killed them so easily. He would call, later today, she told herself vehemently, and everything would be all right again.

At nine o'clock Corrie and Annalise were once again sitting in the edit suite with Colin ready to start the laborious plough through to the end of the programme. As soon as Colin punched up the pictures Corrie could see that he and Annalise had accomplished very little after she'd left the night before, which didn't really surprise Corrie, it just meant that she found it even more difficult to put her heart into what they were doing. All she wanted was for the phone to ring, to hear Cristos's voice telling her nothing had changed. Of course he wouldn't call, she told herself, he'd be filming, so there simply wouldn't be time, but still she continued to hope.

It was probably because she was so distracted by her own dilemma that Corrie didn't at first notice the strained atmosphere in the room. When at last she did she was more than a little baffled by it, since, she realized, it wasn't just Annalise being awkward with her today, Colin was too. Not that he wasn't doing his job, or answering her politely when she spoke to him, it was just that he didn't seem able to meet Corrie's eyes. Surely he couldn't be angry that she'd gone off like that last night, that just wasn't like Colin. Maybe Annalise had said something to him, but then, as Corrie started to watch Annalise a little more closely she noticed something distinctly odd in Annalise's behaviour. Her movements were jerky, almost frantic, her eyes were glittering with a disturbing brilliance and if she laughed at all it was so high-pitched as to make Corrie wince. And she was laughing too much, far too much, at things that just weren't funny. Not that Corrie was ever included in the joke, if anything it was generally at her expense.

At first Corrie thought that Annalise was putting on some kind of show to let her know that it didn't matter a jot to her that things had worked out last night with Cristos, when they obviously hadn't with Luke. But, as the morning wore on and Annalise became noticeably worse, Corrie began to realize that there was a lot more to this strange conduct than false bravado. It was as though Annalise was teetering perilously close to the edge of a precipice while the hand of hysteria crept ever closer, preparing to give her that final push.

'Annalise, are you feeling all right?' Corrie asked in the end, starting in gently.

'Of course I am!' Annalise snapped. 'Why the hell shouldn't I be?'

Corrie shrugged. 'You just seem a bit tense, that's all.'

'Of course I'm tense, I'm trying to get this fucking programme finished, aren't I? But don't you concern yourself about me, I'm sure you've got far more important things on your mind.'

'No I haven't,' Corrie said. 'If something's upsetting you . . .'

'Shut up! Just shut up! Nothing's upsetting me. Nothing that you need concern yourself about anyway. And why should you concern yourself about me? Well, don't, do you hear me? Don't bother about me! I don't want you to. Now let's get on with it!'

If ever Corrie had heard a cry for help that was it, but as Annalise turned back to the monitors Corrie could see that breaking down this barrier of guilt Annalise was shielding behind was going to be anything but easy. Something must have happened though to have brought things to a head like this, and whatever it was must have happened overnight – the question was how was she going to find out?

At last Corrie managed to catch Colin's eye, but reading the question in her own he simply raised his eyebrows and shaking his head turned back to his controls. If he did know what had happened he obviously didn't want to say.

A few minutes later Annalise slammed her hand violently on the desk for the fifth time declaring that Corrie was a fucking idiot and didn't know what she was talking about. Corrie leaned across Annalise to point out something in the background of the picture, and suddenly Annalise's clenched fist hit her full in the face.

'Get away from me, you bitch!' she screamed. 'Just get away!'

'For God's sake!' Corrie gasped, holding her cheek. 'What is going on?'

'Just get out of here! I don't want you near me! It's your fault! It's all your fucking fault!'

'What is? Annalise, wait!' but Annalise was already running out of the door and Colin quickly got up to grab Corrie and pull her back.

'Leave her,' he said. 'Just let her calm down.'

'But what's going on?' Corrie demanded. 'What's my fault?'

'You can probably answer that better than me,' Colin told her, sitting her back into her chair. 'All I know is what happened here after you'd gone last night.'

'Well?' Corrie prompted, as he sat down. 'What did happen?'

After stopping the play-in tape he'd left running Colin turned his chair to face her. 'Quite frankly, Corrie,' he said, 'this is none of my business and I don't want to get involved, but I will tell you this: you'd better get yourself sorted out with Luke Fitzpatrick, and you'd better do it soon, or you're going to send that girl round the bend.'

'What are you talking about?' Corrie cried. 'What's she been telling you?'

'Nothing. She didn't have to, I saw it, heard it for myself. He came in here like some fucking madman . . .'

'Who?'

'Fitzpatrick! Who do you think? He came in last night about five minutes after you'd gone. He was looking for you and when you weren't here I thought he was going to tear the bloody place apart. I've never seen anything like it in my life, and I don't want to ever again. Then when Annalise told him you'd gone off with Bennati . . . Shit, Corrie, I thought he was going to kill her. I had to pull him off her or he would have.'

Corrie was shaking her head, stupefied. 'Why was he looking for me?'

'Why was he looking for you? You tell me.'

'I can't,' Corrie answered, 'I don't know. Didn't he say anything that might have given you a clue?'

'Not a thing.'

'Well why was he so angry that I wasn't here?' Corrie asked, this time more of herself than of Colin.

'Like I said, it's none of my business,' Colin repeated. 'I didn't ask, and I don't want to know. But that girl's in a bad way, and it's to do with you and whatever you've got going with Fitzpatrick.'

Corrie's face hardened. 'I haven't got anything going with Fitzpatrick,' she told him. 'You should have seen that for yourself when Cristos was here last night. Anyway, what happened in the end? Did she go home with Luke . . . ?'

'Oh she went home with him all right. At least she followed him out of here sobbing like her heart would break and pleading with him to wait for her. He just kept yelling at her that he didn't want her, he wanted you . . . And why the fuck had she allowed you to go off with Bennati when you were supposed to be editing here? She was hysterical and he was . . . Well, as I said, he was like a fucking

— 450 —

madman! God knows what happened once they got home, but . . . Well, you've seen what she's like this morning.'

'I'm going to find her,' Corrie said, and ignoring Colin's protests got up and walked out to the main office.

Eventually Corrie found Annalise, hunched in a corner of the stationery cupboard, hugging her knees to her chest and sobbing into them so convulsively it was like her entire body was in spasm.

Closing the door quietly behind her Corrie walked across the narrow space, sat down on the floor beside Annalise and pulled her into her arms. To her relief Annalise didn't resist and as Corrie held her, while she choked and shuddered, Corrie was looking at the rope burns on her wrists and through the mesh of her tights the same burns on her ankles.

After only a few minutes Annalise turned to bury her face in Corrie's shoulder and, like a child, wrapped her arms around Corrie's neck.

'That's it,' Corrie soothed, 'let it all out now. I'm here, I won't let you go.'

'Oh Corrie,' Annalise sobbed. 'Corrie, it was so awful. I should hate you for it, and I keep trying to make myself, but I can't.'

'I'm glad about that,' Corrie smiled. 'I just wish I knew why he was doing it.'

'He said . . . He said . . .'

Annalise's words couldn't get past her sobs and Corrie hugged her saying, 'It's all right, sweetheart, you can tell me later . . .'

Suddenly Annalise's tears were coming faster. 'I'm sorry I hit you,' she gasped. 'Corrie, I didn't mean it. It's not your fault, I know it's not. It's just that he wants you, not me . . . But I know you don't want him. I told him that, and he got so angry . . . Colin had to pull him off me – I thought he was going to kill me, Corrie. His hands were round my neck and it was like . . . It was like he hated me.

And then . . . When we got home last night . . .' Annalise stopped and her eyes rounded with horror. Corrie drew her head back to her shoulder and held her tightly as she started to shake so badly that for a panicked moment Corrie thought she was having some kind of attack.

'What happened when you got home last night?' Corrie asked minutes later.

Annalise lifted her head, and Corrie gently brushed away the hair that was plastered to her cheeks. Annalise's lovely luminous blue eyes, now red-rimmed and sore, were searching Corrie's face. Corrie smiled her encouragement, then lowering her eyes, as though in shame, Annalise whispered,

'He raped me, Corrie.'

'Oh no!' Corrie groaned, closing her eyes as though to block out the horrifying spectacle Annalise's words had conjured.

'I told him that I would let him make love to me,' Annalise went on, 'but he didn't want to. He said he was going to fuck Siobhan, and that I was Siobhan, and he was speaking in this awful Irish voice. I always loved his Irish voice before, but this was so horrible, I was so afraid . . .' She covered her face with her hands. 'Oh Corrie, I can't tell you the things he did to me. They were so degrading, so . . . No, I can't think about it! He said that if you'd been here it would never have happened, but seeing that you weren't he was going to rape me and make me suffer all that Siobhan had suffered . . . He just wasn't making any sense . . . First it was you, then it was Siobhan . . . And he was shouting so loud I thought I was losing my mind. I begged him to tell me who Siobhan was, but he started to rape me and . . .' She was gasping for breath and though Corrie could see how confused she was, she could only guess at the torment that had been inflicted on her body, now reliving itself in her mind.

'If only I knew who she was,' Annalise wept. 'It's all to do with her, I know that. But he's blaming you . . . Why is he blaming you, Corrie? Do you know who she is? If you do, tell me, please!'

'I only wish I did know,' Corrie sighed. 'But you're right it is all to do with her, it has to be. Where is he now?'

'I don't know. He left at the same time as I did this morning. He kept saying he was sorry, that it would never happen again . . . He said I should set a date for the wedding, but I don't want to, Corrie. I can't marry him now, not after what he did to me.'

Corrie rested her head back against the shelf behind her. It was terrible to think of how much Annalise had been suffering while she and Cristos . . . But it was no good thinking that way! What had happened wasn't her fault. She could never have known that Luke would show up that way. But if she'd been there . . . If she'd been there then so too would Cristos and Annalise might not be sitting here now, like the wreck of a child . . . But she was, and Corrie could only thank God that for some reason Annalise had decided to trust her again.

'Corrie?' Annalise whispered tentatively.

'Mmm?'

'It's not true about you and my father, is it?'

It was more a statement than a question and Corrie squeezed her tightly, almost smiling at the way Annalise seemed to have read her thoughts. 'No, it's not true,' she said, and wondered if she should tell Annalise precisely why it couldn't be true. But as soon as the thought came into her head she discarded it – Annalise had enough to cope with right now.

'I never really believed it,' Annalise said. 'But Mummy got me so fired up about it . . . She's like that sometimes and I hate her for it . . . She says things that aren't true . . . But . . . I have to ask this, Corrie, why were you there that night, at the Ritz, with him?'

'I was talking to him about you,' Corrie said. 'I was worried about the way Luke was treating you . . . You see, all those things Luke has said to me – and to you about me . . . Well, I don't even pretend to understand them, but there's something going on inside his head . . . I thought that maybe your father could help, that perhaps he could throw some light on why Luke is like he is.'

'And could he?'

Corrie shook her head. 'Not really. I'm afraid your mother came in at the wrong moment, so we never really got anything sorted. But your father's very worried about you, Annalise. We both are.' She paused, not really knowing whether her next question was a wise one, but in the end decided she must ask it anyway. 'Will you come with me to the police to tell them exactly what Luke did to you last night?' she said.

Almost immediately Annalise shook her head. 'I can't. I don't want to tell anyone, not even you.'

Deciding that now was not the time to try and persuade her, Corrie bit down hard on her disappointment. 'Will you at least stop seeing him?' she said.

'I don't know.'

Again Corrie had to swallow her frustration. The programme they were working on now told her in just about every frame how very difficult, almost impossible, it was to make a woman break away from a man who repeatedly abused her. For a woman like Corrie that was hard to understand, but so it was for any woman who had never been in that situation. All Corrie knew was that she had somehow to make sure that Annalise didn't end up as one of those tragic victims, who not only lost their hearts, but sometimes their lives.

'Would you do something for me?' Corrie asked Annalise. 'Would you take the rest of the day off and go home to your parents? I'll ring your father and tell him you're on your way . . . No, don't worry, I won't tell him what happened . . . Just you go to him, and let him look after you while I finish the programme.'

Fresh tears started in Annalise's eyes. 'I don't deserve you, Corrie.'

Corrie smiled. 'Do you know, sometimes I think I don't deserve me either,' she said. 'But I'm stuck with me, and so are you.'

When she had seen Annalise to her car Corrie ran back up to the office, closed Bob Churchill's door behind her and called Phillip. Fortunately he answered, since Corrie hadn't even begun to work out what she'd say if she got through to Octavia.

'Phillip, it's Corrie,' she said, when she heard his voice. 'Annalise is on her way to you. She's not too good I'm afraid . . .'

'What happened?' Phillip said, his voice stilted with concern.

'Luke, what else? But I think she'll be all right. At least for the time being.'

'What did he do to her?' Phillip demanded.

'I'm not sure, but I think he might have gone far enough this time to destroy whatever it is she feels for him. I'm not certain of that, but I live in hope. Anyway, I've been thinking . . . I don't know if this is feasible, but if you could manage to take her away for a while . . . On a holiday or something . . .'

'I'll do it!'

Corrie almost smiled at his readiness. 'Just one thing, Phillip. Please don't tell her it was my idea, with the way things are, if Octavia gets wind of it then she might end up persuading Annalise that I'm just trying to get her out of the way to further my own ends.'

'OK,' Phillip agreed. 'But what about you, Corrie? We both know that he's trying to involve you, or has he stopped that?'

'No, he hasn't. But the main thing right now is to get Annalise away from him – if she'll go.'

'No, No!' Phillip declared. 'I'm not leaving you behind. You have to come too.'

'I can't. But I'll be all right, I promise you. He won't hurt me, not while . . .' She was going to say not while Cristos is around, but since Phillip knew nothing about Cristos, and Corrie couldn't say for sure if Cristos would still be around, she stopped herself. 'He won't hurt me,' she said firmly.

'Where is he now?'

'I don't know. Just try your best with Annalise,' and before her father could say anything else she rang off.

With a marathon effort, considering how behind schedule they were, Corrie and Colin managed to get the editing finished by eight o'clock that night. It was due to be dubbed on Thursday, meaning that the entire show would be complete in time for the weekend – and Corrie could go to Wiltshire. If there was going to be a weekend in Wiltshire!

Two more days passed and there was still no call from Cristos. Neither was there any sign of Luke. He was in contact with Bob, though, since Bob was constantly complaining about having to relay instructions, but when Corrie casually enquired where Luke was, Bob's response was, 'Don't fucking ask me!'

Annalise was still at her parents' house, where Corrie spoke to her at least three times a day. So far though Phillip hadn't managed to persuade Annalise to go on holiday, but he had succeeded in getting her to agree to a trip up to Scotland with him that weekend to stay with an old aunt of his. Which, Corrie thought, left her even freer at the weekend than she was before, but still that didn't change the fact that Cristos hadn't called her.

'Then bloody well call him,' Paula told her angrily. 'You've got his number, haven't you? You know which hotel he's staying at . . .'

'If he wants me,' Corrie responded tartly, 'then what's to stop him calling me? After all, he was the one who walked out without leaving so much as a note. And he's just too damned fond of doing that.'

'Oh God! Listen to that pride! Just get on the damned phone!'

'No!'

'I don't understand you, Corrie! He tells you he loves you, that there's something special happening between you, and then, just because he goes off early in the morning to start filming you won't ring him.'

'There's more to it than that, and you know it!'

'What, this business about Angelique Warne that you've concocted all on your own? Go down there and ask him about it, for God's sake!'

'I'm not going unless he calls me. And it's already Wednesday, so it doesn't look like he will, does it?'

'So you're going to spend the weekend tearing yourself to pieces over what might have been, holed up there in that studio like a sitting duck for Luke Fitzpatrick . . .'

'No one knows where Luke is,' Corrie interrupted.

'Oh he'll turn up,' Paula said scathingly. 'You can bank on that.'

And she was right, he did, the very next morning, at the office.

When Corrie found the note on her desk asking her to go and see him she was tempted to throw it in the bin, but knowing that she couldn't get out of it that easily, she started towards his office whispering to Alan Fox, 'Do you know where he's been these last few days?'

'Not a clue. Why should I?'

Corrie shook her head. 'No reason.'

'Have you seen him at all this morning?'

Corrie shook her head.

'Then you could be in for a bit of a surprise,' and with a peculiar sort of smile Alan Fox picked up the phone to answer an incoming call.

'Come in,' Luke called, when Corrie knocked.

Corrie pushed the door open and the instant she saw his face she felt her own freeze with shock.

'Is something the matter?' he said.

Was something the matter? Only that he looked like a corpse! That even the tan he must have taken from a sun bed couldn't hide the jaundiced hue of his skin, or the lifelessness of his eyes . . . And his hair! He'd virtually been scalped. 'Are you all right?' she asked before she could stop herself.

'Yes, I'm very well, thank you,' he snapped. 'Come in, close the door.'

'Did you see the programme?' she asked in an effort to sound casual as she turned back to him. 'We finished it on Sunday. It's . . .'

'Annalise informs me that you left the editing session at least two hours early on Saturday,' he said.

'That's right,' Corrie answered.

'Is that all you have to say?'

Corrie looked directly into his yellowed eyes. 'What else is there to say?' she asked, with an ambiguity he couldn't fail to detect.

'I think you should know that Annalise has been pressing me to fire you. You're giving her plenty of grounds, Corrie. If you walk out on an edit session again, I'll do it. You were with Bennati?'

'Yes.'

'Yes,' he repeated. 'Then I think you should know that you're wasting your time. He's not anywhere near over Angelique Warne. He's just using you.'

Corrie gritted her teeth. How could he have known that Angelique Warne would be the one name she didn't want to hear right now? 'I think,' she said, 'that's for me to decide.'

'Oh no,' he barked, 'it'll be Bennati who decides. Just like he was the one to decide when she died.'

'*What!*' Corrie hissed. 'What the hell are you talking about?'

'Ask Bennati.'

'No, I'm asking you! Just how come you know so much about him when he can't stand the very sight of you? That like me he wouldn't trust you any further than he could throw you! And while you're at it, perhaps you'd like to explain what that farcical performance was all about in the edit suite on Saturday night?'

'I came here to find you! You weren't here!'

'I don't call that an explanation. You frightened the life out of Annalise and Colin's calling you a fucking madman. And quite frankly I think you are!'

'You'll be calling me your husband before much longer,' he stated.

At that Corrie was so stunned she couldn't respond at all.

The telephone rang then and snatching it up he snapped a yes into the receiver. Then his voice suddenly softened as he said, 'Yes, it's me.' He listened for some time then said, 'Don't worry, I'll come. I'm getting it sorted now. No, I won't let you down . . . Yes, I understand . . .' then he rang off. 'I'm going away for a while,' he said to Corrie. 'Just a couple of weeks, but I want you to know that when Bennati lets you down you can contact me . . .'

'I don't want to know where to contact you!' Corrie spat. 'Whatever happens between Cristos and me has fuck all to do with you.'

'Like my relationship with Annalise has fuck all to do with you?' he said pointedly.

'What relationship with Annalise? After what you did to her Saturday night I'm frankly amazed and disgusted you've got the gall to face me with that.'

At last Luke showed some signs of discomfort. 'She told you what happened?' he said.

'Not in graphic detail, but I know you raped her! That

you used her body calling her Siobhan and telling her it wouldn't be happening if I'd been here. So what's all this about, Luke? Just who the hell is this Siobhan?'

His momentary unease was over, and with total composure he said, 'So you don't know the actual details?' and he nodded in apparent satisfaction.

'Who is she?' Corrie seethed.

Luke continued to look up at her, then with a smile so pleasant it was almost sinister he said, 'You'll come to me in the end, Corrie.'

Corrie's head started to spin. 'Are you listening to me?' she cried. 'Just watch my lips: I want nothing to do with you, neither does Annalise, as far as both of us are concerned . . .'

'You can go now,' Luke interrupted. 'And be grateful that I'm overlooking the way you're speaking to me. From a subordinate I would never take it, from my future wife I'll suffer it.'

'Is there no getting through to you?' Corrie screamed.

'I'm leaving tonight,' he said, 'I'd like to see what ideas you have for your next programme before I go.'

Corrie had already drawn breath to speak again, but realizing she was wasting her time, she turned and walked out of the door.

That night she was back on the phone to Paula.

'He's insane!' Paula declared. 'He has to be if he thinks you're going to marry him. Have you told your father about this?'

'No. He'll only worry, and to be frank I can do without that right now.'

'Well I expect those prostitutes could have done without being murdered,' Paula responded fiercely.

'For God's sake has the whole world gone mad?' Corrie cried. 'Where did that suddenly come from?'

'From you! Where do you think? It wasn't long ago that you seriously believed he might have killed those women . . . Think back, remind yourself of the way he's tied up Annalise and Felicity – and you, come to that! All those prostitutes were tied up when they were killed. Then look at the way you thought he knew Bobby McIver . . . How he beats up Annalise . . . How he throws a raging fit about you. Add it all together Corrie and what have you got?'

'Paula,' Corrie said, 'as far as Bobby McIver is concerned the police interviewed Luke and cleared him. And plenty of men are into bondage, and beating up women come to that. That doesn't make them . . .'

'Murderers?' Paul finished for her.

Corrie shrieked with exasperation. 'OK, he's weird, he's a pervert, I'll be the first to admit that . . .'

'Then admit what he really is. It's staring you right in the face, Corrie, so why do you keep shying away from it. Just how much danger do you want to put yourself in for Christ's sake?'

'Paula, let's stop this, right now! Luke is going away, he tells me. No, I know what you're going to say, that it doesn't make any difference. But it does. I need some time to think, because my rational mind is telling me that men in his position, as the anchorman of a national current affairs programme, just don't go round killing people. And much less do they interview the investigating officer. OK, I know what I said before, and it's true my irrational mind says that he could have done it . . .'

'Talk it over with Cristos! He's known the man . . .'

'No!'

'Listen to me! You said yourself Luke as good as accused Cristos of being responsible for Angelique Warne's death. Now doesn't that suggest to you that those two men have a history worth knowing about? Cristos might be able to tell you something that could sort this out for you once and for all. And even if he can't, you'll at least be with him at the weekend . . .'

'Paula! Stop! I told you, I want to think about this.'

'All right, have it your way. You think about it all on your own, but you just make sure you don't keep your head buried in the sand for too long, because as far as I can see, Luke going away is only postponing the crisis not avoiding it. And you know as well as I do that there's one hell of a crisis boiling here! So do something, Corrie, speak to someone before it turns into a fucking catastrophe!'

– 23 –

On Friday evening Annalise flew to Scotland with Phillip. Corrie saw them off, assuring them both that she would be all right and promising to call if she wasn't. By now she had managed to calm herself down sufficiently to actually smile at the way she had allowed herself to be carried along by Paula's panic. Not that Paula wasn't making perfect sense – that was, if anything made sense any more – it was just to Corrie's mind there didn't seem much point in getting worked up about Luke when he had taken it upon himself to vanish. She had no idea where he was, and had to confess to being more than a little intrigued, but he'd told Bob that he would be gone for at least two weeks, which for now was all that mattered. At least so far as Luke Fitzpatrick was concerned – for what was bothering Corrie much more as she returned to her studio from the airport, was the fact that she and Cristos had still not contacted each other.

She'd been back in her studio for no more than fifteen minutes when she threw down the book she was reading and started to reach for the phone. This was nonsense! It couldn't go on and if it had to be her who swallowed her pride then she'd damned well do it. Her hand was just about to touch the receiver when suddenly the telephone rang.

Swearing under her breath at having her moment of courage interrupted, Corrie was tempted to let it go on ringing. In the end she picked it up.

'Hello?' she snapped.

'What the hell are you doing there?' Cristos shouted.

'What do you think I'm doing here,' Corrie retorted, matching his tone perfectly while feeling herself start to grin. 'I live here.'

'Don't be obtuse. You're supposed to be here with me.'

'Who says?'

'I say. Now get your Goddammed ass on a train and get down here now.'

'You're taking rather a lot for granted,' she said, glad he couldn't see her right now because her smile was so wide it hurt. 'I mean you haven't even bothered to call me this week, but now it suits you you expect me to come running.'

'I didn't notice you rushing to the horn either,' he barked.

'I wasn't the one who sneaked off without saying goodbye.'

'Trying not to wake you.'

'You could have left a note.'

'Well pardon me, ma'am. Now are you getting on that train or do I have to come get you?'

'I'll get on the train, but you'd better not shout at me like that when I get there or I'll just turn right around and come back again.'

'The hell you will. Now get packing.'

'Cristos,' she said, as he was about to ring off.

'Yes?'

'Weren't you the tiniest bit worried when I didn't call?'

'I've been out of my mind all week.'

'Oh! A bare-faced lie, Bennati!'

'Ask your friend Paula,' he said, and the line went dead.

'All right, all right, I admit it, I did call him,' Paula confessed, 'and yes I did tell him you were having a childish fit of pride. Well someone had to, you were making such a bloody idiot of yourself.'

'I'll forgive you if you can tell me why he didn't ring me – I mean without your help!'

'He didn't ring because, apart from being who he is – which makes him a very busy man – he came all the way up to London last week, whisked you out of the edit suite then spent an entire night satiating your insatiable sexual hunger and telling you how much he loved you, which *you* refused to say in return. He's done all the running, and you've done nothing but lap it up. He's got his pride too, you know! And if you ask me . . .'

'Not so fast,' Corrie interrupted. 'He told you all that?'

'Well, not in so many words. But that was the gist of it. Anyway he's called you now, so stop wasting time and get down there to Wiltshire.'

A little over two hours later Corrie stepped down from the train at Chippenham station into a fog so thick she could barely see further than six feet in front of her. Automatically she pulled her scarf up around her mouth and tugged down her felt hat to keep out the biting cold. It had to be at least five degrees colder than London here, and there hadn't been any of this fog in town either. It was like arriving in another country, she was thinking to herself, as she edged along the platform towards the dim light that looked like it might be an exit. She'd called Cristos, or more precisely Jeannie, to tell them what time train she was coming in on, but there didn't appear to be any sign of anyone.

Then she grinned as she heard someone calling her name from somewhere inside the grey mass. It wasn't Cristos's voice, but it was American. 'Corrie! Corrie Browne, are you there?'

'Over here,' she called, and by using their voices she and the mystery man eventually found each other.

'Hi,' Corrie said, having to hold onto her hat for fear of losing it she had to look so far up at him.

'Hi,' he said, taking her bag, 'I'm Richard, Jeannie's husband. Cristos couldn't come, he had to meet with Bud Winters, the exec. producer who's been chewing everyone's ass off all week. Keep 'em in the Black Tower's what I say. They don't do no good out in the field. Anyway, let's see if we can find the way back to the hotel.'

'Or at least out of the station,' Corrie laughed.

A few minutes later they were in the Mini Jeannie had rented for herself and had grudgingly loaned Richard since she was certain he'd do it some damage.

'She's sending me crazy,' Richard told Corrie, as they inched along the road towards a hazy set of traffic lights. 'Anyone'd think this was a baby not a frigging car – pardon my French, as you English would say.'

Corrie was laughing, mainly because Richard looked so funny sat like that with the steering wheel between his knees. 'Has the weather been like this for long?' she asked.

'All week. Cristos is going about the place having orgasms over it . . .'

'You mean he's pleased!' Corrie interrupted. 'I'd have thought it would make shooting almost impossible.'

'He likes it! Says it's just what he wanted. As far as I'm concerned it's a fucking nightmare. You try lighting a fog – more to the point, you try finding a fucking electrician in a fog!' He grinned. 'But we're getting there. And Bud Winters is only giving himself an ulcer 'cos that's what he's paid for. He loves what he's seen.'

'So tell me all about the scenes you've shot this week,' Corrie said.

As Richard told her, peppering his dialogue with plenty of colourful descriptions, Corrie snuggled deeper into her coat to listen. It wasn't until half and hour had gone by that Richard said, '. . . So that's about where we're up to. And just in case you're interested, we're lost.'

Laughing, Corrie opened up the map she found on the back seat, discovered they were now not too far distant from Bath, and finally managed to navigate them back onto the right road. Over an hour after her train had arrived they finally pulled up outside the Castle Combe Manor House Hotel.

Corrie was already out of the car and trying not to laugh at the way Richard was attempting to untangle himself when Cristos suddenly materialized from the fog.

'Where the hell have you been?' he demanded, glaring down at Richard. 'I was just about to start out looking for you.'

'Give me a break man!' Richard barked, from where he was half-lying half-sitting on the ground. 'She's here now, isn't she? And in case you didn't notice it's foggy out there.'

'Good evening, Cristos,' Corrie said pleasantly. She could only just make out his face, and knew that he was still scowling. Then heaving Richard to his feet, Cristos walked around the car, snatched up Corrie's bag and virtually frog-marched her into the hotel.

Several of the crew were grouped around the burning log fire in the front hall, and looked up as Cristos and Corrie came in. Ignoring them Cristos propelled her right on past them, up the stairs, along a quaint oak-beamed corridor and into his room.

'Through there,' he barked, pointing along a narrow hallway.

Corrie walked on ahead, casting a quick glance to her right as they passed a wide arch which led into a luxurious marble bathroom. Just beyond it was a heavy mahogany door, which, when she opened it, Corrie found led into the most wonderful bedroom suite, with a king size brass bed, a steeply sloping ceiling cluttered with oak beams, all kinds of antique furniture and a huge stone arch leading into the fireplace where a small fire was flickering away.

'Right,' Cristos said, kicking the door closed and spinning her round to face him. 'Don't you ever pull a stunt like that again, do you hear me? I'm not playing games with you, Corrie. I love you, I told you that, and now I'm telling you again. But I sure as hell am not going to tolerate that ridiculous pride of yours coming between us.'

'What about your pride?' Corrie retorted hotly. 'You could have called me.'

'I needed to hear that phone ring, to hear your voice at the other end and know that you had put yourself out enough to find the number and call. You won't tell me you love me, so is that too much to ask?'

'No. But you just quit shouting at me, or I'll leave.'

'I'll do more than shout at you if you take so much as one step towards that door. And stop trying to sound American. You're English. I love you because you're English. I love you because you drive me fucking nuts being English. And what are you laughing at?'

Corrie nodded for him to look behind him.

He turned round to discover Jeannie standing the other side of the bed. 'What the hell are you doing here?' he roared.

'Richard took the key to our room and so's not to bother anyone I was just sitting at your fireplace reading my book,' she shrugged, seemingly unruffled.

'Then get the hell out.'

Obediently she saluted. 'I's a-going, massa.'

She winked at Corrie as she passed, then just before she closed the door she whispered to Cristos, 'That's one hell of a seduction technique you got there, boss,' and as her eyes suddenly widened with alarm she pulled the door quickly together.

'Don't laugh, it only encourages her,' Cristos said turning back to Corrie and grinning despite himself.

'Would you like to kiss me?'

'No.'

'Well that's too bad, because I want to kiss you.' And sliding her arms around his neck she brought his mouth down to hers. He didn't resist, he simply pulled her closer, and not too long after that he was lifting her up onto the bed, which was so high that she insisted it was the only dignified route up she could think of.

Corrie was woken the following morning by a peculiar sounding bell coming from somewhere inside the room. Cristos, she noticed as she pulled herself out from under the blankets, had already gone, and looking around the room trying to work out where the tinny little ring was coming from she vaguely remembered him bending over the bed to kiss her at some unearthly hour of the morning. Smiling to herself she slid off the mattress, spotting as she went the boxed wooden steps beside the bed, and covering herself with Cristos's robe trotted off down the hallway to answer what she now realized was the doorbell.

It was a waiter with a breakfast tray – and a note!

Pointing him to the coffee table in front of the sofa Corrie opened the note to discover that it was a map directing her to the Parsonage Woods location with a scribbled message from Jeannie saying she could join them any time she liked.

Just after ten, clutching the map in her hand and profoundly glad that she had thought to bring her own location gear, Corrie wandered out of the hotel grounds along the cobbled street and into the antiquated village of Castle Combe. The fog was still down so she couldn't see too clearly, but the Market Cross was marked clearly on her map and she guessed that it must be the roofed monument at the centre of the road between the Castle Hotel and White Hart Inn that she was now standing in front of. Dimly she could make out the road that curved down to her right between the quaint little cottages – there wasn't a soul in sight and everything was so still in the eerie silence of dead winter that she could almost feel herself being transported back those many hundreds of years to when the village had first come into existence.

Following the directions on her map she turned in the opposite direction to start up over the hill in search of the Dower House. She was busily bemoaning the fact that she should have come to such an awesomely lovely place at a time when she could hardly see it, when the Dower House was upon her, and crossing the street she began to climb up the narrow muddied footpath into the woods.

She had travelled about fifty yards when a voice called out. 'Hi there! You looking for the set?'

Corrie peered through the mist, and just able to make out a human shape some way ahead called back that she was.

'Keep right on up,' the voice told her, 'but mind how you go, I've spent the best part of the morning on my butt, going up and down that path.'

Corrie could hear the muffled voices even before she reached the small clearing in the woods where Roger, a third assistant was waiting. Down in a dip behind him the location caterers had set up hot coffee and soup amongst the brittle, bare trees and what looked like half the unit were there crammed together, taking advantage of it.

Roger was about to offer Corrie something when a voice crackled over his walkie-talkie saying, 'Quiet over at the coffee, going for a take.'

'Quiet everyone!' Roger bawled.

The response was instantaneous, and Corrie waited for what seemed an eternity as the mist wafted around her, and the cold stung at her feet, before the same voice came back over the radio saying 'We've cut.'

'Where are they actually shooting?' she asked Roger.

'Right up there,' he said pointing into the fog. 'They're

in a field next to the wood. You Corrie Browne, by the way?'

'Yes.'

'Jeannie told me to expect you. You want to go on up now, or you want some coffee?'

'I'll go up now if that's all right,' she said.

When they reached the field and walked blithely through all the notices saying 'No Entry' Corrie saw what must have amounted to two hundred or more men milling about and stomping their feet in the frost-frozen grass. Every one of them was in nineteenth-century military uniform. The spectacle was so dramatic, as the scarlet clad soldiers emerged from the white puffs of mist as though being conjured from bygone days, that Corrie was transfixed. She made an abrupt return to reality though, when a stream of assistants started to ferry in coffee and soup; then being guided through the milieu by a voice at the other end of Roger's walkie-talkie, she and Roger eventually came to where the camera was being mounted on tracks. Cristos was standing nearby with Richard and several others, and an instant grin sprang to Corrie's lips when she saw that besides the moon boots, predictable jeans and ski-anorak, he was wearing a dear-stalker hat with the flaps down over his ears. At that moment he was laughing, and looked so handsome and so ridiculous that Corrie felt an overwhelming urge to hug him. Roger made to call out to him, but Corrie put a hand on his arm saying, 'No, don't interrupt. I'll just wait here.'

She watched for some time, feeling such an inflated sense of pride that it was all she could do to keep the mawkish adoration from her eyes. She wandered a little closer in order to eavesdrop on what he was saying and listened as he explained how he wanted the camera to track against the flow of stampeding feet as a point of view shot.

'It's a cutaway,' he added, 'but keep it going 'cos I'll probably use it more than once,' as he was speaking he was moving closer to Corrie, then turning to her, to her amazement he put an arm around her and kissed her right in front of everyone.

'How you doing?' he murmured, his breath sweeping her face in a white mist.

'Fine. You?'

'Great.'

'Love the hat.'

'Love you.' Then, almost on the instant, she was forgotten as he strode back towards the camera half-listening to the assistant director while shouting for the sound man.

Corrie found herself a convenient spot where she hoped she wouldn't be in the way, but after only a few minutes was being bombarded by people eager to introduce themselves.

'That's what comes of being the director's girl,' a voice behind her said as a junior make-up artist rushed back to the set.

Corrie turned round and almost did a double take when she found herself looking straight at Paige Spencer. Or was it Paige Spencer?

The woman smiled at Corrie's evident confusion. 'I'm Paige's stand-in,' she explained. 'Paige asked me to come over to invite you to her trailer for a coffee. It's right over there,' she added pointing towards a spot which wasn't even visible.

Corrie would have dearly loved to refuse, but not seeing how she could, she gathered up her bag and followed the stand-in into the next field.

'Hi,' Paige said, holding out her hand. She was standing on the steps of her trailer managing to look, Corrie thought, dauntingly majestic. 'I'm Paige Spencer,' she said, 'and you, I guess, are the Corrie Browne everyone's talking about.'

Corrie smiled as she shook Paige's hand, not at all sure she was enjoying being confronted by one of Cristos's past affairs, particularly one so devastatingly beautiful. 'It's very nice to meet you,' she said.

'Come right on in,' Paige said, moving back inside the door.

Once Corrie was seated, and had politely accepted the offer of coffee, Paige came straight to the point.

'I got something here for you,' she said, digging into her pocket. 'It's the address of a doctor I saw in Harley Street. Go see him the minute you get back to London. I was in the clear, thank God. I sure hope you are too, honey.'

'Pardon?' Corrie said, almost choking on her coffee.

Paige rolled her eyes. 'Just what I thought. The son-of-a-bitch didn't tell you either?'

'Tell me what?'

Shaking her head and putting her own coffee down, Paige sat back to fold her arms over the tattered dress she was wearing. 'Hang onto your hat, honey,' she said, ''cos this one's a real bumpy one.' She hesitated a moment, peering at Corrie through narrowed eyes, as though in some way assessing her, then shrugging she said, 'Well, there's no other way of saying it than straight. Bennati's got gonorrhoea.'

Corrie's cup clanged into the saucer. 'He's what?' she gasped.

'Sssh! You might not care who knows, but I sure as hell do. Why else do you think I broke it off with him?'

Corrie was almost smiling now. 'There must be some mistake,' she said, leaning forward to put her coffee down. 'I mean . . .'

'Look, kid,' Paige interrupted, 'I understand you don't want to believe it, hell do you think I did? And I sure am sorry to be the one to break it to you, but we girls've got to stick together. And I'm telling you the bastard's got gonorrhoea – he's spreading it about all over the fucking set.'

To Corrie it was so inconceivable that no matter how

sincere Paige sounded, she simply couldn't bring herself to believe it. But then Paige said the words that sealed it.

'You were waiting for him to call all last week, am I right?'

Corrie tensed.

'Yeah, I thought so. Bud Winters' secretary was here till yesterday – she flew back last night. When did Bennati call you?'

'Last night,' Corrie said dully.

'Are you getting my drift? I tried to tip Sheila off before she went back to the States, but I missed her. You gotta face it, honey, the man's rampant and he's putting it about all over. That's how he got it in the first place.'

The second assistant banged on the door then shouting 'First team up!'

'That's me,' Paige said, getting to her feet. 'You stay finish your coffee – there's a telephone there if you wanna call the doc and get yourself an appointment. Me, I'm suing the bastard once this movie is through,' and she left.

For the rest of the morning Corrie watched in a dull stupor as the action took place in front of her. Carpenters, props men, costume designers, electricians, so many people came over to chat with her, all intrigued to meet the woman Cristos Bennati had invited onto the set, but though Corrie somehow managed to make polite conversation, she was hardly registering what anyone was saying. All she could hear were Paige's words, echoing through her ears.

At lunchtime Cristos came to find her, and putting an arm round her shoulders told her they were going to eat lunch in his trailer. 'I'd kind of prefer it to be just the two of us,' he said, walking her across the field, 'but a couple of the actors want to talk about this afternoon's scenes. And brace yourself, the unit publicist is dropping by too.'

'Why brace myself?' Corrie mumbled.

'Because you should never trust a unit publicist to keep

his mouth shut, even if you tell him his job depends on it. We'll be all over the Sunday press by tomorrow.'

'I see,' Corrie said.

Over lunch Corrie said little and ate even less. She still wasn't sure that she really believed Paige, but if it was true, if he had spent the week with Winters' secretary . . . If he did have gonorrhoea and knowing it had made love to her . . . No, it was unthinkable!

Suddenly she was aware that Cristos was calling a halt to lunch and sending everyone out of the trailer.

'OK,' he said, closing the door and turning back to Corrie, 'let's have it.'

'Have what?'

'Whatever it is that's eating you?'

Seeing no alternative Corrie handed him the note Paige had given her. 'It's the telephone number of a Harley Street doctor,' she explained. 'Paige gave it to me to go and get myself checked out.'

'Checked out for what?' he asked, and looked, Corrie thought, convincingly baffled.

'Gonorrhoea.'

His eyes came up to Corrie's and Corrie faltered as she saw his confusion turning to anger. 'Are you telling me Paige is telling you I've got gonorrhoea?' he said, too quietly.

Corrie nodded. 'She had herself checked out she told me, and she hasn't got it, but . . .'

'Well of course she hasn't got it!' he yelled. 'At least not from me she hasn't. Can't you see what she's doing? She's just trying . . .' He stopped suddenly, and Corrie watched him as he frowned pensively down at the note.

His relationship with Paige had disintegrated pretty rapidly when he was fighting the urge to call Corrie, he was thinking, and the only person who knew that Paige was an obstacle . . .

Slapping the note down on the table he turned and stormed towards the door. 'JEANNIE!' he roared.

Jeannie was perched not far away on a tree stump, idly chatting with the make-up assistants, but on hearing Cristos yelling her name that way, she leapt to her feet, mumbling, 'Holy shit, he's found out!' And turning about face she ran in the opposite direction, never more thankful for fog in her life.

Not until Cristos was safely soaring through the mist on a crane much later in the afternoon did Jeannie venture near the set again. She found Corrie sitting on the steps of the props van, but not wanting to hang around too long she asked Corrie if she felt like going for a walk.

'It's all right,' Corrie laughed, as the two of them left the set behind and started to wander through the winter debris of the woods, 'you don't have to explain to me, I know the truth of it now, but I can't give you any comfort as far as Cristos is concerned, I'm afraid. He was furious, in fact he hasn't quite forgiven me for believing it.'

'Oh shit!' Jeannie groaned, 'I'd better start writing my epitaph now, 'cos I just know he's not going to forgive this one in a hurry. But he's got to understand why I did it.'

'I think he does, he just wishes you might have done it another way,' Corrie chuckled, and linking Jeannie's arm as they slithered about in the slime of dead leaves and mud on the pathway, she added, 'In a way, I suppose I should thank you.'

'I sure wish he'd see it that way,' Jeannie groaned.

They walked in silence for a while then, an archway of stark, brittle branches towering above them, though barely visible through the billowing breath of fog. Melting frost was falling from the trees like rain and nothing but their squelching footsteps interrupted the stillness.

Eventually they reached a stile at the edge of the woods, and after Jeannie had climbed it Corrie stopped to sit on top, saying, 'Jeannie, do you know anything about Cristos's

– for want of another word – friendship with Luke Fitz-patrick? I'm sorry to ask, and I don't want you to be disloyal, but I just don't want to bring it up with him myself.'

'Why?' Jeannie asked.

Corrie shrugged. 'I suppose because everything's so won-derful between Cristos and me right now that I don't want anything to spoil it. And somehow I get the feeling that to ask him about Luke Fitzpatrick would. Or perhaps I should say to ask him about Luke and what Luke knows about Angelique Warne . . . You see, I know Cristos doesn't want to talk about it, and we've more or less made a pact not to ask about each other's past, but I just feel that this is something I ought to know about.'

Sighing and shaking her head Jeannie turned to rest her back against the stile and looked out over the sepia winter landscape that stretched into the valley of mist beyond them. 'I don't know what Luke knows,' she said, 'but whatever it is I don't figure it's the truth. You know, I used to like the guy, but I got to feeling that there's something a tad strange about him. There's got to be for two guys like you and Cristos to get so bugged about him. Anyway, I'm not the one to tell you about Angelique, Cristos is. I will tell you this, though, you got nothing to be afraid of, 'cos in all the years I've known him I've never seen Cristos this smitten. Last night I heard him tell you he loves you, and he means it, Corrie, but this pact of yours is crazy. Don't start out by holding back on him, and don't let him hold back on you, or you ain't going any place together. And that would be kinda sad 'cos I reckon you're both what each other wants.'

'There's going to be plenty of problems though,' Corrie said prosaically. 'Like distance, age . . .'

'What are you talking about?' Jeannie laughed. 'Sure he's older than you, by what, twelve, fourteen years? So what? It's nothing. OK, distance might be a problem, but when two guys love each other they find a way. Did he ever tell you about his folks and what they went through to be together?'

Corrie nodded. 'Have you met them?'

'Sure. They're just terrific. Pop runs a deli and Mom drives the old guy crazy. They love each other like you'd die to still be in love at their age. Cristos is devoted to them. You know his mother wants him to win the Palme d'Or? Oscars ain't good enough for Mrs Bennati. She wants the French one. And Cristos aims to give it to her. It was her encouraged him to go into movies in the first place. Pop Bennati wanted him to take over the deli. 'Course the old guy's prouder of him now than he'll ever admit. Tells him he doesn't bring home that Palme d'Or for his mother he'll leave everything to the daughter.'

'I didn't know Cristos had a sister,' Corrie said.

'Francine. She's a few years younger than him, round thirty-seven I guess. Got herself a great job with one of the banks in New York. Married, no kids. He can't have them, I think Cristos told me once. They're a close family, the Bennatis. Pop wants grandsons.'

'Hang on, hang on, you're going too fast,' Corrie cried, holding up her hands. 'Tell me some of his bad points.'

'You mean you haven't seen enough of them already? Like how temperamental he is? He's a shithead like the rest of us, OK, he's got a bit more talent . . .' Jeannie was laughing, but as she turned to Corrie, Corrie saw her eyes start to widen. 'Shit! Here he comes, which means the unit have got to have broken. Don't let on we've been talking about him, and don't leave me alone with him after that Paige Spencer thing or you'll be coming to my funeral next week.'

Corrie swung her legs back over the stile to watch Cristos approach, holding his eyes and feeling the same intimate smile curve across her own lips.

'You two getting to know each other?' he said, as he reached them. 'Don't believe anything she tells you,' and pulling Corrie down into his arms he kissed her. 'You OK?' he whispered. 'Not bored?'

'Not bored,' she smiled, keeping her face tilted up to his as she circled his waist with her arms.

'Ahem!'

'You still here, Jeannie?' he said, his eyes still on Corrie's.

Jeannie shrugged. 'Guess I'll take a hike,' she said, but as she started down over the hill she turned back when Cristos called out her name.

'Don't think I've forgotten,' he told her.

'No suh, massa,' she answered, making Corrie laugh.

'How's it going out there?' she asked, as he turned back to her.

He grimaced and looked up to what they could see of the leaden sky. 'Fog's clearing, but we're losing light, can't shoot any more today. I've got to see dailies later, but there's still a couple of hours for you and me before. Anything in particular you want to do?'

Corrie grinned. 'Well since you ask . . .' she said with a wry smile.

He raised his eyebrows. 'Right here?'

Corrie laughed. 'Bit cold.' Then standing on tip-toe to reach his mouth, she whispered, 'I'd like to try something different this time.'

'Oh yeah? Like what?' he smiled.

'Like take me back to your room and find out.'

Less than an hour later, with the door firmly locked and the telephone off the hook, Corrie was standing naked against the edge of the massive bed with Cristos's arms draped loosely round her as she told him what she wanted.

He closed his eyes and let his head fall back. 'Shit, Corrie,' he groaned, 'I don't know whether it's that English accent of yours when you say it or 'cos I know you've never done it before, but you're blowing my mind, you know that, don't you?'

'I was hoping you were going to do that to me,' she

smiled, then heaving herself up onto the bed she relaxed back on her elbows to watch him undress.

She waited until he was on the bed beside her, then sliding her arms around him said, 'I'm ready for you now. I don't want to wait.'

He nodded, and gently turning her over, knelt between her legs and lifting her up onto her knees, he pulled her face round to his and kissing her he entered her from behind.

This way he had access to every part of her body, she knew it and he knew it and it was what they both wanted. What neither of them had planned on was coming so quickly.

'God, I love you,' he murmured, as he pulled her into his arms when it was over.

Corrie lifted her face to brush her lips against his cheek, then settling herself back on his shoulder she listened to the still rapid beat of his heart, as she stealed herself to ask the question already burning on her lips. It was as he hooked a leg over hers drawing her closer that she finally said, very tentatively, 'Do you love me enough to tell me about Angelique Warne?'

Instead of the instant withdrawal she had expected she felt his arms tighten around her. 'What do you want to know?' he asked.

Taking heart from his response, Corrie lifted her face to look at him, saying, 'I suppose I'd like to know what really happened between you two . . . If any of those things written in the paper at the time she died were true . . .'

Settling his head more comfortably on the pillow he took a deep breath and after giving her a quick glance he stared up at the ceiling, saying, 'What did Fitzpatrick tell you?'

With a half smile that he'd already guessed that much, Corrie said, 'He told me that you weren't over her. That you were just using me. He said something about you being involved in how she died . . .'

A grim smile crossed Cristos's lips. 'That's what I thought. Did he tell you outright I killed her?'

'No.'

Cristos seemed surprised. 'Well that was sure as hell what he tried to pin on me. The truth is, though, I *was* involved in the way she died, but not in the way Fitzpatrick wants you to believe.'

Corrie listened quietly then to all he told her about the love and then the pain and confusion he had known with Angelique. She reached for his hands when he told her about the baby he would never know for sure was his – she could see that this, more than anything else, would haunt him for a long time to come.

'That's why,' he finished, 'I didn't want to get involved again. I saw how love could destroy a relationship, how wanting more from it than I could offer destroyed Angelique. And I didn't ever want to trust a woman again so's she could do that to me. It sounds kind of selfish, I know, when she's dead, but that's the way it is. Was,' he corrected, looking down at her. 'But I got to tell you this now, Corrie, when I say I love you I mean it, but I'm not making you any promises. I just don't know where we're heading from here . . .'

He stopped when Corrie put her fingers over his lips. 'Don't let's talk about that now,' she said. 'We'll worry about it when we have to.'

With all her heart Corrie wished she could have meant those words, but she didn't. She wanted, so very much, to hear him say that they did have a future, because only then would she risk letting him know how much she loved him.

– 24 –

With the press having got wind of her affair with Cristos, Corrie started to discover what it was like to be famous. Not only did she keep seeing her own face looking back at her whenever she opened a newspaper, but every time she left the office or her studio there were at least three photographers waiting for her and journalists, notebooks in hand, asking her so many questions that she could barely distinguish one from another. Her phone was ringing off the hook inviting her to do interviews for magazines, newspapers, even TV, on both sides of the Atlantic and the amounts of money being offered were staggering – even tempting. But Corrie consistently refused, not only because Cristos so valued his private life, but because she really didn't think that what they had together was anyone else's business.

However the paparazzi were determined that it was everyone's business, and Corrie didn't know whether to laugh or be angry when Paula called her at the office one morning to tell her that somehow the press had discovered where Corrie came from and had been at Amberside taking pictures of the cottage.

'I gave them a short interview,' Paula confessed. 'I hope you don't mind, but they were so insistent, and I found myself saying things before I even knew what I was saying.'

'Like what?' Corrie cried.

'Like what a fantastic person you are and how lucky Bennati is to have met you.'

'Ugh!' Corrie laughed. 'I don't suppose anyone will think you're biased, by any chance? Anyway, thanks for letting me know, but I have to go now there's a call holding for me,' and pushing the appropriate buttons she picked up line six. 'Corrie Browne here.'

'Ah, Miss Browne, I'm calling from *People* magazine in New York. I was hoping, since I'm going to be in the UK next week, that you'd consider doing . . .'

'I'm afraid not,' Corrie interrupted. 'But thank you for asking,' and before the journalist could argue further, or dangle the carrot of untold wealth, she rang off.

Alan Fox was watching her across the desk, and throwing

him a quick smile as she tossed her hair back from her face, Corrie said, 'Haven't *Vogue* been in touch yet, offering me the front cover?'

Laughing, Fox remarked, 'You're handling it pretty well, you know.'

Corrie grinned. 'Well, one gets used to these things, you know,' she said breezily.

'Seriously though,' Fox said, 'do you mind all the attention?'

Corrie shrugged. 'What, you mean like photographs of me getting into a cab, walking out of a door, closing a window, coming out of Waitrose. Did you see the one this morning of me on the bus? Who the hell can be interested in all that stuff?' she laughed. 'But to answer your question, no I don't mind it at the moment, but the novelty is going to wear off pretty soon.'

'What about Cristos? How's he handling it? He rang and left a message earlier, by the way. Said could you remember to take the music cassette down with you?'

'Oh, sure,' Corrie said, glancing at the walkman on her desk. On it was a copy of the composer's tape for *Past Lives Present*. 'Cristos is well used to people trying to dig into his life,' she went on, 'and he hates it. He's just employed an army of security guards to keep the press at bay while he's shooting. And who can blame him when they keep popping up in shot?'

'So, is it serious between you two?' Alan enquired, a little too casually Corrie thought. 'Are you going to give up all this and go to the States?'

'Are you trying get a scoop here, Alan Fox?' she teased. 'Yes, you are, so let's change the subject, because I want to know if you've looked at the treatments I gave you last week.'

'I have,' he said. 'And if you're staying in good old Blighty then I'm with you all the way. You don't want to go public with them yet though?'

'No.'

'Well, you might find this hard to believe, but you can trust me. I'd like to be there with you if you pull it off – and I reckon you will.'

'Thank you,' Corrie said, meaning it.

This conversation with Alan Fox took place on one of the rare occasions Corrie was at the office, for she was spending as much time as she could in Wiltshire. With Annalise still at home recovering from her ordeal the other producers were lining up to take over the available programme slots, and seeing this lull in her schedule as a good opportunity to look further into the possibilities of making three or four special drama-documentaries a year, under the TW banner, Corrie spent all the hours she could observing Cristos and discussing in the minutest of detail how he approached the dramatization of a factual story. Fearing that the two of them didn't have a future together meant that Corrie's ambitions were once again of prime importance to her – not that they had ever ceased to matter, but now she needed them desperately to fill the terrible void there would be in her life once he had returned to Los Angeles. It was all too tempting to fantasize about what she would do were he to ask her to go with him, but in her heart she knew he wouldn't, just as she knew that even if he were to ask she wouldn't go. She hated herself for thinking she might feel differently were he to ask her to marry him, it seemed so parochial and childishly idealistic, but to go and just live with him in a place that she disliked as much as Los Angeles, where she would have no status other than as his girlfriend – and a Hollywood girlfriend at that – was just not what Corrie wanted. But he was asking her to do neither, so rather than dwell on things that would never be, Corrie forced herself to concentrate on what she really was going to do with her life.

Her ultimate goal now was not only to take over TW herself – though she accepted, with her lack of experience, that that couldn't happen for some time – but to get Luke out so that she could eventually run down the current affairs side of the company and concentrate on hard hitting documentaries.

The knowledge she was gaining from Cristos was invaluable and though he didn't actually know the full extent of her ambitions, her desire to do something worthwhile with the air time available to her he supported wholeheartedly. He even started to ask her opinions regarding his own movie, not because he was uncertain himself, but to see what she would come up with and then tell her why her suggestions would or wouldn't work. He taught her so much, like the importance of sound and when and when not to use effects or music; he showed her all kinds of tricks in the rough edit, like what impact it could have to hold onto a shot just a few frames longer or the power of a sudden close up, and then he gave her a portable video camera so that she could try the fly on the wall technique for herself. With regard to budgeting he put her in the hands of his line-producers and accountants, who had set up office in the Shakespeare Room at the front of the Manor House, where Cristos would often find her at the end of the day with her eyes rolling in their sockets at the incredible sums of money being administered.

When Corrie was in London, which she invariably was for transmission and production meetings, she spent her evenings with Phillip and Annalise. By inviting her to his Chelsea home on the evenings Octavia wasn't there, or taking her and Annalise to restaurants or the cinema, Phillip was trying to draw Corrie into his family at the same time as getting Annalise used to the idea of her being there. And in its way it seemed to be working, Corrie reflected with a tenderness bordering on sadness. Though she was growing increasingly fond of her father and half-sister, she was under no illusion as to exactly what role she would be expected to play in their lives. Already they were coming to depend on her in a way she found touching in its genuine desire for approval, but the burden of responsibility it carried, at times weighed heavily.

Phillip himself seemed so desperate to make her his friend that he even confided to her that he was in love with his secretary, thinking that a shared secret might bring them closer together. The worst part of that was how voraciously his eyes had searched Corrie's when he made his confession, making Corrie feel as though he would give Pam up if she asked it. Of course she didn't ask it, and to her relief discovered that she was wrong in thinking that, since Phillip's own relief to discover that Corrie was pleased for him resulted in the added confession that he was glad his affair hadn't brought about their first argument, because, as her father, he really would have had to overrule her where Pam was concerned. That made Corrie smile, and marvel all over again at how two such different men lived inside one body. If only he could bring some of the dynamism and confidence he exuded in the board room – and obviously in his feelings for Pam too – into his family life! But while he was still with Octavia there seemed little chance of that happening, and he wouldn't leave Octavia until he was certain Annalise was well enough to cope with the divorce.

Inevitably, when the subject of Annalise's mental condition came round, so too did the subject of Luke. But every time Corrie asked Phillip to tell her what it was he'd been about to confide to her that night at the Ritz, Phillip would simply dismiss it with a wave of his hand, saying that was all in the past and really didn't matter anymore. Corrie's frustration at that was extreme, since she knew only too well that Luke was very far from being in the past.

Though Annalise appeared a little more stable than she had before going to Scotland, there was no doubt in Corrie's mind that she was starting to pine for Luke. She would never come right out and admit it, but it showed in her eyes every time his name was mentioned, and the fact that after the two weeks he'd said he'd be away Luke had stopped ringing in to the office, meaning that no one was in contact with him now, all too often distressed Annalise to the point of hysteria. Her outbursts were always over trivial things, and Luke's name never passed her lips, but Corrie wasn't deceived.

But it wasn't only the effect Luke was still having on Annalise that told Corrie they were still a long way from being rid of him, it was the effect his disappearance was having on her. She tried hard not to think about it, but his absence, coupled now with his silence, was starting to take on all the menace of a deadly snake coiling itself ready to strike. And the feeling that she herself was his target became even more intense when during his third week of absence the telephone calls started. Most often they were late at night, and there was no way of knowing who they were from, but even when she wasn't there and came to play back her messages later, Corrie knew the calls were from him. There was never anything more than silence, not even a whisper of breath, but those few seconds of blank tape were as unnerving as if he were actually telling her he was coming for her. She tried to put her unease down to paranoia, knowing only too well how many cranks were around, but as time passed and the telephone calls continued she started to become so haunted by the echo of the last words Luke had spoken to her, it was as though he were standing close behind her, whispering in her ear that she would come to him in the end, that she would marry him. And just as insanity seemed to have put its blemish on his mind, so fear started to take a hold on Corrie's. He was out there somewhere, watching her, she could feel it, so strongly at times that she would find herself spinning round in the street to catch him. Of course there was never anyone there, except maybe the press, and Corrie was starting to become profoundly glad of their presence.

She told no one about it, not even Cristos. They'd already

fought over Luke more than once, since Cristos was of the opinion that she should leave TW, start up her own company and get right away from the man. Corrie had explained about Annalise and Phillip then, admitting to who they really were so that Cristos would understand why she couldn't just abandon them. She told him nothing of the things Luke had said to her, neither did she tell him about her earlier suspicions of Luke being involved in the prostitutes' killings. Cristos had enough on his mind trying to complete the movie, and Corrie was determined that she would find a way of handling this without him, since once he had gone she really would be on her own.

It was the day before Cristos was due to fly back to Los Angeles, as Corrie and Jeannie were strolling through Castle Combe together heading for the village post office, that things finally started to draw to a head. The fog had long since been blown away by high winds, which had given Cristos endless continuity nightmares, but somehow they had got through on schedule and now the unit were finishing their last stunt sequence on the weir back in the hotel grounds.

The afternoon was so dull that as the clouds thickened overhead it was as though night were drawing in. Nevertheless Corrie could see the humpback bridge quite clearly from where she was, just as clearly as she could see the lone figure standing on it. Her mind was so full of how she was going to find the courage to handle Cristos's departure the next day, that it wasn't until Jeannie held up a postcard to point something out to Corrie, and Corrie looked at it, that she suddenly registered who it was standing on the bridge.

Her head snapped up as she looked ahead again.

'Something wrong?' Jeannie said, looking up at her.

Corrie's eyes were still fixed on the bridge.

'You in pain or something?' Jeannie said, putting a hand on Corrie's arm. 'Your face is real pale.'

'No, no, I'm fine,' Corrie said, still unable to take her eyes from the bridge.

Looking in the same direction, Jeannie said, 'What is it? Did you see something?' She chuckled. 'Like a ghost?'

Corrie's eyes darted to Jeannie, then forcing herself to smile she said, 'Let's turn back now, Jeannie.'

Jeannie shrugged. 'OK by me. I just want to call in here and post my cards back home. 'Course, I'll be back before them now, but what the hell . . . Coming in?'

'No. No, I'll wait here,' Corrie said, once again turning her eyes to the bridge.

While Jeannie was inside the Post Office Corrie found herself moving further down the street, as though the bridge were some kind of magnet she just couldn't resist. He'd been there, she knew it, she'd seen him with her own eyes, but he'd vanished, like an apparition he'd just melted into thin air. Except he couldn't have, it just wasn't possible, so he had to be there somewhere, lurking in the shadows, pressing himself hard into the bushes, or . . . She swung round, certain she'd heard a footstep behind her, but the street was empty.

She was almost on the bridge now and the air had become so still it was as though even the threatening storm had been paralysed by the atmosphere of menace. A raven suddenly soared up from the river bank, flapping its wings and screeching a raucous cry. Corrie's heart leapt to her throat, but after drawing back in alarm, she found herself once again inching towards the parapet.

As she peered over the edge all she saw was her own distorted reflection in the rushing current, but he was here, somewhere, she could feel it as acutely as if he were touching her.

'Corrie!'

She spun round, her hand flying to her heart. 'Oh, Jeannie!' she cried, 'you gave me the fright of my life.'

'Sorry about that,' Jeannie shrugged, but looking at Corrie curiously she added, 'you're real on edge today . . .'

'I know. It's probably because tomorrow's coming round so quickly,' and taking Jeannie's arm Corrie turned her back up the street towards the Market Cross.

It wasn't until they were outside the Old Rectory, just before the road started to curve to the left, that Corrie nerved herself to glance back. Still the bridge was empty. But she hadn't been seeing things, she was certain of that. Luke Fitzpatrick had been standing there on that bridge.

Twenty minutes later Corrie was back in Cristos's room, trying to sort out what she should wear for the end of shoot party that night when the telephone rang. Even though she'd half been expecting it to, it still made her jump.

Picking up the receiver, and saying nothing herself, Corrie waited for someone to speak. No one did.

'Luke,' she said into the silence. 'Luke, I know it's you.' She waited, but the silence just stretched on. 'Luke!' she cried. 'Say something, for God's sake. I know it's you. I saw you, do you hear me? Now what do you want?'

Still there was nothing – then suddenly she tensed as she thought she heard him breathe. She was about to speak again, when the voice at the other end said,

'Stay away from your father, Corrie.'

Corrie plucked the receiver from her ear, looking at it as if it were playing her some kind of trick. Then speaking into it, she said, '*What?*'

'I'm telling you, you be staying away from your father now.'

'Luke! What are you talking about?'

'Ask him, Corrie. Ask him who was the last person to be seeing those hookers alive?'

'For God's sake, Luke! What are you talking about?'

'Don't you be getting into his bed, now, do you hear me? You just be staying away from him.'

'Luke!' she screamed, dashing a hand to her head. 'He's my father! How the hell can you think . . .'

'To be sure, he's your father. And we don't want him to be doing to you what he's been doing to Annalise, now, do we?'

For a moment Corrie felt like she was losing her mind. 'Luke, you're not making any sense,' she cried. 'What do you mean, what he's been . . .'

'I'll be here to protect you, Corrie. I'll be waiting, and you'll be coming to me soon now . . . Very soon,' and the line went dead.

Corrie was in such a state of agitation as she put the phone down that she could hardly begin to think straight. But she must make herself! She had to get a grip on this panic and control it! But for God's sake what had he meant about Phillip? Why the hell should he think she would go to her own father's bed? She flinched at the repulsion she felt. But what about the prostitutes? Annalise? What did he mean . . . ?

The telephone was in Corrie's hand almost before she knew it. 'Phillip!' she gasped when he answered. 'It's me, Corrie!'

'What's the matter?' he cried, reacting instantly to the distress in her voice. 'What's happened?'

'I've heard from Luke. Where's Annalise?'

'Octavia's just taken her home to pick up some more clothes. Corrie, what's going on? What did he want?'

'He wanted . . .' Should she tell, him? What should she do? But the words were spilling from her mouth almost before she knew it. 'He wanted me to stay away from you,' she blurted.

'*What!*'

'He told me . . . Oh God, Phillip . . . He told me to ask you who was the last person to see the prostitutes alive. Why did he say that? What do you know, Phillip? What is going on?'

'Oh, Jesus Christ!' Phillip groaned. 'I thought it was over. I thought he would leave me alone now. I went to the police, I told them everything I know, but I . . . Oh, Corrie. This is so difficult to explain down the phone.'

'Then I'm coming back to London. Now!'

'No, don't do that. This is your last night with Cristos, and what I have to tell you can wait. I promise you it can.'

'Then explain to me why Luke implied that you were doing things to Annalise . . .'

'Oh Corrie, I don't know what's going on, I swear to you, I don't, but you're not the only one who's heard from him. He was here the other day. I wasn't going to tell you, I couldn't it was too . . . it was too ugly. But he came when Annalise was out with her mother and he accused me . . . Oh Corrie, I never wanted to tell you this . . . He accused me of . . . of sleeping with Annalise. I couldn't believe what he was saying . . . I don't understand it! It's all lies, Corrie . . .'

'Then why is he doing this? You must know, Phillip.'

'But I don't! God knows I wish I did.'

Holding a hand to her head Corrie tried to make herself think rationally. Then from nowhere she suddenly remembered Siobhan.

'Yes, I've heard the name,' Phillip said, 'but only from Luke. He kept mumbling something about someone called Siobhan when he was here the other day.'

'But you don't know who she is?'

'No. I'd never heard of her until then.'

'When he came to you the other day, did he tell you where he'd been all this time?'

'No. But I didn't ask. Should I have? Yes, yes of course I should. Damn it!'

'Do you know where he is now?'

'No. But I can try to find out. I'll call his home, I'll go round there . . .'

Corrie shook her head. 'No, he's not there. He's here. I've seen him.'

'You've seen him? I thought you said he'd telephoned you?'

'Yes he did. After. And he said . . .' Her voice trailed off as she started to feel herself become almost mesmerized by the memory of his words . . . 'He said that I'd be going to him, very soon.'

Too upset to hear the puzzlement in her voice Phillip shouted, 'Don't you go, Corrie! You stay away from him, do you hear me? I'm speaking as your father now, and you'll do as I say. You stay right there with Cristos and don't you move. If Fitzpatrick is there in Castle Combe he can't touch you while you're with Cristos. Are you listening to me?'

'Yes, I'm listening,' Corrie answered. 'But why is he here?' she said. 'Why has he come all this way . . .'

'I don't know, and I don't want to know. I just want to hear you say that the minute you put this phone down you're going to go straight to Cristos and you're going to stay with him until he leaves tomorrow – when I shall be at the airport to bring you back into London myself.'

'OK, I'll do that,' Corrie said, smiling at his near panic-stricken concern. He really did care about her, and just like a father he was giving her orders. It was something she could get used to, she was thinking, as she said a very warm goodbye. Nevertheless, she wasn't going to be taken in that easily, there had to be something behind what Luke had said about Phillip, and she wanted to find out from Luke exactly what it was. And if Luke was right here in Castle Combe . . .

But Luke wasn't in Castle Combe, at least not anymore he wasn't, and in less than four hours, when Corrie learned precisely where he was, she was on the very next train to London, forfeiting her last night with Cristos to spend it with Luke.

The call had come just after eight o'clock, while Cristos was closeted with the actors discussing the extra shots he wanted to do the next morning before they packed up and left for the airport. Corrie was in the bar with Jeannie and several others, glancing nervously over her shoulder every time someone walked in, not really believing Luke would come to the hotel, but half-afraid that he would. Still, she felt safe with Cristos so nearby, so what was there to worry about?

'You're starting to make me dizzy,' Jeannie complained, as Corrie's head spun to the door again. 'He'll be through with Winters any time now . . .' She stopped as she heard Corrie's name.

'There's a personal telephone call for you,' the hotel manager said, 'would you like to take it in reception – there's no one there at present?'

'Thank you,' Corrie said, getting up to follow him out of the bar. It could be Phillip or Annalise trying to get hold of her. And if it was Luke . . . ? Well, she'd just see what he had to say this time.

It turned out to be none of them, and Corrie could hardly believe her ears as the woman's voice at the other end of the line, after confirming that she was speaking to Corrie Browne, told her that she was ringing from Charing Cross Hospital in London where they had just admitted Luke Fitzpatrick.

'He's asking for you,' the woman told her in a tone that couldn't be described as anything other than funereal. 'I think you should come. And without wishing to alarm you, I think you should get here as soon as you can.'

'But what's happened?' Corrie cried.

'I think it's better if I explain when you get here,' the woman answered. 'But you should be aware that his injuries are serious . . . That he's in a critical condition . . .'

'What do you mean? What kind of injuries?'

She heard the woman give a gentle sigh as she seemed

to twitter at the end of the line. 'I'm afraid they were self-inflicted,' she finally answered.

'You mean . . . Are you saying . . . ?'

'Yes, I think you understand what I'm saying,' the woman interrupted. 'He's lost a lot of blood . . . The doctor's with him now . . . We're very much afraid, Miss Browne, that he may not see morning.'

Corrie could feel herself shaking. This was the very last thing she'd expected . . .

She put the phone down gazing distractedly about the room as she tried to decide what to do next. She was on the point of running upstairs to pack when in a blinding flash it suddenly occurred to her that this might be a trick. Turning back to the receptionist, who had come out of the office once Corrie had finished on the phone, Corrie rapidly gave her a list of instructions then ran up to Cristos's room getting there just as the receptionist was putting through the call Corrie had asked for. Corrie felt wretched doing this, especially when she heard a voice answering the phone with,

'Good evening, Charing Cross Hospital.'

And she felt even worse when a few minutes later she had it confirmed that Luke Fitzpatrick had indeed been admitted that night. But she'd had to check, she told herself firmly, because he was quite capable of pulling a stunt as sick as this.

Hastily she scribbled a note for Cristos, threw her things into a bag and ran back downstairs to the bar, grabbing the times of the trains from the receptionist's outstretched hand as she passed.

Jeannie drove her to the station at breakneck speed, getting her there just in the nick of time.

The journey, Corrie knew, was going to take an eternity, and that she should be starting out with a dilemma as to whether or not she should ring Phillip did not bode well for the state of mind she would arrive in. In the end, if only to dispense with the problem, she decided she should ring her father.

The line from the train was dreadful, but Corrie managed to let him know what had happened, and was relieved to hear him say that for the time being they should keep this from Annalise.

'Would you like me to come to the hospital?' Phillip said.

Would she? 'Yes,' she answered, without giving it too much thought. 'But I won't be there for a while yet, the train's only just pulled out of Swindon.'

'Did they tell you why . . .' The line broke up so badly then that Corrie shouted that she would meet him there and rang off.

She sat back down then and started to think about Luke, asking herself over and over why he would want to take his own life. She had no answers, because in truth, she realized now, she knew nothing about him – except that something was terribly wrong with him. But what had happened, she wondered, to make him so bereft of reason that it had dragged him to the point where he'd do this to himself rather than go on . . . She thought back to when she had first known him, asking herself what could be behind his perverse sexuality? Why did he treat Annalise the way he did? Why did he speak with that chilling Irish voice? Who was Siobhan? Where had he been these past weeks? Why did he want her, Corrie? What made him believe that she would marry him? And how on earth was Phillip connected to all this?

The questions were coming at her so fast her head was starting to spin. Had it been him she'd seen on the bridge today? Had he known then he was going to kill himself? Perhaps he was there to take one last look at her before . . . No! Stop! she cried inwardly. This is nonsense! There was so much more to this than his feelings for her . . . And what truth was there in his feelings? He'd deliberately turned any sympathy she might have felt for him to scorn, and any concern to fear. But why? It was as though he just didn't understand about human relationships, his way of handling love was to crush it, abuse it, even to defile it. God knew, Annalise could bear witness to that . . . But what the hell had happened to make him like it? And what was behind those horrible accusations of incest? She closed her eyes. Everything in the end seemed to lead back to her father . . . But why? What had he to do with it all? Was he just the helpless victim of a deranged mind, or had he done something so terrible that he was the very cause of the madness?

Corrie's heart churned as she thought of Cristos then. How she wished he was there with her now. But what was the point in worrying him with her problems when for them it could all be over in less than twenty-four hours? Would they even get to say goodbye now? Already she could feel the pain of losing him. She couldn't imagine that she would ever love anyone as much as she loved him, but telling him that now would change nothing. He would return to Los Angeles the next day, and she would try to carry on without him, working her way to the fulfilment of her ambitions, while trying to pick up the pieces of her life – and the lives that had been shattered by Luke. Dear God, she was already thinking of him in the past tense! It was what she had wanted, of course, to get him out of their lives . . . But not like this, and not before she knew what had incited him to such madness . . .

When at last Corrie arrived at the hospital she was shown the way to go by the casualty receptionist and after walking endless corridors and pushing open countless swing doors, she finally reached the small private ward she'd been directed to.

A nurse was on duty outside, and as soon as Corrie gave her name the nurse smiled. Too happily, Corrie thought, given the circumstances – the muscles in her face were too strained even to attempt a response. But at least, she told herself, as she followed the nurse, the smile told her that Luke must still be alive.

'He's right through here, Miss Browne,' the nurse said, holding open the door.

Thanking her, Corrie stepped into the doorway and looked across to the bed. She stopped so suddenly that it was as though someone had hit her, and a dark anger froze over her heart as she watched the room's two occupants, who were as yet oblivious to her presence. Octavia's back was turned, but Corrie was in no doubt it was her. She watched as Octavia lifted a hand to stroke Luke's face. When Luke tried to stop her Corrie heard Octavia's throaty laugh and the very sound of it was so malignant it seemed to crawl into the deepest recesses of her mind. Her eyes returned to Luke. His face was ravaged, his lips so pale and cracked that they blended almost invisibly with the waxen puffiness of his skin. Then turning his head he saw Corrie standing at the door.

'You came,' he said, his voice as dry and broken as his lips, and as his eyes feasted upon her an indefinable emotion seemed to swirl into their emptiness 'Oh, Corrie, you came.'

Corrie didn't answer, she simply didn't know what to say. She'd been told he was dying, she'd rushed here to be with him because he'd asked for her, *because he was dying* . . .

Octavia was looking at her now and though Corrie wouldn't look back she could feel the pernicious scrutiny of those hideous blue eyes. She had never felt anything like it in her life – it was as though a cloud of pure evil was thickening the air around her. And as a tight band around Corrie's head increased its pressure Corrie cried,

'Just what is going on here?'

'You came,' Luke repeated, holding out a hand.

For the first time Corrie noticed the bandages around his wrists. So he had tried to kill himself . . . *But they had said he was dying* . . . And Octavia! What the hell was Octavia doing here?

'I'm sorry,' Luke said as though reading Corrie's mind, 'I asked them to make it sound worse so's you'd come. I didn't think you would otherwise.'

Without uttering a word Octavia picked up a thick bundle of fur from the chair, and with her eyes still fixed on Corrie she lifted Luke's hand to her lips. Her tongue curled around his fingers, then letting him go abruptly she walked towards Corrie. Keeping her eyes averted Corrie stood to one side leaving her enough room to walk out of the door.

'You saw me today, didn't you?' Luke said as the door closed behind Octavia. 'On the bridge. I willed you to come, do you know that? I willed you to walk down the street at that time, but you brought someone with you. Why did you do that?'

In her stupefaction Corrie could only look at him. It was as though she had walked into a pit of madness, and as the drumming in her head resounded through her ears she felt as though she too was being dragged from the roots of reality. Then the door opened again and the nurse came in, saying the other lady had left something behind. She picked up Octavia's purse, giggled something about hoping Corrie and Luke could make up their differences now, and left the room.

'Did you really mean to kill yourself?' Corrie said when they were alone again.

She watched with morbid fascination as Luke's eyes seemed to glaze over with pain. Then as the bloated lids dropped to mask them, he whispered, 'I don't know.'

'What was Octavia doing here?'

'She was with me when I did it. She called the ambulance and came here with me.'

'Why did you do it?'

As Luke turned his head away, trying to push his face

into the pillows, for the first time in many months Corrie started to sense that terrible sadness in him again. It felt so palpable it was as though she could reach out and touch it. Instinctively she tried to detach herself from it, but it was pulling her in and she was already moving towards him.

'Luke?' she whispered.

'It would have been better if I'd died,' he said, and Corrie's heart contracted at the uncalculable grief in his voice.

'Why are you saying that, Luke? What would have been better?'

His only answer was to shake his head, and then Corrie saw the tears flowing freely from the corners of his eyes into his hair. 'I want you to love me, Corrie,' he said brokenly, 'but I don't know how to make you.'

Sitting on the edge of the bed Corrie lifted his hand into hers. 'Tell me what happened, Luke,' she said softly. 'Tell me what it was that made you like this.'

His eyes were closed, but with no hesitation he said, 'It was you, Corrie. You went off with Bennati . . .'

'No. It was before that,' she said. 'Something happened before that. Was it something to do with Octavia? With my father?'

At that his whole face contorted, as though the pain had become so intense it would rip him apart.

'Which one of them is it?' Corrie pressed.

His head started to move from side to side and saliva began to trickle from his quivering lips. 'What did they do?' Corrie whispered. 'Luke, tell me . . .'

'Oh Corrie,' he cried, grabbing her to him. 'Corrie, make it go away. Please, make it stop!'

'Make what stop? What is it, Luke?'

'Oh, Corrie, help me, please! Love me Corrie. It'll stop if you love me. I know it will.'

'What will? Luke, you have to tell me what it is.'

His arms tightened around her, holding onto her as though to drain the very life from her. 'You have to keep me away from Annalise, Corrie,' he sobbed. 'Will you do that for me? You mustn't let me near her anymore. It's because of her . . .'

'Luke, please! You're not making any sense.'

His body was shaking so violently that Corrie knew she must call for the nurse. But as she extricated herself from his grasp he fell back against the pillows and Corrie saw that he was laughing.

'Luke, for God's sake!' she cried, drawing back in horror. She glanced towards the door, starting to edge towards it. 'Look, you need help. You've got to let someone . . .'

'I need you,' he said, and suddenly his teeth bared in a hideous grin. 'I told you that,' he sniggered. 'Only you can make it stop.'

'Make what stop?' Her voice was a high-pitched thread of nerves.

He pushed his face towards her. '*The incest!*' he hissed.

Corrie jerked back as though he had struck her. She could feel her mouth curling in revulsion and as his sunken eyes blazed manically the blood ran cold in her veins. 'What incest?' she breathed.

'Mine! And yours! And his!'

'What are you talking about?' she cried. 'There isn't any incest!'

'Oh, but to be sure there is, Corrie. Octavia told me! She's told me everything.'

'But she's lying! What she saw at the Ritz had nothing to do with . . .'

His head suddenly twisted away, and Corrie reeled with the shock of seeing his face light up in a beatific smile. Following the direction of his eyes she turned to see her father at the door.

'Hello, Phillip,' Luke said chirpily. 'I didn't realize you were coming too. Do sit down.'

For a moment, as Phillip walked into the room, the sensation that she was losing her mind came over Corrie again. She took a breath to speak, but Luke said,

'Would either of you like a coffee? I'm sure the nurse could rustle one up.'

'No. No thanks,' Corrie mumbled, fighting hard to maintain her grip on reality. She waited until her father was seated, right beside her, then turned back to Luke.

'Phillip's here now,' she said, 'so why don't we see if we can sort out what you were saying before he came in.'

'And what would that be?' Luke enquired.

'You know what you were saying,' Corrie answered through gritted teeth. 'The same as you accused him of when you spoke to me on the phone this afternoon. Now what is it . . .'

'What?' Luke said, wrinkling his nose to show his confusion. 'I didn't speak to you on the telephone this afternoon.'

'Yes, you did.'

'No. You've got that wrong, Corrie. Tonight is the first time I've spoken to you since I saw you in the office.'

'Luke! I heard your voice! You said . . .'

'No,' he said, shaking his head and looking at her with genuine concern, 'it wasn't my voice. I didn't call you today.'

Corrie turned helplessly to Phillip. 'All right then,' she said, turning back to Luke. 'Just before Phillip came in you were saying something about incest . . . "Mine! And yours! And his!" you said. I told you Octavia was lying about what she saw at the Ritz, but there's more to it, isn't there?'

Luke looked at her in profound astonishment. 'Corrie, you seem to have incest on the brain! It's not healthy, you know. In fact, it's not legal either, so I'd forget it if I were you.'

Corrie was so taken aback that an incredulous laugh coughed from her lips. 'I don't believe this,' she muttered to Phillip. Then to Luke, 'What about Annalise? You wanted me to keep you away from Annalise . . .'

Again Luke looked genuinely confused. 'Why would I want you to do that?' he said. 'I'm going to marry her for heaven's sake.'

Corrie just put her head in her hands. 'I give up,' she groaned. 'Either he's mad or I am.'

'Luke,' Phillip said, attempting to take over, 'where have you been these past few weeks?'

Luke tutted and sighed, just like a child who'd been caught out on truancy. 'I took myself off on a holiday,' he said. 'I felt I needed a break. I wasn't far away though, and it was bloody freezing, I'm telling you. Did Annalise miss me? Where is she by the way? Doesn't she know I'm here?'

'Why *are* you here?' Corrie said, leaping on the question.

Luke held up his wrists. 'Come on, Corrie,' he chided.

'OK. Why did you do it?'

'I didn't, someone else did.'

'I'm going to get some air,' Corrie muttered, 'because I don't think I can take much more of this.'

'I'll come with you,' Phillip said, getting to his feet.

As they walked around looking for a coffee machine Corrie filled Phillip in on all that Luke had said up until the time Phillip had arrived. 'And now,' she said, 'he's making like none of it happened.'

'Did Octavia say anything when you saw her?' Phillip asked.

'Not a word. But I'd like to know where the hell she fits into all this.'

'She's been having an affair with Luke almost since Annalise has,' Phillip said, 'so it's no surprise to me that she was here tonight. But that doesn't really answer the question, does it?'

'Luke said she was with him when he tried to kill himself.

Do you think she knows where he's been all this time? Can you ask her?'

'I can try, but I wouldn't hold out too much hope of getting an honest answer.' As he slotted some coins into the machine they'd finally come across Corrie turned to look at him,

'How about an honest answer from you, Phillip?' she said. 'I want to know whatever it is you've been holding back from me these past weeks. I want to know why Luke is accusing you of incest . . . No, I know what he said about Octavia, but when he spoke to me on the phone he said it was happening with Annalise too. So what is Octavia telling him? And why did he tell me to ask you about those prostitutes?'

Phillip nodded, and handing her a coffee said, 'Come on, let's sit down over here. I'm not sure I can answer everything, but what I do know I'll tell you. But you'd better brace yourself, Corrie, because I just don't know what you're going to think of me once you know. But please, try to understand that I'm only human, and that the flesh is weak, as they say, and life with Octavia has never been easy . . .'

Feeling a shudder vibrate through her body as she recalled those few moments with Octavia earlier, Corrie virtually collapsed into a moulded plastic chair and prepared herself to listen to yet another confession from her father. She felt so tired that all she wanted was to turn her back on the whole thing and return to Cristos, but taking Phillip's hand in hers she smiled her encouragement, and prayed to God that this time he wouldn't hold anything back.

'Oh God, what a mess,' she groaned when he'd finished telling her about the prostitutes, in no doubt now that he'd told her the whole truth. 'Anyway, the important thing is, you've been to the police and they've cleared you. So now we have to find out how Luke knows so much about your movements to know that you were with those women not long before they died. Which of course doesn't necessarily mean that he did it himself.'

'No. But it doesn't rule it out either.'

'No, it doesn't does it,' she said wearily.

'And I'm afraid the police have already interviewed him and he's not on their list of suspects,' Phillip added.

'But he's insane, we know that.'

'That's the hardest thing in the world to prove, Corrie, and even if we could that doesn't help much as far as those murders were concerned. Unless he confesses.'

'If he did it. Oh God, we're just going round and round in circles here and I want to go.' She looked at her watch and her heart turned over when she saw the time. 'It's too late now for me to get a train back to Wiltshire . . .' and letting her head fall back against the wall she closed her eyes tightly against the tears. 'I can't believe this is happening . . .' she groaned.

'I think we ought to go and talk to him again,' Phillip said. 'Let's ask him about the . . .' When he stopped Corrie opened her eyes to look at him. 'I don't think you'll have to go back to Wiltshire,' he smiled, and nodded for her to look behind her.

Corrie turned round, and just knew that she was dreaming when she saw Cristos coming along the corridor towards her. But if it was a dream she didn't care, he was the only person in the entire world she wanted to see right now, and thrusting her empty cup at her father she ran to meet him.

'What are you doing here?' she murmured, as he caught her in his arms.

'What do you think? I got your note, Jeannie told me what had happened and which hospital you were at. And the nurse just told me where I could find you. Hello sir,' he added, holding out his hand to Phillip.

'Phillip this is Cristos,' Corrie said, standing to one side as they shook hands, 'and Cristos this is . . . . Phillip. My father.'

'Pleased to meet you at last,' Phillip said. 'I've heard a lot about you . . .' He winced as Corrie trod on his toe. 'Sorry, I've never heard of you,' he corrected, making both Cristos and Corrie laugh.

'So,' Cristos said, 'what's it all about?'

'Don't ask,' Corrie answered. 'It was a false alarm – surprise! surprise! At least he did slit his wrists, but why and how serious he was about it, is anyone's guess.'

'We were just about to go back there and try talking to him again,' Phillip said. 'God knows how far we'll get . . .'

'I think we'll just be wasting our time,' Corrie said, resting her head on Cristos's shoulder and linking her father's arm as they walked back down the corridor.

'If you don't mind, sir,' Cristos said when they reached the private ward, 'I'd like to take Corrie home now. She looks kinda tired, and since there doesn't appear to be any emergency . . .'

'Oh no, I don't mind in the slightest,' Phillip assured him. 'You're right, she does look tired, and you've had quite enough of your last night together spoiled as it is. You go along now, and I'll see if Luke is still awake.'

'I'm sorry,' the nurse interrupted. 'I've strict instructions not to let anyone else in there tonight. However,' she added, looking oddly at Corrie who was still leaning against Cristos, 'he did ask if the young lady would go in and say goodnight before she left, and that I will allow. Two minutes only.'

Corrie looked up at Cristos. 'Do you mind?'

'Yes. But go ahead if you have to.'

The room was in darkness when Corrie let herself in, but in the moonlight from the window she saw Luke turn his head to see who it was. 'I've come to say goodnight,' she said flatly.

'Oh, that's nice of you. Goodnight. Will you be coming again?'

'No.'

'Suit yourself. By the way, did Bennati ask you to go back to Los Angeles with him.'

'That's none of your business.'

'Mmm, I thought not. I told you, he's using you. Anyway I've saved you the pain of a last night together, so you can thank me for that.'

'Thank you,' Corrie said. Let him think what he wanted, it was of no concern to her, and she turned and walked out of the room.

'What I want to know,' Cristos said, as he drove her through the night to her studio, 'is why he called *you* to his deathbed?'

'I don't know,' Corrie answered, sounding as tired as she felt. 'And I don't much care. All that's on my mind right now is you, and how I'm going to cope with saying goodbye tomorrow.'

Reaching for her hand he said, 'How about we deal with that tomorrow?'

'OK,' she said quietly, wondering how, as they seemed to lurch from one crisis to the next with Luke, she was going to be strong enough to support Annalise and her father, when she already knew that it was going to take everything she had to deal with the pain of losing Cristos.

After less than four hours sleep Corrie and Cristos were heading through the first stirrings of dawn back down the M4 to Wiltshire. Corrie was driving while Cristos slept beside her and every time she looked at him the weight of love amassing in her heart grew heavier. They had both been too tired to make love the night before, and she wondered now if they ever would again. As the thought took root a great wave of panic heaved through her chest. She couldn't bear it! She just couldn't live with the thought of never seeing him again. They'd become so close these past few weeks, had shared so much of their lives that there was no point in deluding herself any longer. Without him her ambitions meant nothing. She'd sacrifice them all for him, she'd try to make a go of Los Angeles, if only he'd ask! But she had to face it, he wasn't going to – if he were, he'd have done it by now. She couldn't understand though, if she meant as much to him as he said, how could he let her go so easily?

Vivid, crazy ideas started flashing through her mind. Should she just pack up and go to Los Angeles anyway? Surely he wouldn't turn her away if she did? Perhaps she should beg him to take her. Or maybe she should just crash the car now and they could die together.

She knew it was tiredness that was pushing her mind to the brink of such frenzy, and making a conscious effort to calm herself she tried to concentrate on what had happened at the hospital the night before. Once again, as the image of Octavia sprung before her eyes Corrie felt an icy shiver descend through her body. She struggled to make sense of those few moments and the profound effect they had had upon her, but there was no more coherence to her thoughts than there had been logic to what Luke had said later. All Corrie knew was that there was something going on that was so way beyond her understanding that the fear of it was starting to worm its way to the very core of her reason. How she longed to tell Cristos, to ask him to help her – surely if he knew what was happening he wouldn't leave her here to face it alone. But Corrie knew she would never tell him for in its way it would be tantamount to blackmailing him.

Cristos finally woke as she turned the car from the motorway and began heading through the early morning light towards Castle Combe. 'We here already?' he said, glancing at his watch. 'You must have gone some.'

'I didn't want you to be late,' she said.

He yawned and stretched, then helped himself to one of the peppermints on the dashboard. He sucked it for a minute or two, then taking it from his mouth slipped it into Corrie's. After taking it she looked away quickly before he saw the tears in her eyes. Sharing their peppermints like this was just one of the intimate little habits they had slipped into – almost without thinking. Dear God, why was this happening? Why couldn't they stay together?

'I want you to go right to bed when we get to the hotel,' Cristos told her, leaning back in his seat and locking his hands behind his head.

'But this is our last day together, I want to spend as much of it with you as I can,' Corrie objected. 'Even if it does mean just standing at the edge of the set.'

'Bed!' he said. 'You're beat, and you're emotional. I don't want you there like that. What I want is that you get some sleep so's you've got all your wits about you when we talk later.'

Corrie's stomach seemed to turn itself inside out. 'Talk?' she said. 'What about?'

'You know what about. You and me. We should have done it last night, but now we'll have to do it today. We're not gonna have a lot of time, but we'll find it – and we got to find it before we go to the airport 'cos Jeannie's giving back her Mini car today – she and Richard are coming to Heathrow with us.'

'I'll never be able to sleep,' Corrie murmured.

But she did, albeit fitfully, until she heard the crew clanging about downstairs telling her that they were packing up after their final morning's shoot.

She found Cristos in the makeshift production office, staring thoughtfully up at the frieze of Shakespearean characters while everyone else carried out what was left of their equipment to stack in the waiting lorries.

'You composing me a sonnet?' she smiled, going over to join him.

'No,' he said, 'but I was thinking about you. Let's take a stroll over to the weir, get out of this chaos.'

As they walked through the drizzling rain, with Corrie's arm linked through his and her head resting on his shoulder, Cristos, as he had done so many times this past week, was thinking about how very much she had come to mean to him. He knew he loved her in a way he'd never loved another woman, and it was because of it that he had to be honest with her now, to try to make her understand why things had to be like this – why he wasn't going to ask her to come to LA with him. There were so many reasons why he couldn't, but he didn't want to lay them all on her at once, and now his problem was where to begin.

'You're making me nervous,' Corrie said, when he still hadn't spoken by the time they reached the weir.

'I'm trying to find the right words,' he sighed, looking down into the rushing current. 'But I guess there's no other way of saying it than straight.' He turned to face her and felt the sharp pull of love when he saw the terrible anguish in her eyes. 'I know you're hurting because I haven't talked about our future,' he said, running his fingers over her cheek, 'because you want me to ask you to come with me to . . .'

'That's not true,' Corrie lied. 'You know I've been working hard at . . .'

'Corrie, I know what you've been doing, and God knows I love you for your courage. But it's breaking you up, I can see it. Christ knows, it's not doing a lot for me either. But I can't ask you to come with me – not because I don't want you to, but because . . .' He stopped, dashing a hand through his already dishevelled hair. 'Well to start with I just don't know that I want to make the kind of commitment . . .'

'What commitment? I've never said anything about . . .'

'Corrie, listen to me. You know how I feel about you . . .'

'Do I?'

'Yes! And I know how you feel about me. I wouldn't mind being told, it's true, but I know why you won't tell me. It's because you want to give your whole self when you make that Goddammed statement, and to you giving your whole self means marriage.'

For a while Corrie said nothing, her throat was too choked with misery for the words to come. 'So the bottom line is,' she whispered finally, 'that you don't want to marry me?'

'No,' he said, 'I don't want to marry you.'

The pain cleaved so deep into her heart that it was as though it was pulling her to the ground. She looked past him, out to the countryside and suddenly she wanted to run. She wanted to get away from him, to run so fast and so far that the pain could never catch up.

'Oh Corrie,' he sighed, as he watched her face, 'we've hardly known each other any time . . . It's just too early to be thinking about something like marriage. It's too early even to be thinking of living together. OK, I don't know how well I'm gonna get along without you, but this is one hell of a commitment we're talking about here.'

Corrie shrugged. 'Well, that's it then, isn't it?' she said flatly.

'It doesn't have to be.'

'I think it does.'

'You don't mean that, and you know it.'

'I do, Cristos. How can I even begin to get on with my life if I'm just waiting around for you to make up your mind?'

'I'm not asking you to do that,' he said gently. 'I'm just saying that you're taking it too fast. And ask yourself, in your heart do you really want to come to LA right now? You've still got things to work out with your father. I know that's important to you . . .'

'Yes it is, but that's not the point here is it? The point

is that you don't want me to come with you. You're worried that if I did, and you changed your mind about me then it would be damned difficult to get rid of me when I've come so far and given up so much.'

'Yeah,' he said frankly, 'that's true. But stop putting the whole Goddammed onus on me. Be honest about yourself and your own feelings, Corrie. You don't like Los Angeles, and you know you don't want to live there. That's why we gotta have this time apart to decide what we really want.'

'And if we decide it's each other? The problems seem insurmountable to me. I want marriage and London, you want, well you want movies and Los Angeles.'

'Then if it comes to it we'll both have to make compromises.'

'I know the male idea of compromise,' she said, a trace of irony breaking through her sadness. 'It means you get your own way.'

Chuckling softly he pulled her into his arms to kiss her. 'I love you, Corrie Browne,' he said, 'and that is the last time I'm going to say it until I've heard those words from your lips.'

'Well you seem to have worked out for yourself what would make me say it,' she countered.

'You holding me to ransom here?'

She shook her head. 'I don't know. Maybe. It's not going to work though, is it?'

As he gazed down into her lovely ochre-brown eyes, then smiled at the way the tawny freckles across her nose seemed so vivid and childlike against her anxiously pale skin, he knew he couldn't bring himself to kill all hope in her. If he did, he'd only be lying to himself. 'Not today, no,' he whispered.

Corrie shrugged. 'So you mean that it's not all over for us? That we'll still be in touch?'

Cristos rolled his eyes in exasperation. 'Just when the hell did I say that we wouldn't be? All I'm saying is let's slow down for a while. Let me get the movie edited and into that damned festival then we can sort out us. Is that OK with you?'

'Do I detect here that your movies are always going to come first?'

A quick spark of anger flashed in his eyes. 'Corrie, you know who I am, you know what I do. And if you weren't feeling so bad right now you'd have your own career in better perspective.'

'My career will keep me here in England,' she said, wishing she didn't sound so sour.

'Yeah, I know that. And I know you're gonna really do something with your life – do you think I want to stand in the way of that? It would be the easiest thing in the world to ask you to give it all up for me, and I know that if I did, right now you would. But how would you be feeling six months or a year from now? I can't be everything in your life, Corrie, anymore than you can be everything in mine. So let's be realistic about this. God knows our feet have hardly touched the ground these past four weeks, so maybe it's time they did.' But seeing the tears brimming in her eyes filled him with such a pain of his own that despite all he was saying he very nearly told her in that moment that if she wanted to throw it all up for him, he'd let her. He'd risk what the future would bring, just so long as they could be together now. But he didn't. Instead he cupped her face in his hands and whispered, 'Saying good-bye to you today is going to be one of the hardest things I've ever done, don't make it any harder.'

'I'm sorry,' she said, unable to do anything to stop the tears now. 'It's just that I'm going to miss you so much that right now I want to die.'

'I know,' he murmured, hugging her tight. 'But we'll work it out. Trust me, we'll work something out.'

How could he possibly have known then that in the next few weeks he was going to bitterly regret not giving in to that moment of weakness? If he'd known about Luke, and the full extent of what he was doing to Corrie and her family, then things might have turned out very differently. But Corrie hadn't told him, and now, one way or another, they were all about to suffer the consequences of the pride that had forced Corrie to hold her tongue. But how could even she have known what was waiting to tear their lives apart?

– 25 –

As Phillip drove Corrie out of Heathrow his mind was still caught up by the look on Cristos's face at the moment he had let Corrie go. Any fool could have seen what it was costing him to do it, and Phillip couldn't help wondering why, when he clearly loved her so much, Cristos hadn't asked her to go to Los Angeles with him. A part of Phillip had almost wanted to beg Cristos to take her, at least then one of his daughters would be safe from the danger he felt encroaching upon them. He flinched as he thought of Annalise, but that would have to wait, Corrie just wasn't ready to hear it yet. But that was why the other part of Phillip, the selfish part, was glad Cristos hadn't taken Corrie, because Phillip just didn't know how to handle what was going on in their lives. If he only understood it then perhaps he wouldn't need Corrie so much, but as it was, she appeared to him the only sanity in a world that was slowly but surely disintegrating into disaster.

Glancing over at her he saw that her eyes were closed. As her father he could feel her suffering so acutely that it was as though it was his own heart being flown to the other side of the world. He wished desperately that there was something he could say to make her feel better, even though he knew that nothing would. But that he was there, that his shoulder was available, he knew was of some comfort, and for that he was profoundly grateful.

'It's all right, I'm not asleep,' Corrie said, sensing his eyes on her.

'How are you feeling now?'

'Pretty dreadful, but I suppose I'll live.'

Phillip smiled. 'I very much hope so.'

'Where's Annalise, by the way? I thought she was coming with you.'

Phillip tensed, wishing to God he didn't have to answer that question. But knowing there was no point in holding back on Corrie, and that he would have to tell her sooner or later anyway, he said, 'Annalise is at Luke's apartment with Luke.'

'Oh no!' Corrie groaned, feeling herself shrink away from the words. All she wanted to think about right now was Cristos, but it seemed she just wasn't going to be allowed to, and for a moment she deeply resented the intrusion. But life had to go on, and hadn't she always known that this would happen? 'Why did you let her go?' she asked, more sharply than she'd intended.

'I wasn't there to stop her. She'd already gone by the time I arrived home last night. Luke had called her from the hospital, asking her to go and pick him up. He discharged himself, it seems, only minutes after we'd left.'

'Have you spoken to her?'

'Yes. I've seen her. I went round there today. It was no good, she wouldn't listen to me. Luke's told her that he tried to kill himself because of the way he's been hurting her . . . Anyway, there was no getting Annalise out of there. Luke had an answer for everything I said . . . He accused me of always trying to come between him and Annalise, which is true, and Annalise knows it . . . He said I'd fabricate any kind of story just to poison her mind against him . . .'

'Did you tell her that Octavia was with him when he slit his wrists?'

Phillip shook his head. 'Perhaps I should have, I don't know. But Octavia's her mother, Corrie . . . I did try to tell her though that you were the one he'd called when he was taken to hospital . . . He started to go berserk then, yelling at me that you'd heard it on the news and gone running there to make sure he was dead so that he'd be out of Annalise's life . . . Oh God, I can't remember what he said, but he twisted everything to make it sound as though you and I are in some kind of conspiracy . . . Annalise listened to him, I'm afraid . . . I stayed there until it was time for me to come and collect you, but I didn't get any further. She believed him . . .'

'God, how could she, after the way he's treated her?' Corrie cried angrily. 'I just don't understand her.'

'Neither do I. But as you know I've never been an expert where women and their emotions are concerned.'

He looked so dejected, so thoroughly disgusted with himself that Corrie reached out to squeeze his arm. 'You've done pretty well for me today,' she told him.

'You don't know how much I wish that were true,' he said. 'You've been such a support for Annalise and me these past few months that I just don't know where we'd be without you. But it's not fair on you, Corrie, we shouldn't either of us depend on your strength the way we do. You have your own life to lead, and as much as I want Annalise and me to be a part of it . . .'

'Of course you're a part of it. You always will be.'

'But we put too much pressure on you. Oh, I know you have a fondness for us, but we both make it very difficult for you to respect us. No, please don't deny it, Corrie, because I know it's true. But I'd like to change it, I'd like to do something to make us worthy of your respect. I don't know yet what it will take,' he gave a short laugh, 'your courage and rectitude set a pretty high standard, you know, but I'll get there. And I shall work hard at it. You've brought something into my life that I can't put into words, and though I never want to lose you, I want you to know, that from the bottom of my heart I hope things work out with Cristos the way you want them to. And what's more, I'm going to do all I can to see that they do. Now, how's that for a promise from your ineffectual father?'

'Oh, Phillip,' Corrie laughed, dabbing at her eyes, 'it's a great promise,' though how on earth he thought he was ever going to fulfil it she couldn't even begin to imagine. But it was the sentiment behind the words that mattered, and the touching determination to increase his worth in her eyes.

When they arrived back at Corrie's studio they had a few moments of being father and daughter when Phillip saw the look in her eyes as she seemed to search the place for Cristos. Pulling her into his arms Phillip held her as she cried, telling her to let it all out and soothing her as best he could.

Eventually he went to make some coffee, and was surprised when he heard Corrie pick up the telephone.

'Who are you calling?' he asked.

'Who do you think?'

Phillip was about to tell her he didn't think it was wise when she was already so upset, when Corrie said, 'Annalise, it's me.'

'No, Corrie, I'm not speaking to you,' Annalise said.

'Then let me speak to Luke.'

'No.'

'Put him on now or I'm coming straight round there.'

'You'll be wasting your time because he's not here.'

'Then where is he?'

Annalise didn't answer, and as the silence dragged on Corrie suddenly realized why.

'He's with her, isn't he?' she almost screamed in exasperation. 'He's gone to see Siobhan.'

'Yes, if you must know, he has. But . . .'

'I don't believe you can be this stupid, Annalise! You know what happens every time he sees her and now you're just sitting there . . .'

'It won't happen this time,' Annalise said defiantly. 'He's changed. He's been away to think, and now he knows what he wants. He's got all his frustrations sorted out, he says, and it's me that he wants. So he's gone to end it with Siobhan.'

'End *what* with Siobhan?' And when Annalise didn't answer, 'You see, you don't know!'

'Corrie, stop shouting at me. I'm not a child and I don't have to listen to this.'

'You'll fucking well listen, all right,' Corrie yelled. 'He told you why he tried to kill himself, did he?'

'Because of me. He thought . . .'

'No, Annalise! Not because of you. He did it because he's sick. Because there's something very wrong with him . . .'

'He said you'd say something like that. Now let me tell you this, Corrie. I don't go around the place saying ugly things about Cristos, so you can just damned well stop doing it about Luke!'

'Why do you think I'm saying it, Annalise? Do you think I'd make up something like that?'

'Yes, quite frankly I do. And so does Luke.'

'But why should I? Just give me one good reason why . . .'

'Because you're jealous. Things are working out for Luke and me again, and you've just lost Cristos.'

'Oh, God help me!' Corrie seethed. 'What the hell is the matter with you, Annalise? Just how far does the man have to go before you . . . Do you know that he's accusing your father of incest?'

'Corrie, I'm not listening to any more of these lies. I know Luke has his faults, but you're going too far now. I'll see you at the office tomorrow morning by which time I hope you've had some rest or whatever it is you need to put you in a better mood.'

'Annalise, don't you dare ring off!' But Annalise already had, and as Corrie put down the receiver she sighed to Phillip, 'I see what you mean. It's useless.'

The next morning Luke and Annalise breezed into the office as though they had just come back from a month in the Caribbean. That there appeared to be no bruises on Annalise gave Corrie small comfort, and she, like everyone else, averted her eyes from the bandages on Luke's wrists. No one had made a single reference to them, though Corrie had every intention of doing so, just as soon as she got him alone. She finally managed it just before lunch, when she all but threw his secretary out of the way, and slamming his door behind her rounded on him with 'I don't know what kind of game you're playing, Luke Fitzpatrick, but I want an explanation for Saturday night, and I want it now.'

Using the remote control to flick off the TV set Luke swivelled in his chair to face her. For a long time he simply looked at her, then his eyes moved to the window and followed the mesmeric route of the clouds. At last he said, 'There won't be too much for you to do around here for the next couple of weeks, will there?'

Corrie blinked. 'What do you mean?'

'Well Annalise is going to take some time getting herself back together. I could assign you to another producer for the duration.'

'No, I'm quite happy working on my own projects, thank you. Now, I'd like . . .'

'Yes, I expect you are,' he smiled.

It was the smile not the words that threw Corrie into sudden disarray. He was using it to tell her something, and as his jaundiced eyes peered up into hers she could sense the menace behind them. For a moment she felt strangely lightheaded, as though the oxygen was being sucked away from her lungs. She tried to tear her eyes away, but she was transfixed by the power emanating from him. His smile widened, as though he knew the effect he was having and was enjoying it. Corrie took a step back as somewhere at the root of frozen chaos in her mind she knew that what she was witnessing now in Luke was the same dissolute evil she had sensed in Octavia. Then it was gone and Corrie, as though abruptly freed from a restraining leash, put out a hand to steady herself.

'What's going on?' she murmured. 'Luke . . .' She stopped as he got up from his chair and watched him walk around the desk.

'If you don't mind,' he said, pulling the door open, 'I was about to make a telephone call.'

'No, I'm not leaving until . . .'

'You're leaving now, Corrie. Right this instant,' and gripping her by the arm he manhandled her back into the production office.

That night Corrie told Phillip about those few minutes in Luke's office, wanting to know if he, Phillip, had spoken to Octavia yet. He had, but had got no further than Corrie had with Luke.

Over the next few days Corrie summoned the courage several times to speak to Luke again, but though there was no repeat of what had happened the first time, she knew that her probings were sliding from his implacable exterior as impenetrably as the rain was sliding down the windows outside. He seemed so calm, so frighteningly collected, that he was starting to appear almost inhuman. It was then that Corrie realized it was no longer Luke she was dealing with. The very idea made her fear for her own sanity, but it was like someone else was inside his skin. And the fact that Annalise was repeatedly assuring Corrie that everything was going well with her and Luke, disturbed Corrie even more. It was only a matter of time now, she knew that, though what would happen she couldn't even begin to imagine.

Three intolerable weeks went by. Though Corrie spoke to Cristos every day on the phone, and was in no doubt that he was missing her just as much as she was him, being apart like this was even more insufferable than the waiting game they all seemed to be playing with Luke. There were times when she seemed to be living just to hear Cristos's voice break into the insanity of her world telling her how his editing was coming along, or asking her how her projects were doing. She was working hard, but that her efforts were in the end only going to pull them further apart confused and depressed her even further. She seemed to have no anchor in her life, it was as though she was drifting inexorably away from him towards the sweeping current of disaster. In her heart she knew that if she held out her hand he would pull her back, but somehow she couldn't make herself do it. Nevertheless, she lost count of the times she ended up crying on the telephone. As soon as she did it made her laugh, but she longed to hear him tell her he loved her.

'I told you, not until you do,' he said. 'They're just three words, Corrie, so why torture yourself like this when I already know you love me.'

'I hate it when you're so sure of yourself,' she told him.

'I know you do. But you'll have to live with it.'

'Rather than marry it?'

He laughed. 'Something like that.'

'I hate you.'

'Sure you do.'

Brief as they sometimes were, it was these conversations that kept Corrie going as she continued to miss him more as each day passed. She saw a lot of Phillip, who had tried again to talk to Annalise, going so far as to confirm what Corrie had told her about the way Luke had accused him of incest with her. But Annalise just laughed, telling him that he had got the wrong end of the stick – as everyone did with Luke.

'No one understands him except me,' she would fire off as her parting remark.

Then one night, just as Corrie was packing up to leave the office, Octavia walked in. There was no one else around, and seeming not even to notice Corrie's presence, she stalked straight into Luke's office and closed the door.

From where she was sitting Corrie couldn't hear a thing, so she moved closer, making a pretence of searching for something on Luke's secretary's desk. Still their voices were muffled, so she risked pressing her ear to the door. After just a few minutes she recoiled in disgust.

'Well what sort of things were they saying?' Paula asked when Corrie rang her later.

'I don't want to repeat it,' Corrie said. 'Except I will tell you that he called her a corrupt, evil bitch and she just laughed and said, "keep driving your cock into me, mother-fucker!" '

'Mother-fucker!' Paula cried.

'That's what she called him.'

'You don't mean . . . ? You don't seriously think . . . ?'

'That she's his mother?' Corrie finished. 'How can she be, she's only about five years older than him.'

'So it was just a word she used?'

'It would seem so. But with all his accusations of incest . . .'

'Corrie,' Paula said carefully, 'didn't you tell me she's had a lot of plastic surgery?'

'Yes, I did. And she has, for all the good it's done her. But she's forty-seven, I just checked with Phillip. He has her birth certificate. Not only that he more or less grew up with her.'

'You mean you've told Phillip what you heard?'

'Yes. I told him because . . . Wait for this . . . Annalise rang me when I got in just now to tell me that she, Luke

– 521 –

and Octavia are going to Spain for a two week holiday, tomorrow!'

'My God!' Paula breathed. 'What did Phillip say?'

'He was as appalled as I was. But how is anyone going to stop them? And as Phillip said, if this is the way that Annalise has to find out what her mother's really like, then so be it. We'll just have to make sure we're around to pick up the pieces.'

After a pause, Paula said, 'Has it ever occurred to you how any of this might fit in with what happened to those prostitutes?'

'That's a question Phillip and I rack our brains over just about every time we meet. We can't come up with an answer.'

'But there's one there somewhere,' Paula said.

'I know, it's just finding it.'

It was just over a week after Luke, Octavia and Annalise had flown off to Spain that Corrie received the telephone call that was finally to bring everything to a head. She was at home, idling around watching TV and waiting for the call she knew would come any minute. In fact the phone had rung only a few minutes ago – it had been Annalise calling from Spain to say they were all having a wonderful time, but . . . They'd been cut off then, and Corrie was half afraid that Annalise would ring again and tie up the line before Cristos got through. But when it eventually rang it was Cristos. Though it was in the early morning for him he sounded exhausted.

'Yeah, sure I am,' he sighed, 'I've been here with this pre-mix all night. It's not going so well and I'm not too sure we're going to make it at this rate. I got to tell you, Corrie, that it sure doesn't help with you being over there. I miss you so bad it's creating hell with my concentration.'

Corrie smiled. 'I don't believe it.'

'You better. I want you so much it's driving me crazy. What are you doing to me, woman?'

'Obviously driving you crazy.'

'Damn right you are. Shit, Corrie, can't you say you want me too?'

'I want you, Cristos,' she said softly, 'I want you just as badly.'

'Then come over.'

'For a holiday?'

'Call it what you like, just come.'

'All right,' she said, 'I'll see what I can do.'

The next morning when Corrie asked Bob for the time off he didn't even stop to think about it, 'Why the hell not?' he grumbled. 'Every fucker else around here's on holiday, why should you be any different!'

'I'll book the flight for next Monday, so I'll be here to help out until the end of the week,' Corrie said, trying to sound generous. In fact Paula's baby was being christened on Sunday and Corrie was Godmother, so she wouldn't have gone until Monday anyway.

Then, to her amazement, on Friday afternoon, while she was helping out with telephone calls for another researcher Luke and Annalise walked into the office.

'You weren't due back until next Tuesday,' Corrie said, embracing Annalise. 'What happened?'

'Luke has an appointment he'd forgotten,' Annalise answered, distractedly.

'But everything's all right, isn't it?' Corrie pressed.

'Yes, it's fine,' Annalise answered, walking over to pick up her mail.

But it was obvious it wasn't, and Corrie suddenly felt so resentful she wanted to scream. Why did Annalise have to come back like this now? How could she just go off to Los Angeles and leave her, when things had clearly started to go wrong again? But she would, she told herself, vehemently. Damn it she would.

She started to wonder though, when Luke sent for her, if her leave wasn't about to be cancelled, but to her surprise he simply said,

'Bob tells me you're taking some time off and going to Los Angeles?'

'Yes,' she said, a challenging light springing to her eyes.

'OK. Well, I guess I've given you a hard enough time over Cristos in the past, so how about to make up for it I drive you to the airport.'

'That won't be necessary, thank you,' she said. 'I can take a taxi.'

'Then at least let one of the secretaries book you a car, courtesy of TW – it's the least I can do given the way I've tried to interfere in your life before.'

Shrugging her acceptance Corrie went off to a secretary, then gathering up her belongings left to go to Paula's for the weekend.

As she watched Corrie go Annalise's heart was breaking. Never in her life had she needed Corrie more than she needed her now. But she knew if she were to tell Corrie the real horror of what she had discovered in Spain then Corrie would never go to Cristos, and Annalise didn't want to do that to her. Besides, Corrie staying here would change nothing – it was too late now, nothing in the world could alter what had been done. She thought back to the night, all those months ago, when she had first suspected that her mother was having an affair with Luke. Well she knew now that her mother was, and dropping her head in her hands Annalise felt the tears burn across her eyes. If only it were as simple as that, but it wasn't, and all she could think of was that if she lost Corrie to Cristos now then she wouldn't want to go on living.

Picking up her bag she wandered aimlessly out of the office and down to the street. She had nowhere to go, no one to turn to – she couldn't even tell her father what she had learned because were she to repeat those heinous, vile words she had heard from her own mother's lips, then Annalise knew that Phillip's world would come to an end too.

When Corrie arrived back at her studio on Sunday night there were two messages waiting on her answerphone. The first was from Cristos telling her that Jeannie would pick her up from the airport the next day and take her straight to where he was dubbing. The second was from Phillip saying that he had a meeting near Heathrow in the morning so would come and have a coffee with her before she flew off.

After calling Paula to tell her she'd arrived back safely, Corrie put on some music then set about packing. She was grinning to herself as she wondered whether she would be able to hold off telling Cristos she loved him over the next ten days. Perhaps she wouldn't even try, after all it was a futile game she was playing that was fooling no one, least of all him. Oh what the hell, she laughed to herself, she would tell him, and not only because she so desperately longed to hear him say it again, but because she was just being obtuse in not accepting the fact that she'd already given one hundred per cent of herself to him anyway. Whether or not she said the words couldn't change that, and now she'd had a taste of what it was like not to have the reassurance of hearing them she realized that she didn't want to inflict it on him any longer.

Having reached her decision she was sorely tempted to pick up the telephone and tell him now. But no, she'd wait until they were together, she wanted to see the look in his eyes when she said it.

Before she went to bed she tried calling Annalise, but the answerphones were on at both Luke's and Annalise's. Deciding to try again in the morning Corrie rang off without leaving a message on either machine.

Just after ten the next morning, having woken up in

the night thinking about Annalise, Corrie called the office. Annalise wasn't there so Corrie tried her at home. Again she got the answerphone, but as she started to leave a message, Annalise's voice cut in.

'Yes, of course I'm going in to work today,' Annalise assured her when Corrie asked. 'In fact I was just on my way out of the door.'

'Did you have a good weekend?' Corrie asked.

'Mmm, not bad. How did the Christening go?'

'Beth was wonderful. How come you didn't stay with Luke last night?'

'Oh, we had a bit of a tiff, nothing serious. Anyway, I'd better go seeing as I'm already late, but you have a great time, and don't forget to ring me if you get the chance.'

'I'll do that,' Corrie said, and they rang off.

At her end Annalise, who was hunched into an armchair, gathered her knees into her arms as though trying to collect the crumbling pieces of her life. She was still in her night-gown and doubted she'd get dressed all day. If she did she certainly wouldn't be going to the office. For a moment she was tempted to call Corrie back and ask if she could go with her to LA. But Corrie wouldn't want her there, so Annalise remained as she was – the way she had been the entire weekend, frozen in the nightmare of her life.

At eleven o'clock Corrie's doorbell rang announcing the arrival of the taxi.

'Coming!' Corrie called out, snapping her suitcase shut. She checked around to make sure she had everything, and that all that should be was switched off, then hitting the button to turn on the answerphone she picked up her bags to go. She'd get Phillip to check on Annalise later, she was thinking as she opened the door, and heaving her suitcase onto the top step she turned back again to lock up. At that very moment the telephone rang, and just in case it was Annalise, Corrie ran inside to answer it, but whoever it was rang off before she could get there.

Pressing his foot hard on the accelerator Phillip's car all but flew up over the ramp in Terminal Four's short-term car park. As he swerved around the corner he had to break hard to avoid an old couple with three luggage trollies who were suddenly barring his way. Hooting loudly on the horn Phillip tore past them and squealed the car to a halt in a nearby parking space. Ignoring the pensioners' remonstrations, he pressed the remote on his key chain, locking and alarming the car, then ran towards the stairs. The damned meeting had gone on much longer than he'd expected, and now, if it wasn't too late already, he was going to miss Corrie.

Dashing into the terminal building he took the escalator three steps at a time up to the check-in desks. Pausing to read the TV screens above him, his heart sank when he saw that the last call for the BA 283 to Los Angeles was already up. Still, she was flying first class so might not have gone through yet. But knowing that she almost definitely would have, there was less urgency to his step as he continued to press his way through the crowds.

Twelve hours later Jeannie was at Los Angeles airport watching the arrivals as they filed through from customs. She was searching the faces and smiling to herself as she listened to the British accents of those who passed. She felt like a voyeur as she witnessed the tears and whoops of joy that went along with the greetings, and was so affected by the emotion as it ebbed and flowed around her that she guessed she was probably going to cry when she saw Corrie.

Jeannie waited for over an hour, at first groaning for Corrie that she was getting picked apart by customs. Eventually though, Jeannie's concern took her to the information desk. Some five minutes later it was confirmed that Corrie Browne had, at the last minute, cancelled her flight to Los Angeles.

Jeannie's only hope now was that while she'd been at

the airport Corrie had called Cristos to explain, 'cos if she hadn't Jeannie dreaded to think how Cristos would take the news. Aside from Cristos, Jeannie was the only person in the world who knew that Cristos was intending to ask Corrie to come to Los Angeles and live with him, because only to Jeannie had he confided how bad it had been for him since they'd come back from England. But how much worse it was going to be for him now that Corrie hadn't shown, for in her heart Jeannie knew that Corrie hadn't called Cristos to say she wasn't coming. She'd had more than twelve hours to do it, and if she had then Jeannie would have known long before this – hell, she wouldn't even be at the airport.

When she got back to the lot Jeannie went straight to Cristos's private office and called him on the telephone. It was a while before he left the pre-mix, but when Jeannie saw his face come in through the door she could see he was ready to apologize to Corrie for keeping her waiting. He looked around the room and when his eyes finally settled on Jeannie she saw his dark skin turn pale.

'She didn't come,' he said.

Jeannie shook her head. 'She cancelled her flight.'

Knowing he'd want her to, Jeannie left him alone then, but it was only a few minutes later that she heard him on the telephone, leaving a message on Corrie's answering machine.

'I don't know why you changed your mind,' he said, 'but just call me.'

Two days later Paula and Dave were sitting at the table in their little kitchen in Amberside. Dave was laughing as he was losing the struggle to feed Beth, who was determined to wield the spoon herself, but when he realized that Paula wasn't paying any attention he let go of the spoon and turned himself round to face her.

'I came in from work an hour ago and you still haven't spoken to me yet,' he told her.

Paula started, but when she made to apologize Dave said, 'I take it she didn't ring today either?'

Paula shook her head. 'No. I know you're going to tell me that she's probably too caught up with what's going on over there, but, well she said she'd call as soon as she arrived . . . I didn't expect that, it would have been the middle of the night here, but I thought I'd have heard from her by now.' She paused, looking down at her hands bunched on the table in front of her. 'Dave, I know you're going to say I'm daft or something, but I've just got this feeling that . . . Well, I can't explain it really . . .'

Sighing, Dave said, 'She gave you the number there, didn't she?'

Paula nodded.

'Then use it.'

Two minutes later Paula was listening to the single ringing tone at Cristos's house in the Holmby Hills. When the answerphone clicked on, shy of leaving messages, Paula was about to ring off when she heard Cristos's voice giving a number where he could be contacted. Quickly she dialled again and this time got through to where he was dubbing.

'I'm sorry to bother you,' she said, when he came on the line, 'but I was hoping to speak to Corrie. Is she with you, by any chance? It's Paula here, her friend from England.'

'Paula!' Cristos's voice sounded incredulous.

'Yes. It's just that Corrie said she'd call me when she got to . . .'

'Hang on,' Cristos said, 'you're calling here to speak to Corrie? She's got to have told you that she changed her mind about coming.'

'No,' Paula said, feeling a strange tightening in her chest. 'When did she do that?'

'I don't know. All I know is she cancelled her flight. I've

been trying to get hold of her ever since, I thought she was avoiding me.'

'But why would she do that? She was really looking forward to coming.'

'When did you last speak to her?'

'At the weekend. She was here. Well you know that, you called her here on Saturday.' Suddenly Paula felt the bite of panic. 'Oh my God!' she cried. 'Something's happened to her! I knew it! I could feel it. That was why I rang you.' She turned to find Dave beside her, and taking the receiver from her hand he spoke into it, saying,

'Mr Bennati, it's Dave, Paula's husband here. I take it Corrie's not with you.'

'No,' Cristos answered, and through the thousands of miles of cable Dave could hear the stress in Cristos's voice. 'What time is it there?' Cristos asked.

'Just before six,' Dave answered.

'Right, I'm going to hang up now,' Cristos said, 'I'll get back to you.'

Yelling for everyone in the dubbing theatre to get on with what they were doing, Cristos dialled the TW number. It rang for some time, but then a man's voice answered.

'Who am I speaking to?' Cristos demanded.

'Who are you?' Perkin said testily.

'Never mind that, I want to speak to Corrie Browne.'

'Then you'll have to call her in Los Angeles, won't you?' Perkin responded.

The fear hit Cristos so suddenly it made him queasy. Uppermost in his mind was the night Fitzpatrick had called Corrie to his so-called deathbed. Fuck it, he should have known then that Fitzpatrick was up to something! 'Put me onto Luke Fitzpatrick,' he barked.

'Sorry, he's left for the day. If you want to leave a message . . .'

'No message,' Cristos said, and rang off.

Cristos was thinking so fast now his head was starting to spin, but picking up the phone again he dialled Fitzpatrick's number. Wouldn't he just have known it, the answerphone! He left a message for Luke to call him, then when he got no reply from his own office he got one of the sound assistants to go turf out Jeannie.

Not until midnight Los Angeles time did he finally catch up with Fitzpatrick at the TW offices, by then he had spoken to Paula and Dave again and got the full story of what had been happening to Corrie and her family at Fitzpatrick's hands. Now fear was crawling around his gut like a living animal.

'Where is she?' Cristos demanded the minute he heard Luke's voice at the other end of the line.

'Who?' Luke asked.

'Who the fuck do you think? What have you done to her, you son of a bitch!'

'Hang on, hang on,' Luke said, 'if you're talking about Corrie I thought she was in Los Angeles with you.' Luke's surprise sounded so genuine that for a moment Cristos was thrown.

'Are you telling me she's not there?' Luke said.

'What the fuck do you think I'm telling you! Now where is she?'

'I'm sorry,' Luke said, 'but I don't know. All I know is that she was intending to go to Los Angeles. Shit, I even offered her a lift to the airport myself. She refused, but I can contact the car company she booked through, if that'll help.'

'Do it!' Cristos snapped. 'Better still, give me the number, I'll do it!'

'Hold on,' Luke said, 'I'll have to get it from the secretary who handled it.'

Cristos waited, then, when Luke came back onto the line he scribbled down the number as Luke said, 'if you see her before I do . . .' he hesitated a moment then chuckled, 'yes, I'm sure you will, give her my love. And Annalise's.'

As Luke replaced the receiver he looked up at Annalise who was standing in his doorway. Annalise's eyes mirrored all the pain in her heart, but Luke knew, just as Annalise did, that it was too late now to turn back. Of course Luke had known it for much longer than Annalise had, he'd just never expected Octavia to tell Annalise. Neither, until he had discovered that Corrie was going to LA, had he suspected that Bennati still figured in Corrie's life. But Phillip, the bastard, had taken care of that for him, hadn't he?

As Annalise turned listlessly from the door Luke went to close it before calling Cristos back.

'I think you should know,' he said, when Cristos answered, 'that Corrie's father was due to have coffee with her at the airport before she left.'

As Cristos replaced the receiver he turned to Jeannie and Richard who were sitting in his kitchen with him. Jeannie was on the mobile phone speaking to the London car company. Cristos waited. At last Jeannie thanked the person at the other end then confirmed what they'd all suspected – Corrie had cancelled her car to the airport. Cristos told them then what Luke had said, but even before he had finished he knew what he had to do next. A quick telephone call to Paula gave him the names and numbers he needed.

Phillip Denby was entertaining one of his clients when Detective Inspector Radcliffe and Detective Constable Archer burst into his office. Phillip was so shocked that it took him a moment to comprehend what they were saying.

Neither of them bothered to explain in great detail, but by the time he was frog-marched out of the office he knew he was under arrest. He knew too that it was to do with Corrie, and not the prostitutes.

'I'll call your lawyer,' he heard Pam say.

Cristos looked up as Jeannie came into the dubbing theatre. 'I've got everything you asked for,' she said. 'Names, addresses, credentials. Provisional hotel reservations, hire cars . . .'

'Did you speak with my mother?'

'Yes. Your father's staying behind to mind the shop, she'll get whichever flight you say.'

Cristos nodded then turned back to the dubbing mixer. 'Carry on with this scene,' he said, 'tail the echo over from the last. Try fifty frames. Bring the music in at forty. I'll be back in an hour.'

He walked outside with Jeannie. 'No news?' he said.

Jeannie shook her head. 'I've been trying every half hour. No reply from her home. Paula still hasn't heard anything either.'

'Are the cops telling you anything?'

'Only that they're holding her father.'

Cristos closed his eyes. When he had contacted DI Radcliffe the night before to report the fact that Corrie was missing, the last thing he had expected was that they would go and arrest her father. 'What the fuck is going on over there, Jeannie?' he groaned.

For several hours now DI Radcliffe had been listening to one of his CID officers interrogating Phillip Denby in the next room. DC Archer had been with him all that time, but she'd just popped out to fetch some coffee.

Radcliffe tilted his chair and rested his head on the wall behind him. This was one hell of a fucking mess, he was thinking to himself, and his stomach gave a violent lurch at the unthinkable prospect of finding yet another body on the banks of the Thames. Officers had been on the lookout all day, frogmen were dragging it even now. Nothing had turned up yet, so there was still hope – but where the fuck was Corrie Browne? Forensics were over at her studio now, but when he'd visited there himself earlier it was plain to see that there had been no forced entry and no struggle.

He looked up as DC Archer came back into the room.

'All these months of tailing the bastard,' he said as she handed him a coffee, 'and we lose him the morning Corrie Browne disappears.'

Shaking her head Archer sat down on the wooden bench beside him. 'I think we're going to have to let him go, guv. I mean, those guys he was at the meeting with confirmed he was there right up until eleven forty-five. That puts him in Windsor at the time Corrie disappeared.'

'But where did he go after? No one saw him at the airport, except a couple of old-age pensioners, he claims. And just how the hell are we going to find them without going public on this?'

'Why can't we go public, guv?'

'We will, just as soon as we've spoken to Fitzpatrick. Did you get hold of him?'

'Yes. He's on his way over.'

Radcliffe sighed and scraped his fingers over the stubble on his chin. 'We know it was a man who cancelled both the car and the flight . . . We also know that if Denby is to be believed then most of the evidence points to Fitzpatrick. But what I want to know, is who is trying to put who in the frame here. And why?'

'I don't think we should forget the fact that Corrie Browne suspected Fitzpatrick of knowing Bobby McIver.'

'And neither should we forget that Phillip Denby is her father.'

'Meaning?'

'Meaning that she could have been conspiring with him to put Fitzpatrick in the frame.'

'Oh come on, guv, you don't believe that! If she knew her father had killed those women . . . Well, she just didn't strike me as the type who'd cover up for him, even if he is her father. Especially not over something like that.'

'But we know she had an affair with Fitzpatrick and we know that he broke it off . . .'

'We've only got his word for that, guv. We've never asked Corrie Browne for her side of the story.'

'No, we haven't have we?' Radcliffe sighed, slumping over the table and burying his fingers in his hair. 'The question now is, will we ever be able to ask her?'

Cristos was with Bud Winters in the Black Tower. There were other Universal executives in the office too, but Cristos was the only one on his feet. He was pacing up and down in front of them, informing them that the answer print would be back the day after tomorrow and then he wanted to take it to France and put the finishing touches to it there.

'There's a completion clause to this movie,' one of the faceless suits started to say.

'There's nothing in my contract to say it can't be completed in France,' Cristos roared. 'And that's where it's going to be finished! Are you receiving me? If you fight it I'll just fly Lance Burgess, his assistant and all the dubbing guys out there at my own expense.'

'But even the jury didn't arrive yet,' Bud Winters pointed out. 'What's the rush? We'll get it there.'

'I'm on a flight for London this afternoon,' Cristos stated. 'The others will fly to Nice just as soon as they have the print. I'll join them there. Story over.'

In the end, after much grunting and shaking of heads, it was agreed that Cristos could do it his way. And they would foot the bill – Bennati was too important to them to risk upsetting him.

Cristos went straight to his office, informed Lance that he'd got the go ahead, told him to get everything in motion and two hours later he was on his way to London.

'I just don't fucking believe any of this!' Radcliffe cried, slamming his office door behind himself and DC Archer.

'One of those two bastards knows where that girl is and I can't hold either of them!'

'What's the latest, guv?' one of the other CID officers asked, popping his head round the door.

Radcliffe gave him a thunderous look, so it was left to Archer to explain.

'We just had corroboration from one of Annalise Kapsakis's neighbours that Fitzpatrick *was* outside her house, trying to get in, the morning Corrie disappeared.'

'Does it cover the time she disappeared?' he asked.

'Just about. The neighbour couldn't be exact, but the person we really need to speak to is Annalise Kap . . .' She broke off as Radcliffe's phone rang, then watched his face become more and more taut by the second as he listened to the voice at the other end. 'What is it, guv?' she asked, when he replaced the receiver.

'They've just broken into Kapsakis's flat,' he said, shaking his head incredulously. 'She's overdosed.'

'Oh my God,' Archer breathed. 'How bad is it, do we know?'

'Not yet, she's on her way to hospital now. Come on,' he said, picking up his coat, 'let's get over to the flat. And let's pray to the patron saint of policemen that she's left a suicide note, 'cos if she doesn't·pull through it could be the only way we have of finding out just what the fuck is going on with that family.'

Siobhan was in the room overlooking the sea. The rabbits were playing around her feet, five of them now – Luke had brought three more on his last visit. On her lap was a bunch of dandelions, but it was only Luke's hand that took them to feed the rabbits. Siobhan's eyes were fixed on the rain spattered windows.

Luke was sitting on the floor staring up at her. Once in a while he picked up a rabbit smoothed it then put it down again. Eventually he stood up, slid his hands into his pockets and started to pace the room. 'She was going to see Bennati,' he said, then spun round suddenly and glared at the door. 'Is anyone listening there?' he snapped certain he'd heard a footstep outside.

All was silent.

Rubbing a hand over his unshaven face he walked to the window. 'Octavia told Annalise about you,' he went on quietly, then he smiled a sad and distant smile as he ran a finger through the condensation. 'She told her everything. I told Annalise it was over between you and me. It didn't make any difference. It'll never be over for us though, will it Siobhan?'

He rested his head against the pane looking out at the dull grey sky. The waves lapping the beach were a faraway sound. Siobhan's breathing was so light he could barely hear it. A rabbit hopped across his foot. He looked down, then scooping it up he carried it across the room to Siobhan. 'Is this your favourite?' he said, holding it in front of her face. 'Is this the one you like best?'

Siobhan's eyes remained sightlessly on the window, and as the monstrous rage stirred its unholy power through his gut, Luke's hand tightened around the helpless animal.

'Then why not be having it for dinner?' he snarled.

Cristos's first stop when he arrived in London was Corrie's studio. The two police officers standing duty there went inside with him while he dumped his luggage, but he didn't stay long. He had contacted the police station from Heathrow, so already knew about Annalise, and leaping back into his hire car he headed straight for the hospital.

He found Phillip Denby waiting in a corridor outside the ward. It was debatable which of the two men looked the most strained. 'What news on Annalise?' Cristos asked.

'She'll live,' Phillip answered, tears starting in his eyes. 'I was with her a moment ago, but she won't tell me why she did it. She just keeps asking for Corrie.'

'Oh God!' Cristos groaned. 'Have you told her?'

Phillip shook his head. 'Not yet, no,' and he started to sob.

'Hold on in there,' Cristos said, squeezing his shoulder. 'She'll be all right. They both will,' but in that moment he was very close to breaking himself.

'I thought they were holding you,' Cristos said, as Phillip blew his nose.

'They were. They let me go in the end for lack of evidence.'

'But why the hell did they arrest you in the first place?'

'It's a long story. But it seems they've been tailing me for some time and lost me that morning around the time she disappeared. And when you told them that I was meeting her at the airport . . .'

'Fitzpatrick!' Cristos muttered. 'It was Fitzpatrick who told me you were meeting her. Where is he now, do you know?'

'All I know is that the police have questioned him and let him go. That was hours ago. Maybe it was yesterday – I've lost all track of time.'

As Cristos looked into Phillip's ravaged face he could feel his own panic rising. He loved her so much his entire body ached with the fear of what might have happened to her. Not even in his mind could he bring himself to voice his suspicions, but they were there, driving through his brain like daggers. To think of her knowing even a moment of terror was too agonizing to deal with. He had to find her, dear God, he just had to. She was the whole world to him now, the whole world and more.

'You don't think . . .' Phillip whispered. 'Cristos, you don't think she's . . .'

'For Christ's sake don't say it,' Cristos answered in a strangled voice. 'Don't even think it.'

– 26 –

For days now Corrie had been drifting in and out of consciousness. From time to time when lucidity, like the first
tentative rays of dawn, seeped through the darkened mass
of her mind, she had been dimly aware of someone standing
over her, watching her. She'd tried to speak, knowing what
she wanted to say, but something was preventing her
tongue from moving. In those moments she was trying to
tell Cristos she loved him. But then, as though someone
were clenching a hand, the fingers of light would vanish
and she would find herself once again enclosed in a pit of
total darkness.

Now, as the debilitating layer of numbness started to
peel from her mind again, she parted her eyelids, moaning
softly at the sudden dagger of pain in her head. After a
while, when it had begun to subside, she tried to shift her
body, but the stiffness sent frenzied messages of protest to
her brain. The ache clawing at her stomach, she eventually
realized was hunger, which dimly made her wonder when
it was that she'd last eaten.

Had they given her food on the plane? As the question
coasted through her mind it seemed to take with it another
stratum of the debilitating crust that had formed in her
head like rock. Then panic put its seering finger to the
rawness as she asked herself if the plane had crashed. Was
she lying here, buried in a tangle of metal? Were other
parts of her body strewn somewhere amongst the debris?
She couldn't feel any of them. But she could! She couldn't
move them, but when she tried the pain assured her that
her limbs were still there. Her arms, she realized were

behind her back, and her legs . . . She forced herself to move her feet and felt a pressure tighten on her wrists.

She gave herself some time to think about that, but it wasn't until she attempted to move her swollen tongue and felt it press against the dryness of something that seemed to stretch across her mouth that what had happened to her suddenly revealed itself in all its horrific and blinding clarity.

Luke!

Luke had been there, standing behind her when she'd turned away from the telephone. She hadn't heard him come in, she hadn't even heard him close the door. But he had been there, standing over her, his madman's eyes gleaming.

What had happened then? She must try to think. She had to control this panic and steady the heaving in her chest. They had talked, she remembered that, but what had he said? What was it he had told her?

The pinions on her memory seemed to shift, letting the words through. He had said that she'd left him with no alternative. He had told her that he couldn't allow her to go to Bennati when he needed her himself. Then he had . . . Oh, God . . . He had pulled a piece of paper from his pocket and told her it was a licence for them to get married.

All Corrie could remember after that was the sudden pain that had exploded in her head. Perhaps, she thought now as tears started to burn her blindfolded eyes and the monotonous thud of pain seemed suddenly to intensify, he had fractured her skull.

But how had he got her out of her studio, and down the steps to his car? If he'd carried her, or even dragged her, surely someone would have seen. But they couldn't have, otherwise she wouldn't be here now. But where was she? All she could sense was the dry stench of . . . What was it? Oil? Earth?

Suddenly her whole body froze as from somewhere very

close by she heard a rolling metallic sound. The abrupt splash of sunlight pierced her eyes through the blindfold, and she realized that what she had heard was the opening of something like a garage door. Then there was the metallic sound again and the sunlight vanished – all she could hear now was the soft tread of footsteps coming towards her.

As wave after wave of paralysing terror washed over her images of the murdered prostitutes began racing through her blacked-out eyes. It was here, in this very place, that he had killed them – and each one of them had been trussed in the very manner she was now! And now she was here, and he was stooping over her, his breath warm on her face, his fingers raking through her hair . . .

'Don't be afraid,' he said softly. 'I've brought you some food.'

As he released her mouth Corrie started to choke on her sobs. 'Luke,' she pleaded. 'Luke, please let me go.'

'Sssh,' he said. 'It'll be all right,' and he tugged the blindfold from her eyes.

Corrie's sight was blurred and his face was swathed in shadow, but through the dim light she could see the gleam of his smile – it turned her heart to ice.

'No,' she cried, as his fingers slowly circled her throat. 'No! Luke, please!'

The breath jerked from her body as suddenly his grip tightened and he dragged her up by her neck until she was on her knees in front of him. 'I told you,' he said, 'that you would come to me in the end.'

Corrie was too petrified to speak, but as his lips came down on hers a whimper of pure terror erupted from her throat.

'I don't want to kill you,' he whispered.

'Luke, let me go,' she begged, her voice rasping through the pressure of his fingers. 'Please, let me go.'

'I can't,' he said. 'You'll run to Bennati.'

'No, I'll do anything you say . . . Luke, I swear . . .'

She fell against him as he suddenly released her neck, and hugging her with one arm he slid his other hand into his pocket. 'Here we are,' he said. 'See what we have here.'

Corrie looked down, but in the darkness she couldn't see what he was holding. It was only when she heard the quick spring of metal that she realized it was a knife.

It was nine thirty in the morning when, feeling more tired then he ever had in his life, Cristos slumped onto the sofa in Corrie's studio and pressed the button on the answer machine. Even knowing it was useless, he had been out there all night combing the streets of London looking for her. He had to do it, he had to do something or he was going to drive himself insane.

The messages on the answerphone were all for him, most of them from Jeannie. When they'd finished he let his head fall back onto the cushions and closed his eyes. For a while it seemed as though the merciful arms of sleep were going to carry him to a much needed oblivion, but somehow they couldn't quite reach him.

He had never felt anything like this before in his life. The frustration, the sheer impotence was almost as bad as the fear. He knew he was in danger of losing what little control he still had over himself, and Goddamnit, if he didn't get some sleep soon, he would!

He no longer knew which was worse, the way he blamed himself for not having realized what was going on, or the anger he felt at Corrie for not telling him. But as he sat there, surrounded by her things, feeling her presence so strongly he could almost smell the lemon cleanness of her, could almost touch her sleepy softness and hear the beloved ring of her laughter, he knew that nothing, but nothing could be as bad as this.

The telephone suddenly shrilled into the silence and Cristos jerked himself up to answer it with what he already knew to be a futile hope hammering in his chest. It was Phillip.

'No. No news this end,' Cristos said in answer to Phillip's question. 'What about you? Where are you?'

'At the hospital. They're discharging Annalise later today.'

'That's good,' Cristos said, so numb he couldn't even tell if he meant it. 'Did you tell her about Corrie yet?'

'About half an hour ago. She didn't take it too well. The police are with her now, I know what she's going to tell them, which is why I've come outside to call you.'

'Go on.'

'She's confirmed that Luke was outside her flat around midday on Monday, trying to get in, which I'm afraid coincides with when Corrie went missing. So unless the man can be in two places at once . . .'

For a moment Cristos felt such an overpowering rage that only with superhuman effort did he stop himself hurling the phone across the room. He didn't know how Fitzpatrick had done it, but the bastard had Corrie and nothing anyone said was going to convince Cristos otherwise. What he might have done to Corrie Cristos still couldn't allow himself to think about, but he knew, had there not been detectives dogging every move Fitzpatrick made, then he, Cristos, would likely be up on a murder charge by now. 'Are you sure Annalise isn't just covering for him?' he snapped.

'No, I'm not sure. But I don't think she is. She still won't tell anyone why she took the overdose, but between you and me, I'm fairly certain it's because she found out about her mother's affair with Luke. She's refusing to see either of them. She won't even come home to Chelsea this afternoon – I have to take her to her own flat.'

'Could I talk to her?' Cristos asked. 'Like today. I got to fly to Nice tonight . . .'

'If she's up to it. I'll ask her to call you later.'

At eight o'clock that night, having got no further with Annalise than anyone else had, Cristos was on his way to Nice. He'd left his number in Cannes with Radcliffe, Paula, Annalise and Phillip, making them all swear they'd contact him the minute they heard anything. But the terrible sense of betrayal he felt at leaving was only surpassed by the panic, which had long since taken hold of his fear and incarcerated it in terror.

Exhaustion was etched in every line of Corrie's face. Her body, now propped against the wall, was a weighted mass of agony, and her mind was reaching yearningly towards the elusive haven of sleep. But the bitter cold was biting bone deep arresting her at the brink. Her hands, now unbound, lay uselessly in her lap, her fingers too frozen even to link each other for warmth.

In the moments when Luke had first sliced through her bonds she had been so near to passing out that it had been a while before she'd realized he wasn't going to kill her. Then, as he lit a candle beside her and her eyes had slowly adjusted to the dusty shadows, what she had seen had instilled such indescribable terror in her that her mind had plunged into darkness. Luke had coaxed her back to her senses by spooning water between her cracked lips.

Now he was sitting at the centre of the floor, his legs crossed, his elbows resting on his knees, staring sightlessly into the space between them. Beside him the candle was still flickering a timid glow into the gloom, but its light was strong enough for Corrie to see the wall behind him, to register with her own eyes the reality of what until now had only been a nightmare. He had killed the prostitutes, and he had done it right here in this garage – the evidence was encrusted in the clotted brown stains of dried blood all over the walls and floor. She couldn't allow herself to think of the savagery he must have employed for the blood to have spurted to such a height, if she did she knew her own sanity would be annihilated completely.

A few moments ago she had tried to scream, but just like in a nightmare, no sound had come. Then Luke had told her that it would do no good, no one would hear her.

'Luke,' she said now, her voice so parched the sound barely reached her own ears. 'Luke, you must know that someone will come looking for me . . .'

'They already are,' he said bleakly.

Relief pushed tears into Corrie's eyes – surely someone would speak to Paula and Paula would tell them about Luke. It could only be a matter of time then . . . He was speaking again, but through the turbulence of emotion inside her head Corrie couldn't hear him. She struggled to clear her mind, opening her lips and inhaling the foul stench of the place through mouth and nose.

'. . . so they think I'm in my flat all the time,' he was saying. 'That's why I never stay long with you, in case they knock on the door. I leave the shower running while I'm gone, you see. Or the TV. But don't worry, Corrie, I'll keep coming, I won't leave you here alone any longer than I have to.' He laughed dryly and rubbed his fingers over his eyes. 'I never would have thought it would be so easy,' he said, 'but they make it easy. I just leave through the studio at the back, walk along the lane and get into the old car I used to pick up the prostitutes.'

These words were like a bludgeon on Corrie's already battered senses. But there was worse to come.

'They suspect me, of course,' he said, 'of abducting you, I mean. But Annalise has told them that it couldn't be me.' He sighed, heavily, as though trying to shift the burden of his sadness. 'You see, I was at her house when you went missing. She wouldn't let me in, I knew she wouldn't . . . But I had to be there when you disappeared. And the point is, no one really knows the exact time you did disappear. All they know is that you didn't take the taxi, and you didn't get onto the plane. So after I . . .' his eyes suddenly came up to meet hers. 'I didn't want to hit you, Corrie, I just didn't have any choice. I couldn't take you in the car to Annalise's with me, someone might have seen you, so I had to leave you at your studio. I came back for you, though, once it was dark. I knew I had all that time – the flight to Los Angeles is a long one, it gave me plenty of time.'

'But my father was meeting me . . .' Corrie whispered.

'Yes, you told me that when I came round. But he was late. If he hadn't been . . . Well, he was, so everything turned out all right.'

They sat in silence for a while then. Corrie knew, because there was no sunlight creeping through the cracks around the door that it was night. Did that mean he would be staying longer? Crazy as it seemed she didn't want him to go, she didn't want to be left alone here with the ghosts of the women who had died so violently.

'Why wouldn't Annalise let you in?' she asked, her voice still so hoarse that it scraped on her throat.

'She's angry with me.'

Corrie waited for him to elaborate, but when he didn't she said, 'Because of Octavia? Did she find out about Octavia?'

His head jerked up, then he laughed, suddenly. It was brittle, high-pitched, almost a snigger. 'Yes, you could say that,' he answered. Then suddenly he was on his feet. 'I have to go,' he said, and Corrie saw him slide her blindfold, gag and fresh rope out of his pocket.

'No!' she cried, as he came towards her. 'Please, Luke, no!'

'I'm sorry,' he soothed, 'but I have to.'

'No! I'm begging you, Luke, please don't leave me here. Please, Luke, I'll do anything . . . No!' she screamed as he pushed her face down on the floor. The clasp of her handbag, which was still strapped across her body, dug painfully into her hip. In her mounting hysteria Corrie thought it was the knife, thought that it was beginning, that now was the moment he was going to do the same to her as he had to the prostitutes.

'Luke stop! Please, please, no!' Her voice was still barely more than a croak. 'Luke, don't do it, please!' she begged, as he wrenched her arms behind her.

She realized then that he was using both hands, that whatever it was digging into her wasn't a knife. 'My bag,' she sobbed, 'oh my God, my bag!'

'What this?' Luke said, turning her onto her side and lifting it up. 'Is it hurting you?'

'Yes,' Corrie gasped, unable to see him through her tears.

'There,' he said, laying it on the floor in front of her, 'is that better?'

Dumbly Corrie nodded, but began to sob again as he retied her blindfold. 'I don't want to stay here, Luke,' she choked, 'please don't leave me here.'

'It won't be for much longer,' he said softly. 'I promise you, it won't be long now.'

'Oh Luke, please, please, stop this.'

'Sssh! Sssh!' he said, lifting her head to wrap the gag around behind her. 'I have to deal with Annalise first. I have to make her understand. If I'd lost you, you see, I'd have had to kill her. But this way . . . You're going to help us, Corrie. You're going to help me, and be with me, because I do need help, Corrie. I know that.'

When he had gone Corrie lay on the ground her body shuddering and shivering as the demons of terror swooped through the impenetrable darkness he had left her in. Tears rolled from her eyes, saliva dripped from her mouth and the biting cold spiked every pore of her skin.

The sound of his car had long receded into the distance and she had said many prayers by the time she realized that she had stretched out her legs. Even then the significance of what she had done took some time to register – and when it did the euphoria was so sudden that she could barely sit herself up she was shaking, laughing and crying so hard. He hadn't attached her wrists to her ankles.

She winced, even groaned with the pain as the rope dug into her wrists as she pressed her hands down under buttocks, gingerly pulling herself backwards through the loop of her arms. But her hips were through, and then so too were her legs. Her hands were in front of her!

Fumbling with the edge of her blindfold it was a while before she managed to push it up to her forehead. Then she hooked her deadened fingers into the gag and using her tongue and lips as well, eventually succeeded in freeing her mouth. But when she put the knots on her wrists between her teeth and felt the taut knobbling of the rope she started to cry again.

It took the entire night to loosen the knots, by which time her hands and her face were smeared with blood. But she did free them, and then she set about unfastening her ankles. It seemed to take an eternity. Her fingers were so numbed by the cold she had to keep warming them in her armpits, but eventually she got there, and on unsteady legs she pulled herself up and stumbled towards the door.

For some time now she had been aware of daylight coming through the cracks in the door, and knew that somehow she had to get out of there before Luke came back. But as she confronted the metal barrier between her and freedom, the hopelessness of her situation sucked the feverish adrenalin from her blood and she collapsed sobbing against it. Her knees gave way beneath her and as she slid down the door an incoherent babble of words was bubbling from her lips.

It was only when she felt the jet of chill wind streaming across her legs that she noticed the decayed wooden panel in the upright of the door. Wiping the back of her hand across her eyes she crawled towards it, then taking her bag she smashed it into the rotten wood. It gave out almost immediately. But the space was nowhere near wide enough for her to crawl through, and the panel beside it showed no signs of decay. But she was going to get out, she told herself fiercely, she had to, and a renewed surge of adrenalin flowed through her lending her the strength to kick, hammer, push and pull until the panel was torn from its roots.

Petrified now that Luke would return, she squeezed her shivering, frozen body through the jagged gap out into the rain soaked alley.

As she started to run through the drizzle, stumbling on the cobbles and slipping in the grime of the gutter, she had no conception of the fact that shock had propelled her mind back in time to the point before her ordeal had begun. All she knew was that she was on her way to Cristos. That she was going to tell him she loved him. Which was why, when she finally came to a main road and ran out in front of a taxi to stop it, she told the driver to take her to Heathrow. That's where she'd been heading before all this started, so that's where she must go now, then it would be like it had never happened.

But as she looked down at her battered fingers her eyes suddenly opened wide. Annalise! What was it he had said about Annalise? She couldn't remember, but she knew with a strangely panicked clarity that she couldn't go without Annalise. 'Driver!' she called out, but as she was on the point of giving him Annalise's address it suddenly occurred to her that Luke might be there. She swallowed hard on a fresh onslaught of panic, at last realizing with a frustration bordering on desperation, that she couldn't go to Cristos, at least not yet, she had to go to the police first.

Fifteen minutes later she ran on unsteady legs into Chelsea Police Station. The officer on duty was busily filling in forms and despite the sound of her breathlessness didn't look up straight away.

'What can I do for you?' he asked, distractedly.

'DI Radcliffe,' Corrie gasped. 'Please, I have to see DI Radcliffe.'

The young officer raised his head and his eyes dilated with shock when he recognized the ghostly face looking back at him.

'Inspector!' he yelled, pressing the buzzer to release the security door. 'Inspector, get out here fast! Are you all right?' he said, putting his arms about Corrie to support her. 'Jeez, what happened to you? Where have you been? God, is Radcliffe going to be glad to see you.'

Corrie tried to answer, but relief was coursing so savagely through her veins that she all but collapsed against him. She was safe! She was here at the police station and safe!

Within minutes Radcliffe was down the stairs, followed by DC Archer. 'Mother of God!' Radcliffe gasped when he saw her. 'Get her to the surgeon's room,' he barked to the young PC.

'No! No, I'm all right,' Corrie insisted. 'I have to talk to you. Please!' she added, when she saw him about to argue.

'All right,' he said, taking her from the officer and leading her gently into the inner realms of the station. 'Get the surgeon on stand by,' he added to Archer over his shoulder.

It didn't take Corrie long to tell him what had happened and even before she'd finished a fleet of police cars, sirens blaring, lights flashing, was tearing through the streets of London heading for the TW offices and Luke's apartment. Twice during the interview though Corrie had to be taken out by DC Archer to vomit, but now she was lying on the surgeon's bed, her panic subsided and tears sliding unchecked from her eyes as she thought of Cristos and how desperately she wanted to see him.

'Please!' she begged Radcliffe. 'Please, just let me call him. You see, he was expecting me, in Los Angeles, and he won't know why I didn't come . . . I have to speak . . .'

'He knows why you didn't get there,' Radcliffe soothed her. 'He's been over here himself looking for you.'

'He's been here?' Corrie choked through the constricting emotion in her chest. 'Oh, please, let me go to him. I've told you everything I can . . .'

'I can't let you go, I'm afraid,' Radcliffe smiled. 'But he's in Cannes now getting that movie of his ready for the festival. I've got his number. You just wait here and I'll get it for you. Your father's on his way over, by the way.'

At last Corrie was alone in an office, her hair still damp from the shower, her fingers heavily bandaged from the cuts and bruises she had received during her escape. Dialling was difficult, but after the third attempt she got through to the Majestic Hotel in Cannes.

'Cristos?' she whispered when she heard his voice at the other end.

'Corrie?' he said tentatively. 'Is that you?'

'Cristos! Oh, Cristos!' And suddenly sobs were shuddering so harshly through her body she couldn't speak.

'Corrie!' he cried. 'Oh my God! Are you all right? Where are you?'

'I'm . . . I'm . . . Oh, Cristos . . .'

'Come on, come on,' he said urgently, 'Just tell me where you are, I'll come get you.'

'I'm at the police station. I've told them everything, they're looking for Luke now. Oh Cristos, I want to see you so badly.'

'I'll be right there,' he said. 'I'll get the next flight out.'

'No, you can't do that. The festival is . . .'

'Fuck the festival, Corrie. I'm coming over.'

'No, Cristos, please. Let me come to you. I want to get away from here. I don't want to be anywhere near him now. Let me come, Cristos, please let me . . .'

'But the police are going to need you there, sweetheart.'

'Not now. I can't tell them any more. I'll talk to them, Cristos, I'll make them let me come. Even if it's only for a day. I have to see you.'

'I have to see you too. Oh Corrie! I've been half out of my mind. Are you all right? What did he do to you?'

'I'm all right,' Corrie answered. 'It wasn't so bad really. It was just . . . It was . . .'

'Corrie . . .'

'I was so afraid I'd never see you again.'

'I'm coming over there now,' he declared.

'But the film . . .'

'It's ready.'

'You're lying,' she cried. 'I can tell. I'm not going to let this spoil things for you, Cristos. I'm coming to you.'

'Jeez, but you're stubborn,' he growled. 'Now will you just listen . . .'

'No, you listen. As soon I can get them to let me go I'm coming over there, do you hear me?'

'They're not going to let you go, Corrie,' he argued.

'They *will*! And I want to be there when you win, Cristos. I want to be with you when you pick up that Palme d'Or.'

'Oh, Corrie,' he groaned. 'I love you, do you know that?'

'Yes, I know that. And Cristos . . .' But as she was about to tell him she loved him too there was a knock on the door and Corrie screamed.

'For Christ's sake! What is it?' Cristos cried.

'Nothing,' Corrie laughed shakily, as the door opened and Phillip and Annalise were shown in by Archer. 'My nerves are still on edge, that's all.' Annalise was at her side now, her arms wrapped around Corrie.

'I'll be with you just as soon as I can, Cristos,' Corrie said into the phone. 'I have something to tell you . . . I think you know what it is.'

'I'll be waiting,' he said. 'Just get here as soon as you can.'

When the police broke down the door of Luke's apartment they found the TV blaring and no one at home. Since it was Saturday Radcliffe hadn't expected anyone to be at the TW offices, and he was right. But the security man had handed over the addresses and telephone numbers of all TW's employees and CID officers were spreading out all over London now to go and interview them. Back at the station a constable was onto the licensing centre in Swansea to find out the types and registrations of all vehicles registered in the names of either Luke Fitzpatrick or Bobby McIver. That could well prove to be a needle in the haystack search, but they didn't have much else to go on right now.

Radcliffe himself was on the phone to the doctor who was tending Bobby McIver. 'Just tell McIver we know about Fitzpatrick,' he was saying, his sparse hair on end where he kept agitating it. 'Tell him there's nothing to be afraid of anymore. See if he says anything. If he does, get back to me.'

He banged the phone down as DC Archer walked into his office. 'You've alerted the press?' he said.

Archer nodded. 'Phillip Denby's arrived to take Corrie home. At least, he's taking her to Annalise's where she's going to be staying for the next few days.'

'With a round the clock police guard?'

'Naturally,' Archer confirmed.

The search for Luke went on all that day and into the next, but any lead they gained always ended in a blank. A team of detectives spent hours tearing Luke's apartment to pieces looking for something that could give them a clue as to where he might be, but nothing presented itself. His picture was over the front page of every newspaper, on every news bulletin, but as yet there hadn't been a single sighting.

Phillip was staying at Annalise's too, and though both he and Corrie judged the time right now to tell Annalise who Corrie really was every time they tried to broach the subject it was almost as though Annalise knew what they were going to say but didn't want to hear it.

'Do you think Luke's told her already?' Corrie said.

Phillip shook his head. 'I don't know, he might have. But she loves you so much, Corrie, when she was in the hospital it was only you she wanted, so I can't imagine why she's responding this way. Perhaps she doesn't quite understand what we're trying to tell her . . . Perhaps we should just come right out and say it. We can always explain about Edwina later.'

They agreed to do it that way just as soon as Annalise woke up, but by the time she did Phillip had been called to his office to sign some urgent documents, and Corrie really didn't want to go ahead without him.

She was just ending a call to Cristos when Annalise walked into the room. 'No, you'll have to wait,' she was saying. 'I want to see your face when I tell you. I know, but it won't be long now. I'll be there before the ceremony, I promise. I'll talk to Radcliffe again, see what he says.'

'Why don't you just go?' Annalise said, when Corrie rang off.

Corrie looked up into her pallid face and sighed. 'I wish I could. Oh God, you don't know how much I wish I could. But there's no way of avoiding the police while they're sitting around outside the way they are – and I can't see Radcliffe letting me go yet. Not before they've found . . .'

As Corrie's voice trailed off Annalise turned away. Over the past twenty-four hours no one had mentioned Luke's name in Annalise's hearing and though there was a part of Corrie that wanted to persuade Annalise to talk, another part of her sensed that the pain Annalise had bottled up inside her was so profound that to force her to face it would only be to hurt her all the more.

As bad as this had been for Corrie she couldn't even begin to imagine how it must be for Annalise. To have discovered that the man she loved had so brutally murdered five women; and somehow contrived to have an innocent man arrested, and had all this time been terrorizing her own father while sleeping with her mother was too enormous to comprehend. Yet did Annalise still love him, Corrie wondered. Even after everything? Maybe she did and that was why she couldn't bring herself to speak about him. Perhaps, added to her pain was a shame so deep and so torturous that she couldn't admit to it even to herself. But if she could, if Corrie was only able to reach her . . .

Corrie's eyes suddenly moved back to Annalise. Perhaps there was a way. Perhaps if she could get Annalise as far away from this nightmare as possible, somewhere where she would no longer feel the oppressive presence of the police nor the constant threat of danger . . . If she could persuade Annalise to come to France with her where both she and Cristos could take care of her, maybe then Annalise would let go. If she didn't, and the police didn't catch up with Luke soon, then Corrie was very much afraid of what this unbearable strain would do to Annalise.

'If I go to Cristos,' Corrie said quietly, watching Annalise as she pulled a curtain to one side to look out at the police, 'would you come with me?'

Annalise's eyes widened as she turned back to Corrie. 'Yes,' she said. 'Yes, I'll come with you.'

Corrie's face broke into a smile. 'I'll get on the phone to Radcliffe right now then, shall I?'

'He'll never let us go.'

'I'll make him. I don't know how, but I'll think of something . . .'

'No, stop,' Annalise said as Corrie started to dial. 'Don't call him. Not from here. Call him from the airport, after we've bought the tickets. Just *tell* him we're going . . . He won't be able to stop us.'

'I think he will,' Corrie said, pulling a face. 'But you're right, maybe we should do it from the airport. It'll seem a bit more of a *fait accompli* from there. Of course he'll know what we're up to before we even get to Heathrow. The police outside will want to know where we're going the minute we walk out of the door. Still it's worth a shot . . .'

'Shall we pack?' Annalise said, the ghost of a sparkle lighting the depths of her eyes.

Corrie nodded. 'Yes, let's do that,' she said. 'After we've reserved the tickets.'

When Corrie and Annalise arrived at Heathrow airport, with their police escort, they went straight to pick up their tickets then made for the telephone booths. Annalise was calling Phillip while Corrie tried to get through to Cristos. He wasn't there, but Jeannie was.

'Gee, Corrie,' Jeannie exclaimed, 'you don't know how glad he'll be to hear you're on your way. I'll get right onto him.'

'Will he pick us up from the airport?' Corrie asked.

'Sure he will. If he can't, I'll make sure someone does. Hell, I'll come myself.'

Then, with DC Fulton at her elbow Corrie called Radcliffe.

When DI Radcliffe put the phone down to Corrie he looked across his desk at DC Archer who had been listening in to the call.

'Our lads are out there at the airport, sir,' Archer said, 'shall I get them to bring her in?'

Radcliffe took a deep breath and let it out slowly.

'I think it would be wise, sir.'

'You're right,' Radcliffe said. 'But what am I supposed to do, arrest them? Corrie wants to get out there for that festival.'

'Yes, I know, sir.'

'Then hell, let her go. She's told us all she can, they both have, and they'll be safe enough with Bennati; apart from anything else the damned press are following him wherever he goes – and there's no way Fitzpatrick can get out of this country. We'll fly them back as soon as the awards have been announced. Now, I want you to tell me that some clever-dick on this force has discovered where Fitzpatrick is hiding himself.'

'I wish I could, guv,' Archer said mournfully.

'Well someone's got to know where the hell he is,' Radcliffe declared. 'Corrie Browne walked into this station more than twenty-four hours ago now . . .'

'We've managed to locate the cab driver who picked her up after she escaped,' Archer offered. 'He's on his way over.'

'Good. Any leads yet on the whereabouts of this Siobhan?'

'We're still working on it, sir.'

Radcliffe's lips pursed thoughtfully, as shaking his head he turned his eyes to the window. 'Why is it I get the feeling that the bastard's out there somewhere just biding his time?' he muttered angrily under his breath. 'He's not on the run, he's waiting. And he's waiting for Corrie Browne. So just what the fuck is it that he wants with her? And what in Christ's name did he mean when he told her that he had to deal with Annalise?' He looked up and his eyes were narrowed with intent as he looked at Archer. 'I've got to find him, Ruth, you know that don't you? I've *got* to find the bastard.'

Archer stared helplessly back at his taut face. She knew, as well as Radcliffe did, that it wasn't only his concern for Corrie and Annalise that was driving him now. It was the fact that since Corrie had gone missing his job had been well and truly on the line. As yet not every detail of the case had reached upstairs – like how Corrie Browne herself had tried to warn them about Fitzpatrick all those months ago – but when the top brass found out, and they most certainly would, the shit was sure going to hit the fan. And the added fact that Fitzpatrick was a personal friend of Radcliffe's was going to make matters a whole lot worse.

Both Archer and Radcliffe knew that nothing short of an arrest within the next few hours was going to save Radcliffe's skin now, and the likelihood of that was so minimal as to be virtually non-existent, for it seemed that no one in the world, with the exception of Fitzpatrick himself, knew where he was – or what he was planning to do.

His hands were unsteady as he picked up the parcel beside him. The anger was receding now, coiling back into his gut like an exhausted snake, though lingering remnants of its venom were still poisoning his brain and he took great gulps of air in an effort to cleanse every cell. Tears continued to leak from his eyes – his grief was total, his heart so filled with it that the weight stooped his shoulders.

It was all coming to an end. He was on the point of losing himself for ever, and there was nothing he could do to stop it. He'd tried for so long to fight it, but the moments for himself had become so few, the moments when he yearned for Corrie – like now.

He hadn't made her understand, she hadn't given him the chance and now there was nothing more he could do. The rage was rooted inside him, invading every part of him, eclipsing his mind and governing all that he did. It had crippled him, violated him, and now finally it was obliterating him completely. She might have stopped it, she might have reached out to him and eased the chaos, but she hadn't.

Suddenly he giggled, the sound bursting from his mouth like the discordant cry of a trapped animal. He would die soon, very soon, and he would take Corrie with him. No one could part them then, and in death she would heal his wounds; she would piece together his shattered heart and make him whole again, the way he'd wanted her to in life. She would be his salvation, she would comfort him for all of eternity.

But how could he go before he had released Siobhan?

His precious, darling Siobhan. Her torment was his and his, hers. Only they shared the pain – the pain no one would ever understand. Siobhan had to die, he must do that for her before he left this world. But he couldn't get to her now, there was nothing he could do to free her from her living hell. He'd tried, so many times before, but none of them were Siobhan. To kill those who were like her wasn't enough.

The parcel was open now and as he lifted out the contents he turned to himself in the mirror. His deathly pallor was striped with bands of sunlight, his eyes were red and swollen and saliva foamed at the corners of his mouth. It needn't have been like this – if Corrie had only listened to him, if she'd loved him, she could have saved him. He was going to tell her, he would have told her that day, but when he'd got there she had gone. He'd known then, at the very instant he'd seen the broken panels, that it was over for him.

At first his despair had drowned even the rage. Why had she gone? Why hadn't she understood how much he needed her? Why hadn't she heard his silent cries for help? Of all of them she was the only one who could have saved him. Perhaps, if she'd loved him, she could have saved them all. But it was too late now, she had gone, and as he had knelt there in the rain-spattered street, hunching over the jagged debris of the panels, the monstrous rage had started to slither through his veins.

There had been no time then to go for Annalise, no time to do anything but come here and wait for Corrie. This was where she would come because this was where Bennati was.

And now she was on her way. She would be here soon and she was bringing Annalise with her. His heart contracted as he saw Annalise's face in his mind's eye. How he had hurt her, how he had damaged her – she had tried to kill herself because of what he had done, but they had saved her. No matter, he would end it for her himself. She wouldn't have to live her life the way Siobhan was living hers – oh no, he wouldn't do that to Annalise. He would finish it, the way he should have finished it for Siobhan.

His head dropped as the sobs started to curl agonizingly through his ribs. Would he find the courage for it? Would he be able to end her misery, when like Siobhan, he loved her so much? Annalise, Siobhan, it was so hard to distinguish one from the other now. All he knew was that Corrie stood aloof from it all, untainted by the tragedy, so pure, so caring that in life or in death she would be his salvation.

The plane would land soon, he must go. This wouldn't be easy, so many people to recognize him. But the disguise was there, lying on the table in front of him.

He took one last look at his face in the mirror, knowing that he would probably never see himself again. He'd thought, long ago, that the real bastard was dead. They'd told him he was dead, but they were wrong, he was still alive – Octavia had shown him that. Octavia had shown him that he was the bastard. The same blood ran in his veins, the same perversion tainted his mind. He'd done all that the bastard had done, and worse. He was ruled by the bastard so he was the bastard. And now he would give in to it totally, he would become the man he feared and despised, it was the only way he would be able to find the courage to do what he must.

His last prayer, as his mind started to sink into darkness, was that before setting them all free, God would spare him from harming either Annalise or Corrie the way he had Siobhan.

– 27 –

Radcliffe had spent the past hour in Deptford where the cab driver had picked up Corrie. Just before he'd arrived they had located the garage where Fitzpatrick had been holding her and Radcliffe, still sick to his stomach at what he had seen inside, was now making his way back up the stairs to his office. As he slumped into his chair Archer, who was at her desk in the CID office, put down the telephone and went through.

'There was human hair, teeth, skin all over the place,' he said, as she closed the door. 'And rabbits' carcasses.' He looked up. 'What does it mean, Ruth? What the hell do those rabbits mean?'

Archer shook her head. 'Sir . . .' she began.

'Have Corrie and Annalise arrived in France yet?' he interrupted.

'I was just about . . .'

'I shouldn't have let them go,' Radcliffe went on. 'I want them back here. Tonight. We're going to have to spring a trap for Fitzpatrick, and we'll have to use Corrie Browne . . .'

'I'm sorry, guv,' Archer said, 'but I think it's too late for that.'

There was a sudden swirling queasiness in Radcliffe's gut as he looked back at Archer.

'I've just had Cristos Bennati on the phone,' Archer explained. 'Corrie and Annalise haven't . . . Well, we don't know where they are, sir.'

'What do you mean you don't know where they are?' Radcliffe hissed. 'That plane took off over three hours ago with them on board. Bob Parker called in to confirm it.'

'Yes, sir. I've checked with Air France too, they were definitely on the flight. But as yet we haven't found anyone who saw them get off it.'

'Well they sure as hell didn't sprout wings,' Radcliffe roared. 'So how the fuck could they not get off at the other end?'

'I don't know, sir. Bennati said he waited. He checked with Air France too and got the same answer as I did.

They were on the flight. Bennati assumed he must have missed them in the crowds at Nice airport and that they had got a taxi to his hotel. But they haven't shown up there either, sir.'

'This isn't possible,' Radcliffe muttered. 'It just isn't fucking possible. He couldn't have got out of this country.'

'I've been thinking about that, sir,' Archer replied.

Radcliffe glared up at her. 'Go on,' he said tightly.

'Well, maybe he went before we put a stop on all the air and ferry ports,' she said. 'I mean, he could have gone as soon as he found that Corrie Browne had escaped. He'd have only had an hour or so to do it, but . . .' She shrugged. 'It's just a suggestion, sir.'

'But why would he have gone to France?' Radcliffe snapped. 'Because Bennati is there,' he added, answering his own question.

'Yes sir. He'd know that as soon as she could Corrie would go to Bennati. It's my guess that Fitzpatrick's been there all the time, checking with the airlines just waiting for her to arrive.'

'Well if you're so damned fucking clever,' Radcliffe thundered, 'then how the hell did he get them out of that airport when Bennati himself was standing right there?'

'Bennati, and half the world's press, sir,' Archer corrected him. 'It was chaos at Nice airport when that flight got in, Bennati said. He said too that he was called to the telephone but there was no one at the other end.'

'And just what is Bennati reading into that?' Radcliffe demanded.

'Very likely the same as you are, sir. That it was Fitzpatrick who had called him to the phone in order to get him out of the way.'

'And then what?' Radcliffe seethed. 'Are you seriously asking me to believe that Luke Fitzpatrick walked up to Corrie Browne and Annalise Kapsakis in the middle of Nice airport and offered them a ride into Cannes and they, after all that has happened, said yes please Luke, thank you very much Luke?'

'No, sir.'

'Then what, sir?'

'I'm afraid I don't know, sir.'

'No, nobody fucking knows do they?' Radcliffe cried, burying his face in his hands. 'I just don't believe it. I take it you've informed the French police?'

'Colin's doing that now, sir. But all this is only surmise, sir. It could be that . . .'

She jumped as Radcliffe's chair crashed back against the wall as he leapt to his feet and stormed through to the CID office, shouting at Archer to get him on the next flight to Nice.

'Which one of you fucking morons speaks French?' he roared.

Everyone looked blank.

'Jesus God!' he seethed. 'Then find someone who fucking well does . . .'

'Don't you think we might be jumping the gun, sir,' Archer interrupted. 'I mean they still might turn up. They could have just stopped off to do some shopping . . .'

'He's got them, Archer! You know it, I know it and any minute now the whole fucking world is going to know it. So every one of you better start saying your prayers that those two girls don't turn up on the shores of the Mediterranean in the same state as those prostitutes turned up on the Thames, 'cos if they do . . .'

He didn't finish his sentence because he couldn't. But everyone present knew that whatever happened to Corrie and Annalise now he, Radcliffe, was going to be every bit as responsible as Luke Fitzpatrick. He had bungled this case, he had bungled it so badly that two young women were very likely going to lose their lives because of it.

When Annalise and Corrie had first got into the taxi at

Nice airport Corrie's excitement had been so intense she was on the point of erupting. She could hardly believe that in less than an hour she would be with Cristos. That after the nightmare of the past five days she was at last going to be able to tell him she loved him. A powerful longing had surged through her then as she thought of the way he would kiss her once she'd said it, of his arms encircling her as he pulled her to him, and the tell-tale hardness of his body as it pressed against hers. Would they make love straight away, she'd wondered. Please God they would for once she saw him she knew she wouldn't be able to hold out for long.

Now, an hour and a half after leaving the airport as they weaved through the sun-dazzled French countryside with its dramatic hilltop views of Provençal villages and tantalizing glimpses of the Mediterranean, she was uneasily searching the road signs for any mention of Cannes. So far there had been none.

She didn't know the geography of the Riveria too well, but she did know that Cannes was west of Nice. So why was it that the sea was to their right? She'd already asked the taxi driver that once, but he hadn't understood what she was saying.

She cast her mind nervously back over their arrival at Nice airport. When they'd reached the arrivals lounge it was to find it teeming with press – most every international flight that day was bringing in stars for the festival.

Corrie had scanned the impenetrable mass of faces, then groaned in dismay as she heard someone shout, 'Hey! It's Corrie Browne! Bennati's woman!'

There was a sudden scuffle as all eyes and lenses were directed to Corrie and Annalise, then a British journalist threw himself through the mayhem onto the bar which separated the arriving passengers from the unruly throng. 'Corrie! Corrie!' he yelled. 'Are you here to see Bennati?'

'Oh, no!' Corrie muttered, as the flash bulbs started to pop. 'How on earth are we going to find him in this chaos?'

Her voice was virtually drowned in an airport announcement. Since it was delivered in French neither Corrie nor Annalise understood it.

'Did she say Bennati?' Corrie asked, staggering against Annalise as someone jostled past them. 'I swear she said Bennati.'

'I don't know,' Annalise answered. 'I couldn't hear.'

Corrie peered into the sea of faces again, great splodges of white in front of her eyes from the plethora of flash bulbs still exploding all around her. 'Where is he?' she murmured impatiently.

'Look, over there,' Annalise cried, grabbing Corrie's arm. 'There's a card with your name on it.'

They pushed their way towards the man with the card to find that he spoke no English. However, he gestured for them to go down the steps to their left and elbowing his way through the crowd he kept alongside them until they were out into the lower body of the airport terminal. Using an elaborate form of sign language he explained that the taxi was outside, and in answer to the question did Mr Bennati send him, '*Oui, oui*, Monsieur Bennati.' Then he growled furiously at the journalists who were trying to separate him from Corrie and Annalise, and taking them by their arms he led them outside.

'*Oui, d'accord*,' he smiled happily when Corrie told him the name of Cristos's hotel. '*Monsieur m'a dit. Le Majestic, à Cannes.*'

They should have been there long before now, Corrie was thinking to herself, so what in heaven's name was this taxi-driver up to?

What Bernard Lebrec was doing was following the instructions of the man who had approached him at the airport with five thousand francs and a card with Corrie's name written on it. The man, with shoulder-length black hair, a greying moustache and dark glasses, had introduced himself as Monsieur Bennati and his instructions had been concise; he, Bernard, was to let them think they were going to the hotel in Cannes, but in fact he was to take them into the countryside where he was to double back on himself to the address he was being handed now. He was to take his time over the journey in order to give the man time to get to the destination first. Monsieur Bennati had then explained that he'd bought a villa for his wife and he wanted it to be a surprise.

Deciding that Monsieur Bennati had now had more than sufficient time to get himself from Nice to Cap Ferrat, Bernard Lebrec started to head along the Cap himself, until he reached the address he had been given. As he brought his taxi to a stop in front of a set of vast black iron gates Corrie immediately leaned forward in her seat, saying,

'*Non, non.* We want *L'Hotel Majestic,* in *Cannes.*'

Bernard's reply was in French. The only words Corrie could understand were Monsieur and surprise.

'What's he saying?' she asked, turning nervously to Annalise.

Annalise shook her head, clearly as unsettled as Corrie was.

In the rearview mirror Corrie could see the delight in the driver's face as the gates started to slide open and they made their way up a steep slope through a short avenue of overhanging olive trees. She looked up ahead, able to see the shuttered windows of the white, palatial villa set against the sapphire blue sky and surrounded by majestically soaring palms. They emerged from the sunlight dappled shadows to the foot of a wide oval lawn where small weeping trees bowed over marble statues and fountains. The drive circled around the lawn, and as they veered off to the right, arcing round to the front steps of the villa Corrie became very still.

'I don't like this,' she murmured to Annalise.

'Didn't the driver say something about a surprise?' Annalise answered. But Corrie could sense that Annalise was as tense as she was.

'*Voilà. On est arrivé!*' the driver declared, pulling the car to a halt at the villa's front steps. '*Mesdames, Monsieur vous att . . .*' His voice faltered as he realized that the man standing at the top of the steps wasn't the man who had approached him at the airport.

Corrie looked up and when she saw who was standing there it was as though her heart was being ripped apart by shock and disbelief. 'Drive on,' she screamed to the driver. 'Drive on!'

With profound astonishment, yet automatic reaction, Bernard kicked down the accelerator and roared off around the lawn. Annalise was clinging to Corrie. Corrie, her eyes wild with fright, was sitting on the edge of her seat staring straight ahead and asking herself how this could be happening.

'Oh no!' she cried suddenly. 'No! No! No!' The gates were firmly shut – there was no way out.

'Oh my God!' she gasped, spinning round to look out of the back window as the car stopped. 'Please! Do something! You have to get us away from him!'

Annalise suddenly screamed and buried her head in Corrie's lap. Corrie swung round to see Luke opening the passenger door of the car. Then it was as if the entire world suddenly decelerated into a nightmare of horrific and vivid slow-motion, as ribbons of blood plastered themselves to the windscreen and a fibrous grey substance coated a viscous fountain over Annalise's hair and Corrie's hands.

As the reverberations of the explosion ebbed into the afternoon stillness Corrie's eyes were transfixed by the gun in Luke's hand. He had just blown out the taxi-driver's brains.

Cristos was waiting at the airport with the Sûreté when the next flight came in from London, bringing DI Radcliffe, DC Archer and Phillip Denby. The first moments the two police inspectors came face to face threatened to erupt into pandemonium as both started to shout and neither understood the other. In the end Cristos barked them to silence, and provided the interpretation.

'I don't fucking believe it!' Radcliffe snapped, when Cristos had finished. 'The man's not a fucking magician, he can't just make two grown women vanish into thin air. I take it you've checked your hotel again . . .'

'Of course I have,' Cristos snapped back.

'So how the hell did he get them out of the airport?'

'What does it matter how he got them out, the fact is he did,' Phillip interjected. 'So what are we doing about finding them?'

Radcliffe eyed him nastily. 'How he got them out of the airport matters,' he said. Then turning back to Cristos. 'Ask this frog here what enquiries they've started making.'

'I can answer that for you,' Cristos said. 'They're pulling in all taxi-drivers and hire-car clerks. The crew who flew in on the Air France flight have been detained here at the airport. The Sûreté are right now alerting all TV and radio stations, they've already spoken to the press that are here, and they've wired back to London for photographs.'

'Do the flight crew speak English?'

'As far as I know.'

'Good. Then I'll question them myself. Now, I suggest you return to your hotel in case they do turn up there – take Mr Denby with you, and I'll get to work here. Though how the hell I'm going to make frog-plod understand me, God alone knows.'

As Radcliffe made to turn away Cristos caught his arm and pulled him to one side. 'Why the hell did you let her come?' he asked tightly.

'What?' Radcliffe hissed incredulously. '*You're* asking *me*?'

'You're damned right I'm asking you. I called your office and told someone there to stop her. I was gonna come over there myself tomorrow . . . I didn't want her out of police protection.'

'Then why the fuck didn't you stop her yourself? You knew she was coming . . .'

'She didn't speak to me, she spoke to my assistant. I got right on the phone the minute I knew to tell you to stop her.'

Radcliffe was about to deliver a boiling response when Phillip stepped between them. 'I don't see any point in going over this now,' he said. Let's concentrate on what really matters, shall we?'

Both Cristos and Radcliffe glared at him. Phillip smiled awkwardly, then to Cristos he said, 'I'd like to know what our chances are of finding them. Would you mind interpreting that to the French Inspector . . .'

'He doesn't have to,' Radcliffe interrupted, with blatant hostility, 'I can answer it for you. Our chances at this moment in time are piss poor. France is a big place, Italy is just round the corner. They could be anywhere. What we've got to do is find a lead, like how they got out of this fucking airport. Without it we're up shit creek.'

The second floor veranda, jutting in an expansive semicircle from the back of the villa, was a forest of bougainvillaea, cacti and geraniums. Trailing lobelias coiled a formless route across the white trellis which clung to the exterior walls of the house and a symmetrical array of miniature palms stood like sentries around the sweep of the waist high stone wall. The view out over the sapphire-blue sea, where rich men's yachts glittered in the sunlight, was stupendous and unlimited.

Corrie was seated on a white wooden bench just in front of the sliding glass doors which separated the veranda from the garishly ornate lounge inside. Next to her was a massive wrought iron table to which her feet were tied, but her hands, her mouth and her eyes were unencumbered. Annalise was lying on a hammock chair, her lovely blonde hair tumbling over the edge and her emaciated limbs exposed mercilessly to the sun's searing rays. She was attached to the chair by a rope coiled around her neck.

They had seen almost nothing of Luke since the afternoon before when he'd led them from the taxi back to the house. In those few minutes he had walked silently behind them, only snorting when Annalise had stumbled against Corrie and Corrie had supported her in through the door. He had then gestured for them to go up the stairs, where he had left them in a bedroom, locking the door behind him.

Annalise was so traumatized by the killing of the taxi-driver that she could barely hold herself up, so Corrie had taken her to the shower and sponged the blood and gore from her body, her own still quaking with shock.

At odd intervals throughout the night Luke had returned to the door – Corrie had heard the key grating in the lock, but he didn't come in. Once or twice he yelled out to her that it was all her fault, that she could have helped him, but she'd run away.

'But you'll never run away again,' he cried. 'You're going to save me now, Corrie. You're going to be with me forever.'

Then, just before dawn she had heard him downstairs shouting. Neither she nor Annalise could make out what he was saying, but the agony in his voice was as terrifying as the mocking Irish tones.

He had finally come into the room an hour or so ago now, and made them strip to their underwear. That was when he had put the noose around Annalise's neck. He had looked at Corrie then and somewhere deep in the confusion in his eyes Corrie had sensed a desperation that, despite her fear, had wrenched at her heart.

'Luke,' she said, taking a step towards him, but almost

instantly her arms came up to defend herself as he swung the gun towards her.

'Keep away,' he snarled, and turning to Annalise he pushed her to the floor, keeping hold of the rope like it was a leash. 'You be coming along too now,' he growled at Corrie.

Appalled, Corrie had watched, unable to do anything to stop him as he proceeded to make Annalise crawl on all fours out to the veranda where he had pushed her face into a bowl and made her drink like a dog.

'This,' he hissed back over his shoulder to Corrie, 'is what the bastard did to Siobhan.'

Now, as a gentle breeze rustled the palm fronds, Corrie looked over at Annalise. At that moment the sliding doors opened and Luke walked out onto the veranda.

Corrie looked up at him. His eyes reflected all the torment inside him, but as he gazed down at her she could see that he was unreachable. It was as though he had lost all sense of where, or even who, he was. He lowered his eyes to the gun and started to turn it over in his hand.

'Where did you get it?' Corrie asked quietly.

He looked up in surprise, then smiled. 'Paranoid wealthy Americans. They all keep guns,' he sneered.

Long minutes ticked by, the air so still there might have been no world beyond that terrace.

'Do you intend to use it on us?' Corrie eventually asked.

Annalise whimpered and turned her face into the back of the chair. From Luke there was no response at all.

As the silence moved through an indeterminable time the sun grew hotter and the strain so acute Corrie could feel herself becoming consumed by it. Suddenly she couldn't stand any more. 'What are you waiting for?' she yelled. 'Why don't you just put us out of our misery?'

'Corrie, don't!' Annalise sobbed.

Unruffled by the outburst, Luke sighed and shook his head. 'I don't want to kill you,' he murmured. 'I don't want to do it.' Suddenly his head came up and his grin was obscene. 'Will you be getting hungry now?' he asked.

Annalise turned her frightened eyes to Corrie.

'The police know that you killed the prostitutes,' Corrie said, ignoring his question.

Luke blinked and looked out at the horizon.

Corrie closed her eyes as she thought of the bitter ironies. Of how the prostitutes themselves had chosen TW to support their cause. Of how Luke had interviewed Radcliffe the day Bobby McIver was arrested. Her head came up.

'Who's Bobby McIver?' she asked.

Luke reached out for one of the palms and ran a finger along the spiky leaves. 'My only friend,' he answered.

The heat, the tension, his constantly changing voice was making Corrie's head spin.

'He'd do anything for me,' Luke continued. 'All the other kids tormented and teased him. I was kind to him. He was devoted to me.'

'So devoted that he agreed to take the blame for what you've done?'

'He'll die before he tells them anything. I know he will.'

'But how can you let him . . . ?'

'Does it matter? Does anything matter now?' He took a deep breath. 'I've been setting things in order,' he said. 'I have to make sure that Siobhan is taken care of after I'm gone, you see.'

'Oh God help us,' Annalise moaned, covering her face with her hands.

'Who is Siobhan?' Corrie asked.

Luke blinked, then seemed frozen in a moment of confusion as he looked at Annalise. 'Why to be sure she's lying right there,' he answered.

'But that's not Siobhan. That's Annalise . . .'

'You'll not be fooling me now,' he growled. ''Tis Siobhan right there.'

'No!' Corrie cried. 'Luke, please, listen to me. That's Annalise there. So tell me, who is Siobhan?'

'She's his sister!' Annalise sobbed. 'Siobhan is his sister.'

Luke's head jerked back, as though someone had struck him. Then suddenly he was moving towards Annalise.

'Don't touch me!' she shrieked, cowering back in the chair. 'Keep away from me!'

A mask of feral rage dropped over Luke's face as he grabbed her by the throat.

'Luke! Stop!' Corrie yelled, struggling to break free of the rope.

He spun round. 'And who are you to be giving me orders?' he snarled, thrusting Annalise back on the chair and advancing on Corrie. 'Just who will you be thinking you are to tell me what to do?'

Corrie was pressed hard into a corner of the bench, her head strained back away from him, her whole body shaking with fear. 'Don't hurt her,' she pleaded.

'Why?' he rasped. 'Why shouldn't I hurt her? She's mine to do with as I please. She's mine, do you hear? *Mine!* She's nothing to do with you . . .'

'Luke, stop it, please!' Corrie sobbed.

'Stop it! Stop it!' he shrieked, mimicking her. 'It's too late for that now, Corrie. It's too late to be . . .' He stopped suddenly and cocked his head thoughtfully to one side. Then a strange, knowing smile twisted across his mouth as he turned once again to Annalise.

'You haven't told her, have you?' he said. 'She's not knowing who . . .'

'Shut up!' Annalise seethed. 'Just shut up!'

Luke sniggered and went to sit on the chair with Annalise. For a moment or two he was still, then looking down at her legs he lifted a hand and placed it on her thigh. Annalise recoiled so violently that the chair almost tipped over.

'Don't touch me!' she screeched. 'Don't ever touch me

again or I swear I'll kill you!' Her eyes were gleaming so wildly she looked half deranged, and her fingers were bent like claws ready to attack.

'It'll be rabbit stew for you tonight, now,' he taunted her, picking up the bowl from the floor. 'I'll be serving it to you, right here in your dish and you'll be eating every mouthful now, won't you?'

Annalise's eyes darted to Corrie, and Luke seized the moment to lunge at her. As his full weight hit her Annalise grunted with the pain. He had her arms pinned between their bodies, his legs hooked around hers – she couldn't move. Then his hands slipped around her throat and he started to squeeze the life from her.

Corrie was screaming for him to stop while scrabbling frantically with the knots at her ankles.

'Tell me you'll fuck me and I'll let you go,' Luke seethed into Annalise's face. 'Tell me you want my cock, tell me it's all you ever want . . .'

'Tell him! For Christ's sake, tell him!' Corrie yelled, but Annalise was lying limply beneath him, all the fight gone from her body. 'Annalise!' Corrie screamed. 'Annalise, for God's sake! He's going to kill you! Just tell him!'

Still there was no response from Annalise, then Corrie saw the way she was staring up into Luke's face. She was so calm, so frighteningly still, that were it not for the expression in her eyes she might already have been dead – and the expression chilled Corrie to the very depths of her soul. It was as though Annalise wanted him to kill her, was waiting, almost longing, for the moment when her life would slip away. But until that moment she was going to gaze into the eyes of the man she had loved, right through to the corrupt and tortured void of his mind and let him feel the fathomless depths of her hatred.

'No!' Corrie cried, clawing helplessly at the knots. 'Annalise, don't do this! Annalise! Listen to me . . .'

But Annalise was intent on fuelling his madness with all the loathing in her heart.

Corrie cried out to her again and again, watching helplessly as she started to choke, as her face turned blue. Even in her panicked state Corrie could sense that in some horrific, inexplicable way, this was a battle of wills – but it was one that Annalise was going to lose.

But Corrie was wrong, and she watched in stupefaction as with an inhuman snarl Luke suddenly wrenched himself away, so abruptly that the chair pitched wildly on its chains.

'I'll be having a much better idea,' he said starting towards Corrie, and taking a knife from his pocket he sliced through her bonds. Instinctively Corrie cowered away from him then cried out as he gouged his fingers into her upper arm and dragged her across the veranda. Screwing her hair in his fist he forced her head down to look at Annalise, who was still struggling to heave the air back into her lungs.

'You be telling me now, is she or is she not a beautiful woman?'

'Yes, she's beautiful,' Corrie gasped, wincing against the pain as she twisted her body to try and get away from him.

Luke laughed. 'Ah, now, that's good to be hearing you say that, 'cos you won't mind getting down there with her and fucking her yourself now, will you?'

Corrie's eyes rounded with horror.

'And what'll be the matter with you?' he said, pulling her round so that his face was almost touching hers.

'Luke, stop this!' Corrie pleaded. 'You don't want us . . .'

'Ah, but I do. It'll be you who doesn't want it now Corrie. Or will you just be pretending? Is it that you don't want her to be knowing how you've lusted after her all these months? How you've dreamed of getting your hands on her body? Or putting your tongue in her . . .'

'Luke, for Christ's . . .' She gasped as his hand cracked

across her face, so hard that she staggered back onto Annalise.

'That's it, you be getting onto the bed with her now,' he snickered. 'Put your hand between her legs.'

'Luke . . .'

'Do it!' He slapped her again, bringing the blood spurting from her nose.

Annalise gasped as though it was she who'd been struck. 'Corrie, please! Just do it,' she begged.

'I can't,' Corrie cried.

'You can, *please*.'

Luke was watching them and grinning. 'Do you want to be telling her why you can't do it?' he said to Corrie.

'Stop it!' Annalise yelled. 'Stop tormenting her like this.'

'Do it, or tell her!' Luke snarled at Corrie. 'You be telling her why it is you can't bring yourself to touch her and she'll be telling you why you can.'

'You're sick!' Corrie hissed up at him. 'You're warped, you're . . .'

'Don't you be speaking to me that way, you filthy cunt,' he raged, and his fist smashed into her face splitting her lips wide open.

'Corrie, for God's sake, do as he tells you,' Annalise cried and grabbing Corrie's hand she thrust it between her legs.

'That'll be it now,' Luke grinned, a lascivious light leaping to his eyes. 'Make her rub you.'

As Corrie coughed and gurgled on the blood in her mouth Annalise moved her hand back and forth over her crotch. Luke leaned forward and yanked down her panties. 'Put her fingers in you,' he growled.

'*No!*' Corrie spluttered, jerking her hand away. 'I won't do it!'

Above them Luke was snorting with laughter. 'Is it the incest that's bothering you now, Corrie?'

Corrie's head fell back against the chair and she turned to look at Annalise.

'But Annalise knows all about incest, isn't that right, Annalise? It's why she tried to kill herself, isn't it m'darling?'

'Shut up!' Annalise yelled. 'Just shut up!'

'Annalise, what is it? Tell me . . .'

For a long moment Annalise's eyes blazed up into Luke's, then turning to look at Corrie she said, 'You're not my sister, Corrie. I know you think you are, but you're not.'

Corrie was so confused she could only shake her head. 'But Phillip . . . Phillip's my father,' she said.

'I know,' Annalise said, and as the enormity of the trauma she had suffered engulfed her she pressed a bunched fist to her mouth as if to keep in the stultifying horror of it. 'I know he is,' she whispered. 'But he's not *my* father.'

'What?' Corrie gasped, then seeing the way Annalise was looking up at Luke Corrie spun round to look at him too. Then, as the paralysis of shock started to creep through her body, it was as though the world was trying to suck her into an abyss of endless horror. 'No,' she breathed, starting to pull away from them both. 'No, I don't believe it.'

'It's true,' Annalise said, 'my own mother told me.'

– 28 –

'Bennati?' Radcliffe said into the phone. 'I think you should get yourself over here. Bring Denby with you.'

'What's happened?'

Radcliffe paused. This wasn't something he could tell Bennati over the phone – but there was something he could. 'The frogs have just informed me that a taxi-driver's been missing since yesterday afternoon,' he said. 'He was last seen taking two women who fit Corrie's and Annalise's descriptions out of the airport.'

'What about Fitzpatrick?'

'No mention, but they're working on it. Anyway, there's someone just flown in from London you and Denby ought to meet.'

'Who?'

'A doctor. He's with the frogs now, but he should be finished by the time you get here. We'll be at my hotel,' and he rang off.

Minutes later Cristos and Phillip roared away from the Majestic Hotel in Cristos's hired Peugeot, heading along the Croisette for the autoroute to Nice. Both men's faces were taut and concentrated on the impossibly dense traffic. Cristos held his hand menacingly on the horn and jumped red lights. Behind them a convoy of press, who had dived into their cars the second Cristos and Phillip had leapt into theirs, were creating even more havoc in their efforts to keep up.

'Shit!' Cristos suddenly muttered under his breath.

'What is it?' Phillip asked.

Cristos shook his head and kicking his foot down hard spun the car into the Boulevard Carnot. What he'd just remembered had no relevance to where they were going. He'd forgotten that he was taking his mother to a screening of *Past Lives Present*. But she'd understand. She knew what all this meant to him, and, to quote her, it was one hell of a lot more than the Palme d'Or meant to her.

An hour later, having been alerted by reception, Radcliffe was waiting at the door of his hotel room when Cristos and Phillip stepped out of the lift.

'What's going on?' Cristos wanted to know. 'Did they find the taxi-driver yet?'

'Not yet,' Radcliffe answered, waving them into his room. 'But they're keeping me posted.'

As Cristos, followed by Phillip, walked into the feature-less room a man in his mid-fifties with a head of glossy silver hair and an ungainly, thin body turned from the terrace where he'd been gazing absently into the cluttered street below.

'Doctor Horowitz, Cristos Bennati, Phillip Denby,' Radcliffe said as Horowitz stepped back into the room.

When the three men had shaken hands and all of them, with the exception of Cristos, were seated, Radcliffe said, 'The doctor here read in the papers that we were looking for Fitzpatrick. He got onto the police in London, now he's here to help. He's got something to tell you that, well . . .'

Cristos frowned as a wave of unmistakable discomfort came over Radcliffe – it was almost as though he was wishing that the doctor hadn't bothered.

'You better tell Mr Denby and Mr Bennati what you told me, doctor,' Radcliffe said lamely.

'Yes,' Horowitz said, and removing his half spectacles he raised his sombre grey eyes to Phillip's. 'You have my deepest sympathy for the strain you are undoubtedly under at this time, sir,' he said in his faintly accented voice. 'I only wish that it were in my power to alleviate your anguish. Unfortunately however, I find myself in the position of having to add to it and must therefore ask you to prepare yourself for a shock.'

Panic burned across Phillip's eyes as they darted between Horowitz and Cristos. If the doctor was condoling with him and him alone then it must be . . . 'Annalise!' he cried, starting to get up. 'What is it? What's happened to her?'

'We still don't know,' Radcliffe said, putting a hand on Phillip's shoulder to steady him. He turned to the doctor, 'Just get it over with,' he murmured.

With a grim smile the doctor nodded. 'I'm afraid, Mr Denby, that Annalise, your youngest daughter . . . Well, I'm afraid, she isn't your daughter.'

'*What?*' Cristos hissed.

'What are you talking about?' Phillip cried. He spun round to Radcliffe. 'What's going on?' he demanded. 'Who is this man? How dare you . . .'

'Please,' Radcliffe interrupted, 'hear him out.'

'No! I'm damned if I'm going to sit here and listen to some quack . . .'

'Denby!' Radcliffe said sternly. 'You're not her father. I know you think you are, but you're not. I'm sorry you've had to find out like this, but you'd have had to sooner or later . . .'

Ashen faced and trembling Phillip turned to Cristos.

'You'd better be able to back this up,' Cristos said to Horowitz, his voice dangerously low.

Horowitz glanced at Radcliffe who turned his head away, making it apparent he wished he was anywhere right now other than where he was. 'Finish it,' Radcliffe muttered into his hand.

Horowitz turned back to Phillip. 'Luke Fitzpatrick is Annalise's natural father,' he said flatly.

Cristos's eyes flew to Phillip.

'You're crazy!' Phillip yelled, leaping to his feet. 'The man's crazy!' he roared to Cristos. 'Get him out of here! Just get him away from me before I . . .'

'Denby!' Radcliffe barked, as Philip lunged towards Horowitz. Like a shot he was between the two men and wrestling Phillip back into his chair.

'What are you trying to do to him?' Cristos shouted at Horowitz. 'The girl's been having an affair with Fitzpatrick for over two years . . .'

'I know,' Horowitz said gravely. 'At least I know it now.'

For several moments the two men looked at each other. Cristos's eyes were blazing hostility, the doctor's were a sorrowful insistence of the truth. In the end the doctor stared Cristos down and clasping a hand to his head Cristos turned away. 'I don't believe this,' he muttered. 'I just don't fucking believe it!'

'Would you like some brandy, Mr Denby?' Radcliffe was saying, shaking Phillip's arm. 'Shall I get you something from the bar?'

Phillip was slumped in his chair, his stark white face an effigy of the deepest and most painful confusion. It was as though someone had struck him a death blow and he couldn't work out why it was he was still alive.

'We have brandy right here in the room,' Radcliffe persisted.

'Just get it!' Cristos snapped.

As Radcliffe crossed the room to the mini-bar Horowitz went to Phillip and putting a hand on his arm said, 'I'm sorry, Mr Denby. I'm truly very sorry.'

Phillip blinked, but whether he had heard the words there was no way of telling. He seemed to be lost, floundering in a despair the like of which Cristos couldn't even begin to imagine. However, it revived him a little when, taking the brandy from Radcliffe, Cristos put it to his lips.

'Thanks,' Phillip whispered, taking the glass from Cristos. He tried to make himself smile, but his lips merely contorted in a grimace of bewilderment and pain.

'We don't have to go on with this,' Cristos said, squeezing his shoulder. 'If you want some time . . .'

Phillip shook his head. 'No, I think we'd better hear it. After all, there could be some mistake. I mean, I was there when Annalise was born. I saw her come into the world . . .' It was only then, as Phillip and Cristos looked at each other, that it seemed to occur to either of them that Octavia . . .

'She can't have,' Phillip said, his eyes steeping with horror. He turned to Horowitz. 'No, you see, there *is* a mistake. My wife has always known about Annalise and Luke's affair, she wouldn't have let it continue . . . Jesus Christ! She'd never have let it start if Luke was Annalise's father.'

'I'm afraid, Mr Denby,' Horowitz said soberly, 'that that is precisely what she did do.'

Cristos stared at him aghast. 'Are you saying that Annalise's own mother allowed her to have an affair with Fitzpatrick, *knowing* that she was Fitzpatrick's daughter?'

'Yes, Mr Bennati, that is what I'm saying.'

Cristos turned back to Phillip who was holding his head in his hands. 'What kind of woman are you married to?' Cristos muttered incredulously. 'What kind of fucking mother is she?'

Phillip didn't answer, but no one expected him to. What Octavia had done was beyond any words he could find, that anyone could find.

'Does Annalise know?' Cristos asked Horowitz.

'I don't know,' he answered. 'I wouldn't imagine . . .'

'I think she knows,' Phillip interrupted, and as they all turned to look at him they saw tears pushing their way through his fingers. 'It would explain why she tried to kill herself,' he went on, his voice slurred with emotion. 'It would explain why she's been the way she has since – with her mother and with Luke.'

'Oh Christ,' Cristos murmured.

'I think,' Phillip said, pulling his head up and looking at Horowitz with wide, haunted eyes, 'that you'd better start from the beginning.'

'Yes, of course,' Horowitz said. When he returned to his chair he looked up at Radcliffe and Cristos, as though asking them to sit too. Radcliffe did, but Cristos walked to the window, sliding it closed to drown out the sounds of the traffic.

'I have known Luke Fitzpatrick for some years,' Horowitz began when Cristos turned and leaned his shoulders against the window. 'I have his sister, Siobhan Fitzpatrick, in my clinic.'

'Siobhan?' Phillip interrupted.

'You've heard of her?' Horowitz stated in evident surprise.

Phillip nodded. 'He's rambled about her, we've never known who she was. We didn't know he had a sister.'

'Not many people do,' Horowitz said. 'She's been with me since 1985, when Fitzpatrick first brought her to England, before that she was in a private clinic in Ireland. Fitzpatrick never talks about her, at least I didn't think he did, he never wanted anyone to know.'

'To know what?' Cristos asked when Horowitz paused.

Horowitz glanced at Radcliffe. 'Siobhan Fitzpatrick,' he said, turning back to Phillip and Cristos, 'to all intents and purposes, died over twenty years ago.'

Cristos and Phillip stared at him.

'She died inside,' Horowitz explained, 'because she could no longer face her life. You see, both she and Luke . . .' He took a deep breath. 'Siobhan and Luke were the victims of some of the worst child abuse it has ever been my misfortune to encounter.'

Both Cristos and Phillip looked stunned – this was the last thing either of them had expected to hear.

'What happened to them as children only Luke has been able to tell me,' Horowitz continued, 'Siobhan no longer speaks. Their father, the main perpetrator of the abuse, served a jail sentence for his crimes – he was released in 1985, which was when Luke brought Siobhan to me. The old man is dead now, he died that same year.'

'What about Luke's brothers?' Phillip asked.

Horowitz shook his head. 'He has no brothers. There is only Luke and Siobhan. They grew up on their parents' remote farm in Southern Ireland. Luke is eight years older than his sister, and as far as he can remember there was no abuse before Siobhan was born. It started, he thinks, when Siobhan was around five years old. He can't be sure about her age, all he remembers is that she was very small when he one day caught his father touching her in a way Luke knew wasn't right. When Luke tried to pull Siobhan away his father turned on him and thrashed him until he all but lost consciousness. After that the beatings became increasingly regular – it was something his father enjoyed,

Luke could sense that even then, but the memory that lives most vividly in Luke's mind is that of his mother standing by and watching.

'Very quickly Siobhan too became a victim of their father's violence and their undeserved punishments almost always occurred when the children were tied up with no means of defending themselves. They were tethered in the yard for days on end with leashes around their necks as though they were dogs. They were kept hungry all that time, being given only bowls of water from which they had to drink, again like animals. At the end of it they were forced into the most abhorrent forms of sexual relations with their father in order to eat. Their mother, I think, was too afraid of her husband to intervene, or even to stop him when he forced Luke to have sexual intercourse with her and with Siobhan. This would be anal, as well as vaginal intercourse. During these acts Phillip Fitzpatrick . . .' He paused as Phillip's eyes flickered at the mention of his own name. 'Yes, it is relevant,' Horowitz told him, 'but we will come to it later. To continue . . . During these acts of intercourse Phillip Fitzpatrick would make either his wife or his daughter beg Luke to continue, using language which I don't care much to repeat. Suffice it to say that every obscenity known to Phillip Fitzpatrick was passed on to his children – and the words hit a primal instinct in Luke which, despite his terror and revulsion, brought about an almost feral excitement thus enabling him to perform the degrading acts his father demanded of him. During my sessions with Luke he has told me that it is still often necessary for him, even now, to hear a woman say those words in order for him to be able to make love to her.

'Luke endured this abominable state of affairs until he was sixteen, when he ran away. He went to England, to London. In a city that size he was certain his father would never find him. He got himself a job as a porter at the Savoy – he was a good looking boy, with, despite all that had happened to him, plenty of Irish charm, which was probably what secured him the position. It was without a doubt what gained him the attention of a certain lady who was then residing at the hotel while her London house was being renovated. Her name doesn't matter, Luke professes not to remember it anyway, but what he does remember is the life this woman, who was at least thirty years his senior, introduced him to. It was the life of London's high society – theatre opening nights, royal premieres, charity balls, Ascot, Glyndebourne and so on. They flew off on expensive holidays together to some of the world's more exotic locations, and when she eventually moved back to her own home in Belgravia, she moved Luke in with her. She sent him to elocution lessons to smooth over his Irish accent and a journalism course to improve his mind. She spent the equivalent of a small fortune, dressing him and grooming him . . . and parading him proudly in front of her friends at their exclusive parties. It was at one of these parties that he met the twenty-three-year-old Octavia Farrington Denby.'

As Horowitz stopped Cristos and Radcliffe turned to look at Phillip, but his face was inscrutable. 'Go on,' he said quietly.

'Well, according to Luke,' Horowitz continued, 'he and Octavia were attracted to each other instantly. He didn't know she was married then, but admits that even if he had it wouldn't have stopped him. Whether or not you were at the party yourself, Mr Denby, I imagine is a matter of irrelevance if, what Luke has told me about your wife, is true.'

'Which is?'

Horowitz ran a finger around his collar looking, for the first time, uncomfortable. 'I think,' he said, 'that your wife's morals are perhaps not . . .'

'I think we have already established the fact that my wife has no morals,' Phillip interjected tightly. 'And do let me assure you, doctor, that nothing you can tell me about her promiscuity will surprise me.'

'I see,' Horowitz said flatly. 'Well, so Luke tells me, he and your wife had sexual relations that night in the bathroom of their hostess's home. By this time Luke was eighteen, but his only, shall we say normal, relationship with a woman had been with his mentor. He had never known a woman near to his own age and right from the start he was besotted with your wife. They met every day for the next three weeks, then the situation changed quite dramatically.

'In the two years since Luke had left home he had never stopped thinking about Siobhan. The fact that he had left his sister at the mercy of their father was something for which he never could, and probably never will, forgive himself. And when, just a few weeks into their relationship, Mrs Denby started to illustrate her somewhat unusual sexual preferences, the whole nightmare of Luke's life in Ireland came flooding back to him. Mrs Denby was asking him to do things to her that his father had forced him to do to his mother and Siobhan, and as a result Luke started to become confused and disoriented. At this point he still regarded himself as in love with Mrs Denby and for the first time ever he found himself confiding to someone what had happened to him as a child. Mrs Denby became so aroused by what he was telling her that she made him demonstrate as much of it as he could to her. In other words she started to make him relive it. And the longer he relived it the more confused he became. In the end, though he was still sexually obsessed with Mrs Denby, he came to hate her, and to yearn for Siobhan. When engaged in relations with Mrs Denby he would often believe himself to be with Siobhan, or indeed with his mother, and Mrs Denby did all she could to encourage this illusion. Should he regain his senses and discover that it was in fact neither Mary nor Siobhan Fitzpatrick he was with, Mrs Denby would laugh at him and mock him for his perversions, which invariably led to Luke beating her – which was exactly what Mrs Denby wanted. And as Luke thrashed her she would call him daddy and beg him to stop. This was so reminiscent of what had happened to him before that I believe it was during this time – all those years ago – that Luke's sense of identity first started to merge with his father's.

'Anyway, as I said, his guilt over Siobhan was troubling him a great deal, so much so that he eventually forced himself to return to Ireland. He went . . .'

'Excuse me,' Phillip interrupted, 'but when exactly would that have been? Do you know?'

The doctor's face creased as he searched his memory for dates. 'I believe,' he said slowly, 'that it was in the early summer of '67.'

Phillip nodded then signalled for the doctor to continue.

'Luke returned to Ireland,' Horowitz said, 'with the intention of rescuing Siobhan from their father. And it was what Luke found when he arrived back at the family home that I am now in no doubt was what was responsible for what he later did to the prostitutes.

'He found Siobhan out in the yard locked in a tiny hutch with her pet rabbits. She was still speaking then, though rarely, but when Luke asked she couldn't remember how long she had been there.'

'What age was she then?' Cristos asked.

'Thirteen – in body if not in mind, and I'm sure you will appreciate that her mind was greatly disturbed by now. The only creatures in the world she had had to love since Luke had gone were her rabbits. The only words she ever uttered were to them . . .'

'Wasn't she going to school?' Phillip asked.

Horowitz shook his head. 'She never went to school. Phillip Fitzpatrick got rid of the authorities by telling them he was educating his children himself. Which, to a certain extent, he did. Anyway, as I was saying, the dearest things in the world to Siobhan were her rabbits and when Luke picked her up to carry her into the house she begged him to take the rabbits too. Luke believes that she didn't know who he was, she didn't even seem to care, all that mattered was that she had her rabbits with her. As Luke carried her and her pets into the house his father was watching them from an upstairs window. His mother was in the kitchen and when Luke came in with Siobhan, Mary Fitzpatrick behaved as though the two of them had just come in from playing. Luke was so angry with his mother that he lost control of himself and started to attack her. He couldn't understand how she could have just stood by all those years and allowed her children to be so mercilessly abused. Mary Fitzpatrick did nothing to defend herself, it was her husband who pulled Luke off of her, and before Luke knew what was happening his father had overpowered him to the extent that Luke has no memory of being bound and gagged – all he knows is that when the catastrophic events that led to Siobhan being the way she is now took place, he was strapped to a chair with no means of stopping his father.'

Radcliffe, who had already heard this story once, ran a hand over his haggard face. He wasn't at all sure he wanted to hear it again. Cristos and Phillip were both very still.

'Phillip Fitzpatrick,' Horowitz continued, 'ordered his wife to hold Siobhan down while he took each of her rabbits and, right in front of her, broke their necks. After he had done that he held their bodies over Siobhan letting their blood run onto her.'

'Jesus *Christ*!' Cristos murmured.

'I'm afraid that's not all,' Horowitz said. 'He then made his wife cook the rabbits and forced Siobhan to eat them. Siobhan has never spoken since.'

His final words fell into a heavy, tragic silence as the four men tried to deal with the harrowing pictures Horowitz's words had conjured up. Every one of them was experiencing the same impotent outrage combined with heartrending pity for the little girl whose soul had been murdered by her own father. It was only when a car alarm outside started to scream its ear-piercing cry, as though calling them back to the present, that Radcliffe cleared his throat and turned himself to face Cristos and Phillip.

'There was a detail of the prostitutes' murders we held back,' he said. 'It was that every one of the bodies, besides being covered in its own blood, was covered in rabbit's blood. And the contents of each of the stomachs ... Rabbit.'

Phillip said to Horowitz. 'What happened to Siobhan after that?'

'What happened,' Horowitz said, 'was that Luke informed the police. His father was arrested, Siobhan was taken into care and Mary Fitzpatrick committed suicide. Luke didn't go to his mother's funeral – he hated her for what she had allowed to happen and still does. Himself, he got a job with an Irish newspaper so that he could visit Siobhan regularly, and when she was sixteen he moved her from the care of the authorities to private care, which is where she has been ever since. Over the years Luke has tried everything in his power to bring his sister back to life. He even, with my permission of course, recently brought rabbits to the clinic in the hope of shocking her into a response. The failure upset him greatly. He stayed with me for a time afterwards, which is something I will tell you about in a moment. But knowing what I know now it is my belief that the anger and frustration he experiences at his inability to reach Siobhan has at times vented itself on the prostitutes. You see he wishes his father had killed Siobhan, he has told me frequently. He has even expressed his desire to release Siobhan from her private hell himself. But the truth is, nothing in the world could induce Luke to harm her again. So, in tying up the prostitutes, beating them then killing them, it is very likely that, in his troubled mind, he is imagining himself his father and going through the final act his father never wrought.'

Radcliffe took out a packet of cigarettes and offered one to Cristos. Cristos shook his head and turned to look out of the window, staring at, but not seeing, the triangular stretch of sea at the end of the street.

'It seems,' Phillip said, 'that we've skipped a great deal of time. I mean, the prostitutes weren't killed until last year.'

Horowitz turned back from the mini-bar where he had just helped himself to a mineral water and sat down. 'When Luke took Siobhan to England in 1985,' he said, 'was when he started to pursue a career as a television journalist. As you are all aware he achieved a good deal of success in this – and, since I am the only one of us who knew him at that time, I can tell you that considering the traumas he had suffered as a child, he appeared relatively well-balanced. That is not to say that there were no manifestations of his inner turmoil – there were. He has, by his own admission to me, tried to blackmail many people over the years. He has never done this for personal gain, he has done it out of malice, something he at times finds impossible to control. It is as though he is trying to reap revenge on a world that has cheated him of a normal life. He also, in the past, had occasions when the rage inside him threatened to over-whelm him, but whenever he felt that happening he got on the telephone to me, or indeed came to see me in person. In fact it happened rarely, and usually it was as a result of visiting Siobhan, so he was at the clinic anyway. If it threatened at all during the normal course of a day, it would be because he had spent time dwelling on what happened – so his answer was never to think about it. But of course that just isn't possible, besides which keeping so much emotion suppressed inside was not healthy. But for a while at least it seemed to work – and maybe it would have continued to work, had he not, by the cruellest twist of fate, met Annalise.'

Phillip stirred restlessly, his face had once again become very pale.

'It was Annalise's extraordinary resemblance to Siobhan,' Horowitz continued, 'that first attracted Luke to her. They met, as I'm sure you know, Mr Denby, in a London nightclub. Luke had had a lot to drink, so too had Annalise, but not so much that they forgot to exchange telephone numbers at the end of the evening. Annalise called Luke the next day. He went to her flat; within minutes they were in bed together and within days, for the first time in his life, Luke was in love.

'He'd been seeing Annalise for almost a month by the time he told me about her. He was deeply concerned by her resemblance to Siobhan – afraid that it was Siobhan he was falling in love with and not Annalise. Over the following weeks we spent many hours discussing this, and by the end of it I was of the opinion that what Luke was feeling for Annalise was perfectly normal. Which it was, considering that neither of us at that time knew the truth. Anyway, with your help, Mr Denby, Annalise and Luke went ahead and set up TW productions and you may remember, sir, that it was at the party following the announcement that TW had secured a network slot, that Annalise first introduced Luke to her mother. Luke recognized Mrs Denby immediately, and with the recognition came the horrific realization of why it was that Annalise looked so like Siobhan.

'I am sure you recall, Mr Denby, the way Luke left the party so abruptly that night. He in fact came straight to me. His distress, as I am sure you can imagine, was immeasurable. He stayed with me for three days, by which time I had persuaded him to go and speak to Mrs Denby – though there seemed little doubt of his relationship to

Annalise I felt it necessary that he should find out for certain. Mrs Denby of course confirmed it.

'I don't think I need to explain, gentlemen, that Luke's entire world had been turned inside out. Everything he had striven to forget was once again staring him in the face. And the first love he had ever felt in his life to be totally pure, was of course anything but. Naturally, what tormented him most of all, was that he was doing the same to his own daughter as his father had to Siobhan. Not with the same brutality, of course, but nevertheless he was engaged in a sexual relationship with her. Not only that, Annalise's mother, just as Luke's own mother had, was allowing it to happen. In Mrs Denby's case, she actively encouraged it. And on top of it all, your name, Mr Denby, was the same as his own father's. The coincidences, the shock, the altogether tragic reflections of his own childhood meant that Luke's grip on his sanity became severely jeopardized. He couldn't, and how many of us could?, come to terms with the fact that life had played him such a monstrous trick. He was in love with Annalise, he didn't want to give her up, but knew that he had to. He tried, and until this week I thought he had succeeded. I knew he had continued his affair with Mrs Denby, but only when he came to spend four weeks at the clinic recently, did he tell me what she had been putting him through all this time. Knowing how desperately he was suffering she had been stimulating his confusion over his identity to the point that he truly believed he was his father. The bastard Phillip Fitzpatrick Denby, was what she called him, using your name, Mr Denby, to confuse him all the more. She incited him to torment you or to blackmail you in any way he could. At first Luke resisted, but when Mrs Denby threatened to tell Annalise who he really was, Luke complied. And it didn't take long for his mental state to deteriorate to the point that he no longer knew who he or anyone else was. Of course there were days, even weeks of clarity,

during which he tried to break his relationship with Annalise many times, but never successfully. She was as in love
with him as he was with her, and it seemed not to matter
how cruel he was to her, she wouldn't let him go. And he
simply didn't have the strength to let her go.

'I must emphasize here, gentlemen, that I had no idea
what was happening in Luke's mind or life over this two
year period. He stopped confiding in me at the time he told
me he had ended his relationship with Annalise. It was
only when he came to spend some time at the clinic recently
that I learned of at least some of what had been happening.
He told me that he had been trying to punish you, Mr
Denby, for what had been done to Siobhan. Of course he
didn't tell me how he had been punishing you, but we
know now that it was through the prostitutes. He confessed
to the terrible identity crisis he was having between himself
and his father – and he also told me that he believed, if he
could only get through to Corrie, she could help him.'

Cristos's head came up. 'What's that supposed to mean?'
he said.

Horowitz sighed. 'I think, as far as Luke is concerned,
that Corrie is the only member of Mr Denby's family who
is untainted. I imagine that at first he wanted to seduce
Corrie as a means of tormenting Mr Denby, but as his
state of mind worsened, and I think he knew that it was
deteriorating, he started to view Corrie in a very different
light. You must understand, he can no longer see his life
as being apart from this family, or perhaps I should say,
as being apart from his own nightmare. So his salvation,
he believes, must come from within the family. Or, as it
turns out, must come from Corrie. But he has been unable
to reach Corrie, though he's tried in many convoluted ways
to do so. And, as we know, she is in love with you, Mr
Bennati. I strongly believe that it is because of that, that
Luke's last vestiges of hope – and indeed sanity – died.'

An oppressive silence stretched through the minutes that

followed. Phillip was sitting with his head in his hands, Cristos was still at the window staring sightlessly out at the darkening sky, and Radcliffe was quietly smoking another cigarette. Phillip was the first to speak.

'After Luke returned to Ireland in '67, did he ever go back to London again?'

Horowitz frowned. 'I'm sure he did, many times as a journalist, but he didn't live there again until '85.'

'I see,' Phillip said, and as he spoke it was evident that he was somewhere deep inside his own thoughts. He lifted his eyes to see that they were waiting for him to speak again. 'I was just trying to connect the disappearance of Geraldine Lassiter's gigolo with ... certain other things that happened at that time,' he explained.

Cristos's head came up. 'Who?'

'Geraldine Lassiter, the woman who ... educated him.'

'You remember him then?' Horowitz asked.

'I don't recall ever meeting him, no,' Phillip answered. 'But I knew of his existence. Everyone did.'

'Would you like to tell us what those certain other things were – at the time of his disappearance?' Radcliffe asked.

Phillip shook his head. 'Not yet, no,' he said. 'I'd like to speak to my wife first.'

Every one of them was on the point of protesting, but something in Phillip stopped them.

'Do you remember your wife's affair with Luke?' Horowitz asked.

'Yes, I remember it,' Phillip answered.

Long minutes ticked by as they waited for him to speak again. In the end it was Cristos who broke the silence.

'So where does all this leave us?' he said, turning to Horowitz. 'We still don't know where they are ...'

'I'm afraid that's a question for Mr Radcliffe,' Horowitz answered.

'Then perhaps you should tell us,' Cristos said, knowing that at this stage Radcliffe would be unable to answer the question, 'just what kind of danger you consider them to be in.'

The expression on Horowitz's face as he glanced at Radcliffe was as unsettling for Cristos as it was for Phillip, who was now listening intently. It showed so clearly that Horowitz was seeking Radcliffe's permission as to whether or not he should divulge his worst fears. Radcliffe gave an almost imperceptible nod and Horowitz turned back to Phillip and Cristos.

'I believe that it is Annalise who is in the most immediate danger,' he said. 'Her resemblance to Siobhan will confuse and frustrate him, and if she does know that Luke is her father then her behaviour towards him is likely to be very much on a parallel with the way Siobhan was with her father. Luke could very well respond to that in the way his father did with Siobhan.'

'Oh, God help us,' Phillip breathed, letting his head fall back as he closed his eyes. It was Radcliffe though, who asked the question that had soared to the front of Phillip's mind.

'Phillip Fitzpatrick never went so far as to kill Siobhan,' he said, 'so are you saying that Luke is likely to adhere to that too?'

Horowitz's sallow face became pinched with unease. 'No, I'm afraid I'm not saying that.'

'And Corrie?' Cristos asked, unable to look at Phillip.

The sympathy was clear in Horowitz's silvery eyes as he looked back at Cristos. 'As I said earlier,' he answered, 'Luke has, for some time, been convinced that Corrie's love and compassion was all he needed to make his life whole. This is an irrational conviction, of course, but his mind is very far from rational. He sees Corrie as someone who can heal the damage that has been done to him . . . He feels he needs her, that he can't be without her – in life or in death.'

Fear churned through Cristos's stomach like a vortex. 'What do you mean, in death?' he asked.

Horowitz looked at him, blinking sadly. 'It is my belief that Luke intends to take his own life,' he said. 'If he does then I'm very much afraid that he will take Corrie with him.'

Cristos's face had become very pale, every muscle in his body was taut.

'Please understand, Mr Bennati,' Horowitz continued in a feeble effort to comfort him, 'that I am only surmising. I cannot say for sure what Luke will do.' And it was true, he couldn't. But there was no doubt at all in his mind that Luke had by now lost control completely. There would be no reaching him now, his reason was lost to him forever. There was nothing to be gained from telling Cristos that, for neither man need know the extent to which he, Horowitz, feared that the degradation, abuse and terror of Luke's childhood would be meted out to both Corrie and Annalise before they went to their deaths.

— **29** —

Corrie and Annalise were lying back to back on a vast wooden bed inside the villa. Their hands and feet were bound to each other's, a flimsy cotton sheet covered their near nudity. Some time ago Corrie had heard a distant clock chime midnight and just after there had been the sound of footsteps passing along the corridor outside followed by a door closing nearby. She wondered if Luke had gone to bed too, if he would lay down the gun while he slept – if this could be an opportunity to escape.

She bit down hard on her lip as the futility of her wonderings, the sheer helplessness of their position pushed tears into her eyes. Even if she and Annalise could loosen their bonds, which Corrie knew already they couldn't, the door to their room was locked and the windows were too high for them to jump.

For hours now Corrie had felt her inner strength ebbing. The effort of holding herself together, if only for Annalise's sake, was proving so difficult as to be almost impossible. In her weakened state her desperate longing for Cristos and the yearning to feel herself being lifted into the safety of his arms was growing to such a pitch that she could feel herself drawing ever closer to the brink of panic. But she mustn't allow herself to think of Cristos, she had to push all thoughts of him from her mind. He had no more idea of where she was than she did, and to think of him coming for her was a dangerous fantasy for it was clouding the brutal and stupefying reality of what was happening to her and Annalise.

Luke had kept them out in the blazing sun the entire afternoon while he himself had disappeared inside, or maybe he had even left the villa for a while, Corrie had no way of knowing. What she did know was that she was still, all this time later, reeling from the shock of all that Annalise had learned from her mother while they had been in Spain with Luke. But it wasn't only that Luke was Annalise's father that Corrie was finding so hard to accept, it was the part Octavia herself had played in the whole unspeakable deception.

'Luke says that she's corrupt, that she's rotten right through to her soul . . .' Annalise had said in a voice fractured by the terrible sadness and betrayal she was suffering. 'And how can I doubt that after what she's done? I see her face in my mind's eye and I know that beneath the shallow surface of her oh-so-perfect skin there's nothing more than a festering mass of poison. But whatever she is, whatever evil there is in her, it doesn't change the fact that Luke knew what he was doing. He knew who I was and he never told me. He's tried to excuse himself by reminding me of how many times he tried to break it off between us — it's as though he's blaming me for it all because I wouldn't let him go.' She had looked up at Corrie then with such desperate torment in her eyes that Corrie, who was perched on the edge of the hammock chair, brushed her fingers gently over her face.

'But you didn't know,' Corrie soothed her. 'How could you have known?'

For a while then neither of them said anything. Corrie's eyes wandered across the sea, following the tide to the distant shore. The heat was so oppressive it was soaking through the pores of her skin. It was difficult to move, even to think. The shock, the sheer horror of what had been happening to Annalise these past two years was beyond comprehension. She wanted to find some words of comfort, but what comfort could there ever be for something like this? And what in God's name was going to happen to her now – to either of them?

She looked down as Annalise shuddered, then reached out to her as she struggled to catch her breath through a battery of dry sobs.

'I can't bear it!' Annalise gulped. 'To think that I have to live the rest of my life knowing what I did, what my own mother . . . Oh, Corrie, she laughed when she told me, do you know that? She actually laughed.'

Corrie's face was drawn with pity as she all too vividly envisaged the scene Annalise had had to endure.

'And then . . . Oh God . . .' As Annalise's chest heaved with the pain and revulsion of memory she turned away from Corrie and buried her face in her hands. 'Do you know what she did, Corrie? Oh God, I can hardly believe it even now. She came and stood behind me and she told him he could rape me. She said she'd hold me down for him, and she would make me call him daddy.'

Corrie's eyes closed. She could feel the sun scorching across her back, she could see the blisters starting to form on Annalise's shoulders, smell the pungent sweetness of the flowers, taste the salt in the air. But all of it, just like Annalise's words, seemed so remote from the heart of her senses that it was as though reality had become blurred by the shimmering heat around her.

'And do you know what he did, Corrie?' Annalise said. 'Do you know what Luke did?'

Corrie shook her head.

'He raped me.'

'Oh my God,' Corrie breathed, wishing that her imagination could tear itself free of the images Annalise's words were creating.

'I didn't call him daddy,' Annalise spat, 'but she did! She said it for me! She put on a little girl's voice and shouted "Stop! Daddy, Daddy, stop!" And then she started calling me Siobhan. She called him Phillip . . . She said "Come on Phillip, fuck your daughter, Siobhan. She wants your . . ." ' Annalise's tongue recoiled from the obscenities . . . 'She went on and on and on. She drove him to such a frenzy I don't think he knew who he was, who I was or even who she was. He was laughing and crying and screaming . . . And all the time he was raping me while she held me down.'

'Oh, Annalise,' Corrie murmured.

'When it was over,' Annalise said, 'after she had pulled him out of me so he could finish with her, she told me that Siobhan was his sister. That, so he says, I look exactly like her. That all this time he's been with me in his head he's been screwing his sister *and* his daughter. But not only that, his father's name is Phillip, the same as . . .' Her eyes fell, and Corrie saw the way her mouth trembled.

'Your father's,' Corrie said for her.

Annalise attempted a smile and her eyes were filled with an uncertain gratitude as she looked back at Corrie. 'She was enjoying it, Corrie,' she went on. 'She was loving every minute of it. She must hate me so much to do that to me . . . But she hates everyone, I could see it in her eyes.

And I could see what she was doing. She was deliberately tormenting Luke. She was making him hold me as though I was a baby, and fondle me. And he tried to do it. He tried to make me stop crying by kissing me, by putting his hands all over me . . .' She shuddered violently. 'I got away from them – I ran away, but he caught me. When he dragged me back inside she was sitting there, curled in a chair and looking so superior, so pleased with herself. "You know what brought all this on, don't you?" she said to me. "It's because *you* told him that Corrie Browne was going to Los Angeles, and he's threatening to go back to London to stop her. He wants Corrie Browne," she said. Then to Luke she said, "But you can't have Corrie Browne can you, mother-fucker? She won't want you now, no one wants you now – except me." Luke started to beg me then to get him away from her. He started pawing me, pleading with me not to leave him . . . But I couldn't stand him near me. I never wanted him to touch me again . . . I could still hear her laughing when I ran into my bedroom and locked myself in. And I heard them all night long . . . I don't know what he was doing to her, or she to him, but she kept asking for more . . . And all I could think of was that I wanted to kill her . . . And if I had had the means to do it I know I would have. I hate her, I despise her . . . My own mother . . . And my father . . . But I can't think of him as my father, I'll never be able to think of him as that.'

And neither, Corrie thought now, as she lay in the darkness listening to Annalise's delirious mumblings, would she.

Despite the heat emanating from Annalise's body, Corrie could feel her shivering. Luke had forced her to remain in the sun for so long that day that her delicate skin was now ravaged with blisters and her mind was tortured by the feverish confusion of heatstroke. Again the sheer helplessness of their situation welled up in Corrie, but as the tears trickled from her eyes her own exhaustion settled a smothering blanket over the fear that her conscious mind was losing the struggle to suppress.

Cristos was standing at the vast arched window in his suite at the Majestic watching the first crimson rays of daylight burn the horizon. He had slept fitfully for an hour or two, but now he was wide awake and once again trying to snare the elusive thoughts which had been plaguing him ever since he had left Horowitz the day before. Something the man had said, or was it something Phillip had said, was bothering Cristos, but no matter how many times he re-ran in his mind what they'd told him he couldn't figure out what it was. He was missing something, he was damned sure of it, something vital, but Jesus Christ what was it?

He looked round as the door to the second bedroom of the suite opened and his mother, fastening the belt of her dressing-gown, came into the room.

'Ah, *chéri*,' she sighed, when she saw him. 'No sleep again?'

'Not much, no,' he confessed, slipping an arm around her as she joined him at the window.

'Shall I ring down for some breakfast?' she said, as they both gazed out across the fiery sea.

Cristos shook his head.

'But you must eat,' she told him gently. 'All this worry and no sleep . . .'

'I can't think about food . . .'

'All you can think about is Corrie. I know, *chéri*.'

'Damn it!' Cristos cried, slamming his fist into the wall. 'All I can think about is what that madman might do to her.'

Breaking away from him Mariette went to sit on one of the powdery-pink sofas. 'Come here,' she said, patting the cushion beside her.

Cristos glanced back over his shoulder, but made no attempt to move from where he was standing.

Because he was her son and because she loved him so very much Mariette could feel his pain as though it were her own. 'It'll be all right,' she said softly, trying in vain to comfort him. 'You'll get her back, *chéri*.'

'Mother, don't patronize me,' Cristos snapped. 'You know what she's up against. I told you what the doctor said.'

'But he doesn't know for certain,' Mariette reminded him. 'He was only guessing.'

'And what if he's right? What if Fitzpatrick in his sick mind . . .'

'What if? What if?' Mariette interrupted. 'You must stop torturing yourself like this, Cristos. You can't be any help to her if you don't. Now come, sit here and let's go over it again. Let's see if we can't find out what it is that's bothering you about what the doctor told you.'

'We've been over it and over it, Mother,' Cristos said tightly. 'It's something to do with that woman, Geraldine Lassiter, but Christ knows what.'

'Didn't you say that Phillip was trying to find out where she is now?'

Cristos nodded.

'Then why don't you try to put it out of your mind until . . .'

'Mother!' Cristos seethed.

'Well what purpose is this serving, getting yourself worked into a frenzy . . . You have other commitments here, Cristos. Bud Winters wants you to put in an appearance at the *Palais* tonight . . .'

'If he thinks . . .'

'What he thinks is that a lot of people have worked very hard for you to get this film ready. He thinks you owe it to them to be there for the awards ceremony.'

'Do you seriously think I give a damn what Bud Winters or anyone else thinks when Corrie's out there somewhere . . .'

'Perhaps if you went to the ceremony,' Mariette interrupted smoothly, 'and relaxed a little, you might find that whatever it is you're trying to remember will come to you.'

'Leave it, Mother!' he barked. 'Just leave it,' and before she could say anymore he walked out of the room to go and cool his temper and frustration in the shower.

'Goddammit,' he seethed as the powerful jets of water washed away his tears. The answer was there, it was staring him right in the face, he just knew it, but for the love of Christ he just couldn't reach it.

Tiny slats of sunlight were seeping through the shuttered windows striping the room in which Corrie and Annalise lay. From the chimes of the faraway clock Corrie knew that midday had come and gone some time ago now. She had no idea where Luke was, or what he was doing. He'd come into the room during the early hours, staying only a few seconds, and she'd heard nothing since except Annalise's mumblings and her own sobs as she prayed to God to save them from the terrifying insanity that was imprisoning them.

Annalise was sleeping quietly now and Corrie's entire body ached with cramp. Her mouth was so tender and swollen that just the slightest movement of her lips caused her unbearable pain. Her cheeks were encrusted with tears, her hair matted with blood and perspiration.

There was nothing she could do now to stop herself thinking of Cristos. In her mind she was reliving their moments of tenderness, listening to the gentle lilt in his voice as he told her he loved her. Her heart churned as she recalled the depth of his passion, as she almost felt the sheer strength of him, but with each thought came a wave of excruciating fear that she might never see him again.

As fresh tears started in her eyes she felt a gentle tug at her wrists.

'Corrie? Are you awake?' Annalise whispered.

'Yes,' Corrie answered and felt her throat swell with relief that she was no longer alone. 'How are you feeling?' she asked.

'I don't know. I hurt – all over.' Annalise's voice was parched. 'Where did those rabbits come from?' she asked.

'Luke brought them in during the night.'

'Why?'

'I don't know.'

They both froze as a sudden crash resounded through the house.

'What was that?' Annalise breathed.

Corrie didn't answer.

The noise came again and again, echoing around the polished walls of the villa. Something heavy was being dragged, then glass shattered. Suddenly Luke's voice screamed from below. It reverberated through the house, over and over. There were no words, just the torturous bellowings of a man possessed by a crucifying insanity.

'Oh my God, what's he doing?' Corrie whispered, as Annalise's hands curled into hers.

'I can't bear it,' Annalise sobbed. 'He's going to kill us, Corrie. I know he is.'

'Annalise, stop it,' Corrie said, her chest starting to heave with her own panic. 'We've got to find a way of getting out of here . . .'

'But it's impossible while we're tied up like this.'

'So we have to think of a way to make him untie us.'

'But how?'

'We have to go to the bathroom.'

'But it's right there. He'll be standing there, waiting.'

'Oh Annalise, try to be positive!' Corrie wailed. 'I'll say I want to go, and you have to try to run as soon as his back is turned.'

'But I can't leave you here.'

'You'll have to.'

'No! Let me go to the bathroom . . .'

'Annalise! Just do as I say. It's me he wants, so you have to try and get away.'

'But what if . . .'

Annalise stopped as the door suddenly crashed open and Luke staggered in. His hair was dishevelled, so too were his clothes. He was panting for breath and saliva glistened on his lips. But what froze the blood in Corrie's veins was the madness in his eyes.

'You'll be wanting to eat,' he snarled, and whisking a rabbit from the floor he set it on the tray he was carrying.

'Will this be the one you're wanting?' he said, moving towards Annalise. 'Will this be the one you have your pretty little eyes on?'

'Stop it!' Annalise sobbed, cowering away from him.

'Luke!' Corrie cried nearing hysteria. She couldn't see what was going on, but she didn't have to – the menace in his voice was unmistakable.

'What? You'll not be wanting your favourite pet there, Siobhan?' Luke's voice was slurred with venom.

'Luke! I need to go to the bathroom!' Corrie shouted. 'Luke, please!'

'No!' Annalise suddenly screamed.

Corrie twisted round and her terror and confusion were total as she saw Luke's bloodied hand release the rabbit's head.

'No! No! I can't stand it! I can't stand it!' Annalise choked. 'Please God, help me!'

The blood was now dripping over her face, running into her eyes, her nose and her mouth.

'Now we'll be seeing what you'll do before I feed you,' he grinned, and standing erect he began removing his clothes.

'Anything?' Cristos said as Phillip walked into his room.

Phillip shook his head. In the past two days his shoulders had started to sag, and his handsome face had aged by ten years. 'I've called everyone I can think of who knew

Geraldine. Those who weren't at home I've left messages to call me, the others . . . It seems that no one's in touch with her now.' He looked up. 'Octavia's flying in later today.'

Cristos's face hardened and as his fists clenched his mother put a hand on his arm. 'I take it you asked her if she knew where this Lassiter woman was now,' he snapped.

'Yes, I asked her,' Phillip sighed. 'She said, "dead for all I know." And we have to face it Cristos, she could be.'

Cristos turned away, exhausted by his own anger, but unable to let it go.

Jeannie and Mariette exchanged glances, while Richard handed Phillip a coffee.

'Cristos,' Jeannie began tentatively, 'I got to give the publicity people an answer pretty soon now.'

'It's out of the question, Jeannie,' Cristos told her. 'Now quit hassling me.'

'What's that?' Phillip asked, more for something to say than out of curiosity.

'They want to know if he's going to the ceremony tonight,' Mariette answered. 'And they want him to give a press conference this afternoon.'

'Oh, I see.' He looked at Cristos. 'Maybe you should do it. I mean, life has to go on, and this film is . . .'

'Cristos you got to do it,' Jeannie said, suddenly excited. 'I mean, if you talk to the cameras it'll be broadcast all over the world. You can say you're looking for this Geraldine Lassiter, maybe she'll hear it. Maybe someone she knows will hear it.'

Cristos's eyes shot to hers, but before he could answer the telephone rang. He snatched it up.

'Monsieur Bennati,' the operator said. 'Is Monsieur Denby with you? I have a call for him.'

Cristos turned to Phillip and held out the receiver.

Everyone in the room was very still as Phillip waited for the call to be put through. 'Yes, yes, it's Phillip Denby here. Oh, Dolly, hello how are you? Yes, that's right I left a message ... No, there's no news yet ...' There was a long pause as he listened to what Dolly was saying, then he said, 'I see. Well, thanks very much for calling me back, Dolly. No, that's quite all right, you've been a great help.'

As he hung up he turned to Cristos. 'Dolly Patterson. She knew Geraldine ... All she knows is that Geraldine married someone by the name of Duffel, years ago now, and went to live in the States. New York she thinks. She and Geraldine lost touch in the mid-seventies.'

As despondency crept through the room, Cristos's frown deepened.

'So what do you say to this press conference?' Jeannie said, once again trying to inject hope. 'It'll be sure to be broadcast all over the States, and if she's still living there ...'

But Cristos was shaking his head. 'I don't need a press conference to find her,' he said, his eyes suddenly glittering with urgency. 'In fact I don't need to find her at all,' and grabbing his car keys he ran out of the room.

Luke was standing over them, brandishing the knife he had used to sever their bonds. As the blood eased into their stiffened muscles the pain was unbearable and neither of them could move. Then suddenly Luke grabbed Annalise's arm and with a howl of manic laughter made to throw her from the bed.

'Corrie! Corrie!' Annalise cried, as Corrie scrambled to get a hold on her. But as her hands closed around Corrie's the knife sliced through her forearm. Annalise's cry was followed by another and another as he threw her to the floor, the knife slashing randomly at her defenceless body.

'*Nooo!*' Corrie screamed, but as she made to leap from the bed Luke slammed his fist into her face and she fell back, stunned and blinded by the agony.

The sounds babbling from Luke's lips were an incoherent

stream of mania, as cackling and growling and salivating grotesquely he threw aside the knife and snatched Annalise up by the hair.

'No, no, no,' she sobbed as he dragged her to her feet. Then suddenly he punched her face so hard her whole body left the floor and she crashed against the wall behind her.

She crumpled, like a broken doll and Corrie, dulled and disoriented, tried to force herself up as he bent over Annalise again.

'Luke! No!' she croaked, dragging herself to the edge of the bed, but Luke had already ripped off Annalise's panties.

A torrent of overpowering dizziness swept through Corrie's head. From an immeasurable distance she saw Luke's hands mauling Annalise's lifeless body. Gathering what little strength she had Corrie threw herself against him. He staggered against the wall. She grabbed his hair, yanking his head back. He screamed with pain and she jerked so hard his back arched. Obscenities spewed from his mouth as his hands clamped around her wrists. Corrie wouldn't let go. He screamed again, and sniggered and growled with demonic rage.

Then suddenly he twisted out from under her. He was facing her. Corrie drew her knee back, but as she did he drove his head into her chest. The blow spun her round and sent her crashing against the dressing table. He kicked her feet from under her and she hit the floor hard. Winded and near senseless, she fought for her breath, then his foot slammed into her head, her ribs, her back and as the unbelievable pain consumed her her body went limp.

He turned back to Annalise, panting and snarling. Sweat was dripping from his face, his saliva was stained with blood and a powerful erection protruded from his groin. Annalise was so drugged by pain she could barely see him. She grunted as he seized her by the arms and wrenching her to him he pushed his tongue deep into her mouth.

Curled in a cocoon of agony Corrie's eyes were struggling

to focus on the knife. It was only a few feet away. She tried to move, gasped as a searing pain shot through her, but as Luke threw Annalise onto the bed she made herself try again.

A stream of foul invective coursed from his bloodied lips. He had Annalise by the hair, was trying to force his penis into her mouth. Annalise was gagging and spluttering and using what little strength she had to turn her head away. Her fingers were reaching for his testicles.

Corrie had the knife now. She staggered to her feet, gripping the dressing table as she started to swoon. Her vision was blurred, a blinding pain sliced through her head. She took a step forward, stumbled and fell to her knees.

Suddenly Luke howled. His head swung back, his teeth bared in agony as like giant vices his hands clenched around Annalise's wrists, tearing her away from him.

'Cunt! Filthy, dirty, cunt!' he screamed and drove his fist into her gut.

As he raised his arm again, Corrie lunged. The knife sank into his shoulder, glancing off a bone. He spun round, his sunken eyes blazing like fire, his nostrils quivering with outrage.

Corrie made to thrust again. He caught her arm, twisted it, brought her hand to his mouth and dug in his teeth. As Corrie yelped with pain the knife dropped to the floor.

'Bitch!' he seethed, her blood dripping from his lips. 'Fucking bitch!' And curling his fingers around her throat he charged her back across the room, dashing her head against the wall. He jerked her forward and slammed her back again – again and again. As she started to lose consciousness he clutched her arm and propelled her back to the bed.

She fell awkwardly against Annalise, knocking her to the floor, then dimly she was aware of him rolling her over, pressing her face into the mattress and tearing off her underwear.

'No, no,' she moaned, trying to twist herself free. But she was too weak to fight him now. She felt him gripping her hips, pulling her to her knees. She saw the knife glinting in his hand as he swept it in front of her face. She heard him giggling and bellowing, smelt his putrid breath as he knelt over her – and then she felt the pain.

It was like nothing she had ever felt in her life. It cleaved through her with such brutality it was as though her whole body was being ripped in two. She collapsed beneath him and his entire weight came down on her, and down and down. It was the knife, he was plunging the knife into her! But no! It was there, in his hand, right in front of her. She was so dazed, so ravaged by the agony, her brain was turning numb. It wasn't until he wrenched her arms behind her and started to drive himself frenziedly into her that she realized he was sodomizing her.

Beside her, on the floor, Annalise was trying to drag herself up. Through a haze of indescribable torture Corrie watched her. She could feel the blood trickling over her thighs and his face pressing hard into her neck. His free hand was trying to raise her as he sought an even deeper penetration.

'No,' she mumbled as Annalise's eyes fixed on the knife in his outstretched hand. 'Get help!' Her words were pushed from her mouth by the wild hammering of his body. 'Get help,' she muttered again as Annalise hesitated.

A moment or two later she heard the door open and close. Then suddenly Luke reared up, turned her onto her back and shoved her knees up to her shoulders.

Corrie thought it was never going to end. She had never known such pain or degradation.

Cristos was tearing along the autoroute, his hands clenched on the wheel, his face as taut and white as his knuckles. Beside him Phillip, who had caught up with him in the lift, was every bit as tense.

'I hope to God you're right,' Phillip said, then sucked in his breath sharply as Cristos roared across the three lanes to take the *Nice-Est* exit.

'So do I,' Cristos muttered.

He knew now why Geraldine Lassiter's name had been bothering him. If he'd known her by that name then it would have come to him sooner, but Geraldine Duffel and her husband, Patrick, he did know. And so too did Luke, for it was at one of their parties, right here in the South of France, that Cristos and Luke had first met.

That Fitzpatrick might be there now was a long shot, so long that Cristos was already losing hope. But if Fitzpatrick had kept up with Geraldine over the years then there was a chance she had given him free use of the villa on Cap Ferrat.

'Do you remember where it is?' Phillip asked some fifteen minutes later as Cristos spun the car off the main road and headed onto the Cap.

'More or less,' Cristos answered. 'I'll recognize it when I see it.'

The sea spanned out to their right, acres of tree-studded gardens swept the sloping hillside to their left. Most of the villas weren't visible from the road, but though Cristos slowed at each set of gates he was fairly certain that the one he was looking for was much closer to the apex of the Cap.

At last they reached it, though Cristos thanked God for the name on the mail box, for he knew as he and Phillip got out of the car and stood in front of the vast iron gates that he'd never have recognized it. All they could see of the villa through the forest of trees was the highest windows – every one of them was shuttered and looked as though they'd not been opened for months.

As a deluge of despondency and frustration surged through him, unseen by either him or Phillip, Annalise was wrenching open the front door.

'It was worth a try,' Phillip said, putting a hand on Cristos's shoulder.

'Yeah, I guess so,' Cristos said, averting his head so that Phillip wouldn't see the tears of defeat in his eyes. 'But we gotta get in there. We gotta make sure.'

'Of course,' Phillip said. 'Let's go and see Radcliffe.'

As they walked back to the car Annalise was dragging herself as fast as her injuries would allow across the lawn. She heard a car start and as her heart leapt with hope she pushed herself harder. The sheet she had draped around her caught on a branch. She let it go, floundering down through the undergrowth towards the gates. She had no idea who was in the car, but she could see it now and began to shout.

To her horror it began to pull away.

'No! Wait!' she screamed, stumbling to her knees as her foot hit a root. 'Wait! Please! Wait!' she sobbed, clutching the tree to pull herself up.

She reached the gates just in time to see Cristos's car vanish around the bend. 'No, no, no,' she choked, falling against the gates as despair engulfed her. 'Please God, no.'

It was Corrie who came to pick up her crumpled, defeated body, just as the sun was setting. As she lifted Annalise gently to her feet her own body was still quaking from the trauma it had suffered. Luke stood over them, watching and blinking, the gun in his hand. In the bushes, tucked in behind the wall next to the gates, Corrie could see the front of the taxi. She looked away quickly, sickened by the swarm of hungry flies buzzing around it.

When Luke took them back into the villa he put them in separate rooms. For a while as Corrie lay quietly on the bed, numbed by the shame of what had happened to her, she could hear Annalise next door mumbling incoherently as she talked to the rabbits he had locked in with her. Then she heard Luke enter the room and Annalise started to scream.

Corrie tensed as she heard him slap her. But there was nothing she could do to help Annalise now. Nothing at all.

'No, Luke! Don't! Please, don't kill them!' Annalise's voice carried to her on a current of despair. Then the door opened and closed again, and Corrie heard Luke's heavy tread slowly descending the stairs. After that there was only silence.

It was dark outside when Corrie heard the car. For a fleeting moment a timid hope flared, but there were no voices, only footsteps crunching around the gravel. A few minutes later she heard Luke coming up the stairs.

'Get up,' he said, as he opened the door. 'I'm needing your help.'

'What for?' she asked, and groaned as a savage pain jarred her insides when she tried to move.

'To help me get rid of the body from the taxi,' he answered.

Corrie felt her stomach churn and knew that no matter what, she wouldn't be able to touch the taxi-driver's body. But she was too afraid of Luke to argue, and wincing piteously she gingerly pulled herself from the bed.

'What are you going to do with it?' she asked dully, as she walked ahead of him down the stairs.

'I'll be dumping it over the veranda into the sea,' he answered, and his prosaic tone made Corrie's head swim.

The night was pitch black. The only sound was the distant sough of the waves and the urgent metallic hum of cicadas. Corrie stood at the foot of the steps watching Luke in the dim light from the hall as he moved around the taxi.

'Come here now,' he said, springing the boot open. 'I'll be needing a hand to get it out.'

As Corrie walked forward it was as though her mind had become locked in a timeless vacuum of paralysis. All she knew was that her legs were moving and that her eyes were riveted sightlessly to the amorphous mass of the night.

'Take the legs,' Luke ordered.

A jolt of revulsion leapt through her gut, but with her head averted she reached out in front of her feeling for the legs. She could hear Luke raising the torso and the instant her hands closed over the legs she started to retch. She drew back, staring down at her hands. They were covered in blood. Her face froze with terror as she brought her head up. Then a bloodcurdling scream erupted from her. It wasn't the taxi-driver's body he was holding – it was Annalise's.

'I understand what you're saying,' Radcliffe interrupted Cristos, 'but it's not my territory. If the French-plod say we have to contact the owners first, then that's what we have to do.'

'And if they're in there?' Cristos seethed. 'If this fucking bureaucracy . . .' He broke off as the door opened to admit the burly, Gitane-puffing French inspector.

'*Messieurs,*' Thibault began. '*On a un probléme. Il n'y a pas de réponse . . .*'

Being the only one present who understood French Cristos waited, with mounting fury, for the inspector to finish, then translated.

'He's saying there's no answer from the Duffels' place in New York,' he snapped. 'So they're now trying to locate someone to open up the local *Mairie* to check that the Duffels are still the owners.'

'And if they are, and we still can't get through to them?' Phillip asked testily.

Cristos communicated this to Thibault. 'Then we have to see if we can find someone nearby who might have the keys,' Cristos answered bitterly when Thibault had finished.

'And meanwhile?' Phillip cried. 'What are we supposed to do? Sit around here . . .'

'Hold it! Hold it!' Radcliffe interrupted. 'We don't even

know if they're in there. You said yourself the place looks like it's been deserted for months.'

'Well he sure as hell isn't going to put up a flag of fucking residence, is he?' Cristos shouted.

'*Je reviens*,' Thibault smiled pleasantly, and left the room.

'What did he say?' Phillip snapped.

'He'll be back,' Cristos said.

Long minutes ticked by as the three of them sat there looking out through the glass partition at the hustle and bustle of the police station.

'Aren't you supposed to be at that awards ceremony?' Radcliffe said to Cristos in an effort to break the tension.

'I've had it!' Cristos raged, leaping to his feet. 'I've fucking had it! They're going to open up that villa tonight if I have to use their own fucking guns to shoot the locks off myself,' and he stormed out of the room after Thibault.

The lights were on on the veranda. Beyond was a sea of inky darkness, peppered with the bobbing lights of yachts. Corrie was on the floor huddled up against the wall, shivering and shuddering with mindless terror. Annalise's lifeless body, bound up, beaten and awash with blood was only feet away. Luke was perched on the edge of the wall. He hadn't said anything for some time, but a while ago he'd asked Corrie if she'd care for something to eat. Corrie had been unable to answer. Now, he was just watching her.

At last he moved, gesturing with the gun for her to stand.

Corrie shrank away, but as he started towards her she fumbled her hands up over the wall and clinging to it, shakily pulled herself to her feet.

'Now you be getting onto the wall there,' he said.

Corrie's eyes rounded with horror.

'Get onto the wall!'

Somehow she managed to scramble up until she was kneeling on the narrow ledge. She went no further, if she stood she would fall.

Luke turned away, covering his face with his hands. After a while Corrie realized he was crying. On the wall in front of her was a pool of her own tears, dripping unchecked from her eyes, her nose, her mouth. When finally he looked up his face was like a cadaver. He reached out for Corrie's hand, steadying her as she started to topple. Then very softly, he said,

'It's time for us now, Corrie. Both of us, together. Be getting onto your feet.'

'No,' Corrie sobbed, as he tried to help her. 'Please, please, Luke, don't make me do it.'

'I'm sorry,' he said, gently, 'if there was any other way . . . Now just you be getting up there.'

Clinging to the post beside her, Corrie pulled herself to her feet. 'Luke, please,' she begged. 'You can get help . . .'

'You will help me, Corrie. When we reach the other side . . .'

'Oh Luke,' she choked. 'Luke, please, just listen to me . . .'

'There's nothing you can say now, Corrie. I have to die. After what I've done to my own daughter, I have to.'

'But Luke . . .'

'I didn't know,' he went on dully. 'Not at first. And by the time I did it was too late. I was sleeping with my own daughter.'

'But you could have stopped.'

He shook his head. 'I tried, please believe me, Corrie, I tried. But I was in love with her. I'll always be in love with her. That's why you must come to the other side with us. You have to keep me away from her, Corrie. You have to help me.'

Corrie whimpered as the pathetic plea touched the roots of her heart. 'Luke, what is it?' she gasped. 'Why have you done this? You're so calm now, what made you . . .'

'I've exorcised him, Corrie. I'm rid of him now. I did all he wanted me to do, all he should have done himself . . .'

'Who, Luke? Who are you talking about?'

'My father, of course. I've done to my own daughter now what he did to his. But I finished it. She won't have to live like Siobhan. I've released her.' His eyes came up to Corrie's. 'I know I hurt you, Corrie,' he said, 'but I didn't mean to. I couldn't help myself, please try to understand that. It should have been Annalise, not you . . . Maybe it should have been Siobhan . . . I don't know anymore. All I know is that I need you to help me.'

'But we don't have to die for that,' Corrie said. 'I'll give you my help . . .'

'No.' He was shaking his head. 'You'll go to Cristos and you'll forget about me.'

'That's not true. I want to help you, Luke.'

'Then die with me.'

For a moment, as sobs of desperation shuddered through her her words wouldn't come. 'I don't want to die, Luke,' she pleaded. 'Please, don't make me die.'

'I'm sorry,' he said, and raising the gun he placed it against her temple.

'No! No, no, please!' she sobbed, squeezing her eyes.

'It's all right, I'll be with you,' he murmured, and as his finger tightened on the trigger, the last thing Corrie knew was the sudden jerk of her body as it was lifted from the wall and the resounding echoes of the explosion following her into a void of darkness.

– 30 –

Cristos raised his eyes to look across the room at Paula. Her pretty, girlish face showed the strain she was under and for a moment he was tempted to reach out for her. He resisted the impulse, and was on the point of turning away when she looked up. She smiled, as though to give him reassurance, but her anguish was too deep to disguise.

All of them were having difficulty coming to terms with what had happened, Paula most of all, Cristos thought. The events of the past few days were proving damn near impossible for him to handle but what a chaotic and insane world this must seem to her, who had never travelled far out of Amberside.

He'd called her himself, asking her to come. Hurt him as it did, he had understood when his mother had told him that there was always the chance Corrie wouldn't want him when she came round: that he had to face the fact that Luke might have damaged her so badly she would be unable to face a man again. It had scared him half to death when Horowitz had agreed with his mother, but he had gone ahead and called Paula, since Horowitz and the hospital doctor had agreed that there should be someone there whom Corrie loved and trusted when she regained consciousness.

That they had managed to save her life was, Cristos knew now, nothing short of a miracle. The gun was already at her head, Luke's finger squeezing the trigger, when Inspector Thibault had fired. At the same instant one of his men, who had crept silently across the veranda, had snatched Corrie from the wall.

Hearing the gun shot Cristos and Phillip, who had been made to wait outside, both dashed into the house before the police could stop them. By the time they reached the veranda the officer who had caught Corrie was carrying her inside. Seeing her Cristos knew a moment of such profound terror that unmindful of her injuries he had tried to wrench her away from the policeman.

'It's all right,' the man said, letting Cristos take her, 'she's alive. We got there . . .' He stopped as a cry of unadulterated agony careened eerily over the sea.

'Annalise! Annalise!' Phillip wailed, hugging her to him. 'Oh my God! My darling. Annalise!'

Cristos had buried his face in Corrie's neck as Inspector Thibault gently eased Phillip to his feet while another officer lifted Annalise to carry her down to the ambulances already arriving. Throughout the panicked journey to Nice Cristos had sat with Corrie thanking God for the temper that had forced him to go after Thibault to tell him that he personally would pay for all the damage done to the villa if they would just stop wasting time and break in. Reluctantly Thibault had agreed, but there was no hesitancy in him at all once they had got through the gates – the blood spattered taxi was right outside the door.

Now, as Cristos and Paula sat either side of the hospital bed staring down at Corrie's pale and battered face, their thoughts were running parallel. They'd known, very soon after Corrie had been brought to the hospital, that she would live, but what no one had been able to tell them was what effect the trauma might have on her – or indeed how lasting it would be. They were both aware of what had been done to her, and it was Cristos, Paula knew, who had most to fear from what the future might hold.

Right now Corrie was still under sedation, though an hour or so ago she had begun drifting in and out of consciousness. As yet she had recognized neither of them, but the doctor hadn't shown any surprise at that. It was his hope that Corrie would be with them again some time later that day, he'd said, then he'd left them alone to continue their vigil.

Both Cristos and Paula tensed as once again Corrie stirred. A moment or two later her eyes flickered open, and a look of confusion crossed her face as her eyes struggled for focus.

'Corrie?' Cristos croaked.

She turned her head towards him, and as her brow started to crease he knew that this time she was seeing him.

He smiled awkwardly, lifting her hand and bringing it to his lips, his throat was constricted with fear that she would recoil from him. Then tears rushed to his eyes as he felt the pressure of her fingers closing around his.

'I love you, Corrie Browne,' he said.

She smiled, but as her dry lips parted to answer she heard someone say, 'I love you too.'

Corrie turned, seemed bewildered for a moment at seeing Paula, then suddenly she closed her eyes, her face contorting as though in terrible pain. 'Annalise,' she whispered. 'Where is Annalise?'

'I'll get the doctor,' Paula said.

'Where is Annalise?' Corrie sobbed. 'Where is she?'

'Ssh, it's all right,' Cristos soothed. 'She's right here at the hospital.'

'Is she . . . ? Cristos, tell me, was she . . .'

'She's going to be all right. She's cut pretty bad, and she's suffering from shock, just like you, but . . .'

'But the blood, there was so much blood . . .'

'I'll explain later,' he said. 'But most of it wasn't hers. Now lie still.'

At that moment the doctor came in and Cristos went to join Paula in the corridor. They watched in silence as two nurses went into the room, then Cristos started to pace. They didn't have to wait long before the doctor came out, and both heaved a sigh of relief when they saw he was smiling.

He addressed himself to Cristos since he knew Paula didn't speak French. 'She's insisting she has a bath so the nurses are preparing to give her one now,' he said.

More waiting, such an eternity Cristos didn't think he could stand it, but eventually the nurses came out and told them they could go in.

'The doctor says for a few minutes only,' one of them added.

Cristos looked at Paula.

'Go on,' she said. 'I'll wait here.'

To Cristos's amazement when he walked into the room Corrie was sitting on the edge of the bed putting on her dressing-gown.

'What are you doing?' he cried in alarm.

'I want to see Annalise. Could you take me there? Please,' she added when he started to protest. 'Please, Cristos, I want to see her.'

'Corrie, the doctor didn't say you could get out of bed.'

'I have to see her,' Corrie said, starting to become agitated.

'All right, all right,' Cristos said, putting his hands on her shoulders to calm her, then buttoning the dressing-gown himself, he put an arm around her and started to lead her from the room.

'It's all right, I can manage,' she said, gently shrugging him away.

The pain of her words was like a physical blow, but Cristos lowered his arm and followed her out into the corridor.

Annalise was in the next room. Before they went in Corrie hesitated a moment, looked as though she was going to ask something, then changing her mind pushed open the door and made to walk in. She stopped, stone dead, and when Cristos looked past her it was to see Annalise's deathly face, stitched and bandaged, lying on the pillows and Octavia sitting motionlessly beside her.

Corrie opened her mouth to speak, but her mind had frozen. She turned to Cristos. He shook his head then stood aside as Corrie walked from the room. He was about to close the door behind them when Corrie suddenly spun round and pushed it open again.

'Get her out of here!' she cried. 'Get that woman away from Annalise!'

'Sssh, ssh,' Cristos said, trying to put his arms around her, but Corrie wrenched herself free.

'Get her out!' she screamed. 'Get that bitch away from her!' Then suddenly she was across the room swinging her fists wildly at Octavia. Octavia did nothing to defend herself, it was Cristos who pulled Corrie off.

'Let me go!' Corrie sobbed. 'You don't know what she's done!'

'Hey, hey,' Cristos said, taking a firmer grip on her now. 'Let's just get out of here. Come on,' and holding her by the shoulders he led her back to her own room.

When they got there Corrie sat on the bed and wrapped her arms around her knees, burying her face. After a while, not knowing what else to do, Cristos walked over to the window.

'Do you know?' Corrie said in the end. 'About Luke and Annalise, I mean?'

He turned to look at her and his heart twisted as she deliberately avoided his eyes. 'Yes,' he said.

'And about the part Octavia played in it?'

'Yes.'

'Then why did you stop me?'

'Because it won't prove anything now, sweetheart.'

'Please, don't call me that,' she said, and lowered her head again.

They remained in silence then until Phillip knocked on the door.

'Corrie?' he said tentatively, coming into the room.

She lifted her head.

'Paula came to find me,' he said. 'I was ... Luke's body ... There was no one else to identify it.'

'Oh, Phillip,' Corrie groaned and held her arms out to him.

'I'm sorry,' he said, going to her. 'I should have known ... I should have realized ...'

'No. Don't say that. It wasn't your fault.'

Cristos watched them, the loss etched painfully in his

dark eyes. In the end, as Corrie continued to comfort her father, and he her, Cristos walked quietly from the room.

'You have to talk to her,' Paula said when she and Cristos returned to the Majestic later. 'Maybe you'd like me to do it for you?'

Cristos shook his head. 'No, I don't guess there's a lot of point right now. It's too soon . . .'   .

'But she loves you, Cristos, I know she does. OK, it's still early days and she's got a heck of a lot to get over, but she wants you here, believe me.'

'Did she tell you that?'

'Not in so many words . . . But I know Corrie. I know how she feels about you.'

'Sure. I knew it too, before all this. But you gotta face it, Paula, *I* gotta face it, that what he did to her has scarred her so damned . . .'

'Cristos, you're being defeatist. OK, I'm not saying it's going to be easy, but she needs you. I mean really needs you. Please don't let her down.'

A flash of anger sparked in Cristos's eyes. 'Do you seriously think I'd do that? That I care so little for her I'd just give up? All I'm saying is that I can't speak to her right now. Hell, how can I when she won't let me anywhere near her?'

They were sitting in the hotel bar, untouched drinks on the table between them. Paula was uncomfortably aware of the way people were staring at them, some were even pointing. At any other time she might have felt proud to be seen with Cristos Bennati, but under the circumstances she just wished they'd mind their own damned business. For his part Cristos seemed oblivious to the attention he was receiving, his only thoughts were for Corrie and how the hell he was going to get them through this.

Paula was on the point of speaking again when Jeannie came into the bar and joined them.

'How you doing?' she said to Cristos.

'Just great,' he said flatly.

Jeannie glanced at Paula then taking a deep breath she said, 'Did you want me to cancel your flight home tomorrow?'

Cristos looked up, a deep resentment burning in his eyes.

'I think you should,' Paula answered for him. 'Corrie's not being discharged until Monday.'

Jeannie nodded. 'I'll get onto it. How is she now? Do you reckon they'll let me see her if I go over there?'

'I'm not sure,' Paula said, glancing uneasily at Cristos. 'You could try,' and to her dismay he suddenly got up and walked out of the bar.

'What did I say?' Jeannie asked, watching him go.

'Corrie's refusing to see him.'

'Oh Christ! Me and my big mouth.'

The waiter appeared then and Jeannie ordered herself a straight scotch. 'This sure has been one hell of a week for him,' she remarked dismally. 'Not as bad as for Corrie and Annalise, I know, nothing could be that bad. But did anyone tell you, he didn't get the Palme d'Or? Though I guess he couldn't give a damn about that now.'

'He got the director's award though, didn't he?' Paula said.

'Sure. Don't think he cares too much about that either, though.'

Paula frowned thoughtfully. 'Where's the award now?' she asked after a moment or two.

'His mother's got it.'

'Do you think she'll let me borrow it? Just for a couple of hours.'

'I guess so, but what are you thinking?'

'That if I take it to show Corrie she'll be sure to want to see Cristos then – if only to congratulate him.'

Jeannie shrugged. 'If you think it'll work I'll go talk to Mariette right away.'

But the whole idea back-fired horribly on Paula the following morning, for when she showed Corrie the award
Corrie accused her of trying to lay the blame for the loss
of the Palme d'Or on her.

'And it is my fault,' she shouted, 'I know that, so I don't
need reminding by you, or anyone else. If I hadn't come
here trying to get to him then none of this would have
happened . . .'

'Corrie! No one's saying that. For God's sake how could
you have known . . . ?'

'I couldn't! I didn't! But what difference does that make
now? He hasn't got the Palme d'Or and . . .'

'But what's happened had no bearing on the judges'
decision . . . It's a film, Corrie, some win and some lose.
But he got this award and I felt sure you'd be so proud
you'd want to tell him so yourself.'

Corrie collapsed back against the pillows, covering her
face with her hands. 'I do, Paula,' she whispered, 'Oh God,
I do. But I can't.'

'Why?'

'Because I'm so ashamed. So ashamed, Paula.'

'Oh Corrie,' Paula cried, taking her in her arms. 'There's
nothing to be ashamed about. He loves you and nothing
in the world is going to change that.'

'It is,' Corrie sobbed. 'It will change, because I can't
bear him to touch me. I love him, but I can't . . . Please
try to understand . . . I can't do those things, the things
he'll want me to do . . . not ever again.'

'Sssh, sssh,' Paula soothed. 'He's not going to make you.
He just wants to see you . . .'

Corrie was shaking her head. 'No, I can't stand to see
the hurt in his eyes when he looks at me. I feel it too, but
there's nothing I can do. It's over for us, Paula. We both
have to face that. I'm coming home with you. I want to
be with you, where I'm safe.'

Cristos was waiting outside when Paula eventually left

the room. The dismay in her eyes told him all he needed to know.

'I guess I'll just fly on back to the States then,' he said when Paula told him what had happened. 'I'll leave Monday when she goes back to England.' He smiled bitterly. 'Doesn't seem much point me hanging around though, does there?'

'But you will?'

'Sure I will.'

They both turned as they heard footsteps approaching to see Phillip coming down the corridor towards them.

'How's Annalise?' Paula asked.

'She regained consciousness about an hour ago,' Phillip answered, but the despair in his eyes was apparent.

'She's going to be all right, isn't she?' Cristos asked him. 'The doctor said . . .'

'She hasn't spoken,' Phillip said. 'She won't say a word. It's as though she doesn't even know I'm there.'

'Oh Christ!' Cristos groaned, thinking, as they all were, of Siobhan.

'The doctor says it's probably only temporary,' Phillip went on, 'but with these things no one can say anything for sure.' He rubbed his eyes with his thumb and fingers. 'I'm expecting a telephone call any moment now that might well help. I pray to God it does. But if I'm right and what I think's been happening has, then . . .'

'Then what?' Cristos prompted.

Phillip was a long way away from them, locked somewhere deep inside his thoughts. 'You'll see,' he murmured. 'And so too will Octavia.'

It was the first time since Octavia had arrived in Nice that she and Phillip had been alone together. Until now Phillip knew she had been actively avoiding him, seeing him only at the hospital where she presumed, correctly, that he wouldn't dare to cause a scene. His reluctance was not born of cowardice, however, it was simply that he had a great deal more to say to her than she realized. And for that they needed to be somewhere where they wouldn't be interrupted.

So here they were in this ridiculous room she had taken for herself at the Negresco, with its fur bedspreads and wall-linings, gold laminated bath and velvet chaises-longues. Octavia, in her Christian Dior suit, priceless jewellery and swathed in that hideous perfume, was sitting demurely on the end of the bed. Her ash blonde hair was snared in a pony tail and her surgery tautened face was, as ever, immaculately painted. Phillip was standing at the centre of the room, his face was inscrutable.

'Well,' she said, when all he did was look at her. 'I'm sure you haven't trapped me in here just to gaze at the view. So what do you want?'

'You mean aside from to kill you?'

She snorted and casually patted her hair as she turned her eyes to the window. 'You haven't got the balls for it.'

'I wouldn't count on that, Octavia,' he answered tonelessly. 'In fact I wouldn't count on it at all if I were you.'

'Then why don't you just get on with it?' she said sweetly.

'Believe me, were it not for the fact that Annalise is going to need me, there's nothing in the world that would stop me.'

'Hah!' she sneered. 'Any excuse!' She lifted her chin, revealing her long slender neck. 'Come on, Phillip. Do it!' she challenged. 'Put your hands around my throat and squeeze until you see me go blue in the face, until I beg you for mercy . . .'

'Save your sick fantasies for where they'll be needed, Octavia. Because believe you me they will be where you're going.'

'And just where am I going, Phillip dearest?'

'To hell.'

'Pppfff! Is that the best you can come up with?'

'You're going right to hell,' he said, unruffled. 'And I'm going to make sure of it.'

'And just how are you going to do that?' she smirked, crossing her legs and leaning back on her hands. 'Incidentally,' she added, 'it must please you to know that you *can* father a child. If the Browne girl is yours, that is.'

'She's mine. So is Annalise.'

'Oooh, very noble.'

'Well she isn't Luke's is she?' Phillip asked.

Octavia's limpid blue eyes narrowed.

'Is she?' Phillip repeated.

For a moment or two she held his eyes, so intently he could almost feel the venom leaking out of her. Then a malicious smile curved across her pale pink lips. 'So that's what you're telling yourself, is it?' she said. 'That she isn't his. As usual you're burying your pathetic little head in the sand and pretending . . .'

'The only pretence here, Octavia, is yours. Now let me hear you say it. Annalise is not Luke's daughter.'

'Of course she's his! What the hell do you think this has all been about?'

'I really don't know, Octavia. You tell me.'

'What for? That quack Horowitz told you everything . . .'

'No! He told me what he knew. He told me what you had told Luke, but what he didn't tell me because he didn't know and Luke couldn't remember, is what you're going to tell me now.'

'And just what would that be?'

'That Luke Fitzpatrick walked out of Geraldine Lassiter's on May 19th, 1967.'

Octavia gave a bark of scornful laughter, but her face had turned an ugly shade of grey. It was obvious that Phillip was at last beginning to get to her.

'Shall I tell you how I know that?' he said unable to keep the bitterness from his voice now. 'Shall I tell you why I remember it so clearly? It was the night of my birthday, wasn't·it, Octavia. The night you called off the party you'd talked Geraldine into holding because young lover boy had run out on you both. And unless my memory is failing me, Annalise was born ten months later on March 27th. So unless Luke returned to London sometime during June of '67, it just isn't possible for him to be her father, now is it?'

The careful surgery on Octavia's face had become a travesty. 'He came back,' she rasped.

'Nice try,' he said. 'But you're lying. I've checked with the authorities in Dublin. Luke Fitzpatrick never left the country again after his father was arrested. At least not until 1970 and then he went to the United States – to see Geraldine, I imagine. So now, do you want to tell me you went to Ireland during June of '67?'

'You stupid man!' she spat. 'You pathetic, stupid little man! Do you think that just because Fitzpatrick isn't her father that you are? You're even more . . .'

'So you're admitting that he isn't her father?' Phillip cut in.

'I'm admitting nothing!'

'I think you just did,' he remarked. 'But let me hear it again. Let me hear those words from your own lips, that Luke Fitzpatrick is not Annalise's father.'

'All right,' she sneered, 'he's not her father. Does that satisfy you?'

Phillip's hands were shaking so hard he had to clench them. He was staring down at her with such hatred in his eyes that even Octavia was unnerved. 'So you let that man die thinking he was her father.'

Octavia shrugged.

Phillip knew that he was so close to killing her now that only the police presence he had requested outside would stop him. 'You knew what he'd been through as a child! He told you, and you used it to torment him and satiate yourself. My God, do you realize how sick that makes you?

How contemptible? You led that man through two years of unimaginable hell letting him, no encouraging him, to think he was committing incest until he was driven out of his mind. When all the time you knew . . .' He broke off, so filled with disgust he felt sick. 'How could you have done that, Octavia?' he spat. 'How could you, when he'd already suffered so much? And Annalise, she's your own daughter! They loved each other . . .'

'That's why!' Octavia hissed. 'They loved each other and he was mine. He ran out on me and no one does that! So I got him back. I got him and I kept him. He was never going to be hers.'

'Oh my God,' Phillip muttered.

'But don't start thinking because she's not his that she's yours!' Octavia snarled. 'She could be anyone's. *Anyone's*!

'She's mine,' Phillip said through gritted teeth. 'Do you hear me? Annalise is my daughter. But she's not your daughter, Octavia, because as far as Annalise and I are concerned you no longer exist. As far as any civilized society is concerned you no longer exist. And shall I tell you why?'

Octavia flinched as he suddenly, because he couldn't help himself, raised his fist. 'Why?' she taunted. 'Why, why, why? What is the brave little Phillip going to do?'

'I've already done it,' he said. 'As of now you have nothing. Do you hear that, nothing at all? Which makes you nothing. You can't even pay for this hotel. At least not with money. But you can pay for it with your body. You'll be paying for everything with your body from now on, because you're no longer my wife . . . Ah! Ah! Ah!' he said, holding up a hand as she started to argue. 'There's not a court in the whole of England that would support your claims once they know what you've done. And I'll tell them, Octavia, make no mistake about that.'

'Like hell you will! And drag your precious Annalise through the mud?'

'I'd do it, and so would she.'

'She can't even speak yet, so how the hell do you know that?'

'As a matter of fact she can, but you wouldn't know that would you? You were too busy at the beauty parlour to be bothered about the fact that your own daughter was in danger of spending the rest of her life as a mute. But she won't, not now. Because she knows the truth.'

'So to hell with her reputation?'

'How can that be so when Luke Fitzpatrick wasn't her father? I've left her talking this over with Corrie, and believe you me, Octavia, you have far more to fear from Corrie than you'll ever have from me or Annalise.'

'That stupid little bitch! What the hell can she do to me?'

'You'll find out soon enough. And in the meantime you'd better face it, Octavia, as of now you're a whore. A real whore! It's the only way you'll earn a living because you sure as hell can't do anything else – and believe me, I'll see to it that you never can. I'll have my tabs out for you, Octavia, you'll never escape them. And you're going to suffer, for the rest of your life; because who wants a whore who's approaching fifty who can't afford the plastic surgery anymore? To begin with I can tell you that the manager of this establishment doesn't, so you'd better start working out how you're going to pay the bill. My advice to you is start soliciting now, and while you're doing it remember that there's no one there to save you now, no Luke to stop the sadists going too far, because you've killed him, Octavia. You murdered that man as sure as if your own finger pulled the trigger, and in doing it you've all but destroyed your own daughter.' He started to walk out of the room, but when he reached the door he stopped and turned back. 'Just one last thing before I go. Should you somehow manage to get yourself an airline ticket, don't even think about coming back to Chelsea for your belongings, and don't ever, *ever*, attempt to go near Annalise again. You're finished, Octavia – more than finished, you're dead.'

– 31 –

Past Lives Present was doing well at the box-office. It had opened in the States a month ago to great reviews, and still it was booked out. The press were having a field day with it; it was a controversial movie and as such Cristos had expected it to generate a lot of attention, but all too often it was being mentioned only as an aside to what had happened in the South of France. The mystery surrounding that fateful night had now been relegated to middle pages and features, but his private life was still under siege – it seemed that the entire world wanted to know how his relationship with Corrie Browne stood. There was nothing he could tell them about that, but even if there were, he wouldn't have. His obdurate silence antagonized the press, which was why, he presumed, they had started the rumours about a renewed association with Paige Spencer. The fact that he'd not even seen Paige since returning from Cannes seemed immaterial, but afraid that the unfounded gossip would find its way into the British press he finally issued a statement denying the rumours and saying that he was currently working on a script for a new film which was at this stage still under wraps. All hell had broken loose at that – the press were hungry and on all counts he was denying their carnivorous pens the flesh they craved.

Cristos knew from his regular telephone calls to Paula that Corrie was getting hassled too, but for her it was one hell of a lot worse than for him. Fortunately Paula was doing her best to keep the papers from her so as yet Corrie was unaware that she was suffering the kind of conjecture that would make any decent human being cut off his hands rather than write such outrageous lies. The whole nature of her relationship with Luke was under the microscope, and one particularly vindictive female hack had come dangerously close to accusing Corrie of carrying out the attack on Annalise in a fit of jealousy. Phillip had instantly threatened a law suit and the paper had backed down, printing a two line apology on page eighteen of the next day's issue. After that they turned their attention to Radcliffe, who had been suspended from duty pending an enquiry into his handling of the case.

What was really incensing the press was the fact that a man was dead – and not just any man either, for as a journalist and television personality Luke Fitzpatrick was one of them. They felt they had the right to know what had happened in that villa on Cap Ferrat and they weren't going to let up until they did.

In the end the police came forward with the announcement of Bobby McIver's release. The furore that followed reverberated around the world, since it was now known that Luke Fitzpatrick had killed the prostitutes. Press and public sympathy veered back to Corrie, but under her own instructions they were to be told nothing else.

'She doesn't want any distortions,' Paula told Cristos when he called later that day, 'besides which she feels that it should be Annalise's decision as to how much anyone should be told.'

'How is Annalise?' Cristos asked.

'Getting there, I think. She's still in the clinic. Corrie and Phillip go to see her every day, but I think she could be home soon.'

'And Corrie? How's she doing?'

'Getting better all the time. She went without a sleeping pill last night and, so she says, there were no nightmares. Well, I'd have heard if there were, so . . .'

'Is she still getting the counselling?'

'Oh yes. Three times a week.'

'Is it working?'

'She doesn't talk about it really. At least not to me. I think she does to Phillip though. Why don't you call him, I know he won't mind.'

'It's OK, he called me. She's doing fine with the counselling, I just hoped that maybe she'd said something more to you.'

There was a pause and Paula could sense the strain he was under. The fact that Corrie was refusing to speak to him, had shut him out completely when he needed so badly to help her was, Paula knew, tormenting him beyond endurance.

'I know what you're trying to ask,' she said, her voice imbued with sympathy, 'but I'm sorry, she still hasn't mentioned you. I tried, just this morning, to get her to say something, but . . .' She broke off as she heard the front door open. 'I'll have to go,' she whispered, 'she's just come in. I'll call you again tomorrow.'

'Who was that you were talking to?' Corrie asked, coming into the room.

'Oh, just my mother,' Paula answered.

Corrie turned to look at her, but before she could point out that Paula's mother lived just across the street Paula said,

'How was Annalise today?'

Corrie sighed and collapsed into her mother's favourite armchair. 'Improving, at least physically she is. She wants to come home, but Phillip's afraid that it might still be too early. And I guess, as he's paying, the doctor's only too glad to do what he wants. Anyway, they're taking the stitches out of her legs tomorrow, she's hoping Phillip will change his mind then.'

'Is her counsellor making any headway with her yet?'

Corrie shook her head. 'She's still refusing to talk to anyone about it, except me. And when she does it's like she's obsessed by it. She goes over and over it as though, well I don't know, I suppose it's as though she's trying to find some divine reason for it all.' She sighed wearily. 'If you could see her, Paula, God, it tears your heart apart. She looks half manic, but at the same time she's so lost, so unsure of herself. Well, that's hardly surprising I suppose, but sometimes, when I listen to her reliving every moment of it, I wonder if she'll ever get over it.'

'And what about you?' Paula said gently. 'Do you think you will?'

Corrie gave a dry, mirthless laugh as her eyes wandered about the room. 'Are Uncle Ted and Auntie Hattie coming for dinner tonight?' she asked, pointedly changing the subject.

'I think so,' Paula answered, unable to hide her disappointment. 'Corrie,' she said after a pause. 'Corrie, why won't you . . .'

'No, Paula,' Corrie interrupted. 'I know what you're going to say so please don't.'

'But I'm your best friend, Corrie. I want to help if I can.'

'You are helping by letting me stay here. But I can't discuss it with you, Paula, please try to understand that. I talk to Annalise about it every day, to counsellors three times a week, and to Phillip too. If I start going over it again with you, well, I'll never be talking about anything else, will I? And that doesn't seem to me to be the best way of getting my life back to normal.'

'Does getting back to normal include . . . ?' Paula stopped. Maddeningly she could hear the baby stirring upstairs so now wasn't the time to raise the subject of Cristos. 'Will you go back to London?' she asked.

'Probably. I've been talking things over with Phillip, but we haven't exactly resolved anything yet. Well we can't until we know how Annalise is going to be, or what she wants to do. It looks like he's managed to sell his house, though. Pam's found another, somewhere in Kensington,

Phillip's driving up there now to look at it. There's an independent flat in the basement, Phillip's hoping that Annalise will live there.'

'What about you?'

'I'll go back to my studio, eventually.'

'And TW?'

'Yes, well, we're still discussing what to do about that. Since Phillip has suspended transmissions I doubt it's going to be easy to get the network slot back. Still, that's all in the future. What matters now is that my God-daughter is about to scream the place down.'

A few minutes later Paula was standing over the sink preparing vegetables when Corrie, with the baby resting happily on her hip, came to stand in the doorway. 'Paula,' she said carefully.

'Mmm?'

'Look at me, please. I want to see your eyes when I ask you this question.'

Paula turned. 'This sounds serious,' she remarked curiously.

Corrie looked at her for a long moment, before saying, 'You've been speaking to Cristos, haven't you?' She smiled as the colour in Paula's cheeks deepened. 'Yes, I thought so.'

'He's worried about you, Corrie,' Paula said defensively. 'You can hardly blame him for that, can you?'

'No.'

When Corrie turned away and started pulling faces at Beth Paula thought the subject was going to be dropped, but after a moment or two, with her attention still on the baby, she said, 'How is he?'

The relief and delight in Paula's eyes was ummistakable. 'Having a hard time with the press, he tells me, but his main concern is for you.'

'What do you tell him about me?'

Paula shrugged. 'All kinds of things really.' She waited

a moment, then very tentatively she said, 'Why don't you give him a call?'

'No!' Corrie was adamant. 'No, I can't. I just wanted to know how he was, that's all. I'd better go and change Beth's nappy.'

'Corrie, this can't go on,' Paula said, following her into the sitting room. 'You'll lose him if you carry on like this.'

'I know,' Corrie said quietly. She was kneeling over Beth, who was laughing and gurgling up into her face.

'He loves you so much, Corrie,' Paula persisted, 'and I know you love him. So, please, for both your sakes, call him.'

As Corrie gazed down at the baby the happy fat little face started to blur. 'I want to,' she whispered, her voice so filled with tears it was barely audible. 'Oh, God, Paula, if only you knew how much I want to speak to him.'

'Then why don't you?' Paula pleaded, going to sit on the floor beside her.

'Because I'm afraid. I'm so afraid that it'll never be the same again. That I won't be able to . . . to love him the way he wants me to. Oh Paula!' she sobbed breaking down as Paula pulled her into her arms. 'It's all such a mess and I don't know what to do.'

'Well running away from it isn't going to do any good,' Paula told her gently. 'There's only one person who can help you over this, and that's Cristos.'

'But I've only got to imagine him coming near me to see Luke's face. Those things he did to me, Paula, I don't think they'll ever leave me. It was so . . . Oh God, it was so horrible . . . I keep thinking he's out there somewhere, watching me, and that if I go to Cristos he'll rape me like that again. I know it's nonsense, that he's dead, that it can't ever happen again, but it's like he's haunting me. He won't let me go.'

'And he never will unless you let him go,' Paula said, stroking her hair. 'And the only way you're going to do that is to get on with your life. And to let those who love you help you to put it behind you.'

'It's not as easy as that, though, is it?' Corrie sniffed. 'I mean, there's Annalise to consider. She's been through so much more than I have. What would she do if I went to Cristos?'

'And what will Cristos do if you don't?'

'He'd survive. I'm not so sure about Annalise.'

'But you can't take that burden of responsibility, Corrie. I know she's your sister, and I know too how much you blame yourself for taking her to France, but you have your own life to lead.'

Corrie was shaking her head. 'I can't turn my back on her, Paula. I just can't.'

'All right, but I think you should speak to Cristos and explain it to him. Tell him everything you've told me and I know, I just know it in my heart, that he'll find a way for you to be together.'

'I'll think about it,' Corrie said, drying her eyes on Beth's clean nappy. 'Just give me some more time.'

She spent the next few days with Phillip and Pam at the Denby country house helping them prepare for Annalise's homecoming that weekend. The first night she was there Pam went to bed early leaving her and Phillip talking way into the early hours. For Corrie it was such a welcome release to discuss something other than Luke that she found herself relaxing to the point of genuine laughter as Phillip told her stories of her great-grandmother, Cornelia, who, if his outrageous tales were to be believed, had been quite a character. And, as Corrie listened to him, and they talked about Edwina and her own childhood, she found herself warming to him in a way she never had before. She'd had no idea he could be so witty, or so easy to be with, but he had changed this past month, he was more self-assured, somehow more in control, which Corrie guessed had a great deal to do with being free of Octavia.

Octavia was a subject they had, over the past weeks, discussed in great detail, and, when Annalise came home that weekend it was brought up again. The three of them spent many hours in Phillip's study, though precisely what fate they were planning for Octavia, who had recently sold her story to a tabloid newspaper, Pam had no idea.

'They're locked away in there again today,' she said to Paula on Monday morning, when Paula called around with Beth.

'I take it Annalise has read the story then,' Paula said.

'Oh yes, she read it all right. Every dirty rotten lie of it. How that woman had the nerve to tell those journalists that she had suffered for years at Luke Fitzpatrick's hands, I'll never know. And to say that Phillip has thrown her out because of her infidelity when all she was was a poor, helpless victim of a man who'd terrorized her into doing the things she did, well, I ask you! I can't think for one minute that anyone'll believe it, but I suppose the important thing is that she didn't mention anything about Annalise not being Phillip's daughter. He's received a letter from her though, threatening to reveal even more of the story if he doesn't give her some money soon. I imagine that's what they're discussing now.'

'I see,' Paula said thoughtfully. 'I suppose they'll have to do something or Octavia's going to be blackmailing him for ever. Incidentally, do you think Annalise is Phillip's daughter?'

Pam sighed. 'I doubt even Octavia knows the answer to that, but all that matters right now is that she isn't Luke's. If she had been, well, I'm really not sure she'd have survived it.'

Paula watched her walk across the kitchen to pour them both more coffee. 'How is Annalise now?' she said. 'I saw her on Saturday when she came home, she seemed a bit tired then . . .'

'Annalise,' Pam said, turning around, 'is undergoing

some kind of metamorphosis, if you ask me. Like you said, she was limp and frail when she got home two days ago, since, well it's like someone's turned a light on inside her. God only knows what the three of them are cooking up in there, but whatever it is it's doing that girl a power of good.'

Paula knew, because Corrie had confided in her the night before, precisely what was being discussed in the study, but if no one had told Pam yet then she really didn't feel it was her place to do so. 'Do you think,' she said, 'that Annalise seems as attached to Corrie as she was when she was in the hospital?'

'No doubt about it,' Pam answered without hesitation. 'She may have lost a mother, but she's gained a sister, is the way she sees it, and to her way of thinking that just about makes up for everything. She's devoted to Corrie.'

'I see,' Paula said dully. 'I was afraid you'd say something like that.'

Pam looked surprised at this response, but said nothing until she was sitting back at the table. 'What's on your mind, love?' she asked, her eyes filled with concern. 'If you're thinking that this will change your friendship with Corrie . . .'

'No, no, I can't imagine anything ever changing that,' Paula said. 'It's just that . . . Well, you see, really, in her heart of hearts, Corrie wants to be with Cristos, I know she does. She's still nervous about the after effects of the rape and everything, but he'll get her over that, I'm certain of it, if only she'd give him the chance. And I just know that she would give him the chance if it weren't for Annalise. You see, she's afraid, if she goes to Cristos, of how Annalise might react. I keep trying to tell her that she has her own life to lead, that she mustn't give him up out of a sense of family duty, but . . . Why are you smiling?'

'I don't think you need worry too much about the family duty bit,' Pam laughed. 'Phillip has matters in hand. I don't know if you're aware of how frequently he and Cristos have been speaking on the telephone this past couple of weeks . . . Well, they have. I'm afraid I can't tell you any more than that, but you'll see what I'm talking about soon enough.'

Three days later Phillip picked Cristos up from Heathrow airport and drove him into London.

'Did you tell her yet, that I was coming?' Cristos asked as they sped along the M4.

'No, not yet. I was planning to tell her tonight.'

Cristos nodded. 'Shit,' he grumbled after a moment or two, 'I feel as jittery as a Goddamned schoolboy. Are you sure her counsellor said this was a good idea?'

Phillip chuckled. 'That's what she said, and now is not the time to be telling me you're getting cold feet.'

'Like hell I am. It's just that that daughter of yours can be so Goddamned unpredictable at times.'

Phillip's eyebrows shot up. 'You're the one who was telling me how she would respond,' he pointed out.

'Yeah, well I don't feel quite so sure right now. What if she refuses to see me?'

'She won't. Not once she knows you're already here. Which is why I've held off telling her. I think you should prepare yourself for a wait though, it might take her a day or two to come to terms with the fact that she has to face you.'

But it didn't, for the following morning when Cristos was on the point of going to see Corrie's counsellor Corrie herself called.

'I'm sorry,' she said simply.

'Sorry? What for?'

'For all that I've put you through.'

'Oh Corrie,' he groaned. 'All that matters to me is that you're all right.'

'Is that why you're in London?'

'Yes.'

'But I'm here, in Suffolk.'

For a moment he was silent, hardly daring to hope . . . 'You mean . . . Are you saying . . . ?'

'Cristos, please come,' she whispered.

Throughout the entire train journey he was trying to prepare himself, telling himself that he must treat her gently, must not touch her unless she touched him. One step at a time and it would be all right, he told himself over and over again.

Dave was waiting at the station, his straw hat sitting jauntily on his head as he lolled across the bonnet of his car soaking up the summer sun. They drove through the still, sleepy countryside straight to the cottage where Paula was waiting at the door to greet them.

'She's out in the back garden playing with Beth,' she whispered to Cristos. 'Go on through.'

Cristos's heart was thudding so hard he found himself taking deep breaths to steady it. His hands were clenching and unclenching, and, had he but known it, his long hair was an unruly mess from where he kept dashing his fingers through it. He crossed the sitting room and walked into a pool of sunlight, streaming in through the open kitchen door. His eyes shot to the window, but there was no sign of her. He walked on, out through the door, and then he stopped . . .

She was sitting in a corner of the garden, laughing as the baby mangled a daisy chain in her chubby little fists. She was wearing a pure white cotton dress and her glossy chestnut hair was tumbling over her face. Because of the way the sun was shining down on her she looked almost ethereal, and as she laughed again and it blended with the cheery sounds of birdlife it was as though his whole heart was being torn from its roots. For a while he just watched her, not believing it was possible to love someone this much. Then sensing his eyes on her she looked up and seeing him she smiled. It was almost his undoing. His emotions were so close to the surface that all he wanted was to take her in his arms and smother her with all the love burning inside him. But he couldn't do that, he had to take it real slow, had to be sure she was ready . . . Please God in heaven she would be.

'Hello,' she said, getting to her feet.

'How you doing?' he said softly.

Her smile grew wider, then they both laughed as Paula crept out into the garden to retrieve her daughter.

When Cristos turned back it was to find that Corrie had come half way across the garden.

'You lost some weight,' he said.

She twirled. 'Do you think it suits me?'

'I kinda liked you the way you were.' He winced. 'I'm sorry,' he said, then, after a pause, 'Your father told me he's taking you and Annalise to the Caribbean for a month.'

Corrie nodded. 'We go at the beginning of next week. It's a sort of convalescence, I think.'

'I see.' He looked so dejected that Corrie's heart twisted painfully. Had she really forgotten how impossibly handsome he was, or was it just that her fear of losing him hadn't allowed her to remember? 'Aren't you going to kiss me?' she asked, with not a little coyness.

He seemed so amazed that she laughed.

'I won't break,' she told him.

'Oh Corrie,' he groaned, pulling her into his arms, and as his mouth found the softness of her lips his feelings surged through him with such an intensity as he'd never known before in his life.

'Gosh,' Corrie said shakily when he finally let her go. 'I was going to tell you that you didn't need to treat me any differently than you did before, but it seems I didn't need to.'

The corner of his mouth dropped in a crooked smile, and she felt herself melting all over again as she gazed up at the teasing light in his eyes. 'What changed your mind, about seeing me?' he asked.

'I had to be absolutely sure that I wasn't going to run away from you. That I wasn't going to hurt you by being unable to be the way I was before.'

'And you're sure now?'

'I think so. But I guess we've still got a few things to resolve before it's all over.'

Cristos's insides turned over. 'What do you mean, before it's all over?' he asked, his voice suddenly hoarse.

Corrie shook her head and removed her hands from his shoulders. He watched her as she started to look everywhere but at him. His chest was slowly binding itself into a knot of unbearable foreboding.

'Corrie . . .'

'Cristos . . .'

They spoke at the same time, and smiling uncertainly she took his hand in hers. 'I don't know if anyone's told you,' she said, 'but Doctor Horowitz has been to see me, several times in fact. He's been telling me about Luke's life as a child – and, well, I'd like to go and see Siobhan. Would you take me? We could use Dave's car.'

'Are you sure that's wise? Have you asked Horowitz about it?'

'Yes. I called him this morning, after I called you. He's expecting us. You see, I wanted you to come too.'

'Why?'

'I'll explain later, but will you come?'

When they arrived at the clinic, a small pink solitary house perched up on the cliffs overlooking the sea, a nurse went to fetch Doctor Horowitz who, after offering them tea, which both refused, showed them to Siobhan's room.

'Does she know Luke's dead?' Cristos asked before they went in.

'I told her, yes. There was no reaction I'm afraid.'

Corrie looked up at Cristos, then holding his hand tightly, they went into the sparsely furnished room.

Siobhan was sitting in her usual position by the window, her back turned to the door as she gazed blindly out over the magnificent sea view. Doctor Horowitz went to stand behind the wheelchair, explaining that she could walk, but rarely did. 'You have visitors, Siobhan,' he said to her, and taking the handles of the chair he turned her around.

Corrie gasped, and her grip tightened on Cristos's hand. 'Oh my God,' she murmured. The sunken eyes were blank, the skin was pallid and the shoulder length blonde hair was as lank and lifeless as the emaciated body, but had she not been forewarned Corrie would have truly believed she was looking at Annalise.

'The likeness is quite remarkable, is it not?' Horowitz said.

Cristos was shaking his head. 'And she's not, she really couldn't be . . . ?'

'Annalise's aunt?' Horowitz finished for him. 'I think not. It was just one of life's tragic coincidences, I'm afraid.'

Cristos looked down at Corrie as she let go of his hand and walked slowly across the room. When she reached Siobhan she crouched down in front of her. 'Hello,' she said softly.

Siobhan's staring eyes registered nothing.

'I'm Corrie,' Corrie said, taking Siobhan's limp hands between hers. She glanced at Horowitz and he smiled. She looked back at the empty face and searched her mind for something to say. 'Do you like books, Siobhan?' she asked. 'Perhaps I could bring you some books. I could read to you, if you like. Would you like that?' She looked down as she felt a pressure on her fingers, then looked excitedly towards Horowitz. 'She squeezed my hand,' she said.

Horowitz shook his head. 'A reflex, I'm afraid. It means nothing.'

Corrie stood up. 'There's no one to visit her now, is there?' she said.

Horowitz shook his head. 'But she is well taken care of, Luke's will has seen to that.'

'I should like to visit her,' Corrie said. 'From time to time.'

'You would always be welcome,' Horowitz smiled, 'won't she, Siobhan?'

Corrie turned back to look at the skeletal, inanimate features, so filled with pity her heart ached with it. She looked up then as Cristos came to put an arm round her. His face was taut, his eyes reflecting a pained disbelief at the tragedy that had so cruelly destroyed an innocent life. 'Is there nothing to be done?' he said to Horowitz.

Horowitz shook his head. 'I'm afraid not.'

Corrie and Cristos drove back to Amberside in silence. Seeing Siobhan had had a profound effect on them both, probably Cristos most of all, for he knew now why Corrie had wanted him to come too. But he wasn't going to press her, she would tell him in her own time.

They had dinner with Paula and Dave that night, neither of them saying much about their visit to the clinic, but it was never far from their minds as they laughed and joked with Paula at the lengths she had gone to these past six weeks to get the two of them back together.

'And then, just as I was beginning to make headway, bloody Phillip goes and steals my thunder!' she grumbled. 'Anyway, at least I can say it happened in my garden . . . You can laugh, but I'll bet I make a fortune selling photographs of my little plot out there once everyone knows. I reckon I'll even be able to hire it out for weddings before much longer . . . What are you pulling that face for?' she said to Dave. 'You look like you got a bee up your backside.'

'Subtlety never was your strong point, was it my darling?' Dave said, throwing an ironic look at Cristos. 'Why don't you have some more wine and give someone else a chance?'

Cristos looked at his watch. 'I guess I'd better get going,' he said. 'Phillip'll be sure to wait up for me and it's already late.'

'You'll come again tomorrow?' Paula said, as Corrie got up to walk to the door with him.

'Sure I will,' Cristos smiled.

'Thanks for coming with me today,' Corrie said, as she closed the hall door behind them. 'I know we haven't said much about it yet, but we will, tomorrow.'

Cristos pulled her into his arms. 'You don't know how good it feels just to look at you,' he said, gazing down into her eyes.

'I think I do,' she answered, raising her lips to his.

He kissed her very gently, then started to pull away.

'You don't have to go,' she said. 'You can stay here, if you like. With me,' she added, when all he did was look at her.

'Are you sure?' he murmured, stroking her hair away from her face.

'I want you to hold me,' she said.

'Then I guess I better call your father.'

'We'll get Paula to do that.'

They undressed in the dark, even so Cristos kept his head averted. Moonlight was streaming in through the window and he was afraid that if he saw her he would be unable to control his desire. When he heard her get into bed he was on the point of saying he couldn't go through with it, knowing that his body was going to betray him, but somehow managed to stop himself. She needed him and he wasn't going to let her down. A moment or two later he lay down beside her and almost instantly felt himself tense as her hand sought his.

'Can I put my head on your shoulder?' she whispered after a while.

'Sure.'

As she sat up for him to raise his arm he caught a glimpse of her breasts. Immediately he closed his eyes. He'd thought she would wear something, that her skin wouldn't touch his . . . Then not quite knowing how it happened she was in his arms and he was rolling towards her pulling her to him and feeling the unbearable softness of her nudity. Their lips met and Corrie pushed herself closer.

'Oh God, I'm sorry,' he gasped, suddenly wrenching himself away. His undershorts could do nothing to disguise the treacherous hardness of him.

'It's all right,' Corrie whispered. 'Cristos, please, it's all right. I want you too. I want you very much.'

'Are you sure? Oh, God, Corrie, I don't want to force you . . .'

'Sssh,' she said, putting her fingers over his lips. 'Do you think I'd have got into bed like this if I wasn't sure? So why don't you undress too?'

They made love with such searing tenderness, holding one another so close and never parting for a moment, that by the time it was over both had tears on their cheeks.

'God, I missed you,' Cristos murmured, his lips still on hers.

'I missed you too.'

'Do you feel OK?'

'What do you think?'

He chuckled softly. 'You feel great to me,' and rolling onto his back he pulled her with him.

When finally she slept, her head on his chest and her legs entwined with his, Cristos lay awake for a long time, wanting to be there if the nightmares came. But they didn't, and eventually he too fell asleep.

In the morning when he woke Corrie was sitting on the window seat looking out at the garden. He watched her for a while feeling all the pain that she did at what he knew was running through her mind. He wanted more than anything to put it off, to pretend that everything could go back to the way it was, but it couldn't. Last night had shown them both how desperately they still wanted each other, how very deeply their love ran and how much they needed to be together. But seeing Siobhan had shown them – had shown him, because Corrie had already known – why it just wasn't going to be possible.

Eventually she turned to look at him and smiled with such sadness that he turned away. But there was no point in hiding from it, they had to face it, so getting out of bed, he pulled on his jeans and a shirt and went to stand behind her.

'You ready to talk?' he said, as she leaned back against him and he ran his hands over her shoulders.

'I don't know that I'll ever be ready for this,' she answered, turning her face to kiss his hand. 'Do you know what I'm going to say?'

'I guess.'

'My father told you that he's handing TW over to me and Annalise?'

Cristos nodded.

'Of course neither of us is experienced enough actually to run it, particularly me, so Bob, the exec. producer, will manage things until we're ready to take over.'

'Sounds reasonable,' Cristos remarked. Then, 'Looks like you got a great future ahead of you. Head of your own TV company.'

'Yes,' Corrie sighed. 'Beyond my wildest dreams. Or perhaps it was my wildest dream.'

Cristos turned away and went to sit on the bed. He watched Corrie until finally she turned to face him. 'You're going to do something about Siobhan's life, am I right?' he said.

Her eyes fell to the floor. 'Cristos, you saw her,' she said. 'You saw what damage has been done to her. I know there's nothing I can do to change that, but there is something I can do to help the thousands upon thousands of children who right now, even as we speak, are undergoing some kind of abuse at the hands of an adult. I have to make people understand, to show them that every child in the world needs their protection, whether we are parents ourselves or not. We can't just sit by and pretend it's not happening. It is, and the repercussions go on and on, throughout their lives and into future generations. Phillip and I have been talking this over for weeks, ever since we were in France. We've discussed it with Annalise now too, and she's willing for the whole story to be told. Even her own mother's part in it. Of course it'll stop Octavia's blackmail . . .' Corrie gave a dry laugh. 'Phillip told Octavia the last time he saw her that she had more to fear from me than either him or Annalise. She didn't know what he was talking about then, but she'll find out soon enough. Not that revenge on Octavia is either of our motives, but the exposure will ruin her completely. Annalise doesn't want to be involved in the making of the programme, right now she's saying that she wants no more involvement with TV ever. Maybe she'll change her mind one day, but until then it's up to me. And this is something I have to do, Cristos, you must see that. If I don't then Luke's death, the horrible tragedy of his and Siobhan's lives, will have been in vain.'

Cristos stood up and went to her. She looked up at him as he ran his fingers over her cheek. 'So what you're trying to tell me is that there's no room in your life for us?'

'Oh no, please, don't put it like that. It's just that I can't come to Los Angeles. I have to be here for Annalise, and to try to make some sense of this Godawful mess.'

'So this is goodbye?'

Corrie closed her eyes. 'Please try to understand,' she begged him.

'I do,' he said. Then kissing her gently on the forehead he turned away and started packing up his things.

When he had gone Corrie was inconsolable. Paula tried

to comfort her, but neither of them could say if Corrie had
made the right decision. All Corrie knew was that she
would never, not ever, forget the look in his eyes when he'd
turned away.

— 32 —

Phillip, Corrie and Annalise had been at the Secret Harbour Hotel in Grenada for just over two weeks. It was one
of the island's more exclusive hotels, sprawling across the
hillside on one side of the horse shoe bay looking out on
yachts of all shapes and sizes which sailed in and out of
the moorings each day. The swimming pool, where they
were relaxing now, was in front of the huge Italian-style
villa which housed the hotel's restaurant and bar at the
top of the hill. Below the pool were the hotel rooms, each
like a small villa with their own half-moon terraces jutting
out over the sea.

Corrie and Annalise were both in their bikinis, Phillip
was sitting beside them under an umbrella reading the
paper, Annalise was stretched out in the sun, but Corrie
was sitting up, hugging her knees and staring down at
yet another luxurious yacht as it inched its way into the
harbour.

After a while Phillip put his paper down and looked
across at Corrie. Annalise glanced up at him then she too
looked at Corrie.

'Corrie,' Phillip said, sensing her pain as though it were
a nimbus surrounding her, 'there's no point in trying to
fool yourself any longer, sweetheart. You didn't . . .'

'Please, don't let's go over it again,' Corrie groaned,
burying her face in her arms. 'It's done now, so let's leave
it.'

'No, we won't leave it,' he said firmly. 'I've been thinking, and maybe there is a way you can be with him and still do all you want to do.'

'How? I want to make that programme, more than anything else, I want to make that programme.'

'More than you want Cristos?'

Corrie shook her head.

Annalise looked up at her father, and reading her expression he said, 'I'm going to take a shower, you two talk.'

'Corrie,' Annalise said when Phillip had gone, 'Daddy and I have been talking about this a lot and we think that you feel obligated to make the programme because of us. But you don't have to, really you don't.'

Corrie shook her head. 'I do. I can't run away from it, Annalise, and pretend it never happened. Luke wanted me to help him . . .'

'But Luke's dead, Corrie. Nothing you do can change that.'

'Siobhan isn't dead though, is she? And how many more children are there out there suffering the way she did?'

'A lot, I know. But you're suffering too. And so is Cristos . . .'

'Oh Annalise, I never told him I loved him. I should have told him. I should have . . .'

'Corrie stop doing this to yourself and work out a way to be with him.'

'I've been trying to do that ever since he left, and maybe . . .' she looked at Annalise, then turned away.

'And maybe?' Annalise prompted.

'Nothing.' She didn't want to tell Annalise that she had worked out a way. That she could go to him and do all that she wanted to do, but it would mean leaving Annalise and Phillip. 'Phillip said just now that he'd thought of a way,' she said. 'Do you know what it is?'

Annalise smiled. 'I'll let him tell you.'

Much later in the day they were sitting on Phillip's

balcony sipping cocktails. Phillip and Annalise had just returned from a walk, while Corrie had spent the afternoon alone writing a letter to Cristos she knew she would never send. But writing what she felt in her heart helped her to feel close to him, as though she was speaking to him. She knew she was tormenting herself imagining his responses, but she couldn't stop herself doing it.

'So,' Phillip said, watching her as she twirled the paper umbrella in her drink, 'tell me what's on your mind, what it is you really want to do.'

'I can't,' Corrie answered. 'But I thought you had something to tell me.'

'Yes, I do,' he said.

Corrie looked at him from the corner of her eye then continued to fiddle with the umbrella.

'I am thinking,' Phillip said, 'that you have worked out a way to make this programme and be with Cristos, but it will mean going to America and you don't want to say goodbye to Annalise and me when we've only just come together. Am I right?'

Corrie glanced over at him and he smiled.

'Well, Hollywood's not so far,' he said. 'And we'd both much rather you were there and happy, than with us and miserable, isn't that right, Annalise? And though it might pain you to hear it, TW would survive without you, you know.'

Corrie looked at them, and slowly a smile started to spread across her face. 'You two really have been talking, haven't you?' she said.

Annalise and Phillip exchanged the kind of looks that to Corrie's astute mind spoke volumes. 'If only you knew,' Annalise laughed.

'So does this make it easier for you?' Phillip said.

'I guess it does,' Corrie answered. 'But we have to talk about it some more. I mean . . .'

'There's nothing to talk about, darling. At least not with us. It's Cristos you must talk to.'

Corrie looked at him for a long moment, then suddenly she was on her feet, throwing her arms around him. 'Oh Dad!' she cried. 'I do love him, really I do.'

'I know you do, darling.'

There were tears on his cheeks when she pulled away. 'It's worth giving you up to him just to hear you call me Dad,' he said.

'Dad! Dad, Dad, Dad!' she cried. 'You're the most wonderful dad in the world. Now, are you sure you don't mind me going?'

'Quite sure.'

'Then if it's all right with you I'm going to call him now.'

'It's all right with me, but if I were you . . .' Phillip began, but Corrie had already run around the side of the villa heading off to her own next door.

Jeannie and Richard were in the bedroom of their Sherman Oaks home, packing – and fighting. As fast as Jeannie put things into the suitcase Richard was throwing them out, telling her she didn't need them.

'I know you don't like flying,' Jeannie was saying, 'but you got yourself across to France all right, so now you're gonna just have to . . . Hey! I want that hat,' she cried, catching it as Richard flung it across the room, 'it's my lucky hat.'

'Like your lucky dress, lucky shoes and lucky panties. Why do you need lucky panties? Who are you planning . . . Take it out, Jeannie. You're not leaving any room for my stuff, and get the phone.'

'I'm still watching you,' Jeannie warned as she leaned across the bed to the telephone. 'And put that hat back. Hello,' she barked into the receiver.

'Jeannie! It's Corrie! I've tried all Cristos's numbers and I couldn't get him. Do you know where he is?'

Jeannie spun round to look at Richard. 'Um, uh, hang on a minute,' she said, and putting her hand over the mouthpiece she hissed, 'It's Corrie. She's looking for Cristos. What do I tell her?'

'What he told you to tell her if she called,' Richard answered simply. Then seeing his wife's distraught face, and realizing he was being far too casual about something so important, he got up from the floor and took the phone from her. 'I'll handle it,' he said. 'And don't go near that suitcase. Corrie? Hi, it's Richard. You're looking for Cristos Jeannie told me.'

'Yes, that's right. Do you know where I can find him?'

'Well, yeah, I do, but I can't tell you I'm afraid.'

'What do you mean?'

'Well, he's like gone away. I mean, he's still here in LA, but he's not at his home. And he's kind of left instructions to say that he didn't want to talk to anyone . . .' He paused and winced, 'Most of all you.'

'Oh no!' Corrie cried. 'Oh God, what am I going to do? Are you in contact with him?'

'Kind of.'

'Then give him a message from me, please. Tell him that I've changed my mind. That I want to be with him. That I'll leave England . . . Tell him I love him. Please Richard, would you do that for me?'

'Sure, OK, I'll tell him, but I don't . . .' He looked at the receiver. 'She's rung off,' he said.

Corrie was marching about her room. She wanted to cry but wouldn't let herself. She had to think, but all that was going through her mind was how much she must have hurt him for him to have shut himself away the way he had. She so desperately wanted to make it up to him now, but what could she do? Perhaps she should just get on a plane to LA. But no, if he didn't want to see her then there would be no way of finding him. Maybe, once Richard had given him the message he'd call.

The next morning Corrie was in the shower when the telephone rang. She bumped her shoulder on the bed post, stubbed her toe on her suitcase and tripped over the towel in her haste to get to the phone.

'Am I speaking to Corrie Browne?' said the voice at the other end.

'Cristos!' she cried. 'Oh Cristos! Did you speak to Richard?'

'Yeah, I spoke to Richard.'

'Then you know. You know that . . .'

'Yeah, I know.'

'Do you want to see me?'

'Sure I do.'

'Then I'm coming right there. I'll get the next flight out, I'll be there as quick as I can. And Cristos, Cristos, I . . . No, I'll tell you when I get there.' She rang off and started flying about the room stuffing things into her suitcase. She took her sarong and wrapped it around her, there was no time to dress. Then she remembered she had to book a flight. She got on the phone to reception, asked them to handle it, then heaved her case from the bed and dragged it out onto the balcony.

'A porter,' she said to herself. 'Dad! Annalise! Oh God, I haven't told them I'm going.'

She ran back inside to the telephone. There was no reply from either Annalise or Phillip and she'd already forgotten the porter.

'Damn it!' she muttered as she got to the door. Well, there was nothing else for it, she'd drag the case up to reception herself. She walked outside and picked up the case.

'You going some place?'

Corrie spun round, gasped and dropped her case. Cristos

was standing at the entrance to the balcony, leaning against the door-frame. 'Oh my God!' she cried, and flew into his arms. 'Oh Cristos! Why didn't you tell me . . . Where were you calling from . . . ? How did you get here? Richard said . . .'

'How about one at a time,' he laughed.

She shook her head trying to make sense of everything. 'Five minutes ago you were in LA,' she said.

'Uh-uh. Five minutes ago I was in the lobby.'

'But when did you get here?'

'Ten minutes ago. Now how about you kiss me before the real interrogation starts?'

It was a long embrace and by the time it was over Corrie wasn't at all sure she wanted to know the details until much, much later.

'Hello there, you two,' Phillip called from the next balcony.

Corrie turned to look at her father. She looked at Cristos then back to her father. 'You knew he was here, didn't you?' she said to Phillip. 'You knew all the time . . .'

'I'll leave you to do the explaining,' Phillip grinned at Cristos. 'Annalise and I will be in the restaurant if you want to join us for a late breakfast,' and he disappeared.

'So,' Cristos said, picking up the suitcase and carrying it back into the villa, 'Richard told me you changed your mind. You're coming to Hollywood?'

'Yes. Well, if you still want me,' she answered, following behind him and reaching out to touch him as he put the case on the rack. 'Well, yes, I guess you do or you wouldn't be here. Are you really here? I can't believe you're really here.'

'You want another one of those kisses, just to make sure?'

'Mmm,' she nodded eagerly.

'Well you're gonna have to wait. I want to hear what decisions you've reached.'

'OK. Well, I've thought about it a lot . . . Come and sit

down and I'll tell you. But first I want to know what you and my father have been up to.'

'Just a couple of phone calls. Nothing more,' Cristos grinned, allowing her to lead him to the sofa. 'Now, go on.'

'Well, I thought that I could still make the programme about Siobhan, but I could make it with an American TV company. Of course I would need your help to get in, and I'd need you to point me in the direction of some good writers, and actors of course. Well, actually they'll have to be British. Anyway, child abuse happens all over the world, not just in England. So I thought . . . Cristos you're laughing at me.'

'No, no,' he said, holding up his hands. 'It all sounds great so far. What happens next? After you've made the programme. Providing I can fix you up that is.'

'I haven't thought that far yet,' she confessed. 'And I have to admit it does bother me. I mean, what would I do in Hollywood while you're away making your multi-million-dollar movies?'

'You're asking me?'

'Yes.'

He shrugged. 'I guess you'll be too busy bringing up our kids to think about it.'

She kicked him. 'Be serious.'

'I was being serious. But I guess you're not going to be happy unless you have a career. Maybe you'll find one in American TV.'

Corrie screwed up her nose and he laughed.

'British through and through,' he remarked. 'Think your TV's better than ours, don't you?'

'Yes,' she said frankly.

'But you would make the programme about Siobhan in the States?'

'So that I could be with you, and just so long as it's not sponsored by some ghastly company who want their tasteless product in every shot.'

'I see. What about your father and Annalise?'

'We've talked about it, Phillip said he didn't mind me leaving, but . . .'

'You don't really want to leave them?'

'No. But for you I would.'

He laughed and drew her into his arms. 'I guess I'd better come clean,' he said. 'You don't have to live in Hollywood to be with me, Corrie. You don't even have to make your programme with American TV. You can make it with TW, in London.'

'I don't understand,' Corrie said, suddenly afraid that he was telling her he didn't want her.

'We're going to live in London,' he said.

Corrie stared at him, open-mouthed. 'London?' she repeated.

'That's what I said. I, Corrie Browne, am giving up Hollywood to come to you.'

'No! But you can't do that. What about your films?'

'They make films in Europe, don't they? I speak Italian and French, remember. And I went to film school in London. I've always had a notion to shoot a European movie.'

'You never said before.'

He simply raised his brows.

'You mean you'll give up all that for me?' she said breathlessly.

'Sure. You were going to do it for me.'

'But Cristos, it's different for you. I mean, you're, well, you're you. Everyone in Hollywood wants you.'

'They've had me,' he laughed. 'And I've got another surprise for you. How about I direct your programme for you?'

'You?'

'Yeah, why not?'

'But you don't direct TV. I'll bet you don't even know how to direct video.'

'You're right, I don't. But I can direct film, and take it from me it'll have a far greater impact on film.'

'But you only shoot with 35mm. TW would never be able to run to that sort of budget.'

He looked at her, then slowly she started to laugh.

'Of course, with your name, we'll get all the finance we want.'

He nodded. 'So how about it? You going to give me a job?'

She shook her head in amazement. 'God! What is everyone going to say? Cristos Bennati gives up Hollywood to work in British TV.'

'To make one TV programme,' he corrected her, 'done for cinema release first. Then back to movies.'

She looked at him. 'No,' she said, shaking her head. 'I can't let you do it. I can't let you give up Hollywood. It's your whole life.'

'Jesus, God Almighty, what does a man have to do? I've said I'll come to England . . .'

'No, this is important Cristos, it's . . .'

'Corrie, you're the most difficult, most contrary woman I've ever met in my life. Now to hell with it, will you marry me?'

'No!'

'You damned well will.'

'All right then, I will. But I can't let you . . .'

'Corrie, shut up!'

'I will not.'

'Just do as you're told for once in your Goddammed life!' Corrie grinned.

'Now listen to me. I am coming to London, we are going to find ourselves a house to live in, and in case you don't realize it you just, thirty seconds ago, agreed to marry me. You know what that means don't you?'

For a moment Corrie looked blank, then slowly she started to smile.

'You do. Good. Then let's have it.'

'Just like that? Sitting here like this?'

'Just like that. Sitting here like this.'

'OK. I love you, Bennati.'

'I guess you do at that,' he said, but his eyes were serious now, and pulling her into his arms he kissed her. 'So just how soon are you going to make an honest man of me?' he asked a while later.

'As soon as you like.'

He nodded. 'That's good, because I thought we might do it Saturday.'

'Saturday!'

'Sure. Where are you going?' he said as she headed off towards the telephone.

'To call Paula. I have to tell her. *Saturday!*'

Cristos looked at his watch, then standing up he followed her to the phone and pressed the connectors as she was half way through dialling.

'What are you doing?' she said as he sat down on the bed and pulled her towards him.

'Paula already knows,' he said.

'What? How?'

'Annalise told her, yesterday. And my guess is she and Dave will be landing in Barbados in a couple of hours' time.'

'Barbados!'

'Yep. They'll get a connecting flight to Grenada this evening. They might even meet up with Jeannie and Richard.'

'Jeannie and Richard! Cristos, what has been going on?'

'They're all coming for the wedding. My parents arrive tomorrow.'

Corrie shook her head. It was all too much to take in. 'You were so sure I'd say yes?'

He nodded.

'I hate you.'

'Sure you do.'

'Is there anything else you haven't told me?' she said.

'Yep. We're going to be married on my yacht.'

'Your yacht? But you don't have a yacht.'

'Sure I do. I hired a crew to sail it in from Tortola, it should be here by now. And after the wedding you and I are going to sail off alone for our honeymoon.'

'Do I get any say in this?'

'No.'

'But what am I going to wear?'

'You look mighty fine to me as you are,' he grinned, running his hands over her bottom. 'What you wearing underneath this thing, by the way?'

'Nothing. What are you going to wear?'

'I'll find something.'

'I can't believe it,' Corrie said, sitting down next to him. 'There's been a real conspiracy going on here, hasn't there? But why didn't you tell me what you were planning?'

'I wanted it to be a surprise,' he answered.

'And you say Paula and Dave are coming here? But they don't have the money to . . .' She looked at him. 'You're paying for them, aren't you?'

'I kind of thought you'd want them here when you got married,' he answered. 'But I guess I'll have to stop indulging you this way or I'll end up bankrupt. Now,' he murmured, pulling open her sarong and pushing her back against the pillows, 'tell me you love me again, I've kind of got a taste for hearing . . . Ouch!' he yelled as she suddenly sat bolt upright.

'*Saturday!*' she cried. 'We're getting married on Saturday?'

'I thought that's what we just agreed,' he answered, rubbing his head.

'But today's Wednesday. I don't have time to play around here. There'll be a hundred and one things to do.' She leapt up from the bed. 'Where am I going to get my hair done? What about flowers? Food? Wine? Then there's the vicar. We'll have to find a vicar. Oh, Cristos, why did you . . . ? Cristos! What are you doing? Cristos, put me down. You'll break your back.'

'Corrie,' he said, carrying her back across the room, 'if we're gonna be a team then you better get used to who's giving the orders round here,' and he dropped her onto the bed.

'Oh, I already know that,' she grinned up at him.

He laughed at the mischievous look in her eyes. 'Then tell me you love me.'

'Oh my! You think it's you,' she declared, but as he advanced purposefully towards her she shouted, 'I love you, I love you, I love you.'

'Not bad,' he said, 'but I reckon you could do a whole lot better . . .'

The Mill House

Susan Lewis

Julia Thayne is a valued and loving wife, a successful mother and a beautiful woman. She is everything most other women strive to be. But beneath the surface is a terrible secret that threatens to tear her perfect world apart.

Joshua is Julia's husband – a dynamic, devastatingly handsome man with great style, charisma and humour. He is utterly devoted to his wife and children, but as the ghosts of Julia's past begin to move into their marriage, he finds himself losing the struggle to keep them together. Then two telephone calls change everything.

Julia moves from London to a remote mill house in Cornwall, determined to break free from the past and save her fractured relationship with Josh. But it is here that she makes her own fatal mistake, and once more her marriage is rocked to its very foundation . . .

'Mystery and romance *par excellence*' *Sun*

'Erotic and exciting' *Sunday Times*

arrow books